"Gillespie's grasp of the daily social, religious, and political lives of Germanic tribes and urban Romans alike, and her understanding of the way human deeds are woven by time into myth, keep *The Light Bearer* rooted in historical plausibility . . . keeps the reader engaged . . . *The Light Bearer* taps into one of the most popular themes in historical fiction today, the unsung woman who takes a hand in the shaping of history." —*San Francisco Chronicle*

"Much has been written of the cold-blooded shenanigans of the Roman way of life, but Gillespie weaves her tale in a way that brings new color and excitement to the era . . . [She] gives crisp and detailed descriptions of the fighting methods of the well-trained Roman legions . . . As powerful as Gillespie's action writing can be, she shows a deft and almost musical quality in more passionate interludes . . . Throughout this monumental story, Gillespie constantly increases the excitement and intrigue. There are no flat passages in *The Light Bearer*, only a fast-flowing stream that erupts into a full-scale torrent in the book's conclusion." —*The Washington Post Book World*

"Gillespie immersed herself in the lore and legends of the Roman way of life and emerged with *The Light Bearer* . . . sure to entertain readers in a manner they will not soon forget." —*Orlando Sentinel*

"An intriguing recording of everyday detail, national issues, and more impressively, overarching influences of religion and psychology." —*Publishers Weekly* (starred review)

"Gillespie spent eleven years bringing this magnificent book to completion . . . replete with excitement . . . Gillespie's love of the written word is evident." —*Marina Times*

"A time-capsule journey into a world of richly embroidered adventure . . . Richly flavored with historical references, the plot, action, and painstakingly developed characterizations make it a treasure—even for those who don't put historical tomes high on their reading list[s]. Gillespie's greatest gift is the way she crafts descriptive passages—phrases never sit static on the pages. These words are fluid grace points that translate instantly into living, active images in the reader's imagination." —*Northwest Florida Daily News*

"Auriane is a true heroine, a woman who stands out from the crowd and who makes a journey of growth and discovery. Her innocence and deep faith make her trials more poignant, her choices more stark . . . *The Light Bearer* weaves a strong picture of life in the first centuries . . . There are plenty of details that give a feel for the coarse and glorious realities of the ancient Roman world . . . This is epic historical fiction, centering on one larger-than-life woman." —All About Romance

LADY *of* *the* LIGHT

Donna Gillespie

BERKLEY BOOKS, NEW YORK

THE BERKLEY PUBLISHING GROUP
Published by the Penguin Group
Penguin Group (USA) Inc.
375 Hudson Street, New York, New York 10014, USA
Penguin Group (Canada), 90 Eglinton Avenue East, Suite 700, Toronto, Ontario M4P 2Y3, Canada
(a division of Pearson Penguin Canada Inc.)
Penguin Books Ltd., 80 Strand, London WC2R 0RL, England
Penguin Group Ireland, 25 St. Stephen's Green, Dublin 2, Ireland (a division of Penguin Books Ltd.)
Penguin Group (Australia), 250 Camberwell Road, Camberwell, Victoria 3124, Australia
(a division of Pearson Australia Group Pty. Ltd.)
Penguin Books India Pvt. Ltd., 11 Community Centre, Panchsheel Park, New Delhi—110 017, India
Penguin Group (NZ), Cnr. Airborne and Rosedale Roads, Albany, Auckland 1310, New Zealand
(a division of Pearson New Zealand Ltd.)
Penguin Books (South Africa) (Pty.) Ltd., 24 Sturdee Avenue, Rosebank, Johannesburg 2196,
South Africa

Penguin Books Ltd., Registered Offices: 80 Strand, London WC2R 0RL, England

This book is an original publication of The Berkley Publishing Group.

PRINTING HISTORY
Berkley trade paperback edition / November 2006

Library of Congress Cataloging-in-Publication Data
Gillespie, Donna.
  Lady of the light / Donna Gillespie.—Berkley trade pbk.ed.
    p. cm
  ISBN 0-425-21268-8
  1. Germany—History—To 843—Fiction.   2. Rome—History—Nero, 54–68—Fiction.
3. Women soldiers—Fiction.   I. Title.

PS3557.I37915L33 2006
813'.54—dc22

                                                                              2006048443

PRINTED IN THE UNITED STATES OF AMERICA

10 9 8 7 6 5 4 3 2 1

Acknowledgments

I'd like to give a heartfelt thanks to dear friends who sustained me while I was working on this book—Phyllis Holliday, Julie Whelly, Susan Winslow, Lynn Allen, John Mouw, Eileen Malone, and Janell Moon.

And I owe so much to the insightful comments and suggestions of the members of my writing group as they read through many drafts—Victoria Micu, Karen Caronna, Gene Corning, Ed Gordon, Cliff Young, Leslie Chalmers, Peter Garabedian, Lorrie Blake, and Susan Edmiston. (And to Bart, the writing group's dog. He knows what he did.)

I also want to warmly thank Manfred Ohl, for revitalizing a languishing Muse and convincing me to turn *The Light Bearer* into a trilogy. Here it is at last, Book Two. Just one more to go. Thanks to you.

And I'm profoundly indebted to my editor, Susan Allison, for believing in this book, and to my agent Robert Stricker, for all his efforts to bring this book into the world.

And many, many thanks to two creative and generous Web designers: Barbara Ling and Judy Wilson.

And, as ever, with boundless gratitude to my writing teacher, Leonard Bishop, who first sold me on the crazy idea that I could write a novel.

LADY *of*
the LIGHT

The Roman Province of Germania Superior
104 CE
A Letter to the Emperor

To the August and Beneficent Trajan, Emperor of the Romans, noblest of princes, conqueror of Dacia and, for the fifth time, Consul, into whose divine hands the immortal gods have put our nation,

From your devoted servant Valerius Maximus, Governor at the Fortress of Mogontiacum, Germania Superior,

I am troubled to report that the martial ardor of the Chattian tribe, lately humbled in war, is in these days being rekindled. Though reduced to direst penury, the tribe has amassed a formidable hoard of longswords, said to be secreted into a cave in the West Forest sector of their lands. I am reminded that the historians of war have cautioned us that the barbarian's memory is short when it comes to recalling defeats by Roman might.

To learn who is supplying these longswords I ordered the seizure of ten natives of the region, taking care that the interrogators questioned them separately. One died under the questioning and gave us nothing, but nine gave us matching tales.

There is a benefactor of the Chattian tribe, likely a person of tribal birth who dwells on imperial lands. That none gave us his name even under expert interrogation proves to me they do not know it. This source sends silver coin of an older type, minted in the reign of Nero, before the devaluation, into the hands of hostile Chattian chieftains, who then purchase swords of native Ubian manufacture. The insolent disregard these German savages show of your wise law forbidding them to possess weapons of iron is exceeded only by their cunning, for the swords are transported beyond our imperial border in sacred carts dedicated to their Grain Goddess, which natural piety would render anyone reluctant to search. As all confirm the coin makes but a short day's journey on the rivers, it is likely the malefactor we seek flourishes in the very environs of my own Fortress, not far from the confluence of the rivers Rhenus and Mosella.

His name remains an urgent mystery.

I have commanded the search of all wine-merchants' vessels, for this is the means by which this coin-for-arms is ferried north. And I have let it be popularly known in the province that a sum of one million sesterces will be awarded any freeborn Roman citizen who gives us intelligence that enables us to find and seize this unknown benefactor of the Chattian tribe. That same sum and the citizenship will be given should the person be of native birth; five hundred thousand and his freedom, should the informant be a slave. I pray you think fit to give me your opinion on these actions, as I would have every deed of mine receive the sanction of your divine authority.

On this day we prepare to celebrate the anniversary of your Ascension, through which you did preserve the Empire and the whole of the human race.

Chapter 1

The Province of Germania Superior
105 CE, the Kalends of Aprilis

This was the borderland between worlds. Darkness ebbed up the ravines, and the river Mosella softly sought the wide Rhenus, as it had for aeons. The Mosella held fast to the last light of day, which transformed its sinuous length into a silvered mirror, fathomless as the sky. Flocks of elegant swan-attendants lifted off it like a mist, veiling this serpentine crack between the worlds. The Mosella was loved by those who lived off her, for the river's spirits were said to be generous and mild. As merchant vessels began to light their lamps, a constellation of ruddy stars formed on the river. Along much of the Mosella's serene length, stately villas were mirrored in its stillness, and Roman towns stood as stern guardians of the banks. But in this place was but a towpath edged with meadowsweet grasses, a yew grove, a dusky sky. A day's journey north would take a traveller to the *Limes*, or limits of Empire—the imperial frontier—where an intermittent wall of Roman forts formed a breakwater preserving the still, deep waters of civilization. Beyond that lay world's end, home of the Chattian tribe, a place of no roads, where ancestors' names were not written but sung.

A Chattian woman rode a lean black mare at a steady canter along the beaten towpath that followed the Mosella. She carried a short ashwood spear, the common weapon of her tribe. Medallions of Minerva glinted on her horse's harness—the emblem of the vast Roman estate over which she was mistress. The hood of her cloak had been whipped off by the wind, revealing hair of dark bronze gathered into a single heavy braid at the nape of her neck. Her eyes were steady and gray; in them, the passion of a holy woman mingled with the calm authority of a war-leader, and the sorrows of more than one life. A historian chronicling her life in peace and in war might have filled ten bookrolls. A revered Chattian seeress had foretold she was to be "a thorn in the paw of the Great Wolf"—her people's name for Rome. A Roman nobleman once said of her, "Witness the humor of Providence, imprisoning the soul of a philosopher in a native woman of the northern wastes." A master trainer at a gladiatorial school in Rome had proclaimed of her skill with a sword, "If a cat had human genius it would fight as she fights." An emperor once complained he'd seen twenty-year army veterans with fewer scars. She was called Aurinia by the Romans, Daughter of the Ash by the native hosts she once led in battle, and in her birth village, Auriane.

Close behind her rode her half-grown daughter Avenahar, clad in a short cape fashioned of the skin of a hart she'd hunted herself. Avenahar's gently rounded face was a close copy of her mother's, but fallen under a shadow: Her black-brown eyes, when roused to wrath, turned to hot puddled ink. Her hair, smoothed back into a single, disheveled braid, was the glossy black of wood burnt to a sheen; against it, her brow was pale as the river swans. Auriane's first daughter was a righter of wrongs, a seeker after injustices who often found them. The face she showed the world was brash and unafraid, but as she rode she moved in time with her mother, as a dancer follows music. On this eve, Avenahar was as exhilarated as a maid at a first midsummer festival—never before had her mother taken her on these mysterious night journeys to the shrine.

Both were born in the deep forest; both lived now in a sumptuous riverside villa—the richest and most majestic in all the Roman province of Germania Superior. They were half a family—the native half; at home was Auriane's younger daughter, Arria Juliana, her Roman child, born of her union with the aristocratic Marcus Arrius Julianus, the celebrated statesman who had served as advisor to four Emperors, and planned the assassination of one.

Auriane halted her mare at a way mark of heaped river stones. She was still as a listening elk, straining every sense to determine that no one was about. Were she discovered, this time, there were two lives to be lost—one more treasured than her own.

Nothing but windy silence.

She tied a strip of blue cloth round a low branch of an alder, a signal readily visible to an alert rower on the river. Then she guided her mount onto a nearly overgrown path leading into an old stand of yew trees. There before them loomed a modest marble monument, startling and wan, as though some ghost materialized in their path. Its peaked temple-roof framed three women modeled in high relief, seated in a stately row. This was a shrine dedicated to the Mothers, benign ancestral spirits beloved of all the tribes of Germania. On the offering stone before the lonely monument's base were scattered traces of barley, butter, and cheese. Each Mother cradled a loaf of bread. They looked out on the world with profound patience, their mild countenances opening the mind to dreams of a paradise of bounty and increase under a regal mother's gentle rule. They were women and gods.

Auriane dropped from her mount and placed her spear before the shrine, feeling coated in the warmth shed from the amiable trio of mothers, drawn up into a life larger than her own. The blood that coursed through the Mothers, once mortals with milk-giving breasts, now flowed through her and into her daughter Avenahar. She placed a tied bundle of vervain on the offering stone, and lit it.

The flame perished at once, as if the wind formed a fist and stamped it out.

"The Mothers don't want us here," Avenahar said, more effervescent curiosity in her voice than true concern.

"Nor do our enemies," Auriane said, smiling. "Shall we heed their gods or ours?" Ignoring a sudden prickly sense of disquiet, Auriane began unbuckling the strap that secured two great leather sacks slung across her horse's withers. "Avenahar," she said, holding fast to her daughter's gaze. "I hope you've grown steady enough to hear what I'm about to tell you. You'll be a woman soon and you'll be making your own offerings at our shrines. It's time—" One ponderous sack unexpectedly slipped free of Auriane's grip; its mouth gaped open as it struck the ground. Avenahar saw its contents—dully gleaming silver coins.

The blank startlement in Avenahar's face sharpened gradually into understanding. Her eyes became effulgent with awe. She might have stepped through a portal into some magic mountain full of light.

"By all the nether gods," Avenahar whispered. "*You* are the one—"

"Yes," Auriane said, "I fear it's so."

"—the one everyone's been hunting," Avenahar said. ". . . You—my own mother." Avenahar began to shiver, overfull with a foaming brew of feeling that was one part alarm, nine parts wild joy tamped down.

"I'm surprised it surprises you so," Auriane said with a try at nonchalance. She let the second cumbersome pouch slide to the earth.

"Well, it doesn't, really. But . . . I thought you'd pulled a silk curtain over the horrors committed against our people . . ." Distress overtook Avenahar's face; she feared she'd gravely misstepped. "I mean, I'd always thought it wasn't like you to sit by and do nothing, and . . . I'm gladdened to see I was right! But are you not greatly afraid? The charge against you is the worst they've got, 'enemy of the state . . . '"

Auriane moved close to her daughter's side. "I never stop being afraid," she said then. "But my greatest fear is for my mother." Avenahar knew Auriane referred to the ruthless tribe of invaders overrunning their Chattian people from the north, who pressed ever nearer the village of Auriane's birth, where her aged mother, Athelinda, lived on in her family's hall. Because of Rome's law prohibiting the still-simmering Chattians from possessing weapons of iron, her people were ill-able to defend themselves from these northern marauders. "With that cruel ban, Rome left us like a declawed cat. Sometimes a wrong is perpetrated. And no one acts. Then *we* must. This is how we live, Avenahar. We aren't separate from our kin. It's a law that was old when Rome was a mud hut on a hill."

"Gods, you've escaped detection by Governor, Emperor, and all their spies for . . . how long?"

"Seven years."

"Even Father is hunting you and doesn't know it. This goes to . . . to the top of the world."

"Avenahar, you don't need to stay. Go now, if you wish. And know I love you still."

"Pig feathers. Stand aside so I can get down from this beast and help you."

As Avenahar leaned forward to dismount, a flight of storks flared up behind the shrine, upsailing bodies all speeding grace. They were sentences written across the sky. Auriane studied their outstretched necks, their deeply beating wings, the pattern of their bodies opening out against the dusk like some unfurling fisherman's net.

They flew against their direction of migration. That was ill-omened enough. But Auriane stiffened in disbelief as their formation took the shape of the runic letter her people called *hagalaz*. It warned of a shattering of worlds, the swift destruction of all that is settled and known.

"Avenahar," she said darkly, "stay on your horse. Something evil's about. And it's close."

Sharp disappointment showed in Avenahar's face, as if at an unforgivable betrayal. It caused Auriane to feel she'd failed her daughter in every way it was possible for a mother to fail her offspring.

"I *mean* it, Avenahar. Stop twitching like a tethered hound. Stay ready to gallop home. I'll just finish what I'm about; too many lives depend on this coin—then we'll be off."

Auriane dragged the first of the unwieldy sacks behind the shrine. The sense of knowing oneself as prey is subtle; the moon's eye raises an invisible brow, alert, interested, hungry for a soul. She counted herself that dire omen's cause: For seven years she'd lain in a foreign enemy's bed. By the unbreakable law of the Fates, she'd always known she would one day be called to account.

As she struggled with the second sack, she heard Avenahar splash down to the muddy ground. Auriane gave a small smile and shrug of resignation. *One time out of nine, she does as I say. The fault's mine for trying to instill a natural devotion into her rather than a Roman readiness to obey.*

Avenahar threw her coltish energy into the effort, crow-black hair falling across her face as she leaned against the sack's deadweight. When both pouches were behind the shrine, Auriane pulled aside a flat stone that concealed a hollowed-out place in the earth.

Together, they pushed the sacks into the shallow pit. The money was Marcus Arrius Julianus's, from the proceeds of an estate he'd entrusted to Auriane. *For long, I've taken his wealth and broken his law with it—he who has only been relentlessly kind,* came Auriane's well-worn, shame-ridden thought as she pushed the stone back in place. *But my own mother waits for slaughter while Cheruscan bandit packs overrun our Chattian forests.*

Auriane inclined her head, signaling for Avenahar to do the same.

"Hear me, Old Ones," Auriane intoned, "good givers of all . . . I call on you to watch and ward. Take these coins and speed them on their way—" *I've become a double creature,* Auriane thought, aware of the fineness of Avenahar's hair as a thick ribbon of it loosened from her braid and blew across her face, the vulnerable line of her daughter's throat, and the way fragility and strength were blended in her growing limbs. Auriane reflected on the myriad horrors that could take her child—*any* child—in an instant. *One eggshell life. Would I thrive for a day without her? She's air and sustenance, red mead and nurturing fire. I could go mad.*

". . . and let no foreign eyes fall on this silver," Auriane spoke on, "so it can shield my people from the devastation that comes."

Both mares were in constant motion, jingling their bits. Auriane would have been alarmed by their behavior in any place but this; a grove thick with spirits was likely to cause horses to caper and dance. She kneeled above the pit—this small grave cradling hope of life—and chanted the name of the runic sign that granted protection: *"Algiz . . . algiz . . ."* flattening the sylla-bles into a bone-vibrating hum. As she traced its holy bird-foot shape in the air, her fingers left a trail of living silver in the shape of the rune—whether visible to others or only to her own eyes, she could not have said.

From jarringly near came the crack of stone on stone.

Auriane whipped about to face four men walking in a file, thrashing their way through the hawthorn bushes. All four stopped in place, as surprised to see her as she was to see them, eyes showing white, like frightened horses. A reek drifted from them—of old sweat, bilge water, and fish-stink. Their grimy tunics were tucked up into their belts for flight; they were plastered with mud to their knees. Their hair was cropped close, in the common style of sailors of the imperial fleet.

Auriane saw alarm melt from the eyes of the man who led them, to be replaced by avarice as he recognized a fine opportunity—had he truly come upon two women left foolishly unguarded, wandering about at darkfall? It seemed just enough good fortune to make a man suspicious of ambush.

And wasn't the woman burying something?

Deserters from the navy, Auriane realized. Their base camp was on the river Rhenus. Naval service wasn't counted as glorious as service in the le-gions, and it was commonly claimed Rome inducted robbers and cutthroats to fill out the ranks.

Auriane silently cursed. Her spear lay in front of the shrine, just out of reach. "Get on your horse and *go!*" she commanded Avenahar in their Ger-manic tongue.

"Look, lads, two healthy, strong women!" spat out the man who seemed in authority over them; he had the bare beginnings of a muzzle, and his black beard was just starting to bristle from too many days without a razor.

Auriane was relieved to hear Avenahar's mare clattering off down the towpath, back toward Marcus Julianus's villa, and home. But before the beast vanished in the night, Auriane just managed to see that the mare's gal-lop was loose and erratic, and the reins were flapping free.

Avenahar was not astride the horse.

Auriane fought down the helpless anger she felt. *Of course she won't leave me. She's in the grip of mythic tales. I raised not a girl but a wolf cub. Avenahar has her own fate. But that's an agony to know.*

"This one's of middle years," the sailor said to his fellows, waving dismissively at Auriane, "but she looks hardly used—let's enjoy her here and get rid of her. That tender Niobe, there—*boni amici,* we could get five thousand for her on the block at Treverorum!" Like many in the imperial fleet he was of Syrian birth and his Latin was corrupted by a curious lilt. Auriane didn't understand all at once, so the horror of it stole over her slowly.

"Leave this place or live ever under my curse." Auriane's voice surprised them; it was soft and low but it would carry across a field.

"If you'd curse us," spoke up the slit-eyed brute lumbering up behind the Syrian, his arms as thickly muscled as the men who loaded amphorae onto merchant ships, "you'll have to take your place behind our captain, the whole of the cursed navy, and that stinking river that just tried to swallow us whole."

As he spoke, the bristly-bearded Syrian gestured covertly to his fellows— a signal to fan out and surround the women. Then he unsheathed a short sword, as casually as some bored, cynical priest of Juno raising the mallet to sacrifice the day's tenth lamb.

A sword. All at once Auriane realized her life might end in this place.

She wrestled off her cloak and threw it to the ground, to free her limbs for battle. The improbability of the moment made her feel starkly remote from day-to-day existence; she felt as if she were a masked actor in a drama played out on a stage. Seven years of settled life vanished like a backdrop whisked away between scenes.

All four felt deep surprise at the sight of the tall, sturdily built woman who stood before them, her eyes gently ignited with excitement—as if battle were a song she longed to hear again. Her hair was pulled sleekly back from a high forehead, and she was clad in native male attire—long, belted tunic, leather riding breeches. She was a jarring sight for city-born eyes, for nothing decorative adorned her body, nor was there anything womanly in her manner: Here was grace serving ferocity, beauty married to strength—a marriage faintly appalling to their eyes.

Auriane ebbed backward, moving with the infinite care of a thief easing a hand toward a silk purse, her purpose to retrieve her spear.

But the Syrian moved with her.

As she edged farther from the burial pit, one of their number, a squat creature with straw-colored hair like a dirty horsehair brush, ambled toward it and heaved aside the stone. This man's morose eyes revealed a nature somewhat more reflective than that of his fellows. He dumped the sacks' glittering contents onto the ground and began fondling the silver. "Minerva's eyes!" he exclaimed softly. "What fine old coins!"

"Leave it, Lurio." The Syrian's words came out as a gravelly, monosyllabic grunt. He never took his gaze from Auriane as he slowly crab-stepped around her, body bent forward like a race rider, sword angled toward her throat.

Auriane had no leisure to become alarmed by any conclusions the inquisitive one might be drawing, for the fourth man—she saw only shoulders broad enough to take an ox-yoke—planted himself behind her, blocking her path to her spear. Three of them were ringed about her in a circle that was closed by the shrine. She was trapped.

The one called Lurio ignored them, continuing to examine the coins.

"—not those tinny *new* coins the navy robs us by paying us with; this is fine old silver, solid through and through . . ."

Lurio then regarded Auriane, eyes alive with questions. He had *seen* her somewhere. All at once he remembered: The most wealthy aristocrat of the district, the noble Marcus Arrius Julianus, had gifted the Roman river-town of Confluentes with a theater; Lurio had been in the press of people in the town forum on the day of its dedication. And this woman had been standing beside Marcus Julianus during the ceremony. This was that Chattian savage who'd once warred like a man alongside her rude countrymen, now barely civilized into Julianus's wife, a woman of vast resources—which made it powerfully intriguing she would be creeping out alone at darkfall, burying coins . . . old coins, at that, the sort trusted best by savage northern chiefs. . . .

In his excitement Lurio shivered like a man struck with ague.

The Syrian feinted at Auriane; she flashed aside so smoothly, his eyes widened in startlement.

Behind her, Auriane heard a low whistle. She whipped about to see Avenahar standing ready to cast her the spear.

Good sense had prevailed over Avenahar's first impulse, which was to fall upon them herself in a Wodanic fury; she was wise enough to know she must yield the weapon to her mother. The man planted between them spun about, intending to wrestle the spear from her. But Avenahar was too quick for him; she threw it expertly to Auriane, who, for a lightning-swift instant, regarded her daughter with amazement and love.

Auriane jumped to meet it, and caught it easily in mid-shaft.

Then Auriane swung round to face the Syrian's drawn sword; ghostlight cast by stars slid down the long blade. At the same time, the sailor behind her kicked Avenahar to the ground and began trussing the maid's legs with sail line. This didn't hold her very well, so he sat on her while she thrashed and bucked. The others greeted this with rapid-fire jests in a tapestry of tongues: bright threads of Syriac wound round Germanic dialect punctuated with cheerful obscenities in frontier Latin.

"Fine work, Brico," Auriane called to Avenahar. "For that you've escaped a whipping."

Avenahar was bewildered at first, then realized her mother's intention—*She wants them to think I'm a slave, not her daughter*. Otherwise, the men might hold a blade to Avenahar's throat and demand her mother's compliance.

Auriane felt heart and breath flow into the spear; she was a creature advancing with a retracted claw, a fierce beast poised to protect. While keenly attuned to the Syrian's slightest lapse of attention, she began moving almost imperceptibly into his undefended left side. A direct blow from the Syrian's blade could snap her ashwood spear like a reed.

The Syrian laughed brutishly, dismissively, to conceal his annoyance—he had expected two cringing victims. Instead, he faced a quick-thinking slave girl and a woman who wielded a spear with the seamless ease of a skilled beast-fighter in the arena.

"Put it down, woman." The Syrian's words were angry punches in the air. "I've got steel, you've got wood. There's only one way this can end. So someone's taught you how to hold a spear—it's given you a fool's confidence. You can rot in a ditch where no kin will find you for the pyre, or you can let us have our way."

He executed a diagonal cut that Auriane knew well; it was the first in order of a set all legionary soldiers were taught. He would have been dismayed to know how much he revealed to her by this single, undistinguished display of swordsmanship: The weight of the sword was wrong for him. He didn't know his striking distance. He signaled every move with his eyes before he made it.

Auriane whipped her spear away with what seemed to him more-than-human speed.

"Wretched woman!"

"Farnaces—" The one called Lurio had crept up behind the Syrian. "Don't kill her."

"Shut your mouth or I string you up with sail line."

"Do you know who this is? *She is gold.*"

Curses on all life, Auriane thought. *It was too much to hope that none of them would recognize me.*

"You'll be able to buy a riverside villa with four hundred slaves. That's the woman of the wealthiest man in the province, Marcus Arrius Julianus, who—"

"No time for ransom, we can't tarry here," the Syrian spat out between heaving breaths. "She dies and we take the maid. Give me some aid—you're useless as pot scrapings!" He lunged at Auriane, executing a melodramatic downstroke that, to his amazement, missed her completely and left him looking faintly ridiculous, like some eager Cilician pirate ripping open a lady's bedcurtain from ceiling to floor.

Then he put his whole body into a low horizontal cut. He felt he was striking at smoke.

"Listen, Farnaces, it's not ransom I speak of," Lurio persisted, "but something far grander."

The black-bearded Syrian continued to ignore him.

"You bark after one scrap of meat," Lurio scolded him in a fury, "while just beyond, a sheepfold awaits. For once during your miserable span, harken to a man of wit!"

The Syrian spat at Lurio. His attention shifted from Auriane for but an instant—but it was enough to prove his undoing.

To those who witnessed, it seemed only that she leapt a small distance off the ground and subtly writhed, once, in air—to land light as a lynx, body inclined forward, one knee bent, her movements rapid, fluid, sure as a dancer at a fire festival. Somehow this eyebat-swift maneuver produced two results: She struck the Syrian's sword from his hand with such force it fractured a metacarpal bone. With near simultaneity her spear shot out, its trajectory brutal and short; the fire-hardened point sank deep into the hollow below his shoulder—a place she sought deliberately, her purpose to wound, not to kill. The Syrian had no notion what had happened; he might have been caught by the lashing tail of a dragon. He knew only that his sword was airborne. It plopped in the mud at the feet of the man built thick as an oak stump, who eagerly snatched it up.

In the stunned silence, Avenahar was softly laughing. The man astride her struck her across the face.

"*Maid and Medusa!*" the Syrian cried out as he sank to the mud. Auriane was already straddling him, wrenching her spear free. He lay there gasping like a hooked fish, clutching his freely bleeding shoulder.

Her new opponent faced her with thick legs planted stoutly apart, commanding the space between them like some restless bull. One side of his face was soot-blackened; as he grinned he seemed to wear a stage mask divided into comic and demonic halves. In his eyes was the crackling fire of a madman. He slashed at her with amateurish enthusiasm; he wasn't the swordsman the Syrian was, and Lurio could see the woman knew it.

"Don't fight her, we need only tell the magistrate her name," Lurio shouted as this man executed a flurry of clumsy crosscuts. "You know of the arms-smuggling case that's thwarted every council from this pesthole of a province to the Palace in Rome? You're looking on the woman that's behind it! The bounty's been doubled. It'll keep us for years."

The words struck Auriane a blow that numbed every sense; all became dream-bright and void of meaning, as if she'd heard the pronouncement of a sentence of death. Only long years of training in the art of the sword enabled her to return her whole mind to the man before her.

"We're hunted men—who'd give an ear to our tale?" his sword-wielding confederate called over his shoulder as he sought unsuccessfully to back Auriane against the shrine.

"To Hades with all of you, then." With that, Lurio gave up the effort, and, working more nimbly than seemed possible for his squat, short-limbed frame, began gathering up as many coins as he could. When his bulging leather pouch began to protest and spit them out, he stuffed them into his boots, the leather sheath of his fire-steel, a loose fold of his tunic. The Syrian, fearful he would lose his part of the take, hurried to join in, pressing the cloth of his tunic to his wound while using one hand like a paddle to scoop up coins. Then both turned and fled in opposite directions into the night, Lurio crashing crazily through the hawthorn bushes, the Syrian moving with a shambling gait, making a strange music as each step shifted hundreds of coins.

As Auriane hesitated but an instant, considering bringing down Lurio with her spear, murdering the fugitive sailor for what he knew—and deciding she couldn't—Lurio's sword-wielding comrade seized his moment. He lunged at Auriane, sword aloft in those stevedore's arms for a single, prodigious blow to the head.

"Mother, turn round!" The shriek was Avenahar's, primal and blind.

The swordsman staggered to a stop. They'd been tricked; the maid was no slave.

Never taking his gaze from Auriane, the sailor with the soot-blackened face backed slowly toward Avenahar. He pushed his fellow sailor off the struggling maid and sat on Avenahar himself, putting a thick, scarred arm around her neck and pressing the keen edge of the blade to her throat.

"Drop that spear and come along with us for ransom," he said, spitting through broken brown teeth, "or your comely brat has seen the last of this world."

Had Auriane paused for even an instant, he might have had a chance to make good his threat. Her spear arm lashed out; her body was a whip. The throw was level and merciless as an executioner's. The two men saw only the spear, ripping forth like a bolt from a catapult. It caught the sword-wielding sailor full in his chest, hurling him into the arms of his comrade. He convulsed for a short time as if his ghost struggled out of him in fits and starts, then sank in death. It was done with such precision and ease that the remaining sailor, finding himself with a corpse in his lap, wondered if this night-roaming woman might be no mortal at all but some evil-doing Nixe who wriggled her way here from the glimmering, sprite-ridden depths of the Rhenus. Eyes rounded with spirit-terror, he lurched to his feet and burst into a run, fleeing in the direction of the river.

Auriane and Avenahar were alone with the dead man. The sudden silence was jarring. Auriane heard only her own breath, grabbing for air and life.

Scattered silver coins winked in the starlight like bright drops of blood. Auriane cut the sail line that bound her daughter, slowed by her trembling hands. Then she embraced Avenahar with a gentle ferocity, letting the heat of their bodies bring them back to the living. The need to ward off the cold horror of the night fused them together for long moments. Bewilderment pooled in Avenahar's eyes. Bruises covered her in angry blots; she was muted, indrawn, a candle burning low. Auriane supposed her daughter's giddy dreams of glory bore as much resemblance to this first encounter with battle as a ride through rose-strewn streets in a triumphal chariot might to a romp through the town's sewer.

"Your fate is strong, Avenahar," Auriane said firmly. "Had you obeyed me when I told you to flee off, I'd be greeting the ancestresses right now."

The praise worked as a quick balm, restoring Avenahar to reckless life. "I would never have left you," she said hoarsely. "You spoke the words before—'We help our kin. This is how we live.'"

Auriane affectionately ruffled Avenahar's mud-clotted hair.

Mother and daughter rose together and, each taking a leg, dragged the dead sailor off the path.

"I guess I've outdone you, then," Avenahar said, eyes shining now.

"And how is that?"

"I've lived but thirteen years and I helped you win a victory. You were a decrepit sixteen when you slew your first man."

Auriane smiled wearily at this, while biting back the words she wanted to say—*Do not speak so even in jest, I'll never let you take the oath of a shield maiden—you'll go back to our people as an herb woman or I'll not let you go at all.* "Just tie his laces together, quickly, and we're off from here." This was a custom of her people that prevented the man's ghost from walking among the living.

Auriane turned to wash her native spear in ditchwater. Avenahar caught at her cloak, eyes shining like lamps.

"You slew a man tonight," she whispered. "The Fates have made you a warrior again."

Auriane knelt beside her. "I did only what I had to do, no more. Avenahar, what passed on this night was a catastrophe. That Lurio creature. He *knows.*"

"Let them all know! It's time we warred in the open."

"You disappoint me. I need a steady companion now, not a rampaging hothead. If I cannot find some way to keep this Lurio silent, people will die. And our life at the villa will be—" Her throat tightened painfully. "Start gathering up coins. I'll not leave them scattered about so those rogues can come back and enrich themselves more."

Auriane rose and, in a rapid monotone, spoke the words of a charm over the corpse. She felt like a shattered glass vessel.

My peace is gone . . . a peace I nurtured for seven years. Lost in less time than it takes to plow one row of a barley field.

A chastened Avenahar seemed to hear these thoughts. "That Lurio was a fugitive," she offered. "He'll never dare to show himself before a magistrate."

"Don't be a fool, there are many ways it could be done. Through a second man, for example."

Auriane reached, then, for the sailor's short sword, but her hand stopped as if caught in an invisible net. Because of a vow to a seeress, she hadn't touched a sword of iron in the seven years she'd lived at Julianus's villa. It beckoned, its blade liquid in the starlight. How she lusted to feel the weight, the grip. . . . The sword had been her lyre-string, her voice. But that seeress was the most fearsome and adept in all their lands, and might even be watching them now, through the eye of a swan, a lightflash on the river. She was called Ramis, and her oracles were sought even in Rome.

"Avenahar? The sword—take it and throw it in the river."

Avenahar did not move. She regarded the sword with quiet solemnity, as if it were some door accidentally left open that would take her to a place she was born to be. The haunted determination in her face startled Auriane; it brought to mind maids of old tales who climbed walls or swam rivers at midnight to breach enemy lines in time of war. "No, you may not keep it," Auriane said. "Now, Avenahar. At once!"

Auriane regretted the harshness in her tone when she saw her daughter carefully disguising a limp as she bore the sword off.

Auriane listened until she heard a splash. Then she waded through long grasses to catch her mare, grazing briskly by the river. Before they departed the place, she removed the blue cloth she'd tied round the low branch of the alder, replacing it with one dyed madder-red. This signed to her confederate, a Chattian slave called Grimo who rowed a wine boat, that something had gone gravely awry and he must not venture close; their enemies might well lay a trap for him here.

Somewhere near the river, geese broke out in wild, harsh song, and Auriane started, thinking it the bleat of battle horns.

I've lived through a time of tranquillity that's lasted longer than some lives. Why shouldn't it now be wrested from me violently?

I go home to a different world. One in which I'm naked before a foreign country's law.

Lurio. He will pull down the center-beam of my house.

Chapter 2

Auriane believed the night's misfortunes done. But the Fates' final jest was still to come.

Auriane and Avenahar had less than a mile left to journey before they came to the thorn hedges that ribboned about the main residence and outbuildings of the estate of Marcus Arrius Julianus. The grand villa lay just outside the walled Roman town of Confluentes, close by where the Mosella finished her wanderings and poured into the Rhenus. They trod the paved post road now. Auriane walked; Avenahar sat astride their remaining horse, for she'd sprained her foot while attempting to kick the fugitive sailor senseless. Their hands were stiff from cold; Auriane's leather leggings were studded with brambles. Darkness yielded to a world etched in deep charcoal. Cocks were crowing. The modest fields of the great estate's tenant farmers, necklaced with stone walls, unveiled themselves on either side of the road.

Two hundred paces ahead, something cumbersome and formless swayed gently in elephantine fashion as it separated from the smoking ground mist, a dark living thing that seemed to hover just above the road. For long, its only movement was a strange bellows-like contraction and expansion; it was faintly monstrous, as if the Wyrm that wrapped its serpent-body round the world wove its way inland to haunt men. Perplexed, Auriane studied the apparition through the predawn haze until it resolved itself into a densely packed, slow-moving mass of men and animals.

"That's a hunting expedition," Auriane said. This was a common enough sight; because the well-loved Emperor Trajan enthusiastically pursued the hunt, every man of the province with any ambition to rise felt compelled to conspicuously pursue the sport. "Curses on Nemesis," she added softly. "That's the livery of Volusius Victorinus."

This was the more powerful of the two Roman magistrates at Confluentes. Victorinus was a small-town potentate who had buffed his importance by gifting the provincial town with its gymnasium, its baths, and a new courthouse, supplying each with a heroic statue of himself, sometimes alone, sometimes standing beside his grim-faced wife, Decimina. Relations between Victorinus and the aristocratic Julianus were fraught with distrust. When Julianus quite innocently built Confluentes's theater, not knowing Victorinus had already engaged an *architecturus* to draw plans for a theater of his own, Victorinus saw it as a heinous attempt to supplant him as the "great man" of the district. And within a season, that new theater had mysteriously burned down.

"His outriders have seen us, it's no use turning about. Pull your hood forward. With a scrap of luck he'll pass us by." If Lurio did spill his tale into willing administrative ears, their presence on this road, at this hour, would corroborate the fugitive sailor's story.

"Hunting, is he?" Avenahar muttered. "His slaves will trap the beasts, while our Hercules reclines on down cushions and sloshes down chilled wine while he writes silly poetry on the *subject* of the hunt."

Auriane smiled in amusement, but the gloomy fury behind those words caused her a crawl of uneasiness.

As the train of wagons drew near, the liveried horseman in the lead casually snapped a whip, ordering the women off the the road, blandly assuming that when Victorinus traveled, the road belonged to Victorinus.

"Puffed-up provincial princeling."

"Avenahar—"

"Should it surprise us that a people who've refined cruelty beyond all the known races of the earth should also be the rudest and the laziest?"

"Avenahar!"

"If Nemesis sends him a snorting maddened aurochs on this hunt, I'll dedicate my life to Her worship."

"Avenahar!" Auriane drew the mare to a halt and forced her daughter to meet her gaze. "You will be *quiet* until we're past them. Conserve that spirit of vengeance—you're given only so much of it in a lifetime. Don't waste it on swatting flies."

Avenahar mumbled something that sounded compliant. Auriane pulled the mare down into the muddy field.

Provisions wagons began noisily clattering past; Auriane's quick glance caught jars of pickled delicacies, heart-shaped jugs of pedigreed wines, thick-footed vessels for the finest fish sauce from Hispania. Apparently the magistrate meant not to let a day pass without tickling every culinary whim. Next came a wagon laden with coarser fare for the slaves, followed by four oxcarts bearing heaps of hunting nets, stacks of long spears, and boar spears. The tall Libyan slaves who walked alongside were the skilled hunters who would do the dangerous work of beating the game into nets. Finally came an un-adorned litter bearing a freedman secretary, who would manage Victorinus's correspondence during the hunt. And behind this came Victorinus himself, his litter hoisted high on the shoulders of eight blue-and-gold-liveried Cappadocian bearers. Auriane's contempt matched Avenahar's—what sort of man will not sit a horse, even at a hunt?

That litter would have been laughably gaudy in Rome, but out here with only stunned provincials to take note, she supposed a man could get away with such gilded excess without finding himself ridiculed in vicious couplets scribbled over the town walls.

In twenty heartbeats they were past him.

An owl gusted up from the meadow, soundless as a moth. It swept past the mare's muzzle, giving out its somber cry.

The mare erupted into a series of frog-jumps, rippling sideways, ripping the reins from Auriane's hands. Avenahar lost her knee-grip and hung precariously from the horse's side. The mare crashed into a wagon; a collection of boar spears spilled over the side with a low thunder. The cart's driver cursed and pulled his mules to an abrupt halt, which proved too much for the mules behind—mules and wagons collided. All of Victorinus's Celt hounds started to bark.

"Ho there! Has the world ended?" Victorinus's voice boomed out into the country air—the footfalls of a testy giant. A hand that flashed green fire emerged from fringed curtains of citron-hued silk—an emerald large as a pea adorned the magistrate's ring. With several cutting gestures, he signaled a general halt.

"Have the Titans rained boulders down upon us?" A head was thrust through the curtains—the women saw pale, mottled flesh, smoothly bald but for a scraggly wreath of roan-colored hair. The magistrate was severely shortsighted, and as he turned his head aimlessly from side to side, looking for the cause of the trouble, it put Auriane in mind of the blind, questing head of a worm. A cloud of Oriental scent—sweet, acrid, debilitating—gusted out with him; to Auriane, it was the smell of lethargy. She'd never become accustomed to the fact that these people mixed flower essences with oils, called it *perfume,* and peddled it for indecent amounts of money, ignoring the fact the oils quickly became sour.

He settled his bleary focus on Avenahar. "Calamitous wench. Collect up the mess you caused or be packed off in chains to await your trial."

Auriane gave her daughter a sharp nudge and Avenahar dropped to one knee, gathering up boar spears. Auriane could only guess at what thoughts passed through her daughter's mind; surely they involved Victorinus's feet roasting over a crackling fire.

"Uncover yourself, woman," he said to Auriane. "State your name and farm."

"I'm Auriane, your neighbor to the—"

"Ah!" His manner softened at once. A festering hatred of Marcus Julianus hadn't deterred the magistrate from petitioning tirelessly for a marriage-match between his son, Lucius, and Julianus's nine-year-old daughter, Arria Juliana. Auriane and Julianus would have as soon betrothed their younger daughter to a goat, but planned a diplomatically-phrased refusal. "It's the . . ." He groped for a word that would not offend: *Wife* was not correct; *concubine* too blunt for polite conversation; *beloved of,* too personal—so he abandoned relating her to Marcus Julianus at all. ". . . It's our bold Aurinia, Chattian princess, and her chaste, clever daughter, out ransacking the countryside again." He added amiably to Avenahar, "Leave those, my pretty periwinkle, the slaves will get them."

His eyes brimmed with the marriage question. The hopefulness Auriane saw there disturbed her.

"Volusius Victorinus, do accept my earnest regrets—"

"Come, Avenahar," he said, "I have something for you."

A plague take him, Auriane thought.

"My dear, but that's an odd pattern on your tunica. . . . Here, take this, it's a new volume on the origin of the ancient Libyan breed you admire so much, with the pedigrees of its most celebrated mares. It's penned by my own scribes and specially illustrated."

Avenahar reached for the bookroll as if extending an arm into a bear's cage—leaning close enough for Victorinus to see that her tunica was splattered with mud and blood.

The look of paternal solicitude vanished. "I say, you two are about at an eccentric hour." He looked penetratingly at Auriane. "Where's your second horse? Where are your maidservants and attendants?"

"Save your questions for those brought to your courtroom, magistrate. Our women are not like yours. When we need to, we travel swiftly, and alone."

"Hmm . . . well, you shouldn't be on this road, not without a dozen armed slaves riding alongside you. Just last eve four sailors from the naval trireme *Concordia* murdered their captain and deserted their vessel. They're armed and it's expected they'll be attempting robberies hereabout. Until the local garrison has hunted them all down, you'd best stay safe inside."

Hunted them all down. Auriane managed with effort to maintain a demeanor that was neutral, proud. The fugitives were being actively sought.

Lurio would soon be in their hands.

Victorinus studied the two women for an oddly prolonged moment. Though not counted overly clever by anyone's measure, the magistrate had a boar-hound's senses when it came to discerning attempts to conceal the truth.

"We trust you'll do your duty, magistrate," Auriane said tartly.

"And my answer about the marriage, Aurinia . . ." On that sagging face the eager schoolboy smile looked ridiculous. "It will be soon?"

Your boy will have our Arria in Hades, Auriane wanted to say, but was spared the annoyance of conjuring up a civilized reply because just then, the boy in question, Victorinus's son Lucius, rode up from the back of the train amidst an aggressive hammering of hooves. He was astride a nervous Thracian stallion; its powerfully arched neck was streaked with foam. On its glossy black shoulder was a glistening cut from a whip. The stallion embodied its master's mood; it was as though the same angry genius animated both. Lucius's features at fourteen were a lean, elongated version of his father's, revealing what Victorinus must have looked like before bony prominences became blurred by a comfortable padding of flesh, and empurpled from a lifetime of washing down oily meals with copious quantities of wine.

"What's all this delay, Father?" The boy was like struck flint, sharp-edged, sparking with anger. Lucius gave Avenahar a rancid smile. "I see—it's the holy child, fathered by a god."

Avenahar gave Lucius a look that might have set water to boiling.

But her hands began to shiver. A cruel shot, Auriane thought. To protect Avenahar from the shame surrounding her birth, Auriane hadn't silenced those in their homeland who'd put it about that Avenahar was fathered by the god Wodan. In truth, Avenahar was sired by a Roman slave, a captured legionary soldier who'd labored in the fields of the Chattian farmstead on which Auriane was born.

"Excuse the rough manners of a child," Victorinus amended hurriedly. "He's but a boy with much to learn."

A boy wounded in his pride, Auriane realized, certain then that the lonely, miserable Lucius had somehow intuited, or learned through the talk of household maids, the truth his filmy-eyed father hadn't yet considered— he was not to be given Arria Juliana.

To Auriane, Lucius said, "And if it isn't the war-loving concubine of our own Marcus Julianus."

"Lucius, cease this at once!" came an impotent plea from the father.

"It's tempting to guess at just what the pair of you are doing out here," Lucius spoke on, "as only famous prostitutes and thieves travel this road at night."

"Lucius, beware the Fates," Auriane said, eyes steely, voice low. She gave Avenahar a commanding glance, warning her to silence.

Lucius's voice was a wounded whisper. "You've discarded me already— do you think I do not know?"

"*Lucius!*" Victorinus tried again.

"Arrange a *palla* round the shoulders of a barbarian savage and sit her in a fine villa, and all at once I'm not good enough for her half-breed offspring."

"Lucius, you're not good enough for an ewe in rut," Avenahar broke in.

"Your name's scribbled all over the town's sewer wall," Lucius responded casually. "'Try it with a girl half god.'"

"*You* burned our theater, you envious lout," Avenahar shot back. "Do you think we do not know?"

"Another word, Lucius," Victorinus burst out hotly, "and you'll get more than a whipping!" The magistrate turned to Auriane. "You'd best trim your daughter's slanderous tongue, Aurinia. Rogues from out of town burned down Julianus's theater—my investigations have proved it."

"I'm not afraid of them like you are, Father," Lucius retorted. "Marcus Julianus's day is done. No one of importance cares about philosophy in this age. This is a time for men of valor, not quibblers with a quill who speak against all that's—"

"*Quiet,* every one of you!" Auriane's voice cut cleanly through the rising voices. "Lucius, I do not hear those words. I am sorry for this meeting. Know I bear you two no ill will. Come, Avenahar, we must go."

Victorinus frowned, then turned to his son.

"*Lucius?*" He rolled so far out of the litter that the bearers had to nimbly shift it beneath him to prevent him from tumbling out. "No decision's been made on the matter of that marriage. You spoke as if one *had* been."

"It's true, Victorinus—"

"Avenahar!" came Auriane's vain plea.

"—she'll *never* cross your threshold." Avenahar's words were gleeful slashes of a knife. "I don't know what would cause you to think my mother and father would give our Arria Juliana to such a coarse-bred lout as your son."

Victorinus looked like a man knocked senseless.

"Aurinia? Can this be true?" the magistrate said. "Well, I've been ambushed most cruelly. And here I thought we'd formed a fine family alliance."

"It's true, Victorinus, though I never meant to tell you this way," Auriane replied wearily, striving to keep her voice mild. "Arria's just a child. Among my people we don't give children away in the cradle. And we think it right a girl have some hand in choosing the man she's bound to marry. Don't search for reasons other than this. I am not your enemy, Victorinus."

Lucius seethed like a bubbling pot with the lid bolted down.

"The gods punish hubris, but maybe we won't wait for the gods! Every one of you in that preposterous household had best watch his step. Julianus speaks treason in his lectures at the town academy. He even speaks against Trajan's Great War to come, which will make Alexander's battles look like skirmishes. Know it, you two, Father's written letters to the Secretary in Rome," he sputtered on; this was the Palace official who edited imperial correspondence from the provinces, "in which he's detailed every word of Julianus's infamy, and—"

"*Lucius!*" Victorinus's cheeks were the shade of ripe plums. "The boy lies!"

"I think he tells the truth, Victorinus," Auriane said softly, "but why your surprise that your boy has betrayed you, when you suckled him on poison? I won't seek to harm you over this. It's the custom of my people to choose our opponents only from the strongest."

Auriane was not certain herself what she was doing when she moved to within a hand's breadth of Lucius's powerful, unsettled horse; the boy was amazed that she showed no fear of his stallion. She placed a palm on its muzzle and the agitated animal dropped into stillness, lowering its beautiful head, nuzzling her. Lucius was convinced there was sorcery in that touch.

"You were born on Cybele's day while a mighty storm raged without," she said to the boy. "You never forgave the mother who thought you ugly and frail and didn't want you to live. You never forgot the edge of blackness, so close. It taught you to fear that which you should reverence and sleep when you should be awake. Leave that hall, Lucius, and walk into a greater one. Or you'll be woefully crippled by a mischance of your own making, before this year is done."

Auriane might have thought her words randomly pulled from silence like some madwoman's babble until she saw the deep dread in the boy's eyes, the stupefied look in Victorinus's.

I must have spoken the truth. Gods below, I've no notion how I knew those things.

Father and son regarded her as though she were some force of nature that was not containable, like a river known to regularly flood its banks. Lucius made the "fig" sign at Auriane—thumb projecting from fist—to ward off the evil eye. Then his stallion burst into a choppy gallop that bore him off to the head of the train.

Victorinus finally found his voice. "You'll not like me as an enemy, you necromancing whore."

The magistrate withdrew into the dark of the litter and snapped the curtains closed. Auriane flinched as if he'd slammed a door. Victorinus's train clattered on amidst clouds of dust, torch smoke, and mule stink, until it vanished into the mysteries of the mist.

"Avenahar, your tongue is a menace! You brought us to open declaration of war. Victorinus was already suspicious of why we were abroad at this hour. If that fugitive sailor spills his tale, we're done. At home, a hothead such as you would be counted a curse and driven out of the village!"

Avenahar managed a muted, miserable, "I'm sorry, Mother." Her words held an undertone of relief—at least her mother was speaking to her again. Auriane had walked beside her in silent fury for half the distance between milestones.

"We've made enemies who will remain enemies," Auriane said. "And it was not necessary. Would that you would learn, there are times to fight and times not to fight!"

"I . . . you are right. But that loutish Lucius . . . he provoked me beyond reason."

"A wise woman is never provoked until she so chooses."

"Who *was* my father, then? If I could talk of his noble deeds, I'd have a weapon against such surly oafs."

Auriane felt a sharp stone lodged in her throat.

He was a Roman thrall called Decius, Avenahar, who's now giving battle advice to the chief of the invading Cheruscans, who're overrunning our people and picking our bones . . .

No. To tell her now would be a cruelty.

"Your moon blood comes soon," Auriane said gently, "which means we'll soon be having your womanhood ceremony. When the elderwomen chant your lineage they'll have to name him." *I want you to have more than one mother present when you learn it.*

"Well, he . . . he *was* good and brave, wasn't he?" Avenahar ventured as if reaching into a fire. "He had many war companions . . . and a large hall? That Wodan tale—you didn't concoct it to cover up something terrible?"

Auriane felt a start of queasiness. It seemed that Avenahar, in spite of having hair black as the night sky, hadn't considered the possibility her father might not be Chattian. "He was good and brave when I knew him, Avenahar, and would've given you all he had, had fortune not taken him away. You're too quick to judge men, and quicker still to judge whole nations. Some day, you'll be worthy of knowing your poor father."

They topped a rise. The sun and the estate of Marcus Arrius Julianus revealed themselves together.

Beneath cloud-mountains gold-limned by the sun was a green kingdom by the river, placid and grand. The clusters of outbuildings with red-tiled roofs nestled among neatly combed meadows all yielded to one majestic form—the estate's main house, a two-story brick structure with double rows of glazed windows, fronted by a marble veranda with a noble line of lean, austere Corinthian columns. Its single-storied wings formed an inner court, left open in back to afford a vista of the Mosella; within was a peristyle garden that was a maze of trimmed hedges, flowers chosen for scent, ornamental trees. Connected by a covered walkway was a monumental bathhouse with projecting apsidal rooms, its proud dome ghostly in the morning haze; because of the danger of fire, it had been built apart from the main house. Two rectangular pools surrounded by freestanding columns of Parian marble flanked the main house's wide gravel approach. Within each, high fountains rained multiple cascades over tiers of sea scallops supporting cavorting Nereids twining about thick serpents. The estate's gardens were a patchwork cloth laid over the meadows; here, cabbages, turnips, parsnips, lettuces, and medicinal herbs were grown; in their midst was an artificial pond for geese. Julianus's estate was entirely independent, providing for its two hundred residents, slave and free. Where the forest began were stables for the fine horses raised here, noted for their endurance; the estate provided prized mounts for the Roman cavalry. Alongside the river was a meadow that served as a race course.

Auriane and Avenahar halted at the wrought-iron gate, portal of this small city with its benign co-regents; a doorkeeper within the gatehouse depressed a lever that caused the gate to swing wide. They passed beneath a limestone arch with its keystone adorned with a bas-relief of Minerva, patron deity of the villa—and into another world, watched over by the grand and gentle spirits of this tranquil sovereign state. Packed gravel crunched beneath the mare's hooves as they moved beneath the lyric shadows of hazel trees, used for hurdle-making, and chestnut trees, which provided the villa with charcoal for burning. At the columned entrance they gave their mare to a groom and entered the expensive silence of the vestibule, with its walls sheathed in rare Carystian marble banded in many hues of pale green. Beneath their feet was a mosaic of the Muses so finely wrought it might have been rendered with a paintbrush rather than thousands of minute tesserae. Columns of near-translucent Luna marble, which ringed a softly gurgling atrium fountain, glowed like lamps as they stored dawn light shed from the lightwell. Mother and daughter were met by the household steward Demaratos, who, Auriane knew, was sharply curious about the lateness of their return. The steward raised his brows but faintly, as though reluctant to distort cold, perfect Attic features.

"*Domina,*" he greeted Auriane, inclining his head. "My Lord has asked to see you at once." It was a mystery to Auriane how Demaratos managed to put so much contempt into *Domina.* She knew only that he gave a light, measured pause after the word, as if allowing the household gods time to laugh. Demaratos was of a ruined aristocratic family of Rhodes that had been reduced to one penniless, expensively Greek-educated son. And so he'd sold himself as a slave to a philosopher he admired, counting it a nobler fate

to be an upper servant in a great man's household than a poor-but-free creature forced into the indignities of scratching in dirt for his daily bread. To
the Greek-born Demaratos, Rome itself was barbarous, and Auriane's ori-
gins were so far beneath this, she was not even assigned a rung in his ladder
of social grades. "Two tenant farmers in a boundary dispute await you in the
Records Room," Demaratos spoke on in his polished, precise syllables. "You
shouldn't see them; they're disgracefully dressed. If they can't even find clean
tunics before they come here—"

"I *will* see them. Have them served meat and drink while I have words
with Julianus." She wearied of this constant struggle of wills; the steward
was like some small, steady current flowing against her. No single offense
ever seemed great enough to prompt her to seek redress; it was more an in-
definable cloud of offenses that entered and left a room with him.

Demaratos's bare shrug said: It's not *your* good name you risk, it's *his*.
But he responded with flawless politeness. "He is in the library."

Auriane sent Avenahar off with the children's nurse, so she could attend
to the sprain. A comely Egyptian boy-servant pulled back a folding door,
and Auriane entered the most secret parts of the house. She was sharply conscious of the thickness of the walls, the heating by hypocaust beneath the
floor, the marvelous machinery to mark the hours, the servants for every
small task, the tutors for the children, the stacks of ledgers in the Records
Room listing the yield of estates scattered across five Roman provinces . . .
She'd lived without these things before, and could easily do so again, but had
she the right to wrest from her children what the Fates had given them? *Stop
this! All will be well.*

Hunted them all down, Victorinus had said. From far within the passages'
darkened mirrors, Lurio grinned at her with broken teeth.

Night-shadows still pooled in the cavernous library. Pleasant cedar
scents drifted out. Marcus Julianus was seated facing her, before a work table
that was, she never tired of jesting, so much less orderly than his mind—
documents and correspondence were haphazardly heaped on it, and beneath
them were unrolled strip maps anchored in place with bronze hand lamps.
When he was intently working, he never seemed to think of the danger of
fire. He wore two tunics against the chill—old, worn ones, washed a hundred times. As he studied one of the maps, a young Greek secretary read
aloud from a text that was familiar: "How, then, do we call anything 'my
own'? Merely as we call a bed in an inn 'my own.' If you do not find a bed
then sleep on the ground, and do so with good courage, remembering that

tragedies find a place among the rich, and among kings, and tyrants—" She recognized it as Epictetus, and knew something grievous must be pressing upon him, for he had this philosopher read to him as some might take a draught of wine—to calm the nerves. Behind him she saw an unmade *lectus,* where apparently, he'd briefly rested; he'd passed the night working in the library. She found something solemn and holy in the scene, as if she intruded on some mystery-rite in which he banished spirits of darkness by lifting the lamp of the mind.

He looked up, not startled, instant pleasure showing in his face. It was as if some part of him constantly expected her, as though she never fully left him. He rose at once, and asked the secretary to leave. There was no beauty more compelling to her than the contours of that face, left leaner, more sharply defined by the years, but always emitting the same generosity of spirit. He pulled her close. She ran a hand through his dark, close-cropped hair, recently become flecked with iron gray. Then they held to each other in a comfortable, sustaining embrace that lingered, and she felt the bliss of a babe rocked in sleep as they drew nourishment from one another, pressed together in a way that was both passionate and maternal. In seven years even their most fleeting comings-together had not lost their rapture; between them, a single kind and knowing touch had the power to raise about them a temple of Eros.

He held her at arm's length, his hands on her shoulders, examining her with pride.

"You're a fine argument for having the roads repaired this year."

"Can't I roll in the mud without everyone commenting?"

"What hour is it?" He looked restlessly about, noting with mild surprise the pale glow at a glazed window high in the library's wall. "You're only now returning? Are you well? Was there trouble?"

"We suffered a small accident, nothing at all, really—Avenahar lost her horse. We had to walk the whole distance."

"Did you put flowers on the Mothers' shrine?"

Wariness rose in her like a sap. She'd half forgotten the small fiction invented to cover the night journey, and now it seemed petty and mean to meet his kindness with a lie. She broke his gaze. "We did."

"Why isn't Avenahar bounding right at your side? Something must be wrong."

"At that age, something's always wrong. It's that vile Lucius—he taunted her again."

"A base father produces a base son. I'll send Victorinus a sharp reprimand."

"Marcus, she asked directly again about her real father . . . and my courage broke. Once again, I couldn't tell her."

"Have you ever thought there might be more pain for her in *not* knowing? It only prompts a lively and inventive mind to imagine worse."

"How *could* it be worse? By her measure, Decius is a monster."

She heard a melodious cry muffled through the tapestried passages of the house—a footman, shouting for a *reda*—a travelling carriage—to be brought up. "You're leaving?" The words carried a plaint of dismay.

"It's vexing to me as it is to you, but I've been called to the fortress on an urgent matter." He sat her down upon a cross-legged chair. "Auriane. I need to ask you something before I leave. An odd request, perhaps, but of grave and singular importance." Marcus Julianus was a member of Trajan's Consilium, a council of forty men of various ranks and professions who served as the Emperor's advisors. A panel drawn from it was to meet at the Fortress of Mogontiacum, a half-day's journey south on the post road, to determine if the forts along the river Rhenus could withstand a withdrawal of troops for service in Trajan's coming Dacian campaign. In these times the single nation in Europe able to stand against Rome was the barbarian kingdom of Dacia, far to the east, on the river Danuvius. Trajan had already conquered it once, but once was proving not enough.

"I mean to recommend there's no harm in drawing good numbers of our men from your people's frontier," he said. "Which means matters could get awkward for me if things don't stay quiet there. Which brings us to your Chattian folk. And your old battle companion, Witgern."

Some part of her caved in at the sound of the name. *Witgern, the one candle left burning.* When Auriane was a child in her tribal homeland, Witgern had been the First Companion of her father, Baldemar, the celebrated Chattian chief. Now, Witgern was the sole warrior of her people who still fought for their freedom. He led a rogue Chattian warband called the Wolf Coats, who slept on earth, dressed in wolf skins, and sought vengeance against Rome with small acts of sabotage along the frontier.

"Auriane, have you any influence over him? Could you get him some sort of message to lie quiet, for old time's sake? This would be a wretched time for one of his pranks. It would go hard for your people."

"That would be like finding a ghost. And I don't know if he'd listen—all say the rites have . . . changed him, that he's more beast than man. But his raids are flea bites—he'd never openly attack a Roman fort."

"One of my agents has gotten intelligence that he plans just that, but this one's been wrong before, so—Auriane, what is it?"

The world about her seemed to drift to a soft halt, like an invisible cloak settling into place. Her gaze was caught, then drawn within one of the muted flames of the bronze lamps and she knew that graceful state of fertile emptiness that normally came only after long contemplation of a sacred fire. Exhaustion from the overlong night might have been the cause. The portals normally shut against other worlds blew open—and she was somewhere else. In a cold forest. Where huddled forms draped in skins intoned chants that vibrated the fine bones.

"What is it?" He whispered it this time, drawing her face closer to his, as if to examine what was reflected in her half-shut eyes.

"Marcus, it is already too late."

"What?"

"You can't warn anyone in time. Witgern will attack today, at dusk."

"Where?" He'd learned, by now, not to doubt.

"The fort due north of the springs of the Mattiaci . . . right on the frontier line, the fort whose praefect is named"—she frowned faintly, struggling for it—". . . is named hope."

The last part made no sense to him, but he knew the fort. "By Providence, *why*? That fort's better defended than five others to the northeast."

She shut her eyes completely, striving to see better. "It's something very dear to him . . . to Witgern, I mean . . . I don't know. I can't see more. That is all."

"All right. I must go," he said briskly. "I can be at Mogontiacum by noontide. I'll present this as if it came from regular channels of intelligence so they won't think I've lost one too many spokes in my wheels." He began swiftly gathering up the wax tablets scattered across the writing table. Among them Auriane saw several that bore the familiar, elaborate salutations of a letter to the Emperor. When he saw her questioning look, he said, "Those wouldn't interest you, they're tiresomely dull reading—just copies of letters passed back and forth by the Consilium on that nettlesome matter of the money-for-arms being smuggled over the frontier to your people—"

Her breathing slowed.

"—quite extraordinary that they haven't found him yet . . . It seems the bounty's up to *three* million now for whoever names him, and still we're no closer to knowing. Our poor Maximus is losing his wits, that's the other reason I must go." The Governor at the Fortress of Mogontiacum was a close, fond friend of Julianus's. "He's falling under a hail of criticism because he's failed to ferret out the smuggler, and he fears the Palace will recall him from his governorship a year early because of it. He's starting to panic and make ridiculous arrests. He's even begun questioning women—he brought in several prominent women from the Potters' Guild at Colonia. I've got to go and bring him to reason—Auriane? . . . What is wrong?" He pulled her up to face him.

She considered letting the truth spill out right then, like a sack of stones she ached from carrying—but at the last moment, decided against it.

"It's Victorinus," she said tautly, looking away. "He's learned his son's not getting Arria, and he's in a vengeful temper over it."

Marcus laughed softly. "*That* has you in an anxious state? It was an act of charity even considering him! Surely he never thought—"

"But he did. And he's dangerously angry."

"'Dangerous' and 'Victorinus' do not belong in the same sentence! He's a small, albeit noisy, man, whom we considered only out of politeness. This is a new and uncharacteristic occupation for you," he said teasingly, "to worry over the bite of a fly. One flick of the tail—and it's off!"

I heard once of a horse that died of the bite of an insect. The wound festered. The small can bring down the large.

"There's more to this," he pressed gently. "What haunts you so?"

If her eyes had been a well many fathoms deep, his gaze might have filtered straight through to the bottom. That he did so with kindliness made her feel all the more the cornered beast. *You must tell him,* she prodded herself.

The smuggler you seek? You take her to your bed every night.

No. It would force him into a cruel and impossible corner; he'd be compelled to choose between duty and love. It might well end our life here.

And is there not some chance the whole matter will never come to light?

So she said only, "Perhaps we took a wrong path seven years ago, and living on the borderland is not possible, wasn't meant to be possible . . ."

"Nonsense. I would have no other life but this one here with you." Then he shrugged amiably. "There are no matters before us that can't be attended to, with patience and time."

With arms laced together most naturally, they left the library, talking softly of house matters as they moved toward the waiting carriages.

When he had departed, Auriane slept but a single restless hour, then summoned one of her confidential servants, the Greek secretary who corresponded with the estate by Lugdunum in Gaul, which she held in her name.

She dispatched him to the docks of Confluentes, with instructions to engage the services of a townsman called Aprossius who owned a riverside warehouse that stored cattle hides for the legions. This Aprossius had a secret, second occupation: He was skilled at finding people, and he asked no questions when he took his fee. She would hire him to hunt down Lurio. She would silence the fugitive sailor with a rich bribe, greater than the reward for naming her. It seemed a desperate strategy, but she must try it.

Then she walked to the river, carrying with her a wheel-form brooch of silver that had lain on her mother's breast. This she buried in the earth beneath a wood image of her goddess Fria she'd set up alongside the Mosella's dark, marbled waters; by this, she committed her mother to the embrace of the Mother of all kindred. *Mother, do you know why I do not come myself, to give you protection? It would be a one-way journey that would sever me forever from Marcus and my children. Surely you know I'm prohibited from returning—the Consilium thinks my presence among our people would rouse them to insurrection. No. I must do battle here, in this foreign place that counts my children half-breeds, and myself a kind of elevated slave.*

On returning to the house, Auriane cast an anxious glance into Avenahar's chamber. *How peacefully she sleeps*, Auriane thought—*with a child's trust in the benignity of the world. How different from when she's awake! What will I do with her? She is a fire out of control. She cannot live and marry in this province; she would become like the wild horse that kicks apart its stall. In her, Chattian blood runs stronger. She must one day go home.*

From outside, Auriane could hear gleeful cries; her younger daughter, Arria Juliana, was getting a lesson from the riding master.

That one, I need not worry over; she's a thoroughly Roman child, with no pull toward my people.

But all at once Auriane saw, in that still place that did not know time or distance, a mind-picture deep and sure as that vision of Witgern readied for the attack. But this time it was her quick and audacious Arria she saw, immured within the moldering household of the magistrate, Volusius Victorinus.

Slaves regularly fled off from that estate. No one knew exactly why.

Auriane leaned against the frescoed wall and shut her eyes in revulsion.

This is well—it proves these cursed visions are not true. Because there is no way beneath sun and moon that the vile Lucius will ever have our Arria as bride.

Chapter 3

Marcus Firmius Speratus, centurion of the Eighth Legion *Augusta*, looked with growing unease into the thrashing sea of wind-whipped firs below. He stood on the sentry walk of a frontier fort constructed of turf ramparts stiffened by timbers; the thatched roofs of its corner towers jutted up bravely against the somber sky. His fort was manned by a single century of the Eighth Legion, strengthened by one hundred native auxiliaries. This tiny outpost of Empire was perched at the world's rim; just two hundred paces beyond in the haunted gloom, the Roman world came to an end, and the lands of the savage Chattians began. There, a military trackway, ditch, and wickerwork fence marked the *Limes*, the three-hundred-mile-long frontier line whose humble appearance belied its grand purpose—dividing the known world from the unknown wastes, separating historic time from mythic time.

Light drained rapidly from the sky, and night already had a secure hold on the forest floor. At the tenth hour of this day, his *exploratores,* men of the legionary intelligence system, returned to report they had seen smoke drifting from a sector of land where no Chattian settlements existed. Closer examination proved the smoke issued from a marsh. When Speratus ordered the fort's sheep driven from their forest meadow and confined within the walls for safety, they showed signs of agitation, and they numbered three fewer than they had the day before. The praefect relayed an urgent request for reinforcements, through torch signals passed along a string of signal towers communicating with Mogontiacum, the nearest permanent stone fortress on the river Rhenus. But he could not expect fresh troops to arrive before the tenth hour of the morrow. He'd then sent out a party of volunteers for the dangerous work of digging an additional defensive ditch fitted with sharp stakes, positioned just within javelin range of the fort's north gate. But their work would not be complete before darkness fell on them like a predator.

Surely, he thought, even an Alexandrian Greek, famous as they were for scorning belief in the unseen powers, wouldn't linger in this god-cursed country at night. Out there a man wanted only to hug close to the light of his cookfire until he was rescued by dawn. Too many tales abounded of pale lights moving through the forest accompanied by unearthly singing, of sightings of odd beasts that defied the catalogues of the naturalists, of soldiers who strayed no more than twenty paces from their column, never to be seen again until their polished bones were found in one of the natives' ghastly sacrificial groves. A succession of grim wars beyond the Rhenus had taken Rome this far. The most recent, the Chattian War, had, in his opinion, stretched Roman forces too thinly into this unholy unknown. He knew that in the event of a massive attack, this fort was expected to fall. The long frontier line was thinly patrolled, guarded by thatched watchtowers spaced half a day's march apart. Their best hope would be to hamper the barbarians' progress long enough to allow the legions housed in the great river fortresses time to come to full alert. As Rome was always reluctant to risk Roman lives, many of these small frontier forts were manned by native auxiliaries. Only a quarter of the men under Speratus's command could claim citizen birth. Most were fresh recruits drawn from a local Germanic tribe, the Ubians—hastily trained men who had not yet seen battle.

Just as the softly glowing lamp of a near-full moon eased above the far hills, Speratus began to hear the howls of wolves.

The praefect knew at once these were not the sort that loped about on four legs. New recruits could be fooled. Long service on the frontier taught Speratus to distinguish the cry of the true wolf from that of the man-wolf. With an effort of will he kept his face implacable as a casting in bronze, for the men below were watching him by the light of the windswept torches along the walk.

A sentry stationed by the west tower moved to his side. In the semi-dark, Speratus saw the smooth silhouette of a helmet, a dominant nose jutting like a bent finger pointing downward, eyes that were horizontal arrow slits. This was the soldier most in the praefect's confidence, a veteran of thirty years named Vettius Gratus.

"Curse those clever beasts to the Cimmerian depths," Gratus said. "From the sound, how many would you say?"

The wolfsong grew more poignant. It was a hymn to the great spirits of the forest, a solemn rite in the mystery religion of wolves. It was as though the hills with their ancient hurts found a voice. The cry crossed worlds, charging the dark, illumining the moss with ghostlight, starting a quickening in the earth, prompting the dead to walk. The Chattian warriors were astonishingly skilled in imitating the wolf's rich, emotion-laden wails. With vocal arrangements elaborate as any Greek master of composition's they wove a tapestry of sound, timing their cries so that as one bleak plaint crested and billowed out, a fresh cluster would smoothly ascend, while the oldest drained off in sequence, clinging tenaciously on the night, never fully absorbed into silence. Sometimes the Chattians' howls convinced even the wolves, who would break out in answering cries. Speratus would have found it difficult to explain how he knew these wails issued from men. Some distinctions defy words, yet distinct they are; he knew only that there was a certain sly humanness in the sound.

"No less than three hundred," Speratus said. The turf-and-timber fort suddenly seemed small against the vastness of the forest.

"They're *close,* sir," responded Gratus, "they've crossed the *Limes*—the brutes are half-distance between it and us. Something's not right about this. I've not seen a Chattian band this brazen since before the war." The sentry's hand tightened round his javelin and a taut rope of muscle asserted itself in a thick forearm—javelin practice was the chief leisure activity in this lonely outpost of civilization. "The size of that band . . . it can only be our one-eyed friend—"

"—Witgern."

"Let us give him the heartfelt welcome he deserves."

The Chattian chieftain Witgern was said to be mad, and, according to the credulous on both banks of the Rhenus, had mastered the art of shape-shifting and could assume the form of a wolf. Before his Wolf Coats struck, they performed elaborate rites that freed them from all knowledge of death and infused them with bestial courage.

"Come, Witgern—you pay now for the hart!" the sentry said, speaking loudly enough that two men in the yard below overheard. They turned from the tripod and cauldron from which they were ladling spelt porridge, and raised a shout, *"Revenge for the hart!"*—which was quickly taken up by the whole of the encampment. Last year, Witgern had netted a female red deer in her time of heat and fastened her to a bough near a cave in which he and a number of his Wolf companions lay concealed. Next, they released a fine, strong hart in the path of one of the legionary hunting parties. When the hart scented and sought its mate, the beast brought Speratus's men straight into Witgern's ambush. Two out of twenty had returned to tell the tale.

"Silence! Douse the torches," Firmius Speratus ordered. Through a signal flag borne by a *signifer* stationed on the sentry walk, the praefect ordered every man to ascend to the graveled rampart top, which served as a fighting platform as well as a patrol track. Since the fort was so lightly garrisoned, he knew their best hope was to make a show of numbers on the wall. The legionaries assigned to the six small catapults called *scorpiones* drew back the windlasses of their engines, awaiting the praefect's signal. In a desperate ploy, Speratus ordered a Chattian warrior's cloak hung from the rampart. This signaled that they held a hostage within, and would execute him if attacked. In fact, they had no hostage.

"Permission to speak?" The whisper belonged to a nervous nineteen-year-old Ubian auxiliary.

Speratus nodded brusquely.

"Roughly half the watch ago, when you were below, I'm certain I saw the glint of steel down there."

"Magissus, I'll sever that tongue from your head if you're flapping it without warrant," Firmius Speratus retorted. Since Rome had systematically divested the Chattian tribe of weapons of iron, Witgern fought with fire-hardened spears, clubs, and occasionally, stones. His strength was in his intimate knowledge of the terrain, not his weaponry.

But after a moment of examining the somber deeps, Speratus saw it himself—a beam of cold moonlight moving down a column of iron. There was no denying what he had seen. He'd long known of the coin-for-arms being smuggled into the hands of Chattian chiefs. But most reports claimed the prohibited swords were being hoarded in a cave; for reasons no one fully understood, the natives, to date, had not seemed inclined to take them up. Curiosity rose, along with primitive fright. Why here? Why now?

Moving briskly, neglecting nothing, the praefect inspected the men, who were formed up in two ranks on the rampart. Then he ascended the gate tower so all his men could see him.

He dropped his hand, and six catapult bolts flashed off into the night. There was a tearing of leaves, followed by silence. They had missed their mark.

IN THE ABYSSAL darkness of the forest floor, three hundred Chattian warriors crouched close to the moist, mossy earth. They'd allowed their wails to fade off into darkness. Now they watched the fort with the eyes of wolves, eyes that reflected moon and stars, not human thought. They yearned to spring on prey, to taste its sweet blood in their mouths, but they waited, alert to the signal of Witgern, the Old Wolf. For nine nights they had slept on wolf skins under the growing new moon. For nine days they had shared "raven's bread," the beautiful red mushroom with white warts that ushers in the wolf-spirit. They had chanted the wolf chants, passing leftward around the fire while a tribal seeress sang them into other worlds. Each had fasted until this day's dawn, when they broke it with a meal of wolves' hearts. They knew only their loyalty to brother and sister wolf, and their own boiling fury.

These were the bitterest core of the Chattian tribe's heart, men, and several women, who had deserted home village and kin to live as outlaws. The Chattian Assembly, forced by the war into grudging cooperation with Rome, disavowed all Witgern's acts in the presence of imperial observers. But when the chieftains of the Assembly returned to their villages, they sent out to Witgern's rebel band whatever meat, drink, or hides their families could spare. Witgern had forsaken hoe and plow when he left his clan, and was dependent on this secret largesse.

Witgern had drawn his men into the "swine's head" formation, a long, single rank with the most seasoned wolves at its center. He was seized with a fierce sadness as he gazed upon the fort. So many beloved friends had left him through death in battle, or through capture, that for years now he'd felt a stronger attraction to the netherworld than to this bright middle world of tumult and sorrow. When scarce more than a boy, he had been a companion of the immortal chieftain Baldemar, who held off Rome for a generation, and then of his daughter, Auriane, when she took his band at his death. He counted those the finest days of his life. Now he wanted only for the ghost of Baldemar to let him sleep.

Witgern had learned that Firmius Speratus hoarded within that fort the living relic most cherished by his people.

SPERATUS RUSHED INTO his own quarters, intent on performing one last act. He knew he must accept the likelihood that the fort might be burned.

He hurriedly gathered up all the official documents—stacks of thin wooden sheets on which the year's expense accounts were inscribed in neat, inked lines; his men's service records and the papers stating their time of release; a journal of daily events; letters from the high command at Mogontiacum; and a treasured commendation on vellum he'd received from the Emperor Trajan himself. Hastily he crushed all these into an iron strongbox, feeling in one moment that he singlehandedly preserved a world, a small civilization known only to himself and a few isolated others immured within these frontier forts.

Then he took from its wall mount a gem-encrusted barbarian sword that he'd carried about from camp to camp for years, always believing it brought him good fortune. He'd purchased it in Rome, during the auction of the spoils of the Chattian War. Rough-cut gemstones round its hilt flashed colors of sky, water, and blood. The auctioneer had assured the crowd it once belonged to the most notorious of all Chattian chiefs, Baldemar. Speratus was half-inclined to believe the auctioneer a lying mountebank. But once, in Rome, he'd taken the sword to a naturalist learned in the ways of the northern tribes, who had insisted that such a weapon would only have belonged to a chieftain of highest rank. And Speratus had personally spoken to a soldier who'd been present in the field during the Chattian War's final assault. This man told him that Baldemar's strange, Amazonian daughter, Auriane, who'd taken possession of the sword at her father's death, had lost it on the battlefield when she was captured and taken prisoner. When Firmius Speratus was first posted on the *Limes,* he'd shown the sword to a Chattian battle-seeress, who had broken into tears, begging him to let her have it so she could return it to her people. The savage signs round the hilt, she claimed, spelled out Baldemar's name in runic glyphs, and below this were letters that signified the mountain cat, from which the Chattian tribe took its name. To Firmius

Speratus, the longsword was more than a fine war trophy. He believed it a thing of potent mystery that kept the fort from harm.

Until now.

At the back of his quarters was a small pit intended for burying the silver plate. Into this he placed the sword, then he hastily covered it over with earth.

WITGERN MUTTERED A prayer to the land spirits.

"Old Ones, we are your paws. Old Ones, we are your eyes. We are a proud pack. We feed on victory. Let our blood run strong as we strike in the name of the groves."

"All glory to Sun and Moon," came a whispered response from his men.

"Aid us as we strike in the name of Baldemar, great breaker of rings. Be with us as we strike in the name of Wodan, who brings us every bright gift . . ."

"All glory to Sun and Moon."

Witgern made no effort to check an unwolflike tear that started down a soot-blackened cheek.

". . . aid us as we strike in the name of our living shield, Auriane."

A CONTINENT OF clouds drifted over the moon, snuffing out its light. In the sudden darkness Witgern's men surged forward almost soundlessly over moist fallen leaves, scenting the freshly dug ditch, and flowing around it. A river of wolves rushed toward the fort. The men on the rampart walk heard them before they saw them, alerted to a soft, fast, percussive sound that might have been mistaken for sudden rain. Speratus signaled to the *tubicen,* who gave a single, urgent blast on his long trumpet, and the first round of javelins arced into the void. A dozen of Witgern's men were struck, but most were not, for at that moment the band split like a stream, half seeking the west gate, and half, the east. The *cornicen*'s curved horn gave a deep, hollow moan, calling the men's attention to the standards. They were to fall around to the west and east gates, where Witgern's men were massing like wasps in the double ditches about the fort. The western contingent of Wolf Coats ignited torches and tossed tied bundles of burning straw onto the sentry walk, successfully engaging a quarter of Speratus's men in a frenzied effort to put out the blaze. Simultaneously, the eastern contingent quietly converged on the opposite gate, and pressed against the iron-bound outer door, with its oak planks thick as a man's arm. Their confederate within the fort did not fail them: It fell away, for its heavy crossbar had been removed. Wolf-men collected in the space between the doors, awaiting the sound of a stout iron bolt moving against wood, the signal that the crossbar of the inner door was sliding back.

The Wolf Coats poured in. Witgern was aided by the legionaries' terror as they were confronted with fur-clad Chattian warriors swinging swords like scythes, eyes brilliant with the fire of the draughts, faces and bodies darkened with soot and ash; half engaged them, but great numbers of the untried Ubian auxiliaries dropped from the palisade and fled off into the forest, certain they faced not men, but some deathless spawn of the northern bogs. In less time than it would have taken the soldiers to bring a cauldron of spelt porridge to boil, the fort belonged to Witgern.

FIRMIUS SPERATUS WAS awakened by impossible heat on his face. Was the sun coursing too close to the earth? He lay on his back in his own quarters, bathed in a moist warmth that was comforting until he realized it was his own blood. Slaughterhouse smells, grisly silence—how well he knew these things. It meant a battle was lost.

The barracks blocks were aflame. He knew the direction of the wind.

He would be burned alive.

The doorway filled with a shaggy silhouette, and a near-naked Chattian warrior stepped almost tentatively into Firmius Speratus's quarters. A profusion of hides sprouted from his shoulders like some outlandish dangling mane; about his waist was the fabled wolfskin belt the Chattians believed had the power to transform man into loping beast.

Nemesis. One of the murdering swine stayed behind. Stop hesitating, you stinking brute. Send me quickly to Hades.

Speratus saw the man's face and stifled a scream. In the next instant he realized the warrior was wearing a wolf mask; the leering animal face was painted on crudely carved wood.

The centurion lay utterly still, waiting for death. But the Wolf Coat expressed no interest in him. He removed the mask and crossed at once to the corner of the barracks room, found the place where the earth was freshly disturbed, and began digging with a broken potsherd. Speratus, feeling death pressing close, felt little inclination to wonder how the savage knew precisely where to go. The Wolf warrior half-turned once, while brushing a rope of matted hair from his forehead, and Speratus saw the man's face by the light of the flames that were consuming his fort. It must have once been possessed of some beauty, but was now pitted like stone battered by the elements, and transformed into a Cyclopean horror: Where an eye should have been was a collapsed place; there, the blackened flesh was fisted closed. His good eye was charged with a sad, soulful brilliance. *Witgern.* Legend held he'd put out the eye himself, long ago, when his countrywoman Auriane betrayed him in the matter of a marriage.

Witgern lifted the jeweled sword from its earthen cradle, held it aloft, and began to mutter the words of some savage prayer.

A fresh gust of heat swept in, and Speratus felt like raw dough thrust into a baker's oven. Soon his flesh would crackle and start to rise.

Witgern was weeping over the sword.

Take your loot and get out, you whimpering beast, so I'll have a chance at crawling out of here alive.

Witgern turned about, and the gazes of centurion and barbarian met.

For an oddly long moment Witgern did not move. Speratus saw much in that single eye—mourning tangled about hope, a love of song, the sorrow of one who shouldered on his back the burden of doomed thousands . . . but no, this was an unlettered brute. His fevered mind was conjuring qualities that were not there.

The roof caught fire.

Witgern moved toward Firmius Speratus. *Now I'll die by the blade of my own cursed war relic.* He closed his eyes and prayed to the shade of his dead mother.

But Witgern seized him roughly by his legs—at first he thought the savage wanted his boots. Then the old Wolf warrior dragged him out to the safety of the yard. Witgern left him there, and moments afterward, Speratus heard a crash of timbers as the roof fell in, and the fire, greatest of wolves, swallowed his quarters whole. Then he heard a furious clatter of hooves rapidly retreating through the east gate. Witgern had stolen a horse and was gone, leaving Speratus wondering in his wake—was this a plain act of compassion, or did the famous rebel hope to win mercy for himself, were he ever captured? Did Witgern merely want someone of rank left alive to tell the tale? Or was it because Speratus had long been guardian of what Witgern counted sacred treasure? When he tried to puzzle it out, he felt he peered into a fathomless night sky.

* * *

"IT WAS A night of folly," Firmius Speratus found himself saying three days later, before doubtful-looking members of the Imperial Consilium assembled to investigate the fall of his fort to Witgern. Speratus had made his way back to the Fortress of Mogontiacum on the Rhenus with but a handful of his men. Now he faced an inquisition of dour noblemen in a smoky, windowless accounts room off a colonnaded central courtyard with its geometric graveled walks framing close-clipped box-hedge gardens. All lay within the vast stone fortress that was home to the six thousand men of *Legio XXII Primigenia Pia Fidelis*—the Twenty-second Legion.

He felt like hapless prey dragged back to a bear's cave to be torn in pieces. He knew the governor, Valerius Maximus, would take no particular pleasure in his destruction. Those eyes, set in a doughy face that spoke of contented middle age, were wholly benign, and seemed focused vaguely elsewhere—it was commonly said Maximus regarded his official duties as but irritating stretches between his beloved aurochs hunts with his noble friends. But his two colleagues showed signs of being excited by the scent of a common soldier's blood. One was the young Pomponius Fabatus, barely off mother's milk, ablaze with ambition tempered with no experience, who had gotten his place on the Consilium as a favor to a father who'd detected a conspiracy against the throne. The other was the squat, gnomish Lappius Blaesus, loudest of the "war party" urging the Emperor to invade distant Dacia and bring it under the ever-lengthening wing of empire—that jellied form, Speratus surmised, would roll off onto the ground if you sat him on a cavalry mount. At some point Speratus had begun half-listening, aware only of the horse-sized teeth of the young Fabatus, and how he whinnied when excited—it was easy for him to mentally add ears and make him into a mule. The Mule and the Gnome. These two had, for the last hour, been batting him about like a ball. Two army recorders sat nearby, reed pens scratching over papyrus as they took down every response in camp shorthand. Behind them on a slender pedestal was a heroic bust of Trajan in bronze. The Emperor seemed to be looking straight over all their heads to his new Dacian frontier, emphasizing Speratus's sense of his own extreme unimportance in the grander schemes of empire. He had been charged with keeping the Rhenus frontier quiet, so that greater men than he could prepare to conquer elsewhere. He had failed.

"From the start, all was against us," Speratus spoke on in a monotone. "My half-trained Ubians lost their wits and did nothing but get in our way." The praefect knew, in saying this, he'd ruined the career of the man who'd trained them, but this was a ritual that demanded a sacrifice. Anyway, this man had once tried to ruin him. "They've such a superstitious fear of these wolf-men, that the effect was to triple Witgern's numbers, and so—"

"Wolf-men?" the young Fabatus interrupted. That metallic voice was boring into Speratus's brain like a worm screw. "Explain this."

"They work themselves into a murderous state before battle, howling and dancing and guzzling down mead spiked with wild rosemary," Speratus explained dully. "They believe they *are* wolves. Those *I* saw, however, though exceedingly hairy, were yet men."

This brought tightly controlled smiles of amusement from Blaesus and Fabatus. It was not flattering. Speratus knew they found his country-bred simpleness amusing.

"Let us return to the treacherous envoy who opened the gates," Fabatus pressed on, a jump of militant intensity in his eye. A war-mule, head lowered to trample him. "Firmius Speratus, had you been diligent in following every procedure for securing the fort, this breach would have been impossible."

Speratus was grateful for the poppy juice the fortress's physician had given him for the pain of his wounds; it left him feeling embalmed in a liquid calm, enabling him to stifle a retort that might have cost him his life.

"I swear by the ghost of my father," Speratus said patiently, "that I honored every procedure, and that I . . ."

He was forced to pause when a fourth member of this board of inquiry entered the chamber. Speratus's gaze drifted to him with little interest, then was jolted back for a second look. Who was this man? Everything in his manner suggested might and means held in reserve. He looked as Speratus supposed—in boyhood, at least, before adult cynicism gained sway—a senator *would* look: a man of elegant presentation and uncommon resolve, with the demeanor of one who saw every mundane event in relation to the long sweep of history. His toga appeared as if it had never been worn, and his manners were impeccable as he formally greeted each man in turn. His dark hair was lightly dusted with iron gray. The man's entry had an immediate effect on Speratus's questioners. It was as though someone subtly shifted a balance on a scale, upsetting a relationship between weight and counterweight. Speratus sensed strategies being hastily revised. They sat straighter on their chairs. The august newcomer was hastily provided with a copy of the recorder's transcript of the proceedings thus far, and all waited with taut expectation while he read it. Speratus picked out a name among the muttered words of greeting: *Marcus Arrius Julianus.*

A little tardily, the name and the man before him came together in

Speratus's mind like a thunderclap. He had to stop himself from staring, mouth agape. So this was Marcus Arrius Julianus, of whom he'd heard tales since he was a boy—who had been, for over a generation, the gadfly in the government, who had published banned books in the days of Nero, who openly patronized philosophers who called for the elimination of rulers. Like Hercules, he had battled giants—first, the mad Nero, then the murderous Domitian, as he fought to temper these tyrants' excesses with philosophy. Now he sat upon a misty Olympian peak along with a very few of the Emperor's most acclaimed advisors, and was called the conscience of Trajan's Consilium; Julianus's was the lone voice raised against the coming Dacian war. This must be counted a grave matter indeed, he thought, if Julianus was called to witness.

When Marcus Julianus had finished reading, he, and not the governor, nodded for Speratus to continue. The governor seemed relieved to be quietly handing over the reins to this man.

"—and you may be certain I neglected nothing, my lords," Speratus continued. "I ordered the digging of an additional defensive ditch. I changed the passwords every eve and dawn, and saw to it myself the sentries never neglected to demand it, and I—"

"Then how did one of Witgern's Wolf Coats get mistaken for a lawful envoy from the Chattian assembly?" Fabatus was putting on a fine show now, for Marcus Julianus's benefit. *Perhaps,* Speratus surmised, *the Mule thinks he's seized a chance to hitch a ride on the back of a powerful sponsor and be carried over a few annoying, unnecessary steps in his senatorial career.* "We've five other men to cross-check with. I'd consider well the lie you're hatching; you might be astonished at how swiftly a death sentence can be obtained for giving false information to the Consilium."

"I believe Witgern's spies ambushed our regular envoys and forced the passwords from them," Speratus responded evenly. "I hold this is the only explanation that would satisfy a rational man."

Marcus Julianus raised a hand to stop Fabatus before the young man fired his next bolt.

"I believe you acted well, Firmius Speratus." He had a voice that seized them with a powerful calm; though tempered and brought to fullness in expensive rhetorical schools, it was devoid of the gusty, sonorous self-importance typical of such men. "In reviewing what I see here, I judge you mounted a courageous defense. I do not think you betrayed us; rather, I believe Fortune betrayed you. To rectify that, I'll see that Fortune honors you. The post of praefect of the fort at Aquae Mattiaci has been recently vacated. I'm recommending you be transferred there, as soon as your battle wounds have healed."

If Julianus had struck Fabatus across the face, the great man could not have insulted his junior more pointedly. Not only had Speratus been spared—this was in fact a promotion, for he was put in command of a larger, longer-established fort, situated comfortably farther from the frontier.

Speratus felt as if Theseus snatched him from the path of the Minotaur.

"All these reports suggest wider causes for this disaster," Marcus Julianus spoke on. "But it saves a lot of time, trouble, papyrus, and ink if we heap it all on the head of one man, does it not? That fort was to have been reinforced with a cohort of Batavian cavalry. But our praefect at Aquae Mattiaci detained them for four days so he could employ them in an aurochs hunt. And I don't see it recorded anywhere that this man, Speratus, was awarded both a Civic Crown and a Mural Crown, though this information is readily at hand in this fortress's archives—perhaps an omission intended to make it easier to give him that final push down to Hades?"

"Men have called you an overeducated intellectual bully, Julianus," the gnomish Blaesus broke in with a cultured smile, "and I'm trying very hard not to agree with them."

"Yet you've no reproving words for Fabatus," Julianus retorted, "who just threatened our witness with death. The Emperor has more respect than you two for the ordinary soldier of the ranks. Fabatus, I will make known my displeasure at your conduct."

Fabatus withdrew into wounded silence, dazed at how abruptly his rising fortunes had begun to sink back into the muck. To be admonished by such a man meant the certain ruin of any chance of early advancement.

Speratus felt his appreciation of this man burgeoning into adoration.

"Furthermore," Julianus continued, "I see signs that this attack was anomalous; there's no evidence this presages a larger rebellion—"

"Then, Julianus, you see what you wish to see!" Blaesus struck out then. "Your bias for peace is well-known by all. Conscription's become near impossible out here, because the natives are quoting from *your* discourses against it—such is the mischief wrought by philosophers. And as ever you speak this Chattian enemy's cause with such energy and passion that it calls your motives to question!" This was a common charge made by Julianus's enemies, who claimed that the outlandish barbarian woman whom this man had taken into his household unduly influenced him to speak against the use of harsh measures against her tribe.

"My 'energy and passion,' as you call it, I hope serves only justice," Julianus responded amiably. "First, consider the man: Witgern is afflicted with a sickness his fellow tribesmen call the 'wolf madness'; even his own people keep off from him. None joined him in this raid. Your 'general revolt' seems undermanned. Your 'great effort to push us back to the Rhenus' consisted of a single frantic rush by three hundred rogues maddened with wolf beer. The loyal Chattian chiefs have condemned his attack in their native assembly.

"And," Julianus continued on, "no one's even asked why he struck *this* fort. Its brother forts to the east were not so well fortified. I think Witgern had some other purpose, still obscure to us."

Julianus was silent for a moment, scanning the report. "I see you've neglected to ask our good Firmius Speratus if he observed any looting."

"Five other witnesses have said *no*—is that not enough for you?" Blaesus said with contempt.

"I *did* see looting, my Lord," Speratus said, savoring the annoyance this caused Blaesus. "Witgern thieved a barbarian sword, said to once have belonged to that celebrated Chattian chieftain of the generation before, Baldemar."

The governor was clearly embarrassed he had not asked this question. But Blaesus was of a mind to lock horns until he wore an opponent down; to him, debate was more physical exercise than a test of logic. "So," he said, "they've one more sword in their possession than we thought, Julianus. Have you found the golden fleece?"

"In fact, we have," Julianus replied, smiling easily. "Gentlemen, we need investigate no further. Baldemar's sword is for them a treasure of immense sacred significance. They believe the great chief's spirit lives on in its blade. For many years, they've avidly sought it. Having it in foreign hands—I can only compare it to the horror each of you would feel, should an enemy seize one of our Eagles."

"That's an insolent comparison, Julianus, if not outright sacrilegious!" Blaesus spat out.

"I'm trusting the gods to be more indulgent than you," Julianus replied with an amused smile. "And then there's this, which comes to me now. If you subtract nine days from the day of that attack—which is when Witgern's men began their wolf rites—it's the anniversary of Baldemar's death. Doubtless, on the old chief's death day, they made a vow. When they attacked the fort, they fulfilled that vow. Therefore, I hold a military response would be a sadly unnecessary overreaction to this minor—"

"They carried swords, in contradiction to the ban! You're saying we should do *nothing*?"

"If you need employment for that busy mind, Blaesus," said Julianus, showing the first signs of irritation, "find the source of the silver coin flowing across the frontier. That's how Witgern armed himself. As I've maintained again and again, their hostility's not principally aimed at us in these times, but at the Cheruscan tribe to their north."

"Savages busy killing off other savages instead of harassing us—it's much to our advantage, Blaesus," the governor, Maximus, added. Only Speratus caught the faint wince of distaste those words brought to Marcus Julianus's face—Julianus did not like that line of reasoning.

"Surely a punitive expedition should be launched!"

"I think not," Julianus replied. "They don't have a history of paying much attention to our punitive expeditions—historically, it has almost seemed to strengthen them, like the pruning of vines. I've never believed in the efficiency of rule by terror. For fear vanishes, soon as you depart, and hatred's only redoubled. I hold it's far better to win a nation to us through just dealings, and through hewing to our promises." He was silent a moment, as he calmly regarded each man in turn. "I have no more to say."

"You're too tricky for me, Julianus," Blaesus said then, "but I know a peacemonger when I hear one. Enter into the record that I don't agree with Marcus Julianus. If these attacks continue, *you* can appeal to the Emperor, and answer to the families of the dead."

Now everyone looked expectantly at Maximus, to see what course of action the governor would recommend, for this was legally his jurisdiction—though all knew who the true governor was, when Julianus was present.

"No punitive expedition," Maximus decreed. "We'll send a strong warning to the Chattian Assembly. And we'll put the Chattian hostages to death. That should satisfy the Palace's demand for justice."

As Julianus emerged the victor, Blaesus seemed as amazed as if he'd witnessed a sorcerer's trick. A tribe that had burned a fort and slain most of its men, using swords it was not supposed to possess, was to suffer little more punishment than a warning.

"Might I now speak to the centurion Firmius Speratus in private?" Julianus asked then.

Maximus was mildly surprised at this. "The recorders, too, Julianus?"

"Yes, if you'll allow. I have a message to give this man, from his family. As it's of a disturbing nature, it wouldn't be proper to do so in front of us all."

When they were alone, Speratus asked with urgency, "My Lord, what of my family?"

"Forgive me, that was but a ruse so we could have private words."

Speratus put his head into his hands as he felt a great upsurge of relief.

"I am your lifelong servant, Marcus Julianus," the centurion said at last. "I owe a debt to you that I'm not sure I can repay in this life. Ask what you will, I'll withhold nothing from you."

"You know more than you cared to speak aloud before those men. Why do you think Witgern came for the old chief's sword?"

"Out there they say Baldemar is still alive. Reports keep coming from the hide traders who come back from the West Forest, where his old widow lives on. Something's *certainly* afoot. I wouldn't say it before; I didn't want to throw weight to their side, against you. There's a tale to which I gave scant credence at the time, that Baldemar's ghost commanded Witgern to reclaim his sword, and—"

"Does this ghost urge insurrection against Rome?"

"No. All I hear agrees with you; it's that plundering Cheruscan chief called Chariomer they're arming against, not us. They believe they face extinction. But the troubling bit of it is—" He came to a full stop.

"You must say it. By the ghost of Aeneas I swear I'll not let you be harmed in any way."

"—it's said Baldemar won't lay quiet until Witgern puts Baldemar's sword into the hands of—" Sharp unease contracted his features.

"Nemesis! Enough," Marcus Julianus said quickly, turning away. "I know who you mean." *Into the hands of his only living child, his daughter. Who carried it before.* Auriane.

Though Julianus expected it, still he felt the ground wrench beneath him. The logic of it closed about him—*Of course they would be engineering her return. Her people, once again, are threatened on every side. And they would rally around her like no other.* His features remained composed; Speratus did not guess his torment. But he felt a sick dread that belonged in harsher times, that didn't fit the more sedate world he inhabited now. *For Auriane's sake she must never know this. Her sense of duty to her people would compel her to go back. Gods forgive me, I cannot have it. They ask too much of her. She deserves safety and rest. She's a matron of a villa now, with children . . .*

"I fear I must put that declaration of lifelong servitude to the test at once," Julianus said. "You will speak of this matter to no one. No matter what his field of authority, or his rank. If you would repay me, let it be in the coin of your silence."

"You delivered me from ruin," Speratus replied with fervor. "My allegiance is to you. I'll tell no one. Shall I oath it on our Lord's image?" He nodded toward the bronze bust of Trajan.

"Your word's as good as an oath."

As they rose to depart, Speratus brushed against a drop cloth covering a newly commissioned portrait bust of the governor, Maximus. As it fell away, Julianus saw something that should not be there—a listening hole, drilled close to the floor. He became coldly alert.

That spy-hole had not been there earlier this afternoon—he'd had this room freshly inspected when he'd learned the inquiry would take place here. His own agents regularly re-mapped all the listening holes in this Fortress. Julianus nodded a calm farewell to Speratus. But once he was outside, in the colonnade, he discreetly looked into the unlit adjacent chamber.

It was empty. But had it been, moments before?

And what was that?— On the floor, in the triangle of light projecting into the chamber—a stylus, and a broken bit of the leather thong that had attached it to its wax tablet. Had someone exited in such haste, he dropped it?

A flash of movement caught his eye. One hundred paces ahead, someone was running. The slender figure of a boy clad in a Gallic farmer's short leather cape whipped round a left-angle turn in the colonnade. Pursuit was out of the question: The boy was too far off, and there were a thousand hidden nooks in this fortress into which an agile lad could vanish. Anyway, it was better that whoever had spied upon him didn't know he knew—and he was far from alone. Clerks, accountants, and junior officers hurried past, and Blaesus was lingering in the gardens, facing him as he stood in close conversation with one of the senior tribunes.

All at once Julianus was oblivious to the bright sun of noon, the hurrying slave on some urgent errand who nearly collided with him, the stern splendor of the columned facade of the Presidium, just ahead.

Would Maximus set a spy on me? Impossible. He'd need to ask my advice before he did it. He got his governorship because of me. And he's not of a nature to nurse secret hurts.

And what of that bloated serpent Blaesus, watching me now, while pretending not to? He's never forgiven me for bringing him to prosecution after he wrung dry with creative taxation that unsuspecting province entrusted to his governance. But he's not my equal in power and favor—he'd have to consider that any accusation he hurled at me might rebound back on himself.

The Palace?

Julianus had no illusions; despite Trajan's mildness, his power was as absolute as Domitian's had been, and the specter of violent replacement haunted all rulers, particularly when they were—as Trajan was now— preparing to set out on a distant conquest that could absent them from their capital for years. Julianus knew well that suspicions' fires, if fueled by some act of his, would burn doubly bright. For the Emperor was one of a small cir- cle of men who knew for certain that Marcus Julianus's was the invisible hand behind the assassination of the tyrant Domitian, whose death had ushered in the milder reign of the Emperor Nerva, who had, in turn, adopted Trajan, to assure a smooth succession. The thought would linger in any ruler's mind: The man who engineered such a change of rulers once is capable of doing it again.

He was darkly troubled as he imagined an imperial agent's report:

After Julianus tricked the others into leaving the room by lying about his pur- pose, he gathered intelligence about the plans of our enemy, which he never divulged to the Council. He then caused this Speratus to pledge silence to him, *as though the man owed greater allegiance to Julianus than to his Emperor and Lord.*

The moment would thrive hauntingly at the edges of consciousness in the days to come.

Chapter 4

Auriane held grimly to Arria Juliana's hands, as though to keep her child on earth. Arria fought to hold fast to her nine years; each struggling breath was a hand grasping for purchase on a cliff, staving off a plummet into the world of the shades. The child lay on a *lectus* within the smothering herbal darkness of the villa's sick chamber. Auriane thought of the sad little stand of tilted gravestones alongside the river, marking the brief lives of dozens of the tenant farmers' children, all clustered about Arria's age—a crop of small green shoots snipped short. Children must glide through Hel's realm again and again before they attained the relative safety of adulthood. It had always been so. She took a clay pot of steaming medicine and pressed its bird-beak spout to Arria's dry lips. Auriane had prepared the mixture herself, praying to the Ancestresses while pouring boiling water over leaves of holly, queen-of-the-meadow, and bark of white willow, plants she and Avenahar had collected together while roaming the virgin woodland about the villa. It was helping little.

Not knowing what prompted her, Auriane removed the black leather amulet she wore about her neck always, and placed it on Arria Juliana's breast. In one moment it seemed a rash thing to do. The amulet's power—like the seeress Ramis, who'd given it to her—was unpredictable. It contained earth from the holiest of wells, where Fria, goddess-mother of men, often showed herself to the people; Auriane sometimes thought the amulet a sort of hallowed leash by which the baleful old woman meant to draw her onto the oracular path. Ramis wanted more than that, Auriane darkly suspected, so much more that her mind vigorously pushed the knowledge back into darkness. *She wants me to take her place.* But Auriane did not count herself great-souled enough; all the seeresses of the tribes of Germania called this woman mistress.

She thought it impious to take the amulet off—but perhaps its earth-born holiness could heal.

Arria's dark, thick lashes didn't stir at the touch of the dread thing.

Avenahar was standing expectantly in the chamber door, letter in hand, showing unusual restraint as she waited for her mother to notice her. When Auriane saw that it bore Marcus Julianus's seal, she left Arria with a favorite maidservant, a sturdy young bloom called Brico, born of the Treveran tribe, the quiet Celtic people who'd lived along the Mosella before the coming of Rome. Brico was with child by the steward Demaratos and didn't know that Auriane knew—but that was a problem for another day.

In the passage outside the sick chamber, Auriane and Avenahar read the letter together, after closing the short passage's connecting doors for privacy. Avenahar was a faster reader, having been taught in youth; she read first of Witgern's attack.

She gave a yelp of joy.

"Avenahar! Show a care for your sister."

Avenahar whispered in Chattian, "It's a sign of hope."

"It's a sign of rash stupidity," Auriane answered in their tongue. "All Witgern won us was the murder of the hostages."

"He sprang on them like prey."

"He'll start a war."

"No, read further, Father stopped it. Witgern got to keep his victory." Avenahar then turned to look at her mother, as if at a holy thing. "Mother . . . you named correctly the fort, the day, and the hour."

Auriane regretted having told Avenahar of the prediction she'd given to Marcus. "Never mind, I can't think of that now."

"And you did it without the trance songs—a seeress needs songs to aid her. You just *did* it. This is a prodigy. You even named the praefect . . . this cognomen 'Speratus' is the same word that means 'hoped for' in the Roman tongue."

"Enough. I forbid you to speak on it more."

Before Avenahar came to the end of the passage, she turned and looked beseechingly at her mother. "How long can you deny what you are?"

"Enough!"

As Auriane returned to Arria's room, she felt her whole spirit stiffening in resistance. She sensed a vaulted door swinging open to darkness, revealing a pale, beckoning hand. If she truly possessed such power to see what comes, it belonged to her people—and not returning to them was much like thieving it from them. It was one more sign the Fates required the impossible of her—that she go home and minister to her people.

She returned to the chamber to find the maidservant Brico luminous in her amazement, and Arria babbling, her waxy, purplish lids struggling open. Brico shot up in flustered joy, then looked back, fearfully, at the earth amulet.

"Mistress. That came from the Lady? From Ramis herself?"

Slowly Auriane nodded.

"Arria knows me! She will live! *Domina,* it has brought her back to us."

"It can't be. Nothing heals so quickly."

Arria sat up and stared, full of the befuddled wonderment of a traveler to marvelous places. "I saw awful things," the child said. ". . . They came and came . . . riders in war . . . mountains that turned to monsters."

"It's what a fever does, poor child, it isn't real." Auriane dropped to the bed and embraced Arria as if to crush her. *I'll never let you beyond my sight.*

Had the amulet such power? Suddenly it disturbed Auriane to know it had lain on her own breast all these years, subverting her will, working Ramis's, that somber Lady who'd hunted her like game, all her life.

Just then the bronze bells hung in the passage to ward off evil made their melancholy noise—agitated, insistent.

It sounded like women, calling to her across a lake.

Auriane felt a prickle of spirit-terror. There was no wind in that passage—she'd closed the connecting doors.

All conspires to pull this life apart. I'll not let it. By all the gods, I will never leave this place.

AT MIDMORNING THE following day, a decurion of the Imperial Horse Guard presented himself at the columned entrance to Julianus's villa. The

steward Demaratos found himself eye-to-eye with the embossed image of
Mars on the guardsman's golden cuirass; Horse Guards were selected for size,
drawn mainly from the Batavians, a tribe of Germania. Demaratos disliked
the man at once. The guardsman's gaze was fixed on the air just above Demaratos's head in a way that implied he grappled daily with high mysteries of
state, far beyond the comprehension of a mere country steward.

"I am Marcus Ulpius Secundus," he began, "and I've a letter to deliver to
the master of this estate, from the Secretary to our Divine Lord in Rome."
Though the man had done much to cleanse himself of the marks of native
ancestry—disguising himself behind three names and mimicking closely the
speech of the capitol—the veneer was thin. The red-haired beast was but one
generation removed from kin who pulled flea-ridden blankets to their ears by
a hearthfire with grunting animals stabled near. For all his fine airs, Demaratos
thought, this fellow is just as barbarous as the mistress of this household.

Demaratos made up his mind to make things as difficult as possible for
this Romanized lout. "I fear my lord's not here. He's at Mogontiacum, helping decide where you'll be sent in the coming Dacian war. He's lecturing a
fine group from the Palace, expounding on the beauties of the Age of Gold,
when kings sacrificed themselves to the people, and all lived virtuously without law, but I'm sure you know about these things, being from the Capitol
and all. It starts at the noon hour; if you hurry off now you'll get there just
as Zeus is born." The copper-haired giant refused to look puzzled but Demaratos was satisfied the man knew he'd had his ignorance wagged in his
face. "Or," Demaratos went on smoothly, "you can present your letter to the
Matrona."

"The *Matrona*?" Marcus Julianus had no wife. The guardsman allowed
himself a bare smile, then nipped it short. Demaratos heard clearly: "However you wish to lighten the burden of serving that shameful oddity of a
mistress, I won't object." "No delay, good man," he said. "She'll do. Summon her."

Demaratos hesitated, momentarily distressed—it hadn't occurred to him
the overgroomed brute would consent to giving his message to Auriane. He
recovered himself and managed loftily, "The mistress is . . . practicing. She
spars with wooden swords to heat the blood, to balance the humors of the
body, and to keep her strength."

The guardsman checked a burst of laughter. This country steward would
have him assume this outlandish activity was ordered by a physician. He gave
Demaratos a blank look.

"Of course. Might I disturb her . . . practicing?"

Demaratos felt like a treed cat that could do little but hiss, but he kept his feline dignity.

"You may. But you might want to remove that fine fringed cloak and that gold cuirass, lest she want to spar with you."

The guardsman flushed. It was a dramatic coloring, reddening his face, his neck, his nose, and Demaratos thought it ironic how a flush makes you more visible at the precise moment you'd prefer to disappear.

"Steward, I have never crossed weapons with a woman. This is as much to avoid injury to them as in consideration of the fact that it would not be seemly for a senior member of the Imperial Horse Guard to be seen doing such a disgraceful thing."

"But my lord! She has sparred with far stouter, better-muscled specimens than yourself; in fact she even slew a man twice your size, before all your people!" It pleased Demaratos to wield a double-edged blade, ridiculing both Auriane and this pretentious guardsman.

"Yes, of course. I'm sure she did," the guardsman said carefully, briefly reflecting on a grotesque, half-remembered tale that Julianus had rescued this uncouth woman from condemnation to the arena, where she had competed as a gladiatrix before the mob in the Great Amphitheater in Rome. But he checked a tart reply—why trouble to correct the manners of an ignorant servant, as long as there were none about to witness? He considered briefly that the master and mistress of this household might simply be insane. Julianus was said to be a philosopher, after all, and weren't they all missing a few support beams in their houses? "Just take me to her," he said, for he'd given over his own lathered mount to the villa's grooms, "and I'll deliver the letter and be on my way."

When a freshly saddled mount was brought, the guardsman strode out into the brilliant haze of the morning sun, his plumed helmet adorned with mythic scenes tucked beneath one arm.

"That is a mare." The guardsman said it as if the reason for his objection was self-evident.

"You are correct," Demaratos said politely. "A mare it is."

"I cannot sit a mare."

"It's not so simple to find a mount that will quietly accept an unknown rider, my lord. And, be assured, this is a bold, brave, worthy mare, a battle mare, in fact, who holds the rank of centurion among horses."

"This household has evidently not seen enough of the whip!" The guardsman was gratified by the horrified look this brought to Demaratos's smooth Attic features. He knew, then, this man had never considered such punishment a possibility, amazing as that seemed. Perhaps there was no impudent intent in that response; the man merely made a simpleminded joke? *This is a household of madmen,* the guardsman thought.

He squared his shoulders and announced, "I'll walk."

"It's past a mile."

"And no man can walk it faster than me."

A slender groom, a gentle-natured Treveran boy, proudly marched ahead of them to show the way. They passed the domed bathhouse, and crossed between paddocks in which sleek mares grazed contentedly in silk coats of red-brown, umber, and gold. On a summit above was a small temple to Epona, Goddess of Horses, a deity the guardsman knew well, for she was worshipped by the Roman cavalry—though he disliked sharing his trustworthy Epona with these rude country villains. It made him aware there were no shrines about the estate's main house. Julianus apparently had little use for Jupiter or Mars, and probably worshipped only Providence, like most aristocrats with a taste for philosophy. They strode past the neat farms of the villa's tenants, who grew oats, emmer wheat, and barley; two farmers in their hiplength, hooded leather capes waved familiarly and shouted greetings. *Pert behavior,* the guardsman thought. *This is an estate overrun with impious wretches who don't know their place, and a master is always to blame.*

After a quarter mile—after which Demaratos puffed pitiably and sweated, while the armored man might have been reclining on a couch—they turned off the carriage path and into the forest. There, Demaratos left them. After a time, the guardsman heard the crisp strikes of wood on wood, arrhythmic but precise. The path vanished; their feet sank into the earth's mossy hide.

Before them was a dished place in the earth that formed a crude amphitheater. Nature freely overran the place. Logs had been set about this forest theater, to provide seating for a small audience. Half the places were filled, and the onlookers were an odd mix of stable grooms, house slaves, youths, and maids who he supposed were students from the academy Julianus had founded in the nearby town of Confluentes, as well as a tenant farmer or two. Languishing among them familiarly as a prostitute was a comely black-haired maid, turned out in clothes too fine for a slave—could she be a daughter of this bizarre household? This insolent nymph ruined her tender looks by staring back at him as if he had something to answer for. Next to her was a slight, elfin man he recognized—the fellow had once given a dinner entertainment at a rich house the guardsman frequented in Rome: the satiric poet Milo, the razor-witted waif every man feared, just a little, and every woman wanted to take care of. Milo sprawled casually on a log, gesturing with a chased-silver wine-cup, garbed in an absurd red-and-blue flowered dinner tunic. It surprised the guardsman not at all to find a creature like Milo here, for every oddity in Rome eventually found his way to Marcus Julianus's villa. It burnished a man's reputation to say you'd basked for a time in this temple of learning.

In the natural arena was a tall woman in a short, belted leather tunic, who was bending to help a man to his feet. Auriane, he realized. In her hand was a heavy wooden practice sword, which she held as if it belonged there, like a stylus or a comb.

"Stay here," the young groom said to him. "You must lay down your sword if you would approach closer."

"My patience with this household is at an end. Stand aside. I regret having to deal so firmly with you, but I do not take orders from house slaves." He strode briskly into the cleared enclosure.

Auriane turned to him.

"Perhaps, then, you'll take orders from me." She regarded him with the fierce purity of a Vestal, yet with the barest flicker of humor in her eyes. She seemed oblivious to how outlandish she was, this strange huntress-queen defending her grove. A light sweat glazed her forehead. Bronze hair was drawn back with masculine severity into a braid thick as a man's arm. She wore the dark stain of perspiration on her fawn-skin tunic like some adornment. He found himself faintly appalled, but fascinated.

"Lay down that sword," she said then, "or I'll not take that letter from your hand."

"I wear it even in the presence of the Emperor. Certainly I'll not shed it for a country woman."

"Well then, I'll say you never delivered it. You may even lose your rich pension, Horse Guardsman." In her face was a mix of soberness and playfulness, humor and challenge. The company on the logs burst into laughter. They sound like honking geese in Hades, he thought. Only the bold dark-haired maid wasn't laughing. He saw the sleek-maned she-colt had the same eyes, the same chin, and realized this was indeed the woman's daughter.

Auriane's aspect became gentler. "This is sacred ground, good man, and would be polluted by the presence of iron. I ask as a courtesy, not to challenge you."

"The denizens of this household are uniformly insane." He unsheathed his sword and laid it on the moss.

"A new man, Mars and Bellona be praised! Fight her, fall to her!" The words were Milo's, thrown out musically like verse. Then they chanted all together, "Fight her, fight her!"

"Silence, you villains!" They ignored him.

Auriane raised a hand for silence and they obeyed at once.

"Let me assure myself I have the right woman," the guardsman said. "Are you that same Aurinia of the Chattians brought to Rome in chains after the Emperor Domitian's punitive expedition against your people, who is now the concubine of Marcus Julianus?"

She refused to be goaded. "If you insist on saying it that way, yes, I am."

"This, then, is for you to receive for Marcus Arrius Julianus, from the imperial Secretary in Rome, acting for the Emperor."

"Fight her!" Now they clapped as they chanted the words.

"Some would say he's faint of heart . . ." Milo's needling trill rose above them all. *". . . A sybil said he's full of victories untold. . . . I say he'd better run . . . or he'll wallow in shame when he's old!"*

One of the stable grooms thrust into the guardsman's hands a grimy wooden sword with a sweat-darkened grip.

Angrily, he turned to face them. "I'll not lay this daughter of wild men on the ground just to prove a case that doesn't need proving, before a drunken nest of softlings and sybarites."

Milo stood up on the log, agile as a monkey. A frog-broad smile was touched with horror as he revealed blackened teeth. "You think far too well of yourself, with too little cause, Batavian. *Your* tribe yielded to Rome. It matters not that your master's the Emperor, for it was said by a wise man: 'The slave of a great man is still a slave.' Yet you insult a free woman, of a tribe that did not yield."

That neck's scrawny as a chicken's, the guardsman thought—*one smart twist would snap it.*

"Fight her! Show us what you've got! Fight her!" chorused the others. He did not hear how lighthearted the taunts were; to him, it was the voice of a jury in a capital case, the burning brand that goads a gladiator to strike.

"I debase myself in teaching you this lesson," he said stiffly to Auriane, "but then who's to know, beyond that troop of monkeys over there?"

"As you wish. But they mean you no harm, nor do I."

He removed the heavy gold cuirass. Clad in a belted woolen undertunic, he strode to the center of the enclosure. Auriane turned to face him. The guardsman shifted his hand on the grip and assumed a balanced pose, holding the wooden sword with grim purpose now. In Auriane's eyes he saw a small jump of excitement, as of a racehorse led to the starting rope. He began easing in a circle about her, exhibiting his size, the reach of his arms. She kept herself in range, slowly moving with him, then to his surprise, began pressing in closer—a reckless maneuver, but right for one slight of body, he knew, for with his longer arms he was at a disadvantage in close quarters.

He erupted into motion first, executing a brutal downward cut that played out into nothingness. She scudded sideways like some feather on a breeze. Then this evasive maneuver somehow evolved into an attack, as she seamlessly spun round into a stance so oppressively close they might have embraced, while lashing out with whiplash-fast parries that made him feel closeted, uncomfortable, roped in by subtle argument; he couldn't open out to get a full swing at her. He felt he fought a lynx. He moved backward to give himself room and was not sure of the precise moment when he was no longer doing so voluntarily, but giving ground. Yes, she was *taking* ground and he wasn't sure precisely how; she flashed into openings he didn't know he was leaving, her movements unpredictable as a whipping adder's tail. It was as though her mind somehow fastened onto his and she saw his next stroke as he conceived it.

She struck him in the side with the flat of the sword, bruising a rib.

"That's a strike!" came a shout from the logs.

"It's a kill!" The jubilant shriek was Milo's.

He rushed her then and got control, battering her blade, punishing it with frantic strength. She defended herself with strokes that were startlingly fast, and perplexing—she never quite seemed to meet force with force. It was as though a power were raised up in her by her own movement. And soon enough, he knew she was melting off by design, drawing him to full extension, tiring him. All the while, most aggravatingly, she seemed not to be paying full attention—or rather, her gaze seemed to take in the whole of the field, reducing him to one insignificant part. After a quarter-hour by the water clock he found himself heaving deeply for breath.

His downward cut was masterfully executed—surely, a successful strike to the shoulder. But she whipped her blade up from nowhere. The impact was so blunt and ungiving he felt his wooden weapon struck granite; his teeth slammed together. This was no training-ground maneuver; it was something far stranger. Her whole body had surged forward with the blow, as if all the lifeforce in her flooded into the sword and, oddly, at impact, her attention seemed elsewhere.

Before he had time to assess what she'd done, she was rolling against his side, behind him when she should have been in front. Then she dismantled him in three grand, cursive strokes, like some decisive script written in air—a clipped downward blow to the back of his knees left him slowly sinking. This looped round into a flourish that played into space, to become a crushing horizontal stroke to the forearm. His numbed hand fell open; the wooden sword slid to the ground.

When his senses returned he lay on his back on the moss, too mortified to move, wondering if he could somehow convince them he was dead, so they'd leave him alone.

"She's finished with this one, bring on the next!" The words, all vinegar-and-honey, were Milo's. "Sir, your tribunes should engage *her* to train your Horse Guard!"

He felt his limbs had been set in quicklime.

My career is dust, should word of this fly to Rome. They'll take my horse, my armor, and turn me out, swordless, in a bare tunic, before my assembled cohort. No early retirement, no good civil appointments later, no happy ease basking in imperial appreciation . . .

The wretched Amazon bent over him then, actually meaning to help him up.

"I did not mean to offend," she was saying. "You fought well. Pay no attention to their rude jests." She hesitated, then added, "You must be our guest. Marcus Julianus would want you to pass the night here."

As the Horse Guardsman rose, he studied Milo, that elven nightmare with close-crimped black curls. And Milo, with that wide, guileless, man-boy face, looked back; there was no emotion there, no knowledge of how deeply he had offended. *Would the little wasp pen an epigram about this? Or perhaps this debacle was worthy of a more lengthy work, which would circulate in every great house, every tavern in Rome? I'll see he never gets a chance.*

And I'll see that this ridiculous household, the curse of normal society, of all decent men, pays for its crime.

"I shall take your offer," he replied. If he would silence Milo, he'd have to linger about the villa for a while. It wouldn't be murder. He was only protecting the honor of one of the Empire's most venerable institutions, the Horse Guard.

THE COMPANY BEGAN to rise and drift off, some seeking horses, others meaning to walk. Auriane broke the seal on the imperial letter, face flushed from the bout, mind still afire from the exhilaration of single battle. Avenahar lingered behind the small group; she'd taken up Auriane's discarded wooden sword and was striking ardently at air, imitating strokes she'd seen her mother make; since the incident with the fugitive sailors, Avenahar had been practice-sparring from dawn until noon, every day. Then she dropped the wooden sword and bounded after them, burrowing beneath Auriane's arm.

Avenahar kept her voice as low as she was able, in her excitement. "What was that maneuver you finished him with? That upward blow was uncanny. There was more than your own strength in that. You'll show me how you did it?"

"Yes, Avenahar, but not now . . . tomorrow. That fellow over there bears watching." She nodded toward the Horse Guardsman, who walked at a measured distance from the rest of the company. "He's hungry for something. There's much about him I don't like. Besides, better than half these Horse Guardsmen are informers."

"But all say Trajan allows no informers."

"That's a pretty tale for the commons. This one just knows how to use them discreetly and not offend. If he wants to keep his seat, he'll have informers. Avenahar—!"

Avenahar had snatched the letter from her mother and was rapidly reading. "This is dreadful—"

"Give that to me!"

"I read faster."

"So read something else! I can't believe I raised so unmannerly a daughter."

After moments of tortured progress through the letter, Auriane said, "It's what we feared. That cursed war that's coming, in Dacia . . . Marcus is commanded to go, to be on the Emperor's staff of inner advisors. Our best hope for keeping him home, I suppose, will be if Rome runs out of nations to steal in our lifetimes."

"No, there's plenty more world to snatch—beyond the lands of Parthia lie the mysterious lands of—"

"I need no pert tutor in geography to tell me Dacia's at the ends of the earth. Curses on all life. And Marcus, being Marcus, won't refuse. He'll fear dishonoring his father. This will take him from us for a year. Don't react to this, dearest, that horrible man is looking at you."

The guardsman was watching them carefully, not with simple hatred, as Auriane might have expected, but more with a look of horror and disgust, as of one who opens the stores and finds them crawling with maggots. "That man raises gooseflesh. By the law of guest-friendship we must feed and keep him tonight, but by Hel I want him gone on the morrow, and that's *early* on the morrow. I'll tell the grooms to have his horse and attendants readied by the gate at dawn."

THE DINNER WAS humble—Auriane ordered from the villa's kitchens a first course of saffron quail's eggs, a second of sweet-and-sour turnips seasoned with rue. This was to be followed by a main course of chickens stuffed with olive relish and braised in thyme honey, accompanied by leek and onion tarts; then finally, roast apples filled with almonds. The diners slowly assembled, and had completed the first course while Auriane was still immersed in the daily tasks of the villa—going over the accounts with Demaratos, hearing the household's complaints. In the dark of the library, Auriane listened to another report from the warehouseman Aprossius, who insisted he was so close to Lurio now, he could smell the fish-stink on the fugitive sailor. The sausage vendors of Confluentes had had numerous sightings—mostly of Lurio's back as he sprinted off with their goods. Aprossius then demanded more money of her. Though Auriane suspected she was being milked like a goat, she paid. At least Lurio hadn't presented himself before the magistrate—but Auriane wasn't much encouraged; her deeper senses warned her Lurio wasn't of a nature to let such a fine chance to enrich himself go unexploited.

Lastly, she took a thanksgiving gift to the wooden image of Fria she'd set up by the river, in gratitude for saving Arria's life. After offering one of Arria's jointed wooden dolls to the ever-moving water, she saw that Grimo, rower on the wineship *Isis,* still had left her no sign. Always, he tied a white cloth to the old willow there, to let her know all was well. Now he'd not done so for a quarter course of the moon. It troubled her greatly. The red cloth she had tied there—a second attempt to warn him to desist—hung sadly, rotting off the tree from the assault of the rains.

When Auriane finally joined the diners in the grand *triclinium*—the dining hall reserved for guests—she found Milo putting everyone on edge; her guests savored his mean jokes like delicacies until one struck too close to their own doors. Because he was famous they fought for his attention—a favor hard to grasp as smoke, and as easily lost, until the moment you uttered something you never, never wanted repeated. Auriane had assigned Milo a place on the couch farthest from the Horse Guardsman, stationing herself strategically in between, but Milo respected no couch-order; he was flowing about the room as he acted verses he'd written about a boy-prostitute of the Circus stalls who mortified the high-born in Rome by disguising himself in fashionable stola and wig and invading some tedious, solemn matron's religious rite forbidden to men. Milo's long white hands were graceful as swan's necks as they laced round that sweet, sinuous voice in the gathering dusk. Auriane watched with alert sadness, numbed by the number of things turning to ill of late, seized with a sense that a dark wind blew round this still and beautiful world. She touched Ramis's earth amulet for strength, but suddenly thought it a living thing, and a clever enemy.

THE NIMBLE-TONGUED wretch would need to go to the *latrina* sometime soon, the guardsman judged, given the way he was swilling down Julianus's best wine. He himself had touched scarcely a swallow. One cupful he'd dashed into the chased-silver ice-bowl that chilled the mixing water, so his determination to avoid drunkenness would prick no suspicions. Milo, however, was getting sloppy. Mars and Epona aided him there. The creatures he was forced to dine with reinforced his belief this was a household of madmen: Some appeared to be students from the town who showed signs of desperate poverty, judging from the condition of their shoes, stacked carefully by the door, and by the fact that they came with no slaves. Others appeared to be town tradesmen. Yet they reclined familiarly with a distinguished guest or two from Rome; he recognized the old scholar Marcellinus, of Senatorial rank, who was here, he'd heard somewhere, to complete his twenty-volume work on natural history. Auriane, *Matrona* from Hades, presided over it all not as a decent woman would, but rather like some barbarous chief on a high-seat. She shared in the coarse country jests and passed round cups of some vile, foaming drink—mead, they called it—and once, raised a battle-scarred arm to make toasts. *It's a fatal weakness in Julianus,* the guardsman judged, *to allow this woman such indecencies.* The comely black-haired daughter—*Avenahar* was the coarse name she'd been given—was sneaking unwatered wine while her mother wasn't looking, and the girl's skill at this rivaled her mother's at swordfighting, for this mother had a keen eye for most things. The poor creature has no chance, he thought. That maid might have been groomed to be a great beauty, had Juno given her decent parents. The food he found just fair; the chicken was, after all, a humble bird; a man with Julianus's fortune could dine on peacock brains every night. The house slaves were pert, addressing the mistress without leave. And it seemed no one in all the northern provinces knew how to make an edible olive relish.

Finally, Milo gushed some nonsense in verse about bravely rising to nature's call, legs wobbling like a foal's as he was hoisted up by one of his boy-slaves. The guardsman did not follow immediately after; that surely would have prompted Auriane to investigate. Instead, his groom approached him, as the man had been instructed to earlier, and whispered urgent words in his master's ear. The guardsman excused himself, announcing that he needed to attend to a matter outside. One of his horses had an inflamed pastern and might need to be traded for another. The diners accepted it. But Auriane looked at him as though he'd tried to give her short weight on a bale of wool. He'd have to move quickly.

Once through the vestibule, guardsman and groom walked swiftly along the entrance colonnade; he meant to melt off into the labyrinth of graveled walkways through the peristyle garden, and so, on to the *latrina,* positioned behind the villa's south wing. They passed a chamber off the kitchens where Julianus's servants were gathered about the evening meal, and a quick glance within gave him another surprise: It appeared they were laying into the same fare the guests were enjoying. In a normal household, slaves got the best dishes only at family sacrifices, when all gathered to make offerings to the household gods.

His groom kept pace with him for a time, speaking in a covered voice.

"We've ferreted out an interesting thing or two," the groom said, "though I don't know if it's of much use: I found a cowering native woman stashed in the barn, with a collar reading, 'If I run off, return me to Volusius Victorinus's—"

"That's the most senior of the town magistrates, isn't it? At Confluentes?"

"Right, my lord. He's a man of some importance."

"So, Auriane's helping the magistrate's rightful property alienate itself from him. Not respectable behavior, but not near enough to sink a man like Julianus. You'll have to do better. I want you to stay on a few days here so you'll have more time to root about—feign an illness, a stomach ailment or something, Mercury knows, the food's bad enough. Let them put you up in the barn. But be careful, the woman's suspicious. Has Argaippo brought the horses round?"

"He has."

"Off with you, then. Tell the others, I will meet them at the Confluentes gate at dawn."

The Horse Guardsman halted at the end of the colonnade and paused in a drape of shadow; before him was the *latrina,* a massive, boxlike window-less structure detached from the main house. Within, it was dimly lit by lamps suspended from wrought-iron chains. He faintly discerned two of four marble seats set in a row. Someone exited; it wasn't Milo. He could only assume the elfin versifier was still lurking within.

Just as he made to approach it, he heard light footsteps and women's laughter from the gardens; he was only partly concealed by the rich hangings between the columns of the peristyle. *Fine time for a clutch of housemaids to come by.* He fell back into an adjacent doorway of the main house and was surprised when the thick oaken door easily gave way. Intrigued, he looked about. What was this room? It seemed to be attached to the villa's library, but that door was closed and locked. Documents were strewn everywhere, some spilling onto the floor. It seemed an intensely private place, one, perhaps, that servants never entered, a room for thinking and writing. A place to hoard questionable books, embarrassing letters, texts of damaging speeches, perhaps?

The maids still chattered like jays, just outside the door; he'd be a fool not to see what he could find while he was trapped in here. Hurriedly he took up one bookroll, then another, holding them to the fading light issuing from a single glazed window, growing increasingly frustrated as he waded through texts of lectures designed to send a regular man straight to Morpheus—who could give a fig about Demonax's belief in the rightness of abandoning wealth to live in philosophical poverty? In another, he scanned quickly through, "Seek not that the things which befall you should happen as you wish, but wish the things that happen to be as they are, and you will find tranquillity" . . . but Julianus didn't even write it; someone named Epictetus did. He threw it down in disgust. This was leading nowhere.

But he'd met a man in Rome who had been advertising for some time that he'd pay a fine price for *any* damaging material about Marcus Julianus. He was said to be the agent of the Senator Lappius Blaesus, so the guards-man knew there was good money behind him. He continued to search.

Just as he was ready to give it up, he found his emerald-in-the-straw. He felt a jump of excitement as he came upon a diatribe against all wars of conquest. ". . . how damaging to the commons," he read, "how vain before the ancient philosophers, how hateful in the sight of Providence . . ." He rushed ahead, and realized this, too, was a lecture, given by Julianus at the academy he founded at Confluentes: ". . . In truth, even this coming Dacian campaign, which seems necessary because our territories are attacked by a rebellious king, can be shown to be no more right than theft of a neighbor's house, if one but traces this war back to our republican beginnings, and our seizure of country after country in a path that has finally brought us to Dacia. Think of Illyricum in times of old, said to be 'harboring our enemies,' and conquered by Augustus for reasons that would sound distressingly modern and familiar to our ears . . . where, finally, will peace be made? Off the ends of the earth?"

By Mars's grace, Julianus even mentioned the war by name. *In a lecture.* And if he wasn't mistaken, his enemies might be able to toss an extra log on the fire by adding a charge of defaming the genius of the divine Augustus, as well.

In an ivory canister he found two more copies of the same lecture. He removed one, then found a rolled document in the wall niches, roughly equal in size and thickness, and put this one into the canister so that it would seem nothing was disturbed.

He stuffed his prize into a fold of his tunic and waited as, finally, the carousing housemaids moved on. As he crept toward the *latrina* he saw no sign of Milo. Silently, he cursed. Then he heard the vile versifier's unmistakable laugh, muffled within. Had he tarried to scribble obscene verses on the walls, so all the world would know the great Milo had been there?

A Cupid-faced boy with clothing in disarray stumbled from the *latrina,* to scurry off furtively as vermin when a torch is thrust into a dark room—a household slave, the guardsman realized. Dalliance. So that was what detained the elfin wretch. The guardsman edged into the narrow doorway of the *latrina* and nearly collided with Milo.

The guardsman gave him a brutal shove. Milo careened backward into the gloom of the *latrina;* his head struck a hanging iron lamp. Hot oil splattered over them both. The poet let out a series of melodious shrieks. His cries echoed hideously off the concrete walls, sounding like a water organ pounded upon by a man who'd come unhinged. Greedily, the guardsman got his big hands about Milo's thin neck. Then he felt a hot, fierce pain in his arm. The wretch had a razor. Soon his hands were slipping in some horrid mixture of hot oil and his own blood. He lost his grip. An oily Milo slithered down to the floor and managed to wriggle between the guardsman's legs, all the while continuing his ear-shredding shouts, *"Murder! Murder!"* He continued his squealing cry, even though he was out in the garden now and past all danger. He was rousing the whole household to arms.

The guardsman felt for the stolen letter containing the text of the lecture—yes, it was safely in place.

Then he bolted from the *latrina,* sprinting through a plum orchard, where young Argaippo waited on his nervous black gelding, holding the guardsman's Hispanian stallion, its chest and breech straps flashing with medallions of gold. He was forced to flee like a house thief while that rodent Milo lived on to spread an even worse tale about him. His one hope for keeping his good name was to thoroughly discredit this household, so that no one associated with this den of madmen would ever be believed on any matter, or counted worthy of commanding the respect of decent men.

He put a hand round one of the saddle's four wooden horns and painfully hauled himself up; he was beginning to stiffen up from the blows inflicted by that sword-wielding harpy. Behind him, the household was stirred to great activity: Hounds barked enthusiastically. Shadowed figures gathered in clusters, while others darted through the gardens with torches. His stallion erupted into a gallop. With Argaippo a length behind, the Horse Guardsman set a course for the forest, and a woodcutter's path he'd noticed earlier in the day.

Chapter 5

"*There is a stench about the place,*" Auriane wrote the next day to Marcus, "*since that Horse Guardsman has gone. Evil will come of him. I have it from poor Milo's own lips that the man tried to murder him. Hurry your return. You are dearer to me than my own life.*"

On the following eve, long past the snuffing of the lamps, Auriane was roused from sleep by a tumultuous wind. When she stepped out into the colonnade she saw it again, just as she had the night before—beyond the peristyle gardens, lingering in the somber deeps by the river, was a softly glowing light.

She caught her breath. Last night she'd convinced herself it was the lamp of some merchant craft on the Mosella. Tonight it was clearly something else—steadily it ascended the bank, seeming almost inquisitive as it brushed the ground then arced up to man-height, demanding human attention.

Nothing living would be abroad on this night. But she continued down the colonnade, drawn into the mystery of that phantasmal light. Her nightclothes billowed like a sail. The wind was an outlaw, toppling an urn in the garden, rioting through the orchard, boxing the alders, unleashing ghosts. She sensed legions of the dead clamoring overhead on bloodless horses; on such a night, the wild hunt led by her people's god Wodan would unfurl across the sky.

The fuzzy light continued its evocative dance, edging closer. It blinked as it moved through the orchard and was rhythmically blotted out by trees. Suddenly she realized it was someone with a lamp. Whoever it was approached by the one path that ensured his scent would not rouse the dogs or the horses. Evidently he, she . . . *it* knew the plan of the farm.

I should awaken the grooms, she thought. *It's foolish to meet an intruder alone.*

Once, she glanced toward the stables and saw that one of the grooms *was* there, watching her near the blacker-than-night entrance to the barn.

Good. Let him. He can rouse the others if trouble arises.

Then she realized the light was moving in a pattern familiar as a nod of a head. Could it be? *It was.* That signal was used by the warrior companions of her father, Baldemar, to sign a night approach to comrades. The old sign, once discerned, seemed clear as her feet before her; she couldn't understand why she didn't know it at once. *Gods below, it's someone known to my father.*

Pity, remorse, and amazement jostled within her in a potent mixture. *Feed him.* That was her first thought. She doubled back to the storehouse attached to the villa's kitchens and began stuffing a hemp sack with millet bread, a wheel of hard cheese, sausages from the smokehouse, a glass jar of pickled peas, a jug of good wine—as tears flooded her eyes.

While busy in the storehouse, she never saw the groom as the man darted forward in the dark and began threading his way through rows of concealing box-hedges as he, too, made his way toward the visitor with the lamp.

Returning with her food-offering Auriane felt a yawning dread coiled about a core of relief, as she imagined one might feel when facing death after long illness.

The old world comes for me at last.

News from home could bring no good.

The light had reached the garden; she saw it was a horn lamp, such as are affixed to carriages. It illumined a hooded figure, and the flare of a man's heavy travelling cloak.

"Who's there? Show yourself!" Auriane shouted into the wind. "Have you need of help?"

"A friend! I mean no harm."

That voice shot into forgotten realms in her, infusing breath into withered places. *No. It couldn't be.*

"Are you Auriane?"

That voice!

"Auriane? It's you, isn't it? It's Witgern."

She hesitated, doubtful again. Where was his old valley-filling roar?

"What's the name of the hound my father kept," Auriane said, "his favorite?"

"Shadow," came the ready reply. "Auriane, it's—"

"What is my dead brother's name, and how was he slain?"

"Arnwulf," came an unhesitating reply, "and he was slain in a Roman raid on your father's hall. Why do you doubt me? Auriane, it truly is me, I swear it on your father's sword."

She began running then, losing sausages from the sack as she half stumbled once. She stopped when she was arm's length from him, dropped the food sack, and grasped him by the shoulders.

"Witgern, what in the name of the *gods* are you doing?" A sudden burst of laughter made her anger less convincing. "You're mad to be on this side of the river!"

"I am, perhaps," came a good-natured reply, "but so, too, is the world."

Beneath a woolen hood she saw the warmth of welcome in his single eye, though it burned a little too brightly, like a creature become feral. Ash-colored hair fell across his forehead. The ruined eye was covered with a black silken eyepatch; it lent him the look of a wizard living half in darkness, possessing knowledge of Hel's realms ahead of his time. That angular face hinted of its old refinement though its landscape had become stark, and the corrosion of winds and rain had roughened his flesh to the texture of cowhide. He was shorter than she remembered, but there lingered about him still the spirit of a bemused young poet; had he been born in a Roman town, he would be throwing out lyric lines to a rapt audience, not spears at a relentless enemy. He smelled of the bear's grease he'd rubbed on himself against the damp and cold.

"They'll make a spectacle of your death if they catch you! Do you want to die miserably in some small-town beast show? Have you lost all *sense*?"

"Can we seek a warmer place before you shout yourself hoarse?" He said it grinning.

She retrieved the food sack and pulled him toward the main house, where they found a place beneath the cover of the eaves; there, they sat, with their backs against the wall.

He jumped forward, alarmed.

"There is a fire in the walls."

"It's hot air, not fire. That's just the hypocausts, which give us heat."

Warily, he eased back again, and then he turned to Auriane, cupping a hand beneath her chin. "You're hale and handsome as a swan-maid! So this is where you dwell! A kingly place, worthy of you. I always thought you should be living in a palace. Evidently the gods think so, too."

She started to object that this was no palace, aware suddenly of how much of the world she had seen, how little of it he'd seen, but kept silent. "And you're powerful as a bear!" She said it to salve her sadness at his frailty.

"The sight of you is like spring after a snow-time that froze all the cattle! You're just as I last saw you, and yet forty winters have gone since that spring morning when Ramis caught you, a yowling babe."

"Stop flattering me and eat," she said, spilling the food from the sack before him. From the size of his bites she guessed he hadn't eaten in several days.

"I'll not be driven off?" he asked between attacks on the bread, looking anxiously toward the main house.

"If you mean by Julianus," Auriane replied, "he isn't here. Anyway, he'd never treat as an enemy any man I counted a friend. Let's not put the household's discretion to the test if we don't have to, though. How did you get here?"

"Friends of mine who were forced into one of those new cavalry cohorts, you know, made up of our people and men of our brother-tribes—they dressed me as one of their own and I rode right over the Mogon bridge, at night."

"You didn't! The prize rebel, riding right past the bridge sentries!"

"By Wodan's help I found this place. I was given wrong directions twice. I'll not be long. A few words with you, and the wolf melts back into the forest."

"We are sister and brother through all time!" Brother and sister in battle, she meant, for in youth they'd raided together along the frontier, and starved together during Domitian's war. At its end, he'd meant to die alongside her when the legions drove them from their final fort of refuge, and had his horse not found a rabbit hole and thrown him to the ground as they made their death-charge into the lines of a legion held in reserve, they would have been captured together. Instead, their lives had parted there, and she lived as an expatriate on the comfortable side of the Rhenus.

"I'll get to my purpose," he said, his voice grimmer now. "At the last full moon, the Great Assembly met in secret. They elected me to fetch you—they think I'm the only one smooth-tongued enough to convince you to return. Know this, Auriane: We need you now as at no other time."

She felt her body tautening, as if her flesh had become a shield.

"The Cheruscans have seized seventeen villages," he spoke on. "They've settled in to stay. Your home village lies like easy prey before them."

"And my mother?" she whispered.

"Athelinda's fine. I think the Cheruscan dogs fear her, just a little. They won't overrun the Boar Village until next year. But Auriane, we must go to war." He leaned closer and said in a covered voice, "Thanks to you, we can—your generosity has filled a cave with weapons of iron."

She broke her gaze from his, tense and desolate, beginning to feel herself a beast herded into a narrower and narrower pen.

"We must drive the Cheruscans off now or fall to them evermore," he went on. "The chiefs of our strongest war bands are warring with each other—they won't unite behind one man. I had hopes for that bright-shining son of your father's good companion—Sigibert—but of late there's an ugly tale going round that he plans to marry the invading chief's daughter. The sad truth of it is, we can't raise a force large enough without you. *You* are the only one every faction will follow."

The words shot through her like a javelin, swift, clean, complete—and merciless. She felt she'd been staked to a tree, and left there to writhe. For a time, she could not speak; she could only shake her head, *no*.

"You must know why I attacked that fort."

"That was singularly stupid, Witgern. Do you know that if Marcus Julianus hadn't—"

"I rescued Baldemar's sword from it, Auriane. I saved it from a pitiable life as a Roman war trophy."

"That can't be, no one knew what became of it."

"We watched, we listened, we found it. My band has it safe in their keeping."

"I never expected to hear of it again in this life," she said, with the hush of one who enters a death chamber. "I thought it cast off into a ditch somewhere, or rotting in the earth, or stowed unknown, in some foreign armory . . ."

"I did it so you could return—and take it up."

"But Witgern, a hundred ropes bind me here."

"I have the sword to cut a thousand ropes. Do you want your own Boar Village to be a Cheruscan town? When these Cheruscan lice are in need of money they drag our girl children off from the villages and the maids aren't seen again until they're put on the auction block at Mogontiacum. Can you

sit idle while we stock the Cheruscans' slave trade? We're assembling an army
in secret. When we take the holy images from the groves and go to war, you
must be with us. All say it: The right weapon in the right hand will restore the
world to what it was."

"Well, this is the wrong hand. I left Avenahar once to go to war and it
brought a bitter melancholy to her that's never gone away . . . I think part of
her distrusts me for it to this day. Now you want me to do it again, and this
time, leave *two* babes behind. No. Never again."

But her haunted look told him how divided in mind she was; it encouraged him to press harder.

"Why do you spar every day with a wooden sword? Because you know
your true fate. As for Avenahar and your little Arria Juliana . . . children
must live their parents' fate. It has always been so. You could send for them
in time. As for Marcus Julianus—he's not of our people, Auriane. I ask you
to put the blood of kin before the blood of a foreigner."

"You're angering me, Witgern. You drop a babe into my hands and say,
'Raise it.' You look at this villa that teems with what I love and say, 'Leave it.'
You're thin-witted to think such a thing can be decided in a moment."

"I see things more simply than that. Here is the most potent sword. And
here is Baldemar's daughter. When you want to make a big fire, you bring
pitch to the flames. This I do. I leave you to settle accounts with the spirits."

When she did not answer, his expression hardened. "Well, I see this place
has made you a different creature. You're not one of us anymore."

"That's cruel, Witgern. You ask me to agree, in a night, to unravel my life."

"Ah, I'm doing this badly—I must not be the clever envoy they think I
am. But believe me, Auriane, I *do* know the magnitude of what I ask."

"Why are they so intent upon me? Haven't I trampled on enough sacred
laws to be counted a curse in the flesh? My children have two fathers, and
they're both men of the enemy. I even took Roman citizenship. I've let years
pass without carrying out the rites at the ancestors' graves."

"Make no mistake about it, you *do* have a crop of enemies. There's a seeress who condemns you for those very things—a powerful one, close to Ramis.
But among the warriors, it is different. Some still offer a sacrifice for your return, every spring, on the spot where you were captured. To the common lot
of them you're their victory bearer. Some don't know you from a swan-maid.
And a swan-maid can bed any man she pleases if it suits her purpose or bargain
with the enemy if she sees fit, or for that matter, die and come back to life—"

"But Witgern—"

"Hear me out. To the warriors, it's as though you're one of the Ancestresses already—a fighting Ancestress who will set them free. You've never known your power to give succor. They love you as they love their hearths. They don't think of all *this*"—he waved a hand to indicate the sumptuous estate—"they remember only that after Domitian's war, you won vengeance for all of us when you slew the great traitor who led an army against our back. No one living has matched your deeds, or carried such light. Come with me, Auriane."

Her throat was clenched from grief. Uttering the words felt as painful as being dragged over gravel.

"My answer still must be no."

"You've more wisdom in you than anyone I've known, woman or man, Auriane. But sometimes I think it slows you. You walk through a denser forest than the rest of us, and it conceals what we easily see. Your home is besieged. Our fields are overrun with Cheruscan vermin. How can you turn your back on us?"

"How can I turn my back on my children? And on Marcus, who I *do* count as kin." Miserably, she looked down. "It's a fork in the path, Witgern. Taking either route brings shame on me, for the one abandoned."

But the land is my child, too, some part of her protested. *And I did a shameful thing in leaving it.*

"Don't *think* on it overmuch, Auriane. Just come with me." He waited through silence. "You still refuse, then?"

"I am sorry, Witgern."

"I go, then." He climbed to his feet.

"Stay a little longer!"

"I've no other purpose here. I failed. Farewell."

"How will you get back across the river?"

"It's of little importance now. I go back without you."

"*Witgern!*"

"Oh, I'll give a gift to the river so it won't suck me down, and swim it at night. I'm quite good at eluding frontier patrols. A wolf knows his way."

She embraced him then. "I'm glad at the sight of you, Witgern, dear old friend. But you've slashed open every wound. You leave me desolate. Go in safety. The grace of Fria go with you."

She pressed the remainder of the food on him. He'd gone but a few paces when she ran to catch up with him. "Witgern! A last matter . . . have you heard any news of . . . of Decius?"

"I fear I have, Auriane." For the first time, she saw something hard and merciless flash in his eye. "I'll say only this—his heart is Cheruscan, and he's eagerly bloodied himself." Witgern hesitated, looking somewhat uncomfortable. "Does Avenahar know . . . has she any suspicion that . . ." *That this bloodstained rogue you briefly bedded in bygone days is her father?* she heard in his silence.

"No," Auriane said quickly, looking away. "Her mother is a coward."

THE HORSE GUARDSMAN'S groom lay flat on his stomach beneath a box hedge and didn't move for long moments after the *Matrona* and the notorious rebel had gone their own ways. He'd briefly considered a headlong gallop into Confluentes to roust the magistrate's men from sleep, but good sense told him it was no use. Witgern was adept at moving invisibly through the countryside; the Wolf Coat chief would be well off by the time a search party could be gathered together. The groom had not followed most of what was said—Auriane's native tongue was similar but not identical to the tongue of the Batavian tribe of his birth. But Witgern was here! That was damning enough. This estate was a festering sink of conspiracy. His master had been wise to leave him behind to have a look about. *When he receives this amazing report his gratitude will be so great he'll grant me my freedom.*

ON THE FOLLOWING morn, as Auriane and Avenahar walked swiftly through ground mist, following a path to the practice arena, Avenahar was troubled by the haunted look she saw in her mother's face.

"It's nothing at all," was Auriane's curt reply to a tentative query. *Avenahar, you must never know Witgern was here. I can't have both of you aligned against me. The pull would be too mighty. Witgern would win.*

The crying of my people. The crying of a child. Which is more urgent? Which is my true charge?

Auriane stopped then and removed the amulet of sacred earth from about her neck—certain that it, too, was aligned against her. *It's relentlessly dragging me back to my country. I must get rid of it.*

"You can't take that off; Ramis gave that to you." Avenahar's eyes were black pearls, dissolving in the warmth of her concern.

"I can. You must wear it now." *It will give you protection, when I no longer can.* The certainty that Avenahar would soon need such protection was daily gathering strength within her. "Take it."

"To wear all the time? This is not a jest?"

"I'd hardly jest about such a thing."

"Something *did* happen."

"Never mind. Put it on."

Avenahar stood with arms pinned at her sides, constricted as if bound by invisible cord. She couldn't rob her mother of her most sacred possession. It felt too much like besting her mother—something the part of her that was boisterous, raw, and young ardently wanted. But a deeper, steadier part of her thought acquiring such a prize *this* way a horrible and thankless thing.

"Avenahar, I'll never live in my country again. And home's your direction—that's plain to see. It's right that you wear it. So be it. Don't argue."

Auriane's stern look did not allow disobedience, so Avenahar took it, pulling the thong a little awkwardly over her smooth black hair, feeling she sported with a holy thing—like sneaking on a queen's headdress just to try it, or clambering, just for adventure, onto a temple roof. But as the leather of the amulet touched her skin, Avenahar was certain she felt a small tug, as if the potent thing had already begun pulling her toward a larger fate. In her mind she fled home, to Chattian lands, and took her place among the shadowed heroes and heroines her mother had walked with—a woman revered, not ridiculed, as she doled out counsel in war and peace, who lived as a pivot-point in the life of the villages, not as a shameful oddity, as she would always be in this Roman province. *I'll live even more gloriously the life my mother lived. . . .*

Drunk on strong reveries, Avenahar didn't hear her mother at first.

"Avenahar . . . *Avenahar!* Turn round. You've hurt yourself."

"I don't think so, Mother." Then Avenahar saw the viscerally bright droplet on the gray moss beneath her feet, so brazenly red, teeming with invisible life. Her mother was right. Avenahar looked, baffled, at her unblemished hands, her unscuffed knees. Then she was alert to something strange—a grave and important feeling right down through the center of her, a dull, nudging heaviness in her loins, a bruising pain that seemed to drag her toward the earth. It was a sense like no other, bearing hazed but powerful promises of the pleasures, the vulnerability, a woman's body could know.

"Mother, I think—" Avenahar said, patting her clothes. "I'm not hurt . . . It's . . . ." She was quiet, sensing ancestresses flocking about like unseen doves. The blood-that-carries-souls was their portal back into the world.

"By Fria's love," she heard Auriane whisper. "It has come."

Avenahar felt a bolt of fright. *Blood is there at the beginning, blood is there at the end.* She hugged close to childhood, unready to step away from her mother's encompassing shadow.

"Don't be alarmed, Avenahar, this is good . . . The blood of generations is the means by which you will carry us on, by which we shall not die. Close your eyes."

Avenahar complied, pleased by all this favor and attention. She felt her mother trace on her forehead the runic sign of protection, followed by the sign for strength. Auriane then chanted a quick, quiet prayer to the goddess Hel that made Avenahar feel wrapped in a warm, soft blanket: *"Beautiful one, moving underground, see this daughter who walks with the Sun . . . Let flow from Avenahar all the fruits of the Mother-line. Be gentle with her and take her blood."*

Auriane pulled Avenahar onto a path that descended to the Mosella. "Come this way. You'll wash in the river."

"Now my initiation must take place within the season," Avenahar said, giving a rabbit-leap of joy. "We're going home!"

"Well, for a short time, yes. We've much to do, we'll have to begin readying ourselves for the trip to the Holy Wood. You'll need to finish weaving your womanhood cloak." The grove known as the Holy Wood lay just within Chattian lands, a half-day's ride beyond the *Limes*—the Roman frontier. Avenahar had known all her life that when the blood of generations came she must be initiated on her home ground, in the presence of nine "Mothers," or elderwomen—as it had always been done. Auriane had already laid the initial plans. Because Auriane must be present, too, and a seven-year-old Palace decree barred Auriane from returning to her country, Marcus had called upon the aid of a man much in his debt, Maximus, governor at Mogontiacum, whose jurisdiction they must pass through to enter her lands. When the time came, Maximus had agreed to arrange a covert mother-and-daughter expedition across the frontier. They would remain in Chattian country no more than the nine nights required by the ceremony.

After a time, Avenahar ventured, "Mother, *his* blood is in me, too."

"Your true father. Of course it is."

Avenahar didn't like what she saw in her mother's face then. There was a good tension there sometimes, denoting a soul powerfully trained upon one thing, as when her mother entered a practice arena. And there was *this* tension, full of thoughts of ill, turned back upon herself. So Avenahar didn't press, saying only, "Soon, I'll hear who he is." *He'll be an honorable man who's fought for our freedom,* Avenahar thought, buoyed by the amulet on her breast.

"Yes," Auriane replied. "And I hope you hear it as a woman, not as a child."

Before them then was the glassy surface of the Mosella, still as black marble. But it isn't still, Auriane found herself thinking—the current is there, powerful and invisible. And it ever seeks the Mother River. She thought, then, of how the world's deceptively calm surface was crisscrossed with such strong, unseen currents—one of which tugged relentlessly at her, striving to drag her back toward her sacred groves.

A wild swan, cloud white, more spirit than bird, skimmed low over the black water before it disappeared into the profundity of the ground mist that hung on the air like ritual incense, leaving the Mosella's far bank a holy mystery. A merchant vessel laden with wine barrels bound north startled them as it materialized in near-silence from the fog, its single bank of twenty-two oars flashing out in powerful unison, its dragon-headed prow cutting the water with surprising speed as it moved with the river's muscular flow.

"I'm not sure I like this, Mother," Avenahar said as she bent at the bank to unlace her sandals. "Now, at the moon, I'll have something to hide. And what if it starts at a hunt?"

Avenahar was surprised by the look of affront she saw in her mother's eyes.

"Someone's been passing you counterfeit coin, Avenahar. To have the blood of generations . . . it's *greater* than the hunt."

"But—why, then, does Brico say . . . I once heard Brico say the blood of generations can *curse* a river, that it can cause a river to grow horns, and flood its banks. She says it can stunt a crop. Or keep a cow from giving milk."

"Look at me, Avenahar. You will push what Brico says from your mind."

"All right. But why are you so angry?"

Auriane's face softened at once. Avenahar saw only anxious sadness there now.

"Because she teaches you . . . shame. Avenahar, Brico is full of the ways of iron. When you go home, you'll find something else, the older way, the beautiful way. Know this that I am telling you now, and don't ever forget it—your blood will *bless* the river."

Chapter 6

The first of *Maius* had come. The population of the Roman river-town of Confluentes was swollen to twice its usual size, for these were the days of the rites of Floralia. As the Fire Festival of the Treverans, the Celtic tribe who farmed these hills before Rome claimed them, fell on roughly the same calendar days as the rites of the Roman goddess Flora with her feasts on the green and bawdy games, Confluentes's spring celebration fused Roman and native custom; the result was a provincial hybrid that roused passions to a pitch of gaiety that might not have been achieved by either festival alone. Wine of pale gold from the steep slopes along the Mosella was rolled in barrels down the cobbled streets and dispensed at every street crossing until it flooded into the town's gutters, where it carried along petals of crushed wildflowers. Revelers carried torches in the light of day, in homage to the colors that Flora, Queen of the Flowers, brought to the countryside. Children scattered beans and lupins on the ground—plants that encouraged nature's increase. Bonfires on the high places would keep the countryside illumined into the night, while native farmers ringed about them and offered cakes to the powerful numen of spring. The women of the Basketmakers' Guild wove garlands and gave them out on the steps of the temples. Games progressed outside the town walls—footraces, wrestling matches, and horse races. Since Flora was also a goddess of gardens, and the small game that haunted them were her beloved creatures, maids played at netting hares, or hunting the dormice that scuttled among the grape vines. The townsfolk donned clay masks with beast-faces, linked hands, and danced from fire to fire or feasted in the fields, while young men and women, arms entwined about a hastily chosen lover, ran off to perform the most ancient of rites in the wild precincts of the forest.

Many in the throng of citizens and slaves had massed along the post road, for news had flown from town forum to field that Marcus Julianus's carriages would be passing by the town this day, as he returned from the meetings of the Consilium. A glimpse of a man such as this provided a rare distraction in this tiny tributary of Empire; the old nobility of Rome normally kept a primary residence far nearer the world's center. The sole important personage to whom local folk were accustomed was the magistrate Volusius Victorinus, who, though rich in land, was still one of them. They knew of the hair he'd lost from years of applying overheated curling tongs; they traded jests about his wife Decimina's badly fitting ivory false teeth. Marcus Julianus, by contrast, dwelled high and remote behind his estate's miles of thorn hedges, living a life steeped in esoteric philosophy and the mysteries of grand decisions of state. The lingering tale that Julianus was the conspirator-in-shadow who orchestrated the assassination of the tyrannical Domitian added a dark luminosity to his name; few among them could gaze on such a man without hearing silent flutes and drums.

Victorinus observed the festivities from one of the twin towers that flanked Confluentes's main gate. He was garbed in a flowing linen festival tunic in shades of russet and melon, with a woolen scarf knotted at his throat against the stone chamber's chill. This vantage afforded an excellent view of the town wall's rampart walk and the paved overland road. Victorinus was the festival's sponsor this year, having donated the money for the musicians, the prizes for the athletes, and the boar feast. He sat close by the unshuttered window so the grateful people could hail him from below, passing the time playing a board game called "Robbers" with the decurion of his bodyguard. As the magistrate advanced one of his crystal soldiers to the next marble square, the game was bluntly interrupted by one of the freedmen clerks of his court, a Treveran giant named Cobnertus. A festival wreath held the clerk's crudely chopped blond locks in place as Cobnertus curled himself into a "C" to accommodate himself to the guard chamber's ceiling. His leek-green tunic was too small for him, stretched almost to tearing across a barrel chest. The room was suddenly crowded as he filled it with the eager hopeful-ness of a clumsy, tail-wagging hound.

"My lord Victorinus, I beg a moment. We've just caught a man posing as a priest of Flora at the little temple by the river. Old Lallus, who's supposed to be there, is laid out with bog fever, so this trickster slipped in. He might not've been found out except he was caught palming the coppers the pious townfolk were tossing in as offerings, and I've hurried to tell you—"

Victorinus's gaze remained moodily attached to his crystal game piece, which had, judging from the decurion's alert expression, landed in a danger-ous place. "Why are you nettling me with this today? If he's a slave stow him in the slaves' prison until we learn who his master is. If he's a local man without the citizenship, hold him and we'll have him lashed, after the festival's done—"

"But—"

"—Twenty lashes. That's my verdict. If he's got proof of citizenship, mark him down on the list of citizen offenders and imprison him until I can study his case."

"But my lord, the man's one of the deserters from the naval ship *Concordia*—you know, the ones who murdered their captain!"

That, at least, caused Victorinus to look up from his game.

"You've done well, then, Cobnertus. Lock him up until the next court day; I'll examine him then. You've earned your leisure, good man! Off with you, you're insulting me. I paid a lot for this festival. Find yourself a ripe maid not your wife, have a good draught of our golden nectar, and scamper out into the forest and do us all some good. And leave me in peace to win this game."

The decurion gave a polite but irritated grunt. He was the one who was winning.

"But I've not told you the most *amazing* part of it," Cobnertus pressed on gamely. "This Lurio, that's his name, has an *amazing* tale to tell. He—"

"Don't flog that word to death. Must you stand there? You're broad as a bullock and the youths' footraces are set to start."

Cobnertus hauled himself aside with one overly accommodating side-ways step.

"But my lord Victorinus, this Lurio claims to have uncovered the iden-tity of the famous malefactor who's been smuggling the money-for-arms to the Chattian savages. And the person he accuses, the name will *am*—will greatly surprise you."

Victorinus gave Cobnertus a look that caused the clerk to recoil into wounded innocence.

"Bees in the hives don't work harder than you, Cobnertus, but an ox has more wit. Did you not detect in this man's story a ruse to evade punishment? He's a murderer. He's bargaining for his life. There's as much likelihood he has useful information on this notorious matter of state as there is that your wife is waiting patiently at home for you right now. Don't look so dejected. Give your report to Cletussto there"—he gestured toward one of the solemn secretaries standing by the wall—"and I'll review it when I have time. Now show some merriment, my man!"

Soon after, word was carried to the town that four *redas* bearing the family emblem of Marcus Arrius Julianus—a shield embossed with an image of Minerva—had been sighted passing the First Milestone. More revelers abandoned their feasts and began to surge toward the road.

Almost invisible in this crowd of masked and drunken townsfolk was a young man in a heavy travelling cloak, who hugged the shadows beneath one of the gate towers. His cloak was the same color as the masonry. Its hood was drawn forward. He might have been a bat clinging to the wall, shunning light and human company, as, with growing intensity, he kept his gaze on the stretch of road before him, down which Marcus Julianus's carriages must pass. He emptied his mind as he readied himself for the fearsome task ahead. High above him twenty men of Victorinus's municipal guard were posted, but as the tower's turreted top projected slightly from the base, they could not see him.

Now the throng discerned a line of carriages emerging from the mist, each drawn by two horses hitched abreast, moving at a brisk trot. Spare horses were tied behind each; footmen ran alongside. As they came within a quarter mile of the town's gate the people began to hinder the procession's progress, frustrating the drivers, who had been ordered to refrain from using their whips. Several jogged alongside a black-curtained, gold-embossed carriage, third in line and most distinguished in appearance. They shouted at Julianus and attempted to thrust petitions inside while its driver cursed and threatened them with the butt of his whip.

As the four carriages moved at a smart trot beneath Victorinus's tower, both magistrate and guards' decurion paused in their game and rose to watch.

They were just in time to witness a sight from a draught-laced dream. As Julianus's carriage passed beneath the elm grove that shaded the small temple of Mars, a torch-bearing man wrestled his way through the press of people, and briefly jog-trotted alongside it. He tossed something that looked like three small, smooth stones onto the roof of the carriage, where they broke, proving liquid inside. Immediately after, he threw the torch. Flames bloomed up with startling vigor and brilliance. Instantly they devoured the black curtains. With astonishing swiftness they spread over the wooden frame, engulfing the whole of the carriage—a carriage no longer, but a torch of Hephaestus. The blue-tinged flames were crazily strong, roiling with unnatural fury. The sight was ghastly, impossible—a testy Jupiter might have singled out this particular carriage for a thunderbolt. The horses' frenzied thrashings cracked the carriage's shaft-pole as the beasts fought to escape the ferocious heat. Evil-looking smoke spiraled through the elms.

For long moments the throng was unnaturally still, not certain what they were seeing as the flames rushed skyward in a great gust.

Within that inferno, nothing could be alive.

One strident cry rose above the others: *"They've murdered him!"* A great section of the crowd shifted toward the town's wall for safety, moving as one, like a startled flock of sheep.

Victorinus ordered the trumpeter on the wall to blow a blast, to alert his guards, stationed below. Then he cried out a command to clear everyone away from the flaming carriage. His guards' decurion bolted down the tower's stairs to take charge of his men, while shouting back at Victorinus, "It's Greek fire! Water won't quench it. They must find vinegar!"

Victorinus dispatched a boy attendant to toll the bell that ordered out the town's bucketmen, then turned his attention to the chaotic scene below, scanning the throng for a fleeing assailant. He knew he must be seen to be responding quickly, if he meant to avoid a popular accusation that he'd done too little to apprehend Julianus's murderer. Only later would he give himself leave to rejoice. In the nether regions of his mind, however, wheels were already starting to turn:

It seems the closeted, pampered Arria Juliana has no protector now . . . Perhaps I should apply to be her guardian.

A lone runner separated from the crowd. Victorinus was jolted by the sight of the man's face—black as burnt wood, with great, staring eyes—then realized the fellow had smeared his face with lampblack. He yelped, pointing out the man to the guards below—and now, a dozen townsmen and guards were giving spirited chase, pursuing the assailant into an abandoned flax field that lay south of the Mogontiacum road.

Victorinus's son, Lucius, lurched up the tower stairs then, wailing a tavern song, his face sweaty and flushed. Clamped to his side by one lean, sinewy arm was a frightened-looking Treveran maid.

"Father, you surprise me," he called out merrily to Victorinus, who was leaning from the tower's window, urging on the pursuers with a balled fist. "Your justice is swift as Jupiter's."

Victorinus pulled himself back inside. "Shut your mouth, you impudent young cock. This is not *my* doing, and I forbid you to even think it. I keep within the law. Speak so to anyone and you'll not see a sesterce of your patrimony."

"I apologize, then, Father. What's this elixir that created such a fearsome fire?"

"A thing that's forbidden, except on war vessels. It's a mix of naphtha harvested from the ground, laced with quicklime and sulfur. It's packed into a clay vessel. It must have a fire within it, for flames have a passionate love of it. Poor Marcus Julianus—he has a much more dedicated enemy out there than *I* ever was." He added to himself, "Someone with knowledge of ships, and of naval warfare. . . ."

"Good riddance to the eccentric, bookish fool."

Small in the distance now, the fleeing man shed his cloak with one savage twist of his body and sprinted on. He was a Herculean runner; long, powerful strides pulled him steadily ahead of Victorinus's men. Finally he vaulted a creek and lost himself in the eternal twilight of the mountain ash trees beyond.

Below them, the guards' captain found he could do little to combat the flames. The carriage was like an open forge, too hot for anyone to approach. The town's bucketmen doused the elms with well water so the fire would not spread. In the confusion, no one had yet brought vinegar.

Lamentations arose. Some cried out Julianus's name and tossed Flora's flowers into the flaming carriage. This roaring evidence of murder held many transfixed with an odd reverence. They'd come to gape at a celebrated statesman, never expecting to find themselves witness to his mortal journey's final moments. Their insignificant tributary of Empire felt a little more significant today. Some in the crowd whispered that the fire had such fearsome power because of Auriane—had Julianus not entered into that strange conjoining with an outlandish northern woman snagged in the net of war, had he not formed an amorous alliance that did not even have a proper name, allowing alien gods with gnarled names to pass through his gate, then he might not have perished in such an extraordinary way.

Chapter 7

While the carriage bloomed in flame Auriane sat quietly unaware, tutoring her children in the villa's library. When Auriane taught her daughters, she took them down shadowed paths their Greek and Latin tutors would never tread. She related tales of battle-chiefs who won victories by putting war-fetters on their foes, of land-spirits who saved the harvest when approached with respect and given cakes. She had told them of the birth of the Chattian tribe from the body of a dead giant. In the world Auriane brought to them, leaves rustled with intention, streams coursed with Fria's blood, each mossy stone had its ghost.

As she put questions to them, she saw by turns, Witgern's savage disappointment, Lurio's alert interest as he examined the coins. So she was more irritated than usual with Arria, who always put up a bitter resistance to these lessons.

Arria sat slumped in a matron's basket chair that all but engulfed her. Its wicker back framed that small, wise face like a nimbus around a stubborn little deity. Her feet didn't touch the floor, and she swung her legs in boredom, while sneaking peeks at a cheaply made bookroll flattened out beneath her ivory study box, which wasn't as well concealed as she thought it was. She'd spent an hour by the water-clock readying herself for these lessons, and Auriane thought her aim was, in part, to shield herself from them by clothing herself in aristocratic Romanness. Her heat-pressed aquamarine tunica embroidered with vermilion trim draped to hennaed toenails, revealing remarkably unscuffed sandals. She'd had the *ornatrix* style her hair with a tight row of curls in front, and long ringlets behind, captured into a net of gold thread. To Auriane the effect was sad and odd; a girl of nine, even by Roman custom, wasn't expected to bend and curb her nature; her hair was normally left loose and free. Sadder still for Auriane was that Arria had cast aside her Chattian name and answered only to her Roman name. Auriane never objected to these small self-assertions; she'd brought her children to a borderland between worlds, and long ago decided to let each daughter's allegiance be her own affair.

Avenahar had spent no more time to ready herself than it takes to beat the fleas out of a saddle-blanket and throw it on a mule. Spurning furniture, she sprawled on the mosaic floor next to her sister, elbows resting on a portrait of the Greek philosopher Anaximander, amidst soiled bookrolls that might have been blasted about by storm winds. Her sandals looked as though a goat had chewed on them. Her short brown tunica was a record on cloth of all she'd done of late, stained with oils used for conditioning leather, blood from helping with the birth of a calf, and slime from the well she'd shimmied down, to clear it of branches. She *had* stood still long enough to allow Brico to run a few strokes through her hair; it was a black silk curtain drawn across her face as she bent over her wax tablet. Only about her hair did Avenahar have a measure of vanity; Auriane supposed it because her older daughter counted herself Chattian through and through, and to a woman of the tribes, hair was sacred treasure, and a cloak of power.

"A stranger presents himself at your hall, begging food and help," Auriane asked them. "He is bloodied, and tales have come to you of an ambush and murder nearby. What must you do?"

"Take him in and shelter him from his foes, for the law of guest-friendship demands you keep a wayfarer well, even if he's a fleeing murderer," Avenahar replied effortlessly, from behind her hair.

With each question, Arria pretended her older sister had spoken up too quickly for her.

"What passed in this season, and on this day, in the time of your grandfathers?"

"Our grandfather Baldemar destroyed the Roman fort at Aquae Mattiaci and claimed as a war-prize the javelin of a first centurion."

"Arria. Will you let your sister answer every time?" Auriane said it neutrally, but hurt edged in, in spite of herself.

Arria's head sagged in a child's parody of misery, and she mumbled, "Why must I learn of people who live in dirt?"

"I tire of this, day after day, Arria."

Arria went limp as silk cloth, feigning weariness unto death.

"Arria, sit up. You have a Mother-line. You will learn of *all* the spirits that made you or you'll grow into an ignorant woman."

Arria contorted her face in the usual manner of a thoroughly disgusted girl of nine. "Your people are nothing but dirty, beaten beggars."

"They are your people as well." Auriane felt a momentary jolt of shame at the quiver of vulnerability in her voice.

"They're *not* my people. Don't say they are! Everyone makes cruel jokes about us because you say that. Avenahar loves them so well—let her study them!"

"When Witgern's army is at your door," came Avenahar's supple retort, "then, maybe, you'll have respect for the history of our people."

"Be silent, both of you!" Auriane felt a dark, ugly twist of misery within, as though Arria were trying to saw herself away from her with a serrated blade.

"Let me see what *you* learn of," Avenahar said then, leaping up, eyes sparking with playful malice. With a whip-fast motion, she snatched off the bookroll Arria had been secretly reading.

"Give me that!" came the younger child's piercing shriek as she twisted off the basket chair, ripping the fine tunica on the wickerwork in a frantic effort to retrieve the bookroll.

"Mother, look at this!" Avenahar said gleefully. "She'll pick through Roman garbage to get one tasty scrap of gossip! It's the *Acta Inepta* for the month of *Aprilis*—" The *Acta Inepta,* or "Doings of Fools," was a popular satirist's play on the name of the Palace bulletin posted daily at Rome, the *Acta Diurna*—"Events of the Day."

"—and here we have"—Avenahar nimbly bounded to her feet to keep it out of Arria's reach—"momentous events, well worthy of study! Scantia is divorcing Gaius Apronius, solely so she can ruin his career. But it is just as well, since all her children were sired by his footmen. The Emperor's favorite boys held a midnight contest to see who looked best dressed as Helen of

Troy . . ." Arria sprang on top of Avenahar then, a wildcat onto prey, and both children fell hard to the floor.

"Enough of this!" Auriane's voice grabbed them and held them fast. Her children froze in mid-struggle, with Avenahar's leg hooked about Arria's waist as her elder daughter strove to push herself off from her sister.

I'll have no more of this, ever, Auriane thought then. *Arria is as the gods have made her. I can do nothing. There must be a deeper purpose here, subtler than my blighted yearnings and knowings.*

On realizing this, strangely, Auriane found the misery swiftly drained out of her like poison from a tipped phial. And then an odd, striking peace flooded about her, a rapture she'd felt strongly before only in the presence of Ramis. It was as though the old seeress somehow blessed this understanding.

"Arria Juliana, stand up," Auriane said, feeling softer, more certain, within. The girl disentangled herself from Avenahar and stood like a small soldier at attention, ropes of hair from the ruined coiffure springing free in riotous coils. *I love the pride and belligerence in her eye,* Auriane thought. *It does not matter anymore that it does not serve what I serve.*

"You're free, Arria," Auriane said. "You no longer have to study my people. I give you over to your Greek and Latin tutors. From this day forward, I free you from serving your Mother-line." Arria knew enough of Chattian customs to understand this meant she was absolved of all duty to worship her mother's deities, and somewhere within those soft gray eyes was a primitive start of alarm.

"Isn't this what you want?" Auriane said, perplexed, expecting Arria would feel more like a load of manure had been lifted from her back. "I know not what else to do. Go now. Irenaeus comes today; I'll have him read to you from Herodotus."

Like a long-penned horse that can't readily accept that there's no longer a fence about the meadow, Arria did not move. She was discovering what the horse discovers—there's security in that fence. It encloses a known world. She fastened the gaze of those lucid owl-eyes onto her mother, in that deep-knowing way that always jolted Auriane into wondering—just who is mother and who is daughter here? Then, as if reaching out to touch a possibly-hot grill, Arria ventured, "That's well. Very well! But . . . are you angry, Mother?"

"Oh, no, she's jolly as a wineship's drunken steersman, you wretched brat, you—"

"Avenahar, be quiet! No, Arria, I'm not angry. I'm . . . relieved. The spirits of Rome are stronger in you than the spirits of my people. Do you not want to go?"

Avenahar was staring at Arria with raw triumph in her eyes, so the younger girl put on a brash show of certainty. "Yes," she said bravely, holding her copy of the *Acta Inepta* close to her body as if it were a shield. Then she backed out of the room, wondering, by turns, if this were a ruse, if her sister had somehow bested her, if her mother still loved her. Then she turned and fled from the library, leaving Auriane equally confused; a solution that had seemed a kindness now seemed harsh and extreme.

What have I done? My children are wild horses galloping in opposite directions while lashed to me.

Avenahar crawled up into Arria Juliana's huge basket chair, a complacent victor taking possession of territory she'd just won.

Into the sad silence, Auriane said, "Avenahar, I'm going to read to you from the life of Ramis," because she felt, suddenly, a great urgency to do so. "Listen well. Afterward I'll ask you to repeat to me as much of it as you remember."

"But you said I needed to be at least twenty to begin to make sense of her."

Auriane was rattling a bronze key as she unlocked a cedar cupboard and drew out a rolled manuscript. "Time's an enemy; I don't know how much of it we have left. She's great as kings, yet few know the tale of her beginnings. Her story must be passed on."

"That's the book you've been dictating!" The words came in an eager hush.

"It is. But remember, this is only an account of her life. You can't learn her teachings from words on papyrus. A person might read them at the wrong time. Or might not hear them as they were meant, and twist her into something else. Her teachings can only be passed from living mind to living mind."

Auriane settled herself and gave the papyrus volume a few turns, unrolling it just enough so that she could see the first column of script. The marble-sheathed chamber about her dissolved away. She sat on well-trodden earth, face gleaming from the heat of a hearth fire.

"I tell you now of Ramis," she began, letting the words roll out in the lulling rhythms of a songmaker, "and of all her marvelous deeds of knowing. For if it is instructive to study the rise of greatness, it is wise to study her.

"She sprang from the rudest, yet rose to become more celebrated than any woman or man of all the tribes of the north. A word from her mouth can send a nation into war. Her counsel has stayed the hands of Roman legates. In her fiftieth year the lots were cast and she became the Veleda—first seeress over all the tribes. For those who don't live among us, this title means, the 'One Who Sees'—not the future, as is commonly thought, but the true nature of earthly life.

"She was conceived at the Eastre rites and sired by no mortal father. The village of her birth was the Ram's Eye, where the folk were so poor they fed off middens. Ramis's mother, Radegund, shared a goat with four neighbors. The man who called himself her father did not own a sword. One twilight when she was a ragged maid of nine she was grinding herbs in her village's mead shed. In poured a light not shed by fire or sun, for it cast no shadows. She felt someone standing behind her. Fright blinded her and she wanted to dash off to her mother. At dusk other worlds mingle with ours. By force of will she stilled herself and slowly turned about.

"In the doorway stood a ghastly hag so withered she might have known two hundred winters. She smelled of grave earth. Her flesh was blue, her hair dry as parched grass. Most unsettling were her hands, for they resembled nothing human; they were the claws of a falcon. This woman of other worlds cradled a white cat."

Intent on the tale, Avenahar shifted too far forward in the wicker chair and caught herself just before she tumbled onto the mosaic floor.

"The old woman demanded milk for her cat, which was stringy and starved. Famine was on the land. The she-goat Ramis's family shared had been driven off by a rogue war band; the last jug of its milk lay buried to its neck in the cold earth, at the back of the shed. Ramis fetched it and poured into a pan all the milk they had. One of our elders once asked her what evil took her, that she would feed a beast and leave her family to starve, and Ramis replied it was because in that moment she knew there was but one fire in all the world, and that the ogre of scarcity itself was nothing but shadows cast by our stunted knowings. No sooner had the cat lapped up all the milk than the old woman's face became changeable as the surface of a wind-ruffled lake; she was by turns a pearl-cheeked maid with coppery hair; a bearing mother; a bald crone wrapped in a rotting shroud. And the clay jar had, through some divine art, refilled itself—it brimmed with milk.

"The nine-year-old child fell to her knees and asked the strange woman who she was. She said a name that was beautiful, that called forth tears, but Ramis said she could not recollect it even just after she heard it, for it was not uttered in a human tongue; it came out in all the sounds of the world: forest rustles, rushing wind, children's cries.

"But the woman's next words Ramis remembered with stark clarity, as if they had been inscribed in runes on a stick:

"'Ramis, daughter of Radegund. I charge you to touch the living torch to the one that grows cold. And you will bear it on as long as you live, and give it over to the next of your line.'"

"What does it mean, Mother?" Avenahar asked.

"That knowledge of the world's true nature ever hovers at the edge of forgetfulness, and that Ramis was here to preserve it. This is the true purpose of the high seeresses our people call the Holy Nine—not to lead festivals or give birth oracles or counsel chiefs in war, as most people think, but to save the near-lost knowings given down to us from the Time of Peace and Wandering when all ate at one board. We're not in an age in which we can bring this back; we're in a time of shadows, with more to come—so one torch burns alone in each generation. And then," Auriane said, returning to the document, "before Ramis's eyes, this changeable spectre vanished like the moon before day."

"Who *was* she?"

"Ramis would never tell me, but perhaps the white cat tells the tale."

"Our Lady keeps a white cat . . . one of her divine daughters? Or maybe it was . . ." She'd meant to say, *Fria herself*, but dropped into silence because Brico was standing in the library's entranceway, clutching the door frame for support. The young maidservant was in startling disarray; masses of red-gold hair had tumbled down into a swollen face blotched from sobbing. Auriane and Avenahar stared at her, feeling shaken awake from enchanted sleep.

"Brico! It's all right, come in."

The girl edged toward them, her manner both unobtrusive and urgent. She started to speak but lost her courage and looked down, pulling fretfully at the linen cloth of her tunica.

"What is it?" Auriane asked gently.

"I am sorry . . . forgive me . . . but you must know . . . our lord Marcus Julianus has been attacked by an assassin. His carriage was set afire!"

Chapter 8

Auriane slowly rose to her feet.

"Does he live?"

In answer Brico wrenched herself about to face the frescoed wall, crushed the cloth of the tunica to her eyes, and shook her head violently, *No.*

Auriane commanded Avenahar to stay where she was and strode swiftly out, whipping aside the heavy curtain, her steps resounding urgently on the marble. All the dove-spirit in her had vanished; now she spread the long wings of a hawk. Within, she felt only battle readiness.

Outside the villa's grand, colonnaded entranceway, stunned servants were collecting by the dozens, in great silence; the only sound came from an infant boy in the arms of one of the maids, who cried desperately and hard, as if he could not get enough air.

Demaratos found her. "We will tend to this, *Domina*"—this once, he spoke the word with no trace of contempt—"and see to bringing him home."

"No, Demaratos. I'll tend to it. Have them bring out my horse."

"But the throng! They've turned into a herd of wild beasts."

"I've ridden through worse. Go quickly!"

While she waited, a heaving sea of grief welled up in her, and she shivered with the mighty effort of erecting a dam against it. *Not now. I must show courage or I'll throw the household into despair.*

Burned alive.

No. He is too great a spirit to be so easily consumed. He would fight his way out—he always has. He defied and outlived two tyrants. Surely a mere hired assassin could not get the better of him. Everyone is mistaken.

No. There were too many witnesses. There can be no mistake. The thought taunted, again and again, in moments separate and horrific as sword thrusts. Hammer blows of grief nearly struck her to her knees; she wanted to melt to the ground and mingle with mute earth.

Cocreator of a kingdom with no king, beloved companion in all I do. We are a potion of minds, twin forces never meant to be separate in this life. My love is a fierce and adamant beast. It belongs to the wild, not to this civilized world.

And if I have a seeress's powers, why did I not foresee this?

Two of the humbler carriages from Julianus's returning train had found their way home, and their teams of two horses hitched abreast were advancing down the wide carriageway at a swift trot, hooves crunching noisily in gravel. Avenahar and Arria, all enmity forgotten, tucked themselves beneath Auriane's arms so that mother and daughters seemed fused into one monument to grief. Auriane felt a harsh remorse for having sent Arria off, and clung more tightly to her younger daughter than to Avenahar, lest the girl fear she'd lost a mother as well as a father.

Numbly, Auriane was aware that their guest from Rome, the aged scholar Gaius Asinius Marcellinus, had emerged from his suite of rooms and was standing beside her, urgently seeking her ear. "My good Aurinia," he was saying, and she was drawn to the concern in his voice, seeing but not seeing fleshy, ink-stained fingers, the smooth dome of his head, a deeply furrowed brow. "I'll send out a letter at once, and secure protection for you. As you know, my son is powerful at home in the Court of Inheritance. I will do all I can to see the estate's not seized."

"You are most kind. But . . ." She paused, quietening, feeling caught, then, in the unseen currents, and when she spoke, it was as though an alien certainty inserted itself into her, from possession by some spirit larger than her own. "Wait with your letter. It might not be necessary."

"I assure you, it *is*. False heirs are likely to come forward in the settling of any estate grand as this one, and as this one's now in the hands of a—a woman foreign born, they *certainly* will."

"My situation would be dire—were Julianus truly dead."

"But . . . madam . . . all say he is!" Now he regarded her with unease, wondering if the loss of Julianus had taken her mind.

Arria Juliana heard none of this, and silently cried. But Avenahar was very still, watching Auriane with acute interest.

Auriane's attention was diverted by the second carriage, which should have followed the first onto the connecting gravel road that led to the stables; instead, its driver kept it on the wide roadway that led directly to the main house. An outraged groom chased it for a time, shouting, "*Halt!* Where are you going? Turn about!" The carriageman calmly ignored him.

While all looked on, baffled, Auriane began walking, then running, to meet the carriage, not certain herself what propelled her forward.

He always has outwitted his enemies.

The driver pulled the horses to a halt before her. The black-curtained door of the *reda* swung open. And then, looking none the worse for wear, his tunic and travelling cloak hardly singed, Marcus Julianus dropped lightly to the gravel walk, looking mildly impatient, and full of his usual trust the world was in order.

The household, after a short, startled pause, erupted into loud clapping, as if at the happy climax of a theater performance.

Auriane stood mute and still, tears streaming from her eyes. For a suspended moment she feasted on the sight of him, marveling at the machinery of the Fates. *Great Fria be praised. It's unsettling to know how necessary he has become.* Somewhere within, her trust in the power of her knowings settled, and began to root.

"You clever rogue!" she said hoarsely, feeling like a sacrificial beast snatched, almost too late, from beneath the mallet of a priest.

"Nemesis! You did not know!" he said softly, as he swiftly closed the distance between them, and seized her shoulders in a fierce grip, horror and pity in his face. He realized then that the official messenger from Victorinus bearing news of his death must have made it through the roiling throng—but not his private messenger with news of the truth. "This is dreadful!"

She crushed herself against him, laughing, while he buried a hand in her braided hair. "You nearly sent me to the ancestors," she mumbled into his cloak. Warmth returned haltingly to her limbs as she fed, like one half-starved, on the closeness of him. "No matter, it's all come out well, praise to Sun and Moon."

All at once shy of her audience, she broke away from him and together they walked toward the main house, but her hand found his within the secrecy of the folds of their cloaks, and he clasped it in a tight, sustaining grip.

"Don't praise Sun and Moon too highly," he said, "for there *is* a tragedy here—to our good poet Peregrinus, who's lost a thousand volumes of his newest works."

"You had his books in your carriage—"

"Yes, and right now they're a blackened heap of ashes that look rather as his critics would have them look. I'll have to have them all recopied. He'll never find another patron—no one but me seems to be able to see his occasional flights of lyric brilliance."

"Then you knew you were being hunted."

He responded with a look of bare acknowledgment, but made no reply.

"What have you not told me?" Auriane said quietly, looking straight ahead.

"Ah, much has passed, and many urgent matters have come up that I'd like your opinion on . . ."

"You aren't going to answer me, are you?"

He maintained a neutral expression as they walked past Gaius Marcellinus, whose initial grin of amazement and delight at finding Julianus alive had faded off; he studied Auriane with penetrating curiosity. Somehow this strange foreign woman had known Julianus was alive.

"How is our dear Gaius Asinius?" Marcus said affably. "He looks like he has indigestion. Has Avenahar burned down the barn yet?"

"You're *determined* not to answer me."

Arria had, with a mouse-quick dodge-and-run maneuver, escaped her nurse; she captured her father's other arm and was happily trying to climb him like a tree. She was his child through all her soul—as Avenahar was Auriane's own. Marcus got to one knee, ardently gathered the child close, then produced from his cloak fresh copies of the *Acta Inepta.* Arria ran off with them, suddenly content.

Then he enclosed Auriane's hands in both of his, and said only, "Wait while I dismiss everyone and meet me in the north dining hall—no, the south library alcove, it's more private."

"MY GREATEST ENEMY is alive," Marcus Julianus said when they were alone in the library alcove. He was seated on an ivory-footed *lectus,* a small bed with a carved frame of terebinth wood inset with tortoiseshell, and held untouched a chased silver cup filled with a well-watered sample of the pale local wine. Auriane slowly paced, head down, her own cup held distractedly as she closely followed his words. Servants had left an oval platter of delicacies—small bites of hare-liver pâté formed in the shape of fish, figpeckers in coriander sauce; despite the clever presentation, the sight of it made her stomach feel like a shivering aspic.

"But we *know* all your enemies are alive," she said. "Livianus of the Praetorian Guard, and that brute Lappius Blaesus, and all those horned bulls who are pushing so hard for the war in Dacia—they're flourishing and well."

"I'm not speaking of *this* toothless crop. It takes a tyrant to breed real enemies. To the credit of our lord Trajan, men today scarcely know what enemies are. I mean a man from another time."

A hush of dread came to her voice. "One of the partisans of Domitian?"

"Yes. I mean Domitian's old fanatic-loyalist Praetorian Guards' praefect, Casperius Aelianus—"

Auriane stopped so abruptly she sloshed amber wine drops onto the travertine floor. A long-sealed cellar door creaked open and out billowed a fetid gust; she sensed something hideous slithering toward them in the dark. "Gods below," she whispered, "the man who commanded the cruel torture and execution of the conspirators who carried out your orders . . ."

For so long, they'd believed no one was left alive to avenge Domitian's assassination.

"Yes, *that* Aelianus, but to be precise, I mean his equally fanatic son of the same name."

Slowly, she sat beside him. "But Marcus, that isn't possible—unless he assumed dolphin shape. He's dead. He drowned, along with all the others." The son of the loyalist Praetorian praefect Casperius Aelianus, along with a hundred of the tyrant Domitian's most notorious informers—men who had, for years, misused their power, bringing false charges that sent men to cruel deaths—had been punished by the Emperor Trajan as soon as the new ruler ascended the throne: First Trajan ordered them exhibited like common brigands before the populace in the Great Amphitheater, so their victims' families could shout abuse at them. All expected Trajan would give them to the wild beasts. But Trajan punished the criminals in a novel way; their new Emperor was a blunt and plain-spoken man, but because of this, many said this proved his poetry was in his acts: He ordered the informers taken down to the Tiber, where they were put on a rudderless ship that was towed far out to sea then left to drift, until the craft was dashed apart by the fury of ocean storms. Trajan let the gods of wind and water slay them, while his own hands remained clean of their blood.

"Casperius Aelianus the Younger lives on, Auriane. Neptune neglected to gulp this one man down. Perhaps he clung to broken-up timbers and drifted ashore, who knows? My own belief is that he washed onto land at Sicily, because there, my agents learned he murdered a caretaker of a great seaside estate, threatened the slaves and enriched himself off the farm, before the owner, who didn't live there and didn't know, could set the authorities on him. We've evidence, too, that he visited his ancestral estate in Apulia, which was shut up and awaiting auction, and took only such things as a son would take—personal letters of his father's, family portraits, a seal ring, bills of sale, and the like. He was far too clever to try to reclaim his father's wealth, however. He then made his way north, to our neighbor-province of Gallia Belgica, where he took a false name and used his stolen wealth to establish an estate near Augusta Treverorum. He has prospered well. He's alive, Auriane—the man who believes I murdered Domitian, his patron and god, and slew his own father, and made him a hated outcast. Alive and living for no other purpose but the chance to punish me for murdering his beloved Master and God."

"You've known of this for some time, Marcus. Am I a child, that you kept this from me?" Soon as she said it, the irony of these words stung her like the cut of a whip. *And who am I to accuse him? I, who can't tell him I have been, for years, secretly shifting his money across the frontier?*

"Utter nonsense!" He put down his cup and clamped his hands protectively about her shoulders. "All I wanted was for your life here not be shadowed by this. I wanted to see how you'd flourish in tranquillity, if given the haven you so richly merited."

"I'm sorry for that; I should not have said it. You tried, with great good will, and if you couldn't do it, none could have." *Our tranquillity was doomed from the start,* came words she couldn't speak. *I brought the high winds and storm with me.* Then came a quick image of Witgern huddled in the snow, while she was nestled in warmth. Of her aged mother, Athelinda, facing the invading Cheruscan chief called Chariomer—*while I linger over hare-liver pâté in the shape of fish. How could any daughter of my people have acted otherwise?*

"How did you know this son of Aelianus would strike now?" she asked.

"He sold the estate quite suddenly, and disappeared from the sight of my spies. As you know, there's no better time to strike at a man than when he's travelling."

"By now, he knows he didn't succeed." She looked at him. "He'll try again."

"At least he's shown his hand. We will just have to move about with care, and always under guard."

"Always under guard? When Avenahar and I go hunting, or visiting the town?"

"I fear so, Auriane. He'll continue to strike at me. He has a madman's determination crossed with an athlete's skill and endurance, and he's disturbingly careless of his own life. And worse: Because of the hatred he's nursed for so many years, he's as likely to strike at you."

After a moment drawn into thought, he added, "Because of this, I'll have to refuse Trajan's summons to go to Dacia. I can't abandon you here to this."

At this, she was pricked by an obscure alarm. "Marcus, *can* such a request be refused? Is it not, despite its mild language, really a command that must be obeyed?"

"You are right. It won't endear me to the ruler of the known world. But I fear it must be so."

"And we came here to live a plain, unfettered life, and raise happy children, well off from the horrors of tyrants and wars."

"Madness, I know, but life isn't a wall painting. It's more a swift river of clouds, constantly changing shape. Perhaps I sowed my doom in Rome. 'Assassination' is a word that manages to sound cleaner and grander than 'murder.' I *did* cause a man's death. And worse, others were punished for it, not I . . . and punished horribly. Perhaps only now, after eight years, has Nemesis found me for retribution."

"'*Caused a man's death*'?! Marcus, any sensible man would say you brought justice to a murderer. A murderer of many! Nemesis worked *through* you—and she would not slaughter her own! Your remorse is a demon that over the years has fed and gotten fat on your kindly nature. I will not listen to this!"

He laughed softly. "I believe your lack of tolerance for my remorse has kept me from becoming a madman."

He cradled her face in his hands and the world drifted to a dulcet halt. "How would I have thrived all these years, without that still flame in your eyes drawing me back to what's true?"

In the gardens beyond the glazed window's gauzy glow a stable boy idled with a shepherd's pipe; it sounded like a life lived beneath endless sunset. Or something grand, gently unraveling. She moved with those descending notes as she collapsed against him in a great soul-exhaustion, her head nestled beneath his chin. Most naturally, most knowingly, he began kissing the back of her neck, each press of the lips more insistent than the one before, reaching deeper into her—until she felt her flesh begin to melt off, and there was nothing left of her but a shivering puddle, a sensitized yearning shot through with that need that was so welcome, so incapacitating. Tears pooled in her eyes as he released the pins of her tunica. The fine cloth slid down and collected round her hips, leaving her half naked like some sturdy Venus in pale Luna marble. She struggled to get his woolen tunic off him, and then they were pressed heart to heart, skin to skin, and every part of her flashed open. Even now she felt a spark of the illicit when they lay abed entwined, as if they were lovers married to others, seeking one another in a darkened colonnade. It might have been because the whole of his world, from the aristocracy of Rome to neighboring farm folk, disapproved of the high place she occupied in his life. It made her feel she swam a rough river to get to him.

Through this, he managed to draw closed the heavy curtain that draped the alcove. Moving in time with the woeful pipe, they caved back together onto the *lectus,* and all the fury beyond the walls was gone. But as they gratefully joined, no exquisite playing on the skin, no worshipful touch, no mingling of the deepest waters was enough to banish her sense of being prey to encroaching darkness. *Hunted like game,* she thought. *Both of us.*

A POST RIDER cantered up the graveled walk to the villa of Marcus Julianus, soon as Flora's festival was done. As was Demaratos's habit, he turned over the day's correspondence to Auriane.

At the bottom of a neat stack of folded and tied wax tablets was one that shot her into cold darkness. The wax seal placed over the knotted string tied about the tablet was stamped with the imprint of Volusius Victorinus's signet-ring.

She broke the seal and unfolded the tablet's three wooden leaves. It was a summons, ordering her to appear in Victorinus's court in the town of Confluentes, at noon on the morrow.

Lurio. Aprossius has failed me. The fugitive sailor's gone to the magistrate— why else would Victorinus summon me?

I must go, and contrive some way to keep Victorinus silent about this. Which means I'll need to concoct a false reason to give to Marcus, for the journey into the town. I grow ever more enmeshed in my own web.

And now, a spider is roused to my struggles.

ON THAT SAME eve, Auriane came upon Avenahar unexpectedly in the forest amphitheater, sparring with one of the grooms.

Avenahar whipped about, alarmed as one caught carrying out a forbidden rite; the groom shot through her defense and she got a blow on the thigh with the flat of his wooden blade. The frightened groom backed off, ready to flee when he saw Auriane. Auriane did not know what she was seeing; Avenahar seemed to wield a column of light.

Auriane felt a melting terror, thinking it another unwanted vision—this one, fine and precise as a fever dream. *Is this, then, my daughter's future?*

Avenahar had a short sword in hand; the steel blade hoarded the reddening sun so that it glowed like the heart of a furnace.

"Avenahar," Auriane said, *"where did you get that?"*

Defiance warred in Avenahar's face with a many-shaded sadness; she was woman-grown, then, but unknown—someone else's child, another country's daughter, all that tamped-down determination disturbingly visible.

"It's the fugitive sailor's sword," Avenahar said in an alto voice Auriane scarce knew. "I threw a log in the river that day—not the sword." She added, with a belligerent lift of the head, "So now you know. Punish me."

The burning sword. It still felt like an omen, even though Auriane knew its natural cause.

"You brazenly disobeyed me. You've had that out here in the wood, all this time? How did you hide it on the way home?"

"I put it into one of the emptied sacks while you weren't looking."

"So even as the magistrate halted us—you had a concealed sword, which is a forbidden thing, and would've made us look all the guiltier, were it found—where are your wits? It takes more than a womanhood ceremony to make you one!"

"I am sorry for it." But Auriane could see that Avenahar's only regret was for her mother's disappointment. "It was as though an evil wight possessed me." After a moment, she added, "I've become adept with it. Would you like to—"

"Throw it in the river. This time do it without fail or I'll forbid you to come here more."

Avenahar jogged off with it at once, alert to something in her mother's voice not to be trifled with.

Auriane felt an errant pride in her daughter, then. *I, too, was defiant at her age of life, but with it always came a portion of shame. Shame will never cling to Avenahar as it did to me. I raised a daughter who knows her innocence. In this matter I've succeeded, if in nothing else!*

"Mother, I can help us," Avenahar said on her return. "All our troubles at home are the doing of that Chariomer and his raiding gaggle of bandits. His rape of our country left you no choice but to break a Roman law. I mean to take the oath of a shield maiden when I go back, and gather together all the disheartened . . ." Her fine fervor dissolved into uncertainty. "Your mind has flown; you aren't even listening!"

Victorinus is awash in riches, Auriane had been thinking. *What can I offer such a man to keep him silent?*

"Why do you not see what I am?" Avenahar pressed on plaintively.

"What makes you think I don't? I see a heedless hothead. Avenahar, that life holds none of the beauty you're dreaming into it. Cold and want, misery from wounds, early death—are these things glorious? And in the end, you discover you're battling not the enemy—but Fria herself."

"I want . . . an important life. As yours was. Here, I will always be an outcast. I would *belong* somewhere."

"I want you to oath a thing to me, right now, on that amulet of earth, in case death comes to me . . . sooner rather than later . . . that when you're fully grown you'll go home and apprentice yourself to an herb woman. You're far cannier than most, in those arts. And you'll shun weapons of war."

"I won't do it. An oath's a dread thing. I'll not make one I can't keep."

Chapter 9

The interior of the courthouse at Confluentes was somber at noon. Auriane felt muted and small as she passed between the solemn stone women flanking the entranceway, Roma and *Iustitia,* Justice, their rippling marble garments frozen for the ages in midbillow. The vast basilica held all the color and noise of the town's Forum at bay; as she stepped into the formal gloom, her footfalls sounded as hollow and solitary as if she'd entered a mausoleum. Upon entering the long nave she reached to her throat to touch Ramis's amulet, following long habit—but her hand closed round emptiness, and she felt a momentary sink of regret that she'd passed it on to Avenahar. She moved between rows of thick columns of red porphyry—smooth, voiceless trees standing at relentless attention. High clerestory windows emitted a sallow, autumnal light. Beneath them, running the length of the walls, was a rhythmic motif of green scrolls carved in bas-relief against a field of gold. Beneath her feet a black-and-white mosaic of interlaced vines reduced all the comforting chaos of nature to measured, still geometry. The basilica played grandly on the senses but she was ever conscious it was not alive. A living house was made of materials that lived once—willow withies, grasses, oakwood. It had breath; the winds were free to stir in it. This was a shuttered temple, a stone grove.

The magistrate followed her progress down the nave with stony patience, eyes bright and malign as some troll beneath a bridge. A troll in a soiled toga, she saw as her vision began to adjust to the stale twilight. Like all provincial courthouses, this one was meant to convey the grandeur and permanence of Roman law. But the effect was spoiled somewhat by Roman law's representative, Victorinus, propped sloppily atop his chair of office, a globular amphora of a man with ears like jug handles and a protruding lower lip. He had a frightful welt near his left eyebrow, given him by one Venusta, citizen of the town, who'd hurled a peach stone at him when she'd taken a dislike to his judgment in the matter of the theft of her cook-pan, and he'd combed one scraggly lock forward in an attempt to disguise it. Encountering him in this austerely beautiful gallery was like finding a soup stain on a perfectly penned manuscript.

She halted before the tribunal, feet sinking into a carpet of sea-green wool. There was an iron distance in the magistrate's eyes; they were void of all memory of any past pretense of friendship. She thought it odd Victorinus's sizable staff of clerks was nowhere in evidence, not even that amiable oaf Cobnertus. Nor was there so much as a single slave secretary posted near to record the proceedings. Whatever Victorinus planned, he wanted no witnesses.

The spider is alone as it awaits the fly.

"I am here, Victorinus. Though I'm not sure why I'm here."

"Ah—Queen Aurinia has swept down from her country throne to delight our little town. I trust you are well."

"Do you? At our last meeting you called me a necromancing whore."

"It's vexing to have one's words thrown back at one, rather like hearing some overzealous accountant tell you everything you spent last year. Where is Avenahar? I wanted her here, too. I've a gift for her coming birthday."

"What is it you want, Victorinus?"

"To deliver her gift in person—it's of such a nature, it can't be delivered by messenger. I was compelled to ask you here, as you never seem ready to offer hospitality to me—all those prominent guests who're regularly welcomed at Marcus Julianus's dinner banquets, and it seems *this* guest is always prominently missing. That's not a way to cultivate the representatives of the law, Aurinia—whom, I assure you, you're soon going to want in your camp."

The fright she felt was physical and sharp. Somewhere within, she was a hapless creature scrabbling for purchase on a steep trail. But from long experience with single battle her gaze had a wrestler's strength, and she held him fast with it.

"I'll not be batted about like some cat's ball, Victorinus. Inform me of whatever it is by letter when you finally see fit to come to your purpose."

She turned and strode off down the basilica's central aisle, her sky-blue cloak unfurling in her wake as her angry steps echoed crisply on stone.

He saw his hope was vain that his courthouse would have a humbling effect—she might as well have come upon him naked in a bath.

"Here is Avenahar's gift!" he called out to her retreating back.

Auriane's steps slowed, tension sabotaging every muscle.

"I mean to give her"—he paused, savoring her torment—"the security of knowing she'll still have a mother—that is, if you come my way, and make no trouble."

She spun about, the light of a lioness in her eye. "You adder in the straw. Explain yourself."

"Let us say a fish bearing a fascinating tale has swum into my net . . . a fish named Lurio."

Lurio. The name shot up from the murk of nightmares, livid and horrible.

"What explanation do you have for burying coins near the Eleventh Milestone, behind a shrine to the Mothers, on the eve of the Kalends of *Aprilis?*"

"You flatter yourself beyond reason, magistrate," she said softly, "to think I would reveal my affairs to you."

"Perhaps your insolence will be tempered when I tell you we have more than Lurio's identification of you—though, in a case so notorious, I'm certain the Palace's requirement for three freeborn witnesses would be waived. A medallion of Minerva torn from a horse's harness, such as are worn only by mounts from Julianus's estate, was found there on the ground—proving someone from your farm *did* haunt that remote place, and that some sort of struggle ensued, as this Lurio claims—"

"No wise judge would count that firm evidence."

"Ah, you know my methods little—in laying out a banquet, I save the best dish for last. I posted guards there day and night, to see who came down the river seeking your hoard. You must know, Auriane, I have arrested Grimo, rower on the *Isis,* a wineship out of Rigodulum. He named you under torture, Auriane. Your traitorous days have ended."

The abyss claimed her.

"This Grimo was feeble," Victorinus spoke on, "and he expired under the torture, but he proved quite the babbling coward before he went. He gave us more than enough to destroy you."

She knew he meant to goad her into a show of pity and revulsion, thus demonstrating her connection with this man, and with immense effort, she maintained a look of detachment. But in her mind's eye she traced on air the runic sign of rebirth for poor Grimo. *Fria, cradle him in death. Though he had an oar in his hand, not a spear, he died a warrior in this war that does not end. See him off to the shining sky.*

"Well then, Victorinus. If you have what you need, why call me here at all? Deliver me up to the Imperial Council and collect your three million sesterces for my blood."

Her mind was in ferment as she spoke—she must get word at once to the hide trader at Mogontiacum, a man called Axsillius, to whom Grimo passed on the coin, in case poor Grimo had named him as well. . . .

"You've got courage even if you lack all the regular charms one holds dear to womanhood." His wan smile vanished. "Hear me through. I have in this letter here the whole record of my gathered evidence. Fast as I can get it through the post to Rome, the ministers of our Lord Trajan will be reading this with amazement—and gratitude to me."

He motioned for her to come closer; she did not move.

"But know this, it does not have to be so—" His voice altered subtly, sounding more sly, almost ashamed, and her animal senses caught a foul whiff, evidence of a new sort of danger.

"—for consider, Aurinia, I am already a very wealthy man . . . perhaps that three million sesterces isn't much more to me than one more string of sea-pearls round a high-born matron's neck . . . Suppose there is something else I want even more."

He leaned farther out of his chair. "I'm ready, even now, to commend this letter to the fire," he said, extending an arm and holding the rolled papyrus high above the five flames of a pottery lamp, "if you'll sign this document here, betrothing your second-born daughter, Arria Juliana, to my son, Lucius."

"Have you lost all *memory* of honor? I didn't think your shamelessness could still astound me."

"Yield her, Aurinia . . ." He tried to infuse a victor's amused complacency into his smile but his eyes betrayed him; they had a look of pleading, and they smoldered with the fire of a man who sees one thing, desires one thing, in all the world. One finger intimately caressed the edge of the document, as though it were the flesh of a woman who stirred the blood. Auriane felt sickness rising in her throat. ". . . and perhaps then, your crime will remain secret between us."

"Have you no fear of Nemesis? That's no true marriage! You'd have me exchange my child for my freedom, like some hostage of war. Your country may have been founded upon women who were forced, but my daughter Arria is no Sabine bride who'll turn about in a year and come to love the man who seized her and dragged her to his marriage bed. Even if I agreed, do you imagine Marcus Julianus would? That he would gladly turn over his only child-in-the-blood to a man who must extort a bride for his wretch of a son because he can't get one any other way?"

"Julianus? Ah, I imagine that with your witch's tongue you could get him to agree to anything you wished. *Yield her.*"

She took a step closer. "If your case against me is so unshakable, then why give it up? It's difficult to believe you'd toss off three million sesterces *and* the glory this would shower on you. Why cheat your masters of so valuable a criminal as myself?"

He had no answer for this; a shade seemed to drop over his eyes.

"What's wrong with your case, Victorinus? Perhaps you did catch Grimo, but, inconveniently, he died without naming me? Or maybe you're calculating just how little weight the Palace will attach to a case prepared by a wriggling worm such as yourself?"

"Play with your doubts, Aurinia, they're all you have. I assure you, Grimo named you."

"And I say you are a liar."

"And I don't imagine, with your low birth, you'll be allowed to choose the manner of your death. Then there's the matter of whose money it was. Poor Julianus—I'll wager he'll think twice before he drags more barbarian baggage home from the wars. I don't know if you duped *him* as well, but no one in official places will believe Marcus Julianus wholly innocent in this matter."

"Victorinus, you are faithless to everyone, even to the men you serve. You've nothing to bargain *with*. Bargaining supposes a man possesses a measure of honor."

She whipped about and, once again, swiftly walked away.

He rose from his seat, fists clenched as he realized he was losing what he sought. "You whinnying mare, I will have you!" There was a slight warble in his voice, as if he sang through a hollow reed. "And before I turn you over to higher justice, I'll see you stripped naked and whipped before the whole of the town!"

She halted abruptly, turned round, and closely examined his face.

"It's *you* you want her for," she said in a low voice. It was a guess that felt certain, born of all she sensed about the man. "Not your son, Lucius. The marriage is just a means to have her close."

"You are wrong. I want her for my son." But his eyes told her otherwise. She felt she had surprised a lizard when she looked into them—something small, dark, and clammy streaked for cover.

Despoilers of children, she thought. *When your people take brides at twelve,* she supposed, *a girl of nine must look near ripe.* Among her own people, it was counted shameful, unmanly even, for a man to lie with a woman of less than twenty years. But here, she knew, to take a maid less than half that age was counted but a minor vice, like swilling down too much wine in the wrong company.

My babe, my tender bud not yet opened, set to be plucked off and devoured . . .
My betrayal of Marcus has exposed my child to a monster.

"I leave you no choice, Aurinia," Victorinus said softly. "Yield her."

In her own country Auriane had witnessed ritual cursings; she decided to gamble that she could imitate the practice convincingly enough. From a leather pouch hung from her belt she got a pinch of common goatweed, an herbal powder she used in everyday rituals of blessing. With a flourish, she flung it high, as though it were a seeress's cursing powders.

"You venomous Circe . . . what are you doing?"

As the greenish-brown cloud drifted down over her she began intoning a chant, employing the Chattian tongue. *"May you be cursed in blood and eyes . . . may you be twisted in every limb—"*

"What's this barbarous cant? Stop at once!" After a frantic search on his person, the magistrate produced a small bell and rang it with frenzied motions, believing the tinny bell tones had the power to ward off evil.

"—may your vitals turn to putrid rot . . . may Hel tangle thought and memory. I reverse your name. May—" As she intoned these words, with swift, swordlike precision she traced runic letters in the air. The magistrate knew her people possessed a dreaded secret alphabet, used solely for warding, cursing, and spells.

He believed it was a death curse. Fear of sorcery was the fine fracture in the stone on which she tapped to crack him open.

"Guard!" His dry croak did not carry to the guard chamber.

"And should you make any more attempts to snatch her, Hel will take you off within the moon," she finished in clear Latin so he would understand.

She regarded him in solemn quiet for a moment, while the goatweed cloud drifted off, leaving a sharp, evil silence in its wake. Victorinus sat stiff and still on his cross-legged magistrate's chair, his torso twisted about like a man in the grip of a a quick-acting poison.

"I suggest you keep your letter," she said then. "You'll need something to wipe the drool from your chin with, when you think of my daughter. Good day, Victorinus."

YIELD HER. VICTORINUS'S words ground into Auriane's mind like a mortar into a pestle.

"What did Victorinus want?" Avenahar asked as she saw Auriane emerge from the law basilica looking stricken but adamant. The hood of a magenta-hued cloak lay against Avenahar's darkly shining hair, and her arms glittered with adornments of gold; these bright woman's things, so rarely donned, seemed only to increase her natural boldness. Mother and daughter spoke in their Germanic tongue to conceal their words from their retinue—four stout grooms from the villa who served as bodyguards and way-clearers. The small party wove their way through the town forum's crowds, through spring air infused with the delicate aroma from the hot-drink stands ladling out spiced, watered wine. They sought the gem-cutters' stalls, where Avenahar would choose a sardonyx ring, which they would have engraved for her as a gift from Marcus Julianus for her birthday—this was the purpose she'd given him for her journey into town today.

"He wanted Arria," came Auriane's terse, distracted reply.

"Gods below, a chicken has more wit," Avenahar said, failing to check a burst of laughter that bent her double, "and a horsefly less persistence! The man must get some carnal pleasure from hearing you utter the word *no*. Was that all?"

"No, Avenahar," Auriane answered, grief stifling her voice to a whisper. "It wasn't. He knows everything. Or enough to destroy us, anyway. He's interrogated Lurio."

To Auriane's surprise her daughter seemed more intrigued than intimidated, as if presented with an especially challenging move in a board game. "My counsel's to tell Father. It's his country and his law. We've not the means to battle this alone."

We've not the means. Auriane needed to force back a smile. This was Avenahar's recently forged new self, afire with brash confidence since the blood-of-life had come. Avenahar now carried a set of keys to the house. She went alone to the wooden image of Fria by the river, to make her own offerings. And she'd begun questioning her mother's judgment with all the insouciance of a favorite pupil who trusts her teacher will see it not as combativeness but as an admirable willingness to ride full-tilt at a problem.

"It is not so simple, Avenahar. Well as I know and love him, still I cannot guess what he'll do when he learns this. I need time to warn those who still need to be warned. If there is a way I can avoid burdening him, let it be so. And just perhaps, if the Fates are decently kind—I've terrified Victorinus into silence."

Auriane found she did not believe it as she said it.

Chapter 10

The old chief sat still as a wooden idol on his high seat. In his right hand he held an iron standard topped with an image of a stag in flight.

This was the same spring day, but far to the north of Julianus's villa, in a valley civilization did not know. Lost in Germania Libera's rolling oceans of forests, this pine-rimmed river valley was a destination that would have been, had passable roads existed, fourteen days' ride past the Roman frontier. The chief was called Chariomer, and he was lord over the Cheruscans, a north Germanic people who had been enemies of Auriane's Chattian tribe for one hundred raiding seasons and more. He had assembled his war companions in a freshly captured longhouse that had become his seat only yesterday, when his army surprised and seized this Chattian settlement. The bodies of the village's folk lay unmourned and unburned, scattered across the emmer fields, or abandoned to the gloom of the forest where his men had fallen upon them as they tried to flee. Rome called him "King" Chariomer because he sought hereditary rule, but he bore no more resemblance to what literate southern peoples called a king than a dozen other skin-draped battle chiefs struggling for overlordship in the turbulent north. An untrimmed beard of sandy brown threaded with gray trailed down to a massive, gold-plated belt. Eyes the color of dirty snow stared out from great, bony sockets. A long and haggard face was broken by jutting cheekbones; beneath them graying skin slack as overstretched cloth caved in to form cadaverous hollows. The ermine skins wrapped about him concealed a body more wasted than battle-trim, after the steady erosion of sixty winters. Behind him hung a tapestry woven in shades of ocher, russet, and moss green, depicting himself blessing a stag to be offered to the god; eleven skilled weaving-women directed by his now-dead wife had labored two years in its creation.

The two hundred young warriors seated before him on benches running the length of the hearth fire waited in solemn anticipation for the brother-making ceremony to begin—a rite that would transform these new-won companions into war-brothers, bound to die for one another. The old chief knew well he hadn't won these warriors' devotion in the traditional way, through displays of prowess in battle. These fierce hawks jostled for place in his hall only because the Roman Great King called Trajan, lord over lands Chariomer would never know, had begun pouring gold into his coffers again—his reward for harrying the Chattian dogs and not letting them rest. The Roman gold had come by muleback a quarter-moon ago, and it was enough to keep hundreds of war companions sworn to him for many seasons to come.

Now, the Fates stood ready to make good for all the troubles they'd given him—exile by his own people, a wife who'd birthed only daughters, the mysterious ten-year-old slaying of the young man who had been his sworn-son by a shield maid called Auriane, daughter of the Chattian chief Baldemar. Through the years he'd lived in hiding, seeress after seeress had warned him the elder gods were punishing him for imitating Roman customs—drinking wine until he fell down; conspiring to pass on his ancestral lands in the Hart country to a son instead of a daughter; assembling his bewildered companions on a parade ground and inspecting their weapons, as though he were some centurion over soldiers rather than a chief over free men. But his victories over the Chattians told the truth of it—he was a hero who brought gifts hitherto unknown to the people, one greatly loved of Wodan, to whom he'd regularly offered his best horse, his finest haunch of meat.

Chariomer nodded to his songmaker and silvery music began shivering off the strings of a harp, falling on the company like a soft, trickling rain. Chariomer detested the music of harpists, which sounded to him like tears. He preferred horns and drums and instruments that made the blood rush, and thought the whole race of harpists parasites on others' goodwill. But harpists made stories and the grandness of this occasion demanded one.

Chariomer lifted the iron stag-standard and beat it loudly, twice, on the planked floor. Four thralls stepped into the smoky twilight of the hall, their backs bent beneath the weight of a linden shield heaped with red-gold coins— Trajan's gold, sent in gratitude for the services Chariomer performed for Rome. The company of warriors watched as if they witnessed some prodigy— the torches affixed to the longhouse's walls infused the treasure with a living light; it seemed some dragon's hoard, emitting balefire.

Those nearest Chariomer heard him grunt in irritation. Something about the treasure-procession displeased him.

Or some*one,* as it proved—a fifth thrall had fallen in behind the shield-bearers, ambling along with a jaunty step. The bearded, ring-girded company along the fire watched his progress with eyes narrowed in bafflement. The interloper grinned a grin that suggested the world might prosper, if only it followed his advice. He was a man obviously not bred in the north: Mediterranean-dark eyes glimmered with cynical good humor. His face was carefully clean-shaven, exposing a strong, square chin. He was short in stature, and close-cropped black hair flecked with silver was trained forward in the Roman fashion. As the four treasure-bearers set the shield on the floor with a resonant *thud* next to Chariomer's booted feet, the brazen fellow strode right up to their king and gave a bow like some actor in a farce, seeming so untouched by the solemnity of the rite, he might have just helped haul a sack of turnips to market.

This man was Decius, once a Roman legionary soldier—that same Decius who was the blood-father of Avenahar.

Chariomer's frown deepened as Decius leaned close, employing a broken Germanic that lapsed into Latin at his convenience.

"There's a bit of a problem here, O august and kingly one."

Chariomer just stared at him, disoriented by the interruption.

"Can't trust a Vestal these days," Decius continued. "I'm afraid a few of these *aurei* aren't full weight."

Chariomer gave a grunt of discontent, trapped between a fierce interest in all matters that touched on his payment, and a need to maintain dignity.

"Some jokester stashed a few sham coins at the bottom," Decius spoke on, "and, I'll own, they're a fiendishly good copy of the real thing. You can't let them use you this way, old friend. I'd be no chief advisor worth keeping if I didn't press you to send an embassy back to the Aquae Mattiaci fort at once to tell them just how strongly—"

Chariomer brought the standard down smartly on the wooden planking while roaring, *"Begone, Hel-cursed nithling."* It mortified everyone but Decius.

Decius bowed deeply. "Ever wanting to please," he said lightly, then gave a shrug that expressed tolerance for a cranky child. As he moved off he placed one of the offending coins on the whetstone by the king's seat. This was too much for the old chief, whose gaze was drawn to it as if pulled by a cord; he greedily examined it before he caught himself and angrily tossed the sham coin back with the others heaped at his feet.

Decius cheerfully took himself out, his free and easy strides contrasting oddly with the quiet shuffle of his fellow thralls, trailing after him. The company of warriors followed this exit with blank looks, as if Decius had been a winged dragon dropped into their midst. What spell had this foreign wretch put on their testy chief, that Chariomer allowed a thrall such liberties?

When Decius was gone Chariomer called out the name of his daughter, Elza.

The solemn office of handing round the mead horn to the companions was always performed by a woman, most often the chief's wedded wife. Only women knew the spells that called down the gods into the mead and could make it stand for blood, so that warriors who were not kin became brothers. But since Chariomer's wife had died nine winters ago and negotiations for a new wife were not yet complete, the rite would need to be performed by Elza, the last living woman of his family.

A young woman slim and tentative as a deer paused in the longhouse's wide doorway. She was clad in a cloak dyed forest-green with flowerheads of reeds; beneath was a madder-red dress with green embroidered hem. The men's talk died off; even the harpist's fingers stumbled and stopped as all turned round to gape. Elza seemed a spirit-girl, standing there. A sliver of sunlight breaking through thatch illumined her copper hair, just visible beneath the hood of her cloak, creating a nimbus of fuzzy light about the crown of her head. Her lucid eyes were wide and wondering, swift and sad; they drew one in with the steady force of a quiet compulsion, as to some game of guessing the depth of an uncannily clear spring. Though most would have counted Elza plain of feature, that face was mobile and expressive, reminding those who looked on her that there were qualities other than beauty that could bind a gaze to a woman's face. In her right hand was a long, exquisitely curved aurochs horn with a gem-set silver mount. It had known the touch of her great-grandmother's hands.

Meaning to encourage her to approach, her father gave her a small, tight smile, motioning with an exaggerated gesture, as if to one who spoke a foreign tongue. He knew this daughter little. She was raised by his late wife's women-thralls, and he'd never turned more than the most cursory attention to her. He interpreted her tautness, her hesitation, as maidenly timidity.

It was not. It was anticipatory excitement.

Elza began to walk with ceremonial slowness down the length of the hearthfire. Its flames swelled as she passed, as if in homage, and the men believed the ancestral spirits living in the hearth were greeting the daughter who loved them. Her eloquent eyes made her seem a doe among wolves, but the impression was untrue. The set of her small mouth, the tension in her jaw, revealed her nature better. She was one to see a matter through, no matter how it hurt her. From earliest girlhood Elza had learned she would get nothing in this harsh world unless she injured another to get it—she'd watched her poor mother do the same.

On this day she had a fearsome deed to carry out.

The small, shivering stones of amber in her pendant earrings and the silver sieve-spoons hung from her girdle made music as she walked—lulling sounds that contrasted with the tension in the hall, which steadily, inexorably grew, like the tautening of a rope with the turning of a winch. For this girl of nineteen summers held great power in her hands, if only for a fleeting moment. Elza was keenly aware of how these men feared her. Fatal violence might erupt if she handed the mead horn round in the wrong order. She might call a man a thief and this company would be bound to treat him as one. She could speak a charge of cowardice against any one of them, which might send him off on a quest that could kill him. Women knew how to speak the words that festered in the flesh and slowly destroyed a man. And this power was doubly potent when a woman carried out the brother-making ceremony, when so many denizens of the unseen world hovered close.

Elza counted this power-of-the-word as her sword and shield. Her mother had taught her to be merciless with it.

She halted before the mead-cask and with a practiced dip of her arm, filled the horn. She had brewed the mead herself using more than fifty herbs, some brought by expeditions to faraway lands. Each plant added its own subtle force; their powers fused to produce a brew so fearsome in its potency it could transform strangers into kin.

Then she stood before the high seat, a supple young daughter facing a father who watched her like a gaunt, aging wolf.

She began whispering words of an invocation old as the stones beneath the hall. By giving the horn to her father first, she confirmed him as war chief over this band. It was a sight that a man ignorant of the ways of the tribes might have found astonishing—a ruthless, battle-scarred old man placing the weight of his future days in the palm of a half-grown maid.

Her invocation ceased. Within, she readied herself for vengeance.

Elza did not want to be handed in marriage to any man of his band, for she despised them all as the murderers of her mother. One of them, with her father's assistance, had poisoned her mother, Theudolind—Elza had long known it was no common childbed death. Her mother had just given birth to a third girl-child, inciting Chariomer to murderous wrath. Her mother had had no chance: Never trusted because she was Chattian, her marriage had been a torment, the result of one brief, long-ago attempt to make a Chattian alliance.

And so Elza had made her own marriage plans in secret. She had seen the young Chattian war-chief Sigibert but once, and sought him in part because he seemed everything her father was not—noble even to the lowly, ready to risk wealth and freedom to aid his friends, and truly loved by his war companions. The match was impossible in these times; the two tribes were at war. A high-placed seeress might mandate it in an oracle, however, and Elza had managed to lure one into her camp—Sawitha, one of the seeresses of the Holy Nine, second in eminence only to Ramis herself. What Elza planned next would seal her alliance with Sawitha. In exchange, Sawitha had promised to open the way to the foreign marriage Elza so fervently wanted.

Chariomer raised his hand to take the horn.

But Elza held it just beyond her father's reach. Chariomer refused to humiliate himself by pitching his body forward and straining to take it. His anticipatory hand was left suspended there, half opened.

"*Elza!*" he said in a whisper meant only for her. But those seated nearest heard him over the softly popping fire. "You're not so old I can't have you beaten!"

Elza met his eyes calmly. His posture began to look ridiculous.

"Do you see this brooch I wear, Father?" Her voice was clear and mild. She indicated the raven's-head brooch that fastened the green cloak.

His hand sank to his side. "No, I don't. I see only the flicking of a she-serpent's tongue. You Nixe's daughter . . . *give me that!*"

She took a half step farther from him.

"It's my dead brother's brooch, Father. The brooch of your adopted son, Odberht."

She was gratified by the ember of fear that appeared in her father's eyes, steadily growing brighter.

"You clearly didn't get enough thrashings as a girl. That's impossible. Odberht died in a far-off land, felled by another woman's treachery. No one ever recovered his brooch."

Her father's words were true. Elza's brooch was a fair copy of one she remembered. But it would not hinder her purpose.

"Odberht gave it to me when I was little," she smoothly lied, "before he marched south for you so long ago, to attack the Chattians at your command. Now your murdered son has only me to speak for him."

"He was no son of the blood!" Ceremonial dignity fled; his voice was wheezy and shrill. "He was a Roman son. It is not the same!" Because Chariomer's wife had borne only daughters, he had adopted the young man called Odberht after the Roman fashion, using a modified version of his people's blood-brother ceremony.

"Ah. But Father, many saw you declare him a son, before the gods."

"Elza, stop this, I *beg* you," he said, probing for a vein of sympathy in her, "and you've my word I'll speak of this with you, later. I'll find you whatever husband you want. Just *give me that!*" Spittle dribbled down his chin.

She eased her eyes half closed. Her voice was ululating, high, like some seeress crying over the wind.

"Chariomer. You bear the wolf's head and your blood is poison. You have dishonored every brave man here." The power in Elza's voice was startling; it carried all the hope-fueled ferocity of the tormented animal seeking one chance to break free. "I cannot look over our fields with gladness until my brother, Odberht, is avenged. His blood cries out from the ground. I charge you in the name of Wodan, avenge his death or be despised by all good men."

Elza pulled back the hood of her cloak and removed the bone comb that secured her hair. The men round the hearthfire murmured in alarm. Some shielded their eyes, or sputtered imprecations to the lesser gods. Chariomer looked like a corpse frozen in the snow—flesh gray, mouth gaped open, left hand curled like a claw.

"Daughter of trolls . . . what have you done!"

Elza's thick copper hair had been hastily, crudely cropped off. She had cut it herself, without the aid of her looking-glass. It lay sadly on her head like some coverlet nibbled by rats, clipped so short that it curled about her ears. To the assembled men the sight was repugnant, obscene. A woman's holiness resided in her hair; it bound the greater family to the gods. It was as if Elza had vandalized the village temple out of spite.

"And, Father," she finished, "as my brother, Odberht, was not slain with honorable weapons of war, but was strangled with an enemy woman's hair—I have shorn mine off."

At this a few in the company of warriors exchanged questioning looks. But many knew this disturbing tale. During the Chattian War, Chariomer's adopted son, Odberht, had been captured by the legions and dragged to Rome to be used as a fighting-slave, or gladiator, as some knew they were called. Auriane, daughter of the enemy chieftain Baldemar, had suffered the same fate. In the name of the Chattian tribe, Auriane had sworn vengeance against Odberht because the young man led a force of Cheruscans against her tribe's back. The fragmented story had filtered back many seasons later: In that distant place Auriane met Chariomer's sworn-son in single battle, in a sacred enclosure where fighting-slaves slew each other for the pleasure of their sun god. After a battle to a standstill in which he divested her of her sword, this shield maiden daughter of Baldemar used her long hair as rope and strangled him. Men touched talismans at the memory.

Chariomer rose unsteadily to his feet.

"Daughter, I command you, grow it back!"

Elza's low, husky laugh was so like her mother's, Chariomer thought his slain wife's ghost had taken possession of his daughter. "Who listens to a war-chief who's failed to avenge his kin? I'll grow it back when you swear vengeance against Auriane, before all your men."

"In your madness you've taken no heed of the fact that Auriane's living in Roman lands now, under the protection of one of their high chiefs."

"Ah, but she'll be here soon," Elza responded. "She has a daughter approaching her moon-time. They'll need to come here to proclaim the daughter's womanhood."

Chariomer saw that his objections, his hesitation, were a mistake. Many watched him doubtfully, thinking it somewhat thickheaded of him not to have anticipated Elza's challenge. Others looked like men discovering midway across a river that they'd climbed aboard a leaking boat. They could not pledge to follow such a man. "Why doesn't he just declare?" came a growl from along the hearthfire.

This was the hornet's nest that, for so long, Chariomer had no desire to thrust a sword into—for once he slew Auriane, every man of the sons of her father's companions would then come for *him*. This was the curse of vengeance. It was never complete.

Elza had destroyed him.

When Chariomer spoke, his words came out in the bare, whispery voice of a man cut down half throttled from a sacrificial tree.

"I do now swear before Wodan to avenge my son, Odberht—"

"Louder, Father. Those on the low benches can't hear you."

"—by the slaying of Auriane of the Chattians, daughter of Baldemar, who was born at the Village of the Boar, and to carry this out under the sun, with honorable weapons of war." He refused to look at Elza as he spoke. "And, I pledge every man of you before me to aid me in this quest."

Along the hearthfire, men's faces began to relax.

"Hail, brothers!" Chariomer spoke on, with a weak show of cheerfulness. "He who drinks with me now shares my blood, through this world and through the next."

"For one bloodstream runs through us all." Elza spoke the ritual response. "Gold-friend of men, dispenser of treasure, you are our Lord, and all here are kin."

She handed her father the god-infused mead. Chariomer wrest the horn from her so roughly that half spilled on the planking—a thing Elza counted ill-omened for herself. The mead was holy, and that was her own luck and fortune sloshed like waste-water onto the floor.

"Miserable she-spawn," Chariomer whispered to her before he took a generous draught. "I oath one more thing: Cries of regret for this betrayal will be the last words on your lips!"

Her father was a killer of women, capable of making good his threat. But Elza felt no terror as she took the horn from him, refilled it, then turned gracefully as a dancer to offer it to the man who was first among the companions. For she had the protection of a powerful tribal seeress now, and could flee from her father's vengeance. She would steal off on this very eve and stay at the seeress's sanctuary until the marriage with Sigibert could be arranged.

As the First Companion rose to his feet and repeated the formula of the oath, proclaiming himself everyone's brother and finishing with a promise to murder Auriane, Elza strove not to worry over the foul omen—the mead that was her blood, still glistening on the floor. For she'd set her course well. And the seeress, a woman called Sawitha, would praise her and love her, when she learned her harsh will had been done. It was this Sawitha who so keenly desired Auriane's death. Sawitha meant to take the staff of the Veleda. And she was tormented by the suspicion that the ever-unpredictable Ramis meant to pass her oracular staff to Auriane.

Resting in the stillness pooled in the wake of her fine victory, Elza felt a fleeting throb of disgust, realizing that the purest, simplest part of her detested Sawitha, thought Auriane more nobly fit to become the Veleda, and believed this outcome sad and wrong.

But the moment soon vanished. After all, she judged, such sad and wrong things were the way of the world, brought about because the Fates preferred to tangle their skeins so that their purposes were impossible to track with the mind.

Chapter 11

In his time as a soldier Decius had gotten every decoration the Army had to give, even the *corona civica* for saving the life of a brother-in-arms. And that one was trickiest of all, because first one of your brothers-in-arms had to admit you'd saved him. His course in the army had been bright and short as a comet. A brave man didn't have to fear a stretch of peace on the German frontier; constant opportunities to show valor helped lift him to the rank of centurion when he was only twenty-three. He supposed all this brazen good fortune must have irritated Fortuna, for he'd had the coveted centurion's vine-stick but a month when a horde of Chattian savages fell on his men as they were digging the foundation for a fort. That marked the day he was plucked forever from all that was sensible and good. He was taken captive along with all his men, and he alone escaped the sacrificial grove, saved by the bookroll they found on his person, which—Minerva be praised for his scholarly bent—caused them to take him for some sort of seer. Fortunately his father had long since been ferried over the Styx. It would have done the old man to death to know how his son's fortunes had flipped about, how a man of property had *become* property, that he who was scion of ten generations of proud Tuscan farmers was now the slave of mead-swilling barbarians.

His Chattian hosts had been a nervous and excitable lot who made a great show of hating Rome while enthusiastically mimicking her tactics. He'd been used rather rudely by them until the day he'd caught the eye of the maiden daughter of their chief, a rather more advanced creature among them called Auriane, oversupplied with a most unbarbarianlike quality, curiosity. Somehow this maid had gotten her father, Baldemar, to see the wisdom of keeping a learned and civilized man like himself about. And so he, Decius, had kept himself alive by enlightening His Chieftainship on fine points of Roman strategy. Unfortunately this earned him no love from his Roman countrymen, who called him "Decius the Traitor" if they spoke of him at all, but he preferred that to what the Chattians now called him— Decius the Swift, earned after he outdistanced a whole Chattian assembly on the night it was learned he'd gotten Auriane with child.

On that night he'd escaped a foot's breadth ahead of his life, he hadn't considered that Fortuna might have lifted him from the stewpot only so she could drop him on the grill.

He had fled north, of course—fleeing back into Roman territory would have earned him one of a variety of clever punishments the army had invented for deserters. But he'd only succeeded in falling into the clutches of a fresh pack of unlettered brutes, these of the Cheruscan tribe. These were not much different from the first pack, except Cheruscans had no scruples about cooperating with Rome, and had taken to calling the fur-draped beast who led them a king. Chariomer was his name, and that was whose not-so-tender care he was in now. Chariomer's seat was a palace of thatch that lay in a mountain fastness in the Hart country, many cold, wet days' ride north of Auriane's people. "Don't be deceived," Decius had told his drinking-friend, a travelling trader called Iarbas, "a king in this place has neither scepter nor kingdom, nor manners, or plumbing. The wretches who hail him such also call horse blood wine, and a boiled calf's head a feast."

So he was reduced once again to playing the savage mind like a cithara to stay alive. Chariomer at first treated him as a slave, but with patience Decius taught the old king to call him "chief advisor"—no easy task, for he'd observed that once barbarians learned a thing one way, that was it. He'd read various theories of why this was, and favored that of the naturalist Eutychus, who put forth that the barbarian mind was rendered sluggish by the cold. As Decius's advice won the king a victory or two, Chariomer was lavish with his gifts. And Decius had been clever in making the best of his dismal plight. On the grounds of the old king's palisaded compound, using scraps the trader Iarbas brought him from afar, he, Decius, had rebuilt civilization. He'd constructed a real *house,* no mud-smeared hut—with a stone foundation, an atrium with a votive bust of Vespasian, Emperor when he was last a free man, and fully enclosed *rooms,* not just places sectioned off with wickerwork. And no cattle stabled inside to drop dung everywhere. He'd even built himself a pool, a wise thing to have because Chariomer's cooks managed to burn down at least two longhouses a year. The water didn't yet run off properly from the rock-lined *impluvium,* but the chief engineer was still studying the problem. He had a growing collection of bronze lamps. And a limestone Apollo of unknown provenance, missing a hand and a foot, which he counted a fair personification of himself—lack of materials left him feeling he had one hand; imprisonment in this compound was akin to having one foot. And he'd patched together a good imitation of a steam heating system beneath his wood floor, using lead pipes taken from burned villas and a couple of iron cauldrons. It so confounded and amazed Chariomer that the old king had had him copy it for his own hall. But dearest of all to Decius was his library. Iarbas had a standing order from Decius to purchase anything new and interesting on any subject that he might find in the bookstalls in the Roman settlements along the river Rhenus, and there was no celebrated historian or naturalist whose recent works he did not possess.

Still, the sour-tempered old king did everything but chain him like a hound, and Decius never forgot he was a prisoner. Not that there were many places to flee off to when you'd made rabid enemies of both Rome *and* the Chattians—all the land belonged to one, and most of the folk hereabouts had sworn allegiance to the other. It didn't surprise Decius that he'd tumbled into this new snare because of a woman—the aforementioned Auriane. Ever since he'd donned his toga of manhood, women had followed him shamelessly, comforted him, confounded him. While still in the army he'd made a name for himself as the only man of his unit whose maids never demanded coin in recompense—indeed, they stalked him right back to his barracks. But *this* time, he couldn't banish the woman from his mind. Not only was she their fairest daughter—perhaps their *only* fair daughter, barbarians not normally being given to producing them—but a passable swordswoman as well— much thanks to himself, who'd patiently tutored her in the art for years. She certainly had done an excellent job of covering his back on that night the Chattians chased him off. Iarbas once told him he didn't understand why

Decius kept mulling over this lone specimen of the female race. "Providence gives to some a powerful genius," he'd somewhat lamely explained, "and it's not for us to know why. All I can say is, I'm with this maid or that, and I see *her* watching me scornfully. She overwhelms the one you're with."

Of course Decius had heard she'd long since taken up with a better man than he was. He tried very hard to be sensible about that. It did *not* sadden him. Indeed, when the memories pummeled him he pushed them off and congratulated her for having done extraordinarily well for herself. No, it did not sadden him . . . but he never forgot that this haunting creature had loved him once, had bred herself to him of her own free will, leaving him ever after to ponder just what sort of child had come from this crossing of a formidable she-warrior with an outstanding, decorated soldier like himself.

A lust to find out had helped keep him alive these many years in this bookless, bathless waste. The fruit of that fugitive love he knew only by the taunting mystery of her name—*Avenahar.*

"Some with a nasty turn of thought," Iarbas goaded him once after they shared almost a full goatskin of his vile wormwood wine, "would say you want the daughter just because you can't have *her.*" And he'd replied that his vices were of a more plebeian sort—he was willing to leave incest to emperors and gods. It was the mother's spirit he wanted about, and he believed there was bound to be a good measure of it served up in the daughter. For years, this one desire left him restless with an unaccountable grief. He was determined to see his only known child before he was tossed on the pyre. *Known* child. The unknown ones could go off and populate a province without his guidance for all he cared.

He wanted more than her name.

In his fourteenth year of captivity, life took yet another wretched turn. Chariomer began his so-called conquest of the Chattians, pressing farther south, dragging an increasingly unwilling Decius with him. He was pried from his comfortable Roman house and compelled to partake in savageries that had little purpose beyond spreading the terror of Chariomer's name. Now Decius had a second desire, equal to the first—to flee this flea-ridden king's side before *all* his hair was gray—he liked it the way it was now, just elegantly silvered at the sides. Lately, he'd begun committing the one sort of sabotage that was safe: While reading Rome's directives to Chariomer, he began omitting passages. Once, he'd left out an imperial order to level a village believed to be supplying Witgern, the Wolf Coat chief. Decius told Iarbas he did such things because he believed Auriane's people had suffered enough. Only to himself did he admit the true reason: Now that his daughter, Avenahar, was on the cusp of being old enough to understand, he wanted her to think well of him.

He was convinced Avenahar could be brought to see his side of things.

Then came the day Iarbas brought him the wonderful scrap of news he'd given up all hope of hearing while he lived.

It happened just a few days after that recent night he'd helped Elza escape. *That* had been a harrowing caper—Elza had balked at crawling under those smelly cattle hides, and he'd thought her mewling would wake the world. And Chariomer's sentries came so close to searching the wagon, the memory still made him break into a sweat. Had he been punished lightly for helping her fly, they might have contented themselves with merely drowning him in the bogs. He certainly hoped that later, if ever he needed Elza's aid, she would remember this.

It was midmorning, a cold and brilliant day. Iarbas blew his signature trumpet blast before he came within spear-casting distance of the village, and soon the trader was ambling beneath the gate, followed by his entourage of six slaves and ten mules. Their packs hung slack and empty, for this was close to the northerly terminus of his route. Iarbas was a crafty and nimble fellow who tried to buff his glory by claiming to be a spy for the Twenty-second Legion, but he was in truth an itinerant junk dealer. Many years ago he had been a standard-bearer in the Ubian native auxiliaries, before he was run out of the cavalry over some nasty disagreement about the size of a bribe to his centurion, so he was as close to a brother-in-arms as Decius was likely to find in this place.

Decius had gotten word that Iarbas would come on this day, and he'd ordered his kitchen staff to prepare a fine meal. Yes, he even had a kitchen staff, and he'd brought it with him, along with as many of the comforts of his beloved house as he could pack on muleback. It lessened the sting of abandoning that fine wilderness nest.

Iarbas clamped his arms around Decius in a bearish embrace. Decius had always thought Iarbas an odd but friendly specimen. The trader had the rude, roughened features of a cut purse, yet that face was appealingly rounded, like a child's. A twisted half-smile hinted that he waited for you to catch on to some dark jest he'd been playing for some time. A broader smile made him look as though he'd stashed apples in his cheeks. Missing teeth outnumbered the ones he had left. And his hair looked as though it were trying to escape his head. Nero would have been envious of those frisky curls—no hot curling tongs necessary there. Take away the bristling beard, Decius thought, and you were left with a male Medusa, an amiable Gorgon.

"I've some fine, fine news for you, old friend," Iarbas said, "but let me wet my tongue before I tell it."

Decius was absorbed in examining Iarbas's remaining wares. "You've got few books in here, Iarbas. By the new moon I'll have these read and be wanting more."

"Begging your pardon. I had more, but I got robbed. Is there another oddity like you tucked away up here somewhere? They got a whole mule-load. They pinched my silver-and-jet and my best glass, too, but the books I find most mystifying. Unless they're thatching houses with them or feeding papyrus to the goats, what in Hades's name are they doing with them?"

"I *have* seen them cut them up for amulets," Decius said as they began the short journey to his temporary home in this captured village—a wooden outbuilding not much larger than a horse stall, which had served as a hide storehouse. It lay behind the thatched longhouse Chariomer claimed as his own.

"Amulets, you say?" Iarbas pulled on his beard. The trader lurched along with head slightly cocked; some long-ago injury caused him to walk as if he bore up under a heavy load, meditating on each step. "You shouldn't have told me that . . . There might be more to be made selling the books to them than to you. A bit dangerous journeying this far, anyway . . ."

"You've the loyalty of a sewer rat, Iarbas. If I dropped dead beside you, you'd auction off my cloak." Decius clapped him on the back.

"Not if I couldn't get enough for it. Then I'd roll you into that well over there to poison the water and get revenge on this camp—some of them haven't paid me in over a year."

As they passed Chariomer's hall, starkly empty but for the single weaving-woman working on an upright loom set in the light of the doorway, Iarbas said, "Where's His Royal Chieftainship? I brought the red leather boots he ordered. They'll look ridiculous on him—don't laugh when he puts them on. I want to get paid this time."

"I'll try. He's on a boar hunt. Took the whole barking pack with him, too, thank all the gods."

Iarbas looked meaningfully toward the wooden palisade, the open gate, then to the rampant, beckoning forest beyond. "When do they come back? Decius, your guard's gone. Sprout wings and fly, old friend."

"Open your eyes, Iarbas. Look in that tree. Not that one, *that* one."

Iarbas's bleary gaze settled on a scraggly fir with wooden steps nailed to the trunk at crazy angles, then moved up until he saw a shadowed form heavy enough to bend a branch.

"*One* man, Decius?" Iarbas said. "That's all it takes to keep you leashed?"

"One man with a horn, Iarbas—and mighty lungs. He's got one blast for fire, another that means 'suspicious-looking strangers approaching,' and another, just for *me*."

"But how quick can they get back here to grab you?"

"It rouses the whole countryside, not just Chariomer's men. No one hereabouts would be mad enough to shelter me. They all know who I belong to and they fear him like the plague."

At the door of Decius's quarters, Iarbas peered within at a pair of bronze lamps in the shape of many-branched trees. "Gods, Decius," Iarbas exclaimed, "you took your house with you!" The trader's eyes adjusted further. "You even brought the table!" The "table" was a low dining table that had cost the wealthy provincial from whose riverside villa it had been stolen at least a half million. Its citrus-wood top, which Decius reverently kept buffed to a high shine, had the pattern serious collectors called "the peacock's tail." It had been a gift from the king, after Chariomer successfully retook a salt spring from the Chattians, acting on Decius's inestimable military advice.

Iarbas entered, stepping over an entranceway mosaic of badly mismatched tiles that showed a stiff-backed dog with bulging eyes, and the barely readable warning, CAVE CANEM—BEWARE OF THE DOG.

"You don't have a dog, Decius," Iarbas commented needlessly.

"Don't be contrary. I'm fond of it. My father's house had one like it."

"A fiendishly clever fellow you are, old friend!" Iarbas said as he stepped within. "You capture all the creature comforts of the Governor's Palace, wherever you go!"

"You haven't heard the wind howling about here at night."

They settled themselves about his fine table, already set with a silver wine service, eating knives, and silver spoons. His guests had to recline on hen-feather cushions set on the planked floor, but that worked well enough.

"I hope you've brought a good appetite," Decius said. "I've got pickled artichokes I've been saving for months, and my cooks have roasted a pheasant stuffed with bayberries. And I sent for the bread you like—what they bake here would send a ship to the bottom."

Two aged and cheerful Ubian women carried in the first course from the cooking shed. These serving women had several times drawn from the trader the surprised comment that they seemed truly fond of Decius, jesting with him, seeming delighted when he liked what they prepared. Decius supposed one didn't see that often, hereabouts. Not that the tribes were cruel to their thralls; actually, it was against their native law to strike them—and Rome couldn't claim that. But they didn't quite acknowledge them as fellow beings, either.

"Decius," Iarbas said at last, when he'd assuaged most of his hunger, "on the way here I fell in with one of those fellows who runs supplies to the Wolf Coats—you know, a tree branch doesn't fall in the forest without them knowing it. He told me something that'll make you prick up your ears. Your Chattian warrior-maid-turned-villa-matron is coming to the Holy Wood, at the edge of the West Forest. She brings her—*your*—daughter, for the maid's womanhood rite."

Decius found himself in a rare state—amazed to complete silence. If a ballista stone weighing half a talent had just crushed his roof he probably wouldn't have noticed. In the next moment he felt like an old fire-mountain starting to rumble to life again. But the excitement he grappled with was all muddied up with a sadness debilitating as bog fever.

Both mother and daughter could still do that to him. An irritating thing to admit.

Lastly, Decius felt something else he hadn't for a long time, with Auriane tucked safely away in her aristocrat's villa—fear for her life.

When his tongue unfroze, Decius sent off the kitchen staff, telling them to take along a jug of his best wine and what was left of the dinner, and finish them off in the yard.

He turned to Iarbas. "Are you *certain?*" An idiot's response, he chided himself.

"They've already chosen the elderwomen and arranged their passage. Three Chattian maids are to be initiated at once. Avenahar's one of the three, I swear it on my mother."

As his mind turned like the wheel of a crane, he supposed he stared a little too long at his half-eaten fried squash, because next he heard Iarbas saying somewhat plaintively, "Speak, Decius—you're worrying me. I hope you're not planning something foolish. Don't forget, every fort on the Frontier still has standing orders to put you in chains. I like you the way you are, with limbs still attached."

It was true. The military could be stubborn about some things. It couldn't be said the Roman Army knew how to forgive. And it didn't seem to matter to them either that, technically now, he was aiding their ally.

"There's a thing you don't know, Iarbas. Auriane's not safe here. Just four days ago, Chariomer declared vengeance on her, before all his men."

"You're jesting. He's too lazy to do such a thing."

"He was goaded to it by his daughter, Elza. Now *there's* an Agrippina in furs. She's far more dangerous than he is. It was all slightly ridiculous—at least, until you told me Auriane was coming here. I must admit, this causes me a spot of queasiness."

"Gods, what was her purpose?"

"Elza's? To lift herself out of this cesspool by means of an intelligent marriage. And destroy her father in the bargain. You need to have studied the barbarian mind before it makes any sense. She's got ambitions to marry Sigibert, you see, the son of old Sigwulf, of the companions of Auriane's father, Baldemar. Impossible, of course. For that, she needs Sawitha, you know, that bloody-minded seeress no one likes. Who'd only help Elza if Elza helped *her*—"

"—by setting Auriane up for murder," Iarbas finished, catching on, "so Sawitha, not Auriane, can be named successor to Ramis."

"You do have a grasp of barbarian politics. Iarbas, you must warn Auriane."

"I suppose, I'm going that way anyway, I could—"

"She must be told to quit this country as soon as possible. She must look to her back while she's here. Chariomer just took two hundred new men into his band, and that, added to what he's got . . . let's see . . . that's over four hundred, and every one of them has sworn an oath to separate her spirit from her mortal form. You can't fail me in this, Iarbas. Ten *aurei* are yours for doing it, good fellow."

Decius knew the trader would balk at asking a friend for money, but knew, too, how precarious Iarbas's financial health was. Last year, Iarbas had lost his accounts books in a river flood that drowned one of his mules—and with them, his only record of what everyone owed him. "I'll do it, Decius," he said at last. "Keep your gold."

"Take the gold, I insist on it." Decius got to his feet. "Iarbas, wait just a moment."

"Long as you're feeding me I'm not going anywhere."

Decius looked about until he remembered where his strongbox was, then returned carrying a square of yellow silk, on which lay a fibula—an ornate brooch for securing a cloak—fashioned of purest white gold. It was shaped as a circle that was completed where the heads of two serpents met; their eyes were sapphires. Where the pin was attached, it was set with an irregularly formed pearl, the largest Iarbas had ever seen. The sight caused the trader's eyes to become fogged over with what Decius could describe only as avaricious awe. Mercury Himself might have materialized before him.

"That thing's worth more than your dining table," Iarbas said. "Chariomer give *that* to you, too? Now I understand why you don't run away."

"Not the king, his dead wife. She loved me."

"I hope you don't want me to take that anywhere."

"I do, Iarbas."

"I'm a junk dealer. You've said so yourself. I get robbed all the time."

"We'll sew it into the lining of your cloak."

That silenced Iarbas; who could wrestle that cloak from the fleas?

"What if I'm murdered and dumped in a river, cloak and all?"

"I'll take my chances. You're my one true friend, Iarbas. Now that's an advantage that comes with *some* responsibility." He was smiling as he said it, but Iarbas's frown only deepened. "Take this to Avenahar," Decius pressed. "Twenty *aurei*. Don't argue."

"But . . . how do I get near a maid during the ceremony? They'll beat me off with switches."

"Sometime during it, she'll be commanded to go off alone. That's the way it's done. Approach her then. Mind, mother and daughter don't look much alike. Avenahar looks more like me—black hair, black eyes—at least, I've heard it said. You'll know her when you see her. Tell her the brooch is a gift from her true father . . . just a small assurance of my goodwill toward her."

He wasn't sure in the dim light, but he thought Iarbas's eyes were looking a bit watery. Perhaps it was his own eyes, and he was remembering it wrong.

"Tell her that her father wants to see her, Iarbas. He has to escape first, of course, but that's not her problem. Perhaps she'll find she has some affection for me stored somewhere in her maidenly heart. Her mother certainly did. We'll meet at a place . . . at a place I haven't worked out yet."

"But Decius . . ."

Decius cringed. He saw signs that Iarbas was trying to be gentle.

". . . You endanger her just by being near her. You know, Chariomer's blood debt *could* be extended to cover the daughter. I've known of cases. His men might follow you and harm her. And the Chattians hate you as much as your own people do—it might make trouble for the maid."

Iarbas was right, of course, but Decius supposed that too much time in this dripping wilderness had left him more than a little mad. "I have it," he said. "We'll arrange to meet at the house of Auriane's mother, Athelinda. It's natural our daughter would journey there to see her own grandmother. Athelinda's homestead is sacred ground. No one would carry out an act of war there."

"And how many times have you told me, escape's impossible?"

"When inspired I can do amazing things. Until now, I didn't have a great reason to risk life and limb to get away."

"Decius, I've never known you to be so light-headed. You're worrying me. And I must ask you something else. Has it occurred to you that . . . that Avenahar might not want to see you? After all, your being her parent hasn't exactly made life easier for her, or done her much good that I can see."

"I'm her kith and kin, Iarbas. I *know* I can win her. There's never been a single specimen of the female race I couldn't bring into my camp, if I really tried. It's a bounty of Venus I was gifted with at birth." He grinned.

"When you say it, I believe it."

For a moment, Decius forgot Iarbas was there.

Avenahar. The suckling Auriane gave birth to on Ramis's island was probably now as tall as he was—maybe taller, from the influence of her barbarian blood. She must be the very image of her sturdy mother on that day so long ago when Auriane came to him, to wring what she could out of him. *What do I want to do? Live those days over? And what will* she *see, when she sees me? An old man battered by winters and years. A face once that of a daring Cynic jester, twisted into that of a tired, acid-filled curmudgeon. Time's river's flowed over my face for too many years, carving deeper and deeper cleavages . . .*

But when a man's got no future, I suppose the past swallows him up.

He was only half aware Iarbas was speaking to him. "I'll do it, Decius. But keep your payment. Don't insult an old friend."

Chapter 12

Rome
Seven days before the Kalends of Junius, 105 CE

The month of *Maius* was near to a close, and Rome had formally declared war upon Dacia. In a chamber of the Domus Augustana, the private wing of the new imperial palace built into the eastern ridge of the Palatine Hill in Rome, the Emperor Trajan prepared to meet in secret with his Consilium. Historians claimed that eight centuries ago on this very summit, beneath the same azure sky, the humble grass hut of Romulus had stood, and the people of Rome believed it had always been a place of rulers—today's were just better housed. Rising from the hill now was a labyrinthian, multitiered glory of pillared porches and ascending porticoes that might have made Romulus feel he'd been snatched off to some shining otherworld. This present house for Roman kings featured octagonal reception rooms with ethereally painted walls that haunted the eye, peristyle courts with waterfalls rippling down stairs into pools of gold-glass mosaic, banqueting rooms sheathed in polychrome marbles rising to ceilings fretted with ivory, and crowning it all, a complexity of gables and domes, the gilded roof tiles creating an impression that some divine hand lavished liquid gold over the whole.

In a most interior room of the Domus Augustana, two youths of the Imperial Pantomime Troupe searched about in the gloom for a terra-cotta lamp. The windowless chamber was a storage room for the troupe's costumes.

The elder of the two, a young man called Pylades, found the lamp, lit it, and knelt upon the floor. His torso was encased in a smooth-fitting tunic of rose-colored wool, revealing a tapered form sinuous as a slender urn. He was flushed and damp from a dress rehearsal and his artfully curved lips still bore traces of cosmetic cinnabar's harsh orange-red—he'd just danced the part of Achilles disguised as a maiden. His silken, honey-gold locks and blond brows contrasted oddly with eyes of soft slate; it appeared as though a band of mysterious shadow played round his eyes, a striking effect that had worked its quiet sorcery on an Emperor. Pylades was known from the Circus stalls to the Palatine Hill as the current boy-favorite of the Emperor Trajan. Rome counted the young pantomime actor one of the two forgivable vices of the "Iron Soldier," as Trajan was commonly called. The other, a fondness for downing stultifying quantities of wine, he had acquired in the marching camps and partook of openly. The Emperor's trysts with Pylades were carried out with such secrecy that his discretion brought him universal praise. "Zeus should be careful of his pretty Ganymede when Trajan is about," was the worst that whisperers would say of him.

The lamp flame flared and the chamber glittered, alive with fragile iridescence. Butterflies of light winked through the gloom as the fireglow played off crowns for kings, gossamer wings of thinnest silk, silverine chitons, and brazen breastplates for heroes.

Pylades removed a thin rectangular tile from the chamber's floor. Through an aperture the length of a man's foot but no wider than a finger, the boy could see down into the chamber below. He leaned close and saw a section of travertine floor, a scattering of cross-legged ivory chairs, the polished top of an antique Egyptian writing table.

This was the private council chamber of the Emperor Trajan.

The youths had a second occupation: They were spies in the pay of Marcus Arrius Julianus.

The boy kneeling next to Pylades was Apion, a novice in the pantomime troupe but not to the listening boys' trade; Apion had pressed an ear to the wall for his master since he was nine. He didn't know the day of his birth, but by his own calculations, he was at least fifteen. Apion eagerly waited for Pylades to make a place for him so he, too, could look, but for an uncomfortably prolonged moment Pylades pretended he wasn't there.

Since yesterday's eve the younger boy had noticed Pylades behaving oddly toward him.

"They come!" Pylades whispered excitedly, more to himself than to Apion.

Pylades smoldered still at the memory of last eve's dinner performance in the grand *triclinium* of the new Palace, when the Emperor's glance had wavered as he watched Pylades dance, then was drawn firmly as if pulled by a rope to agile Apion, with his flexible waist, boneless limbs, eyes of bittersweet black that begged the world to care for him. The Emperor had called Apion to his couch and kept the boy there through the length of a song, tracing his fingers over those stubborn lips, and had gifted Apion with the brilliant feather mask that hung on the wall above them now. The moment was all the more intolerable to Pylades because he had just celebrated his nineteenth birthday, and was hovering at the cusp of the next age of life. Once a youth attained full manhood, a great and powerful man was expected to set him adrift, for then, a tryst with him was a less forgivable vice. Daily, Pylades expected Trajan would summon him no more.

"You tyrant, let me see!" Apion whispered. The younger boy shouldered his way in.

They heard the rumble of a door drawn back, multiple footsteps, men's neutral murmurs. The strip of room below them was filled, suddenly, with the tops of men's heads. Both boys had become adept at recognizing Rome's great men from above, and they expertly sorted out the scene below. The servants they ignored. There—with a round skull and hair like iron shavings, the man prone to quick, brutish movements that made Apion think of an angry boxer caught in a net—that was Titus Claudius Livianus, the more influential of the two praefects of the Praetorian Guard.

And there, easing into his seat with the casualness of one who counted the Palace a second home, his body matronly in its soft decline—the man with a smooth knob of a head, oyster-shell ears that projected from it boldly, and strong, sun-browned hands that moved with the cleverness of a mime as they collected together everyone's thoughts—that was the Emperor's old friend from his home city in faraway Hispania, Lucius Licinius Sura.

And there, settled in place sloppily as a grain sack, with his ebbing fringe of black hair, the small, mean head of a wasp, set as a comical afterthought on that overflowing body—that was the Senator Lappius Blaesus. This was the man Marcus Julianus had set them to watch. Blaesus kept himself at a taut distance from the other two, as if he'd not yet been initiated into this august company, but expected he would be, soon.

A fourth chair was significantly empty. After a tense, protracted moment, this chair disappeared beneath a man whose movements were possessed of such gravity and grace, Apion thought there must beat in that breast not a heart, but a military drum. His thatch of thick, gray hair curled a bit, as if in protest against how sternly it was trained forward. His towering form had the breadth and muscle tone of a discus thrower; he needed a larger chair. That impressive, bony brow, Apion knew, sheltered vigilant eyes that made a man think very carefully about every word he spoke. A complexion darker than most from a life lived under the sun made it easy to imagine he was, indeed, a man of iron. That lean face, with its high cheekbones and flat planes, smooth as armor, was possessed of but one outlandish feature—a great, tuberose nose, red-veined from the ravages of wine. Attached to such a man as this, however, even that nose managed to keep its dignity. That was the Emperor, Marcus Ulpius Trajan.

Pylades indicated the Emperor's old friend Licinius Sura, and whispered to Apion, "I can't believe that man was once the Emperor's lover . . . too fat, too slow, too bookish, too dull!" Pylades did a faint mimic of such a man as he spoke.

"He wasn't then!" Apion replied indignantly. Their whispers were obscured by the men's greetings, the scraping of chair legs over marble. "Sura was still in the hands of a tutor in those days, and the Emperor not much older."

Pylades stared darkly at Apion, making much of how fervently the younger boy came to the Emperor's defense in matters of love. Then he said, "Apion, you never told me—how came you to be Marcus Julianus's man?"

The question sounded slightly odd to Apion; perhaps it was Pylades's timing. *As you are, too,* Apion thought. *And why think of loyalties* now, *at this time when we're most vulnerable to discovery?* Marcus Julianus's spy network was as vast and intricate as the Palace's, and Apion felt great pride in being part of it.

"I swear you know this already," Apion answered irritably. "He restored my parents to their home after my island's procurator imprisoned my father on a wicked, false charge. I would lay down my life for the man. Fix that meddlesome snout on Blaesus, not on me." For reasons they hoped to uncover today, Blaesus had, of late, greatly stepped up his efforts to destroy Marcus Julianus.

The council had not yet begun; Licinius Sura was speaking rapidly to one of the servants while the Emperor began to unroll and read a lengthy document that Livianus, the Guards' praefect, had pressed on him. Apion squinted, but it was penned in spy's shorthand and he made nothing of it.

"Ah, Julianus!" Pylades whispered. "None of Rome's women are good enough for him. For that matter, neither is Rome."

Apion's discomfort increased, but he kept his demeanor calm. Never before had he heard Pylades speak slightingly of his true master.

"The first time Julianus summoned me," Pylades whispered on, "I thought . . . oh how I hoped!—but my exultant flutterings were cruelly crushed. The man's tastes run entirely to women. And strange foreign women, at that."

Below them, the servants had departed. The four heads drew closer together. Apion wondered again over Pylades's sourness, his sudden agitation. Did the older boy fear he was set to lose his golden fortune? To Apion, it didn't seem possible. Pylades had basked in the imperial sun for over two years, and to Apion that was an impressive stretch of time, long enough to make Pylades's place in the divine bed seem dependable as sunrise itself.

Pylades snuffed out the lamp; the only light in the chamber was that which softly filtered up from below. The boys dropped into stillness, paying close attention now. In their trade they depended wholly on well-schooled memories; committing words to a wax tablet would have greatly increased their danger.

The first voice they heard was the Emperor's.

"Were that there were two of me! I shouldn't have to abandon all these labors, half done." It was a glorious, full-throated voice meant for the windy expanses of a parade ground.

"*Grand,* is he not?" Pylades whispered right in Apion's ear. "He sounds like that even in the bedchamber, Apion. It's not an actor's role for him."

Apion silenced him with a cutting gesture. It was quieter down there now. Pylades would have them both found out and destroyed.

"You must trust matters into other men's hands more than you do." This came from the Emperor's friend Licinius Sura, whose expressive hands were gesturing hopefully, suggesting his were the ideal hands to trust. "You've chosen capable men. The donatives will be paid. The architects will proceed. Your Forum will dwarf Augustus's. I've arranged to have any amendments to the plans sent along to you. No harm will come from this sudden departure. It will be as though you never left Rome."

The Emperor spoke brisk words addressed to the room at large. "Early June is late to set out." Apion knew he referred to his date of departure from

Rome for the second Dacian war. "Three months into the campaigning season—it leaves us time to reinforce the bridges and no more; the main attack won't come until spring. Which gives the Dacians another year to gather allies." Trajan turned abruptly to the Praetorian praefect. "Tell us why you called us, Livianus. I trust this touches on the war. I've no time for matters that don't."

Following Trajan's victory, early in his reign, over the far eastern kingdom of Dacia, the Dacian king Decabalus had proved remarkably quick to forget he'd lost the war; he'd hardly waited for Trajan's triumphal procession to end before he'd begun rebuilding his fortifications. Yesterday the fateful dispatch had come: Decabalus and his Dacian army had crossed the river Danuvius and broken into the Roman province of Moesia. This morn, the Senate had proclaimed Decabalus an Enemy of Rome. Four days after the Kalends of the month of *Junius,* Trajan would sail from the harbor of Ancona and begin his march into Dacia.

"With all respect, my Lord, this *does* touch on the war," the Praetorian praefect replied. "More specifically, on the safety of the dangerous Chattian frontier you must leave at your back."

"I have a dependable report assuring me that region will remain stable for two years," the Emperor replied.

Blaesus nudged in bluntly then. "And whose counsel was that?"

His words were met with thick silence. Everyone knew whose counsel it was: Marcus Julianus's. It was not a question so much as an accusation.

The Praetorian praefect aimed a curt gesture at Blaesus—visible to the boys above, but not to the Emperor—warning Blaesus he was moving in too quickly. "The intelligence I give you has two parts, my Lord," the praefect Livianus smoothly continued. "The first part concerns this turbulent Chattian frontier, which we're forced to leave lightly garrisoned. The second part . . . concerns a man."

The Guards' praefect then put several rolled documents onto the Egyptian writing table. "These dispatches from Germania are alarming, the more so since this notorious malefactor who's been arming the Chattians all these years has never been found, and—"

"That should concern you no more," the Emperor broke in, lifting a hand. "Our esteemed Governor Maximus insists he's close to bringing this person to justice."

"Ah, but the horse may already be out of the barn. Look at these dispatches, they tell a tale of increasing Chattian boldness—two of our observers were murdered in a drunken fracas at one of their tribal law-assemblies. And note that here, a common soldier of the Eighth Augusta, who was hunting in Chattian territory while on leave from duty, was kidnapped and 'tried' by one of the Chattians' barbarous tribunals, for the supposed 'crime' of looting treasures from one of their sacred lakes. The Chattians condemned a Roman soldier with that virgin prophetess Ramis acting as judge. And none of our loyalists stopped it. And note here that—"

"That frontier is Nemesis's crown," the Emperor interrupted. "The mantic woman you speak of, Ramis—her sway over these simple folk has become too great. You will order her arrest."

Livianus nodded. "It shall be done. And there's also this: During the rebel Witgern's recent attack, his band was armed with swords—swords it's been illegal for this tribe to possess since the first year of your reign. Somehow this fact got buried beneath mountains of . . . of a certain man's rhetoric." Livianus's voice dropped to a soft growl; Apion had to grope for his next words. "Which brings us to the matter of a man . . . an ever so subtle man, who keeps counseling us to ignore all these clear signs of insurrection."

Apion saw Lappius Blaesus move his head closer to the Praetorian praefect's; the boy read close complicity between the two. Blaesus was alert as some carrion creature waiting for a larger beast to bring down the game so it could feast. Apion could not abide Blaesus, who he believed would prosecute his own mother if he thought the fame showered on him by the trial would cause his speeches to be memorized by students in rhetorical schools, and get him raised to the post of city praetor.

"This man we speak of has long been blessed with your friendship," the Praetorian praefect continued, "which causes us great sadness for what we must tell you now. In the inquiry after the rebel Witgern attacked, twenty men of your Council were in strong agreement about the seriousness of these recent threats to the security of Germania's frontier, and—"

"—Julianus's is the *one* report that contradicts," Blaesus finished for him, giving dread weight to each word.

A long silence followed; to Apion, it had a foul smell. Not even the mild-mannered Sura raised an objection. Apion felt the first prickle of horror. In the language of these men, failure to speak up in a man's defense amounted to a strong condemnation.

Apion felt himself in the grip of a waking dream, so intently was he listening. He never noticed that Pylades was ignoring the drama below and staring at *him*.

Below them, the Emperor spoke on with challenge in his tone. "I must confess myself surprised by what you imply. This is *Marcus Julianus*. In the past, he has been correct with his every recommendation. He has an impressive record of saving us much in troops and supplies. Twenty disagreed, you say? It would take twenty men of the Council just to equal him in learning."

Apion saw the Guards' praefect visibly contract; the boy sensed aggravated ill-feeling over the high esteem in which Trajan had always held Marcus Julianus.

The praefect Livianus continued, "That is so . . . and doubtless, it's *not* because of compromised loyalties, springing from the fact that Julianus took one of these Chattian savages to his breast, that he consistently counsels a light hand against this tribe—"

"Just give me this new evidence!" The chill in the Emperor's voice caused Apion to feel one brief spasm of relief.

"Here is a private letter Julianus wrote—"

"I do not look at private letters!" It was a voice to annihilate all but the steadiest of men. Apion had to grudgingly admire the Guards' praefect's courage.

"Of course," the praefect Livianus smoothly continued on, "but *this* letter—well, I won't bore you with it, because I see how this offends you, so I'll just leave it here so you can look at it later . . . Just know it was culled right from Julianus's own library, by one of your most loyal Horse Guardsmen, a fine man who only this morning passed it on to me—but more on him later. In it, Julianus says the Dacian war's our fault. And be aware, these base ideas are also the text of a *lecture* Julianus gave. To eager, attentive students. In a public place. At Confluentes, a small, but influential town—"

"*Enough!* I don't care what philosophers think."

The Praetorian praefect Livianus placed the letter on the Egyptian writing table, close by the Emperor. To Apion's dismay, Trajan did not push it away despite that fine display of imperial wrath. The boy sensed that Livianus had hooked his fish.

The praefect Livianus rapidly spoke on. "Julianus met alone with the commander of the fort attacked by Witgern's Wolf Coats—after first concocting some lie to trick the other Consilium members into leaving the room. He drew information from this fort's praefect, a man called Speratus, that he never passed on to the Consilium. And—it grieves me to tell you of such impiety—he swore this Speratus to silence. Julianus got a man to swear allegiance to *himself*, over *you*."

Apion read the Emperor's silence as evidence of true surprise, as when a man strikes a wall in the dark.

After considering this for long moments, Trajan said, "What information was withheld?" Now Apion heard weary sadness in the imperial voice.

"That the rebel Witgern broke into that fort to steal the sword that belonged to the Chattians' old hero-chief, Baldemar. Julianus learned the rebel has hatched a plot to put that sword into the hands of some new war chief. Our informant did not discern the name. Now our Governor there, Maximus, he's a good man but he couldn't be expected to know what to make of this peculiar theft. But Julianus *does*. He has described in his published works on the nature of these northern savages how they believe the soul of a sword's former owner dwells on in the blade. He *knows* Baldemar's sword's a rallying point for rebellion."

"Now, *that's* a thing to report," Blaesus broke in. "The Chattian savages are resurrecting the old rogue."

Trajan was rapt as a sentry alerted to an enemy's approach. Apion could feel the fine, sharp edge of his concern.

"I'd want to hear Julianus's version of this first," the Emperor said at last. But to Apion, Trajan's protest lacked his usual firmness. *This is more than one day's work,* the boy thought with accumulating dread. Doubts these men had planted before this day had sprouted, flourished, and were ready for harvesting. *What clever scoundrels Livianus and Blaesus are,* the boy thought. *There's no better time to reap the ruin of a powerful man than when an Emperor must turn his back on his Capitol for a long campaign.*

"To hear whatever tricky defense he'd have at hand?" the praefect Livianus replied. "I know *I* can't outparry him. He'd probably tell you they're arming against that King Chariomer and his Cheruscans, not against us. But given that the Chattians are unpredictable as a herd of bolting horses, this does nothing to ease *my* concern. But then, I'm just a plain, simple soldier who sees the matter as our noble grandfathers would."

The Emperor's heavy silence was not encouraging to Apion.

"This is new for Julianus," Livianus pressed on. "He's never before *acted* on his eccentric beliefs." The Emperor gave him a hard look. Livianus amended, "I mean only, we've known, all along, how Julianus lectures at that Academy of his that 'the time of Rome's expansion is done,' and how he dissects and discards, in the worst Stoic fashion, the base of every authority you've ever claimed—but I know you don't listen to *that* sort of evidence, so—"

"He's out there assembling a party of opposition in the provinces!" Blaesus broke in hotly. Apion observed that the two men had distinct roles: Livianus marched in the vanguard, cutting swaths with broad, clean strokes. Then Blaesus scurried in under the Guards' praefect's cover, to deliver the blow that was messy and brutish. The Emperor's old friend Sura seemed present only to observe, or perhaps Trajan brought him here to serve as a sort of anchor, to moor these men's vengeful flights.

Blaesus then added, while nodding significantly toward the letter, "And we must remember Julianus's history, my Lord. Before he turned against Domitian, he began by *speaking* against him."

"What I tell you next," Livianus pressed on, dropping his voice again, "we found difficult to credit at first. It comes from that same loyal Horse Guardsman I mentioned before. His name is Marcus Ulpius Secundus and he is a decorated soldier. The rebel Witgern was welcomed on Julianus's estate."

The silence that followed was thunderous.

A queasiness rose in Apion's throat; he feared he'd lose his morning porridge. *This cannot be true,* the boy thought. *These faithless men are spewing lies.*

"This is proved?" Trajan's voice was taut, emotionless.

"I fear the source is impeccable. Witgern came to Julianus's villa in the dead of night to meet in cabal with its mistress. He was welcomed as if he were an old friend by that woman Julianus lives in concubinage with, and was given food and shelter." Livianus paused just long enough to allow the Emperor to absorb the enormity of this, then added, "I fear Marcus Arrius Julianus is *not our friend.*"

Blaesus spoke up then. "In light of his displays of treasonable disloyalty to you, my Lord, it should surprise us little that Julianus refuses to accompany you to Dacia." Blaesus handed Trajan a gilded wax tablet; Apion could see it was an elegantly penned letter.

Trajan read aloud Marcus Julianus's brief, polite refusal to join him on the Dacian campaign. Apion marveled at how every word of that courteous, mildly phrased letter sounded decidedly sinister, against the backdrop of suspicion these men had prepared.

Apion knew well the shape of the concerns that would be on any ruler's mind at this time: the inadvisability of departing for a long war while leaving behind a powerful man you can't trust. Once, Apion saw the Emperor briefly put a hand to his temple, as if this were too much for even a strong man to bear.

The Praetorian praefect Livianus spoke. "This is an awkward matter, my

Lord. The hopeful news is that we've the means to handle this cleanly and quietly. There's no need to worry over leaving a dangerous source of instability at your back. You've worries enough. My Lord, you need only free us . . . to do what we must."

The silence that followed was difficult for Apion to read, for the Emperor's encompassing spirit housed multiple souls, some of which harbored conflicting aims: One part of him seemed wreathed in a god's omnipotence as he shouldered the burden of the world, and strove to bring well-being and justice to its peoples. Another part was a tough, plain soldier who could nip every appetite and stow every desire, if necessary, to forge himself into a man able to inspire an army to march half a world away and die for him. And yet another part was a practical ruler, ever aware that the man who holds absolute power is never secure. And then there was the generous part that would rather perish in fire before he'd fail to show gallantry to a friend.

"Julianus has the great good fortune to be your good friend, but sadly, he's no friend of the state," Livianus said then, intuiting the nature of the Emperor's reluctance. "I'm relieved that it's *you* confronted with this dilemma, and not myself—for you, like the god Augustus, have always had a heroic ability to put the safety of the country ahead of all private affections."

"Sura?" The emperor turned to his old friend.

But Sura made a dismissive gesture, indicating he would leave the matter to them. Apion knew Licinius Sura found the whole matter odious, but all had already progressed too far. These were not ordinary times, and it was dangerous to speak for Julianus while the Emperor's mind was still not known.

The stifling silence stretched on. To Apion, it signaled agreement.

Unexpectedly, the Emperor said, his voice iron-cold, "I do not condemn men without a trial."

The Praetorian praefect was ready for this. "Of *course* not," he said with matching indignation. Then he straightened, looked away, and muttered with the emotion-laden exasperation of a stage-actor, "And the gods know it's not our fault, but the treacherous Dacian king's, that there is *no time for a trial*."

"I owe him much," Trajan said finally. *I owe him my throne,* Apion heard in those words. "He opened the way to the age we live in now. I wouldn't deserve rulership, were I such a man as that." Trajan dragged forth these words with a sad, simple openness, and it seemed to Apion he subtly transmitted a plea—

Tell me how to rid myself of him.

Tell me how I can do it, and yet at the same time, not do it.

Apion glanced briefly at Pylades, curious to see what the older boy was making of all this, but Pylades's fit of moodiness hadn't passed—he was putting all his attention into fidgeting with the gold braid on one of the costumes. The Praetorian praefect Livianus spoke again, and Apion forgot Pylades.

"What if it were another man's deed, and all could clearly see that this was so? What if it were done by a man known to despise Marcus Julianus so much, a man *so ready* to destroy him—no one would believe it was not this man's plot from the start?"

Apion felt a jolt of disbelief. The silence that followed was peculiar; he couldn't read it. Was Trajan intrigued, or horrified?

"Am I correct in understanding," the Emperor said at last, "you refer to Casperius Aelianus's son, who lusts to avenge the assassination of Domitian?"

Apion's fright grew. *Why is he even acknowledging this monstrous plan?*

"I am," the Guards' praefect Livianus replied. "The very man who, conveniently, has made one clumsy attempt already, and before a crowd of thousands, when he tried to immolate Marcus Julianus in his carriage," Livianus whispered. "Let this young Aelianus be the weapon . . . the means."

"You're quite sure it *was* this younger Aelianus who made a torch out of Julianus's carriage?" Sura interjected then. The Emperor sat in regal, distant quiet, as if he did not want to touch such a shameful plan with any part of himself, even his voice.   .

"We are. In fact, we've made contact with him already," Blaesus replied. At this, Sura sharply withdrew. This was a rash thing to have done, an even rasher thing to admit.

The next voice was Trajan's. "This is despicable. I am ashamed."

"Shame is deadly at this altitude, my Lord," Livianus responded. "Natural law's not the same for a ruler—that, I scarcely need tell you. I remind you, you'll be gone for *two years*."

The Emperor said, "You'd employ our enemy to destroy our friend."

"That's no way to put it!" Livianus objected. "We're just clearing a way for a mad dog. You know this young hothead will keep trying to finish Julianus anyway—we'll just increase the odds that he succeeds. I'll see this Casperius Aelianus is given money, and we'll install him in a minor post at the Mogontiacum Fortress. It will all be done by local men. There will be so many men buffering the deed from the Capitol—it will be a broken, twisted trail no one will follow to the Palace."

"You and Dio are on opposite sides of a perch," Trajan said with a lightness that brought a fresh queasiness to Apion's stomach. The Emperor referred to the court philosopher, Dio Chrysotom, who had of late been giving windy, sleep-inviting lectures on the necessity of displaying courage in the practice of virtue. Apion sensed that by acknowledging the man, Trajan was disarming him.

"Dio puffs words into the air and gets nothing done," the Praetorian praefect said. "I get the cart to market."

"I will not say yes to this. . . ." the Emperor said, his words trailing off into tension.

The Praetorian praefect Livianus leaned close to the Emperor, his whisper soft and eager as a lover's.

"But you won't say no?"

Apion's chest tightened so that he could scarce get a breath. He watched, amazed, while Trajan removed the diamond ring of office given him by the Emperor Nerva when that Emperor had adopted him as his son, and placed the ring on the table. His meaning was clear: *I cannot wear this while committing so shameful an act.*

"Just don't say *no*," Livianus went on in that oddly seductive voice, "and we'll quietly go about our work. You need know no more about it."

This next round of silence was a death warrant for Apion's master. Hot tears puddled in the boy's eyes. His gentle spirit did not blame Trajan; it would not have occurred to him to question the deeds of such a majestic man, so charged with Olympian purposes. To Apion, this was more a matter of one god setting out to slay another, and his reflex was to deflect an arrow aimed at a man he loved.

For long, the boy could not move. He was sweating. He felt he was in the clutches of ague.

Below him, the tension broke suddenly, as if someone cut a taut rope. Finding they had no more to say, the men began drifting to their feet—first the Emperor, then the others, while trading banalities about the health of wives, the vacillating fortunes of children.

If I were fleet as a heron, Apion thought, *I could fly to Julianus and give him warning tonight.*

Then Apion was jolted from one nightmare and pitched into another. He looked about the small room.

Pylades was gone.

Apion found the loose tile and clicked it into place. He fumbled for a sulphur match, relit the lamp, and began exploring the room while softly calling out Pylades's name—even though the hollow emptiness he felt all about told him the truth.

The fright that gripped him now was of a different sort—keen and immediate as a blade pressed to the neck.

Pylades had abandoned him. Was he vengeful enough to betray him to the guards of the watch?

He was.

How had Pylades melted off so silently? Through the trapdoor onto the practice stage, Apion guessed.

Then Apion saw that Pylades had taken the feather mask from the wall and savaged it. All that was left of Apion's gift from the Emperor were sad drifts of vermilion and gold feathers.

Pylades was mad. He meant to slay a rival in love.

Apion opened the door leading to the vaulted passage behind the costume chamber, listening acutely for the tramp of guard-steps as he paused between the guttering flames of two wall sconces shaped as griffin's heads. In his belt was a silver dagger. Its blade was not sharp; it was but a prop he used in performances. But it would do for his purpose.

So Pylades believes he can cast off Marcus Julianus with scarcely a thought, and toss me away like table leavings?

Now Apion did hear the distant staccato of heavy-booted feet, the rhythmic jingling of keys on an iron ring—four guards, he judged, approaching at a trot. Fright shot him into another world. Then all at once fear was faraway and small, and Apion felt he drifted like a ghost as he moved down the passage, away from the sounds of the guards. He made no attempt to outrun them. In his fury he no longer cared if he died.

His dagger had passions of its own, and it sought Pylades's throat.

"There! Just ahead! Get him!" The harsh shouts reverberated all about the stone passage, resembling the yips of excited dogs. He guessed they were a hundred paces behind him.

When Apion came to the spiral stair tread that led to the galleries below, he found Pylades lingering behind a basalt column. As Apion had guessed, Pylades had not gone far; the older boy had been unable to resist the sight of Apion's destruction.

Apion hurled his slender body at Pylades, mighty in his fury. The older boy was thrown backward by Apion's weight. Apion's silver knife was a ravening talon raking open Pylades's soft wool tunic; dark stains appeared in many places on the rose-colored cloth. Entwined about one another like serpents, the boys fell into a silk-embroidered curtain closing off a portico. The curtain was torn free; it billowed down on top of them.

The guards circled them with swords drawn, frustrated as hounds at bay, shouting at them to get to their feet. They must take Apion alive, if they were ever to learn who the spying boy's master was. And they dared not injure Pylades and risk the Emperor's wrath for maiming his favorite.

"Proditor perfide!" came Apion's raw cry. "Loathsome betrayer." The most damning words in Apion's world burst from a molten heart. Apion fought his way atop the older boy. Pylades got a desperate grip on Apion's wrists. The younger boy's knife strained toward Pylades's throat. Pylades's arms shuddered with effort as gradually, he began losing strength. In several heartbeats Pylades would be dead.

The guards knew they must act at once. One seized Apion's legs and pulled hard. Simultaneously, a second guard, using the flat of his sword's blade, delivered a sharp blow to the side of Apion's head, meaning to stun the boy.

The guard misjudged the strength of his blow.

Apion was dying but he did not know it. He thought he'd taken horse, and was speeding north. Apion had never learned to ride but he was riding now, travelling at reckless speed over the post roads, through a string of towns, through fields, through verdure—crossing an Empire bafflingly vast, seeking a villa on a northern river. He must warn Marcus Julianus.

Marcus Julianus. There's no one else to tell you that they mean to kill you. I shall not fail you in this. You'll be so proud of me, you'll adopt me as your son. . . .

He galloped on until he rode into warm, sentient light, heard the laughter of the wild woodland goddesses his mother loved, felt the lapping of nurturant water as he swam his steed across a river that had no bottom. Still galloping, he surged onward through liquid tranquillity, into a world where betrayal had no meaning. And then he galloped no more.

Chapter 13

Four days after the Kalends of Junius

"My man in Victorinus's house just came with the news," Auriane said to Avenahar. "We are finished. Victorinus's 'evidence' has been sent."

At the villa of Marcus Julianus, Auriane and Avenahar were racing the mares, an annual event held on the estate to determine which horses would be kept for breeding and which would be sold in the horse markets at Confluentes. They approached a changing station at the far end of the meadow, close by the glassy shimmer of the Mosella's narrow course. There, a groom waited with two fresh horses; sunlight played along the sculpted ridges of their shoulders, coursed round sleek, tapered flanks; their coats were bright as bronze vessels against the lustrous silk of sea-green meadow grasses. In a household aswarm with servants, this proved Auriane's first chance to take counsel with Avenahar alone. She was astride a losing mare, a lean, bony horse of Hispanian stock, deflated from exertion, walking with slack steps, its lowered neck streaked with lather. Avenahar's winning bay had dark shading round the eyes that gave the beast a look of great equine wisdom. Beneath the red-tiled eaves of the villa's north wall, a collection of grooms and household slaves had gathered to watch. Auriane was just able to discern that Marcus and Arria Juliana had joined them; a servant held a fringed blue sunshade over Arria's head. Normally Auriane would have felt warm pleasure at the sight of the family momentarily joined—but not today.

"He lost his fear of your death curse?" Avenahar asked.

"Stay calm and don't show agitation in your face. It all happened thiswise." Auriane reached down to stroke her mare's neck—an unconscious gesture meant to console the beast for losing the race. "Four nights past, Victorinus ate a tainted clam. He thought he was dying because of my curse."

Avenahar bowed her head as she nipped short a burst of laughter. She recovered herself, mumbling, "Sorry, Mother."

"His wife, Decimina, ran shrieking all about the house, tearing her clothes, and all the slaves began lamenting—"

"Sham tears! I'll wager his poor mistreated tenant farmers made thanksgiving sacrifices!"

"Shssh! Listen. Victorinus turned a sickly shade of green, and collapsed onto his couch. He called his son, Lucius, to his bedside. Victorinus told the boy he was dying, because of *me*—"

"I do want to commend that clam."

"Be silent and listen! Victorinus, of course, wanted vengeance on us. As his dying wish, he commanded Lucius to send off the evidence, a thing that apparently, until then, he had not done, still hopeful, I suppose, that I'd give in and betroth Arria to his boy. Anyway, Lucius has done so. Dying wish, indeed! Two days later our clam-eater is hale and healthy again, and back at what he does best—tormenting small shopkeepers in his courtroom."

The mares shied as one at an eruption of blackbirds from the meadow grass. When they were brought under control, Auriane went on. "Avenahar, this means we've a month and a half, at most, before that evidence makes its way to Rome. Our enemy's not Volusius Victorinus anymore—it's the pride of the most ruthless nation the gods ever brought forth. And the wrath of a man who *is* a god, their Emperor—"

"But Marcus—"

"—doesn't fear emperors, I know, and even humbled one once, but Avenahar, he uses reason, not sorcery. We must not tell him yet—first I get *you* to safety."

"But what of *you*?"

"I stand and fight."

"You stand and die!"

"No more of this! I would never leave Arria and Marcus."

"You'll go down with this ship and drown, like a dutiful sea-captain," Avenahar said in a bitter voice, looking away. "This isn't what you wanted, is it, Mother?" she whispered. Avenahar stole a look at her mother, and saw Auriane stiffen slightly, as if from a knife thrust. Avenahar felt keenly her mother's haunted yearnings. "You want to go *home*." She spoke the word *home* as if it were the Fields of Elysium. "In your secret mind you've always wanted it, and I've always known it. Your secret hand reaches for a sword. I see it. You want to lead a great raid and get our lands back from the Cheruscans. Tell me the truth. And what better time to depart this place than now?"

"What's that vile machine they torture slaves with, that pulls you apart, joint by joint? The rack," Auriane whispered. "Must my own daughter put me upon it?" She could not understand how a fierce and blind need to remain at the villa could be housed within her side by side with that strong pull to go home and reclaim the land—but it did.

"You and I belong where we took first milk," Avenahar pressed on. "I despise saying this but I think your counsel is clouded by love."

"Well, that's amusing!—coming from a maid who hasn't yet loved. It doesn't cloud counsel, it reshapes it."

"This country . . . it's poisonous. You see only Marcus, who's fine and good. The gods alone know how he got that way, living among these people. All is twisted and backward among them. Here, it's the men who're *boldest*, the soldiers of the ranks who fight on the frontier, who're treated like slaves. No champion's portion for them—"

"Avenahar, not now—"

"—while the men with no battle-mettle at all, noblemen who give commands but do not fight, live within thick-walled houses while slaves spoon delicacies into their mouths. These people are false to their gods, and false to the brave." She captured Auriane's gaze. "Let's flee off from the ceremony. Let's just *not come back*."

"Rein in those bolting horses, my little spitfire. You're half right. One of us will flee from it. You. Directly after the rites in the Holy Wood, you'll travel to my mother's hall and stay with Athelinda for a few seasons—just for safety. Athelinda is your grandmother, it's good she should know you before she leaves this life. I won't see your life endangered for what I've done."

"Madness. I won't go off without you." Avenahar bit her lip and cast her gaze down.

Auriane reached across the space between horses and gathered up Avenahar's hand. "Dearest, you must. Our life-threads are entwined, can't you see? We'll be woven together again, in time. You're never alone, Avenahar; the Ancestresses are with you. Lift your head up, now. Look peaceable and gay, everyone's watching."

"Mother, I want you to know . . . if the Fates do separate us, *I will become you.* Whatever you have left undone, I will finish. I'll strike for you. Your mother, your home village—I'll find a way to protect them."

"Nobly said, but you're too untried to know what those words mean."

They came to the shed at the meadow's far end and gave the wearied mares over to the groom. Auriane grasped her fresh mare by the mane and withers and sprang up in a beautiful bound, without the aid of the mounting block. Avenahar, with much enthusiasm but less grace, did likewise. The strong young mares surged toward the starting mark, making a frenzied music with their bits as they capered sideways at a frustrated half-gallop, protesting the tight restraint of the reins, which drew their slender necks into exquisite arches. The course would take them round the breadth of the grassy meadow, bounded by forest, main house, and river.

The mares burst from the mark. Clods of earth sailed high in the air. Auriane felt like a stone hurled from a sling. She joyed in power unleashed, the drama of smooth, rapidly lengthening strides. Both horses attacked the path with an unquenchable appetite for running; they were mated ecstatically to the wind. It was as if they'd been too long denied their natural right to fly. *They are some beautiful machinery of the gods,* Auriane thought, *formed so we'd know the limitlessness of speed and grace.*

The mares were so evenly matched, they might have been tethered together at the bit. Iron hooves battered the dirt path as they rushed at a blind curve around a thick stand of alders, where the track bent close to the deep forest at the beginning of the Slate Hills. Both mares leaned steeply into the sharp curve in the track. Avenahar's mare, who held the inside position, edged her dark muzzle slightly ahead.

Then before them was the impossible—a pile of building stones freshly deposited on the track, as if some careless giant dropped a fistful of them. The frightful obstruction was already so close there was no time for horse or rider to plan an evasive move. They had not even a moment to wonder who might have done this. Both horses left the ground, propelling themselves over the tumble of stones, stretching their bodies in flight to lengthen their leap when, while airborne, they realized the length of the obstacle.

Both beasts wrenched their hindquarters to the side to avoid nicking their hooves on stone. Auriane's mare landed on a patch of soft earth; with a few inelegant frog-hops, her horse got safely over the remaining stones. Avenahar's mount struck rock, and was slammed to its knees. The mare's hindquarters flew up; the beast was flung onto its back. Avenahar was launched into a thicket. The broken mare got up with one mighty lurch, then began turning in aimless circles, limping pitifully amidst the rockfall.

Auriane brought her mare around and cantered to Avenahar's side.

"I'm well, Mother, don't bother with me," Avenahar shouted, noisily fighting her way out of the thicket. "Look about! Whoever did this can't be far!"

Auriane scanned the meadow, studying the russet-and-violet shadows pooled along the treeline at the forest's edge. At last she saw something, just entering the drape of shadow—was that an ox-drawn quarryman's cart? Yes. It lurched crazily over the uneven ground, bumping along like some hurrying turtle. She remembered that she'd seen an ox cart laden with building stones abandoned not far from the course, where the tenant farmers were constructing a wall—apparently, someone had seized it for his own devices. She kicked her mare's sides. She was an arrow shot at her quarry.

Ox cart and driver would soon be lost in the cleft of a shallow ravine. She supposed whoever it was had gambled that the victims of this prank would be too stunned to pursue. Auriane pushed the mare harder than she had during the race. The cart's driver realized, suddenly, his cart's progress was not fast enough; he sprang from the seat and began sprinting for the forest. As the young man fled from her with a strange stride that shifted him swiftly along like some running stork, Auriane saw a familiar thin neck widening into sloped shoulders.

Lucius.

He was close to freedom. As Auriane's mare whipped past the cart, the boy took the creek in one elongated stride and sped on, nearly falling once in the thick matting of silverweed on the far bank. Then he pitched himself headfirst into the wood, and to safety. The forest in that place was treacherous with rock slides, rendering it impassible on horseback. So she let go the hope of catching him, realizing it was enough to have identified him. She had, as well, the cart for evidence. Galloping at an easier pace, she returned for the bruised, bleeding Avenahar. Astride one mare, mother and daughter crossed the meadow, seeking the main house.

Marcus rushed up and caught her horse's rein, his face taut with concern. Auriane related the tale in clipped, brief sentences, while pointing toward the forest. As she spoke, she saw him slowly overtaken with an anger she'd seen but rarely in their life together—thunderous, but quiet, a rage of many parts, possessed of a finality that promised it would not be discharged fully until someone was punished.

Abruptly he turned from her and began striding purposefully down the covered walkway that gave onto the villa's columned porch. "Marcus—?" she called out after him.

He slowed, but only to say, "I mean to see this does not happen again."

As she dropped from her horse, she heard him giving brisk orders to Demaratos, then to the decurion of grooms. After she'd dispatched a man to see if the fallen mare could be saved, she made her way to the vestibule and was just in time to see Marcus departing, in the company of his first secretary. The carriagemen's whips cracked; two teams of sleek, silken bays hitched to two elegant *redas* broke into motion, accompanied by running footmen and ten armed grooms on horseback. *He means to go now, to bring Victorinus to account.* A queasiness rose in her throat. Any gratification she might have felt at this swift justice was snuffed out by her sudden fear that matters had shot irreparably beyond her control.

JULIANUS'S JOURNEY TO Victorinus's riverside estate required but a quarter hour by the water-clock; the magistrate's villa was adjacent to theirs, separated by a half-mile-wide strip of uncultivated land. This was the eleventh hour of day; the town court would be shut up for the night. The magistrate was a man of regular habits, and Julianus judged it near certain Victorinus would be at home, dining alone or with clients and friends.

His carriages halted before the thick columns of green porphyry that fronted the main house of Victorinus's rambling, red-tiled villa. The entryway's heavy double doors were pulled wide, exposing the vestibule. Within, two rows of interior columns were garlanded with ivy to welcome the evening's dinner guests. The startled doorkeeper stared, baffled, at the rich *redas* with their emblems of Minerva carved into the sides, the footmen, the grooms, wondering what great eminence had been invited—and why he hadn't been informed.

"Bring your master out, and at once," Julianus spoke from the carriage, "if he wants to keep his post as magistrate."

The doorkeeper's look of affront shifted to astonishment as he recognized the august visitor framed within the parted drapes of the fine *reda*.

The Hermit-King, as his master called him, deigning to pay a visit here? He vanished within, while Julianus waited with gathering impatience. The vestibule's mosaic floor was visible through the open doors, the reds blood-red, the blues iridescent in the late-afternoon glow sifting from the lightwell above. In a better temper he might have had leisure to marvel at the vulgarity of Victorinus's choice of subject: Most entryway mosaics depicted solemn tableaus, often mythic, always remote from day-on-day life, chosen from standard designs offered by the mosaicist's shop. Victorinus's showed the magistrate himself, rendered with the crudeness of a child's drawing. The figure's head was a flattened globe resembling a partly squashed melon; one odd, outsized arm was stiffly extended as the magistrate was depicted gifting the town of Confluentes with its gymnasium.

Victorinus soon emerged, wagging his head and protesting, ". . . but I've got guests! How does he dare—" His azure-and-saffron silk dinner gown had slipped, exposing a knobby shoulder. Close beside him was his usher, the slave whose duty was to aid a master's memory by announcing guests' names; Victorinus had refused to believe the doorkeeper, and couldn't trust his own poor eyesight. The magistrate still had a dinner napkin tucked beneath his chin. An agile serving-boy appeared from the darkness beyond, adroitly picked it off, and disappeared. From the interior of the house came the lowing of pipes, the fast shake of tambourines, the wild yelps of guests. His wife, Decimina, gusted in on his wake, her stola billowing like an unraveling shroud. A pearl diadem was lodged at an angle in preposterous hair; Julianus supposed many blonde serving maids had sacrificed their locks in the construction of this edifice of curls, all for the sake of a style one dynasty out of date. Daylight was ruthless to this woman, highlighting the cracking paint that whitened her face; the chalky unguent had pasted her row of tight, even, ocean-wave curls to her forehead. She seemed a thing returned from the dead as she hovered there behind her husband, glaring imperiously, certain he would say something to embarrass her.

"Volusius Victorinus, stand out here where I can look at you."

Decimina put a painted paw on Victorinus's shoulder to stop him. He carefully removed it with hands still greasy from his meal. Then, warily, he edged out onto the columned porch. He put Julianus in mind of trapped vermin alert to any crevice through which it might wriggle off.

"This is most irregular, Julianus," Victorinus said, squinting to get a better look at the well-kept carriages, the neatly attired footmen, the shadowed

man watching him with quiet wrath from within the *reda*. "Could you not
have chosen a time amenable to us both?"

"There's no amenable time for murderous pranks, Victorinus. Your son,
Lucius, has played his last."

"I've no notion whatever what you're speaking of."

"Your son set out to gravely injure Auriane and my daughter. This isn't
the first time; it's just the worst. Your ill will and envy have made him what
he is—as a father lives, so does the son. Answer for him!"

"His *daughter*," Decimina whispered with wicked glee, from behind Victorinus. "What man of substance adopts a daughter whose father is unknown?"

"I . . . I'll see the boy whipped," Victorinus offered. "Soon as he's . . .
he's out somewhere now, hunting grouse—"

"I want better than that, Victorinus. He's not to take himself within
sight of the walls of my estate."

A curious guest materialized in the shadows beside Decimina. "Victorinus, Decimina, you're missing a good story—" the newcomer began, before
Decimina, with a slightly panicked look in her face, tried to turn him round
and steer him back into the dining room. Julianus noted that this guest spoke
in the crisp, precise syllables of the Latin of the capital, not the softly corrupted speech of the provinces. The guest refused to cooperate, and he and
Decimina were locked in an odd tussle while Decimina pleaded with him in
a loud whisper. Victorinus, too, was dismayed that the intruder was witnessing this exchange, seeming trapped between his fear of Julianus and a need
to maintain dignity before the man behind him.

"Agreed. And if that's all, Marcus Julianus, you'll have to excuse me
now; I've got high-born folk inside, and—"

"It isn't. I want Lucius to make a public apology on the oration platform
in Confluentes's forum," Julianus continued, "with you standing beside him.
You don't seem to be able to curb him on your own. Perhaps if the whole
town has knowledge of this, they can help you keep watch on him, and his
evil mischief can be controlled."

The thought came to Victorinus then—*Julianus has been badly compromised by his woman's perfidy—need I take this beating at all?*

Fearing Victorinus would capitulate, Decimina crept up behind him.
"We are ruined, *ruined*," she whispered loudly, while miming tearing out her
hair, "because my husband is a coward!"

This proved effective. Victorinus took a bold step closer to Julianus.

"That's a humiliation, Julianus, and nothing more. I'll do the first, as I must, as a father, but I'll be poleaxed if I'll do the second!"

"It can't be helped, Victorinus," Julianus said sharply. "I want the boy's mischief exposed to the town. And I want it done before the Ides of *Augustus*."

Had the magistrate and Julianus been speaking in private, all might have ended there. However, the curious guest behind him was Victorinus's uncle, with whom he was trying to engineer his return to Rome and, hopefully, a post of honor. An offense given to one member of the greater family was given to all. He could not let his esteemed uncle witness him consenting to look the fool before the populace of his own town. Victorinus was like some unwilling gladiator, goaded with firebrands to keep on with the bout.

"We'll do *none* of those things, Marcus Julianus." His eyes glinted with the blank courage of the boar veering into the charge. "And who are you to threaten *us*? It's time you learned it, Julianus—that she-animal you call *wife* has ruined you! It's my pleasure to tell you, if you don't know it already—your Aurinia is the very villain everyone's been trying to catch, who's been smuggling arms-money over the frontier."

"You'll curb that lying tongue if you value your freedom."

"She's the traitor with three million on her head! And I've the proof of it! Traitor, who harbors traitors, who are you to mete out punishment to an honest man?"

"The ravings of an intemperate, choleric man. I'll hear no more."

"Maybe it's a bit more than that, Julianus. Your woman's been arming those barking savages who are her kin, and has been, for years. I've got evidence. As we speak, it's making its way to Rome."

Now that Victorinus had purged himself, regular good sense returned with a snap. He was aware, suddenly, of Julianus regarding him with the steady wrath of a calm avenger. The boar-glint faded off. What had he done? He was but a provincial magistrate, facing a man whose connections and means were far beyond his own.

When Julianus spoke, his voice was almost gentle, but it did nothing to quell Victorinus's unease.

"Perhaps you've simply gone mad, Victorinus. I do not know, or care. But for now, just know this: Your days as magistrate are done."

The carriagemen's whips cracked; the proud bays broke into a stately canter. The party departed down the wide, graveled carriageway, to the accompaniment of Decimina's wails. Julianus could still hear her when he'd covered half the distance home.

On the brief journey, he had leisure to ponder Victorinus's words. Was it possible the magistrate spoke the truth?

It was.

But would Auriane keep such a thing secret from him?

Certainly not.

But what, then, inspired Victorinus's boldness, his brash certainty?

I've never wished to know the result of any test that might pit Auriane's loyalty to her people against her love for me. And does not an unwillingness to know some grave and telling thing often foment disaster, at the last?

On his return, he went at once to his Records Room and drafted a letter to the Secretary of Imperial Correspondence in Rome, who sorted all incoming letters from the northern provinces. With a very few lines, Marcus Julianus cut out the ground from beneath Victorinus, first summarizing the Florentius affair, in which the magistrate had taken a bribe from the owner of a nearby limestone quarry accused of causing the deaths of ten soldiers assigned there who'd been crushed in a rockfall; Victorinus had managed it so that the case was never brought to trial. He also charged that Victorinus had misdirected funds allocated by the Treasury for "Public Entertainments," using this public money to add a race course to his villa. *If half the provincial magistrates were as corrupt as this one,* he mused, *we'd do better to settle disputes as primitives do, through combat.* Though Julianus had a good store of offenses to choose from, he stopped there, determining that it was better to do too little than too much; this was the sort of weapon that kept its potency through light, infrequent use.

He then commanded one of his messengers to carry the letter to the posting station, so a post rider could be off with it at dawn. His seal on the letter would ensure the swiftest delivery.

Then he asked Demaratos to send Auriane to him.

AURIANE FELT A pressing sense of dread as she made her way to the villa's Records Room. A waiting tension lay over the house. Night had fallen and darkness poured in everywhere, flooding the chambers, flowing into the halls. The still flames of the row of hanging lamps above her in the passage were small, brave islands of warmth.

She had been going over accounts with the horsemaster, and she was still clad in a mud-stained deerskin tunica belted with a hemp rope. Her chestnut hair was loosened, falling about her shoulders. Grass and straw had caught in it, and she knew she looked more like a woodwife of the forest than a matron of a villa.

As she approached the atrium, she threw back the heavy olivine-colored curtain that draped the doorkeeper's alcove, flushing a flustered Demaratos from his favorite listening post. This was one time when she did not want to be overheard. She caught a look of sharp disappointment in the steward's face, for spoiling his evening's entertainment. Demaratos quickly recovered his Greek manners and began some belligerent explanation, but she walked away from him before he was through.

And then she stood before Marcus Julianus in the Records Room. He sat before a gilt-legged accounts table, his head bent over a row of wax tablets. Behind him was the bronze cupboard that held the waxen masks of his ancestors, which he'd carried with him from his great house in Rome, and a marble portrait bust of his father, whose cold, shrewd features made it difficult for Auriane to believe the man had truly felt much love for his son. How different their faces, she thought, though the gods obviously cast both from one mold: The father seemed to look down a long, narrow corridor, while not approving of what he saw at its end. The son's look had no such fixedness; it embraced a long stretch of horizon.

With a start of dismay she recognized the procurator's report he studied so intently: It was from the estate and vineyard outside Lugdunum, capital city of Gaul, which he had put in her name. Never before had he taken an interest in it.

She was keenly aware, suddenly, of the comforting sound of the rushing water of the atrium fountain. *Water flowing inside.* She tried to recapture how wondrous that had been, when first she came here—to have a tame river running all over the house. It reminded her that she lived and raised her children in an earthly paradise. Unfortunately, that paradise was an island. One step outside and darkness began. She would ever be a stranger in this world, with its lives played out indoors amidst unnatural quiet, its pallid festivals, its myriad strange gods, its thick stone walls that brutally divided the great from the humble—and its women, who lived clothed in a shame infused into the heart at birth. They behaved like citizens of a defeated country, keeping desires bridled, counsel muzzled, steps shortened, ambitions shuttered, or forced through a maze of others. And yet, this villa was a harbor, preserving the only tranquillity she had ever known, and she felt herself braced to fight to the death to preserve it.

"I am here, Marcus."

The familiar comfort of his face was painful to look upon. *This must be why the Fates do not want enemies to lie together. In the end, there must always be a betrayal, either of the birth-country or the country taken anew.*

He looked up. The flames of the bronze candelabrum illuminated a gray solemnity in that well-loved face, a weariness of the world that brought forth a rush of sympathy in her.

"Auriane," he said quietly, "Victorinus will soon be ruined because of what I have just done, but it's only justice, and no more than what that scoundrel deserves. But he has made a charge against you that I pray before every god is not true.

"He claims *you* are the notorious malefactor whom all seek, on whose head Maximus has put three million. He says he's in possession of proof. Tell me it's not so, and I'll see Victorinus not only ruined, but prosecuted for a false charge as well."

She found herself suddenly emptied of a lifetime of reasons, acutely aware only that she'd grievously wounded someone she never wanted to hurt. Her gaze fled his, taking refuge in the lamp flame's reflection in the mirror gloss of the tiger-cypress table top.

"I can't tell you that," she whispered, "because it is true."

I have done it, she thought, *poisoned a rare communion, murdered a magnificent devotion . . .*

He dropped his head into his hands.

"You may well have destroyed our life here," he said.

"I know it," she whispered.

"Surely this is some madman's jest or some drunken dream. I feel the dupe in a farce!" He met and strongly held her gaze. "Why did I have to learn it from that lout Victorinus, and not from you?"

"I couldn't bring myself to force a cruel choice upon you, between your people and me. I wanted our love left in peace."

"This is a thing that tears us from our very moorings. It risks us all. Gods above and below, I believe I could have understood anything but this!"

"Marcus, it's my own mother who's set to be taken hostage. My own kin who've been pounced upon by this Cheruscan beast. What are my people to defend themselves with? Stones?"

"Auriane, no enemy still festering from the wounds of war, living right on our border, can be left under arms. It's the most fundamental point of military strategy, why can't you understand—"

"But my kin, my land, they are not separate from me. Our earth, it owns us—I'm attached to it still as if by a birth string. How could I abandon them?"

Wearily, he broke away from her gaze. "I'm sorry but I feel played false . . . betrayed . . . betrayed that you did not tell me, and that this was carried on for so long."

"But Marcus, this is the very sort of matter we agreed, from the first, never to speak of. You're bound to your law, I'm bound to ours. We always said that if we aired every question between your people and mine, we'd live our lives facing each other across a battlefield. Please know I never would have willingly brought you harm. Before our gods I had no choice."

"I've done the tricks of an acrobat trying to understand your gods and your ways. Because I've seen the world through your mind's eye, we took no marriage vow, you hunt in the forest as well as overseeing the house and teach the children your history as well as ours. But of what use is *my* understanding in this matter, anyway? It's hardly going to help you! It is brutally evident now, you cherish your people above our life here. You've savaged my trust and my love."

An animal grief seized her then, a bitter-cold misery that flooded down into the farthest roots of her spirit, full of the bleakness of the babe torn from its mother, the mother torn from the babe.

He is my country, too. What have I done?

Edging her way round the table, approaching him with a caution alien to their life together, she whispered, "*Marcus . . . ?* Love of kin, love for you . . . they are one thing, I couldn't set one over the other. Please . . . look at me." She extended a hand across the chasm between them, wanting to rejoin their souls again, but stopped, not knowing if she could bear it if he rudely brushed her hand away.

His face was a cold cliff. Her hand dropped heavily to her side.

I have broken the law of guest-friendship, she thought. *I must pay the ring-price for this. Otherwise I disgrace my family.*

"Marcus."

Alert to a dark solemnity in her voice, he turned to meet her gaze.

"I am a guest-friend who betrayed the trust of a host," she said simply. "A noble host from whom I've taken much. And so, I've turned my greatest friend into an enemy. I've disgraced my clan. You would be right to drive me off. I will go."

"What is this foolishness?" The simple earnestness in her words dismayed him. She meant it truly. "Auriane! Never! You are as harsh a mistress to yourself as your northern winters are cold." He dragged her numbed body toward him and held to her tightly, as if striving to bring life-warmth to one frozen in the snow. "Don't speak so. Let us stop all this." They clung to one another while he ran a gentling hand through her hair. "Let's fight on one side," he said, "let's not battle each other. Let us put our minds to devising a way to secure your safety."

Together, they turned to look at the records tablet from the provincial estate and vineyard outside Lugdunum. His purpose in giving her full ownership of this estate was to preserve the rich fortune he planned to leave Arria Juliana and Avenahar. Because both children were illegitimate by Roman reckoning, under the laws of inheritance they could only receive a legacy from their mother.

"Come, let me understand exactly what it is you did. First, how much of this does Victorinus know?"

"He captured my man Grimo, and tortured him. Grimo knew enough to seal my fate. Victorinus has a witness, who saw us burying the coin, and—"

"*Us? Avenahar* was with you? She'll be judged as harshly as you, as your accomplice. This tragedy has birthed more tragedy."

"I know it well, and I'll let no harm come to her. I'll shield her with my life, if need be." She indicated one of the neatly penned lines of figures. "I had my procurator draw off one quarter of the proceeds of the farm," she continued, "and instead of reinvesting it in more land, he brought it to the money changers at Lugdunum, and had it converted into old silver, Nero's silver, when it was last full weight. He left it at Lugdunum's bank until I could send an agent out to receive it. I buried it myself at agreed-upon places, along the river. The wineship *Isis* actually belongs to me, purchased under a false name; we invented a shipper who supposedly lives at Lugdunum. My man Axsillius received it at the native settlement where the Mosella flows into the Rhenus. Getting it over the Roman frontier was hardest—we had to put it into the sacred wagons that go round the fields at first thaw, bearing our Lady Fria's image—"

"Yes, Maximus ferreted out that part—by Charon, you were clever. Continue."

"From there, it was taken to the Chattian Assembly and given into the hands of the three strongest Chattian chiefs. They then purchased longswords from the arms dealers of our brother-tribe, the Ubians. The swords are stored in a cave, in our lands; I don't know where, exactly. Witgern guards it. Victorinus threatened me with his evidence, but I believed his purpose was to force me to betroth Arria to his son. I thought lust was a draught that numbed his wits—I didn't think he'd have the mettle to send it. *He* wants Arria, Marcus. For *himself*."

"He'll be fortunate to keep the tunic on his back when I've had done with him." Marcus put his hands to his temples, and sank slowly onto his cross-legged chair. "By the foul tricks of Providence, this is the worst of times to be accused of such a thing—at the start of this far-eastern war. Trajan might well believe I had knowledge."

"Let me go before the Governor at Mogontiacum and take this all upon myself."

"No. You can't go and confess, it will only incite greater passion against you. I'll have to trust that my past deeds on behalf of the state will be remembered, and will shield me."

His face solemn with grief, he fervently met her gaze. "But for you, Auriane, there is no shield." He took her hands in his. "We must look for ways to preserve your life. You are a dead woman unless you flee the country."

"I know it."

"In the face of the very real possibility that I can't undo this, a journey must be planned for you. We must arrange to send both of you somewhere beyond the reach of our law." He frowned, thinking rapidly. "You know of Caledonia, in the northern reaches of the Isle of Britannia? It's a wild land that has never been brought into the Empire. It's been used as a refuge from tyrants, in times past. The climate there is similar to yours, and naturalists say the folk there come from the same stock. Perhaps this place would be more amenable to you than—"

"Caledonia? What is Caledonia? I know nothing of this place. I won't hide in an outland full of strangers. Marcus, if I flee off, I go nowhere but home."

"And the patrols will pick you up within a day." His gaze held hers with the iron inflexibility of a wrestler's hold. "Auriane, you must listen to me. You've no full knowledge of what you've set yourself against. Caledonia it must be, if we are to preserve your life!"

She wrenched her hands free and took a step away from him. In her anguish, she'd torn at her hair, and she watched him with bold eyes from behind a fall of rumpled locks that obscured her face like some half-drawn curtain. In that moment she looked remote to him, a woman governed by alien promptings, unknown tides. "Marcus," she said with soft ferocity, "either I stay here. Or I go home. Or I give myself to the gods."

"We cannot argue over this! You must live! Do you think I can stand idly by while you *both* walk into destruction? This is all horrible enough without you battling the only reasonable solution!"

"I'll not go off from Arria. I'll not be split apart from my own child!"

"It can't be helped, Auriane. For now, it must be so. Perhaps it won't be forever. Arria is a Roman child—she'll flourish far better here than in your country. I'll send off letters to Rome and finish the marriage negotiations at once, so she'll be taken care of, no matter what happens to us. Arria will be well. Not so, you . . . what tragedy has come . . ."

"Marcus—what of Avenahar's womanhood ceremony? Its time is but eight days off."

"I'm sorry, Auriane—"

"We cannot deny Avenahar her initiation!"

"This is folly! Why cannot you see, you both must flee!"

Auriane turned from him, drawn into wretched silence; she was a soul blindly battling river currents, not accepting them, and for long moments she listened to the atrium fountain's sad trickle in the darkness. The atrium was somber as a cave because the servants needed to venture past the Records Room to light its lamps—and thus far none had dared.

Then she happened to think of something else. She turned round again, and tightly grasped his hands.

"Marcus . . . we'd go away together, of course? You would come *with* me?"

This caught him by surprise—she felt him tauten.

He disengaged himself from her, turned away, and for long, would not reply.

"That is not possible," he said at last.

"And *why* is it not possible?" she said, her voice growing hoarse.

"You don't understand," he replied, choosing his words with care. "I have complicated and pressing duties here—"

"More pressing than us living on, joined as one?"

"Auriane, you don't understand, I'm the head of my family now, and must watch over them all—"

"But . . . *I* am your family. As you are mine."

"Of course, but matters are different among my people. Auriane, that would be *exile*. Under a good and fair ruler, exile is the harshest punishment ever meted out to a member of the Senatorial class. That's because it severs us from everything that gives us life—the country where grandparents are buried, the masks of ancestors . . . the family's guardian spirits . . . the sacred relics of the past, the books on which our lives are written, and all that exercises the mind . . . It takes us from the very sun. I would lose even my citizenship. That's the fate of a Roman no longer living within the *imperium,* whether voluntarily or not. I could never so dishonor my mother and father."

"But *I* exiled myself for *you*."

"You should have been an advocate! Yes, you did. And look at the ill fortune it's brought upon us."

"Do you not see, Marcus, that for all those reasons you just said you must stay—if I go anywhere, it must be back to my people? My mother is there. My father is buried there."

"No, Auriane. You must go where I say. Your enemies have grown too numerous, on both sides of the Rhenus." His voice rose to oratorical strength. "I want our children to have a living mother!"

"I want our children to have an *honorable* mother."

"To Hades with your honor," he said sharply, "if it takes you to your grave!"

"To Hades with *you,* if you deny Avenahar her womanhood ceremony."

For long moments, their gazes locked; her eyes were fevered with determination and hurt; his, fogged with anguish. They were two exhausted opponents dropping into troubled rest, after battling to a draw.

Finally he said in a voice of lead, "I am so stricken with grief, I can scarce think on what must be done. Our children, ourselves, set to be rent apart . . . this is much akin to going to our deaths. Leave me now, to think on this."

"I will go. But I leave you with this one bit of counsel—I am a free woman. Not a slave."

"And who treats you as a slave?" he said with startled affront.

"I must say it only because among your people, the difference is not always readily apparent."

"*Who treats you as a slave?*" Affront flashed into outrage.

"Anyone who compels me to go where I mean not to go."

"Madness. What a sad madness. Leave me!"

FOR A DAY and a night they had no words for one another. A sickly quiet lay over the estate. Demaratos, soon after Auriane had banished him from the alcove, had been lured back again by the sound of rising voices. And so the household knew at once of the rift between master and mistress and went about their duties in grim, guarded silence. Slaves of ruptured households lived in fear of being dispersed.

That night, long after Marcus had retired, Auriane halted at the door of their bedchamber. His words, *you've savaged my trust and my love,* left her emptied, mute; she felt like a fire smothered under damp sand.

And so she exiled herself to one of the guest chambers. He did not inquire. Her desolation deepened.

As she lay in wakefulness, she thought something foul must have been coiled in the pit of her heart since birth—how else could the act of aiding her people have brought those she loved to destruction? And she marveled that somehow that ancient sense of her own evil was never completely conquered. It was like smoke—close off one aperture and it found another.

Sleep brought dreams that raged like a tempest. Behind them, she thought she heard Ramis, laughing. The old seeress fed off ruptured worlds. *Did she lay some curse on my life here in order to force me back to my country—and to her?*

Dawn came, and it was a day of small horrors. Marcus sequestered himself in the library, wrapped in the mysteries of plans he didn't disclose, writing a series of letters, sending out and receiving messengers. *Arranging passage,* she supposed. Arria Juliana, though she had been told nothing, was so unsettled she would take no food. Once, Auriane caught Brico stuffing clothing into travelling trunks—her own, and Avenahar's. Apparently Marcus had ordered this. Auriane told the flustered girl to stop. When Avenahar learned she was to have no womanhood ceremony, she tore herself from her mother, her eyes wild and lost. Moments later, Auriane discovered that Avenahar's womanhood cloak was missing from the weaving room. Guessing her daughter's purpose—Avenahar had run away once before, when she was nine, and hadn't returned for three days—Auriane rushed outside and saw Avenahar taking long, fierce strides toward the stables. Fortunately her daughter was too distraught for stealth. Auriane set out in pursuit, and caught Avenahar's horse by the rein as she was galloping for the villa's arched gate.

ON THE NEXT night, Auriane came again to the bedchamber she and Marcus had shared for seven years. She knew he lay awake in the dark, though he spoke no words of greeting. In all their life together, she had always stayed with him through the night, though this was not usual in aristocratic Roman houses. Normally, husband and wife came together for love, then returned to their small, separate chambers. "How singly your people live," she'd said when first they'd come here, "stowing themselves in bare, comfortless boxes at night—one body, one room. How like a burial chamber. Among my people, we sleep alone only in death." His people never considered that a person's soul might not end at her skin, that a family's spirit might flow together in one wide river course. She knew this separateness embraced his people's every thought, enabling them to make small, unfettered decisions, so unlike the broad, slow, encompassing ones, common to her people. How different this separateness was from her world, where one longhouse might be packed with a hundred bodies, human and beast, family and friend. For her sake, he had defied custom, and they had pulled two high, narrow Roman beds together. Two bodies, one room. But the cleft had always been there, in the dark, a divide that never allowed her to forget she was among strangers.

"Is my greatest friend my enemy still?" she said, her voice venturing out into the dark. She felt herself an animal stretching out its neck for the sacrificial blade.

"Of course not." Words like a warm blanket. "Come here."

She found his hand, warm and welcome as a hearth fire. Gently she gathered that hand up, feeling a powerful welling of relief that melted her down onto the *lectus,* where she happily burrowed in against him, making a nest, and lay in great contentment with her head upon his chest. For long moments they drifted on something deep and ancient that flooded over all the careful knowings of the mind.

"I don't know why you've forgiven me," she mumbled after a time.

"By any fair reckoning the fault's as much mine. The gods tempted me with happiness and I greedily snatched it up, and came here with you. Didn't I know your nature from the first, how adamantine your passion . . . How could I ever have thought to remake you, or even have wanted to, since that hallowed devotion was the very thing I loved?"

She guessed, from these stilted and lofty words, that he'd sought the consolations of philosophy while she'd sought the solace of Fria. *Yes, it has been a feast of days,* she thought as his hand gently invaded the opening of her tunica, finding her bare back, venturing round to an unbound breast. *I haven't murdered a great communion,* she realized, delighting in the progress of his hand, strongly willing him on, feeling herself a spreading rose falling open, startled anew at the eloquence of his touch—always, it seemed to combine the knowledge of each previous touch. There was a library for the senses in those hands, a wrenching record of all their days. She sought him like one starved, pressing her whole body against his. His skin felt like hot silk. She joined with him then, in a world grown soft and brilliant again, and they were one in the dark, beautifully one, and his generosity seemed the only balm; lack of hope bound them together so tightly that when pleasure came, she nearly cried out in pain.

Afterward, they lay wakeful for a long time, molded together. She was aware, then, of that irritating cleft between the beds, realizing it formed the shape of the runic letter that signified *ice*—and cold isolation. It had lain there between them all these years, sly and silent, prying them apart with its harmful runic magic . . .

"Marcus, you cannot deny Avenahar her womanhood ceremony. Today she tried to run away."

"I was told of this, and I think I was wrong on that matter. It *has* all been arranged—all those concessions I made to Maximus—and it comes so soon. I suppose we could get Avenahar through that, and then on to safety, before all of this all comes down on your heads."

"This is well, very well. Avenahar will be grateful."

After a moment's silent thought, he said, "When you and Avenahar go, we'll travel together, as far as Mogontiacum. Today, during all this, Maximus sent me an urgent message, something odd. It seems the Emperor has ordered him to summon the prophetess Ramis to the Fortress for questioning."

The utterance of that name nudged her into another world.

"Ramis?" she said softly. "She's to be *summoned,* like some disobedient servant? That would make a fine scene for a farce. Why?"

"She tried a Roman citizen. She convened a native court and condemned to death one of our soldiers up there, a man the Chattians claim looted treasure from one of your sacred lakes. Maximus wants me there beside him when he confronts your dread high priestess on the dais. The poor man's at his wits' end—he has no idea how to handle such an interview."

"He's frightened of her, you mean. I've never known a mortal man who wasn't. Except for the utterly foolish . . . or the mad . . . or you."

"Fine company you've put me in." He smiled in the dark, and smoothed back her hair.

"Marcus, you don't fear her, just a little?"

"Someone has to keep their head."

"No, truly. You can question her as if she were an ordinary woman?"

"When negotiations begin I think only of the facts of the matter at hand, and all men and women are as one to me. Maybe it's a form of shortsightedness. My poor old father was the same."

"You do not do yourself enough credit. There's a core of steadiness in you that's not in others. And others readily give you faith, because they recognize a rare spirit who won't abuse it." Auriane hesitated in silence for a moment, then said, "Marcus, this morning as I stood by the river I felt something else that's ill, a thing that lies separate from all this. I sensed about you, danger from an animal."

He was silent—a sharp, knowing silence.

"Heavy and dark, with a smell of musk. Perhaps it's nothing. *Marcus?*"

"By all the gods, you can be alarming at times, Auriane."

"What is it?"

"One of the concessions Maximus pried out of me was, he got me to agree to go with him on one of his infamous aurochs hunts."

"To hunt a great bull? But you despise that sort of thing."

"He's been beseeching me for years. It will please him greatly, and I didn't think it would harm me overmuch."

"You once called the hunt 'a vicious means for a chair-riding quill-pusher gone to fat to prove he still has his mettle.'"

"Your damnable memory. You will quote me into a corner."

"Have you turned somewhat from that position?" she said, managing a smile in the darkness.

"I'll be on the sidelines, just to please him. I won't be harmed. He's done a lot for us. He takes a great risk, helping you and Avenahar across the frontier. Anyway, a man should try everything, at least once."

Feeling drunken on the warmth of this renewed closeness, she decided to make a final try for accord. "Marcus, do you see now that if you cannot turn this matter round, that Avenahar and I must go nowhere but *home*? This Caledonia . . . its spirits do not know me."

He was uncomfortably silent. The air between them seemed to stiffen.

"But one thing matters—that you and Avenahar live," he said finally. "We must open an escape route for you, and keep it in place. You've got to understand that it's not in my nature to quietly watch while both you and Avenahar are dragged to execution. I've decided to travel to the Dacian camp and force an audience with the Emperor—face to face, I've a better chance of softening his wrath toward you. But Auriane, I want you in safety when I do it—in case I fail."

Something broke within her then, as if she'd struck a granite center within him. She accepted, then, that they would never come to agree on this matter. She lay trapped in the grief this brought, feeling herself a jug cracked against a wall, with its waters trickling out.

I must forge a way around him. I am a warrior again. What I plan, I plan alone.

She half heard him as he spoke on.

"I love you more than my life, and I abhor the thought of you fettered in any way. But cannot you see, that in this matter, you simply have no choice?"

"You are right," she said, wedging herself more comfortably against him. He entirely mistook her meaning—*You are right,* she meant, *I've no choice but to flee home. At the end of Avenahar's nine-day ceremony, I, too, will journey to the hall of my mother.* The fledgling decision hung there, bright with the strangeness of turning life upon its head, and leaden with sadness.

Chapter 14

This was the same summer's eve. In the small native village that served the Fortress of Mogontiacum was a rotting tavern built at the end of a dock that projected into the waters of the Rhenus. The whole structure leaned downstream, as if straining to go with the river's current. Within, two men met in the humid, dim-lit room at the back reserved for gamblers. One wore a traveller's *paenula* with its ample hood pulled forward, so none might know him. The other was the young man loyal to the assassinated Domitian, who so ardently sought vengeance upon Marcus Julianus.

The hooded man spoke first. "You're going on an aurochs hunt."

The young Aelianus, eyes watering from the smoke of cheap lamp oil, could not tell if this was an agent he'd encountered before. Though that voice—softly rasping, strangely calming—was familiar. The midnight hour was well behind them and Telethusa, the tavern's proprietress, ever careful with oil, had snuffed out every lamp but one. Some claimed this wasn't thrift, but to ensure that she couldn't see clearly all that went on within, so she could never be called before a magistrate as witness. Her tavern was a haunt for cutpurses and fugitive slaves as well as bargemen and sailors of the imperial fleet.

From behind a stand of wine jars on the brickwork serving-bar that divided the tavern's front room from this fetid back room, Telethusa watched them distrustfully as if they were slaves carrying a stack of her best dishware.

The young man knew she'd already guessed they were planning a murder.

He didn't need to ask which aurochs hunt. Everyone along the river knew of the great hunts staged by the Governor, Maximus—that grand game played out by the lords of the world as they vied with one another to win the laurel that fell to the noble hunter who made the fatal thrust into the beast. It was an event that employed hundreds of slaves and skilled natives from the local Celtic and Germanic settlements. Maximus's hunts always stimulated much gambling along the docks, as taverners laid wagers on which aristocratic hunter would bring the fearsome beast down. The young man even knew the aurochs they sought. The aurochs is a colossus among bulls, the most formidable known to naturalists, and this particular beast was a murderous rogue Maximus had hunted unsuccessfully ever since he took command of the Fortress. Its coat was of a color never before seen—a ghastly white. He'd heard that the soldiers of the frontier forts thought it could only be slain by a man half-god, such as Hercules was.

"This must be some jest," Aelianus replied to the hooded man while nervously running thick, ink-stained fingers through wiry, dark blond hair. "I've never hunted anything larger than boar."

"It doesn't matter. It's not the aurochs you'll be hunting."

"I'm a *clerk* by profession now. I look up soldiers' records. Not that I'm less a man for it, understand. That amphora there, by the door—I can hoist it with one hand. And I've finished off half a dozen worthless men no one needs to know about. But this is a beast that's slain twelve skilled hunters and thirty slaves. The Chattian savages won't even take it on. Believe me, I want the same thing you want. But with respect, I can think of a dozen other ways to get this task done, without putting myself in the path of horned death."

"Then let your betters think for you. Our man's got guards about him, always. We've got you to thank for that. This hunt will be the one time he won't. Now, listen well—this will be somewhat more difficult than setting an unguarded carriage afire before a crowd of stupefied country farmers. But we're wagering you've the mettle to carry it through."

The young man carefully disguised his amazement. He should have expected the agent would know about his botched attack on Julianus's carriage. These hooded men who came to him seemed to be able to tell him what he'd dined on a year ago on the fifth day of *Junius,* or when he'd last spit in a well.

The man-in-shadow made a curt gesture to Telethusa, commanding her to bring them another *sextarius* of her hot wine. Telethusa waited a good length of time before she moved away from the hot drink bar, disdain in the bold arch of her sharply downturned mouth. She was a woman of rambling proportions; masses of graying hair were scarce contained by a tightly tied Greek headband. Gold hoops suspended from her ears were adorned with a single pearl. She was a freedwoman who'd begun life in a Gaditan dancing troupe—the famous erotic dancers from Gades in Hispania—and she'd bought this tavern with her slave's savings. As the years thickened her in girth they'd added gravity to her dancer's grace. She approached at her own speed, with slow, proud rolls of her hips, to let them know she wasn't a servant. The young man was momentarily fascinated by her; she advanced upon them so complexly, like tentacles under water or cold honey ribboning thickly from a jar, while her hips shimmied faintly as if from the memory of the tremor of reed pipes, and the fringe on the hem of that close-cut tunica danced on its own to an opposing rhythm. He'd never bedded a Gaditan dancing girl, and he found himself wondering how much he'd have to shake out of his purse to make her shake that way just for him.

Telethusa set the clay wine jug down with a rude *thunk*—she was wearied of them and they were staying too late. A rat burst from the straw, startled by the impact, causing Aelianus to reflect that all the care the proprietress put into painting, plucking, and buffing her person must have diverted her energies from improving this pesthole.

The hooded agent caught Telethusa by the heavy gold chain that hung from her neck. For a prolonged moment he held her fast, by a golden leash. Slowly he twisted the chain, until it constricted her throat. The young man guessed Telethusa must have seen something brutally cold in the agent's eyes, for the proud proprietress's eyes began to fog with fear.

Somehow, the sight pleased him.

"There'll be no more of that," the hooded man said in a voice that was mother-soft. "We stay until we're through. No one else comes in."

She nodded faintly, and he released her. Then she ebbed away from them, controlling her fury as she retreated to her post. It was suddenly so quiet they could hear the soft, suctioning sounds of water lapping round the pilings of the docks. The young man's hand was stiff with tension as he produced a leather pouch and shook its contents into his battered silver travelling cup. He was adding his own purifying spices to the tavern's wine—cumin, fennel, and wormwood. In a stinking hole like this, who knew what might have died in the wine cask?

"Are you losing your courage, Casperius Aelianus?"

The agent lingered cruelly over his name. Hearing it spoken caused the young man to feel vulnerable as a clam prised from its shell. Officially, "Casperius Aelianus" was among the shades—that young man had drowned, executed in that horrific shipwreck at the advent of Trajan's reign. He still remembered the screams of his fellow condemned men as they died in a squall that blew up fiercely soon after their ship had been set adrift, as if in response to their imperial executioner's wishes. Their only crime, he'd often reflected, was dutifully carrying out the commands of the Emperor Domitian, as they were bound to do by oath. He'd been reborn as Attius Ferox, promising young man with powerful sponsors in Rome, recommended to the Governor at Mogontiacum for a good post at the Fortress's treasury offices, managing the monies deposited in the legionaries' compulsory savings bank. The young man born Casperius Aelianus, now Attius Ferox, was not certain whom these Palace agents served—these all-providing helpers who always seemed to appear just when he ran out of patrons, money, or luck—and he suspected that if he even asked, he risked death. He'd convinced himself they must issue from a reputed faction of the Praetorian Guard who still vowed in secret to avenge the assassination of Domitian.

"Losing my courage? Never," Aelianus answered him. "Not while I live on this earth . . . and Marcus Arrius Julianus lives on it, too."

The agent's voice was flat, cold, without a trace of grace, amusement, or pity. "We can get your fee doubled, if you're much troubled over danger from the bull."

"Triple it." A little blustering couldn't hurt his standing with these men.

The agent hesitated but a moment, then crisply replied, "You have it."

With that, the young man felt a door swing shut behind him. Before him was a maddened horned beast. Suddenly he'd no desire to finish the fried chickpea cake on its greasy tin plate.

"Here are the names of the men who'll take part in this year's hunt."

Swiftly, the hooded man recited ten noble names. "You're certain none of these men has ever seen your face?"

"I've told you, I was but a lad of fourteen when our great Lord Domitian was foully murdered. A man who's been in Hades long as I have changes greatly in aspect. Maximus didn't even recognize me—and he was a good friend of my father's."

"Julianus's informants have good descriptions of you," the agent said then, "so tomorrow we're sending a barber and an *ornatrix* to you, to fit you with false hair and darken your brows—"

"You speak of a *wig*? Like a woman's?"

"The most feared commander of all, Hannibal, didn't disdain to wear wigs to fool his would-be assassins, and you're hardly the man he was. Keep silent and listen. Two of Maximus's beast-handlers will be ours; they'll maneuver our man away from the party, and protect you from the animal. But you will have to get in close. Tomorrow you'll have your first meeting with your confederates. You're an excellent horseman, but you'll need to practice with the heavier hunting spear they use, and so on the morrow, you'll . . ."

An hour by the water-clock passed as the agent described precisely how it would be done. At the last, young Aelianus, now Attius Ferox, found a moment to voice the objection that had troubled him from the first. "I lust to do this thing. But how do we get our man out there? He doesn't hunt. Marcus Julianus despises the hunt."

"He does, this time. This will be his first hunt, and his last."

"EVERYTHING'S WRONG, ISN'T it? Is it something I've done?"

The question was Arria Juliana's. It was night. Auriane knelt before her by the brickwork arch of the great hearth in the villa's kitchens; the girl's solemn face, round as a moon poised in darkness, was tinted red-gold from the glow of the still-glimmering charcoal fire.

"No, of course not!" Auriane replied. "We're going on a journey, that's all. Father, a shorter journey. Myself and your sister . . . a longer journey. Philomela stays here with you, of course." Philomela was Arria's aged Greek nurse. "All will be well." Impulsively she pulled Arria close, holding to her daughter with a fervor meant to imprint love so deeply the child would know it well even when her mother was gone. And stop the spreading bleakness she felt inside. Then Auriane broke away, realizing how strongly she was conveying her desperation.

"A long journey." Arria repeated her mother's words without judgment, which sharpened Auriane's despair. Arria's eyes were trusting vessels, awaiting what Auriane put into them. In that moment Auriane thought battle simpler to face than her daughter's lucid, softly engulfing eyes.

"I said long*er*, not *long,*" Auriane corrected. "I'll be back . . . soon." The lie had an acrid taste, but the dictates of a mother's kindness demanded it. She felt the words might not have been spoken, for all the effect they had on Arria. The lie dissolved immediately in those great, round seer's eyes.

"Arria, I have some things I must tell you. I do face dangers, though I expect to overcome them. And you know, Arria, the Fates never tell us everything, and so, we must think of what would happen . . . if I didn't. Just to *think* of it, mind you. So I must tell you some marriage-things, even though you'll not need to know them for six years or more to come."

"You have chosen a man for me."

"Yes. But only with your blessing. And it doesn't mean you can't choose someone else, when you're old enough to know about that. But Father will help you there, so don't worry over it now. Here is his portrait." She gave to Arria a portrait of a boy, small enough to cup in the hand, painted with delicate detail in tempera on wood. "He's studious, and in good health, and he has his honorable career all plotted out for him. He's sixteen now, so he's not terribly much older than you. He is the youngest son of the brother of Cornelius Palma, who a few years ago served as coruler with the Emperor—"

"*Consul,* mother," she said, as the raw delight of a child handed a fine present came into her eyes. "And his father's a man who's great, among the Emperor's friends. He's the one *I* chose."

Auriane felt a rush of relief. "Keep his picture near your breast and it will cause love to develop. But if love doesn't grow, or if it turns out, in time, that we . . . made a mistake, know this: It's the way of Marcus's people that another choice can be made for you, even after the horn's been shared, the oaths given, and the bridal rite complete, so don't worry—"

"*Divorce.* And we don't share horns. You've forgotten, Mother, you've told me about all this."

"Of course," Auriane said, privately amused for one quick instant by Arria's confidence in these matters. "But as I said, it's a long way off, and Father will be here. But I thought it right that, as your mother, I be the one to give you his picture. Now, come with me. There's something else that's very important."

Auriane got a sulphur match from her belt and lit a terra-cotta hand lamp. A cook's boy pulled back a door for them. Auriane led Arria across a stone walkway to the herb storeroom, just outside the kitchens. Arria walked beside her, grim and upright, taking large, firm steps, feeling important because her mother was telling her important things, which in turn helped her accept all this with courage. Within the pungent dark of the storeroom, Auriane took from a high shelf a tightly sealed, green glass jar filled with seeds, and a corked glass phial that contained a dark sap.

"These are seeds of the rue plant, which can be found almost anywhere. And this is Cyrenaic juice from the silphium plant, which is found almost nowhere. It grows in a faraway hot place, and it's very costly, with good reason—there's little of it left in the world. But a good herbmistress can usually get it for you, if you pay her handsomely enough."

The girl seemed lulled into a trance by the sound of her mother's words. *She's listening with her whole spirit*, Auriane thought. *She hears the dread in my voice*.

"These plants have the power to keep you from bearing. This is very important, Arria. After the blood-of-life comes, if ever you don't wish a babe to grow in you, you take a chick pea–sized dose of this," she said, indicating the Cyrenaic juice, "and a pinch of rue seeds, early in your moon. You choose the time to bear. You are no one's servant. Do you understand?"

Arria nodded solemnly.

"The next thing I must tell you is this. Even though I know you think little of my people, I want you to remember this: You spring from warriors. Your grandfather is Baldemar, greatest of them all, who kept his people free for a generation. Your mother was one, too—she couldn't keep her people free anymore, but she *did* win vengeance in single battle against Odberht, the enemy who betrayed us and led an army against our back. And so, you, too, are a warrior, even if you never lift a weapon, which I don't suppose you will! . . . But know, Arria, you have that fire in you."

Arria gave her mother another solemn, slow nod.

"Be kind to the weak. Let none steal your honor. And remember, nothing is ever as it first seems. And that life is never done. And that your mother is with you always."

"You must be going far," Arria mumbled, looking at the floor. Auriane lifted her easily—she was so fine-made and small, yet strong—and settled the child into her lap.

"Not far. And not for long," she whispered through a throat thick with sadness. *Fria, let it be the truth*. "I love you more than my life, Arria."

* * *

JULIANUS'S FLEET OF four *redas* moved at a fast trot over the post road, through a brooding morning tense with withheld rain. Auriane pressed close against him, feeling a thorn was embedded in her heart as she struggled to raise up an indwelling strength, as on any battle's dawn.

At the Fortress of Mogontiacum, Julianus would remain, to be a party to the treaties being made, and to the interrogation of Ramis; from there, Auriane and Avenahar would journey on alone. In a *reda* bearing the Governor's emblem, accompanied by an escort of four cavalrymen, mother and daughter would pass through the Empire's northern gate, and then, as far as the roads were passable, on to the Holy Wood. Maximus had provided Auriane and Avenahar with false documents identifying them as Gallic natives, mother and daughter, given leave to travel to a marriage.

It could not be that Julianus had made one plan, and she, another. The more she thought on her sad stratagem, the more firmly she pressed against him. The opposing thoughts—*What have I wrought?* and *But how could I have done otherwise?*—swung to and fro in her like a slow bell clapper ringing tidings of doom. *What I plan is not only against your wish, Marcus; it's against my own. I want only for our life to be what it was—an idyll by a river.*

She felt herself a voyager into nowhere.

Avenahar managed somehow to sleep among the cushions and coverlets spread about on the carriage's floor, despite the fact that the *reda* shook them like grain in a winnowing pan. *The deep peace of the young,* Auriane marveled. *And what's to become of that peace when, on the last day of the ceremony, my overproud daughter hears Decius named as her father?*

Through these thoughts she saw again, with needling clarity, Victorinus's moist mouth, his eyes fogged with carnal passion, on that day in the basilica. "We'll send Arria off soon," she said tensely, once, to Marcus, "to have speech with her groom?"

"As soon as next year's thaw allows travel to Rome," came Marcus's distracted reply; he was studying copies of every agreement ever struck between Rome and the Chattians.

"I feel dangers closing about you, coming with the black creep of a tide at night. Why do you not ask the Emperor's protection in the matter of this young fanatic who loves Domitian?"

"Someone powerful is helping that young fanatic get about. It intrigues me. First, I would learn *who.* You trouble yourself needlessly. Trajan does not carry out secret crimes, nor does he ruin men clandestinely. If he's displeased, you know it in clear terms, and at once. You must not worry over me." He turned to her then, sensing something dark in her silence, and with passionate sadness, enclosed her hands in his. "You must not suffer so. Your leaving won't be forever."

She averted her gaze to look into the shadowed green redoubts of the passing forest, veiling her plan, certain it was brazenly visible in her eyes.

Chapter 15

Auriane and Avenahar trailed the procession of women and girls as they climbed a rock-strewn path up a nameless summit. Gray-robed elderwomen led the way. The late afternoon sun bathed them in amber light. Warm earth cupped their bare feet. They meant to gain the Holy Wood by dusk; then, the nine-night-long ceremony would begin. All the tribes of Germania favored night over day for the convening of sacred assemblies; in childhood, Auriane was told this was because, "Night came first; day was created."

Gunora, most senior of the elderwomen, strode forcefully at the head of the file, her knotted staff striking out at the slope like some stiff third leg, her weighty gray braid swinging grandly from side to side. She was bulky as a bear in her dress of calfskin hides. Her broad, seamed face was bound in fierce quiet; those slitted eyes emitted a peace deep and trackless as the forest. Gunora's kinswomen vigorously kept pace, despite the fact that each had more winters behind than ahead of her. Their strong faces spoke of rites most of the folk had forgotten. They numbered eight; Auriane, climbing alongside them, would complete the circle of nine. The elderwomen carried out a role that was dying among the people: that of Grandmother, who ed-ucated girls. At other times, they raised root vegetables and emmer wheat in the holy fields within Ramis's summer sanctuary. *These women are trees,* Auri-ane thought; *they live from season to season, gripping to the old ways with roots so deep, they surely break into Hel's caverns. The maids they teach are the supple fast-growing branches, who must learn that they pull their life-spirit from what is an-cient, below.*

Behind the elderwomen came the three maids: Avenahar, Ivalde, Hildigun.

Avenahar was attacking the hillside with strong, young strides, and Auri-ane thought her daughter looked fine, noble, and determined in the brick-red cloak she had woven for the ceremony. Ivalde, born in the small settlement below, was a girl with pleading eyes, pale hair, and paler skin, an indrawn creature of twelve summers who always knew when a calf would be born. Hildigun was the daughter of a celebrated seeress, who, like Avenahar, had been fostered for a time at Ramis's sanctuary; she was a girl large for her age, heavy of bone, with handsome, masculine features, and, Auriane saw, an in-trusive way of pretending to know what she did not. These maids would be initiated by the Old Ceremony, passed down from the Time of Peace and Wandering, an age only Ramis's women remembered, when it was said "the spear was sharpened only for the boar." The Old Ceremony bore more re-semblance to the rites of initiation into the order of village priestesses than to the common womanhood rites of the Chattian tribe, in which a maid dis-played skills at brewing and working the loom, her readiness for marriage and bearing children. It was claimed that this was because, in the Time of Peace and Wandering, becoming a woman was not so unlike becoming a priestess. Its purposes were to test oracular powers and strength of mind, and to open a way to the knowings that would come with greater age.

Auriane realized they were being followed. One lithe, long-maned man, then another, limbs naked but for heavy, gray battle cloaks, tracked the party at a measured distance—Chattian warriors moving smoothly as foxes, threading in and out of sight. She caught up with Gunora to ask why. "Yes. I asked them," was Gunora's cryptic response. "They stand watch." *Stand watch?* Auriane wondered. *At a womanhood ceremony in peaceful country, within shouting distance of my cavalry escort camped outside the village below?*

They came to a high place; the Holy Wood lay at the bottom of a great bowl formed by a ring of hills. Auriane halted, absorbing her first sentinel's view of her lands. The lean profile of the long, quiet hill enclosing the valley had the smooth elegance of bone; beyond, the heaving gray-green ocean of forest swelled and dipped like music, falling back until it dissolved into gold-fired haze. Fertile tranquillity lay over all like a mist. She felt she'd outdistanced the separateness, the sadness, of cities. For all its vastness her forest home was a house, and the family it housed, small.

Her body stiffened as she saw something on a far hill, flaring brighter than the haze; from it issued a furiously roiling coil of smoke, dark as a scream. "Gunora," she said in a low voice. "Something's afire. That's a burning settlement."

Gunora squinted, and shrugged. "I see nothing but clouds and sun."

As Auriane continued to stare, whatever it was flashed off like light-spectres playing on a lake. *I must have been mistaken.*

Gunora frowned, lost in calculation. She seized Auriane by the arm. "Auriane. There *is* something there—but you couldn't have seen it, it's too far off. Where you pointed, if you journeyed straight for perhaps three days—that's where Chariomer the Cheruscan is camped."

Auriane fell into an iron-bound silence, feeling swollen with sorrow for them all. *Chariomer. I destroyed the life I loved to stop you, and still you taunt me with your coming. How I loathe what I've done.*

Gunora was still watching Auriane with guarded amazement as the party dropped into the steep descent. Their downward progress hastened the fall of the sun. It was as though they dropped into a cauldron that swiftly filled with night, a fertile bowl where all would be stirred into something new and unknown. For succor Auriane found herself watching Avenahar, who was galloping down the hill with huge, exuberant bounds. *Her bright hopefulness is the only balm,* Auriane thought, *for the stifled hopes I carry inside. Was that ever the way, with a daughter?*

The Holy Wood closed over them. It was a grove of old beeches that hid in its most secret places a cave, a pool, a hallowed stone. A chill wind flowed through the sky-reaching branches—a river on high, composed of familiar souls. A soundless flutter of yellow leaves drifted down on dwindling shafts of light, and she felt it was a greeting. Gray-violet shadows were sprinkled with the blood-red leaves of wild cherry. The air was humid, welcoming, and rich with the sweet, fungal aroma of many layers of moldering leaves over yielding loam. Mud oozed beneath their bare feet, as if the tender ground were bruised and bleeding. The place was beautiful but haunted. Inviting, but strange. Scattered here and there were looming clusters of outsized mushrooms that had sprung high after last night's rain, tiny ghosts frozen in silent shouts of surprise, their pale caps like miniature skulls. Fragrances of death and fertility were richly mingled in the ground's perfume. Elven presences skulked shyly in the somber places. Sad Ancestresses' woody faces peered down from the high branches. Affixed on a beech trunk was the moss-mottled skull of a mountain cat, peering down on them from eternity—the spirit animal of the Chattian tribe, standing watch forever.

And looking on, above, emitting its swift-gathering power, was the crisp, white-gold sliver of a new moon, nine days off full.

Moving quickly to take advantage of the last of the light, the elderwomen began dragging the timber and brush that had been chopped and stacked earlier. First they built a bonfire. Each wood had been chosen for its particular power: The smoke of birch aided birth, and all that grew swiftly. Oak gave strength. Pine, long life. Gunora kindled it in the ancient way, by vigorously rubbing woods from a fire-tree that grew in Ramis's sanctuary. She called it the Middle Fire and proclaimed that it would not go out for nine nights.

In a ring about the fire, they constructed nine rough shelters of interlaced beechwood branches. The maids built their own brushwood huts, outside this circle. The three initiates were instructed not to speak. Another of the elderwomen, Walberga, a gaunt-faced woman who moved about in stately silence, kindled a smaller fire beyond the circle of brushwood shelters. Over it she set a tripod, from which she suspended a bronze cauldron. Auriane helped her haul water from the spring that fed the pool, then watched as Walberga prepared a soup that would last through the nine nights. Walberga put in leeks, onions, turnips, dried venison, and thirteen grains, as well as herbs with the power to lure guardian spirits. Auriane saw she also put in secret things—the vertebrae of a wolf, stones inscribed with helpful signs. The soup would get richer and stronger, through the days. Outside the circle of huts, Walberga set up a stout post carved with avertive runes, to keep at bay harmful spirits loose in the forest.

The sun was snuffed out behind the fringe of firs that rimmed the wood. Night came with enthusiasm. A fragrant, twisting rope of steam connected the cauldron to the sable-black, star-dusted sky.

Late in the eve, after Gunora had performed the opening sacrifice and sent the three maids to sit out before the pool, the nine women sat about the fire, passing a mead horn and telling stories. As the talk began to drift down,

Auriane leaned close to Gunora and confessed her fear of the ceremony's last day, when Avenahar would hear Decius named as her father.

Gunora's response gave her no comfort.

"It will bring her sorrow," the elderwoman responded bluntly. "She must know her sorrows. That is why she is here."

Auriane asked again about the warriors who had been posted as guardians.

"They are for you." Firelight cast harsh shadows on Gunora's dour face; she looked like an angry old man. She frowned more deeply. "You do not know?"

"Whatever scraps of news I get of our people come rarely, and late."

"Just over one moon past, Chariomer declared vengeance on you. His four hundred companions did likewise. He knows you're here. It's not impossible they might send a lone adventurer to this place, to do the deed and take the glory."

There was little room in Auriane just then for the full measure of horror this might have brought; she felt only a great, debilitating resignation. This was, after all, to be expected. Her long-ago act of vengeance stalked her like a wolf.

"I wonder only that Chariomer waited so long," Auriane said at last.

"He's no true warrior, just a small and ruthless man. He needed to be goaded."

"I must get Avenahar away from here—it's not safe for her, either."

"She's being well looked after. Those men keeping watch are warriors of the companions of young Sigibert, son of Sigwulf who followed your father, Baldemar. They are devoted to you. They carry no weapons, because Rome is so close. But they're adept at killing with whatever they find on the ground."

"Who goaded Chariomer, after so long?"

Gunora leaned closer, and said in a covered voice, "None know *this* part but you and I—and I just learned it myself. The seeress Sawitha's behind it all. She seduced Chariomer's daughter, Elza, into her camp, and got Elza to play the part of goader. Sawitha wants you dead, Auriane—I suppose it's to be expected. She lusts to carry Ramis's staff. Sawitha's fear of you is a measure of your power." Gunora dropped her voice still more, and Auriane had to grope for her words. "A power I saw today, I must tell you. Up there on the hill, Auriane—you had a vision in day. That is rare. And to my mind, your gift's a particular one—you see what threatens the land."

Auriane found this too much to consider, just then. "It's all such monstrous madness," she whispered. "No one wants Ramis's staff less than I do."

"It's no matter of your *wanting*. The path to Ramis was set for you at birth."

"There are quite a few who don't agree, Gunora. I've violated more sacred laws than there are trees in this grove, and I've every intention of violating a few more. I don't suppose it would help matters if I just sent Sawitha a message, telling her she can *have* the cursed office. I've no wish to sit where Ramis sits."

"That's not the way of things. Ramis chooses. Not you. Not I. Ramis and the Fates. I was sent a dream of you, Auriane, right before you came. I saw nine fires. These were for the nine years you have wandered in a foreign land. For this year, there was no fire. On this year, you either die, or return to us."

AVENAHAR, IVALDE, AND Hildigun sat on freshly flayed cowhides, before the pool. Its surface was a mystery in the starlight, black and still as well water. They had been commanded to keep their gazes fixed upon it throughout the night.

The maids had been ordered to fast for a day, and by now, hunger was a claw digging into Avenahar's stomach. She knew she must put her whole spirit into a mighty effort to do well, if she was to do honor to her mother. The thought goaded her, again and again: *And when your mother's more than mortal, this requires more-than-mortal effort.* She stared searchingly into the rustling darkness, but no marvelous knowings came—she saw only the ungiving night. The pool was a bald, unblinking eye, mocking her, telling her nothing. She knew no moments of grace, only the stiffness brought by the ever on-stretching time of sitting, as she became more cold, more hungry, more wet. A panicked sadness began to settle over her: More than this was expected of Auriane's daughter. As the long night progressed, Avenahar became near certain that the black and fathomless pool harbored monsters. She resolved to sit still and be eaten by them, if necessary. She could not disgrace herself, or her mother. . . .

Avenahar had arrived in this place with a victor's confidence, but by nightfall she felt chastened and small. The elderwomen seemed to reserve their most damning glares for her. She thought she'd acquitted herself adequately through the opening rites. But during the spells for protection, she'd been reluctant to taste the wolf's blood. The other maids were accustomed to such things; she was not. Gunora had become so indignant over this, Avenahar feared she'd be banished from the rites. And once, she'd overheard Hildigun refer to her as "that coddled villa whelp," uttered with such contempt that Avenahar felt a bolt of shame for the warm floors on which she'd walked, the marble-encased ease in which she'd grown to womanhood. Ivalde and Hildigun knew all the living, changing tales being passed about the Chattian villages. The tales Avenahar knew were mummified fragments preserved in bookrolls. And both her fellow initiates had exhibited marked gifts for divining. Avenahar was beginning to believe her own spirit-eye was blind.

And once, after surprising Hildigun in close conversation with Ivalde, Avenahar thought she'd heard herself called the "child of a Roman slave." This she found both horrifying and peculiar, and she concluded, finally, she must have misheard Hildigun's words.

Dawn poured into this low place, rendering the pool harmless again. Avenahar felt a wash of relief; now it was just an outsized coin, round, flat, and metallic, as it reflected a cold, iron sky. Soon after first light, an elderwoman who had just returned from the village with more provisions dropped a loaf of freshly baked bread on the path behind the girls, not more than ten steps from their sitting-out place. All three could smell it; to the fasting maids, the moist aroma was seductive as a Nix's song. Avenahar shut her eyes; with excruciating clarity, she tasted its comforting, nutty softness.

No one was about. Avenahar heard Ivalde stirring from her place. With the stealth of a squirrel Ivalde edged toward the bread and seized it. She first offered some to Avenahar and Hildigun. After both silently refused it, Ivalde bit into it like a beast and devoured the whole loaf herself. When Gunora returned to lead them back to the fire, Hildigun told the elderwoman of Ivalde's disobedience.

Avenahar was surprised by Gunora's response. "You have broken silence," Gunora interrupted Hildigun, iron in her voice. When a flustered Hildigun protested that Gunora had just told them they could speak, Gunora said, "No. You have broken a greater silence." Abruptly, she walked away. Avenahar noted carefully that Gunora seemed far more displeased with Hildigun, so quick to betray another's weakness, than she was with Ivalde, who had succumbed to hunger. Avenahar knew, then, they were not being tested in an ordinary way. She began to suspect the bread had been dropped near them purposefully.

Soon after, as they trod the path back to the fire, Gunora saw the glint of a bronze medallion Avenahar was wearing, which she'd bartered for in the village beyond the hill, to the dismay of her mother. It depicted the head of a wolf; the villagers claimed it had fallen from the harness of Witgern's horse.

"You must not wear that in this place," Gunora told her, after holding it close to examine it. "It carries the taint of killing."

"It carries the taint of freedom," Avenahar said, facing Gunora with a proud, quiet lift of her head. "In all the world, only Witgern fights for us. I won't take it off."

For tense moments, Avenahar gamely resisted the elderwoman's baleful glare. Gunora had a face like a balled fist, blunt and pugnacious. Her worst damning looks would be good for igniting tinder, Avenahar thought. At the last, it was as though Gunora's gaze had greater muscular strength; Avenahar felt she'd been mentally thrown to the ground. With an angry flourish, Avenahar removed the medallion, then strode off to bury it beneath a tree for later retrieval.

She didn't know Gunora was pleased with her and was smiling privately at her back.

Ah, yes, the fire is there, Gunora was thinking. *But because she doesn't know where to direct it, it burns out.*

The nights and days turned, and more tests and teachings were given. They were taught the proper prayers to utter while lighting a hearthfire. They were shown how to summon the Ancestresses, and the rudiments of reading their will in fluttering leaves. They heard tales of the deeds of the great seeresses. One day, they were sent into the forest to hunt for the Nine Herbs, then asked to explain the nature of the goddess or god sovereign over each. Avenahar knew the Nine Herbs from her mother's lessons, but because she did not have a close knowledge of this land, she was last to find them. So it was with every task given; she walked many steps behind her two sisters.

I dishonor my mother and I disgrace myself. The thought came more strongly with each day. *How could I ever have thought myself worthy to live the grand and illustrious life she lived?*

The soup got richer. The moon swelled. The Middle Fire roared.

* * *

FOR AURIANE, THE time was a prayer offered to the Ancestresses. Through the days, she strove with all her mind to give strength to Avenahar. But at night, in the solitude of her leafy shelter, she felt a cold so great it burned, as if she had been cast naked onto a snowbank. She'd not passed many nights sleeping singly, these last seven years. She fought and failed to conjure the presence of Marcus, pressed close, warm as a noontide sun. She felt she'd bedded down in a stone sarcophagus as words she wanted to say to him in the night echoed hollowly back to her. In the intelligent dark of the forest night, both alternatives—yielding to his plan or following her own— were the same: brutal, grotesque, impossible. She knew, then, that she and Marcus had grown together like old vines, with branches fused and all their fine tendrils intricately interwoven.

On the sixth day of the ceremony, a rider came from the village of the Boar—her mother's village—bearing the response Auriane had been await-ing from her mother, Athelinda. The message the boy spoke was stark and bare, but Auriane clearly heard questing and longing in the empty spaces be-tween her mother's words:

"I am well if you are well. Yes, both come. Do not take the West Forest track. Dangers await that you do not know. Come by the rivers. Stay in the deep forest. Do not come to the Hall; I am being watched. When you arrive, don't despair at what you see; all is not lost, we have helpers in the forest. We look over the fields with gladness because you return."

ON THE SEVENTH day, Avenahar, Ivalde, and Hildigun were dressed in the skins of boars, and taken at dusk to the low cave that overlooked the pool. There they would sit through the night within the living darkness of this earthen temple. Before Gunora left them, she offered to each girl a horn brimming with a drink she called the "mead of remembering." Gunora told them she had called up the great Boar Spirit; the maids were to ride the Boar down to the realms below. Avenahar felt a gathering unease as they were told that ancestors so distant as to have no names would come to have speech with them. The three were to remember what visions might come of a future life, so they could tell the elderwomen and seek their advice.

The maids found their places in the cave and settled onto their cowhides, positioned too far apart to draw comfort from one another's presence. As night shadows edged toward the cave's mouth, eager to join with the greater blackness within the cave, each maid faced that encroaching tide alone.

When the sun abandoned them and they were engulfed, Avenahar fought panic. Damp cave walls pressed close. She felt she was wedged at the bottom of a well. Scaled hands would reach out and pull her into a clammy embrace.

And what was happening *behind* them? The back of the cave was horribly alive. Avenahar broke into a light sweat. Caves harbored bottomless shafts to the world below; all manner of unholy things might seep up through rocky crevices.

Ivalde's occasional muffled whimpers further fed Avenahar's terrors.

When Avenahar finally discerned fragile starlight filtering in through the mouth of the cave, her mind reached for it and clung to that pale light, as if to the hand of a rescuer.

Then she heard a furtive crackling sound, just outside the cave.

What night-creature crept close? Some gnome formed of living rock, coming to punish them for driving him out of his cave?

Or was it something without the sense to be furtive, something . . . *dead*? The walking dead were abundant in these woodland places, far from the protective rites regularly performed in the villages.

Her breathing became shallower; she drew in her shoulders in an instinctive attempt to conceal herself. She was seated closest to the cave's mouth; the thing out there wasn't more than ten steps off from her.

She heard the crackle of another cautious step; then whatever it was, man or ghoul, halted again.

A tear of fright came. This was too much to bear.

"Avenahar."

A ghoul that knew her name?

A ghastly shape was silhouetted against the stars—a head that seemed to sprout snakes. The man-thing lurched toward her.

Avenahar shrieked.

Chaos descended. From above came barking shouts from the warriors positioned on the ridge as they spilled down toward the cave. From very close came the snapping, crashing sounds of someone making a sloppy retreat. Light jerked crazily through trees as elderwomen bearing torches hurried to the cave.

Then Gunora and Walberga were there, and, Avenahar was most relieved to see, her mother. After Avenahar had told it all, Gunora asked, "You're certain it was not a night vision?"

"It was a man. I could smell him, he reeked of horsehides and rot. He knew my name! He was right *there—*"

While the elderwomen questioned her and comforted her, the warriors from Sigibert's band searched about in the dark outside the cave. They found nothing. For the rest of the night, the warrior-sentinels took places closer to the cave. Avenahar returned to her cowhide, and the maids were left again in darkness. Avenahar's mind was in ferment. What had he wanted of her?

And no sooner were they alone than Avenahar heard Hildigun's low, husky laugh. Evidently the older girl thought Avenahar betrayed weakness by crying out. Avenahar felt a flash of wrath but kept silent. She had not thought any sort of laurel was to be won in a womanhood ceremony, but Hildigun apparently did—and Hildigun seemed certain that laurel would fall to her.

I'll not cry out again, no matter what I see. She was determined to be at home in the night. It felt like a physical effort. "Night was first mother of the world," she told herself, imagining Auriane would be proud of her for thinking that. After a time, Avenahar realized these thoughts were busying her, but bringing her no peace. A deep, dragging hopelessness settled over her as she stared out miserably into darkness. The night expanded to a month, then shrank to a moment, while she waited with growing impatience for a vision of future days that refused to come.

Maybe I have no future days, she thought as she stared at all that taunting, visionless blackness. *The spirits of this land do not want me.*

I've no right to be here.

Perhaps Auriane isn't even my true mother.

For comfort, she found herself fumbling in her tunic for the amulet of earth that Auriane had passed on to her. She held tightly to the smooth, well-worn pouch of leather that had known the touch of Ramis herself.

She gave a small gasp of amazement. It felt warm. Surely her fevered senses deceived her.

But that warmth lent her the steadiness to try a method of contemplation her mother had taught her, which Auriane had learned from the great prophetess. It was called the Ritual of Fire; it was a way of banishing all word-knowledge through envisioning fire, and becoming pure, empty memory. Avenahar's first attempts were unsteady, but gradually, they gained momentum. Her strenuous imaginings conjured frail flames, pale but definite—they had their own life.

Something gently collapsed in her mind. Common words had no meaning. Enemy . . . tribe . . . cave . . . stars . . . the names of things were noises. It was terrifying in a way Avenahar could not have described, like losing a horizon line that ran, not just from sea to sea, but through every thought birthed by the mind. But she didn't struggle against it. After a time, she felt soundless rhythms coiling up from deep in the earth, then passing through her body; she'd been taken up into a great, thumping heart. She was seized with a rapture of the mind that was keen and extravagant and full of hope. Now she had no fear of somber places; she *was* the dark. She was turning and diving in the pool below. She beat long wings and glided low over night-drenched hills. The cave, the rocks, the shadowed trees emitted a furry ghostlight that beckoned her to a home she'd forgotten.

After an unknown stretch of time, Avenahar began to realize there *was* a fire. Out there, before the cave.

Avenahar felt its heat.

She distinctly heard a log shift. And smelled the rich, sweetly astringent, cleansing smell of burning pine.

Had she tumbled into the world of the dead? Was this just some powerful dream?

No. Her eyes were watering.

Why did Ivalde and Hildigun not see it? Were they asleep? She opened her mouth to speak to them, but found herself mute as a beast.

Gradually, she discerned elongated shadows moving round that fire. Oddly, she felt no fear. Slowly, the forms solidified into women, surging gracefully around the fire, swaying, dancing. Two wore masks—the gold-plated head of a sow, a falcon's head. They took brazen, ground-eating steps, moving with a wild assurance close to recklessness; they shouldered the world aside as they lunged and spun. It suggested a nature that could be war-like as easily as gentle. It was also full of a marked carnal joy—as though the women were coupling with the air. There was something deeply foreign about the way these women moved, and this alone gave Avenahar an instinctive sense of the reality of what she saw: She couldn't have invented what she had never before seen. Compared to these women, the women she'd known in the province moved in ways that were cramped, muted, restrained, ashamed.

As she saw them more clearly, Avenahar began to believe these were foreign women, possibly from a hot place. Their clothing was odd. It didn't cover them well; they were as exposed as Syrian dancing girls, naked but for shell necklets, and skirts such as she had never seen—they fell only to the knees and were fashioned of dangling ropes. At the bottom of each cord was a knot weighted with fittings of gold; these caught the firelight, clicking together to create a rippling rhythm. Their rope skirts swung with authority, showing the women's nether parts as they danced. Those skirts looked dangerous. All at once Avenahar understood that these women were not foreign at all—at least, not to this place. They were only foreign to this time. They had lived here, in this Holy Wood, not tens, not hundreds, but *thousands* of seasons ago.

She counted them. *Nine.*

She felt a veiled presence behind them, powerful, beneficent, watching like the moon. Avenahar felt it was somehow Ramis, but not Ramis; the source of her power, perhaps.

The unknown presence seemed to put words directly into her mind: *We are here, we have always been here. We weave in and out of the world.*

The fire vanished. Avenahar was aware once more of the cave, of extravagant warmth shedding from her body, of a sense of security, of stableness so encompassing she would not have feared being cast from a cliff onto sharp rocks. Ivalde had ceased her muffled whimpering, and Avenahar sensed her vision had somehow nourished Ivalde as well.

When the elderwomen came to fetch them in the morning, Avenahar emerged from the cave feeling tender and raw as a newborn freshly pulled into a waiting world. All returned to the Middle Fire. The maids took their places before the elderwomen.

As the memory of what she had seen began to settle more firmly into her mind, Avenahar found she wanted to push it away. She listened warily as Hildigun and Ivalde described their visions: a stag that spoke in human voice, a shining village in the sky. Avenahar was certain there was something peculiar about her own vision, an unacceptable strangeness that somehow spoke of a strangeness nestled at the core of herself.

She looked tensely from one face to another as the elderwomen waited for her to speak.

"Avenahar, whatever it was," Auriane prompted her gently, "it's not *yours*. It comes from gods."

Avenahar's tale came out all at once. She described her rapture, the shining sow's mask, the golden life pouring out from the dance. She told of the tall, veiled presence behind them. She lingered long over attempts to describe those powerful rope skirts that clicked and swayed.

The women were deeply silent. Gunora seemed to have fallen in a trance of amazement, her downturned mouth half opened. Walberga's eyes shone; a tear began to course down one age-mottled cheek.

Avenahar began to wonder if she had gravely displeased them in some way.

"You saw them," Gunora said at last.

Avenahar did not understand. But she guessed from Auriane's face that her mother was beginning to grasp it.

"The first nine sisters, from *aeons* ago," Gunora said, "from the Time of Peace and Wandering."

"You saw how very old we are," Walberga added. "You saw that which we work to preserve and keep holy, that which is in danger of being lost."

Gunora turned to Auriane. "I've never known a maid to see them."

"I've scarce known one who is adept to see them," added another of the elderwomen.

Avenahar looked on in mild amazement as the elderwomen gathered round her mother and conferred in low voices. The three maids grew restless sitting before the fire, while the elderwomen's barely audible talk continued on. Once, Walberga's voice rose above the others to say, "Ramis must be told. You cannot deny any longer, Auriane, what lives in your line." When the conclave came to a close, the elderwomen ordered the maids to return to their shelters.

In spite of how unsettled her mother seemed, Avenahar felt she'd been given a crown. She wore it in light-headed ignorance, for she scarce knew what to deduce from all this. She cared only that she was a despised outsider no longer.

But as she made her way to her small brushwood hut, she passed Hildigun and Ivalde huddled in close talk that died off abruptly at her approach. Hildigun turned about and challengingly met Avenahar's gaze, that handsome, stubborn face communicating some unfocused threat.

Avenahar sensed envy turned to poison, for the admiring attention her vision had brought her.

A SHORT TIME afterward, Auriane returned to the cave to examine in day-light the place where the intruder had approached her daughter.

She found crushed grasses, and a man's sandal-print in the mud. Her daughter had spoken the truth.

And there, sun-bright on the ground, was a golden brooch so unweath-ered it seemed brought forth by magic; indeed, it was as polished as if just filched from a wealthy matron's jewel casket. It was of ring-form design; a pair of serpents' heads with sapphire eyes completed the circle. Where the pin was fastened it was inset with an extravagant pearl. Certainly, the intruder dropped it in his flight. The fibula had a fine, sharp point, but it hardly seemed a likely choice for a weapon. Auriane showed it to Gunora, who was equally baffled.

"I'll set a watch there," Gunora said. "That bauble's worth a year's harvest. Whoever lost that thing may return for it."

As AURIANE ROUSED herself from sleep on the rite's ninth and final day, she felt bowed beneath a load of dread, before she remembered why.

The day of the naming of ancestors.

The day my newly proud daughter hears the name of the hated foreigner who fathered her.

Gunora had sent the three maids off to wash themselves in the pool. In preparation for the culmination of the ceremony, Auriane and the elderwomen began dragging more pine logs to the Middle Fire.

While the women were decking the low branches of the trees with flowering wreaths, very near in the forest, they heard men's staccato laughter and animated jests.

Two young Chattian warriors burst through the underbrush, grinning triumphantly. Red-blond hair fell in tangled masses to shoulders draped in marten-skin cloaks; beaten silver rings glinted on scarred, muscle-roped arms. Their sentinels, Auriane realized. Between them, they dragged an unhappy-looking man with the chubby face of an infant and hair that sprouted from his head in oily serpent-coils.

The elderwomen gaped.

One man called out gaily, "This is what returned for your golden bauble! He looks harmless enough. Unless he's got a lady's hairpin stashed on him somewhere."

"What shall we do with him, Gunora?" the bristle-bearded one cried out. "Nail him to a tree with golden nails, since he likes gold so much?" They pushed the quivering man to the ground at Gunora's feet.

Auriane and Gunora helped him to stand, brushed him off, then sat him before the fire and began to put questions to him.

"An *assassin*?" the befuddled-looking fellow said, shaking his head so emphatically the serpent-coils swung about. "I don't even own a dagger. I'm a Ubian junk dealer. My name's Iarbas; ask any dozen traders who travel the West Forest road, they all know me. I only wanted to—"

"I should curse you with death for intruding on a maid in her silence," Gunora said. "You polluted the rites."

Auriane saw the man had tied dried mugwort round his ankles, a remedy for tired feet commonly used by far-travellers, and she gave a faint nod to Gunora, signing that she thought the man was telling the truth.

"I meant no harm! I only wanted words with Avenahar—I've a dire message for her, to give her mother, and I've got a—"

"This is Auriane," Gunora broke in. "Have your words with her."

The man's brooding, red-rimmed eyes widened considerably. "*You* are—" Iarbas began, became flustered, and stopped. Auriane grew uncomfortable as the odd fellow studied her face with great care, as if trying to fit her into stories he'd heard. With a jolt he remembered himself, and inclined his head. "I am most honored to meet a woman I've heard spoken of as a queen, throughout these lands. I was sent by another, the man who is Avenahar's father—"

"Oh, curses on all the gods," Auriane said.

"—who just wants to set eyes on his only child before—"

"I regret, but you must leave," Auriane said. "You do more harm than you know. We'll give you meat and drink and see you safely on your way."

"I beg you, hear me out. Decius meant to come himself, but couldn't— he'd hatched a clever escape plan, but that lord who holds him found out and—"

"Chariomer, you mean, who all say Decius helps?"

"The very one, but you shouldn't lay his crimes at poor Decius's door. Decius is his prisoner, Lady, and he suffers from Chariomer's displeasure as we speak. He sent me to warn you, Chariomer's oathed all his men to slay you. And he sends Avenahar a rich gift, as a token of his goodwill, but"—he looked pitiably bewildered as his gaze moved from Gunora to Auriane— "this isn't coming out well: I seem to have lost it."

"Is this what you lost?" Auriane rose, and returned with the fibula.

"Praises to Rosmerta, you have it!"

"Take it, Iarbas—" Auriane said.

"You are nobly kind."

"—and give it back to him."

Iarbas's face deflated like a punctured wineskin. "I can't do that. He depends on me as a friend, to do this thing for him." He looked so helplessly distressed, Auriane felt a welling of pity.

"Iarbas, I must attend to my child," she said more gently. "Avenahar is proud. Decius must understand that. I hope he's well. But tell him, if he has any true tenderness for her, he'll stay far away from her. He'll let her have a chance to be known as an honorable woman."

"He wants only to look on the beauty of his daughter. At least give her the gift, and tell her it's from her father."

The brooch glinted in the morning sun, as if innocently begging her acceptance, as though it were Decius's fading voice, trying to reach her through the years. Decius, who'd troubled himself to dispatch this man to warn her. It seemed small and mean to refuse. Slowly she nodded in agreement.

When they'd sent Iarbas off with dried venison, a bread loaf, and a skin of mead, Auriane went to Avenahar's hut and put Decius's golden fibula into her daughter's goatskin sack. Later, she would devise some way to tell Avenahar whose gift it was.

I'VE DONE WELL!—the words surged joyously in Avenahar's blood as she caught a root and pulled herself, naked, from the pool, dried her fall of thick, crow-black hair with a woolen cloth, then put on a tunic of clean white linen.

I belong here, I do indeed belong. . . .

From beyond the trees she heard the dark, doomful pounding of a drum, a big, brazen, stomping sound like the footfalls of giantesses. It was a rhythm of many parts, the sound of all nature on the move. She felt caught up in something fated and large, forced forward by a powerful expulsive thrust, like the final convulsions of a birth, propelled into a drama that could not be halted until nature had had her way.

Her sister-maidens were already ascending the path from the pool. They spoke to each other in low voices, paying her no mind, but the rapture brought by the elderwomen's praise of her vision blunted the misery Avenahar might have felt at being excluded from this fond fellowship. Happily, she climbed after them, lengthening her strides to catch up.

As she crowned the rise, she saw that Ivalde and Hildigun had halted to wait for her. Avenahar would, long after, remember the matching looks of bright menace in their eyes. Hildigun looked down from her sturdy height, her square chin lifted. Pale, uncertain Ivalde was glaring at her with a belligerence that, to Avenahar, felt borrowed; for reasons Avenahar did not know, Ivalde had chosen to make Hildigun's enemies her own.

"You're preening about this place like some fine cock, Avenahar," Hildigun said, her voice rich and low, "as if no one around here knows you were fathered by a Roman dog."

Avenahar felt the blood drain from her like wine from a tipped chalice.

"What filth spews from your mouth?" she whispered. Through some deep knowing, Avenahar sensed something dangerous in Hildigun's words. A numbness formed around her heart that spread slowly to her throat, her limbs.

"Why, how could anyone *not* know," Ivalde joined in, "with her ugly black hair telling it all! Go back and wash your hair, Avenahar."

Avenahar's warrior nature reared up then, and a strengthening madness began to steal over her.

"By the gods, you two are fools," Avenahar said, taking a smooth, strong step toward them. "By those words you insult my mother."

"It's true, Avenahar," Hildigun said. "If you hadn't fled off to a foreign land, you'd have heard it yourself, many times, by now. Your mother lay with a murdering Roman swine called Decius and the result was you. So you can stop strutting about as if you're nobler than us!"

Something burst in Avenahar's heart. She left the ground like a lynx, striking Hildigun somewhere about her midsection. Hildigun was pitched backward, and they fell together into grass and mud. Avenahar clawed at that proud, pleased mouth, while Hildigun fought to shield her face. Through a fog of fury, Avenahar was only gradually aware that Gunora was standing above them—a storming giantess ringed with thunderclouds, ready to hurl down a bolt.

"Get up! You dishonor the rites. You are not women, you are addlepated children. I should send all three of you home in disgrace!"

Gunora looked longest and most penetratingly at Avenahar, seeming to assume she was the perpetrator. Then the three maids followed meekly in single file behind her. Avenahar was left struggling to contain all the storm and thunder in her breast, feeling imprisoned within the ceremony now. Until it was complete, she could ask no questions of her mother, would have no outlet for the molten mix of rage, confusion, and grief roiling in her.

As the maids were brought before the Middle Fire, Avenahar scarce saw how the waiting grove had been transformed for them. A hanging forest of garlands woven from flowers of bloodroot and moonwort drooped from the low limbs of trees; the small blooms were scattered stars of golden yellow and rose. The air was heavy-laden with the scents of honey and fresh hay, from the smoke-herbs Gunora had cast into the bonfire—dried sweet clover to gladden minds, benevolent mullein to push back evil in the unseen world. The elderwomen, including her mother, were dove-white in their rope-belted linen shifts; their heads were adorned with wreaths of flowering goatweed, the glory of midsummer. One of the elderwomen played a bone flute; the warm, trembling tones gushed out strongly, drawing guardian ghosts from moist green shadows. Walberga continued to beat the drum, a sound abstracted, yet alert. The glade was, at once, solemn and gay. A shyly emerging sun shone through wet leaves and they sparkled like gemstones, flashing yellow-green against the watery translucence of a slate-and-blue sky.

Avenahar scarce was aware, too, that onlookers had come: As this was the ninth and final day, a collection of village women had travelled over the hill to watch from a respectful distance. Afterward, there would be feasting, storymaking, and dancing.

AURIANE WAS ALARMED by the stricken look in Avenahar's face, the slash of a mud stain on her white linen tunic. She looked questioningly at her daughter.

But Avenahar would not meet her eyes.

The three maids stood before the fire, their hair tumbling free—one head of sun-gilt russet, one of red honey, one of shining black. Gunora, near as thick in girth as she was tall, faced them with her back to the fire, her bellicose features grim and closed, her cloak whipping in gusts of heat. Auriane and the elderwomen sat on flayed hides, behind the maids. One elderwoman rose and placed chaplets woven of wolfsbane and ground ivy on each girl's head, plants that helped a woman see the invisible world. Another hummed an incantation while circling the maids three times, sprinkling their heads with boar's ashes. The ropes of flute tones wheeled out, looping loosely, lazily, about the patient drum beats. Gradually the far-ranging flute song began to tighten, moving in more urgent circles, causing all in the grove to feel roped in, bound ever more closely together.

Then flute and drum were silent, leaving them awash in the soughing of leaves, a clear quiet so steeped in peace that Auriane thought this was how the forest must have felt before Rome came. *When no one told us where we could settle, when the movement of peoples was like a sea, flowing everywhere. Soon, we'll be feasting and laughing over it all. Why am I braced in every muscle? Why do I feel a long night pressing close?*

Gunora approached Hildigun and began speaking into the silence, a slight warble in her voice.

"Hildigun, daughter of Udo, you stand before the Ancestresses on this day . . ." The invocation stretched on for long moments, halting only when Gunora offered Hildigun a loaf of bread kneaded with water from a holy spring, baked with nine grains. Hildigun took a careful bite from the oval loaf; the bread united her with Fria as giver of all sustenance. Gunora then drew out her seeress's dagger with its broken point, which stood for the Fates's power to start life with the cutting of the birth string and to end it with the severing of the final thread. With the dagger, she traced runic signs above Hildigun's head, writing growth, strength, and protection in the air. Next, she commanded Hildigun to take her child's clothing and place them in the fire, along with a bit of cloth darkened with her first blood. Gunora then sang Hildigun's lineage; the line of mothers wended backward for twenty generations. The line of fathers broke off after only five; as always, fewer were known. Finally, Gunora placed a blue mantle around Hildigun's shoulders, and the maid owned the right to sit among elderwomen.

Gunora repeated the ritual with Ivalde. As Auriane listened, she found herself proudly studying her daughter's neatly made body, visible through the thin linen sheath—subtly narrowed waist, bare bloom of hips; it put Auriane in mind of a slender, sinuously curved wheel-made pot. *She is beautiful and strong and her life heals mine. How can evil come of this day?*

Ivalde took her place among the elderwomen.

"Avenahar, come before the gods," Gunora intoned.

Avenahar was blessed, and offered the bread, and bid to throw her child's things into the fire.

"Avenahar, noble and bright, is brought before the guardians of forest and grove. She comes from all and she comes from one . . ."

As Gunora spoke the lineage, her voice seemed to follow a soundless drum. "Auriane is her mother, and she is called Daughter of the Ash. Athelinda is Auriane's mother, and she is called the Wise in Council. Gandrida was Athelinda's mother, and she is called Gandrida the Sorceress. Avenahar, first of that name, was Gandrida's mother, and she is called . . ."

As THE MARCH of mothers continued, Avenahar could feel Hildigun and Ivalde watching her, their fierce interest like a blast of heat on the back of her neck. Avenahar clung to a hope her tormenters were simply wrong—or perhaps, playing some vicious game wrought of envy. Gunora would embarrass them when she named Avenahar's father, who might be some poor Chattian landsman, perhaps, but a good and proud man nevertheless.

Gunora intoned, "Of fathers, she has but one who is known, for he was birthed in a far, foreign land . . ."

Avenahar drew in a tight breath. This was akin to being lashed to a hill-top tree, awaiting the strike of lightning.

Unseen in the sun-bright sky, the moon came to fullness.

"Her father is Decius of the Roman tribe, suckled by a she-wolf in lands far south. . . ."

Auriane never heard Gunora's next words—she saw only her daughter. Avenahar's body convulsed as if someone tugged sharply on a rope about her neck. An animal whimper came from her. Avenahar looked like a thing broken in two, suspended there, head bent forward, dark hair tumbled in her face.

Auriane rose to her feet, thinking only to somehow give comfort. Gunora was steadying Avenahar with a firm hand on each shoulder, whispering words Auriane could not hear.

At this time you will need more than one mother, Auriane had told her daughter once.

A hundred mothers might not have been enough.

From behind her, Auriane heard a slurred snort, as of sharply suppressed laughter. Hildigun.

Then came whispered words, audible in a sudden silence. "Who'd believe the daughter of a Roman murderer would've dared come here." Ivalde.

Their smiles vanished when they realized they'd been overheard.

Auriane turned to them, feeling herself not a woman, but fire.

The avenging passion in Auriane's eyes held everyone transfixed. Sharp silence collected. The ceremony had twisted off course. The elderwomen stared in blank surprise, not sure what Auriane meant to do.

"Hildigun. Ivalde," Auriane said softly. "Gunora proclaimed you women, but I never will. I say you don't deserve to walk among human creatures. Leave this place."

Leave this place? Hildigun looked to Gunora for help, then to each of the elderwomen in turn, but got no response from those impassive faces. What was this? Were they to go home?

"Perhaps you'll live long enough to know, one day," Auriane went on, "what it is that makes a woman noble. It is not a father. It is not a tribe. It's the nobility that lives in your deeds. Go from here!"

Hildigun and Ivalde rose uncertainly to their feet, not knowing what to do. No one spoke. The two edged off to collect up their possessions, still waiting for some mollifying words, some counter-command, from Gunora, from anyone.

But Gunora had decided not to interfere with a mother's vengeance. Hildigun and Ivalde were fully born into the tribe now; they must settle their own accounts with Auriane, as one tribeswoman would with another. And the others, following Gunora's lead, kept silence.

Gunora waited until the two chastened maids were well away from the fire, then returned her attention to Avenahar.

"We take Avenahar to our hearth a woman," Gunora said gently, arranging the blue mantle around Avenahar's shoulders.

Avenahar was an isolated figure, stiff and still as a boundary post, her head wilted forward. The blue mantle fluttered sadly, looking too large for her.

Auriane cautiously came up beside her.

"Avenahar . . . dear child . . . do you see, now, why I couldn't tell you before this day? You needed to be stronger. You needed to be a woman to hear it."

Gunora put a firm hand beneath Avenahar's chin and lifted it so that their gazes met. "The blood of your mothers is strong, Avenahar—easily strong enough to cleanse away the blood of that father. Listen to me. You would not have been given that great vision, were you not greatly loved of the gods."

Avenahar turned then to look at Auriane. "Why, Mother?" She looked like some urchin who begs on temple steps, eyes tremulous, imprecating. "You should have torn me from your womb. You should have drowned me in the bogs at my birth."

The words were scalding broth flung in Auriane's face.

"No, Avenahar," she whispered. "How could I have, when I loved you before you were even born."

"Is this truly so, or have I fallen into a nightmare?" Avenahar said. "My father's a man of the people who destroyed us . . . and not the best of them, as . . . as Marcus Julianus is, but the vilest of them. I'm not even Chattian, then, not fully, as you let me believe. I am like some mule, with a horse mother and a jackass father. At home at the villa, I'm an outcast . . . and now I don't belong in this country, either. I belong nowhere. Why did you never tell me?"

"I hadn't the heart to savage your pride when you were at too tender an age to bear it," Auriane whispered.

Avenahar collapsed slowly to her knees before her mother, her hands covering her face. "I can't live with his poison blood in me. It burns like fire." Several deep sobs came from her. She scooped up a handful of earth and smeared it on her face, as women in mourning did. Then she looked up at her mother with her frightful, dirt-smeared face. "Did you give me life as some cruel jest?"

"*Avenahar!*"

Auriane dropped to her knees and seized Avenahar by her shoulders. "This is madness. You must calm your hatreds before they kill you. You were midwifed by Ramis. Would she have done so if your blood were poison? Decius was no monster! I knew him as nobly kind."

"*Kind?* He's helped Chariomer slaughter his way through half our lands!"

"Avenahar, I cannot speak for what he's done since. It's beyond my kenning, too. I only know that in desperate times, long ago, he sheltered me when no one else would. But for him I would have died. But for him, I would never have become adept with a sword. But for him—ah, you're too young to know these things, how can I bring you to understand—"

"Get off from me!"

She flung Auriane's hands from her shoulders.

"Put your head up, Avenahar," Auriane said, rising to her feet, her voice stern. "I will not have this. Wipe the dirt from your face. Gunora has just told you his blood cannot harm you. You dishonor a great elderwoman if you don't give weight to her counsel."

"You lay with a Roman thrall and bore his babe, and you speak to me of dishonor?"

Auriane knew dimly that her arm flashed out and she slapped Avenahar across the face. Never before had she struck her daughter. She looked, horrified, at the fast-blooming crimson blotch on Avenahar's cheek.

Avenahar rose and backed a few steps away, one hand raised, protecting her face. As surprise ebbed off and rage rushed back in, she met her mother's gaze with a look that was bold and unafraid, feeling vindicated by the slap—it strengthened all her swift-forming assumptions.

Avenahar then turned and strode off, the blue mantle slipping from one shoulder, stumbling once as she made her way through a gauntlet of concerned elderwomen. Then she disappeared into her brushwood shelter.

Auriane started to follow. Gunora put out a hand to stop her.

"It might not be wise, now, to crowd her with so many mothers."

Walberga came close, and said, "There's much child in her yet, Auriane. Let the storm subside. It will be well."

Auriane stood mute, feeling covered with stinging nettles, filled suddenly with a dreary, stagnant shame she thought she'd purged from her spirit long ago. *Avenahar reacts rightly to that crime I committed as a maid. I defied sacred law when I lay with Decius so long ago.*

Gunora sensed the shape of Auriane's thoughts, and offered, "She loves you, Auriane. A day or so ago when you were off somewhere, she told me an amusing tale of how you humiliated some arrogant Horse Guard who came to your villa. It was easy to see, her pride in you is wide as the earth."

Auriane was not much comforted. In dark silence, she sat before the bonfire. Gunora sat wordlessly beside her through most of the day. Beneath layers of misery, Auriane was grateful for this.

As dusk came, the elderwomen began breaking camp, preparing to travel over the hill to the small settlement of ten longhouses and join in the less-than-gay feast of celebration that had already begun—Avenahar's despair, and Hildigun's and Ivalde's banishment in disgrace had left an inauspicious gloom over the ceremony's end. When the elderwomen departed, Gunora stayed behind with Auriane.

Gunora left a millet loaf and a pan of soup outside Avenahar's hut. Avenahar did not touch them.

Wrapped in a rough wool coverlet, Auriane did not stir from her place as nightfall came; eventually Gunora fell off to sleep. Poised high above was a full moon in majesty, pitiless, victorious, swollen with covert designs as it flooded its waxen light into the grove. But Auriane saw only the now-untended initiation fire as it burned itself out, feeling lulled somehow by its slow death. When the night was more than half gone, Auriane, too, dropped into sleep, curled before the fire.

After unknown hours had passed, Auriane found herself suddenly awake. The stars were still bright, but a halo of charcoal gray hovered above the eastern forest. She did not know what had awakened her. Perhaps it was that there was too much silence about.

Barefoot, and still groggy with sleep, Auriane made her way to her daughter's brushwood hut. She had prepared no words to say. Her stomach seemed made of aspic. Her whole soul felt sick. Her head hammered painfully as if something large in there fought its way out. Her mouth felt full of dust.

"Avenahar?" She bent to peer inside, staring into darkness for long moments, while time seemed to stretch and contract.

The hut was empty.

It meant nothing. It meant everything. Auriane got a glowing brand from the fire, to better see within.

Avenahar was gone.

There are two kinds of emptiness, she realized then. There is incidental emptiness, in which the space still strongly holds the spirit of the absent person. Then there is an emptiness full of intent, that jolts the heart to desperate attention.

She saw that Avenahar's womanhood cloak and her goathide sack of possessions were gone, as well. Only then did she feel herself poised for a plummet into limitless dark.

She awakened Gunora.

"Ah, this is ill," Gunora said. Both women began examining the ground about the brushwood shelter, looking for some telltale sign. While Auriane walked a slow circuit of the forest all about, calling out Avenahar's name, Gunora settled herself on a cowhide before Avenahar's hut, and lifted her gaze to the crowns of the beeches. She dropped at once into that bright, still state in which she heard the language of the leaves.

When Auriane's search yielded nothing, she returned to Gunora.

"It is ill, indeed," Gunora said, using her staff to rise cumbersomely to her feet. "I cannot feel Avenahar's ghost. She has already gone far, though whether in distance or in mind, the forest would not say."

"Curses on all the gods—what if she's taken her horse? Gunora, I must go ahead of you, and see."

Without pausing to collect her belongings, Auriane set out swiftly over the hill. Their horses were tethered just outside the small village at the hill's base, in the glade by the brook, where their cavalry escort camped.

Three of the cavalrymen were attending to morning tasks: One strapped on his armor; one mended a bit of harness; another noisily rattled tin mess cups before their cookfire as he prepared their breakfast gruel. She passed them with scarce a word, and came to the roped enclosure where their mounts were kept.

Avenahar's lean roan mare was there, happily tearing at hay. Auriane felt a small surge of relief. Avenahar was on foot. She couldn't have gotten very far. Auriane realized it would have been impossible to saddle and bridle a horse and bring it out of the enclosure without rousing the cavalrymen.

Just then, the fourth cavalryman tramped out of the forest behind the roped enclosure, clad in the long woolen tunic they wore beneath their armor. He looked angry enough to join a tavern brawl. He shouted to his comrades that the villagers were thieves—he would see the men crucified, and the women sold into slavery.

After Auriane managed to stem his choleric outburst, she learned he'd tethered his horse outside the enclosure last night, leaving the stallion on a long rope, for this was a noble beast that needed more grazing room than the ordinary horse. And now, his beautiful Apulian stallion, which had cost him half his yearly pay, was gone, along with the handsome boy-groom charged with keeping watch over the proud animal.

"You will leave the village in peace," Auriane said curtly. "I know its folk well, they don't steal horses. Your groom's fled in fear of you. My daughter has your horse."

Chapter 16

Auriane's mare splashed noisily through the shallow stream, throwing up showers of shattered crystal. The hoof prints of the cavalryman's stolen stallion had led to this stream, then vanished.

Auriane's hopes first began to founder when she realized Avenahar had been clever enough to ride in the stream.

By now, she's had time to travel far.

But where would she go? She has no knowledge of our rivers and trackways, little understanding of all one must know to thrive alone in the deep forest. Boldness and determination are not enough. She'll be overtaken by some war band and slain for that fine horse she stole. Or dragged off to be the slave-concubine of a petty chief.

Or she'll be found by Chariomer's men and slain in vengeance.

Even now she might be lying alone in the forest, her leg broken, waiting for night, and wolves.

Auriane remembered suddenly that she'd stashed Decius's golden fibula in Avenahar's goatskin sack. *At least, she has a thing of value—if she's still alive to barter it.* Auriane thought it odd that the despised Decius's extravagant gift had become the whole of her daughter's patrimony.

The sun rose to midheaven while Auriane scanned the stream's stony banks, keenly alert for prints in the mud, broken branches, trampled grass, a bit of torn cloth—anything that might reveal where her daughter had turned off into the forest. But studying those banks was like reading some endlessly unrolling volume that proved relentlessly blank. She'd assumed Avenahar would have the good sense to ride in this direction—the opposite way would take her closer to the villages overrun by the Cheruscans. But as the sun eased into the western part of the sky and still she saw no telltale signs, Auriane was forced to consider the possibility she'd spent most of the day riding in the wrong direction.

Panic compressed her heart. With a sharp pull on the bit Auriane swung the mare about; a rope of blood-flecked foam streaked the tall chestnut horse's lathered neck. She began retracing her route, urging the mare to a weary canter. Tears blurred her vision.

Even now you might be lying, trussed and gagged, in the bed of some slave trader's wagon.

The agony of being roasted alive could scarce be greater than this.

Her nurturing, mist-wreathed forest home had become a brooding dragon, lusting to devour her daughter. How swiftly, how utterly all else was forgotten, she realized as she peered with diminishing hope into tree trunks receding far into gloom, felt the cold, empty enmity of that massive, unending forest. It was a warped, taunting dream-place from a nightmare. Its leafy sighs were death-rattles. She had no thought now for the troubles that pressed about her, or the darkness collecting about Marcus. Adrift, too, was her plan to flee off to her mother's hall. In all the world, there was only Avenahar lost. She was but a ghost in search of her daughter.

At dusk she returned to the small settlement, too tired to weep. From Gunora's grim face, she knew the elderwoman had had no better success. Gunora had passed the day at the longhouse of the village alewife, sending out messages to neighboring villages, organizing a band of folk to help with the search.

At dawn the following day, the collection of youths, maids, farm wives, and field thralls that Gunora had assembled split into four parties. Auriane, at the head of one of these, rode deep into the danger-fraught northerly direction, inquiring at villages, halting travellers on the trackways, closely examining river fords. As the sun descended on the second day she began to see Avenahar's shining hair in the glistening black-green water of rushing streams, to hear her voice in the bright talk of water over stones. She never stopped crying out Avenahar's name, lest her daughter be lying somewhere, unable to move about. Auriane returned to the village at darkfall, too hoarse to speak.

The four cavalrymen who had escorted them across the frontier refused to take part in the search, claiming they could not exceed the orders given them by their centurion. As the nine days of their assignment stretched to eleven, they became sharply restless, pressing Auriane to return with them to the Fortress of Mogontiacum.

On the third day of searching, one of the parties discovered an overturned hide trader's cart alongside the great West Forest track. The spear they worked free from the corpse of the murdered driver incited much talk; Gunora identified the runes cut into its shaft as Chariomer's victory formula.

If any man of Chariomer's travelled this far in advance of the Cheruscan invaders, Auriane thought, *he could only have been hunting for me. Or my daughter.*

That eve, in the village alewife's longhouse, Auriane and Gunora conferred by the hearthfire.

"I've alerted all Sigibert's men," Gunora was saying. "Every hunting party they send out will search. The seeresses of the summer sanctuary know now—they'll carry news of this wherever they travel. By next moon the Great Assembly will be told, and those who come can take word to—"

"That's too many days off," Auriane said suddenly, rising restlessly to her feet and moving to the longhouse's door to look out into the thick darkness. "We can't gather the people before then. They won't come if the moon isn't full."

The sunny shrieks of the alewife's children interrupted them then; at the far end of the hearthfire, they were playing with a tame red squirrel. One child's laughter was so like Arria's, it was like a brand laid on Auriane's heart. *Arria. Avenahar. Will we ever sit round one fire again?*

"Gunora, I must go back to the Fortress."

Gunora grew sharply quiet, lower lip protruding decisively as she bridled her disapproval. "Ah." The word was a soft grunt. "This, then, is how you end." Auriane had told Gunora of the coming criminal charge against her, and of her plan to stay at her mother's hall. "You are handed one fine chance to escape your Roman accusers—and you spurn it."

"Gunora! Do you not see, I have no choice!" Auriane dropped down beside Gunora again, meeting the old woman's gently damning eyes. "I've got to enlist Marcus Julianus's help. Our efforts are pitiful compared to what he could command into being. He can have the Governor send cavalry detachments into every village of our people. He can cause messengers to be sent to every Roman fort. He can send an alert to a thousand watchtowers. He can have the Governor put out an edict that my daughter's not to be harmed. Gunora, I have decided it. I return on the morrow."

Gunora seemed to gaze upon something sorrowful in the distance. "Remember my dream of nine fires. No fire for this year. Auriane, you must not go back there."

But Gunora's admonition was a whisper in a windstorm. Later, as Auriane drifted into a fitful sleep on a scattering of hay and bedstraw by the hearthfire, she strove mightily to envision Avenahar living and free, in spite of a small, troubling thought that kept nibbling at her like rats—*if that's so, then why haven't cold and hunger driven her back to the only world she knows?*

Only when Auriane was half lodged in dreams did she acknowledge another reason for returning to the Fortress: The Governor had summoned Ramis before his military tribunal for questioning. And that interrogation was set for four nights from this day. The thought of beseeching Ramis's help intoxicated Auriane with hope; she felt like someone sealed into a tomb who'd broken open an aperture and gotten the first whiff of unbearably sweet air.

If I throw myself on her mercy maybe she'll help me. Her powers, like wind, are far-travelling and invisible. She knows what lies beneath the lake. She gave Avenahar her water-blessing and her name. And she travelled on a long journey to pull me from my own mother's womb. Surely she has some love left for me . . .

But it's equally likely her displeasure's soured into loathing, for all these years I've turned my back on her, luxuriating in a rich villa on foreign ground.

The great prophetess was, in these times, so drawn into her mysteries, none dared approach her unless summoned. But Auriane had heard it said that if Ramis was petitioned while travelling, she never sent anyone off without an oracle or a blessing.

Surely, Auriane thought, *the fearsome old seeress is my best hope.*

THE AUROCHS HUNT would commence the next day at dawn.

The Governor's great hunt engaged over two hundred men, slave and free, from professional beast-handlers and native game-beaters, to net-men, wagon masters, weapons masters, and grooms, and the battalions of slaves who shouldered the provisions. A half-day's journey from the Fortress of Mogontiacum on the Rhenus had brought the vast hunt company to a melancholy forest the Chattians called Wodanswood, a hilly wild place free of villages, presided over by the god Wodan, lord of magic; here, the game-beaters had sighted the pale beast. The Chattians had abandoned this country to the dark elves, and told tales of ghostlights that came at night, to lead men off high promontories to their deaths. This was a land that scarce knew it belonged to imperial Rome, and the city-born hunters supposed it had changed little since the days of Saturn.

The professional animal-baiters set out for this country four days in advance of the hunt party, to track the famous aurochs the Governor sought. Mostly men of nomadic Libyan tribes, they were seasoned hunters who had provided Indian tigers and Mesopotamian lions for the beastfighting school in Rome. They were aided by men of the local tribes, who knew this aurochs's favorite watering holes, the muddy places in which it liked to wallow, its favorite paths through the forest. Broken tree limbs less skilled hunters might have ignored, the tribesmen recognized as sites where the great bull had groomed itself by rubbing its hide against a trunk. On the morn of the third day of tracking, the hunters had sighted the infamous beast, drinking at a pool. The native hunters had never known the aurochs's shaggy coat to stray from shades of black-brown, but this beast's coat was dead-white, like the bone in the field, the flesh of the corpse, killing snow, or ghosts. The native hunters believed it a spirit conjured by the seeresses who dwelled in caves in this wood, and claimed it had dragon's blood in its heart. Every hunt party sent against it had ended in wails for the dead. The Governor thought his hunt would end differently only because earlier expeditions had never committed so many men, nor had they planned each detail with his thoroughness.

The animal-baiters employed a Roman method of rendering the beast tractable—drugging its watering hole with quantities of wine. Then they frightened it with trumpet blasts while game-beaters wielding thonged whips weighted with clay balls drove it toward the long meadow, where the high officials from the Fortress of Mogontiacum, lords of the world out for a day's diversion, awaited the dawn of the hunt.

On the hunt's eve the forty tents of the Governor's party were laid out with military precision at one end of the nameless meadow. The tent of the Governor was grandest in scale. Within, Marcus Arrius Julianus was his honored guest, along with the Mogontiacum Fortress's two senior tribunes, young noblemen required to complete two years of military service before beginning their long climb to the Senate. In adjacent tents, fellow huntsmen, officials from the Governor's staff, were taking their evening meal. Set in neat rows behind them were the humbler tents of the personal slaves and grooms. Their many cookfires formed even ranks and files of warm, shimmering lights strung out across a field of night; these little fires seemed the only light in the world as Cimmerian darkness closed over the vast forest.

The four noblemen in the Governor's tent reclined before a sumptuous country feast—soft cheese in reed baskets, preserved citrons, honey frittatas, wild mushrooms grilled with fish sauce. Behind them was a small shrine to Hercules, the most beloved god of this reign, scarce separate in the minds of Rome's more credulous citizens from their Emperor Trajan; an offering of bloody boar flesh lay before the stone image. Incense curled from the altar, leaving a pungent odor of piety, thick and unmoving in the air. Just outside the entrance of the Governor's tent, Maximus's chief cook roasted a boar on a spit, basting it with silphium and rue.

Slaves had lit the bronze lamps scattered about the low table. Twilight was an indrawn breath.

"Good friend, I've a thing to ask of you," Marcus Julianus was saying to the Governor. A nervous Gallic serving maid dressed in leather hunting attire entered the tent wielding a platter too large for her; on it was an island of boar meat in a steaming lake of juices. Julianus paused briefly in his talk to steady the platter, and help her make a place for it on the table.

"Near Confluentes dwells a petty man of ungovernable appetites," Julianus spoke on, "a former magistrate called Volusius Victorinus, whom I've ruined. I won't trouble you with *that* story. But I worry that this fellow might be spiteful enough to try some mischief against my daughter Arria, in my absence. She's well cared for now—she has a good household about her, and nurses who love her. And my estate is well guarded. However—" Julianus needed to lean closer to Maximus in order to be heard; the voices of the two tribunes were becoming more florid and aggressive with each round of the wine jug.

"—should it happen that I lose my life, and should some misfortune befall Auriane as well—it would ease my mind greatly to know you were watching over the estate."

"Of course," Maximus replied, frowning in mild surprise. "But we face an aurochs tomorrow, not Hannibal. And that adventuring wife of yours is probably more a danger *to* the countryside than it is to her!"

Marcus Julianus cast a restless glance toward the living darkness outside the opening of the tent, beyond the cookfires, where dusk gathered thickly among the old oaks and beeches, turning forest pathways into sunless caverns.

"Her party's two days late in returning," he said in a voice grown grim. He fiercely regretted having capitulated to the womanhood ceremony.

"Ah, they probably had some trouble with their passage," Maximus said. "It's rough country. But it's peaceful country. And we gave them my four best Batavians."

They were forced to silence as the blustering words of the senior tribune took over the tent. To Julianus, both were forgettable young men, matched in self-love and blindness to all the world but the small scrap of it on which they stood. The man's name was Camillus, and he was holding forth on the grandeur of the hunt.

"And why *do* we hunt dangerous beasts, when we do not need the meat?"

Because we're an empire in middle age, in terror of losing our mettle, an irritated Julianus answered in the silence of his mind.

"Consider that it's only the noble who pursue the hunt," the tribune rumbled on, "for overcoming a great beast requires a man be living a noble life, an existence not defiled by laboring over daily bread, and endless, tedious scurrying about to meet animal needs. A life with the hands free leaves the spirit free to ascend, to grapple with higher things. A humble country farmer might snare a hare or two. A slave, a woman, does not hunt at all. The slave's hands are too busy. A woman is . . . too undisciplined, too full of unmanly timidity. Most likely, she'd be in complicity with the beast. Nor do idle, luxury-loving foreigners have a great passion for it. Consider the Egyptians, for they further prove my case—aeons ago, princes of Egypt *did* passionately pursue the hunt. And these ancient days coincided naturally with Egypt's days of greatest battle-glory. Witness, too, the present-day slothfulness of the Greeks—"

Thank all the gods I'm not being asked to respond to that windy effusion of self-congratulatory nonsense, Julianus thought.

"—and how the tyrant Domitian only hunted animals that were tame," the oratorical assault continued. "He shot his arrows from a safe place, within a hunting garden stocked with captive beasts. And did not this mockery of hunting parallel a mockery of a rule? Then see how our lord Trajan hunts in places that are remote and wild. One shouldn't be surprised that the one proved unfit to rule, while the other has proved more remarkably fit than any other." To Julianus's dismay, Camillus shifted his attention to Maximus and himself.

"Marcus Julianus. You haven't told us who you're wagering on for the kill."

Julianus turned to meet a square, fleshy face painfully overripe from drink, a forehead lightly beaded with sweat in spite of the chill, eyes fogged with wine and complacency, and brimming with assumptions—chief among which was that some sort of close camaraderie existed between them. He wore a fine white tunic with gold-embroidered hem; it had slipped to expose his shoulder, revealing a bunched mass of young muscle on the threshold of going to fat.

"I'll lay my money on the aurochs," Julianus replied quietly.

The tribune gave a clipped, abrasive laugh. "You're quite the jester. I didn't know it."

"It seems an eminently sensible choice to me, considering the beast's record. Fifty thousand on the aurochs."

Maximus nudged him. "As your good friend it's comforting to know you're in such a robust financial health you can toss off a small fortune."

"You know, I do find it odd," the young tribune said then, assuming a reflective expression that bore a closer resemblance to a wince of pain. "You're no hunter at all, Julianus. I saw how you stood apart when we gave our offering to Hercules. Yet you had the mettle to face down two tyrants. I wonder . . . can you be the single example that defeats my case?"

The Governor frowned at this line of inquiry and gave his young subordinate a bare shake of the head that meant, *Mind that careless tongue.*

Camillus's senses were too blunted by drink to notice. "But perhaps it isn't so odd after all. You *do* lecture on and on about peaceful containment. Perhaps, philosophers who counsel us to coddle our enemies are also in complicity with the beast—"

"Be silent, Camillus, or you'll get no favorable report from me." Maximus's voice was iron-cold.

"We're in the wilderness," Camillus protested. "Surely, here a man's free to speak his mind."

Marcus Julianus raised a hand, smiling amiably. "He's broached a fair question," Julianus said. "I take no insult from being held to favor dignified containment over massacre of our neighbors. I wonder if men will always count the unfettered exercise of strength to be just in the sight of the gods—perhaps we've been in the grip of a long blindness. When Rome conquered Syracuse, reflect on the legionary soldier who slew the great Syracusan mathematician Archimedes, father of so many marvelous engines and machines. Rome won that day. But who was truly the stronger? Today we don't know that soldier's name. And every schoolboy knows the name of Archimedes.

Feats of arms seem to leave nothing permanent inscribed on the tablet of man—perhaps it's why I've always found Nemesis more to my taste than Hercules. She finds justice for those who can't seek it for themselves. She prods the phlegmatic into thinking on what they've done."

The young man lifted the wine jug while fixing sour eyes on Julianus. "Mars be thanked, my father didn't believe a son should be taught philosophy. I empty this jug to his wisdom." His colleague, a thin, wolfish young man of darker Hispanian complexion, laughed silently into his cup.

After the two conversations drifted apart again, Julianus overheard fragments of Camillus's talk as he consulted a list he'd made on a wax tablet: ". . . two wagers on Sabinus in the next tent . . . twenty wise wagers on our illustrious Governor . . . one insane wager on the aurochs . . ."

Out in the deep forest, far, but not too far, Marcus Julianus heard a wolf howl most eloquently—an intelligent sound, old as the moon.

THE GREAT, SHAGGY bull paused in a muddy pool. It lowered its bearded head and gave a bellow of protest at finding itself tricked into the midst of cruel, vile-smelling humankind. The effects of its drugging had long since worn off; it was left with only its rage. Dark stripes of blood streaked down from its massive, humped back to its belly, from wounds made by weighted whips. Hunters' lances slanted from its sides like long, heavy quills.

For the better part of the day, the party of Jovian hunters had been harrying the great aurochs and wearing it down. The sun had travelled past the peak of noon and the hunt was moving into its final, mortal moments.

A hunter's net had been strung across the meadow for the length of a quarter mile. This long net, the one human intrusion on the landscape, this lone specimen of artifice, managed somehow to have a most natural beauty: It rippled with the seductive grace of a water snake, and occasionally, inspired by the wind, bowed along its whole length as if straining to fly.

The eight noble hunters were positioned in a two-tiered semicircle about the beast; the undulating net closed the open side of this human pen. The strangely white creature before them seemed some apparition condensed from ground fog. It showed no signs of wearying. The famous white coat, at a closer look, proved mottled with blotches of pale gray. Its horns were a natural wonder of fluid curves, flaring outward, then inclining forward and upward, to finish with a smooth, inward flourish. Its ears, muzzle, and tasseled tail darkened dramatically to black, as did the tips of its horns, and its feet to the fetlock; these dark points lent the massive, top-heavy beast a strangely discordant delicacy, a fierce grace.

It arched its head downward and roared, stabbing one beautifully curved horn into the earth, throwing up clods.

Maximus and the three most seasoned huntsmen were positioned in the inner semicircle. Marcus Julianus was positioned in the outer one, closest to the net. The skilled Libyan beast-fighters were placed by the forest's edge, beyond the hunters' sight. They were to enter the field only if Maximus and his friends lost control of the aurochs; otherwise, they would be stealing the kill from their noble masters. As the men waited for Maximus's signal, their mounts capered in place, unnerved by the musky smells of the bull.

The Governor dropped a colored cloth, and the eight hunters galloped forward as one.

Marcus Julianus moved with them. He kept a short rein on his horse, finding his reluctance had risen to a new pitch. He carried two hunting lances, with which he'd become adept in practice, but today they were mostly for safety; he had no intention of depriving the Governor of the kill. By mid afternoon, as the aurochs's agony stretched on, Julianus found himself, more and more, as Camillus had put it the eve before, "in complicity with the beast." *This is ignoble*. Before him, the great bull was motionless as a marble monument as the eight hunters rushed at it. *This first hunt will be my last*. Between a jumble of horses' hindquarters, Julianus saw the Governor skillfully positioning himself to cast his lance, aiming between the third and fourth ribs, the killing place. *The aurochs has rightly won. We should let it go.*

At the precise instant Maximus's lance flashed out, the bull made a nimble half-turn—a creature heavy as a standing-stone suddenly agile as a hart. It veered off with startling speed in a direction no one expected, bursting through their lines. The careening beast crashed into the flank of Camillus's tall chestnut stallion, slamming the horse to the ground. Young man and mount rolled in the long grasses. The aurochs shot off amidst thunder; once again, it was free.

The Libyan beast-fighters stretched their hands to the sky, praying for the help of native gods. This aurochs's cunning and endurance were as unnatural as its whiteness; it should have fallen by now. It was some unknown god that chose to take the form of a bull. They agreed among themselves that it would not be slain until it had taken a noble life.

*   *   *

ON THE FAR side of the long net, a tall native woman in deerskin breeches and cloak of rough undyed wool made her way among the servants' tents. She presented herself to the decurion of slaves, asking to be taken to Marcus Julianus.

Auriane and her cavalry escort had ridden as far as the bridge-head fort across the river from Mogontiacum when she'd learned the hunt was in progress. She'd dismissed the escort, passed a night at the *mansio,* then set out for this meadow alone, after a day and a night of little sleep and no food. The slaves' decurion would only repeat Maximus's order that no one was to cross to the other side of that net. Auriane felt a slow madness stealing over her limbs as she prepared to wait for this odd, overplanned Roman hunt to come to an end.

Does Avenahar live? Dully she watched the distant riders, near lost in the long grasses, heard the occasional shriek of a brass trumpet, the undertones of low, dusky grunting from the earth-born monster, the hard hammering of hooves as horses swept like a swift tide from one side of the meadow to another. *The likelihood dwindles, day by day.* Once, she recognized Marcus Julianus's dappled-gray mount by the distinctive arch of its neck; moments later, he galloped close enough so that she could see his face. *Few men look so noble on a horse!* she thought, strengthened by the sight of him, full of a vaulting hope—but all too soon, it fled.

Avenahar, I did not know you were the sun. A mother should perish from the earth before a daughter. Or else who will welcome that daughter to the Ancestresses?

THE EIGHT HUNTSMEN wheeled their mounts about and gave chase as the aurochs thundered away from the net. The Governor's bay stallion shot in the lead, crashing through the grasses. A bruised but uninjured Camillus was close behind, astride a fresh mount. Maximus urged his agitated, sweat-darkened stallion alongside the bull and steadied himself for another throw of the lance. This shot was high, grazing the hard hide of the bull's back. The aurochs surged onward with its strange, heavy, rocking gallop, until game-beaters at the far end of the meadow rose up from the grasses and drove it back toward the net.

Moving at a fluid and ponderous slow-beat trot, the pale bull seemed perversely obedient as it ambled back into the hunters' midst; its languorous gait suggested surrender. It halted and began rhythmically shaking its head. As the hunters tightened their circle, the oddly submissive monster remained very still, watching them with great care, showing the whites of its eyes in a slightly mad but most expressive manner. To the hunters, it was disturbing—the creature seemed to know them, to be laying plans. The wind drew in a breath; the net softly deflated. From the direction of the distant camp came the whimper of a Celt hound wounded earlier in the day by a boar that now hung, skinned, over drifting smoke. The aurochs and all the earth seemed to await the best moment to catch the noble hunters off guard.

Then the bull swung itself round like a heavy boom, once more its gloriously unpredictable self. It thundered straight for Julianus—a mountain in motion, a barreling behemoth unstoppable as a cart full of boulders careening downhill. Its eyes were bright with ire; it thought Julianus the author of all its hurts. Snorting, chuffing sounds came from it with the impact of each heavy stride.

Marcus Julianus's panicked horse scuttled backward. He gathered his wits just in time to manage a swift, hard throw of the lance, embedding it deep in the bull's heavily muscled shoulder. This fresh strike had no immediate effect; he might have thrust a toothpick into the beast. But an instant before the monster would have collided with his mount, it slung its bulk around, and rotated twice—the crazed motion of a beast in pain.

Then it made an erratic, arrow-quick dart between the hunters' lines and sped off, the strange, sloped bulk hurtling along with remarkable speed as it careened into a portion of the meadow where no game-beaters were positioned. Maximus held his bay stallion in check; the horse did a liquid dance-in-place while the Governor signaled angrily to the game-beaters, commanding them to come round and close up the open place. It had required a grueling morning's work to position the beast for the kill; now all was set to be lost.

The aurochs never slowed as it burst upon a hunter's trackway that ran alongside the meadow's edge. A few more ground-grabbing strides and it would be lost in the forest.

Then the hunters discerned a distant human figure, nearly in the beast's path—one of the grooms. The man was on foot, returning to the hunt camp from some errand. The bull shifted direction slightly and bore down on the groom, turning all its wrath on this lone specimen of its two-legged tormentors. It caught the helpless slave on its horns and flung him into the air as if he were a straw doll. No one was near to give aid.

To Maximus's astonishment, Marcus Julianus wheeled his dappled mount about and urged it to a gallop, rushing to the aid of the fallen slave.

"Dogs of Cerberus, what's he doing?" Camillus shouted in a fury, bringing his horse up beside Maximus's. "He'll drive it farther off, he'll dash what we've spent half a day setting up." To himself, he muttered, "Never bring a philosopher along on a hunt." *The eccentric pedant,* he thought. *I could buy five slaves like that one, with what this magnificent beast's hide is worth.*

"Hurry, my Lord, he'll steal your kill," cried out a hunter who had placed a large wager on Maximus. But the Governor wasn't willing to forgo dignity to chase after strayed quarry.

As Julianus's horse flashed past Maximus, the Governor saw his friend's normally mild features hardened into a look of grim purpose. Julianus's flying dappled-gray cleaved the grass, while Julianus himself was bent low over its neck, moving easily with the horse's powerful strides. Maximus was more amused than angry, marveling somewhat at this quietly intense, city-bred man-of-ideas suddenly turned hunter, and for an instant he considered that perhaps the philosopher's life *could* adapt a man to any exigency, if it could so instantly transform his scholarly friend into a swift and deadly predator.

When Marcus Julianus had closed the better part of the distance between the hunters and the strayed bull, a second huntsman shot off in Julianus's wake. This was a fellow called Attius Ferox, who'd arrived at the campsite only that morning; the hunters knew him as the newly appointed official in charge of the legionary savings bank. The tribune Camillus shouted angry expletives at his fleeing back; their formation was reduced to chaos. The Governor frowned, puzzled that this Ferox, a man of scant experience in the hunt, would display such eagerness to aid in the rescue.

Julianus galloped between the great bull and the fallen slave, hoping to confuse it and redirect its fury. The injured groom lay unmoving in the long grasses. The aurochs loomed taller than Julianus's horse. The mammoth bull had ceased mauling the body of the groom and began pawing at the earth, its doleful eye on Julianus as it emitted a series of dark, irritated grunts.

Marcus Julianus brought his nervous horse as close to those heaving, bleeding sides as he dared. But he never had a chance to hurl his lance. The aurochs gave a cry like a blast on a war horn and slung its bulk at him; with a quick twist of its head, one long horn tore open the belly of Julianus's horse. The dappled gelding towered upward, forelegs clawing at the sky, then toppled onto its back. Julianus flung himself free. To the distant hunters it appeared as though both Julianus and horse were submerged beneath a sea of long grasses.

The dappled gelding struggled weakly to rise, then ceased its efforts. Julianus found himself stunned, but with no broken bones. Crouching, he crept toward his swiftly dying horse, meaning to use the poor beast as a shield, snatching a brief moment to look once, heartsick, at the long, ragged slash in its belly that laid gray ribs bare. The aurochs was so close, he could see deeply into the labyrinth of one mad eye. The reek of musk, damp fur, and rot enveloped him. His second lance lay just beyond reach. He had only the dagger in his belt.

From somewhere unknown, a poignant shout of protest arose. It could have been an eagle's cry, except it was edged with human passion.

It came from afar—beyond the net.

Julianus stole the briefest look in that direction and was surprised to see that a distant rider had climbed aboard what was, surely, his own spare horse—another desert-bred dappled-gray, out of the same dam as his slain mount. The rider, though impeded by grooms grasping the reins to stop him, was urging the horse to a gallop on a course straight for himself and the au- rochs. It made no sense—no mortal horse could clear that net.

The same quick look revealed that help was coming from several quarters. Closest at hand, one of the hunters—what was his name?—Attius Ferox?— rushed for him at good speed. Well behind him, roughly half the hunt party, Maximus in the lead, approached at what seemed to Julianus's fevered mind an excruciatingly slow pace. And two separate parties of game-beaters armed with nets and goads fanned out across the meadow, coming even more slowly on foot.

The bull bore down on him; he might have been trapped beneath a plummeting ten-talent block of marble. The body of his horse wouldn't even slow it. He would be pounded to pudding beneath anvil-sized hooves.

Julianus whipped off his cloak.

When the bull was one stride short of trampling him, he cast his cloak at the lowered head. It caught on curved horns, then molded itself about the beast's head and shoulders. The aurochs jammed both forelegs into the earth and gave a shrill bellow of surprise. It became a bovine pendulum, loosely swinging its ponderous head to free itself of the insulting piece of cloth.

From the edge of his vision Marcus Julianus saw that the young treasury official, Attius Ferox, had dropped from his horse and was running to his aid. Even in the chaos of that moment, as Julianus was shouting into the wind— *"No—too dangerous—wait until the rest come up"*—he sensed something odd in this rescue. But he dared not take his eyes from the blinded colossus be- fore him.

Julianus was judging the distance between himself and his lost lance when he felt a powerful blow between his shoulder blades. *What in the name of the gods—?* It jammed the breath from his body. In one disoriented instant he thought: *Has the monster split itself in two?* Was its twin goring him from behind?

No, it was Attius Ferox, gone mad.

Numbness flashed down his arms. Then came a tearing pain like scalding water, a deep drag of agony across his back.

Julianus twisted round to face his attacker, his own upraised dagger poised to rake flesh. Ferox's blade came down a second time, sinking into Julianus's shoulder, catching in bone.

Julianus twisted free and seized the younger man by his muscular forearms, striving to contain him. The two were locked in mortal struggle, each restraining the other's blade as survival was thrown upon brute strength and will.

Ferox was the stronger; steadily, hungrily, his dagger edged toward Julianus's throat.

This cannot be my end. It's too senseless.

"What madness takes you!" Julianus gasped, arms shivering with the effort of striving to push the younger man off. *But are not most ends senseless, even when we choose the hours of our deaths?* Ferox continued to steadily overwhelm him. Julianus felt blood coursing down to his collarbone as the young man's blade pricked flesh near the windpipe. Ferox's eyes were sightless with a rage so unbreachable, so certain of itself—so impervious to appeal—it inspired its own sort of horror.

"Murderer . . . of . . . my . . . Lord!" Ferox forced out the words through deep, heaving gasps for air.

Casperius Aelianus.

Of course. All will count my death the work of the aurochs.

This man did not fit his informants' description, but he scarce had leisure to wonder over this.

Neither man was aware of the earthy grunting of the frustrated bull. Huge forehooves sank to the fetlock in moist ground as the beast continued its elaborate efforts to free itself from the cloak, dragging one horn along the ground, grunting and lowering itself to its knees, then comically flinging its head skyward, as if taken with fits. Marcus Julianus was conscious only of a simple and primitive desire for life. As he collected his wits, something stubborn as bedrock rose up in him. He refused to be forced down into darkness. He wouldn't leave the world before leading his children into adulthood. He wouldn't go where Auriane was not. The doggedness of this fellow and his perverse allegiances filled him with fury—and fresh strength flashed into his limbs.

He lashed out with a mule-kick to Aelianus's knee; it broke the younger man's hold on his wrists. Without a halt in motion Julianus brought up his own knee and delivered a battering-ram blow to Aelianus's stomach. The younger man folded and fell forward, mouth gaped wide as breath left his body. Julianus managed then to tear the dagger from Aelianus's hand; he flung it far into the rippling grasses. As Aelianus collapsed onto the lifeless body of the horse, Julianus grasped a lock of the young man's hair, suspecting, now, how Aelianus had disguised himself. And Julianus found himself holding what looked like a small, dark pelt. False hair. The freshly exposed close-cropped straw-blond hair beneath *was* true to his informants' report.

The man who so lusted for his death was possessed of an almost Apollonian beauty, even with the blood drained from his face. His short, muscular body rolled off the belly of Julianus's horse, coming to rest beneath the muzzle of the aurochs. Simultaneously, the bull, with a final, mighty toss of its head, freed itself from the cloak. The woolen cloak drifted down, blanketing Aelianus's body.

The aurochs bellowed, then turned all its fury on the cloak. It raked the cloth with one horn, then the other, and pawed at it with iron hooves. Blood bloomed on the cloak. The young man flailed his arms, which excited the bull all the more. Julianus shouted at the aurochs and waved his own arms in an attempt to draw its attention from the bloodied man at its feet—enemy that Casperius Aelianus was, no human creature deserved to perish this way.

Maximus cantered close then; Camillus, Sabinus, and the rest of the hunt party were just behind. The sight of the man they knew as Attius Ferox, mangled and groaning beneath the forehooves of the bull, caused all to feel doom closing round like a god's fist. It was all the more ghastly, concealed beneath the cloak.

Four hunters flowed about the bull, lances in position. Maximus dropped from his horse and dragged the young man out of the path of hooves and horns. Julianus limped off to retrieve his lance. Aelianus's dagger seemed still lodged in his back; each step caused him to feel some fiend gave it a twist.

Maximus was then aware of furious motion just beyond the billowing and receding hunter's net. A dappled stallion hurtled toward them with raw fury unleashed, like water from a burst dam. Its rider was was almost invisible; in his hand was an upraised spear. What did this man think he was doing? Only a winged horse could clear that net.

When Julianus looked, he felt a surge of love and dismay. It was, indeed, his spare horse. Astride it was Auriane.

When did she come to the camp? She doesn't know she's charging, full-tilt, into forbidden ground—these men will not want her aid.

For a moment no longer than a heartbeat or two, Julianus watched, transfixed, as Auriane and her mount came up to the twisting net. She reined in the horse slightly. Julianus understood: She studied its motion, feeling for the rhythm of its billowing, so she could send her mount over it at the precise moment it sagged low enough for the horse to clear it; her sense of such things was precise as an acrobat's. Horse and rider shot forward at a moment that seemed randomly chosen—and the net sagged obligingly to the height of her horse's withers. The dappled gray rose like a crane; woman and beast were one creature, and that creature flew. The horse's leap was a wave that crested then crashed to earth, to be lost in the grass sea.

When they reappeared, Maximus, too, recognized Auriane. She rode with the grace of a desert nomad. She was a bird of prey skimming low over the grass.

The aurochs broke into frenzy. A leftward lunge and swipe of a long horn hamstrung Sabinus's mount; it bucked violently and Sabinus was flung ingloriously over his horse's head. A rightward lurch, a lumbering stride— and the tip of a horn caught in the leather strapping of Camillus's boot; he was tossed over the bull's shoulder, onto the grass. In a bare instant, the aurochs had unhorsed two hunters.

Julianus pierced the bull's shoulder with his lance, lodging it in bone; he held desperately to the thin, bowing shaft, in a futile attempt to hold the beast in place. Men's shouts battered his ears. Through the chaos of blindly struggling men, the reek of sweat and blood, a pitch of horror that recalled for Julianus his single, long-ago experience on a battlefield, he knew the bull was swiftly, efficiently savaging the fallen Sabinus. Camillus saw the fate of his fellow hunter and bolted off in primitive fright, sprinting like an Olympic runner. His flight took him vaguely in the direction of other humans—the approaching beast-fighters. Excited by the sight of the running man, the great, pale beast launched itself in that direction, closing on Camillus like an avalanche. It laid him flat; moans of dismay came from the approaching beast-fighters as the bull ravaged Camillus with hoof and horn. Several fled off in spirit-terror. Day had turned to endless night. All felt the rank, stifling breath of the gods of slaughter.

This bloody work done, the bull paused, blowing pinkish steam, then barreled toward Maximus. The Governor's weapons were spent. Escape was impossible. It would roll over him like thunder. The long grasses were littered with the fallen. Maximus remained dignified and still, bracing himself for a terrible death.

Auriane shot into their midst.

Her flying horse cleaved a diagonal line between Maximus and the bull. The noble hunters watched with blank surprise as, with swift and casual ease, she curbed her dappled mount's exuberant flight and began cantering in ever-tightening circles about the aurochs, while her horse threw up clods of earth to the sky. It was as though she bound the bull with invisible ropes. She was so steady in the presence of the earth-born monster, none thought to question what sort of help could come from a lone woman armed with a fire-hardened spear. Chestnut hair flew from her loosened braid; as she circled the white bull she was some sylph riding the mist, a creature that resembled nothing they knew from civilized life, an emanation of ancient days—Atalanta of myth, or the fighting maidens that somehow always flourished in history's remote shadows.

And Julianus, who believed only in Providence, found himself praying. He beseeched the most ancient spirits of the earth, Juno and Diana, protectresses of women, to see this did not end with her lying horribly mangled in the grass.

The aurochs's strangely knowing, brightly malicious eyes were fixed only on Auriane now. The mammoth bull attempted to turn with her, becoming confused, angered, and dizzied by her circling. When her circle had become quite small, with a dancer's precision she pulled her horse to a nimble halt-and-turn. Auriane faced the bull's flank. As her mount half reared, she smoothly rose up in the saddle; fluid as a lynx whipping off its mark, her spear-arm flashed out.

It was as though her spear and the heart of the beast were already joined in the minds of the Fates.

She found the killing place. A new sound came from it—an unnaturally shrill, bleating cry, an earth-born creature's protest against the sky. It rotated like a mill pole, crushing grass.

In its dying it made a final try for vengeance, bursting toward the last three hunters still astride their mounts. As these scattered in three directions,

Auriane gave chase, then galloped alongside the bull, bringing her mount so close that horse and aurochs nearly touched at the shoulder.

What they witnessed next, the game-beaters would still be speaking of when they reached trembling old age. While her wild-eyed, frightened horse fought the reins, Auriane reached out and grasped the rank beast's hair, at the withers. Then she drew herself onto the monster's back.

The aurochs halted all at once. Raising its shaggy head, it lowed to the sky, in what appeared to all like outraged disbelief.

She was impossibly astride, riding an eruption of nature, whirled about on a wind demon, seeming small and lost as she clung to the massive humped back of the great bull. She moved with its madness, never struggling against it as the drunkenly lurching beast slung her from side to side.

Now she was safe from the horns.

Some saw the flash of a bronze dagger in her hand as she dropped down along one muscled shoulder, clinging to coarse fur until she was able to reach the wheezing throat and strike out with her blade. The aurochs's forelegs buckled. The powerful hind legs straightened, then shuddered violently in a way that spoke of dying. The mammoth body quaked as a final river of rage gushed through it.

Marcus Julianus ran toward the dying animal, fearful Auriane would be crushed when it fell. But as the aurochs began to heave downward, Auriane threw herself free, and landed on her feet in the deep grass. Soon after, the beast crashed to the ground, heavily as a toppled pillar. It rolled once and flopped still, a great white bloody ruin, its mighty flanks heaving like a bellows, the motion fainter and fainter as the earth drank its heated blood.

All about was a dread silence, such as might come after a violent windstorm scatters a village. Though the sun still flared in the western sky, clotted thunderclouds thickened directly above, bringing an unholy darkness, as though Wodan pulled a shroud over his meadow. The mangled and the dead were everywhere. The slave had perished, as had Sabinus, along with two game-beaters the beast brought down earlier in the day. The man they knew as Attius Ferox, horribly trampled beneath the cloak, was nearer death than life. The moaning Camillus had frightful wounds, but the field physicians thought he had a chance of life. Four slain horses lay scattered about in the grass.

In this bright, strange quiet, Auriane moved toward the lifeless hill of flesh, and began softly uttering words over the aurochs, to appease its spirit.

The silence was finally broken by the Libyan slaves, who burst all at once into raucous cheers, and blew blasts on their hunt trumpets. In the wilderness, the slaves were more exuberant than they might have been within the formal precincts of the fortress. "She is clothed with the sun!" Auriane heard one man cry. A party of them surged forward, laughing, flowing round the bull's corpse. Several produced knives and began rapidly skinning the beast.

Auriane was uncomfortably aware, then, of everyone's attention fixed upon her, and saw the varied shades of feeling her intervention had inspired. She'd blundered into a society not her own, ripped the threads of its invisible web. In the eyes of the Libyan beast-fighters were only raw amazement and joy. And the several Chattian hunters among them studied her with great intensity, eyes fired with a pride that brought her a strengthening gladness—after two barren days of helplessness, she'd roused proud spirits, she'd won a victory. She believed this would, in turn, lend strength and luck to Avenahar.

But among the Roman hunters, she saw guarded relief soured with sharp annoyance—and even shame among some, powerful enough that they would not meet her gaze. In the face of one man was brittle hatred undisguised.

And then she looked at Marcus Julianus, and forgot every one of them.

He swiftly made his way toward her, fear for her melting off to leave only joy-filled relief, a drunken love of Providence, and a vaulting pride in her, all his own. Of his countrymen, he alone would have given her an Olympic crown. She loved him fiercely in that moment, for that great generosity of spirit.

Then she saw how his tunic was reddened so that he wore a mantle of blood. "Marcus, it struck you. Turn about, let me see."

"Not the bull," Marcus said softly. "There, on the litter. Casperius Aelianus the avenger, in the flesh. Yes, that's him. Don't look. I'll be well, he missed his mark. And from the looks of him, he won't get a chance to try again. Say nothing of it, now."

"But how did he—"

"Not now."

Maximus was shouting hoarsely for more litters, and bandages. The noble hunters were ebbing back toward the camp with the dazed steps of walking dead men. One man of the party, face chalk-white with rage, vented his wrath on the Libyan beast-fighters, promising to see every man of them flogged to death, for their slowness in coming to the noble hunters' aid. Several fell to their knees before him, begging for their lives.

Auriane and Marcus closed in an embrace, then, that was a marvel to them both, and full of fevered reverence; she basked in a holy moment between them that was a balm to the world's indifference.

"How come you to be here?" Marcus whispered finally, still holding tightly to her, stroking her mangled braid, then gently sorting the loosened strands of her hair. To his embarrassment, he found he was struggling against tears.

"Avenahar is gone. I had to find you at once, to—"

"Gone?"

"She fled off from the womanhood ceremony. I've hunted her for two days. She left in the most frightful fit of melancholic wrath I've ever seen."

"Madness! It was when she heard Decius named as her father?"

"It was." Auriane looked away, fighting shame, her throat tightening. "My babe is out there alone. I don't know if she lives."

"Domina, the hooves and the horns are yours!" interrupted the tanned, grinning beast-fighter with gold rings in his ears, who was chief over them.

Numbly, Auriane nodded to thank him.

"Domina, you made fools of us!" These words were spoken by Maximus, who strode up beside them just then. Mockery and praise were mingled in his voice in a way that was confusing to Auriane. She turned to look at him, and saw he said it with a broad smile, as if he handed her a small gift.

She gave him a grave, cautious smile of acknowledgment.

"I must know the lineage of that horse!" called out another of the hunters as he rode past them at a trot, gesturing toward Auriane's mount, which was being led off by one of the grooms. "It leaps like a hare and flies like a falcon!" Auriane realized he couldn't acknowledge her greater skill in the hunt, so he behaved as though the honor belonged to the horse.

Marcus Julianus put an arm about Auriane's shoulders and with Maximus beside them, they moved slowly toward the hunt camp. As the tribune Camillus was carried past them on a wickerwork litter, he lifted a blackened hand, ordering the slaves who bore him to halt. Addressing Maximus, the tribune whispered through a crushed throat, "Who brought down the bull?"

When Maximus silently indicated Auriane, Camillus wrenched his head about to look at the tall woman standing close by Marcus Julianus; she regarded him with earnest gray eyes, face flushed from wind and exertion. He squinted. Where had *she* come from, this comely native woman in a bloodied leather tunic, her long hair matted with mud, and that faintly barbarous mien of calm strength? He concluded that he must have been misunderstood.

"No, I mean—who among our party delivered the fatal blow? Who wins their wager?"

"No one," Maximus patiently explained, "for no one wagered on *her*. This Diana you see before you is your victorious hunter, and the slayer of the bull. She killed it with a native spear."

"That's an odd jest, my Lord. That's impossible."

Auriane felt a hot rush of rage, but kept silent. Marcus tightened his grip on her shoulder to underscore his alliance with her.

"That, before all the gods, is the truth, Camillus," Maximus said quietly.

Camillus stared at Maximus, then at Marcus Julianus, as if the two had conspired in some crude joke. Then, abruptly, he seemed to lose all interest in the matter.

"The aurochs got away from us then," Camillus said finally. "No one slew it."

"Did that war-loving Chattian Amazon really steal our kill?" came a grand exclamation from another man of the hunt party, walking behind them.

Marcus angrily whipped about to face this man; Auriane saw, to her dismay, the sudden movement caused his wound to bleed more.

"If she were as base and ignoble as you," Julianus said, "she would have let the bull have its way with you. I would that she had—the world would be cleansed of one blind, complacent strutting cock."

Maximus burst out laughing. "Today's sad play was well worth it, to finally see you angry, Julianus!"

The Governor turned, then, to Auriane. "*Domina* Aurinia, you did, indeed, aid us greatly." Auriane felt quiet amazement. It was one matter to hear a servant call her *domina*. But a man such as Maximus would only use that form of address for Julianus's legitimate wife. She knew this was the highest praise he knew how to give her.

"You have done us a great service on this day. You do credit to your native people, who understand these great beasts where we do not. You saved my life, and his, as well," he said, indicating the man Julianus just chastised, "though he's not wise enough to admit it. As the son of illustrious fathers, it's my duty to do a great service for you in return. It happens to be my fondest wish, as well. I don't know what I could give you that so generous a husband as this could not, but think on it, Aurinia—you need not answer me today."

Auriane was faintly uncomfortable through this stilted tribute, but collected herself enough to say, "I can answer you now."

Marcus Julianus braced himself, hoping she wouldn't ask for something Maximus couldn't give.

"I would like two things," she said, watching him him gently, solemnly, while the wind blew long chestnut strands across her face.

The Governor smiled, encouraging her.

"Have mercy on the slaves who failed you today," she said. "I want no more blood shed because of this day."

Maximus considered this and nodded slowly, finding it reasonable.

"And," she continued, "I would like a company of men to command—mixed cavalry and foot soldiers, your very best from the Fortress—so that I might ride at their head—"

Julianus winced; it was too soon after that harrowing hunt for such a severe test of the resilience of Maximus's sense of humor.

"—and lead them in a hunt for my daughter. She's run off. I've got to find her before the forest slays her."

"Consider the first request fulfilled, Aurinia," Maximus said graciously; a quick flash of amusement in his eyes softened the formal precision in his manner. "But before I turn over the Roman Army to you, can we discuss this matter over a fine meal?"

Chapter 17

The Fortress of Mogontiacum

On the following day Marcus Julianus insisted upon interrogating the dying Aelianus himself, with no recorders present. Maximus greeted this with grave doubts; this was a man who'd tried to murder Julianus twice, inspired by purest hatred—what did he hope learn from this madman?

The Mogontiacum Fortress's hospital was a timber-and-stonework structure built in a rectangular shape about a vast courtyard. A slave-assistant to the First Physician greeted Julianus at its casualty reception center, and he was led over white marble tiles that glowed orange in the light of the four arched brick hearths along one wall, in which physicians purified their wound probes and surgeons' tools. Beyond was a skylit operating room, empty now. They passed preparation rooms, where battalions of slaves were making ointments from animal fat, lead salts, and resins. The brisk, muffled staccato produced by a row of assistants pounding herbs was the sole sound as they entered the corridor opening to the hospital's sixty wards, which flanked the whole of the circulating passageway. Each of these consisted of two private rooms and a latrine. Any cries that might have issued from the patients' rooms were muted by double-timbered walls built between corridor and wards. Long ago, army physicians had learned that illnesses did not spread so quickly if the patients were put into separate chambers. Julianus's eyes watered in the smoke of fumigants. The air was pleasantly oppressive with the insistent pungency of myrrh, but a faint stench of blood, tainted humors, and corruption hovered darkly beneath.

Casperius Aelianus had been taken to the row of wards reserved for officers. His sickroom was twice the size of a common soldier's room, its walls gaudily abloom with paintings rendered in red and blue encaustic. The chamber was bare but for the bed on which Aelianus lay and a bench for a physician. The smell of wound medicines was thick and sweet on the air— pine resin, oils of cinnamon, and cassia. Aelianus's half-opened eyes sought nothing more from the world; they put Julianus in mind of scummy pools at the bottom of a trench. His mouth was slack, his breathing staggered.

"I sewed him well, even the muscles inside," the physician's assistant, a prim Greek, said blandly as he made to depart, "but the blood has stagnated. He has the perforation that kills in a day and a night."

Julianus knew enough of medical science to know this meant the stomach or colon was pierced. "Wait. He suffers," Julianus said. "Is that the balm?" He indicated a squat jar of thick green glass on the floor by the bed. "Give him more of that."

"You'll not get any answers out of him if I do," the young assistant objected. It contained a decoction of henbane and poppy juice. "The *hyoscyamus*"—he used the physician's name for henbane—"brings forgetfulness."

"Do it anyway," Julianus replied, too dismayed by the dire scene to say it diplomatically. His own recently dressed wound was pulsing viciously. The physician tilted the young man's head to aid swallowing, and spooned some of the liquid into his mouth. Then Julianus waved him off, and sat next to the dying man.

"I am Marcus Arrius Julianus."

The scummed-over eyes opened a fraction wider. Along the length of his body, Julianus saw a tightening of muscles.

Somehow he managed to lift his head. Then he spat out the mixture the physician's assistant had given him. Much of it splattered onto Julianus's tunic.

"That was a balm, not poison," Julianus said. "Why would I hasten your end now? To what purpose?"

The young man made no reply.

"I've come because I'm greatly curious about you."

"I'll tell you nothing," Casperius Aelianus breathed, easing his eyes closed. The words issued from him like poison fumes. "Murderer . . . of my Lord."

"I am not your enemy. For that matter, I was not *his* enemy," Julianus said, referring to the assassinated Emperor this man so loved. "Not truly. I want the truth, and I'm prepared to be generous in exchange for it."

Aelianus turned his head defiantly to the wall.

"You are resourceful and possessed of much courage. My agents could not keep up with you. A pity, I could have used a man like you in my service." He paused, then pressed on with quiet persistence. "You are the man who set fire to my carriage."

Long moments passed in which he sensed a struggle within the young man: Talk to this enemy and be known a little, for something, before he perished? Or stay proud to the end and die in dignified silence? Julianus had time to study the frightful painting of the goddess Hygeia on the wall, her eyes huge and staring, her form so primitively rendered it appeared her arms were not attached to her torso. Had the military architect used native painters, who copied works of —

"I might be that man."

"You gave a false name and false record of your past to Maximus."

"It . . . was . . . necessary." Each word seemed to require a separate effort.

"You are Casperius Aelianus, son of the Praetorian Guards' praefect, who remained loyal to Domitian."

"I have the great honor . . . to be his son. He . . . alone . . . understood the import of a sacred oath of loyalty . . ."

"Yes, well, I question if loyalty's such a fine quality in and of itself, divorced from the reality of what or whom one is loyal to."

"My Lord Domitian held . . . *order* in his hands. He loved us . . . He knew us . . ."

"He was a monster. But there's nothing to be gained by batting about the finer points of his character now."

". . . He gave us . . . donatives and gifts . . ."

"He gave the Praetorian Guard and army donatives and gifts."

". . . and if he was cruel . . . men like you forced him to it . . . by belittling his divine authority with twisted philosopher's babble. You've no faith . . . You hate what the gods love. He was kind . . . he helped the families . . . of men fallen on hard times . . ."

"He helped only those who held swords in their hands, Aelianus. The rest fell to the sword. Or to wild dogs in the arena."

"Serpent-tongue, your words are filth! For you, I was paraded in the Great Amphitheater like an animal. For you, I have no patrons and friends. For you, I was towed out in a boat to drown. Marcus Arrius Julianus . . . I lived through that shipwreck only so I could stand on your grave." He fell silent, then seemed to speak to someone else in the chamber, visible only to him. "I am sorry . . . What the sea storm couldn't do, a wild bull did . . ."

"I must disagree with one thing you said—it seems you *do* have patrons and friends. Wealthy, powerful ones. Someone got you from place to place, secured you a good post. Someone wanted you to succeed. I know you've no reason to tell me these things, but consider, there's one thing I can offer a dying man—generous aid to those you leave behind. Ask for someone of your family, if you wish, or a freedman, or a friend. I care not for the cost. Just tell me who paid your fares and set you in place."

"You're a faithless man. And I'll be dead. Why would I trust you to grant what I ask?"

Julianus felt a start of anger, but stifled it. "My word's been good enough for four Emperors, Aelianus—it will have to be good enough for you. And I haven't heard of anyone else making you such an offer."

The young man's expression altered then, softening somewhat, like a reflection gently blurred when water is disturbed. "That *was* a balm," he said wonderingly. He apparently had not spit all of the mixture out.

"Of course. I said it was."

Aelianus was silent, still reluctant to speak of things private and close. But the draught was separating him from his wrath while it roused an appetite for conversation. "I have a son, newborn . . ." he said finally, "gotten on a freedwoman. I was sending them money. I've no family left—you've seen to that. My son and this freedwoman, they'll be beggars, left on the mercy of the countryside when I'm gone. I wouldn't ask a murderer like you to send them a sesterce. But if you could see that they're informed of my death. I have some clothing and slaves and horse gear that could be turned into cash for them."

Marcus Julianus struggled against his old enemy—incapacitating remorse. *This man, enemy or no, is my victim,* he thought; *in planning Domitian's death and opening the way for a new ruler, I set in motion the events that crushed him . . .*

Julianus was silent for a time, doing calculations in his mind. "Tell me where they live. I'll send my man to the bank at Lugdunum. There, mother and son will find a sum of sixteen million set aside for them—one for each year the boy lives, until he comes of age."

"You must think me a fool. No man does this for an enemy."

"Perhaps I do it for justice. Enemy or no, you were caught up in a chain of actions originated by me. I do not know *how* to convince you, beyond what I have already said. But know this—I've done as much for the families of my fellow conspirators, who suffered so much for doing my bidding."

Aelianus was silent for too long, a stubborn, armored quiet that could not be breached.

"I'll waste no more of your final moments, then." Julianus paused to retrieve a woolen coverlet that had fallen to the floor and replaced it over the young man's feet. Then he rose to go.

"Wait," came a whisper. "What was that cursed question, again?"

Julianus sat down again on the bench. "Who paid your passage from Lugdunum?"

"There was a supposed legacy . . . from a freedman of my father's, a man emancipated many years ago, when I was a babe. For some reason I had to come *here* to claim it. That was strange—and indeed, you would have thought he believed me dead, after the shipwreck; he'd no way to know I survived. But the sum was desperately needed, so I took it."

"And the post? Maximus got a letter recommending you, from the Governor's staff at Lugdunum in Gaul; it bore a seal you couldn't have duplicated. You have influential friends. How and where did you acquire them?"

"Perhaps our murdered Lord was better loved than you know."

"Enough of that. Every man who might have been involved in this counts Domitian a bald-headed Nero. You're getting aid *not* for your political beliefs—which you share with a dozen others in the world, none of them in important posts—but because of your means to your end. Someone who laughs at your opinions but loves your methods. What of the horses you recently acquired? Who provided them?"

"I won them at dice at the Bacchus tavern, at one of the post stops on the way, Dumnissus, I believe it was."

"That did not seem odd to you?"

"They're serious about dice at that tavern. Fine beasts, but they eat a lot. My own horse had been stolen at the last *mansio*. I was lucky to get them.

You're looking for something that's not there, Julianus. Now I've answered your questions—does my son still get the money?"

"Your horse is stolen on your journey here to murder me. And almost immediately, you're supplied with two more. It's hard to believe that wouldn't make you wonder. You won them from the tavern owner?"

"No, the praefect of the posting station."

"The imperial post? Not the town station?"

"Yes." Wariness came into his eye. "I tell you too much. You'll cheat me, I'll get nothing for this."

"Shall I call a notary to this room, now, and write out a statement for the sum of sixteen million?"

But Aelianus's spirit seemed to have slipped off to another place, as if testing its readiness to fly off from its mortal housing. When sight returned to his eyes, he almost seemed to have forgotten who Marcus Julianus was, and now he spoke without reserve.

"There's much about *all* this that's been odd . . . the hooded men who come to me, who know so much . . . but I never know their names, so I've none to give you—"

Hooded men? Julianus felt a sharp chill.

"Let us return to these horses."

"I won them early in the eve, and strangely, this station praefect showed no interest in playing more, after that. You'd think he'd be eager to try to win them back. Next morning he said he had ownership papers to give me. He left the room once, and while he was gone, I saw something. My name on a document. My *true* name. *That* roused me."

Julianus tensed, sensing the truth was close.

"All I managed to read, before he came back, was a signature. It was 'Nabis'—written in a clear and simple hand, like a child's."

This struck Julianus like a bolt. But he somehow preserved his neutral mien. "You're quite certain of that?"

"It was writ large, with a flourish. I'm certain." The name would have meant little except to one privy to the secret workings of the government. Nabis was the secretary to the centurion of the Imperial Couriers, a body of specially-trained legionary soldiers stationed at the Castra Peregrina in Rome, who acted as messengers between the provincial Governors and the capital. Most thought their duties confined to securing grain requisitions for the army, but they were in truth the Emperor's internal security force, directly beneath the control of Livianus, praefect of the Praetorian Guard. Julianus had seen documents this secretary had signed; his hand was clear, the letters formed with childish care.

The Couriers—and Livianus—could not have moved against him without the Emperor's approval.

Aelianus was an arrow in a bow pulled by the Emperor himself.

In the light of day it seemed impossible. But this, surely, was something fomented in the dark.

Marcus Julianus rose to his feet. "The payments will be made, Aelianus, whether you've faith in me or not. Give me the names of mother and child, and their town and district."

When Julianus had copied the names onto a wax tablet, the young man said, "Why do you not despise me, Marcus Julianus?"

Julianus thought on this for a moment, and then replied, "Because when a man hates something, he stops *seeing* that thing. I've had a lifelong aversion to all unalloyed sentiments; they've always seemed so—oversimple. For life then becomes *one* thing, instead of many things. We stop knowing the glories of the variousness of creation. That is all. Die in peace, Aelianus."

Aelianus's spirit fled off.

And Marcus Julianus was alone with the knowledge that the most powerful man on earth plotted his death.

Chapter 18

Red-gold afternoon sun turned the Rhenus into a brazen highway, comfortably wide, a golden route by which the prophetess would come. On this day's eve, the Governor would interrogate Ramis. Already, a mass of local tribal folk gathered along the riverbank in a great, pacific sea, each hoping to be first to sight the single-oared merchant's galley bearing the revered high seeress.

"Auriane, you must flee, or perish. You cannot tarry here any longer." The words were Marcus Julianus's. Auriane stood in the tapestried door-way of a guest chamber that opened onto the Mogontiacum Fortress's courtyard garden, with its maze of close-clipped box hedges. From some-where beyond the courtyard, the sternly resonant blows of an armorer's hammer sectioned off each moment in slow-march time, a reminder that this verdant pocket of close-managed beauty was an island of incongruity within a vast military outpost where over six thousand legionary soldiers were quartered.

"I will not leave this fortress before Avenahar is found," she replied.

She was bound in a despairing silence that unnerved him. Her eyes were a place of cold ash. The search Maximus launched for Avenahar was in its second day. They'd learned nothing.

Avenahar might have vanished off the earth.

"Within ten days," he tried again, "given favorable winds, the confessions Victorinus extracted against you will be the talk of the Consilium. I must see you safely off before *I* go."

Her eyes glistened, and he thought, *That's at least some sort of response.* Encouraged, he gently shook her shoulders, as if to rouse her to life again. "You've another child at home who needs you alive!" As they spoke, the barge that would take her down river delayed its departure, awaiting her; from there, a galley would take her over the dark Western Sea to the far place of many tribes, only recently discovered to be an island — Britannia, from where she would travel overland to wild Caledonia, the traditional place of refuge.

"Your Maximus pushes me aside like a housemaid. I am Avenahar's blood-kin. To be chief over those who search is my right."

"You cannot expect them to tolerate a woman of rank riding among them like a soldier — it too greatly violates custom."

"I do not want rank then," she said, voice rising with passion and hurt, "if it means sitting in a house while others do battle for you. I'll wear no *palla*—" She tore off her matron's cloak and threw it to the floor.

"Auriane!"

"—and I'll not be called *Domina*. I'll never be a sheep in a pen, no matter how 'honorable' your people call it. I would give insult to my family."

"You see injury where none is meant," he said, starting to feel helpless before her agony. "Maximus has done much. He's assigned men to this search he can't really spare."

"Your people don't know our forests, while I was born to them. I've survived in our hills without food, and under siege. Yet your Governor would have me sit idle in a chamber, while his men-marching-all-together blunder out into a country they don't understand, to search for a girl who means nothing to them, who's run away because she fears she's one of them!"

"Well, it does sound absurd, put like that! But you forget, we're in the grip of more than one plight!"

"I no longer care if your people try me and condemn me."

"*I* care. It would be akin to being rent apart on the rack!"

At this, all that was brittle and braced within her broke apart. She saw him again, and their spirits touched. And he saw straight within her — to her vulnerability, her terror. Like one lifting an injured lamb, he gathered her close.

"They will find her," he whispered fervently into her hair.

"But will they find her alive?"

"Stop this! Whatever spirit enabled you to slay an aurochs, it lives in her, too." He tightened his embrace, then bent his head and kissed her on the mouth with such delicate care that a carnal wanting edged with a burn of desperation welled up in her. Both seized on one thought—but neither drew the other toward the bed, content to merely bask in Eros's shadow; it granted a fleeting grace that quelled thoughts of future days.

"Most likely she's hiding somewhere," he said, "terrified to come home because she fears you're angry with her. Some kindly farm wife is spooning gruel into her mouth as we speak."

"What will you say to the Emperor when you get to that far place?" she asked after a doleful silence.

"I sow my doom if I let on I know his was the hand that struck. I must help him disguise his role, while at the same time, I reclaim his faith in me—when I don't know why he lost that faith to begin with. I suspect the involvement of Blaesus, but I cannot prove it."

"You'll not win clemency for me, no matter what you tell him."

"Auriane, I must try. I'll be entering a victorious Roman camp. It doesn't require an augur to see which way this war will go; Dacia's a barbarian empire that does not even possess a standing army. I'll arrive to laurel-draped javelins. In the celebratory air, he'll be inclined to mercy."

"Marcus, the Fates get irritated with us when we stop fearing them."

He smiled companionably at this. "There's something odd, I forgot to tell you. The hooves and horns of that great aurochs? Someone stole them."

"*Stole* them?"

"It's believed one of the Chattian hunters spirited them off."

"This is ill, that aurochs had a powerful ghost. And I am now part of its fate. Harmful magic can be worked against me with its remains."

"Philosophy's the best cure for that," he responded amiably. "Read Lucretius, he puts forth how the wonders of nature can be taken for conjurations of gods, if—"

A soft rapping at the corridor entrance to their quarters brought them to silence. "My lord." The grimly apologetic face of Maximus's Greek chamberlain appeared in the dark void of the doorway. "A quarter-hour ago, the prophetess's boat was sighted passing Bingium. You're asked to make ready."

Marcus nodded; the chamberlain vanished.

Ramis, Auriane thought. *Dark mother who's stalked me my whole life.* She felt the fluttering and noise of an obscure excitement, as of bats rushing up at the flinging open of a long-shut-up passage of the mind. The time when Ramis had wanted her as apprentice seemed distant as Caledonia.

"Remember all I've ever told you of her, Marcus. Don't let the Governor try to stand between her and her gods, and it will go well."

He answered her with, "In the morn, whether Avenahar's found or no, you board that boat and go."

WHEN MARCUS HAD departed, Auriane waited until she could no longer hear his footsteps. Then she called softly to Brico.

Brico bounded from her alcove, light as a squirrel. Her face was ruddy with vigorous life; she counted this a rare adventure. With a keen-bladed determination that contrasted with her luxuriously cushioned softness, the maidservant pulled from a trunk a long-sleeved woolen tunic, thick woolen breeches, and a leather shoulder-cape that fastened down the front with thin thongs. Swiftly Auriane put them on. The cape came only to the hips; its peaked hood could be pulled forward to hide the face. This was the common costume of the Gallic farmer; its humble silhouette rendered its wearer almost invisible.

This was the safest way to move among an unruly throng at night.

Auriane then inclined her head before the rough-carved image of Fria she'd set in an alcove, feeling she gave herself over to the intelligent winds, the cunning forces flowing underground. "Great Lady of the moon and mountains," she ended her short plea, "let Ramis look on me with kindness."

Throughout this Brico stood solemn as a soldier, but about her mouth were signs of a barely-contained grin. Journeying away from the villa had already restored her vigor, Auriane saw. Brico had arrived at the Fortress only yesterday. She'd lost the child she carried by Demaratos through a malicious accident: As the pair rode round the estate in a wagon, inspecting the fields, the children of Victorinus's tenant farmers had hurled stones at them, calling them "slaves of a barbarian whore." The pony bolted; the wagon overturned in a ditch; Brico's babe was delivered dead. As no balms had eased her melancholia, Demaratos thought a journey might cure her, and sent her here to attend Auriane.

"Now, douse the lamps," Auriane said.

Brico began snuffing out the myriad flames of an iron candelabrum. "Do you think she'll help us?" she asked, squirrel-bright eyes on Auriane.

"With Ramis it's a throw of the dice. She *was* midwife to Avenahar's birth. But I know for certain, she won't unless I ask her." They entered the portico with its long march of alcoves inhabited by stone gods.

"She doesn't give you shivers?" Brico gave Auriane a grave look from beneath her hood. "I heard she once imprisoned a man in a tree. Just yesterday you said Avenahar's running off was probably because of her curse."

"Forget my words of yesterday, I was half mad. You can stay here, Brico, if you'd rather not come."

"Never! I've dreamt of seeing Ramis ever since I was this tall"—she extended a hand—"and heard that tale of how she called a wolf to swallow the moon."

AURIANE AND BRICO left the Mogontiacum Fortress through the gate used by merchants, and followed the road that arched down to the docks. The pair passed a shipwright's yard, where the frame of an unfinished hull loomed above them like giants' bones. The bleeding sun held to its final moments of dominion, then surrendered, and the sky's vault of mystic violet transformed the river into a spirit road into another world as it held the last of the light. Never had Auriane been so aware of how full of potent mystery was the dusk; she felt the brush of ghosts across her face. Corridors hovered open between the worlds of flesh and spirit; there lay horror; there also lay hope.

The throng was thickest around the stone quay where Ramis's boat would dock. The crowd was remarkable for its silence. It proved a mingling of women and men of many subject tribes, some of whom had travelled far. Thousands of the Aresaces, the Celtic people who dwelled in the shadow of the Fortress, stood shoulder to shoulder with Germanic Ubians and Mattiacans from across the river, and a scattering of her own Chattian countrymen. Even among the Romanized tribes dwelling west of the great river, the old prophetess carried great authority, and was thought by some to be a living deity.

Foreign smells lay on the air, gentle and strong: The women of the Aresaces prized Mediterranean luxuries; the nard and cinnamon in their perfumes made her feel she'd entered a southern garden. Auriane looked far down the river, but saw nothing but silvered water teeming with every sort of craft—the swift and beautiful double-oared liburnians of the Roman Navy, passenger ferries with their linen squaresails unfurled, merchant ships with their stems carved into animal heads, their hulls painted in bold bands of red, yellow, and blue. Two warships of the imperial fleet, the *Pax* and the *Armata,* rocked gently at the docks; they'd been ordered to stand by, in case the throng became unmanageable. A detachment from the Twenty-second

Legion lined the way Ramis would walk, strengthened by a century of the Governor's own Batavian Horse Guards, and one hundred mounted archers. There was no hint of rebellion in the people's eyes, but she supposed it was their numbers the Governor found troubling, coupled with a suspicion that on this night the people were under Ramis's control, not Rome's: A nod from her, and these long-docile tribespeople might toss off a generation of friendship and bend down to pick up stones from the bank.

Ahead, the crowd thickened, as those who depended on the river for their livelihoods—stevedores, caulkers, the boys who dove to recover lost cargo, sandmen who handled the ships' ballast—left their labors. Auriane and Brico found a place among the men and women massed on the steps of a small temple of Hercules; Ramis's route would take her close, and the temple's upper steps gave a fine view of the river and the quay.

Brico, with the keen eyes of youth, saw it first: A torchlit boat of elegant shape separating from the mass of other craft, approaching the dock with magisterial slowness, submitting in small spurts to the pulls of a single row of oarsmen struggling against the powerful current of the river. As it drew closer Auriane saw it was bedecked with thousands of flowers; the aft cabin was curtained in mystery. High above, a floating island of clouds moved off to reveal a white-gold moon in decline, balefully gibbous now, softly misshapen in its dying, just robust enough to command a place in the sky. *It shines with the tranquillity of a spirit that knows it will live again,* she thought. But that expiring moon disturbed her, seeming a portent of ill.

As Ramis's boat drew nearer, Auriane and Brico saw a thing that was marvelous. Among the press of people close by the riverbank, a fragile fire bloomed, doubled itself, then began to flow along the riverside. This slow-rippling, living fireglow kept pace in an ever-lengthening line with the flower-bedecked boat of the prophetess. The on-flowing flame was a glory in the dusk, an exquisite, warm beauty in the somber half-light. Auriane drew in a breath, baffled and awed. Only gradually did she realize what they were seeing: The folk formed up along the bank carried unlit torches. As Ramis's ship came abreast of them, a burning torch was touched to one that was cold, and in this fashion the light kept pace with her, so that the prophetess moved with a growing line of fire spreading majestically into the deepening dusk. It was as though Ramis held dominion over fire; her movement over water pulled light into the gloom. It roused the spirit-terrors of Maximus's soldiers; it reminded all who witnessed that there were other kinds of power, older than the sword, other empires in the country of thought and dreams.

The disarmed tribespeople had chosen this way to say to their Roman masters: *Beware, she has our devotion. Do not treat her roughly, do not humiliate her.*

That rippling light pulled Auriane straight into times she did not want to remember: sitting before Ramis in her island sanctuary, performing the Ritual of Fire, while Avenahar lay within her, unborn. *Ramis touched her living torch to me. I let it go out. I wanted safety and Marcus and peace.* "Your desires are idols, worshipped blindly," she remembered Ramis saying to her on that day.

She has ways of bringing her apprentices home.

The mad thought came then that *every* trouble ringed about her was Ramis's curse, from Victorinus to the loss of Avenahar, to the horror and mystery of that high-placed attempt to murder Marcus. Ramis had always said that only a woman stripped of her robes and pitched out of the nest of all she knows will continue a quest for clear sight.

Brico, sensing Auriane's distress, gathered up her mistress's hand and held it, as a child will comfort a parent.

When the boat's artfully-curved silhouette came abreast of the quay, Auriane saw the craft was an old wine merchant's galley converted for the prophetess's use. The stem was carved into playful volutes that culminated in the head of a goose, a creature counted a messenger between the living and the dead. In graceful majesty the sternpost arched high over the aft cabin. The draped cabin that housed Ramis was blanketed in garlands. The vessel's name, *Libertas,* hadn't been removed from the bow; Auriane supposed both the goose figurehead and the galley's name had been considered by Ramis's women when they made the ship their own. For Ramis, too, was counted an emissary between life and death, and the old seeress was said to bring the one true freedom.

As the galley approached the Fortress's dock, the oarsmen raised their oars high, and the exquisite craft with its lacy silhouette glided in like a swan with upraised wings. Smoke from burning sage and marjoram scudded out over the still water. The goosehead prow slid soundlessly between the quay's twin snowy images of Neptune looming spectrally from the stone dock. People stretched out their hands to the great priestess they could not yet see, proffering pipe clay images of their native goddesses and softly calling Ramis's name.

A dock crew lowered a plank onto the galley. Two white-robed girls carrying pots of smoldering herbs descended from the craft; chaplets adorned their heads and their dark hair flowed free. They were from the sacred order of maids who sang the spirit-songs as Ramis gave her oracles. A third maiden attendant emerged from the cabin with a length of white linen, to spread over the mud where Ramis would walk. So deep was the hush, Auriane heard the tinkling of temple bells drifting from the ship, a sound like children's ghosts, laughing.

The crowd's murmurs were punctuated with the occasional wails of babes. Some tossed wildflowers onto the muddy path Ramis would tread. Many of the native faces in the throng were malnourished and thin, or scarred from disease. Some were borne on litters. Their eyes were vague with hope-lessness, or keenly alight with hope.

Auriane turned to Brico and saw a trance-state had settled over the maid-servant. Her lips were parted faintly; she was intensely awake and alive, in some other world. She seemed prepared to see Ramis turn into a swan.

"She'll give me another child. And this one will thrive," Brico said when she saw Auriane looking at her.

Auriane was not certain Ramis could do such a thing, but wasn't about to churn the waters of such a pure devotion. *Perhaps my own certainties got blurred from having lived a life in more than one world.* In these times Auriane found herself less stirred by Ramis's wondrous acts, and more drawn to the old prophetess's masterful detachment in the face of life and death.

A fourth figure emerged from the deerskin-draped cabin. This was a peaceable-looking woman of middle years; a wreath of wildflowers lay on her gray head. Soft cries of *Ave!* started up among the throng; some thought this the prophetess herself. But she carried a plain yew-wood staff, not the brass-bound staff of the Veleda. This proved to be a woman called Algifu, of the Holy Nine, the most revered sisterhood of seeresses in all the northlands, who answered only to Ramis. It was usual for one of their number to accompany the great prophetess when she travelled. This woman, too, started up the path.

The throng's attention was fixed so raptly on the cabin, they might have watched some acrobat quivering on a tightrope. Many flinched at a crash out on the water, as if a river Nix had slapped his scaly tail on the surface. A ner-vous Horse Guardsman drew his sword. But it was only an oarsman throw-ing out the galley's anchor.

A stern, sweet tone floated out over the water, rippling like a silken bridal veil; a white-cloaked attendant flanking the cabin played a bird-bone flute. A second fluteblower joined her, and the tone enriched into a sharp, chilling harmony that opened a door to archaic remembrances, softening the texture of the night. Wordlessly all were seduced into a world infinitely older than this one. The fluteblowers beckoned and calmed the land spirits. They stepped from the boat and followed Algifu.

At the cabin door, all saw a flash of silver.

A woman emerged with slow grace from the deerskin-draped cabin. Even when this mystery was still in shadow, people sensed she seemed quieter than the others, and it was a curious stillness that spread out wide as the river. Soft murmurs arose; then came a silence that prickled the skin. Brico's hand tightened on Auriane's.

The people saw that she carried a staff nearly as tall as she was, amber-studded, and deeply incised with runic signs—the staff of the Veleda.

The silence was mighty. Two torchbearing attendants came up beside her, and illumined the face of Ramis.

Hers was a visage so stark and strong, it would impress a memory that would remain in the minds of those who saw her this night even if fifty more years of life were left to them. The old prophetess's face had the forbidding beauty of snowy escarpments, the cold authority of an alabaster temple image—until one saw there was so much living sorrow hovering about her eyes. In her great age, her skull asserted itself strongly through the skin as though death pressed hard into life, but still her beauty was the sort that made one think of the perfect architecture of the human face. Deftly-carved cheekbones accentuated haunted hollows below; an arched mouth was sculpted with stern grace. Her silver-and-bronze hair was collected into a massive braid that recalled nothing feminine, but rather, ship's cable, thick serpents, rope to hang a man. On her high, smooth brow was a silver ornament in the shape of a sickle moon, suspended from a circlet on her head. Those hooded eyes were wells of memory that saw equally the visible and invisible.

Soft cries came; they rose to a roar that pressed painfully on the ear. Within the Principia of the Fortress, Maximus heard it on his dais, and frowned deeply. They came perilously close to courting this strange woman like some soon-to-be-crowned queen.

The legionaries tightened their ranks and looked to their signal flags, braced for an order to push back the throng.

But Ramis raised her staff, and it was as if she pressed quiet on the crowd. The Roman guard marveled at this. With slow dignity she inclined her head and began descending the plank, moving with the careful fragility of extreme age. She wore a heavy cloak of lambskin, dyed the strong blue of the sky and lined with white cat's fur; the cat was beloved of Fria, the goddess she served. The cloak's hem was studded with gemstones that glowed like small, dark moons. Using her staff, she made her way to the dock. Auriane had never known the exact number of her years, but as Ramis was said to have been in her third decade of life when Nero ascended the throne, she judged the old prophetess must have passed her eightieth winter. This simple calculation caused Auriane to revere her the more, for Ramis was such a woman that every year added another chamber to the vast library that was her mind.

What she must now know, Auriane thought.

As Ramis gained the bank, a native woman in the throng managed to force her way between the line of legionary soldiers. She fell on her knees before Ramis, and spread out a handful of earth at the prophetess's feet. The woman shouted into the silence; Auriane could hear her words without difficulty.

"This earth is from the grave of my son! Great Veleda, tell me what world he lives in!"

Two legionaries seized the woman and began to drag her back.

"Let her be!" Ramis's voice was lilting as a bee's flight, but it cut the air, fine and strong. Under the spell of that certainty the soldiers dropped the woman. Clutching the ground, she looked up at Ramis.

Ramis placed her palm on the woman's forehead. Those nearest reported that the old seeress began to hum—an odd, earthy, atonal music, more elemental than human. Others insisted this sound rose up from the ground. Some would later claim to have seen a pale, man-shaped light crouching near the woman, a spirit-thing that hesitated, then joined with the prostrate petitioner. Wherever Ramis walked, no one afterward ever agreed on what they had witnessed. When Ramis spoke, it was surprising to Auriane how well that crystal voice carried on the chill air.

"Rise, Ivixa, basketmaker of the Aresaces. I see your son. He goes about with you everywhere." No one could say how Ramis knew this woman's name, trade, and tribe. She traced runic letters in the air, hands knitting the space too rapidly for Auriane to read their meaning. "I send all sorrow from you. Go and light nine candles. The last one burning, that is you. Your son is midwife to your rebirth. Return to your home village and heal them. You can now see future days in water and silver."

The woman shook violently as if seized by a spirit. But when she rose and turned about, her face showed the peace of another world—Auriane felt it, recognized it, desired it. It seemed to Auriane all in the crowd were ghosts; only this woman lived. The transformation of the woman brought a variety of reactions from those who saw—fierce envy, bafflement, anger, fear.

Auriane felt a quiet amazement steal over her. *Ramis has powers she had not before. Why did I abandon this? What else in all this Middle World is so important as this? I've been flung off a great wheel into darkness. No, I have not—there is no off. I'm the wheel and the darkness.*

The crowd became frenzied, as if someone had cast a fortune in golden coins onto the ground. Many surged toward Ramis, shouting questions and requests. This time they didn't obey when she raised her staff. A decurion of the Horse Guard shouted an order; a scarlet signal flag shot up among the line of mounted men. Thirty Horse Guards, using the shafts of their lances, began driving the throng away from the bank, pushing them back as far as the warehouses. Simultaneously, in a double file, ten Horse Guardsmen approached Ramis, lances held low; as one, they halted, turned about, then stood ready to open a way for her.

At that time, soldiers cleared the steps of the small Temple of Hercules. Auriane had to drag Brico from her place, while she whimpered and struggled, for now all chance of approaching the prophetess was lost.

Auriane and Brico were drawn into the chaos of the crowd. They soon became separated, carried apart in opposing eddies of people. Auriane set out in pursuit, fearing that Brico, in her determination to approach Ramis, might get into a battle with the soldiers.

Auriane could no longer see what was happening about Ramis, but later she would hear it told and retold: The Governor had provided six litters to carry Ramis and her women to the Principia of the Fortress. Ramis regarded the comely litter-bearers in their tightly-fitted tunics embroidered with gold, the enclosed chairs with their silk curtains, their jumbles of cushions, and announced, "We will walk."

The decurion of the Horse Guard protested that the way was long; she would tire and the Governor would grow impatient. Ramis answered that they would ride in the litters only if the bearers were given their freedom.

The decurion objected that he had no authority to do this. Ramis persisted, and the decurion relented only because he feared she might take ship and depart, leaving him to be called to account for the prophetess's failure to appear before the tribunal. All this was curious to Auriane, for she had never heard Ramis speak of slaves or the proper treatment of them. Perhaps she saw slavery as not natural to man, as did Marcus and a very few others among his people, or perhaps she went further, impossibly further, and thought it should be forbidden altogether. Auriane felt for a moment she heard cries in tongues unknown; here was another closed chamber of the old seeress's mind.

The progress of the litters was slow as a boat ploughing through a reed-filled lake. Auriane strove only to rescue Brico now—she counted the night's original purpose lost. She wouldn't let herself know the misery this caused her, how it threw her back onto her own dwindling reserves of courage. She realized then how the loss of her daughter had caused her to want a mother tonight.

Brico appeared and disappeared; Auriane managed to get a hand on the girl once, but it was like trying to grasp a carp in a pool. Brico was drunken on the crowd's excitement, the haunted night; she burrowed into the throng like a mole, earning curses and blows. The movement of the mass of people was forcing them in circles. Did the fortress lie this way, or the river? Clouds extinguished the sickly gibbous moon; only the flashing of guardsmen's torches showed the way. As she chased Brico, Auriane began to fancy she followed a deer through an uncertain forest, its white tail flashing mockingly as it lured her into another world.

Then Auriane found herself staggering into the space the guardsmen had cleared for the procession of litters. Just ahead she saw Brico, darting with deer-grace toward a litter somewhere in the middle of the line of six. The maid couldn't have known where she was going much better than Auriane had, yet somehow, in her madness, she'd found Ramis.

Auriane halted, transfixed, as she saw a white hand emerge from Ramis's litter, a palm pressed to Brico's forehead.

A fertilizing hand? Had balefire flickered round that hand, or was it just the light of a guardsman's torch, behind them? Was a life-spark passing into the girl's body before her eyes? Or did it mean only that the next time she lay with Demaratos his seed would be strengthened and she'd be delivered of a strong child that would thrive?

Auriane rushed up to claim the enraptured girl, full of fearful images of mortals coming too near to gods and blazing up in fire. The hand that quickened, if held too long, could kill.

She caught Brico as the young woman's knees began to buckle. And looked up to see the muzzle of a horse, bright trefoil pendants on the breast strap of a harness, the hard glitter in the eyes of a young Batavian guardsman. His long hair was twisted into a figure-eight knot just above his right

ear, the fashion among this elite force of native-bred horsemen. "Move off!"
he shouted, prodding Brico with the leaf-shaped blade of his lance, tearing
her leather cape. Blood spread down the sleeve of Brico's woolen undertunic.

"Leave her be!" Auriane cried to him.

The cutting blade of his lance flashed out again. Auriane caught it in both
hands, just behind the blade, and twisted it, while throwing all her weight on
the shaft. The lance was wrenched from his hand. His horse half reared.

"Daughter of a whore!" He drew his double-edged cavalry sword.

Auriane shot up and seized the guardsman by his dangling, hobnail-
booted foot.

"Sheath it, or I pull you from your horse."

"Miserable hogspawn!" But alarm showed in the guardsman's eyes. A
horse soldier possessed many advantages, and one great disadvantage—the
ease with which he could be pulled from his mount.

This awkward stalemate lasted for a heartbeat or two while the guardsman leaned precariously from the saddle with Auriane fastened to his leg, his
sword useless because he couldn't effectively position himself.

"Stop this, now," came a bell-clear voice behind them. "Auriane. Let
him go."

Ramis spoke from behind old dreams.

Auriane let the guardsman's leg drop.

"No brawling in my presence," Ramis spoke on. "Young man, cease battering these two. Ride off and behave yourself."

The guardsman righted himself on his horse, anger put out like a doused
fire, eyes hazed with mild befuddlement. Auriane, too, felt pleasantly disoriented, as if the air were warm, liquid amber, and she were gently seeping out
into a sentient sea of souls, into which flowed all who were present—for an
instant, she even felt she flitted about the prickly passages of the guardsman's
mind—and was aware, suddenly, that this was some glamour worked by
Ramis.

"Go now," Ramis prompted the newly released horseman. He kicked his
mount and trotted briskly off, leaving Auriane to wonder: Had some blood-
cooling spell travelled on Ramis's voice? Or had she just compellingly awakened some image of this guardsman's own mother, hovering huge from dim
days before the gods put language into his mouth—a mother who, like
Ramis, would be an aged native woman?

Their decurion cantered close, shouting, waving Auriane and Brico off
with his vine stick. But this man recognized Auriane; hesitation showed in

his face. The native woman Marcus Julianus had taken into his household would need to be treated with greater diplomacy.

Behind her, Auriane heard Ramis laughing, in beautiful, clear notes.

"Auriane. Turn round and give me greeting. I'd forgotten how amusing you can be."

Brico got to her feet, legs splayed like a foal's. Auriane whispered, "Stay still here, hold the cloth like this, to staunch the bleeding." Then she turned to face Ramis. The prophetess's litter rested on the shoulders of eight tall men; Ramis's face was poised above her like some watchful moon. Auriane felt the gaze of those hooded eyes penetrating straight through to the back of her skull.

"Lady, we must move on," the Guards' decurion said to Ramis. "You shouldn't keep His Eminence waiting."

Ramis's laugh was husky, earthy. "My good man, his waiting doesn't cease when I arrive. Tell him I can't come so quickly these days. I'm too old. Anyway, I'd miss the fine scenery along the way."

"You're a quarter-hour late by the water-clock already and it would not do to offend—"

"Young man! You're quite sure what's important here? Beware. Life's a confusing play, after all, with its trifles praised, its heroes disguised, its grand moments unknown." Ramis added in a tone of command, "I will have words with this woman and you will keep silent."

The decurion spat a curse, but said, "Be swift about it." Not about to let them forget his presence, he positioned his horse so the beast's head and clanking bit were thrust between Auriane and Ramis.

"My Lady," Auriane said, inclining her head, "I give you greeting in the name of the Ancestresses—"

"Yes, stop trying to join them every chance you get, would you? They don't want you yet. Given your nature, though, it's well to keep on good terms with them."

"Please, I've come to beg your help in finding—"

"Many years ago, I told you to go out and play in the world," Ramis smoothly interrupted, her voice cold and inflexible as a steel blade. "And so you did. But you forgot to come back. Rest is life, when it's needed. Rest is poison, when it's not."

Auriane stood numbed and speechless, feeling she'd been expertly disarmed somehow. Ramis pointed a bony finger at her. "Giving my amulet to

Avenahar—that was pitiful. Being apprenticed to me is not something you retire from, like a cobbler from his trade."

"It's Avenahar I must ask you of," Auriane rushed on, too unnerved to wonder how Ramis knew she'd rid herself of the amulet. "She's run off. If you've any love left for my family, can you help me—"

"That's most unmannerly, young man," Ramis said sharply to the decurion. "Can you manage it so your horse's whiskers aren't tickling our faces?"

The guardsman muttered some half-audible insulting description of them both, but he did rein his horse back two steps.

Her baleful gaze swept back to Auriane. "You thought, when you settled in your fine villa, your sorrows were done." Auriane had all but forgotten Ramis's unnerving habit of penetrating without preamble into the mind's most private chambers. "You paid a great debt, you believed," Ramis continued, "and now, surely, you owe no one. And should be able to dwell peacefully on your mountaintop forever. Like a rock. But remember, Auriane, Fria does not collect, or pay, in a coin we recognize."

"I—I don't know of such things anymore . . . You were midwife to Avenahar's birth, can you help me!"

Just ahead, a portion of the crowd broke into riot as shouted insults between people of the Mattiacans and the Chattians erupted into blows. It did not take much drink to bring out these neighboring peoples' traditional hatred of one another: The Mattiacans counted the Chattians brigands who thieved from their neighbors; the Chattians called the Mattiacans lap dogs of Rome. The Guards' decurion left them, trotting off briskly in that direction, almost feeling he'd been rescued—here was a proper excuse for this ridiculous delay, one less likely to get him demoted in rank.

Ramis waved a hand after him. "He won't be missed." Then, as an eagle seizes prey, she said to Auriane, "I want you to cease dictating those books of my life."

This is madness, there is no time, this is not what I came here to speak of . . .

But Auriane found herself lulled, immobilized as some fly enmeshed in spider's silk; that strange stillness shed by Ramis scrambled the proper order of the world, dissolved the stratagems of reason.

"But your name will be dust," Auriane found herself replying.

"Less than dust. Dust can be seen."

"You *want* to vanish from the earth?"

"Because a thing is not seen doesn't mean it has vanished. There's no need to assemble a word-picture of me for their world. There is another world in which my image will be clear as a full moon reflected in a pool."

"Very well, whatever you wish . . . but please," Auriane said, grasping tightly to the extravagant ornamentation on the side of the litter, "do you know if Avenahar lives!"

"Oh, she lives. It's *you* I worry over. You scurry off to a cozy Roman farm and bury yourself in it—a living woman immured in a sarcophagus. You were meant to shelter thousands, not three, or four."

Auriane felt a stifling panic rising in her throat. The scuffle that barred their way was starting to run down; soon, the Horse Guards would have it quelled. *This maddening woman will be be whisked off by the bearers before I get an answer.*

"Where must I go then, to bring her home?"

Avenahar lives. Auriane's relief was like a plunge into hot water on a frigid day. Her mind frog-jumped ahead through the days; she half forgot where she was. *I will fetch her myself. What a homecoming we will have! But she'll get a stern talking-to over this that she won't soon forget . . .*

"You can't bring her home," Ramis said, "for she is in no place."

"I don't understand . . . You said she was living."

"Oh, she's most alive. And she's right where she's meant to be."

"Stop gaming with me!"

"She has joined Witgern's Wolf Coats."

Auriane had heard it said that when run through by a javelin, one feels nothing—the senses, the heart, the mind, are struck blind. It is almost merciful. Unfortunately, she felt that way but briefly; then a thousand worms of terror awakened and began boring relentlessly into her heart. *Fria, no. A thousand deaths await her.*

"She has run off to school, Auriane," Ramis said more gently. "She's fled to her academy. It's time. You did much the same, at her age. Have you forgotten?"

"Have you no pity! Joining a hunted rebel and his draught-maddened pack of fugitives is not *school*!"

"Oh, for her, it's the best of schools. Her spirit's much like yours at her age—only broken out in a rash. She must play out that inherited rage to its end."

"This is madness! You must give her sanctuary!"

Ramis was silent a beat too long, as if to give Auriane time to listen to herself. There was no flicker of emotion in that enigmatic face. Then she whispered, "I won't tear the fair web spun by one far greater than I."

"You care naught for any of us! Of what use are you!"

"Your true enemy, Auriane, is the part of you that you fancy is most reasonable—that's so certain it knows what's right. You're disappointing me. How, by the powers, did you lull yourself into thinking the world *wouldn't* fall apart? Didn't it, before? Doesn't it always?"

Auriane shrank back from the litter and dropped her head into her hands. Above her, Ramis was speaking words she scarce had ears for.

"This is the last time of turning, Auriane, your final chance to die to this world, and follow me."

A subtle certainty settled into place, and Auriane said softly, "You knew I would be waiting for you here."

"Oh, I thought there was a good chance. You didn't really think I came all this way just to be chastised by His Pomposity, did you?"

The decurion of the Horse Guard cantered toward them on his lathered, wild-eyed mount; his leather knee-breeches and gilt cuirass were splattered with blood. Auriane doubted it was his own.

"Forward!" With his lance, he indicated the cleared way ahead.

"You've always sought refuge, Auriane. First, it drove you to war—only in battle did you find peace. Now it drives you to too much peace. You must want clear sight more than refuge. Listen to me. You are one of the fires of this land. Rarely do I see transcendent beauty in a will to fight, but it is so, in you. You must ignite again. You must prepare, now, to be what I am."

"You speak as if I were free as a maid. I would never desert my children."

"Ah. But you've done so already, by deserting your true nature."

"Move *forward*!" the guardsman shouted hoarsely.

"The lily opens. Don't try to close it by main force." Ramis looked ahead. "A pity. I must go."

Ramis dropped the litter's curtain.

Auriane wanted to sink to the mud and sob until all the desolation was washed out of her, but was seized with a strong sense, then, of her father watching her from the Sky Hall; she could not shame him. So she stood stiffly, unable to move, while the throng buffeted her.

Ramis's silver-crowned head emerged a final time.

"Auriane. Rivers are the borderlands between worlds. If you do nothing a river will decide."

"A curse on you! Speak words I can understand!" This brought quick, horrified looks from those standing near.

But Ramis showed no sign of offense. She calmly signaled to the bearers, and the eight tall men straightened themselves as one, as though beneath the control of a single mechanism. With beautifully matched steps they moved up the slope. The litters of Ramis's women broke into motion, too; the bearers carried them swiftly forward in a smooth then halting rhythm, just above the crowd, so it appeared as though the six litters were being rowed through a sea of heads.

Auriane started off in pursuit. But masses of people flowed together in the litters' wake, hindering her, and she was engulfed once more in her mind's relentless night. The ground-shaking truth that Ramis still wished for her to one day carry the Veleda's staff hovered somewhere beyond misery's edge—what could that matter, now? Her family was to be torn apart like a loaf of bread at a feast. Marcus lay under fatal suspicion, and she, by her own hand, had destroyed herself.

And Avenahar had leapt astride a dragon.

RAMIS WALKED DOWN the central aisle of the Principia of Mogontiacum, the massive basilican-form structure that dominated the square of headquarters buildings within the Fortress. The mammoth stone hall served as court, place of assembly, and shrine for the legionary standards. Darkfall transformed its vaulted interior into a yawning cavern selectively illumined by small, regularly-spaced puddles of light cast by wall sconces. Ramis moved between a double row of monumental columns that were lost in darkness where they met the roof. Four maiden attendants walked before her, bearing pottery bowls of smoldering mullein. Soldiers of the Twenty-second Legion in parade dress were posted along the walls; coronas of firelight outlined their upright javelins.

Many had heard tales of this greatest of northern sybils but few had looked upon her. Those assembled on benches below the tribunal strained to see as she approached amidst gusts of smoke, the music of the bronze implements that hung from her belt, the crisp tapping of her staff on stone. She presented a sight jarring to Roman eyes, with her bulky cloak and hairy calfskin boots, her adornments worn not to beautify but to confer authority: The heavy silver sickle-moon at her forehead flashed a quiet warning. An amulet of black leather strung from a thong seemed some dark leather heart at her throat. From her hide belt dangled pouches of herbs—potent poisons, they imagined, that would turn a man livid in less time than it took to haul water from a well.

She gained the cross-hall of the nave and ascended the low platform that had been prepared for her. Few doubted, then, the charge that she had condemned a legionary soldier for looting treasure from one of her sacred lakes—this was the face of a woman who could pronounce a sentence of death. Her platform and chair had been set so that Ramis faced the Governor levelly—Ramis's women had insisted on this during negotiations for this meeting. The maiden attendants took places flanking her. Unlike Ramis, who had made past journeys to this place, her women were bewildered by this hollow, man-made mountain, the wealth of gold on the legionaries' helmets and breastplates, the bold geometry of the mosaic floor, and the whole of this vast, bustling city devoted to war that was the Fortress of Mogontiacum.

Her three inquisitors were seated before her on cross-legged chairs atop a dais. In the center was the Governor, Maximus, whose normally sagging, affable features were hardened into a formal mask. At his left, one of the junior tribunes watched Ramis with bovine vacancy; he sat in for Camillus, who still lay between life and death after the goring dealt him by the aurochs. And to his right was Marcus Julianus, sitting poised and alert, if somewhat stiffly from the pain of his injuries; Julianus alone was not in military dress. Rising elegantly behind them was the *sacellum*, the marble shrine with peaked roof that housed the golden eagle standard of the Twenty-second Legion; a stone screen shielded it from view. Flanking the dais were rows of recorders skilled in short-hand writing. Ranked behind them was a detachment of the Governor's Grooms, thirty stoutly-made men recruited from the provinces whose duties included requisitioning horses for the army, and making arrests.

The symmetry of the scene of the tribunal was odd, to the women's eyes—even the drape of the Governor's heavy military cloak had not been left to chance; it fell too evenly from his shoulders, and was arranged with studied grace where it broke on contact with the floor. He sat as if a vise were clamped to his head as he gazed down an imaginary line bisecting the Principia.

The audience was split into two parts, with the best benches given over to the staff of the legionary headquarters, Palace observers, and leading townsfolk from the native settlement that served the Fortress. On more distant benches by the wall was the small party of Chattians with whom the Governor had been in parley throughout the day—rough-clad men with unshorn beards, long hair, eyes intent as birds of prey, who looked uncultivated and wild in this polished hall, like some errant patch of bramble-ridden waste ground in the midst of a manicured garden. Chief over them was the rising young war-leader Sigibert, comely of aspect, with red-blond hair swept back from a commanding brow—that same Sigibert who was so desired by Elza as husband. For the delegation, it had been a day of onerous concessions: They'd been compelled to agree to leave five more miles of unsown land between tribal lands and the frontier of the Empire, and to yield double last year's number of young men to supply a new native auxiliary unit that was being formed. With Ramis's arrival Sigibert felt like a soldier who sees the arrival of reinforcements at the end of a long day of bitter fighting.

A herald sang out the names of the prophetess and the men on the tribunal, his voice fluid and muscular as the vaults and turns of an acrobat.

"I greet you Ramis, prophetess of the Chattians, called the Veleda," the Governor said without emotion.

Ramis addressed each man in turn, ending with, "I greet you, Valerius Maximus, well esteemed among the lords of the known world." Her bare stress on the word *known* seemed to shrink the Empire to the size of a barley field, while bringing unwelcome attention to the vastness of what lay beyond.

Ramis watched the three men without expectation, and with infinite patience, her eyes still pools, active, awake, while she sat proud as a falcon. They saw a strange and elegant crone, her look lordly but quiet as she shed a tranquillity that was a rich balm on the air. The Governor began to believe this formidable woman would be content to meditate on his face for an hour, should he make no effort to speak. It was as if time, and the world, moved more slowly for her. He found her noble in a darkly foreign way, but felt no reverence. He held fast to attitudes instilled by a Greek education, certain she was no more than an inspired charlatan who played skillfully as a citharist on tribal superstitions.

The tribune found her cooly authoritative manner an irritant—he didn't understand her and didn't want to; she was the sort of woman who belonged nowhere in his world. However, he'd once known a man who died from the spells of an Etruscan witch, and so he watched her with some wariness.

As for Marcus Julianus, he was seized with the surprise of his life. Before a word had escaped her mouth, he knew he looked upon someone of unusual attainments. At first, he read it as evidence of the fiercest Stoic will he had ever encountered: She *made* herself impregnable to Fortune's storms, through the practice of some philosophical regimen unknown. She had forged her strength through a long lifetime. But how? From where came that brilliant silence? He was astounded to realize she'd done no more than utter a brief greeting, and yet the very air in the vast chamber seemed softly luminous, and many in the room looked as if they had just arisen from gentle sleep. He judged that everything this woman did was conscious, not because she was desirous of others' surrender but for obscure reasons, having to do with her gods. He had seen a tranquillity so potent only once before, as a youth: in the face of his old Cynic teacher Isodorus, that wise, babbling madman living under bridges, on the eve before Nero had him thrown to the wild dogs. *Is this the one who "lives as in the days of Saturn, when all ate at one board," as foretold by Isodorus in his last madness? I should have known to expect much of this woman,* he chided himself. *I should have taken on faith that Auriane wouldn't have expended her reverence lightly.*

The Governor addressed her first. "I trust your journey was well."

A bare smile came to her face—a slight brightening of the moon. "It was smooth, as river journeys usually are. And how very many fine new villas you have built along the banks! What *industry* your people show. There were not half so many, just forty summers ago."

Maximus nodded faintly, with no lessening of his reserve. Marcus Julianus suppressed a small smile of amusement; she spoke of Rome's achievements as the works of precocious children.

"That would have been," Ramis continued thoughtfully in that sharp, clear voice, "in the time of your father." She looked directly at Julianus. "Marcus Arrius Julianus the Elder."

The Governor heard: *I treated with your father, Julianus. I was busily arranging the world you enjoy today when all of you were still babes.* But Julianus heard it only as a pleasant reminder of his father's connection with this unusual woman.

Ramis seemed to have selected Julianus out, bypassing the other two men as if they held lesser significance—the Governor possessing some, the tribune, none. "He was an able man, your father," she said, plucking words from a void with great deliberation. She had some trick of making every word count for three. "I have here a written copy in your Latin tongue of my last treaty with him." She produced from her robes a slender bronze canister with silver chasing, and held it up for them to see.

The Governor frowned in annoyance and shifted in his seat. That treaty had been broken many times by Rome—and the conniving woman knew it, he thought. Even to have brought it here was an insolent act. Marcus Julianus felt only admiration for her boldness. In the humble seats, the young chief Sigibert grinned broadly once, caught himself, and resumed his look of fierce quiet.

Julianus rushed in before the Governor could utter a tart reply. "And he spoke well of you, Lady. He said you were sensible and fair, and of penetrating judgment—" The Governor half turned to Julianus, his irritation visible. *What in the name of Nemesis are you doing? Flattering her into even greater willfulness?*

"—and that you never failed to keep your sworn word," Julianus finished.

Maximus remembered, then, that the old treaty stipulated she was not to give priestly judgments within the *imperium*—the lands within Roman control—and relaxed slightly as he realized what Julianus's purpose was.

She smiled, and faintly nodded. "I try to keep to it, gentlemen. Your soldier who desecrated our lake was in the Aldermeadow, a place which does, indeed, lie within Chattian lands."

"You are wrong," the Governor said. "That is imperial land, since Domitian's Chattian campaign."

She held up the bronze canister. "A war that violated this very treaty, Julianus the Elder's last with me. Rome, by what's promised here, sits there wrongfully. It seems your people write treaties on waste paper."

"Insolence and trickery will not serve you, madam." The tribune spoke for the first time. But his anger was a damp torch that would not ignite—her strange calm unnerved him, caused him to feel kingdom and cosmos were shimmering, preparing to melt into a new shape.

She regarded him with boredom, then returned her gaze to the Governor. "Not that it matters, overmuch, in my world," she said, making a graceful dismissive gesture. "You're here, you're there, it's the nature of your people to push others off their lands, a habit I don't soon expect you to break." Her voice rose up powerfully, filling the gallery. "But because you can separate men from their own soil does not mean you can do the same with gods. I am the guardian of sacred law, gentlemen. And in the end, I did not judge him: I left his sentence to the Fates."

"This 'judgment' was criminal and impious," the Governor retorted. "You threw him on the mercy of the forest and he perished of cold and attacks of animals. No citizen of Rome should be used so. You had no authority to chastise him. You—a non-citizen, a woman of a subdued tribe—have *no* rights in this matter. This is what you fail to comprehend."

She interrupted him with a soft clucking sound, as if chiding a child. "But my dear Maximus, our worlds don't touch. You're hurling javelins into the sea. Calm yourself . . . What lies beneath? . . . golden stillness, only golden stillness . . ." She cast the words out like a net that flared, settled, and softened; Marcus Julianus would not have believed it, were he not here to witness—had she henbane on the voice? ". . . anyway, you should love my sentence," she continued, "for it was markedly similar to your august Trajan's own, when he put the evildoers who served Domitian on that rudderless ship and let Neptune work out their fates."

"I warn you, you're tumbling into a pit!" This touched the Governor's favorite wound, one he aggravated and nursed. "You dare compare yourself to a civilized ruler of a world larger than you will ever know, a man before whom even Greece with all its accumulated wisdom bows, even Egypt with all its venerable history—a man who sits alongside the Capitoline gods!"

"Yes." It was said with modest surprise that he would think it a thing to wonder over. "We were both born of woman. We both speak for many peoples." Her eyes became less gentle. "And we both make laws."

In a controlled fury, the Governor snatched a tablet handed him by one of his recorders. "One year ago you were commanded to elevate the loyal Sigibert, here today with us, above the other Chattian chiefs, by means of delivering to your people favorable oracles concerning him. You have failed to do so."

Marcus Julianus briefly shut his eyes in embarrassment. Maximus had not told him he would frame the charge that way. Astonishment showed in the face of Sigibert on his distant bench, but he mastered it quickly.

"People believe my oracles come from the elder gods," Ramis said. "How disappointed they would be to know they only come from Maximus."

"I warn you to hew to the solemnity of this discussion!" Maximus responded. "Don't tell me that's not, in truth, what you do—produce expedient pronouncements accompanied by incense and music, in a voice well-timbred for theatrical effect. You tell your listeners whatever you consider most politic. If I'm wrong surely you could manage it, once. If you wished." He leaned forward slightly. "To refuse to do so is to use your great influence against us."

She smiled at this, and Marcus Julianus alone saw it was the smile of a mother at the charming deceits of a child.

The smile vanished. "Speak your purpose, my lord Governor. You want me to promote this man," she nodded toward Sigibert, "above other Chattian chiefs because a troublesome tribe is simpler to control if you have but a single neck to yoke."

"Lady, I would advise you not to—"

"You are creating overlords among us, through the seduction of your gifts. In my youth, there was one such; now, because of Rome's constant meddling in our affairs, they are much more common. Witness this Cheruscan called Chariomer, growing like a canker on the body of our tribe. I see this leading us, several generations hence, straight into what my people have never had before—hereditary nobles. Like you. Your most heinous weapon against us is not the ballista or catapult, but your art in leading us into imitating you." Firelight played off her brass-bound staff, the silver circlet, her eyes; she glimmered like a night sky. "No, I won't help you. You want one leader; I insist on many. Anyway, the Veleda does not promote chiefs; this is a Roman thought, believed only because it has been repeated so many times. My good man, I only promote *sight*."

Maximus nodded curtly to the judicial recorders. "We duly record another act of insubordination."

Marcus Julianus was disturbed by the increasingly hostile nature of the interview. At the same time, he found himself more and more ignited with curiosity about her. In Ramis, he sensed a critical volume unread, a living storehouse of surprising connections between obscure points of knowledge, a mind that might link, underground, the divergent philosophies he'd investigated all his life. Maximus was beginning to look like a man who dug through nuggets of gold to get to a bale of straw.

Marcus Julianus raised a hand to silence Maximus, and said, "Tell me, Lady, what you meant by the last words you spoke?"

Again, Ramis regarded Marcus Julianus with great attention, as if he were the only man present with whom it was possible to have meaningful speech.

"That is what 'Veleda' means: the 'one who sees'—through walls of earth and stone thickened with centuries of belief, straight through to the true nature of earthly life. How astonished you would be, good man, confronted by the civilization of the unseen! What seems fixed before you is, in fact, infinitely various. The very bedrock on which this fortress sits is not solid. It is alive. Your deathless spirit, in truth, lacks nothing. This is why all pursuits bring grief—and why I counsel abandoning them. You knew these things in the blood before you grew out of tender childhood, and got caught up in the narrower and narrower passages of your world's labyrinths . . . and you can know them again."

The tribune looked elaborately bored; idly he stroked a stylus he held against his chin. Maximus's eyes had become hard and blank as an executioner's.

But Marcus Julianus regarded Ramis so intently, he appeared to have gone into a light trance.

"To the matter at hand," Maximus said then. "Ramis of the Chattians, you are also accused of —"

"Just one moment, good man!" Her words cut him off cleanly as a sword stroke. Julianus reflected, *she gets off with that only because she has no fixed place in Maximus's hierarchy of persons; she haunts the spaces in between.* "I have something to say, just to Julianus."

Ramis quietly returned her gaze to Julianus's.

"I know you," she said in a voice that came like music to the beat of a drum, as though the oracular state were beginning to drift over her. "You have worked so very hard, all your life, to determine what wisdom is. As if it were a thing hidden from you somewhere. And you could discover it by reaping and storing more and yet more knowledge in that fine and noble mind of yours. Poor man, you could have the whole of the Library of Alexandria in your head and still not have wisdom. Consider that when a man has a nightmare, or a powerful dream . . . does another know its power from having it described to him in words?" She pointed a long, slender finger at him. "Wisdom cannot be taught. It can only be *remembered*."

Julianus's face was solemn with amazement. "Lady," he whispered. "Those last words. They are from Socrates."

"Well, yes . . . but they're not just his, though he used them to good effect. Forget whose words they are. Just keep them near."

"But how in the name of the gods do you know of —"

Maximus loudly cleared his throat. "Might I have my courtroom back? I've heard enough philosophy to last me to the end of this reign. Ramis, we commanded you to halt the criminal activities of the rebel Witgern—and you made no effort to do so."

"Why would I ask Witgern to throw his wolf coat into the fire," she replied, "when you only want him quiet so you're free to go off and commit mayhem elsewhere? You wish me to bring peace here, so you can plunder that far-off land. Dacia, I believe it is called? Why would you think I feel less for the Dacians than I do for you?" Her gaze settled on him mildly, and with kindness. "A pity no one ever informed you that I will not do such things."

Maximus scarcely seemed to hear this; he sat forward, keenly focused on her as if she were the target of a javelin throw.

"Today your long life of undermining us comes to an end. You, Ramis of the Chattians, are accused of supplying money to the Chattians for the purchase of arms—"

The air seemed to rush from the room.

"—which you saw transported across the frontier of the Empire into Chattian lands, in contradiction of law, where your confederates put these weapons of iron into the hands of enemy chiefs. This is an offense capital in nature, and subject to the supreme penalty."

Marcus Julianus required a moment to believe it. Maximus had told him nothing of any plan to lay this long-unsolved crime at Ramis's door.

The chief called Sigibert leapt to his feet.

"This is treachery! This was not the charge! You tricked her here!"

He did not even know he was shouting in his own Germanic tongue; the Governor regarded him blankly. "Take that man off," he commanded.

Four of the Governor's Grooms fell out of their rank and began half prodding, half dragging Sigibert toward the courtyard while he hammered the air with shouts that echoed grotesquely in the vast stone gallery.

When silence returned, Maximus said, "Do you admit to guilt or do you say you are innocent?"

"Your purpose is not justice but to rid yourself of a burr under your saddles. Long as I live, I mean to make it impossible for you to have one chief who can be tucked into the folds of your togas."

Maximus planned this from the first, Julianus realized suddenly. *In fact, the entire afternoon parley—in which he conceded nothing to the Chattians, and which could have been accomplished through messages—was, no doubt, a ruse to get her here. He couldn't tell me of his intentions because he knew I would never approve of her arrest.*

And, he's wrong. *But I can't prove it to him without destroying Auriane.*

Auriane, who, through foul fortune, is still here, within the Fortress.

Marcus Julianus leaned toward the Governor and said in a low voice, "We must recess. I want to look at your evidence."

Maximus ignored him. "Do you admit guilt or deny it?"

"Neither." She spoke the word as if she moved an unimportant piece one square forward on a game board. It caused Julianus a fresh seizure of horror. *Surely she knows she is fighting for her life?*

Perhaps she does not care.

I must help her.

"My Lady," Marcus Julianus addressed her, "last month we apprehended a man called Anniolus, who confessed to having been the man who drove the sacred carts in which the arms were concealed. He claims you mean to make arguments to secure his release."

Ramis realized Julianus made a roughly-patched-together attempt to ex-onerate her, by demonstrating to Maximus that she did not know this critical link in the chain died under interrogation shortly after his apprehension. Ap-preciation glimmered in her eyes.

"My dear Julianus, there would be no use in that unless the Fates raised him from the dead."

Julianus was saddened and alarmed; she would not let him aid her. He hurriedly scratched a note on a wax tablet and passed it to Maximus—

We must recess. She is martyring herself. This woman lives in near-poverty. The person we seek has vast resources.

But Maximus was proud of his case, and its solution promised him re-lease from the mounting pressures put on him by the Palace to root out this famous malefactor. He scratched a note in reply: *Hear me through.*

"We believe that you, Ramis, did encourage the women of the Potters' Guild of the town of Colonia Agrippinensis to collect donations of silver for your purpose, in the amount of . . ." He talked on into the horrible si-lence, each word miring the Chattian delegation in greater dismay. When he came to: ". . . and they employed one Eppia Silvana, freedwoman of Chat-tian birth, to requisition carts for transport . . ." Julianus, now visibly losing patience, vigorously shook his head and wrote—*No. I questioned this woman and dismissed her. She is a notorious fabricator who claims to have committed crimes for the sake of the disturbance it causes.*

This time Maximus pushed the tablet aside without reading it, irritated that it was apparent to all that Marcus Julianus was raising objections. Max-imus had hoped Julianus would greet his findings with admiration. What er-rant spasm of eccentricity drove his exasperating mentor to undo all his labors?

". . . who has confessed under expert interrogation," Maximus contin-ued, "that these weapons were to be disbursed to Chattian chiefs, including Witgern, who has turned them upon us already, when he laid waste to our fort under the command of Firmius Speratus."

Julianus, frustrated, furious, made a final try, and hurriedly scribbled, writing half-legibly now:

This is a holy woman who cannot touch iron. She would have nothing to do with its transport. Someone has given you false information. We must recess.

* * *

"—AND SHE IS to die." The youth, a son of one of Julianus's grooms, finished his tale just as his heaving breaths began to slow. The lithe-limbed boy
had sprinted the gravelled distance from the Principia to the Governor's residence, where Auriane awaited him; earlier she'd dispatched him to the tribunal to glean what he could. The boy told it feveredly and all out of order;
twice she'd had to stop him, calm him, and get him to start again.

"You've done well," she said finally. "You can go." She pressed a *denar-
ius,* moist and warm from her hand, into his.

When he was gone, Auriane felt washed clean of all sorrow, as if her
mind were a chalice that could hold only so much of it and the contents of
an amphora had been poured in. She'd scarce had time to assimilate the news
that Avenahar was with Witgern. It was as though the bloodcourse connecting head and heart had been severed, leaving an otherworldly detachment,
tranquil as falling snow. She sensed something unnatural in her calm, feeling
her ghost rode on air just above her body as she moved to the writing alcove
Marcus used for dictating letters, and sat before an elegant table on delicate,
deer-form legs. This fresh disaster was, oddly, almost a relief, perhaps just
because it left the path ahead so clear.

Nothing mattered but that she set things to right.

She retrieved a stylus from among the drifts of papyrus and found a
brass-bound wax tablet, clean of letters. With painful slowness, she wrote,
pausing once as she heard the ominous swell of distant voices—the native
populace was evidently learning the same news she'd just been given. Auriane understood now why it had been necessary to post so many soldiers
along Ramis's route. But even the people's cries didn't disturb the still surface of this fantastic tranquillity—*is this a dim flicker of what the immortal gods
know every day?* she wondered once. *Or have I fallen victim to some spell?*

She got her plain cloak of undyed wool from its peg and fastened it with
a silver brooch in the shape of a wheel, mate of one her mother, Athelinda,
wore; it reminded her that her family, both the living and the dead, walked
with her. Then she called out for Brico.

The maidservant came slowly from her alcove, stumbling once on the
front of her long tunica, her full face swollen with sleep.

"You're going out?" Brico asked. Then she heard the people's thunder
beyond the walls. "Something's wrong. What is it?" Her eyes were immense
and shining.

"Yes, I must go out. Don't stay awake for me, there's no need."

"If you go out, I go with you!" Brico wasn't entirely surprised something dreadful had passed, for the presence of Ramis was dangerous; her touch was the crooked finger of lightning, illumining, searing, leaving a swath of mysterious destruction to be discovered in the light of morning.

"No, Brico. You're scarce awake and you've had enough adventuring for one night. But listen to me now. When Marcus Julianus returns, don't fail to tell him at once what's befallen Avenahar. Then, I have a task for you." She gave Brico the wax tablet, now folded and neatly tied. "There's a seeress here with Ramis, named Algifu. I want you to give her this, and—"

"Me—ask to see a seeress? Why not *you*? Where will you be?"

"You must not ask that, or even think about it."

With a fierce twist Brico turned away, shoulders heaving as she quietly cried.

"Brico, please, be of good courage. None of us has time to be afraid. You must do this thing and not wonder over me. I'll be well." She put her hands on Brico's shoulders. "They say Algifu is kind. She won't harm you. You must ask her to give this to Witgern, the Wolf Coat chief."

"To Witgern." Brico said the words as if they were devoid of meaning.

"Yes. Put it in a safe place, for now. Do it on the morrow." Witgern's band shifted about like the winds, but Auriane believed a member of the Holy Nine would know how to find him.

Brico took the tablet in both hands, as if fearful of dropping it.

Witgern would not be able to read what she'd written, but he had occasional commerce with Gallic traders, most of whom were literate. The short message would remind him of their old and dear blood-friendship, close as the bond between husband and wife. She begged him to conduct Avenahar to a safe place; she named the Holy Wood. From there, men sent by Marcus Julianus would collect Avenahar, and take her to him. Auriane swore on her honor as daughter of Baldemar that this would be carried out with great discretion; he need not fear an ambush.

Feeling borne along on a river-current of Ancestresses, Auriane departed the guest chamber, passed through a haze of smoke drifting from an altar dedicated to the Governor's household gods, then on into the night. Torches still burned around the Principia. It was the third hour of darkness.

The sounds of turmoil from beyond the Fortress's walls were louder now; the cries resembled the mourning wails of wolves. Clots of smoke blew over the crenelated rampart; there was burning in the native village. As she approached the triple-arched entranceway of the Principia, she saw a knot of her Chattian countrymen gathered outside its doors—the tribal delegation.

She quickened her pace and pulled forward the hood of her cloak, but one tall, bearded warrior hailed her, then another. None of these had ever seen the daughter of Baldemar but they knew she was here, and so had little trouble deducing that this tall native woman with bronze hair, her eyes gently molten with grief, was Auriane. If they had doubts, the wheelform brooch quelled them.

A well-favored young man among them brazenly put himself in her way, feet planted apart. His face haunted her; it was insistently familiar.

"Auriane? It must be."

"Yes. I am sorry, I've no time for—"

"Auriane!" He grasped her strongly by the shoulders. "It is truly you! We're departing for home. You must come with us."

"Gods below, you are known to me."

"It's my father, Sigwulf, you knew, slain beside you so long ago."

She tamped down a fresh start of sadness, but beneath it lingered a stronger faith in the rebirth of souls. "I'm gladdened your father lives on in so fine a man." She pulled away from him. "I'll greet Baldemar for you."

Sigibert caught her cloak as she strode off, and she dragged him like some unwilling hound on a lead.

"We would win back the old world!" he called out. "Chariomer and his Cheruscan brigands will fatten the crows. Auriane, were you to come with me now, I would give over the whole of my warband to you. *'Greet Baldemar'*? What do you mean by that?"

She made no reply.

"You're not going in there?" he said then. "Only treachery awaits inside."

"I must, if I'm to get Ramis back for you." She wrestled herself free from him and strode on.

"Auriane!" She did not slow. *"'Daughter of the Ash, lead us out!'"* At the sound of the battle cry from long ago, Auriane became very still.

"Sigibert, you foolish dreamer, get out of here now before he arrests you all." Prompted by the realization she sensed a wound in this young man that for a reason she couldn't name called to mind her lost daughter. She came closer and said, "You can help me, Sigibert. The Wolf Coats have my daughter Avenahar. Watch over her as best you can. It's my last wish, you can't fail me in this. Tell her—what I do now, I do for her."

A desolate Sigibert found himself staring helplessly at her fluttering, rapidly retreating cloak.

At the door of the Principia, a clerk of the headquarters staff lowered his banner-draped lance, signaling her to halt. She told him she had information bearing on the case. He dispatched a junior clerk to relay this to Maximus, and she was given leave to approach the tribunal.

She felt she wasn't walking so much as drifting as she moved toward the dais like some wind-driven leaf. Only Maximus remained, and he was rising to leave. Later she would learn that Marcus Julianus had quit the tribunal in outrage, not wanting to be a party to this deception. She could still smell the holy incense of the seeresses, lingering like the black perfume of a funeral's wake. She found the absence of Ramis strange and unsettling. Had the Governor's Grooms actually laid profane hands upon the Veleda and put her under arrest? There was something repugnant, obscene in the mental picture of Ramis taken into custody; some part of her thought it impossible.

Maximus smiled paternally at her approach. "It is our female Hercules!" He sounded like giants shouting from mountain to mountain as his voice travelled hollowly about the stone hall. "Has Julianus told you I have written a letter to the Emperor describing your singular deed?" But his gaiety was wan.

As he better discerned Auriane's face, the fond smile was replaced with a puzzled but forbearing look.

Maximus's curiosity sharpened further as she halted beneath his seat. In one mad moment he felt he looked at many women, all living in her eyes— Ancestresses. He saw another sort of strength in her then, that of elements that conquer in time, as water, through constancy, carves stone. She was a creature flexible and strong as a young tree, this confounding native woman who had casually leapt on the back of an aurochs, who watched him now as though she stood before some altar of sacrifice. The candelabra flames illumined two soft, steady points of light in her eyes; they were made of silvered glass, lit from within. *By Charon,* he thought, *when one looks upon this woman, one thinks the gods likely to exist.*

"State your name." It was a formality for the recorders. Reed pens scraped over papyrus.

Then she said, "Valerius Maximus, I am the woman you seek."

"My dear Aurinia . . . what are you saying?"

"I am the criminal you've sought for seven years. And I can prove it so. Ramis is innocent."

After a sharp moment of hesitation, he said dismissively, "Perhaps you should speak of this matter first with Julianus."

"Do *not* speak to me as if I were a child!" Her words split the silence like a whip crack. It startled him; he sat straighter in his seat.

"I know it all," she went on, "how new-minted *denarii* were exchanged for older, full-weight coins at the bank at Lugdunum, the names of the captains of the vessels used for transport, how the wagons were secured, who got it across the frontier—for I'm the one who planned it. Give Ramis her freedom. Take me and let her go. Or you commit a woeful mistake for which your gods will punish you."

Maximus's eyes began to harden as he rapidly considered that what she claimed could well be true. She seemed a woman of entirely too simple and direct a nature to concoct elaborate lies. And she *had* been a dedicated enemy of Rome, long before she'd ever entered Julianus's household—had it been wise to assume her allegiances had so thoroughly turned, after a few short years of civilized life? He'd been careless. He'd let Julianus's eminence act as a shield, deflecting all suspicion from this woman.

"And . . . Marcus Julianus . . . ?" he said finally, the words left unspoken too dreadful to voice.

"I carried this out entirely without his knowing. I will swear to this by every god."

"That is not possible."

"Do not be a fool, it is possible."

"Mind your speech! You're too unsophisticated to know when you give offense, or I'd punish you for that. Where could you have gotten access to these great sums of money, without him knowing it?"

She told him. Maximus's expression became increasingly clouded. These were most unwelcome words. Her singular boldness had saved his life. The thought of putting this exemplary native woman in chains appalled him. Tensely he tapped a stylus against the same wax tablet Julianus had earlier thrust into his hands.

"I think you confess to this only to save your prophetess." It was almost a plea.

"No. And I suspect you've got it turned about. There's a good chance Ramis allowed you to believe in her guilt, in order to save *me*."

He found himself suddenly depleted of objections. As he looked on her now, her comeliness began to distort in his view, until it became the frightful beauty of the bright serpent flowing prettily, bearing poison.

"This is a sad madness, it is too much to consider in one sitting. Leave me to think on this."

"And had I not been found out this spring by the magistrate at

Confluentes, I'd be arming my people still. You may cross-check with him; his name is Volusius Victorinus. As we speak, he sends his evidence to Rome."

"If this all be so, then you are Nemesis's own emanation." His voice had grown soft and ruthless. "At best, you've cost me time and trouble. At worst, your act has grievously harmed a noble man, and has led to the death of good soldiers. Your gods preserve you if these things be true."

"You must do Ramis no harm! Tell me you will release her!"

"Take her off," he said to the Grooms. "Hold her in the guard tower."

Chapter 19

When the sentry announced Marcus Julianus, Auriane felt the cold, hollow readiness of the soldier rudely roused at dawn by a war trumpet.

From her prison's narrow window she could see a brown-green expanse of parade ground with its guardian images of Victory with upraised spear, of Mars in flowing garments, hovering weightlessly above their plinths. She had been watching the training of a detachment of the Twenty-second Legion, soon to be dispatched to the Dacian war. They drilled in pairs. One man was armed with the *falx*, the dreaded scythelike sword carried by the Dacian nobles; the other defended himself with the short sword of the legionary soldier. She had heard it said that because of the terrible penetrating force of the *falx*, the Palace had revived the use of a stronger mail armor of antique type that Rome had not used for generations, and ordered the legionaries' shields stiffened with extra planks of wood. *That is how Rome has extended herself so—by refashioning herself to fit each new enemy. My people would have hotly refused to do such a thing. They would have counted the Dacian falx a dark sign from this god or that, brought on by some family misdeed, then faced it naked of armor, to*

retrieve more of their honor. Ramis always spoke of the strength that came from be-
ing mutable as water; does this mean she privately thinks her own people fools?

Such thoughts were a fire-break against what she did not want to see—
Ramis brought to execution. Avenahar torn apart in the wild.

And Marcus's fury. *Doubtless, he means to take leave of me forever.*

He stood in the open doorway, eyes afire with the silent shout—*Why?*
There was a solemn distance in his face, uncomfortably close to the expression
in the portrait bust of his father. He was unshaven and haggard, eyes bruised
with sleeplessness. And he was clad in tattered gray mourning clothes. With
an unpleasant start she realized he wore them in mourning for her.

Auriane wore the same cloak she'd donned before the tribunal, and she'd
not been given enough water to wash. She drew off from him, humiliated by
how defeated and soiled she must look.

"I could not let her die for me," she whispered.

"I came to take my leave," came words in the flat voice of an officious
stranger. "I've settled affairs at the villa. Tomorrow I set out on the journey
to Dacia, in the company of the cohort you see practicing there."

"I care if no one else in the world understands," she said then, "but I
must have *you* know why I did this thing. I was born to stand by the gate and
protect—the Fates know why. And you are the same. So I'd hoped you'd
understand."

He put his hands gently on her shoulders. "I return in spring," he said.
"The journey will be mostly by oared galley, down the Danuvius. Where the
river forms a spur into Dacian lands, Pontes, it's called—there, the Emperor
assembles his army of invasion. I'll winter there. What hope have I of softening his wrath toward you after that complete confession? Little or none.
And now, I'll be making a plea before a man who suspects *me* of treason. But
that's the bed we now lie in."

This massive effort of self-control frightened her; she was uncertain
what lay beneath.

"As you say," she said, edging off again, feeling intensely, unpleasantly
alone. "That is well, then." She felt she poked at the dying embers of their
common hearth. "Will . . . will we meet again, in this life?"

"I am not a sybil! Ask the woman you sacrificed us for!"

"Ah, that's better. I like your anger more than your nothing-at-all."

"You forced my hand—do not expect me to be pleased. The one *fortunate* part of all this is that Avenahar's run off with a hunted rebel with a
price on his head even greater than the price on yours. At least, we know

where she is—more or less. At least, the law cannot get to her—that is, not yet!"

"Marcus, no king, no spirit that dwells among the living or the dead could have kept me silent while this woman who stands at our people's heart was accused falsely of a deed committed by me."

"I knew your nobility would slay us one day. A man cannot serve two masters. One is always wronged. You straddle two worlds, and you're struck down by the halfhearted faith you give to each. Our being together was ill-starred from the start."

"Marcus. In my place, you, too, would have come forward with the truth. You're adamant in giving faith to what you love and it's for this we've always given each other so much honor." She felt herself a vessel breaking into fine shatter-lines, ready to crack apart. "How can you call so dear a time ill-starred?"

"Gods. Let us stop this." It was a cry of grief. He pulled her to him like a man in famine times who comes upon sustaining bread. In this matter his words were against his heart, and he knew it. The courage she'd exhibited in going alone before the tribunal shored him up immensely against the cold caprices of the world.

She felt she embraced a lightning-struck oak.

She gathered her strength for the fearful question.

"What have they done with Ramis?"

"Nothing, yet. She's being held in a chamber not unlike this one. Maximus believes you. He overreached himself. Your people have lit fires all over the hills. He knows that if he harms her, the Chattians and their allies will make war—and they could do some damage, even in their weakened state. He doesn't have the men to handle it. He rushed ahead in this matter, without consulting me."

"He has no reason to hold her here!"

"Auriane, you saved her life. You couldn't have preserved her freedom. He would have found a way to detain her, just or unjust. The order to arrest her came from the Palace. Maximus thought the ruse necessary—had your people suspected he planned to hold her, they would have cleverly hidden her away somewhere where Rome would never have found her."

"And will he keep her here until she dies?"

"No. But she's to be taken far from your people. Her influence is too great. She will suffer the same fate as that Veleda who served before her, in the reign of Vespasian—she'll be sent to Rome to live out her span on a modest pension, far from any mischief she might work among your people."

"Sent to Rome. What madness. She is a woman of the forest." She tensely met his gaze. "He *did* release Ramis's women?"

"Yes, all but two maidens, to attend her."

"My message got out, then."

"The message you gave Brico? Yes. But Auriane, know this, mad as it must seem—just now, Avenahar is probably safer where she is."

"She's in a war camp!"

"She has a chance of life. You're battling in a *sine missio*." He referred to the form of gladiatorial combat in which no combatant was allowed to survive. "Auriane, we must speak, now, of what's to be done for you."

Together, they sat on the straw-stuffed mattress; the supporting wooden frame gave a forlorn creak. "Listen with care. When I'm gone, they will try you, and they will, no doubt, condemn you."

"Yes," she said quietly. *I will be executed on the block. Like the ten hostages after Witgern's attack. It happens commonly. I will be one more. A quick, clean death. There was no sword stroke I could not defend against. Except this one.*

He pulled a rolled papyrus document from a bronze canister. "This is your grant of citizenship from the Emperor Nerva. It's but an exemplum, a certified copy of an original document. It's inscribed with a lettermark, here, that indicates the location of the master copy in my archives, back at the villa. Demaratos knows how to retrieve the original. Remember this, should this be stolen or destroyed. Maximus will know what this is. You are going to appeal, which is your right—I've explained that already. This alone won't save you, of course, but it will gain you some time, until *I* can do so. Do not tell anyone you have this—wait for the trial."

Gravely, she nodded.

"Appeal will mean to the Emperor, of course, who—bad chance for the Palace's court, better chance for us—will still be in Dacia. It will greatly annoy everyone concerned, but they'll have no choice but to follow the letter of the law and send you there—the case is too famous. Do not lose heart."

"Marcus, Arria must know nothing of any of this. If the Emperor does now count you an enemy, her groom's family won't want her anymore. They'll break off the betrothal. It will destroy her one place of refuge."

"Cease tormenting yourself. Arria will be married at the proper age, with due ceremony and ample dowry even if neither of us survives. If I can see to nothing else, I'll see to that."

They rose together, and he readied himself to depart. "Auriane," he asked suddenly. "Do you know how Ramis was schooled?"

"She interests you?" She realized this gladdened her.

"She is a surpassing mystery."

"Did I not always tell you?"

"It's one thing to hear of it and entirely another thing to witness, for it engages every sense, not just the mind."

"She herself had a teacher, another great seeress who died before Nero ruled."

"That hardly explains it. She has the speech of philosophers. When they took her off I followed to make certain they didn't misuse her, and I put questions to her. Her every reply raised up more mysteries. She is a Pythagorean. She describes the deathless spirit just as they do, and its passing on from one life to the next. She spoke even of the Age of Gold and the Age of Iron. She knows their disciplines—she once kept silence for five years. How can this be? This woman has never seen these texts—indeed, she cannot read, and has lived all her life far from any academy, where only the peace of the forest could have taught her."

"Is it so unthinkable? Our seeresses have always taught of the hidden soul-truths. And in ages past they were far-journeyers, more than today— though they seem to have been forgotten by your people's tale-keepers. Have you ever thought, Marcus, that you may have it all turned about? That when human creatures left their earth dwellings and moved into stone houses, they may have brought this knowledge with them? That perhaps your Pitta . . . Pitha—"

"Pythagoras."

"—may have taken *his* knowledge from *her*?—her sister seeresses, I mean, of aeons past?"

"You turn civilization on its head but at this dismal hour it looks better that way. Her jailers think her some sort of high magician who could walk through walls. But for me it's something else: She does not just *speak* these things. This woman truly *lives in another world*. She seems present among us but she's not. And, by all the gods, Auriane, every sense tells me it's a better world."

"I know it. My people call it the place-of-no-sorrowing."

"I would study her if I didn't have to depart. A pity to come upon such a wonder when we're both so close to being damned."

The darkening chamber was melancholy as an abandoned house when ghosts start to stir. There came a dry flutter of wings, an owl's cheerless call.

"Auriane . . . matters are grave . . . for you, I mean, graver than I have said."

"I'm ready for what comes," she whispered. "We had our feast of days." A lightflash of a smile crossed her face. "I'll be a ghost over Avenahar's shoulder, over Arria's—over yours. You'll have a guardian spirit." She crushed her face against his rough cheek. Her kiss was fervid, sad, a protest against the brutal finality of his going, but he met it in a way that was rich with consolation, and for long they drank of each other in deep final drafts, enough to last out the somber, uncertain months. They drifted on sorrow, emptied of words and hope, and she didn't know she was mumbling, ". . . We are closer than kin, closer even than mother and babe . . ."

"There is no other creature like you on this earth," he said hoarsely into her hair.

As she held to him she saw that the pooled blackness over his shoulder wasn't so empty as it seemed. There was a quickening at its core. She stiffened, and drew in a breath. Though fainter than starlight, images boiled out of the void, swarming, coalescing, forming. She heard a rush of air and a slashing of boughs, men's shouts. She saw a king—the Dacian king?—fresh from murder, a bloody *falx* in his hand, and behind him, an empty horizon broken only by the movements of tribes who lived their lives on horses.

"What is it?" he whispered darkly, not wanting to know.

"Marcus. You go into another world."

"You could call Dacia that," he said uneasily.

And I don't know if it's of the living or of the dead. "There's . . . a good chance I'll not see you again in this life."

"Nonsense. Do as we've planned and I will see you in Dacia. I promise it before every god, Auriane, that however far I go, even into other worlds, I will find you."

Chapter 20

As Avenahar gained the high point of the summit she felt joyous enough to fly, and intimate with the loneliness all about. The sky was a field of cold blue traversed by puffs of rushing clouds. The hills fell off in ever-paler hues of gray-green, to become ghost hills at the horizon's edge. Ground mist shrouded the valleys' somber recesses, alive with the furtive dartings of the unseen world—always there, just out of sight. A wind affectionately ruffled the grasses and set into undulating motion the golden carpets of aromatic flowers. Here Fria was a close, kind sister.

After one and a half cycles of the moon with Witgern's band, Avenahar was lean as a wild mare. Her face and arms were tanned nut-brown from long days spent beneath the northern sun. Her hair, when they'd found her, had been so matted with burdock burrs there was no help for the mess but to crop it; the remains were torn dark silk, hanging short and blunt as a boy's. She wore a waist-length deerskin cape over a baggy tunic woven of nettle fibers, belted with rope; Witgern's provisions women had tossed into a cess trench the muddy remains of her womanhood cloak, and the fine, tablet-woven tunica she'd worn from the villa. But for the wilted wreath of blue verbena flowers caught in her hair, she might have been a gangling youth as she stood on the hilltop, surveying the land as though she'd conquered it.

A woman with sagging jowls climbed up beside Avenahar and surveyed her kingdom. This was Ragnhild, the herb woman who travelled with Witgern's band. She had the indrawn shoulders of a woman shy of her fellow creatures, and could be stubbornly mute in most company. But her small eyes were sharp as pins—she knew what she knew, and when she spoke of those things, all shyness vanished. Wind whipped her cloak back magisterially and tugged at her dove-gray hair, pulling it free from a snail-coil at the nape of her neck, blowing it across her durable face. She scented the wind like a horse.

"I smell burning," Ragnhild said. Avenahar sniffed. She smelled nothing.

"Ragnhild," Avenahar asked then, "these plants . . . wolfsbane, golden woundwort, Bride of the Sun . . . they're what we gather before battle." Ever since word had filtered to them of the Governor's treacherous seizure of Ramis, Avenahar knew Witgern had been laying plans for some mysterious, reputedly dangerous expedition that would cost Rome much in men and supplies.

"You've been listening better than I thought. We'll know what that's about when we're meant to. Move along, sluggard, we're nearly there."

Avenahar romped down the hill, sinking into soil like cake. Ragnhild scuttled briskly after. "Slow down, Peregrina," the old woman called out. "Town life's dashed your patience." Avenahar had plucked the name "Peregrina" from a tale she'd read in a book of fables, about a brave girl who'd saved a town from pirates. Avenahar had let the Wolf Coats believe she was a fugitive slave, a wardrobe maid from a villa on the Great River, who'd fled a nervous mistress lethally fast with an iron hairpin. Witgern alone knew the truth, and Avenahar prayed no one else would deduce it—she wasn't eager to put the war band's tolerance to the test. In the last month, she hadn't wanted to be known as either parent's child: As Auriane's daughter, no mettle she displayed would ever be counted her own. As Decius's child—that was too fearful to imagine.

They might well decide to sacrifice her to the gods.

"I found it—wolfsbane," Avenahar called out with extravagant pride. She charged into a field of flame-colored flowers and began happily tearing at flower heads.

"Stop that! Be gentle, just take the petals—like this." Ragnhild began stripping petals with precision, delicacy, and formidable efficiency. "Don't injure my pretties. Do you know why she's the best balm for sword wounds? Because she's got a bit of sun captured inside her. What heals better than the sun? It means she's got the Lady herself inside her. Look how fine and bright her heads are." Ragnhild had nothing but gentle thoughts for plants. Avenahar was amused to see how plants excited her and people didn't—though their ailments sometimes did. Her neck projected from her shoulders at an equine angle, from a lifetime spent examining the ground, where her sly children, the roots, fungi, and flowers, hid from her. Ragnhild filled her wicker hamper long before Avenahar did. The herb woman's hands were hard, smooth, and curled like claws; she could pull up an angelica root without a spade. She claimed it was because she first won the trust of the plant. Ragnhild answered to no one but the land spirits. If Witgern ever offended her, she would be off, and Witgern knew it.

"Does wolfsbane grow here without help?" Avenahar asked.

"No. This is one of my gardens. Other women use it, too, though, so we'll just take what we need, no more." Ragnhild frowned. "Peregrina? What are you looking at?"

"There—on that hill."

Near the peak of a neighboring hill was a point of fire that steadily grew, until it seemed to open like the baleful eye of an awakening giant dwelling in the hill. Then it was a fiery blade thrust up against stark blue.

"A need-fire's been lit," Ragnhild said. "That's close by the Boar Village. They always seem to get foul news first."

"The Boar Village?" Avenahar whispered. "We're that near?" She felt an unpleasant tug, as if she'd dropped an anchor in deep water and couldn't happily sail on any more. Her throat tightened. There, Baldemar's hall stood; there, Auriane was born. And there, Auriane's aged mother, Athelinda, lived on still. She wanted to go there and draw in the spirits of the wells, the old hall, to drink in whatever elixir had given her mother such uncommon battle luck, and set her on a course of deeds that left a star-path still reflected in the eyes of the people of this country. Perhaps there, Avenahar thought, she would belong, as the mountain ash belonged—and could forget she was a woman of split soul, that the blood of a foreign murderer polluted her heart. A tangle of needs jostled within Avenahar—to best her mother, to hurt her, to have her adoration. All had Auriane at their center, however, like some maypole Avenahar was bound to circle round, first in one direction, then the other. And Avenahar knew, then, that running off was doing little to heal her hurt—she'd just been living off the succor of inflicting an equal wound on her mother.

On the hill behind them, a second fire found feeble life, and grew steadily stronger.

"Another one," Avenahar said wonderingly. "Something dreadful's happened."

"Let's get to the stores, and back to camp."

More excited by all this than frightened, Avenahar followed Ragnhild down the path to the cave where the old woman stored her medicines.

"Is it Chariomer's army, do you think?" Avenahar asked. The two women were uncomfortably far from Witgern's encampment, and they had no weapons.

"No, we'd hear horns. Anyway, it's too late in the raiding season." Ragnhild's face contracted as if she'd put something bitter into her mouth. "We can expect *that* scourge to reach these hills by next spring, though."

In the past month, Avenahar had begun to see the Chattian tribe's plight with merciless clarity. Once, while ranging far for herbs, she and Ragnhild had come upon a village in the Cheruscans' wake; the precincts before the temple were heaped with unburned dead. Black blood on skin turned to hide; a babe that had starved beside its slain mother—she couldn't banish these horrors from memory. Chariomer's army had massacred them just after harvest time; this was how his war band supplied itself with fruits and grains for the winter, for the Cheruscan chief's own provisions women had abandoned him over some dispute. *Chariomer, with Decius at his side.* The swords Auriane courted ruin to send, said to be hidden in a cave in Witgern's keeping, were the Chattians' single frail hope that Chariomer might one day be driven off. But Avenahar drove off, soon as they came, all thoughts that might enhance her mother's glory—for these days, despising her mother was the fuel that kept her warm.

As Avenahar and Ragnhild spilled down the hill, they saw more fires' unsteady blooms, manifesting near, then far, shimmering awake like the first stars of evening. The whole of the land was ablaze with protest.

Avenahar was seized with an unaccountable certainty she did not want to know what was wrong, that it would strike her to her knees.

"Ragnhild . . . you are not at all frightened?"

"I was at the Ram's Eye when Chariomer butchered even the she-goats. I climbed down a well. The dead were thrown in on top of me. After such a thing, all else is but the prick of a bone pin."

This suppressed Avenahar to quiet. "I am sorry, Ragnhild. That's the village where Ramis was born, is it not?"

"It was. My, you know much about us, *Peregrina*." Ragnhild slowed, and slyly slid her gaze toward Avenahar.

Avenahar drew in a breath. Had the old woman deduced who she was?

"They've taken from us every*thing,* every *place* that is holy," Ragnhild went on. "It could never have happened in Baldemar's day. The folk here about don't understand why Auriane never came home. Maybe that's why all this has happened, maybe her desertion cursed us."

Is she laying out bait? Does she know I'm not of a nature to let a dart thrown at my mother go unmet? "Perhaps she had . . . a good reason. Perhaps she was trapped where she was, by her honor. Perhaps she does plan to return."

"Is *that* it. You're full of answers today, villa-child. I tell you though, when a babe cries out for its mother, it doesn't reason why." Ragnhild shrugged, and began nimbly striding on again, following a deer track that led to her root cave. Stinging smoke bit the backs of their throats; both women held a corner of their cloaks over their noses.

Then Avenahar burst out with the question that had been swelling within her ever since the Wolf Coats had found her. "Ragnhild . . . what do people here say of the fact that . . . that Auriane lay with the Roman thrall Decius?"

Ragnhild stopped so abruptly that Avenahar collided with her.

"I should take a willow switch to you."

But Ragnhild softened her gaze when she saw Avenahar's distress. She made a dismissive gesture. "I know some folk say that, Peregrina, but you must understand, these are liars who hate us. Auriane's child was fathered by Wodan."

Avenahar fought to convey nothing with her face. Living as long as she had in territories held by Rome, where even rough countrymen drank in with mother's milk a small dose of cynicism about the gods, she'd half forgotten there were sober men and women in this world who thought a child could be fathered by a god.

"Ragnhild, do most people here believe . . . I mean, *know* what you know, concerning this matter?"

"Most do, but there's a sorry lot that don't. There are even some who'd slay her for it. But the true people, the good and pious folk, know Auriane incapable of doing such a thing."

Avenahar bit back a response. She knew this assessment couldn't be all that accurate—at her womanhood ceremony, it had seemed everyone knew the truth. But it would be unmannerly to speak against the words of an elderwoman and host.

Ragnhild followed a path almost invisible to Avenahar, who could only find the root cave by looking above, to the rotting red cloths Ragnhild long ago tied in the trees to mark the way. Finally they were halted by a lichen-covered rockface pitted with small hollows that oozed a sticky substance; Ragnhild regularly smeared butter and honey into the boulder's pocked surface as offerings to the woodwives and elves, so they wouldn't be inclined to venture farther and steal her treasures. They moved along the wall of stone until the rock split, then followed this narrowing crevice until they found themselves enveloped in the earthy darkness of the root cave, and pleasantly smothered in its sweet pungence. Ragnhild needed a secure central place to store her medicines while she roved with the migratory war band. Every surface of the interior was draped with herbs, some desiccated, some still fresh; many hung from hemp ropes strung just beneath the cave's roof, so that the cavern seemed to drip with plants.

They dumped their flowers and leaves into the willow-withy baskets at the back of the cave. Then Ragnhild began gathering up a sackful of what Avenahar had heard the old woman call "misery bread"—not bread at all, Avenahar discovered, but a thin, hardy, whitish-brown root that tasted somewhat like parsnips. "We'll need more of this," Ragnhild said as she hoisted the sack to her shoulder.

"You told me that's for starving times."

"Trading that fine stallion of yours fetched us quite a bit but you couldn't expect it to keep us forever."

"But what of the food gift Witgern was promised?"

"The village that promised us this time? The Four got there first." Ragnhild shrugged. "It happens now and again." Seeing Avenahar's look of bafflement, she added, "That's four cavalrymen of the frontier patrols who ride in a pack—Rome's scavenging dogs. They make the circuit of the villages and demand what they want, usually portables, buried silver and such. They sell it to supplement their army pay. If the folk are slow to give, they burn the granary."

This sort of story was growing familiar: Roman patrols unable to control themselves among a beaten and humbled populace. It puzzled and disturbed Avenahar that most people seemed to accept it, like crop-destroying hail.

But Avenahar said nothing, and she, too, gathered up a sackful of misery bread. Then she carefully scanned the cave's floor in the half-light, relieved to see nothing amiss. The first time Ragnhild had brought her here, they'd found something darkly unsettling near the back of the cave—a dagger with a broken point, tied about with a strip of white cloth secured with wolf's hair. Ragnhild had told her it was a curse worked against the owner of the cloth—the working of a knowledgeable seeress. The old woman had been deeply alarmed; she believed only her apprentice herb women knew of this cave. Then Avenahar had realized it was woolen cloth of a finer weave than one ever saw in this country, with a tablet-woven border. And she knew, with dull terror settling on her stomach, that it was a torn bit of the tunica she'd been wearing when Witgern's band found her.

Someone in this country wasn't pleased she was here.

But on this day she discerned no sign of an intrusion. And so they set out for the Wolf camp. The way was long; the sun began to sink. They waded through a shifting sea of blue chicory flowers, then plunged into a twilit grove of mountain ash, the wise and beloved tree from which, Ragnhild had told her, the first man was formed. They passed a wolf skull nailed to a tree; Avenahar felt the gaze of its captive ghost tracking their progress.

Then they found themselves in the midst of Witgern's encampment, as if it had sprung up from the ground. The Wolf Coats' tents were set out in no order, like a rockfall among the trees; when Witgern's men moved, they moved in a swarm. Some had made shelters that were no more than a deer hide lashed to a triangular frame set against a trunk. Others had dug into the earth like dogs and pulled a hide over the hollowed-out place, or made a nest at the base of a tree. The camp was deserted but for an occasional sentry posted among the trees. Avenahar was mystified by this until they heard the stark keening of a priestess issuing from deep in the grove. A sacrifice was taking place. They followed the sound, threading their way through strewn bedding and goathide sacks. The band's possessions were portable and few; Wolf Coats wore their wealth on their arms, as beautifully-wrought silver rings of varying weights, or about their throats, as necklets of precious amber. There was a bare simplicity about their society that had, at first, made their lives appear chaotic to Avenahar. Among them, men were not so neatly divided into the humble and the powerful as were the folk of the Roman province. A man of prestige, famous for some bold deed, might be asked first for his opinion in council, but when they carried out their rituals, all drank from one horn. Only gradually did she perceive that they were caught in an invisible web of law, whose radial threads connected back to a belief that a war band shared one soul. And as she observed them longer, she saw traits to admire: Theft was almost unknown among them; Avenahar sometimes thought they might kill a man before they would steal from him. They were ferociously protective of friends, and good to the few thralls they kept, a kindliness of disposition that originated with Witgern, whose nature was disseminated throughout the whole band. But most important to Avenahar, they lived by war, and were remorseless enemies of Rome. Among them, vengeance was a holy rite; they believed it could restore a slain man's spirit to the greater soul of his family. They despised what she despised and acted upon it with a swiftness that cleansed the blood. This fitted her temper so neatly—like two halves of a broken vessel brought together again—that she was willing to overlook some things, such as the filthiness of many of them, or their frequent bickering over trifles, such as whether Witgern or Sigibert had a greater collection of captured Roman cavalry medallions. The Wolf Coats lived like wild pigs, but they were free.

One bearded sentry, then another, watched the women with great silence. Two nodded respectfully at Ragnhild. Avenahar might have been a stray dog.

They passed a beardless sentry—a youth. No, one of the band's eleven women, Avenahar realized after a discreet second look. Her head was wrapped in a length of brown wool; her small face was weathered to a coppery sheen. The scarred pelt of a gray wolf hung from her shoulders. This maiden Wolf Coat was scarce older than Avenahar, but she seemed of no age; her closed expression suggested she'd never allowed a childish thought free play in her mind. She stood still as a temple god, ash spear upright in a calloused hand. In selecting his companions, Witgern was said to consider only whether a candidate was truly possessed of the wolf spirit. The band's women had performed tests of valor as rigorous as the men's—the single-handed slaying of a boar; the seizure of some prize from deep within an enemy camp. They, too, had endured the trial in which they were buried in earth to the waist, given a small round shield, and made to defend themselves against a rain of spears. The women were famed for having no thought for safety—often they were first to scale a palisade or last to retreat, and Avenahar suspected this was because, mingled with their wolf frenzy, there was a measure of anger that some expected less of them.

Avenahar nodded hopefully to the fiercely silent maid, who ignored her.

Greenish light filtered down from the boughs. In spite of the band's indifference, Avenahar felt content as a horse on a plain in this country, and was filled with an unaccountable sense that this land wanted her.

As Avenahar passed between two tents, a stout, leather-laced leg projected across her path—and she was airborne. She landed hard on her chest and hands. Her face ploughed into rotted leaves.

"No goat meat for you, villa-whelp," came a thick, lazy voice behind her. "Risk nothing, get nothing."

After lying numbed and senseless for a time, she turned about to see the youthful but ruined face of a Wolf Coat. His upper lip was cleft with a puckered scar that cleared a path through a red mustache, then travelled up to one eye, the result of a dagger cut that hadn't been properly stitched. Matted red hair did not quite cover a bare place on his head where a Roman javelin had partly scalped him. His lips glistened with the wild rosemary mead that all of them had been quaffing since dawn as he watched her with truculent, glassy-eyed satisfaction.

Ragnhild appeared suddenly from behind a tent. The draught-dazed warrior jerked to attention; he'd thought Avenahar was alone.

"Listen well, Hrolf, you wriggling malt worm," Ragnhild said, pushing her face close to his. "This is my herb woman. You will not molest her."

Hrolf scuttled backward until he was pressed hard against an ash trunk. Ragnhild moved with him.

"My eyes grow feebler these days as I stir the worts into your brew," Ragnhild muttered right into his ear. "It grows harder to tell the wild parsley from the water hemlock."

The Wolf Coat mumbled something half coherent while fumbling in his clothes for the figwort amulet he wore for protection against sorcery.

Ragnhild ambled off, calling out, "May you get a wound that festers." Avenahar found herself warmly pleased that Ragnhild had struck a blow for her. And amazed afresh at the fearful respect the old woman commanded. Avenahar had seen at once that elderwomen in this country wielded a natural authority that matrons in the provincial town of Confluentes did not. They had an ability to change the way things were done, the power to impress their wills on all domains of life, from hearth, to altar, to battlefield. She thought it partly because all in this place believed women stood closer to the gods, and partly because of their near-universal command of the witches' arts, which they employed at every passage, from the ceremonies that gave strength to the babe in the cradle to the incantations that guided the spirit after death. At Confluentes she'd once seen a pack of boys, sons of the town's

Roman officials, steal pears from an old woman's fruit stall. It would never happen here. In this land, to offend a crone was to risk ridicule, starvation, and death.

Nevertheless, the Wolf warrior's words cleaved her heart; she knew he spoke thoughts harbored by many.

They came to the place of sacrifice. The warriors of Witgern's band were seated on wolf pelts, massed in a semicircle about a small clearing with a shallow pit at its center; most were obscured behind the sluggish smoke of the sacrificial fire lazing low over the ground. A bone flute's golden brown notes wended through the trees with the torpid slowness of a sleepy dancer; the rich lament poured a warm glaze over the scene. A dirty-robed, barefoot priestess moved in a fluid circle about the pit, droning an entreaty to Donar the Thunderer, who had hurled a bolt yesterday that set an oak ablaze in their midst. Her long hair was loose, and hung in her face. The blood of a goat darkened the bottom of the pit; a Wolf Coat was dragging the flayed carcass toward a spit. When it was roasted, the band would partake of the flesh in a communion feast.

Avenahar and Ragnhild quietly moved past them, toward four provisions wagons that seemed wedged among the trees. There they saw a young maid with arms thin as sticks, pale hair, and even paler freckled skin, clad in a sad cloak patched with big, naive stitches; she wrestled with an unwieldy sack of grain. This was Ermenhild, a daughter of one of the provisions women, an independent tribal society that grew grain for the warbands. She had been kind to Avenahar, who supposed it was because Ermenhild was of humble status among these women, and so felt comradeship with another who stood outside.

Avenahar broke into a trot. "There are need-fires all over the hills!"

"You've not heard it yet?" The heavy sack bent Ermenhild's thin body like a bow as she let it slide to the ground. In bitter quiet she looked toward the open forest, as if this were her private grief. "The fires are for Auriane."

Avenahar felt a flash of numbness, as if pricked by a poison dart. "Is she . . . living still?" Avenahar managed.

"Yes, but she's a prisoner. No one understands it. It's said she's confessed to some Roman crime. It's thought to be the end for her."

Avenahar felt her spirit slip from her body, neatly as a hand from a glove. She knew then she'd somehow sensed the shape of what had passed, before Ermenhild spoke—as if so dreadful a thing could not happen without sending out invisible messengers.

The iron jaws had closed about her mother, and soon would mangle her alive. Ragnhild caught Avenahar as her knees buckled. Aided by Ermenhild, Ragnhild guided Avenahar toward the herb women's tents.

Ragnhild's portable dwelling consisted of three walls and a roof constructed of willow-withy mats lashed together and covered over with hides; the open side faced her cookfire. Bearskins thickly blanketed the ground within. She helped Avenahar to sit before her fire. When Avenahar shuddered like someone taken with palsy, Ragnhild wrapped her in several coverlets and began humming charm songs. Once, she forced on Avenahar a strong broth brewed from goatweed and all-heal, which was the herb woman's balm for anguish.

Avenahar was buffeted about on a heaving sea. Her mother *was* the world, in some way Avenahar could not name, the broad stage on which her own life was played. In one moment she felt intoxicated by a certainty all would be well. Auriane might go off, but she always returned—as when Avenahar was a babe, and Auriane had left her to go to war. But then in the next, Avenahar knew only that her running away was the cause of this evil turn of fate. And she wanted to snuff herself out like a candle. She willed that the light rain, falling now, would dissolve her flesh and mingle her with the earth.

From the distant songs, the women knew the sacrifice had been consumed. At nightfall, when they heard the wolf-chants begin, Ragnhild took Avenahar by the chin and gently held her gaze.

Avenahar's face was flushed from the potent soup Ragnhild had given her; she felt she rolled on an ocean of fog.

"If we are to be of any use to one another," Ragnhild said, "we must stop the play-acting. I know you are Avenahar."

Avenahar felt one sickening jolt, as if a step had given way beneath her. But then she felt relief—maintaining the false identity had begun to weary her.

"How did . . . did Witgern tell you?"

"No. I just knew. You know, if you'd even once said, 'Peregrina' while thinking, 'Avenahar', it's 'Avenahar' I'd hear."

"Gods below . . . who else knows?"

"The elder provisions women. At new moon the forests a day's ride south of here were overrun with Roman patrols searching for Auriane's daughter. Then we find a girl with hair black as jet in extra-fine clothes, riding a horse fit for a chief. Anyway, anyone who's ever set eyes on your noble mother would see her in your face."

"So . . . many were out looking for me?"

"What did you expect?" Ragnhild shook her head chidingly. "No deed ever plays itself out without intruding on the fates of multitudes of others, knocking them off course, either a little or a lot, for good or for ill. And how much more so, a grievous deed such as your running off. The young! They never pause to think of that."

"Why didn't you tell me you knew?"

"You seemed to need to hide."

"Why didn't you turn me over to the patrols?"

"That's Witgern's domain. You're not a plant—that's mine."

"You'll keep my secret before the others?"

"I think I can keep remembering to say 'Peregrina.' I've managed this long."

"What's to be done? We cannot let my mother die!"

"It's a Roman place. We have no power there."

"Ragnhild, I must go back there . . . and do whatever I can, to—"

"And storm the walls, and lose your own life? No. You must live. You are god-born, and you bring us strength and luck. You're with *us* now, like it or not, secure as if you were our prisoner."

A fresh grief seized Avenahar. She realized then she'd been harboring a belief that going back to her mother was always possible. Now, clearly, it was not. Without intending it, she'd blundered into a place with no return path. Six days ago, a messenger from one of the Holy Nine had found her way into the Wolf camp, bearing a wax tablet on which was inscribed an urgent letter in Auriane's hand, asking Witgern to conduct Avenahar to the Holy Wood. And Avenahar, at the time still full of loathing and brash confidence, had not even shown the tablet to Witgern; she'd tossed it into the stream.

How easy that had been to do, when she'd thought the choice her own. This was no Elysian forest-world now; it was a blasted plain, empty of her mother.

"And will Witgern do nothing?" Avenahar started struggling sluggishly to her feet.

"Sit down, where do you think you're going? First, he'll carry out what he already plans. He's promised this secret expedition will strike a grievous blow to Rome. It will restore balance in the unseen world."

"Vengeance? That is well, but it does nothing to save her!"

"Avenahar, try to ease your mind a bit. I knew your mother from old." Ragnhild's voice was soft, warbling, comforting. "The Fates own her acts. They watch her like the shepherd his sheep. They'll open a way for her."

What an ignorant old woman, the savage thought came to Avenahar. *Ragnhild knows every rock and root, but this, she does not understand.* "No way will open. She goes to her death," Avenahar whispered.

"Don't take power from the Fates or they'll avenge themselves on you." Ragnhild looked slyly about, as though those mighty women might be listening.

"We should go to war."

"You're full of plans today! Our strongest war chiefs stay in their halls, accusing each other of treachery with Rome. And you've forgotten we've got the Cheruscans clamped onto our backs like a lynx. There are times, child, when you can do nothing but wait."

Avenahar caved forward, dropped her head into her hands and wept. Ragnhild watched kindly, until all Avenahar's tears were spent.

"Avenahar. I have wanted to ask you something, ever since the night we found you. You were trying to give yourself to the gods. Why?"

Because it's true Decius is my father. But if I told you, you wouldn't believe it anyway.

Or maybe you would, *this time—which would be worse.* "No, Ragnhild. I'd only fallen to the ground from exhaustion."

"You were found lying against a tree on a bitter-cold night, with no cover and no weapon, and you'd let that fine black stallion loose with all your possessions tied to the saddle. No one who means to stay in the world does that."

"No, Ragnhild, I—" Avenahar gave it up; Ragnhild was watching her as if she were trying to cheat at dice.

"All right," Avenahar whispered. "You're right. I was."

"An honorable woman doesn't do that without a good reason." Ragnhild pressed on sternly. "Why would you run off from so noble a mother, and give her grief?"

On that night, she'd slid from the stolen stallion's broad, strong back after riding all day, straight north. The beast had wanted to run; both horse and rider had exulted in speeding swiftly to nowhere. The horse was a ship, sailing north under the stars. The powerful stallion had slowed at last, in this twilit grove of mountain ash. Avenahar had meant to let the wolves and the cold have her. *I belong nowhere. As a ghost, perhaps I'll be welcome here. As a spirit, I could stay.*

Avenahar knew she must concoct a suitable reason, if she hoped to silence Ragnhild's—and everyone's—questions. She couldn't meet Ragnhild's eyes as she mumbled, "My Roman father, Marcus Julianus, planned to marry me to a piggish lout of a man against my will." She felt she'd fouled her tongue—surely the Fates would avenge this base slander of Julianus.

Fortunately Ragnhild's normally keen senses suffered a lapse. She slowly shook her head in sympathetic understanding.

"Ah. Romans have no shame. A woman has a right to refuse a father's choice of husband, everyone knows that. Sleep now, Avenahar."

Avenahar obeyed at once; she'd grown weary, and was eager to avoid further questions. She crawled to the back of the hut and curled like a puppy among the woolen coverlets. Ragnhild topped off the heap with a bearskin.

But before she fell off asleep, her hand crept into her possessions sack and she pulled out the marvel—an exquisite serpent-form fibula inset with sapphires and a single, great pearl. On her first night after her rescue, this impossible thing had simply been *there* when next she'd looked into the sack, a mysterious beauty shedding its muted magic, its presence a severe test of her occasional doubts about the immortal gods' interest in human affairs. She was certain it was put there by some good spirit of the forest, and it comforted her.

She pressed her lips to it, put it back into the sack, then dropped swiftly into blackness, greatly relieved to leave the world for a time.

As Avenahar descended deeper into dreams, she began to hear a soft pulse of skin drums. Her spirit edged toward the sound. She imagined it the heart of the world, promising succor was to be found somewhere. Ages fell off like sloughing snake skin and she plummeted downward, to find herself in a bright cave where there was a fire. Condensing from dream-darkness were the same nine women who had come to her at her initiation ceremony. Nine pairs of knowing eyes, each transmitting a different quality of strength. Their voiceless speech took shape in her mind.

Regard, Avenahar. We are long dead. Yet we live.

Avenahar felt the sustaining warmth of close kin pressed about.

You are the stone on which we inscribe. You are your own mother. We declare you our own blood.

Then they commanded her to go outside the cave, and see what she saw.

Avenahar obeyed. Before her was a low plain where mist pooled to form a white lake. Onto the plain came a hart; its branched horns were imprecating hands reaching to the sky. A mountain cat shot from the mist, and was astride it like a rider. She saw savage writhings, white teeth. But the mountain cat was feeble and starved. Wolves came to help, streaming through mist. Fleetingly, she saw through wolf eyes, felt a blow to her side as the wolves were mangled beneath the great hart's hooves. As hart and mountain cat sank together beneath the mist, both bearing terrible wounds, she once more overlooked the plain, suffused with a numbing sorrow. She waded into the fog, meaning to help the injured creatures.

And found herself returning to the women in the cave instead, understanding that this would aid them more. As she entered, one of the nine women rose, smiling, and gave her a yew staff and a crown of vervain.

Avenahar awakened with a jolt when the sun was already high. The hut was empty—*of course,* she thought, *it is so late in the morning, Ragnhild's already gone out somewhere.*

Fria save my mother, was her first miserable thought as the waking world claimed her again. But she was surprised to find that the vise-grip of horror that had come with yesterday's news had lessened somewhat. That potent dream—surely it was the cause. It coated everything in its beauty and mercy. The nine elders' presence was so close, she smelled the smoke of burning mullein clinging to their clothes. The dream was gently provocative. She sensed it prodded her somewhere necessary, and that if she yielded to it, she would give strength to her mother.

As Avenahar rose and made her way to the stream, she found herself full of the exuberance of the strong stallion that had carried her here.

For the first time since she'd run off, she ardently wanted to live on.

If Auriane were not in the world, then she *must* be, was somehow required to be. It was the only way to defy Auriane's death, and embrace the Fates as sisters. And soon as she knew this, desire for the fate she'd nurtured through childhood began to flood back: She would fight for the land. She would win vengeance for all the Chattian dead.

And she would cleanse the poison of Decius from her blood.

As Avenahar washed briskly in the frigid stream, wincing at the cold, then began beating the dirt from her cloak, she strove to remember the elderwomen's words. The dream was, at first, hazed in memory, but the morning's forming light solidified it, and with it, her certainties. By noon, her course was set. Had not the elderwoman said, *You are your own mother*? The plain she'd seen was a battlefield. The hart, surely, was the Cheruscans, for this was their spirit-animal; Chariomer himself was said to have been fed by a hind, when he was a babe. The mountain cat was her own Chattian tribe. The wolves were Witgern's band. And she had been one of them—she felt an ache in her side where the hart's hoof had struck her.

Ramis had said of Auriane, at her birth, *You will be a living shield.*

Surely I have inherited that fate.

The Wolf Coats' women numbered eleven. She must see that number raised to twelve.

When she returned to the willow-withy shelter, Ragnhild was there, depositing an armful of tinder onto the ground near her fire. The old woman was alert to the bright purpose in Avenahar's eyes.

"Where are you going?" Ragnhild asked, frowning.

"I must see Witgern."

Something shifted in Ragnhild's eyes; in them was a sorrowful darkness Avenahar had never seen there before. "He's not here."

"But I've heard he hasn't left his tent since yesterday morn."

"And I hear traitorous thoughts clamoring in your mind. Why must you see him?"

"Because I must! How can you say he's not here?"

"He is a slender gray wolf, loping south to scout the forts, and learn when they're most poorly defended."

"You've the power to see him when he spirit-travels?"

"Yes. And do not forget—you are my herb woman."

Avenahar looked down. "Ragnhild, I have had a . . . a telling dream. It is what must be."

"Traitor."

The word tore at her. Avenahar bit back a protest, then turned about and strode down the path toward Witgern's tent.

As Avenahar tramped through the camp, she passed knots of men speaking of the news that had come this morning: One of the Roman observers sent into Chattian country to report on the tribal assemblies had been lured from his escort and murdered; it was a reprisal for the Governor's condemnation of Auriane.

When she reached the stream, she followed it until she came to a place where the shallow, stone-strewn waters were broken by a small island. On it was pitched a sturdily made tent fashioned of goat leather. Its peaked roof was fastened down by ropes; the rectangular interior was designed to house eight soldiers. Avenahar recognized it as the standard issue of the Roman Army. Witgern had made it his own by painting moons, stars, and protective runic signs on its sides. Nine Wolf Coats were posted about it as sentries.

She crossed a log bridge over a short stretch of rushing water. Ash leaves drifted from above.

"It's the villa princess!" one sentry called out gaily.

"What's the trouble, the maid too slow bringing the sauce for your misery bread?"

"She's come to complain we forgot to stoke the fires for her hot bath."

"Or that the ground's too hard," called out another. "Someone fetch her a cushion."

Avenahar approached the one sentry who hadn't grinned through these taunts, and begged for a word with Witgern.

"He can't be troubled by the likes of you. Off with you, now."

So she settled herself in, just outside the opening of the tent. Witgern would have to come out sometime. The sentries glared threateningly at first, but soon grew used to her presence and let her be.

The sun travelled across the first quarter of the afternoon sky. Within the tent, she heard men's voices in three different pitches. Avenahar's legs began to ache from sitting. Just as she was ready to give up in weariness, two Wolf Coats emerged from the tent, ignoring her as they briskly strode past.

Now Witgern was alone. Avenahar got to her feet.

One of the sentries whipped his ash spear across the opening, barring the way.

"I see a stray wolf-cub out there," came Witgern's amused voice from within the tent. "Let her in."

Chapter 21

At first Avenahar saw only the hazed shaft of sunlight slanting from the smoke hole cut into the tent, and a glowing worm of light that was an herb fire. As her eyes made darkness their home, gradually she discerned Witgern. He sat cross-legged on a wolf skin, regarding her with a peaceful vagueness in his eye. Looking on that fine-boned old face, she thought of beauty collapsing, of gently ruined grace. Ash-hued locks long enough to break at his shoulders were neatly combed back from a broad, high forehead. The ruined eye was a mystery beneath a black woolen patch. Wodan, the seer-god worshipped by his men, also had one eye, and most saw it not as an affliction but as an open door to the world of helpful spirits. For a fleeting moment—was it just the smoke-daemons riding upward on the column of light?—Avenahar thought she saw a wolf face materializing over Witgern's features, a furry countenance with golden eyes, brimming with wolf-qualities—shyness, mournfulness, ferocity.

Witgern gestured for her to sit. For a man who lived not much better than a beast, he was meticulous in his habits: He'd washed his hair clean in a preparation the people called Batavian soap—goat fat mixed with ashes of beechwood. A neatly combed beard was remarkably free of all evidence of his last meal. The cloth of his brown cloak was worn smooth from many washings over stones. A warrior's ring of beaten silver gleamed dully on his spear arm. Fragrant leaves of coltsfoot made his fire most pleasant; he breathed this herb for a cough that had lingered through summer. His tent was bare, but for his lindenwood shield painted with images of the Sun and Moon, a possessions sack, and a great clay jar of salt, a thing so precious that it was always in Witgern's keeping.

"Avenahar." He said it seemingly for the enjoyment of her name's rhythm, letting it rouse hosts of leisurely memories. She fidgeted, not knowing when it was proper to speak. He seemed to have drifted off. She felt like an overfull grain sack ready to burst. Finally he nodded, encouraging her, saying, "Silence the part of you that sorts things out. Let your immortal part speak."

She wasn't sure what he meant. He waited, patient, amused, while she struggled over how to begin.

"Witgern . . . I am grateful to you for giving me to Ragnhild as her helper. She's taught me much of the ways of the plants, and one day I hope—" She stopped. "And what is so amusing?"

"Nothing," he said, mastering the smile. It was her guile—her strategy of expressing gratefulness first, to soften him toward whatever she planned to ask—carried out with such childlike earnestness, it didn't offend him. "Speak on."

The interruption caused her to lose her place, but she plunged on. "At home I practiced every day with the native spear, and in the last year, with a sword of steel. Last spring I even saved my mother's life, when we were attacked by fugitive sailors on the river road. And as it's my own blood that's in peril, it's my place to avenge. After all, I—"

He raised a hand for silence.

"Let me quicken the pace or we'll never be off at dawn tomorrow. My answer is no. This much, I owe your mother." Such a look of anguish came into Avenahar's face that he added, "This I owe to *you*. Do you not see why?"

"No. I do not see."

"Avenahar, you are not your mother. Now, don't take it ill, I did not mean it that way—"

"How could I not take it ill? I will show you, I *am* my mother."

"Avenahar, the tests are arduous. You're scarce fourteen. You've never slain a man, you've never suffered through a winter in a war camp."

"But you have a war companion who's twelve."

"He was reared very differently from you, orphaned at six, stealing food to live, and never a day without a spear in his hand since."

"I will perform the tests. I will raid with you or I will die."

"You are not ready. Truthfully, I do not know if you will ever be ready."

"You are wrong, Witgern. And I've had a dream that proves it."

As she related the dream, Witgern frowned thoughtfully and pulled at his beard; he was often inclined to count the intelligence culled in dreams of greater worth than information gathered in waking life. Finally, he said, "That is a dreadful, powerful dream, Avenahar. It causes me to quake in fear for us, that both Cheruscan hart and Chattian cat were grievously injured. However, the young can fashion meanings to fit ardent wishes. I am not so certain what *your* part was. I would tell it to a seeress. Gunora comes through these valleys, next moon; let her interpret it. But today I can only follow my own senses as to your fitness to be a Wolf."

"You, too, think me a coddled villa-child."

"No," he said firmly. "That is very far from what I think. Sit still. Can you stop twitching about and *not speak*, for the time it takes to milk a goat? Your impetuousness forces a meaning into my words that is not there."

Avenahar stilled herself by main force, fixing her gaze on the dirt floor near his feet. Witgern smiled faintly; she didn't look as though she could remain that way for long.

"You don't know what a narrow, bitter road this one is," Witgern said. "We Wolves are condemned to the wild and barren places, because we've been permitted to live nowhere else. You were reared in a larger world, and that makes you too large for this world. What I mean is, you've a questing mind that's been opened to the vastness of things—you've been schooled in sums, the arts of writing and of understanding what people of old have written, and this changes the spirit. You've the ghosts of other peoples, other ways, living in you. You do have a fire in you, but it's a fire of knowing, of swaying minds. I do not think you were made for warring."

He raised a hand to stay a protest, and continued, "This is not an ill thing. There are so many other noble paths in this world.

"I think, Avenahar, you won't let yourself see how you are different from your mother because you believe that to be unlike her is to be somehow worse, or perhaps even to be scarce worthy of life. You see the glory given your mother. But there is noisy renown and there is quiet renown, and even unknown renown, all of which are equal before the gods, for is it not somewhat mad to suppose our greatness increases with the number of people who witness it? No, it's just *there*, like a silver ring, whether people know it's there or not, and it's more valuable than salt, and you carry it always, even into other worlds, Avenahar.

"I once saw Thrusnelda of the village of the Boar walk right into a village known to be cursed," he continued, "when no other priestess dared, for it meant defying the battle chief who'd cursed it. But she didn't care, because the people within were sick and she had the knowledge to help them. This sort of courage—to stand against a small or great evil when it blocks your path—is one of your greatest fires.

"There's also this, Avenahar: We face torture if we're captured. We fight men better armed than we are. No, I cannot allow it, for the love I bear your mother. You should live to marry one day, and carry on Auriane's line. I'll protect you long as you want to stay in this camp, but you will not raid with us. Stay by Ragnhild. Let her teach you healing. That will lead you to your fate."

Avenahar would not meet his eyes. *He is wrong*. Adding to her distress was the memory of Auriane telling her, "You are far cannier than most, in the herb woman's arts." She put up a stone wall round her mind so neither of them could get in.

Without warning, the sorrow of yesterday's news closed about her, and she dropped her head into her hands. "My mother . . . I cannot bear it . . . what will they do to her . . . ?"

"Avenahar, Avenahar," Witgern said, finding her hands, clasping them strongly in his. "None of us know. We will do all we can to lend her strength. But in the end, know this: Your mother and I have faced such calamities before. Life is not long, poor child. And she and I have survived far longer than most. You must remember there is an eternity in the halls of the gods, and we'll all be there some day."

She started to tell him she would either be a Wolf Coat or laid out on a pyre, but summoned the strength to force herself to silence. Far better to keep her purposes veiled. They would grow stronger that way.

"Go now," he said gently. "I have to prepare for our departure."

After a taut moment of hesitation, she asked, "Witgern, can you tell me for certain you haven't refused me because . . . because of Decius?"

He laughed an open, free laugh.

"Now, what is so amusing?" she asked.

"I cannot seem to rid myself of that mountebank! First he took the woman I wanted, and now he takes our villages, his only coin a lack of scruples, and warfare-knowledge learned from books. He's just not that important, Avenahar. In this band we have men fathered by murderers and thralls, and men who'd stop their ears if you threatened to tell them who their father was. I've always held the mother's blood runs stronger." He shrugged and smiled wistfully. "If Baldemar had had his way, so long ago, *I* would have been your father. You know, he chose me as Auriane's husband."

Avenahar was silent, momentarily paralyzed by the oddness of that thought. In that case, who would she be? Born to someone else? Or still herself—only more content?

"How greatly I would have preferred that," she said softly. "But I think you're alone in those mild thoughts of Decius. I fear to think what your men would do to me, if they knew."

"Of course, there's always a quarrelsome lot looking for people to blame for their troubles, and I do have a few of them here. But these men are oathed to me. They dare not injure those I protect."

She rose to go, but paused a final time. "I should return to my mother. I should share her prison, and her fate."

"I forbid you to speak so," he said with soft ferocity. "She did not give you life so you could rush off to destruction. No doubt, her one comfort in these times is knowing that you live on."

As AVENAHAR RETURNED to Ragnhild's shelter, she felt a fierce ache as she witnessed the band's preparations for war. She passed a Wolf Coat who was naming before a seeress those of his fellows who were to receive his possessions, were he slain. This man's face, so solemn with death-knowledge, further roused Avenahar's curiosity about the nature of their expedition, still secret from all but Witgern's inner circle of Wolves. Farther into the camp, another shaggy group was gathered about a fire; each, in turn, committed to the flames some small offering to Wodan. One among them—another of the Wolf Coats' women—wore a wolf skull as a headdress. While chanting the god's praise in a voice that poured from her as though some great creature were lowing, she held aloft a bronze belt buckle and dropped it into the fire. Avenahar had heard the men speak this woman's name; it was Gondul. She was lithe and proud of aspect, with features boldly carved like an image cut in wood, her eyes incongruously wise and sad. How easily she walked with these wolves. Avenahar felt a hollowed-out sorrow, believing, just then, she would never be one of them.

Ragnhild brought Avenahar her share of this night's meal. All the provisions women had to give them this eve was a thin soup in which floated nettles, sorrel, leaves of purslane, a few sad bits of barley. And along with it, misery bread. They sat and ate before the old woman's fire. Two young herb women, also Ragnhild's apprentices, sat huddled in hooded cloaks on the other side of the fire, making their own talk.

Avenahar was hungry and gratefully took the cracked wooden bowl, spilling hot, watery broth onto her hands. At the bottom of the bowl she found . . . pebbles.

"Leave them, Av—Peregrina," Ragnhild said as Avenahar began to pick them out with distaste. "They strengthen the bones."

Ragnhild had steamed the misery bread; Avenahar bit into it with a crunch. Ragnhild herself ate none of it; she would partake only of soups and gruel. Gradually Avenahar had realized this was because Ragnhild suffered from an affliction of many her age, in this country—severely worn-down teeth. When Avenahar once watched the provisions women grind einkorn wheat to make their hard, flat bread, she thought she'd uncovered the cause: The flour was never cleared of particles from the grindstone. When Avenahar had tried to convince them this was a harmful thing, she was tartly told to tend to her own matters.

"Ragnhild, do you know anything of what Witgern plans?"

Ragnhild brusquely shook her head, genuinely uninterested. What Avenahar had managed to learn only puzzled her the more; one man spoke of a plan to raise a mighty howl from the forest near a bend in the river Moenus. She failed to understand what harm this could do to the enemy.

"We've had this same soup for five days," Avenahar said then. "Each night it gets thinner."

"I'm sorry it isn't villa fare." Ragnhild tipped her bowl and emptied it with a fast, efficient series of slurps, then wiped her chin on her cloak. "The men had no time to hunt. Ermenhild set out nets today; perhaps she got something. Even a hare or a vole enriches the broth. Don't think of it. Just eat."

"I'm not complaining, I'm just noticing that since I've been with you, the rations have gotten steadily more meager."

"Well, it isn't your fault, Peregrina, if you're going to take that upon yourself, too. I told you, the Four came again." Ragnhild ambled over to the back of her hut and returned with something precious cupped in one hand. "Here. Acorns. I was saving them for you. Eat them, they fill you up."

"Keep your acorns. I don't mind, really." After a moment, Avenahar asked, "Cannot Witgern stop them? The Four, I mean?"

"They're just one problem of many. Anyway, they have hostages.

They threaten to kill their hostages if we complain about them to a Roman authority."

"Hostages? At their fort?" Avenahar set down her bowl. "Ragnhild, things are not done that way among those people. There may well be hostages held at their home fort. But these four cavalrymen can't be men of rank, if they're on a patrol—they would have no power over the handling of hostages. They would report to a centurion, who reports to a camp praefect, who has that power. And since they're breaking their own regulations, I doubt they'd be eager to give any report at all."

"It's no matter anyway. They've done it, they're gone, we eat soup."

As FIRST LIGHT illumined the creamy mist pooled among the ash trees and the red deer began to stir, the Wolf Coats doused their fires, covered them over with earth, and shouldered their possessions. Clothed in great silence, they began to move off through the forest. The journey to the regions of the river Moenus, a middle-sized river that flowed into the wide Rhenus, would require two days. The Wolf Coats led the way, followed by Ragnhild and her apprentices, travelling with six provisions women. The women's stores had been loaded onto sturdy ponies; wagons would only slow them. The Wolf Coats stayed well off from the traders' tracks, pathways that led to villages and popular places for fording streams; they were a shadow-band, flooding into obscure valleys, flowing from meadow to meadow. By nightfall they came to country where pathways were better travelled. And on the second day, villages became more common; here the folk had commerce with the Roman forts. At dusk, Ragnhild and the provisions women fell back and camped in a thick forest of beeches. Just one hill beyond was the slope that led down to the Moenus. This was a dangerous part of its course; here, it flowed close alongside the *Limes*, the ever-onstretching ditch and wickerwork fence that marked the limits of Empire, with its regularly-spaced watchtowers and legionary patrols.

In preparation for battle, the Wolf Coats darkened their faces and limbs with soot and ashes and hummed the names of victory-runes over their spears. They shared the "raven's bread" to draw in the Wolf spirit, while Witgern prayed over them. Then they melted off on their mysterious expedition.

As night deepened, the women heard faintly once, from the direction of the river, the swelling and fading of wolf cries; to Avenahar's ears, they sounded fearfully agitated. Then the women heard no more. After two days

Avenahar saw sharp concern in Ermenhild's eyes. Surely all had perished or been taken captive. But when Avenahar spoke her fears to Ragnhild, the old woman reminded her that this country offered many places that were wild, still, where wolves might hide, and that Witgern had studied the habits of the patrols along the *Limes*, and knew how to elude them.

On the third night, at staggered times, Wolf Coats began straggling back into camp. They did not look like victors. They looked like men who had been caught up in the fist of a giant and roughly hurled aside. Ragnhild set up shelters for the wounded and began by dividing them into two groups—those who she judged might live and those who would surely die. Ragnhild took the most difficult cases into her own care. While Avenahar was preparing lengths of wool for compresses, burning her hands on bronze pots as she boiled water for draughts, or staggering about under the weight of wounded men, she managed to learn in fragments that the Wolf Coats had been pursued by cavalry, then were forced to split off from one another so more might escape.

At midday, when Ragnhild became overwhelmed with critical cases, she gave entirely into Avenahar's care a grievously wounded young man called Hagbard. "This one can't be helped," Ragnhild pronounced out of Hagbard's hearing. "Note the coloring of the flesh about his wounds, and their odor. That smell is death. Four days, no more. You'll ease his passage to the Sky Hall. You know what to do?"

Avenahar nodded bravely, though she found his fearfully mutilated hand frightful to look upon. Once she got him to the shelter, she started by giving him draughts of henbane and all-heal, for his misery, and blood-heating broths to warm his body, which hadn't fully expelled the cold after he nearly drowned in the dark waters of the Moenus. Without deliberating on it much, she began dressing a gaping wound in the young man's side, using herbal formulae partly of her own devising, partly remembered from medical books in Julianus's library. As she pressed the wolfsbane compresses to his wounds, it seemed knowledge rushed into her hands. She found herself remembering charm songs Auriane had taught her, and would chant them with one palm on his forehead, the other on the amulet of earth her mother had given her. Sometimes, she just sat for long with her hands around his, thinking the gods into him.

Euphoria brought by the draughts inspired him to talk, and soon Hagbard came forth with the full tale. Avenahar, on hearing it, judged the expedition a complete, and probably fortunate, failure—it accomplished so little, with luck it wouldn't provoke Rome to launch a punitive attack. In fact, she wondered if Rome would notice.

Witgern's covert plan proved to be an act of sabotage on a trestle bridge spanning the Moenus. Through intelligence gathered from his spies, Witgern had learned the precise day that a detachment of one thousand men—a cohort from the regular legion stationed at the Fortress at Bonna on the Rhenus, with five hundred Arabian archers—would cross this bridge before beginning the overland stretch of the long journey to Dacia, where they were to join the great foreign war Rome was waging. As night fell, two Wolf Coats garbed in stolen legionary armor slew the sentries posted by the bridge's approach. Then, twenty men who had volunteered for this dangerous work, Hagbard among them, crept onto the bridge and began their labors. The greater part of the band stayed in a protected place in a wood, where they raised wolf cries through the night to distract the attention of legionaries posted at the small bridgehead fort. The twenty lowered themselves down into the bridge's wooden trestlework arches. Working through most of a moonless night, they sawed through the wood of the trestles, between the bridge's second and third stone piers. This was carried out while dangling in darkness, high above the rushing water. Three plummeted into the river and drowned.

Hagbard had fallen, too, but had eluded the Nixes and hauled himself out. While night still shielded them, the saboteurs rejoined the main body. As soon as dawn illumined the forest, Roman cavalry were dispatched in pursuit. A grim battle ensued in a beech forest. Hagbard's left hand had been pinned to a tree by a cavalryman's lance; he'd saved himself from death beneath the cavalryman's sword by tearing his hand free, then plunging into a part of the forest too thick for a horse to pass.

By midday Hagbard had found himself split off from his companions, huddled on a bramble-covered rise that gave a view of the bridge across the Moenus. And so he was witness to the grand Roman parade as it gradually began to appear on the river road—a thousand armored men, flanked by massive cavalry horses, their plumed riders bearing brightly colored flags, a startling sight against a land left bleak and brown by coming winter. The detachment moved onto the bridge. It was then, Hagbard said, he knew Witgern was the victim of the cold, unpredictable humor of Wodan.

For the bridge refused to collapse.

The Wolf Coats had lost nineteen of their own men to the long lances, and left them as food for ravens. Avenahar heard all this in sad amazement, for a short distance off in the forest, Witgern's men gave themselves over to mead-soaked rejoicing that lasted through the night, as they celebrated their "victory." They seemed to believe this dubious blow they'd struck would somehow prod the Governor into releasing Auriane. Avenahar could not see the use of it, and occasionally wondered if she was among fools, then felt mean and ungrateful for thinking these things.

Late into the following day, while her wounded charge was sleeping in draught-cushioned contentment, Avenahar took Hagbard's spear and stole off to a remote meadow. She practiced with the native spear until dark came, hurling it hard at ever more distant trees. The next day, she did the same. On the third afternoon, she made off with Ragnhild's sleepy dun horse, a good-natured-enough beast except that it refused to move faster than a lumbering trot, and would slyly attempt to pull at grass at a rider's first lapse of attention. Sometimes, with great effort, she got the horse to canter, and she would cast the spear at targets she'd marked on trees. Slowly, she felt strength begin to flow up strongly like spring sap, and she was drunken on its rising. Her muscles awakened; her limbs began to remember the long hours of practice with her mother. This was her passage to freedom. Avenahar needed to invent many excuses for Ragnhild, to explain why the poor horse was so tired.

She knew she must find some fearful task to carry out, something marvelous enough to inspire the Wolves to welcome her into the band. Somewhere beneath all her bold intentions was a child's terror. And dark mind-pictures of her mother's fast-approaching fate. Grand plans helped keep these things at bay.

On their ninth day at the encampment by the river, Ragnhild came to Hagbard's shelter to ask Avenahar about some pot of bear's-fat ointment she couldn't find. And Ragnhild caught sight of a thin, unkempt, but very much alive Hagbard, hair hanging in a clumped, dirty mane, tunic fluttering from a skeletal frame as he disappeared with fragile steps round a bend in the path.

Ragnhild stopped in mid-word, mouth locked open. "He is *walking about*?"

"But you said moving about is good for strengthening the blood, once the worst danger has—"

"Peregrina," Ragnhild said, clamping one strong claw about Avenahar's shoulder. "Stop shrinking off, I'm not angry—I'm closer to a faint of amazement. What did you do for him?"

"I . . . I don't remember."

"You will sit there until you tell me."

"I bathed him in thyme water, as Roman physicians do. For cleansing the wound I think I made a centaury compound, from Celsus I guess it was, and to make him sleep I used a formula I got from a book of Soranus, who—"

"These were your teachers, where you came from?"

"Well, not exactly . . . at home I had lots of volumes on the medical arts."

"Volumes? Written things? These are dead medicine women who have written their secrets? I have heard of that."

"Yes, Ragnhild, except—"

"What *else*?"

"Well, I also used my mother's charm songs, and—"

"The wound in his side, that bared the bone of the rib—how did you close it?"

"I stitched it with my hair."

"Gods below. This is extraordinary. Avenahar, let me see your hands."

"Shh—you used my name!"

"Don't worry, there's no one about." She took Avenahar's unwilling hands and pried them open. After studying them with care, she announced, "You have the Lady in your hands. It is the power of your line."

"That's well, then. Did you find the bear's-fat ointment?"

"Avenahar! This is a great god-gift!"

"A gift's not so great if it isn't the one you want."

Ragnhild regarded Avenahar as though she had tossed a sack of silver onto a midden.

Avenahar stubbornly met Ragnhild's gaze. Then she looked down, mumbling, "These are avenging hands, not healing hands."

After a time, Ragnhild gave a shrug, and sadness swept across her face as she rose to her feet to go.

As the tale of Hagbard's recovery was related throughout the Wolf band, Avenahar found the men's praise of her medical skills increasingly irritating. The best part of it was that Hagbard became a strong ally, and this caused many in the band to treat her less like a stray dog. But better still was Hagbard's gift: In thankfulness for his recovery, he told her to select whatever she might want from his possessions.

Avenahar chose a wooden sword.

Hagbard had two, which he kept for practice sparring. They were carved of ashwood by a skilled woodcrafter, made of two pieces joined together between blade and hilt, and they were carefully balanced and weighted to feel, in the hand, like a sword of iron.

After a cycle of the moon, when the survivors were strong enough to journey, and those who'd died of wounds had been given over to local priestesses to be burned, all decamped for the familiar grove of mountain ash, which was one of Witgern's wintering places. Avenahar found the home grove little changed, except the nights were sharply colder, the sun was shy and remote, and naked branches bristled against a dead gray sky. Avenahar felt bleak as that sky; while camping in the southern places, she'd held out a strong hope she would get news of her mother.

They had scarce been in the winter camp for a day when the war chief called Sigibert rode into their midst.

"WHY DOES WITGERN welcome him?" Avenahar whispered to Ragnhild. They'd picked marsh mushrooms that day, and they sat before Ragnhild's shelter, laying the mushrooms out to dry on a wickerwork frame. A warrior on horseback was approaching at a stately pace through the ash trees; he carried himself like a man from hero tales as he wended his way though camp with his war companions following him in a file. "I'd think they'd drive him off with stones. Sigibert concedes everything when he makes treaties with the Governor."

"He's not what he seems, Peregrina," Ragnhild replied.

Avenahar saw how warmly Witgern's men greeted this visitor. He'd obviously been among them before.

"But he's betrothed to Chariomer's daughter, Elza!"

"That betrothal just might be so Rome is better confused by him, child, and so, will trust him better and reveal to him more of her plans."

Avenahar briefly wondered what sort of man would go so far as to take a wife among the enemy, just to keep his loyalties obscured. Who could trust such a wife, whose first loyalty would always be to her own clan?

"You might as well know it; he has a close alliance with Witgern," Ragnhild said. "Sigibert comes about here more and more of late, to hold council. Next year will be the year, I think."

Avenahar knew Ragnhild spoke of Witgern's long-nursed hope of uniting the Chattian factions and waging a great war that would push Chariomer off their lands forever.

Sigibert was closer now as his graceful stallion, bred of an exquisite southern strain, threaded its way through ragged shelters as though it picked its way through lilies, nodding its beautifully tapered head. She stared at him in open wonder; in the past two months she'd seen no one so richly attired. A cloak sewn of squares of many hues of woad-dyed blue swept from his shoulders and onto the rump of his mount like some kingly train; on his bared arms were massive, richly-worked rings of silver. His town-made boots surely came from the finest provincial workshop. His hair flowed down in a noble mane; its color matched the coat of his glossy chestnut stallion. Avenahar was stirred by the beauty of them both; he caused her to think of the sun, full of brazen light, and she found that she didn't want to stop watching either the man or the horse. Their compelling harmony of movement and form put her into a pleasant trance. He was younger than most of his men, but had attracted a great retinue of companions because his father was Sigwulf, slain long ago beside Auriane in the Chattian War, placed now among the lesser gods. Avenahar caught bits of his speech; he was gathering men for a boar hunt. He displayed so much broad confidence before his men, and seemed so much a man the gods loved, she believed any plan he wrought would win them glory.

As he rode past her, one sweeping glance encompassed Ragnhild's shelter.

And Sigibert found his attention riveted upon a gaunt, haunted wood sprite with rough-cropped hair, who stared back at him with bold eyes. He pulled his mount to an abrupt halt.

Curtly, he motioned to Avenahar to rise and approach.

Fascinated as a bird before the flash of a mirror, Avenahar came close, and stood before his elegant stallion. For reasons Avenahar didn't know, she gave no ear to a small, sharp voice within, insisting she take care lest she be recognized. She sensed obscure pathways opening up into a greater world, leading off to pleasant gardens unknown. For the first time since joining Witgern's band, she felt a burn of humiliation at the thought of her mangled hair, and cursed the burdock burrs. She found herself reaching protectively for locks that were not there. What could this fine, proud man want?

But his eyes were not kind. They had a metallic glint. He settled his gaze somewhere just above her head, in a way that was most insulting.

"Is this the best you can do for your mother, Avenahar?"

It was the roar of a man with lion-spirit in him. Actors who played gods in the stage plays at Confluentes had voices like that.

He'd trumpeted her name for all to hear.

"To flee off like some idle-headed, ungrateful brat," he spoke on, "and give her yet more torment?"

She was so startled by the insult, she was only distantly aware of those around her exchanging startled looks, muttering, *Avenahar? This is Avenahar?*

"How dare you," Avenahar said softly. "Speak when you know what you're speaking of, and not before, lest you look the fool before all your men."

She turned about and began marching swiftly away from him.

"But your running away has only brought her shame," he called after her, blustering now, his aim less sure, "just when she needs the strength of kin about her, who—"

Avenahar paused and whipped about.

"You know nothing, yet you keep talking. It's a weakness in men who're given too much too soon, after having worked for it too little. Maybe one day wisdom will curb your foolish mouth. For myself, I plan to earn the glory I get."

When he'd collected his wits after the unexpected rebuke, he burst into free, full-throated laughter; he was of a nature to take pleasure in the sight of any creature putting up a vigorous defense.

Avenahar locked her gaze to the ground as she pushed herself to walk faster, seized with a need to find Witgern. *Now they know. . . .* She almost tripped on a root. Many had risen to their feet to get a better look at her, and they milled about, impeding her progress. Ragnhild strove to follow her for a time, but couldn't keep up. Murmured questions broke out here and there, and a peculiar, thoughtful quiet fell over the band; each person's wonderment had its distinct character. She stole occasional looks at them: Many studied her face in simple surprise, while nodding to their fellows. "It is no wonder she cured Hagbard," she heard one man's voice above others.

But as she crossed through the part of the encampment that lay closer to the stream, she began to see darker looks, accusing stares. She could guess the shape of their thoughts: *You and your mother chose Roman comforts over your kin.* She caught the musk of hatred on the air.

Spawn of a murderer. Decius's daughter. She felt like crockery smashed in pieces; each picked up a piece, supposing it all of her.

If I cannot stay here, where, then, can I go?

What an arrogant, unthinking lout this Sigibert is. Why would Witgern join forces with such a man?

Her way was blocked by a press of men; among them, she saw the ruined face of Hrolf, who had tormented her before. A thick-faced man, flushed scarlet from draught-spiked mead, caught her by the shoulders and twisted her about, displaying her for his fellows to see. A loathsome reek drifted from him.

"Good companions!" he shouted. "Look what's been foisted upon us. A whelp half-Roman, sired by Chariomer's pet dog."

Terror caused a weakness to sweep over her. She had no ready retort; they'd found her out. She hung limply in his hands, feeling like a condemned criminal suspended from a cross, dangling in final pain and humiliation.

"It's no wonder our luck's been cursed," came a low mutter.

"She's the reason the bridge didn't collapse!" a man cried out.

"Let her go, you carrion," came a calmer voice—but this man was too far off to give aid.

"Is she a good enough sacrifice?" bellowed the man who held her, "or will she pollute the altar? Shall we take a life, for the ones taken?"

He dropped her then; Avenahar landed off-balance and fell backward into mead-soaked mud. The flushed-face man straddled her drunkenly, wildfire in his eyes as he began energetically kicking her. Two of his fellows rushed to join in, but they became entangled with one another, and fell on top of her. Avenahar thought she would suffocate in mire.

From somewhere, Avenahar heard the crisp, fast rhythm of cantering hooves. Suddenly there were fish everywhere—heavy, silvery, and slick, plopping fast in the mud, rapidly piling up about her.

Fish?

It startled her attackers into forgetting their purpose; they clambered to their feet. Above her, Avenahar saw Sigibert on his tall stallion; in one hand he held an upended wicker basket. He'd seized a basket of fish from the bed of a provisions wagon—nothing better had been close at hand—and dumped the contents on the brawling men.

A freed Avenahar got, trembling, to her feet.

"Don't help me, you arrogant blockhead." She picked up a fish and hurled it into Sigibert's face. "Go chase your boar-pig."

As she forged her way onward, once again, she heard Sigibert's open, free laughter behind her. Lodged somewhere in the older, steadier parts of her was gratitude, even amazement, for the rescue. And, in spite of herself, she recognized his laughter as that of someone nobly good-hearted. She noted, too, that it continued an instant too long—as if to hold her there.

She found Witgern sitting outside his tent, in the company of a senior provisions woman called Ethelberga; both peacefully watched the stream as they discussed something of import. They seemed oblivious to the fact that she'd nearly been offered in sacrifice.

"Witgern." Heaving for breath, Avenahar burst between them. "That strutting cock you joined forces with has spread my secret to the far ends of the earth. Give him my thanks!"

Witgern focused on her gradually, seeming to rise slowly through soft layers of sleep. Finally he said, "Avenahar, sit. If that's not too much like putting a storm in a bottle. This is good. Now my men know who you are."

"*Good,* you say. Yes, it gives them a *good* reason to roast me alive! When you avenge my death, strike down Sigibert. He'll be the cause, surely as if he struck the blow himself."

Ethelberga smiled wanly, benignly.

"He's not a bad man," Witgern said placatingly. "He talks faster than he thinks, but he always regrets it later. Quiet yourself a moment. I have something to tell you. You know, Sigibert just came from the south, and—"

"I don't want to be Decius's daughter anymore!"

"Avenahar, stop this at once." Witgern pulled her closer to him, and put his hands on her shoulders with a most maternal kindness. "It will be well. Is it not better to be completely free from the burden of pretense? It just means we'll have to hide you better from those who would harm you. You must not go out alone into the forest anymore—"

"If I could fight for us, then maybe they wouldn't treat me like a scourge."

"No. Now, more than ever, you must live. Listen to me. Despise Sigibert if you must, but he does hold your mother in great esteem, and he has journeyed long to give me, in person, some grave news of her."

This dropped Avenahar through a trapdoor into another world. The insults, the fish, were forgotten.

"Does she live?" Avenahar scarce recognized her own thready voice. She felt like a prisoner at the place of beheading, extending her neck over the mysteries of the abyss.

"She lives, yes. And while she lives, so does hope. But they've had a trial for her, at the fortress. They say she's transgressed a law laid down by their Emperor. They've condemned her to death."

Avenahar made no sound; she just sat forward, grasped her hands about her knees, and trembled.

"But for reasons we don't understand," Witgern continued, "they haven't yet carried out the sentence. We are trying to discover what this means. Perhaps they fear us. Ah, if only Auriane had come with me, last spring . . . ! But the very best you can do for her, child, is to stay alive and find your fate."

* * *

AVENAHAR AWAKENED THE next day to an oddly altered world. Many met her gaze now as she passed, nodding faintly, or speaking her name; overnight she'd shed the role of barely tolerated outlander and taken on that of close kin, and for some, of living talisman. Now they saw the ghosts of others living in her—Baldemar, her grandfather, who'd kept them free for a generation; Athelinda, her grandmother, still giving counsel from the village of the Boar. If her persecutors pressed too close, she would find Hagbard or others lingering nearby, ready to protect her. To the herb women, all that mattered was that she was the daughter of Auriane. They would call her to their fire and ask her opinion on matters, small or great. But acceptance wasn't as sweet as Avenahar expected—*was anything, ever?* a growing part of her began to wonder. And the smoke of hatred still smoldered darkly, at the edges of the camp. Hrolf and those of like mind were held in tenuous check only by Witgern's will.

Sigibert stayed for a day and hunted with Witgern's men, but departed for home on the next, for word had come that a force that splintered off from Chariomer's army had laid siege to his farm and hall. As he departed the Wolf camp, he rode out of his way so that he would pass near Ragnhild's shelter. He met Avenahar's gaze from a small distance, and a wordless truce passed between them. The intensity of Sigibert's look confused her; she saw kindly interest there, blended with something she didn't understand, that was rich, strange, encompassing; it left her feeling a clandestine excitement, a languorous yearning. There was sorrow in his look, too, and apology. She smiled somewhat wistfully, and nodded at him.

She wondered, afterward, about that peculiar drunkenness in the flesh, that sense of filling pleasantly with warm water—that could be inspired by no more than the sound of his voice. *Gods below, is this desire? So, the flesh can desire when the spirit does not. For I'm quite sure I don't want him.*

Mother. You could tell me if this were a dangerous mystery, or nothing at all. And if you've ever known such a thing. It's you I want. He can go to Hades. This is brutal beyond bearing.

That eve, the provisions women brought them news of the latest outrage committed by the Four. The cavalrymen had seized the half-grown daughter of a village priest of Wodan, to sell at the small slave market by Mogontiacum.

Avenahar left Ragnhild's shelter to listen at Hagbard's fire. She felt a bolt of excitement, for this time, it seemed the Four's destination was known. The cavalrymen were overheard to speak of journeying to a village called the

Raven's Nest, where it was rumored silver had been thrown into the local spring, as an offering to its sprite. This village lay less than a half-day's ride from Witgern's winter encampment.

Avenahar sat for a time in agitated quiet with her rapidly fermenting plans. Hagbard smiled at her questioningly once, wondering at her silence.

Then she took leave of them and walked down to the stream, listening for the voice of her mother in the softly rushing water. *Do you see me? Are you well?* She pulled the earth amulet from beneath her tunic and pressed it to her cheek. High above, a white-gold moon swelling to fullness was a softly effulgent glory against the chill, clear lavender of the sky. *Is this not my charge?*

She sensed only beautiful silence from the stream, the moon, the wood spirits.

Then she started at a subtle movement across the stream. Among a stand of crooked, lichen-mottled elder trees, an old she-wolf, much battered from her hunts, was walking with a delicate limp. She was the color of the dusk. She halted, and fixed her messenger-eyes on Avenahar. They were formed of the same white-gold matter as the moon. They glowed with deep-forest knowings.

Yes, this is your charge.

I have my test, Avenahar thought as she walked back to Hagbard's fire.

I will destroy the Four.

"RAGNHILD," AVENAHAR ANNOUNCED on the following morning, "I must leave the camp for a time."

Ragnhild, bone needle in hand, halted in her work of stitching up a tear in her best woolen cloak. Her deeply seamed face appeared more ravaged in the thin purity of early morning light. Avenahar hesitated, feeling she had committed a grotesque cruelty, then forced herself to speak on. "I'm going to earn my place among the Wolf Coats. I mean to hunt down the Four. And stop their marauding, forever."

Ragnhild made no protest; she just cocked her head slightly, considering these words, sadness accumulating in her eyes.

Feeling awkward in the silence, Avenahar ventured, "Surely you knew, always . . . that I was never an herb woman."

Ragnhild shifted the cloak slightly so the sun fell on her work, and returned to rapidly, expertly, pulling the spun wool through the coarse cloth. Words sprang from her unexpectedly.

"I'm not a fool, Avenahar. I know you've been stealing off to practice-spar with Hagbard. But four trained soldiers against one maid? Why not save them the trouble and just draw a dagger across your own throat?"

Avenahar was amazed that Ragnhild launched no greater protest than this; there was even a measure of grim acceptance beneath those words. But then she considered that Ragnhild probably expected that any daughter of Auriane's would seek an unusual fate. This all made Avenahar increasingly uncomfortable, and she went on weakly, "I'll get their horses, Ragnhild. Your dun's worn out. I promise you a younger, stronger mount that will carry you far."

"And bring me a few whiskers from Wodan's horse while you're about it." She angrily put down her work. "You insult me, trying to win me with a gift."

Avenahar fought tears.

Ragnhild looked at her then; the old woman's eyes were suppurating wounds. "Avenahar. You have a medicine woman's hands. Not so many have this gift. Yet you toss it off like old soup bones."

"They are going to kill my mother," Avenahar said passionately. "As a warrior I've some hope of helping her. Or at least, of *avenging* her, if it comes to that, for by every god, avenge her I will."

Ragnhild returned to her sewing, making small, tight, angry stitches. "You have no faith in the powers."

"I do, Ragnhild. I was taught to love Fria as a mother. What I do, I do in adoration of her. Please . . . I've trusted you enough to tell you . . . don't betray me to Witgern."

"That would be like standing in the way of the wind. So be it, then, the Fates have you now."

Ragnhild's words made Avenahar feel a small door had been shut in her face, and locked.

"I . . . I am grateful for all your teaching, Ragnhild. You must know it."

But Ragnhild said only, "You shouldn't ride out alone. You've got a lively crop of enemies lurking about. Remember what we found in the cave. Somewhere hereabouts is a seeress who wishes you ill."

"I won't be alone. I've already asked Hagbard to come as witness."

"You should wait a few years before you start feeding the ravens."

"The women of my family come into their fate young."

"Indeed . . . it gets younger with each generation! Doesn't the test require three witnesses?"

"If this goes as I've planned it, I'll have everyone in the village as witnesses." She hesitated, then went on, "I have to declare my intention to two more. Who else can I trust with this?"

Ragnhild considered for a moment, then named two young members of the band who were loyal to her because she had recommended them to Witgern. Then she put down the cloak she was stitching.

"If you really mean to do this thing, Avenahar, you must do it right. You'll need the Wolf herbs. Can you listen well when I tell you how to take them? They are sacred, and dangerous. You must sing the right words over them. Men have died from not taking them as they were told."

"I'll listen well," Avenahar said softly. "Can I have the dun for two days, so I can catch up to my quarry?"

"So I have to lose a horse to get one."

"I swear on Fria's brightness I'll fetch you a new beast without losing the old one."

After Ragnhild reluctantly agreed, she was silent so long, Avenahar thought the old woman would speak of the matter no more. Avenahar watched the sun climb higher, alternately struggling for peace and assailing herself for being harsh. She wondered how long she would need to endure this bitter misery knotted painfully in her chest. Flies began to buzz around the leavings from last night's soup pot.

When Ragnhild said finally, "I have a gift," Avenahar was startled by her voice. Ragnhild began rooting about in her medicine bags, muttering steadily beneath her breath as she was nearly defeated by the disorderly profusion of chipped clay pots half-filled with greasy ointments, worn shoes, broken glass, and other oddments she'd collected for barter. "Ah!" she said at last, and offered to Avenahar something unidentifiable dangling from a leather thong. "Keep this on. Like this, let it fall near the heart. It's a wolf's paw. It was given me by my mother. She'll think you're one of us and she'll protect you."

"But this is for a daughter. Your mother will know."

"I've lost both my daughters and I'm a barren field. If you won't wear it, who will?"

"I thank you, Ragnhild. I dedicate my victory to you."

"Never lose your dread of the powers."

Avenahar nodded, unable to speak.

Ragnhild leaned forward and whispered right in Avenahar's ear. "And tell Ermenhild where you want to be burned."

"Yes . . . of course," Avenahar said as if she'd already thought of this— but Ragnhild saw the furtive start of terror in her eyes.

"If you don't plan for your pyre, you're not showing respect for the

Fates. Tell her, so she can tell the priestess. The Boar Village would be a good place, since your mother was born there."

"You are right," Avenahar said, still battling against the horror of this, striving to think only of the better life to be won.

Avenahar then sought out Ermenhild, who gave her a cattle horn and a skin of mead for mixing the battle draughts, and the pelt of a black wolf. Ermenhild also gave her food for the journey—several flat, brittle loaves baked of einkorn wheat, slightly burnt as always, and goat cheese wrapped in cloth.

Later, when Ragnhild gave her the sacred herbs, Avenahar was surprised to discover that the celebrated "raven's bread" used in so many Wolf rituals was a pretty, spotted mushroom. She had often seen clusters of them as bright, bloody sprinkles scattered through the autumn woods, never suspecting they were the secret thing that called up wolf storms within. When fresh picked, they had beautiful red caps with white warts; seeresses claimed they were colored so by the red-flecked foam of Wodan's horse as the god's eight-legged steed plunged through the night clouds in midwinter. Ragnhild carefully explained the power of each herb. More than once, Ragnhild cautioned Avenahar to take no more than the common dose for a child, as this was her first time.

AVENAHAR AND HAGBARD set out separately for the Raven's Nest, then met on the traders' track, across the valley. Too many questions might be raised, were they seen journeying off together. Ragnhild let it be known that she'd dispatched Avenahar to the root cave. So she might better pass through the country in safety, Avenahar garbed herself in a village priestess's gray hooded robe. She and Hagbard took turns riding Ragnhild's stocky dun horse.

They hadn't travelled far when Avenahar saw the old she-wolf again, on an escarpment above. Avenahar marveled that the horse was not frightened, then realized the beast must have become somewhat accustomed to wolf scent, from often being made to carry the pelts on its back. The she-wolf, colored like stone and earth, moved low over the ground in her swinging trot. Then she halted and regarded them kindly with her keen, white-gold eyes, set at an angle that lent her a look of wise discernment. With her tufted cheeks, she resembled a whiskered man.

Eyes of the moon. Eyes of her mother. Avenahar felt a new warmth, a fresh gush of certainty.

"The wolf spirit knows we are here," Hagbard said with more reverence than she'd ever heard from him. "This is good."

The she-wolf broke into a slinky gallop, a wolf-stream rippling, flowing over the broken ground, following them for a time for reasons of her own before vanishing back into her world.

Chapter 22

The horse's jolting trot made Avenahar feel like dice shaken in a cup. By the time she and Hagbard reached the valley they sought, the shadows stretched long, and a chill moon five days off full watched them with a cold, neutral eye. The village called the Raven's Nest lay in the gray-blue shade of a fold in a valley thick with tall pines. It was home to ten families; their longhouses were arranged like spokes in a wheel about an oasthouse for fermenting mead and a small wooden temple of Wodan. Dotted about the yard were several squat, lumpish dome-shaped clay ovens that glowed eerily but invitingly in the gathering dark; a village potter was still hard at work. Somewhere within, a babe howled. Suspended from a pole projecting above the settlement's palisade was a horsehide, with the skull and flayed flesh from the legs still attached, a forlorn thing making a ragged outline against the sky. From the look of it, Avenahar judged, it was an old sacrifice; who could offer something so dear, today?

Two torches by the settlement's gate gusted tauntingly in an evening wind.

Avenahar found a place in the forest where she was concealed by wild briar shrubs, but had a view of the village's sagging wooden gate. She hid the robes in which she'd disguised herself, then drew the black wolf pelt about her shoulders and fastened it with a thorn.

Hagbard pulled on a battered bronze bell that hung from the gate, and soon a man with a strong crop of gray hair and a hunter's horn slung across his chest emerged from a longhouse and exchanged words with him. Hagbard, as they had planned, claimed to be a traveller seeking a night's shelter. Among the northern tribes, to refuse a night's hospitality was unthinkable— openhandedness to strangers was considered a sign of nobility, and it was unmannerly to closely question a traveller's purpose. So Hagbard was taken into one of the longhouses and given a place round the fire, and their dun horse was given hay. The family offered him porridge and mead, then afterward he was given a comfortable bed of straw among the cattle and sheep stabled at the thatched dwelling's east end. All through the eve Hagbard listened with close attention to the family's talk, asking discreet questions about the Four. The cavalrymen had been put up more lavishly in the longhouse of the village's brewer, across the walkway from his own lodging. Later, Hagbard managed a strategic trip to the cess trench just beyond the back gate, which took him past the enclosure where the Four's horses were penned, and the shed where they kept their tack and armor.

The night was clear and still, and Avenahar from her place beyond the village's surrounding hawthorn hedge could hear the sounds of loud, careless carousing, cries of despair over a dice game.

Hagbard stole from his straw bed in the still-time before dawn. Avenahar followed his shadowed, spindle-legged form as he moved stealthily through the yard, tossed a scrap to a hound to keep it from barking, then shimmied beneath the gate, flexible as a sapling, careful not to sound the bell.

"All four are here, in the brewer's house," Hagbard whispered, eyes shining with what he'd learned. His oddly gentle face, scant beard growth, and fumbling manner made him seem he would ever be a boy, but there was a firm determination beneath his acts. "They're armed as regulars, not auxiliaries. They're not wearing the solid cuirasses. They wear the metal-like cloth, you know, that's open at the sides, and it falls to here—"

"Slitted mail armor," Avenahar said, nodding encouragingly.

"Yes, that's it, and from what I saw of their scabbards, they've got the regular-issue, long cavalry swords. And such horses! You've got to see these strapping beasts. They make ours look like skinny ponies."

Avenahar nodded gratefully.

"And they do leave today," he continued, "sometime this coming morn."

"'Sometime in the morn' is near as you could get it?"

"I could hardly ask them outright, could I? And I saw bulging leather sacks, that buckled on—full, no doubt, with what they've thieved from these people."

"Very good, that will slow them." After putting several questions to him about the horses' harness, she asked, "Did you see the maid they seized?"

"No, I suppose they're keeping her close and secure, in the house where they're lodged."

"I thank you, Hagbard. You've helped me greatly. If I live through this I'll praise you everywhere."

She cracked open the hard bread and divided the goat cheese, and they ate. Almost reverently, Hagbard brought forth a delicacy and offered it to her—a withered, yellow apple stuffed with honeyed nuts, which had been roasted in a clay oven. Another guest at last night's meal, a traveller like himself, had passed a basket of them around. She found it sorely tempting, but knew he was unaccustomed to such treats, while she thought she'd probably had more than her share, in her life at Julianus's villa. "You have it all, Hagbard. I can't eat more."

Hagbard carefully returned the roast apple to his sack to save for later; neither knew how long they would need to wait. Then Avenahar clasped her hands tightly about his, and whispered, "Go in strength." Hagbard then set out for an old beech tree he'd chosen earlier, and took a position on a comfortable lower branch that afforded him a broad view of the overland trackway and the valley.

Avenahar began the ritual that would transform her into a wolf.

In a soft voice that never rose above the soughing of the trees, she began singing the one simple wolf chant that she knew. The musical syllables invoked the living qualities of the wolf. Interspersed between the memorized verses, she reminded the Wolf-spirit who she was, of the deeds of her mother, of her grandfather Baldemar. Gradually the repetitive sound eased her gracefully into another world. It was a wordless place of smell and touch, of flight and flowing; it had no roads leading up to it, no roads leading away.

Then she poured mead into the horn and added the contents of the first pouch, an herbal mix of which wild rosemary was the principal part. This was the drink called frenzy mead. Ragnhild had claimed it could turn a gentle farm wife into a grinning ogress, and warned that too much of it could bring on vicious cramps. Avenahar took one timid swallow.

She poured more mead into the horn and broke in the smallest amount of the raven's bread, which had the power to bring sharp, clear knowing, and the senses of a wolf. She raised the horn to the field of stars while singing the Wolf words Ragnhild taught her, and asked for the protection of Wodan, guardian god of Witgern's band. Ragnhild had instructed her to take three swallows. Avenahar took two cautious ones, then poured out the rest in a circle about her, as she'd seen Ragnhild do once, to ward off hungry spirits that might come in the night.

Last, she took from her leather sack a shining black berry Ragnhild called "wolf cherry." She felt its dark strength as she held it in her palm. These were grown by the female battle spirits called the Choosers, who harvested the bravest dead from the battlefield. Wolf cherry was said to fill you with the mettle of a god. It was famous everywhere and had many names. Some called it "rage berry," others, "eye of the wolf." In the east, they called it Lady of the Forest. In the south, belladonna. A man might eat three or four before a raid. She ate one.

She resumed the wolf chant, relishing the sounds of the odd, knotted words, which Ragnhild had told her were from a tongue passed down from the Time of Ice. Avenahar was skeptical of this, unsure how anyone could know such a thing, but she struggled to believe, lest the Wolf-spirit think her a profane, town-bred child. If her doubts offended the Wolf, it might refuse to come.

No. Something was here.

There was an attentive stillness all about, an intelligent quiet, as something tall as the pines examined her with keen, golden eyes. The very air pricked its ears and sniffed. She heard the soft snap of branches from the light, furtive pressure of invisible paws. The scent of damp fur was a night perfume, warming her, welcoming her.

A hot wind rushed through her, fusing the wolf pelt to her back. She felt a great ghost not in human shape wrestling within her, as though struggling to fit itself into her body. A bolt of frightful strength rushed in, as if powers above the human were forced into her like air from a bellows. If she wanted, she could skim light and fast over rocky ground, paws scarcely touching the earth. She could leap a palisade. She was suffused with . . . not rage so much as a lust for furious movement, a driving need to leap on quarry, as if all life were contained there. Blood would taste like wine. A different pair of eyes were fixed over hers. Eyes made of moon matter.

She knew why the Wolf Coats performed this ritual before a raid—this "rage" drove fear before it as the sun drives the night.

She lived in a blaze of day. She wanted to snap her jaws. The pack was with her.

Her mind stretched broad and far as the sky; she felt firmly anchored to the four horizons; it was impossible to fall or die.

She was not one wolf, but many.

Then quite suddenly, she saw the beauty: The hills about were garbed exquisitely; strings of jewels lay on the land's cloaks of living russet and mystic green, their hues luminous, even in darkness. The land breathed; she breathed with it. Greenness washed over her—green had a taste. All slyly glowed with hidden gold. Was this the gold of Fria she'd heard tales of, that most could not see? The purslane carpeting the forest floor was colored gloriously as the plumage of the peacocks she'd seen in villa gardens. The forest gently rose and fell with rolling waves of multicolored life. The beauty was painful; warmth flooded to her face, and her eyes watered with grateful tears. She believed this beauty was there always, but that most human creatures, drawn up in ever-narrowing circles of life, simply stopped seeing it.

Now the somber avenues between the trees were crowded with mischievous, softly glowing elfin beings. The seeresses spoke truly, Avenahar realized—the forest teemed with hidden life.

Malign presences were there as well. A frigid wind blew through her. She sensed sour ghosts gliding up through fissures in the ground. She heard the voices of the Choosers, arguing about her. A reverberating shriek sounded in her mind, and she felt Hel shifting, moving, deep in the earth.

To banish her terror Avenahar pressed her mother's earth amulet to her heart and struggled to conjure Auriane before her. For a moment, she succeeded. But her mother's hands disintegrated into a flax field rifled by wind, her eyes into cornflowers. The despairing thought came, *She has abandoned me again, as she did when I was a babe.* Avenahar knew this old emptiness as a chamber deep below her in the earth, from which other passages branched off, to ultimately lead her to this place—where she was a Wolf in the forest, hungrily watching a village gate.

In Auriane's place was a hooded, black-cloaked Ancestress. Avenahar did not want her there. There was a foulness about her, part scent, part feeling. Her presence was suffocating. Avenahar felt life choked off, mortifying like a dead limb. The hooded one identified herself as Avenahar's great-grandmother Hertha, who'd immolated herself by walking into a burning hall. The spectre's mind clamped over hers. Avenahar was flushed with panic, sensing she had pried open a gate she could not close. *Is her ghost here truly? Or have I dosed myself with too much wolf medicine?*

Avenahar, the spectre's voiceless words came to her. *Your mother abandoned the work of winning vengeance. You will take it up again.*

The presence's pull was darkly seductive, and Avenahar felt herself fearfully yielding, as someone half starved might be pulled toward a steaming soup, despite knowing it was seasoned with water hemlock.

The spirits want me, Avenahar thought. *I am greater than my mother. Where she failed I will be victorious. Vengeance closes all wounds.*

Morning was close. The sky was not soft black anymore; it was a deep charcoal that lightened to scallop-pink along the eastern horizon.

A brief, hard rain came, as if a stopcock in the sky were opened then shut again. It left Avenahar's wolf skin damp and wet.

But she scarcely minded, for now she belonged as the wild briars belonged. She was growing hairs. And dog teeth. Her hearing embraced every leaf crackle. Her sense of smell was mighty; fingers of smell-sense rivered far out into the wood, hesitating over the odor of red deer droppings, a female, just a short lope away, then streaking off farther to explore the carcass of a badger. Somewhere close, a vein of water moved through the earth. The dankness of a stream lay heavily over everything—how intrusive and potent was the smell of life-giving water! Laden on the wind was a confusion of aromas carried from afar, too complex for an inexperienced wolf to sort out—of a traveller edging along on muleback, of burning moss, of venison roasting. The air was so rich with scent-messages, it was savory as a stew.

A sallow sun poured its sickly light onto the road. Avenahar heard morning stirrings in the village: the serious ring of hammering, children's shrieks of raw joy, the uncomfortable moans of milk-swollen cows, the clunking of a bucket bumping down into a well.

Now she smelled *them,* in the village. Her quarry. Their peculiar mansweat was mingled with the sweeter fragrance of horses, the dead smell of tanned leather. She had no words for their sour tang; she knew only that it was distinct from her tribespeople's smell. She heard the soft burble of the villagers' voices, overlaid by the pushing, jarring talk of the Four—their words made small wounds in the air.

A tired-looking woman bearing a babe in a sling appeared at the village gate; her dirty linen dress dragged in the mud as she slowly pushed it open.

The four cavalrymen rode out in a single file, their mounts moving at a brisk walk. The short but formidable parade was a brutish reminder of where power lay on earth. Their heavy lances were angled forward, the evil leaf-bladed heads like ships' prows. The bronze nose pieces of the horses' harness and the flexible mail *hamata* encasing the men's torsos glinted darkly in the sun. On their left arms the men bore oblong, iron-bound shields; on their near side, the pommels of swords projected warningly from their sheaths. Their garish colors were jarring against the soft green landscape—red martingales with gilt fringe, studded with glittering Medusa heads; four-horned saddles of crimson leather double-cinched over saddlecloths of harsh blue. The horses' forelocks were tightly plaited so that they stood upright, like a single horn. Those horses were proportioned to heroes. The heroes astride them, however, seemed bored by their own invincibility.

One rider led a shaggy pony on a long lead; with its shorter legs, the smaller animal was forced to a hurried trot to keep apace. Astride was a reedy girl of perhaps ten summers. She slumped forward; fawn-colored hair fell into her face. Once she straightened, and Avenahar saw her ashen lips. Her hands were bound before her with cord.

Avenahar watched with golden eyes. Her senses existed only for her quarry. The Four were a single disjointed, sixteen-legged beast, a creature both awkward, with its detachable armored parts, and exceedingly dangerous, with its four terrible talons—their swords. The segmented beast ambled loosely onward with its ridiculous sixteen-legged walk, a creature all sourness, sloppy inattention, and soft underbelly.

She felt no fear.

Her mind was empty of plans. Wolf wisdom would flow in, moment by moment. She waited patiently while they passed. Then she eased down from her place.

In a slinky trot, on four long, strong legs, she moved out onto the beautiful meadow where the Choosers lived.

The tired woman by the gate jerked awake. Who was that running at a crouch, falling in behind the Four—a youth slight of form, a maid? The woman watched Avenahar's progress with sharp interest. She said nothing to warn the Four, for this was her quarry, too.

Avenahar let herself be pulled into the cavalrymen's wake while staying off the road, mingling herself with the grasses. The horses did not catch her scent; she was protected by the direction of the wind.

The Four passed by Hagbard, concealed in his tree. The horses knew he was there; they questioned Hagbard with head-tosses and snorts, and tried hard to inform their riders—it was all so clear to Avenahar. But the cavalrymen paid no mind to the urgent horse talk.

Now Avenahar could see the trefoil design on the shield carried by the last man in the file. As she quietly closed the distance, she groped for the horse she would take. The last horse was a dispirited roan whose head sagged too close to the path. This beast was not hers; he was too resigned. She darted into the skull of the next one; this horse thought only of biting the horse ahead of him. It was unpleasant being inside this one so she leapfrogged into the skull of the handsome bay lead horse. This was a sensible, fair animal that liked his fellows, but wanted to outrun them. He pulled hard against the bit, annoying his rider, straining for freedom. This was the horse she would take.

But the lead horse's rider was the most stoutly-made man of the party. Bear-shoulders sloped down to scarred upper arms, lumpy with muscle like a wrestler in the palaestra, and on to hairy red hands clamped onto the reins. He swayed a bit; he was too large for the horse. Still, she felt no fear. Great was the frenzy-root. Unconquerable was the Lady of the Forest.

She broke into an easy lope, flowing close to the trailing horse and rider; the Wolf caused her to seize this horse's tail. She held to it, working hard to calm the beast with her mind, to let it know she meant it no harm. She pulled herself forward, and then, moving with great silence, she arced so smoothly, so easily onto this horse's haunches that she felt she was *falling*.

This was glorious.

A shriek escaped her lips. It was no wolf howl, but a shout in the Chattian tongue—*Vengeance*.

There came a turmoil of turning horses, barking men. The segmented beast was one creature no more; it splintered into four parts, each spinning in chaos. The highly-trained cavalry mounts lurched beyond their riders' control, skittering backward, eyes wild with too much white. They thought a living wolf had dropped into their midst. Avenahar hadn't considered the terror that might be wrought by the musky reek of a wolf pelt, dampened in the rain.

All played out with great swiftness, but to Avenahar, it was broken into slow, deliberate parts. She braced herself by grasping the rear horns of the saddle, jammed a foot beneath the cavalryman's right knee, then drew her leg sharply upward. It was so unexpected, it succeeded; the startled man was pitched leftward. Pulled by the weight of his shield, he toppled awkwardly to the hard-packed ground. It was not a good fall. That one moved no more.

Avenahar scrambled into the saddle, then retrieved and tautened the reins. She was a ravening beast.

"Halt! Beware! Attack!" Only now did she hear their shouts scoring the air like trumpet blasts. Their maddened horses were a tangled skein that rapidly grew more so; the pony's lead line broke and the unconcerned beast merrily trotted off, bearing the captive girl down the roadway ahead. Amidst the tumultuous storm of agitated horses one cavalryman managed to unsheathe his sword and position his mount for a strike. He drew back his arm for a crosscut that would have embedded the blade in Avenahar's spine.

Avenahar never knew. Her mount twisted upward, forehooves scrambling in air; the finely honed steel sunk harmlessly into the thick cushioning of the saddle. She let herself fall from the beast's vertical back, onto the broad rump of her attacker's mount; before she'd settled in place, she was already slashing furiously at him with her small flint knife. She was many wolves, snapping exuberantly, borne aloft on the rapture of the hunt.

"Seize him!" They were flustered dogs trying to outbark each other.

"It's a *maid*," she heard one shout, the stress on the word expressing disappointment, contempt—and ever-new surprise. Though an occasional battle maid was a common enough sight in rogue warbands, it never seemed to impress well upon soldiers' memories; she supposed it was because a man in a strange land sees what he expects to see.

"Hades—get the she-beast off me!" The man with whom Avenahar had hitched a ride wrenched himself about in the saddle, sword arm lifted, but he wasn't properly positioned to strike. Avenahar's dagger was a ravening claw, catching on the iron mail of his *hamata,* snaring itself in the thick wool of a military cloak, biting deep into the exposed back of a neck.

Spewing curses, he threw himself from the saddle to escape this stinging Fury, this gadfly in the shape of a maid. As he dropped to the ground, Avenahar, with a whip-fast movement, got a grip on his sword arm just below the elbow. The force of his fall pulled his arm in a direction it wasn't meant to go. He yelped eloquently. His grip on the sword slackened. She cut herself on the blade as she fumbled for the pommel of the cavalry sword—then it was hers.

Sheer madness won it for her. Now they faced a Fury with a sword.

The hexagonal grip was still warm; it seemed to melt into her hand. Her wolf frenzy married muscle and mind and she adjusted at once to the sword's weight, its balance. She executed a downward cut for the joy of it. The fine blade jumped sensitively through air, moving with a curious unpredictability, as though it had its own ghost. The stoutly made cavalryman launched his mount toward her, his own blade raised like a scythe. Some part of her was astonished to find herself responding with the casualness of a veteran, snaking her sword up beneath his. Their blades met in air with a bell-clear *clang*. Sparks showered down. From behind her came frenzied shouts, as at a horse race near the finish—*the villagers,* she realized. They'd massed at the gate to urge her on to victory.

Without a break in motion, she looped the blade downward—it moved beautifully, as though she ran a fine quill over glass—and severed the bay stallion's right rein. The horse rolled back on its haunches and spun leftward, following the pressure of the remaining rein. The cavalryman raked his sword in air. The man she'd just unseated rushed at her then, meaning to seize her by the leg. She drove him back with a mule kick to the face.

At the same instant, the bay stallion collided with her mount, shoulder to shoulder. Avenahar tore off the wolf pelt, caught the bay by the remaining rein and flung the pelt at her chosen stallion, some part of her apologizing to the poor beast as she did so. The pelt settled onto the bay stallion's fiercely bowed neck.

The bay erupted into a mad, blind horse dance, bucking erratically as oil droplets popping on a hot griddle. Somehow through this, Avenahar managed to keep her grip on the long rein. The wolf pelt dropped off. A final spasm in air—and the cavalryman flew over the bay's head. Avenahar drew the stallion close, caught one of the saddle horns, and pulled herself aboard.

She had her horse! Sitting on the throne of Jupiter couldn't have been more dizzying.

The fourth and only uninjured man of the party had dropped from his uncontrollable mount. Calmly, steadily, he took aim at Avenahar with his lance.

Look behind!—the villagers cried out in warning.

But Avenahar's stallion was paying no heed to her attempts to guide it with a single rein; it continued performing a slightly less energetic version of its wolf-pelt dance. The cavalryman's arm snapped forward; the heavy missile shot forth, fast and straight as an arrow from a bow.

The bay bolted. One of the villagers had struck its haunches with a well-aimed stone.

Avenahar clung to the plaited mane as her nervous prize hurtled down the road. The cavalryman's lance whipped over the stallion's hindquarters, skipped off an outcropping of rock, and skidded into the long grasses.

Good sense might have prompted her to keep on going, but the Wolf madness knew nothing of good sense. Pulling and jerking on the remaining rein, Avenahar forced the protesting bay stallion around in a great arc that took her into the meadow. With much frustrated head-tossing the stallion yielded, slowing to a back-jolting canter punctuated by random kicks of rage. When her horse was aligned with her quarry, she urged the stallion to full gallop. The cavalrymen became, then, Rome and all its crimes. They'd wrested her from her mother, as a babe. She would scour the land of them forever.

Two of the party lay unmoving on the roadway. The two still fit for battle stood together, braced against her, shields to the fore. Spirit-terror had undermined them; this madwoman called up tales of death-dealing swan-maids who could take any shape. No mere maid could have brought such destruction to four professional soldiers.

Avenahar's stallion barreled toward them to the accompaniment of a rhythmic, driving victory chant. She stole a glance in the direction of the gate. The village's full population of forty or so shook fists in the air, urging her on.

The cry, *Vengeance,* shot from her throat; her blade was a hawk descending, all swift grace. An iron-bound shield whipped upward to meet her sword. The mighty impact almost tore the weapon from her grip. The force of her horse's motion knocked the cavalryman from his feet; he sprawled onto his back.

This shattered the courage of the last man standing, who had no taste for battling this maddened spectre while injured and alone. He threw down his shield and began to jog-trot dazedly toward the wood. His comrade crawled from beneath his own shield and followed after, limping rapidly on a sprained foot; together they scrambled up the embankment.

Avenahar gave chase for a time, but when they broke into the forest, she let them go.

She was victor. As soon as she knew it, her will to do battle deflated all at once, like some billowing banner when the wind dies.

There came a quiet suffused with gold.

It was filled suddenly with the villagers' clamorous shouts. She felt she was clad in shining garments. This was the finest of days.

I am my mother. Glories will be mine.

The bay stallion shied from the severed rein, lifting its knees as though it walked through a field of spikes. Avenahar dropped from its back. She felt like a snapped lyre string. Exhaustion dragged her toward the earth; she wanted to curl up and rest in the arms of the warm, mothering sun.

But she had matters to attend to. She examined the first man who'd fallen. There was no help for him—he lay in an odd posture; she suspected his neck was broken. She moved to inspect the wounds of the second man, who was propelling himself along with his arms, seeking the side of the road, oozing onward in caterpillar fashion.

Hagbard dropped from his tree, laughing so hard he swaggered as he walked. He clamped his hands about her shoulders. "Avenahar, you were a wolf with wings. I've never seen the like. None will believe this!"

"We'll have to let one horse go," Avenahar said, nodding toward the cavalrymen's horses, peacefully pulling at grass in the meadow as if nothing of importance had happened, "to carry the wounded man back to their fort." Her people did not keep prisoners. And here was one more man to spread the tale of her marvelous deed. Hagbard nodded gamely at her, grinning.

Then he turned about, and vomited on the side of the road.

"Hagbard?!"

"It is nothing, I'm fine."

"You don't look fine. You look as if you've had a bit of the wolf medicine yourself. The wrong dose."

"It really is nothing. I'll go chase down the maid, I don't think the pony went far. Avenahar, I'm fine, stop looking at me."

"All right then . . . we'll arrange for the maid to be returned to her home village, and then we must—"

The villagers flooded through the gate. They came down the path in a boisterous herd, jostling one another.

Victory was hers, and they had seen! She swelled with love for them, and imagined their adoration of her. She decided she would award one of these fine horses to them, as well as half the captured treasure.

If only her mother were here to witness.

As they jogged closer in a disorderly mass, the Lady of the Forest still drenched all in beauty. Avenahar did not see the murder-lust in their eyes.

And Hagbard saw nothing at all, for he had doubled over again, emptying everything he'd eaten yesterday into the ditch.

The wan-faced woman's expression was eager and alive.

They come to do me homage. Avenahar would celebrate with them tonight, before she returned to camp.

She was momentarily puzzled when villagers trotted straight past her. Some brandished stone axes.

Too late, she realized their purpose.

"No! You curse yourselves! *No!*"

The villagers swarmed over the wounded man like wasps. Avenahar sprinted after them, crying out at Hagbard to help her. Axes were lifted against the sky. They struck blows she couldn't see, but her mind's images were bright, searing, horrible; she felt her own skin being split like cloth. She seized a woman by the arm, pulled hard at a man's shoulders, and managed, finally, to drag a child away from the feeding—yes, it was a *feeding,* she thought.

It was no use.

She circled them, imprecating, entreating, as her voice became hoarse. But they were feasters after a winter famine.

Behind the terrible noise they made, the sound of her own pleas, Avenahar heard a crackling fire and unhallowed laughter that seemed to seep up from the ground. The portals opened by the raven's bread were still thrown wide; things of night swarmed into the day. The land darkened under the cloud-shadow of an Ancestress. She sensed her great-grandmother Hertha standing over her, tall as the firs, hair unfurling in gusting flames. Her voice was wind rushing through an abandoned house. *Vengeance is holy, it gives life to the clan.*

She lives and she rejoices. I have released her into the world.

THE WOLF COATS watched in silence as the unlikely parade moved quietly into camp—Avenahar, astride a war horse spirited of eye, heavy of bone, leading two mounts of equally grand proportions. Long cavalrymen's shields were lashed to their saddles; their trappings, glowing with embossed bronze fittings, were glorious as a field of evening stars. The sight caused some to break into laughter, as though at a fiendishly clever jest. And then came Hagbard, no longer able to sit upright on a horse; he slumped forward along the neck of the docile dun. None knew what to make of it.

Then three elders from the Raven's Nest solemnly recounted Avenahar's deed.

In the joyous pandemonium that followed, Avenahar was a captive; they dragged her from her horse and carried her to Witgern's tent, then handed her from fire to fire, forcing her to tell the tale again and again. The Four's weapons and armor were heaped in the center of camp, and the Wolf Coats studied them as though they were volumes in a library, running hands over the beautifully crafted saddles, mumbling words of amazement over the complicated strapping of the harness, playfully hoisting the iron-bound shields to their shoulders and practice-sparring with their fellows. One cavalry mount Avenahar had gifted already to the villagers. The resigned roan she presented to Ragnhild, to carry her burdens. Witgern claimed the slender chestnut stallion, so his messengers could ride swiftly. But the formidable bay was her own. Witgern insisted that it could not be otherwise; a holy madness had won this horse for her, and their spirits were already joined.

There was no joy in their return for Hagbard, however. When Ragnhild saw his condition, she sent a runner to fetch a seeress from Ramis's Summer Sanctuary. Avenahar was alarmed to learn that Ragnhild thought Hagbard's affliction so beyond her own powers.

"I've no strength to tell it again, let me pass," Avenahar protested as she finally escaped the band's aggressive adoration. As she fought her way to Ragnhild's shelter, others began to tell the tale for her, and she heard small blurrings of the truth. She supposed that within a year she wouldn't recognize the story as her own.

"The roan . . . you don't like him?" Avenahar asked Ragnhild.

Ragnhild just stared into her fire, in a way that saddened Avenahar. "He's fine enough," she responded finally, her features seeming to sag more than usual. Avenahar realized then that Ragnhild had prayed she would fail—but somehow still return alive and well.

"How is Hagbard?" Avenahar asked, frowning. "Has he improved at all?"

"He worsens. It is a mystery. He's got the best of care on its way now, the *very* best. The Holy Nine are staying at the Summer Sanctuary."

"Why now, almost in winter? Would one of them actually come here?"

"There's to be a convening, you know, because Ramis was taken from us. And no, they wouldn't, not just for poor Hagbard—they'll send an apprentice."

"Why are you so certain you can't help him?"

"I suspect a potent poison. The Nine are more learned in these arts than anyone in the land."

Avenahar nodded slowly, absorbing these words, then crawled dispiritedly to the back of the hut where Ragnhild kept a small food store.

"Avenahar, what is wrong?"

"The whole of the world," Avenahar muttered as she pawed through Ragnhild's food baskets, "and every stupid blade of grass, every cursed rock and tree in this beastly world. I've been to a place so vile I want to bury the memory under a mountain. But I can't."

"What's this jabber? Why are you taking my food? Avenahar, look at me.

You are blessed, many times over. You have the fate you wished for. Now they'll initiate you as a Wolf. What sort of fool cries and complains after something so glorious?"

"It's glorious as mud. I've proved myself the world's best horse thief, maybe."

"Sometimes I wonder if you *are* your mother's daughter."

"I won't be a Wolf."

"Have you lost all sense?" Ragnhild wedged herself between Avenahar and the stores. "What is wrong with you?"

"Ragnhild, please! I need to go off for a time, and I need a bit of food."

"Running away—again? Always running away."

Avenahar glared at her.

Ragnhild laughed, unimpressed. "If you sat in one place long enough, maybe things would sort themselves out."

Fast as a fox, Avenahar snatched a loaf of hard bread, then nimbly scuttled backward, out of the shelter.

"Avenahar!"

But Avenahar was already making light, quick progress down the trail.

THE ENCAMPMENT DROPPED into quiet when word was given out that Witgern would address his Wolves.

After a leisurely paean to Avenahar's victory, Witgern concluded by saying, "Friends. The spirits are signing that they will open a way for us. The Fates mean to give us victories now. As a lone Wolf scattered and destroyed the Four, so we, though weakened and small, are now strong enough to take back our land from the Cheruscans. Now we can unite our warring chiefs. Next year's raiding season—we go out, full and strong, against Chariomer!"

"The mountain cat slays the hart!" came a stray shout.

"Then finally, Rome." Witgern's mild voice floated out serenely. "Once Chariomer's driven off, we'll reclaim every scrap of land stolen from us by the Scourge of the South."

The clatter of spears struck against shields sent a cloud of starlings gusting from the boughs above, thick as dust shaken from a blanket. When all had quietened somewhat, Witgern signaled to Ragnhild. "Bring Avenahar to us."

Ragnhild glowered at him. "That would be a fine trick. She's run away."

* * *

THE APPRENTICE SENT by the Holy Nine sat in silence astride her small ghost-pale horse. The beast's bridle shivered with amulets of silver. Ragnhild found herself puzzled by the woman's garb; Ramis's followers spurned wealth, and this apprentice was attired as a chieftain's daughter. A cloak of reed-dyed green that draped to the pony's knees was fastened with a falcon's-head brooch inset with gemstones worth more than Ragnhild's new horse.

The apprentice's maiden attendants spoke her needs; Ragnhild never even learned the woman's name. Within the shadowed recesses of the lamb-skin hood of her cloak, Ragnhild discerned the smooth, bold features of a woman of perhaps twenty, with a narrow, handsome face, waxen skin, great, exploring eyes. Those eyes pulled all into them and held them there, like stilled whirlpools. Something about her put Ragnhild in mind of a thing both deftly curved and sharp, like the silver-mounted horn at her belt.

The maiden attendants drove the well-wishers from Hagbard's shelter, and even commanded Ragnhild to go, claiming the spell their silent mistress needed to perform for Hagbard required her to be alone with him.

The apprentice dismounted and entered Hagbard's shelter, while her attendants stood guard, allowing no one to stray too close. She examined Hagbard with a sharp, professional gaze, turning his damp body once, noting the lividity of his skin, his lusterless eyes, then prying open his mouth and studying the color of his tongue. Finally, she nodded, satisfied, as if all were as she expected, then she seated herself beside him, watching him with detachment.

Hagbard had lost the ability to speak. He stared at her, eyes silently begging help.

Alarm began to show in his face as he realized she meant to do nothing.

"Hagbard," she said finally, her voice clear, bored. "Did you, perchance, out there in the wood with Avenahar, eat an apple?"

Slowly, he nodded, his beseeching eyes beginning to fog with fright.

"Your tongue burns? You've voided all you've eaten?"

He mewled in assent, then moaned something that matched the intonation of, *Help me.*

"Ah, there's nothing to be done. There's enough akony root in you to fell three men, really—I'm surprised you're still living. I am Elza, daughter of Chariomer, apprentice to Sawitha. When I make my kill potions, they kill."

He emitted a higher-pitched moan of protest.

"It wasn't for you; it was meant for Avenahar."

Hagbard struggled to sit up, his eyes sparking like a fire sputtering a final time before it surrenders to darkness.

She pushed him firmly back onto the straw bed.

"You two scamps forgot to consider that some among Ermenhild's sisters answer to me. I'm sorry about your death, Hagbard, but you're of little matter; you were but a fallen log in Sawitha's path. You're dying in the place of one whose fate is, evidently, much stronger than yours."

His moan said, more with the eyes than the voice, *Why?*

She leaned closer, smoothing back his wet hair with a gesture Hagbard found repellent, void as it was of affection. "To show the people that Auriane's line has no power and no luck. Only Sawitha is blessed enough to put her hand upon Ramis's staff." She shook her head, and smiled. "It was your misfortune to have had anything to do with Auriane's wretched spawn. Sawitha warned Witgern not to give that brat meat and mead. He disobeyed. Sawitha gives measure for measure."

Still Elza tarried, puzzled by how tenaciously Hagbard clung to life. The Raven's Nest villager who'd also partaken of her poison fruit had died more quickly. She inspected the amulets he wore, wondering if he were under the protection of some spirit unknown to her, but found nothing unusual. Then his breaths quickened, in the way that signified dying. "Have a good journey, Hagbard," came her sibilant whisper. "Tell Hel you know me, and she'll treat you well."

Elza then rose and lifted her hands above him in blessing. She was unconcerned by the fact that her intended victim still lived; alone among the women of Ramis's sanctuary, Elza had no fear of Sawitha. Her voice tolled out strongly—"Hagbard, I commend you to the immortal Fates, older than all the gods. Hagbard, lie in Fria's fields. All glory to Sun and Moon."

"AVENAHAR. I WANT to hear the tale from your own mouth," Witgern said. Avenahar had wandered back into camp after two days of sitting out in the forest. She stood in Witgern's tent, gaze fastened firmly to the ground.

Witgern found her altered in some small but significant way, and wondered if his knowledge of her confounding battle-feat was acting as a sorcerer's glass that warps and enlarges what the eyes see. She was young enough to be growing still, and he would have laid down coin that she'd grown taller in the last two months. Her dark, shining hair was smoothed sleekly back and captured into a short braid—it was finally long enough—and this somehow lent her a calm, self-possessed look; he doubted she was aware of it. She was a nimble young version of her mother, a supple she-wolf, proud and gentle, glossy black fur shining under the sun. *It is odd*, he thought, *to see, all at once, how a maid will look in full womanhood.*

"I don't want to tell it any more," she said, meeting his gaze. "And I won't be a Wolf."

"Now that you've turned my mind, yours turns the other way! You've been given powerful signs, strong as the shining sun. You cannot spurn them."

"What really happened to poor Hagbard?"

"The seeress said he drank water poisoned by elves."

"I drank the same water he did. It makes no sense. He was cursed because my deed was cursed. I shall wither next."

"Nonsense. Yours, Avenahar, was the most glorious battle-test any among us has carried out in the seven years since I gathered this band together. And the seizure of these swords . . ." He looked at the three cavalry swords, their long, thin blades blankly reflecting light from the opening of the tent. "These are things of great power, because of the way you won them. We have a weapon direct from their hands, which we can turn against them. You've given us a measure of hope. Where do you see evil in this?"

"They murdered one of the cavalrymen," she whispered, looking away. "The villagers. They savaged him while he lay wounded on the road. He gestured to me for help."

"But Avenahar—"

"I know. I despise them, too. I think I hate them more than anyone does . . . but when this man lay defenseless at my feet, begging for help, somehow he became something else . . . I don't know *why* that made it different, but it did. And I cannot pluck the picture from my eyes."

"This part was not unknown to me. The villagers sought vengeance, Avenahar. And they carried it out under the sun. Vengeance isn't murder."

"What, then, of the rightful shame all should feel at striking one who has fallen? It is like feasting on the dead."

"Life with your mother has confused you. In ancient days, when enemies were honorable . . . those were less confusing times. Living apart from our people has taught you different notions of where clan lines are drawn."

"Witgern, when it was over, I saw . . . an evil Ancestress. She was somehow captive, and I set her free."

"Avenahar, the raven's bread can trick you into seeing what's not there, if it's your first time. *Battle* is what you saw. When songmakers sing of battle, they show us a . . . a serene and noble skeleton, washed clean of blood, empty of cries. You saw it as it is, and many say this is somewhat like a first sip of a poisonous draught. You sip a little more, the body strengthens itself — and it sickens you less. Sip still more — and you kill like a wolf."

Avenahar said nothing, emptied of every desire except to go home.

"Trust my will, Avenahar. Begin your initiation into the band."

Witgern took her hand in a strong grip. "Do you know the ways of wolves, Avenahar? I watch them. Like men in a war band, they have different tasks. One is the boldest of the pack, and leaps first on the prey. Another stands guard. One, always a she-wolf, decides where the den will be. One clearly commands, with pricked ears and raised tail. And one lays strategy.

"You will be such a one that lays strategy. When you are fully grown, and steadier, and have performed all the tests, I will take you in as one of my inner council."

At this, Avenahar felt such a bolt of joy—and was so genuinely amazed—that the memory of the horror grew softer and dimmer. She felt she fluttered in confusion between two worlds.

"Witgern. Before, you said to me, 'You are not your mother.' Do you now . . . think you were wrong?"

"Your nature's a puzzle. I see you still think that to be unlike her is to be somehow less! *Whatever* you are, the Fates are making you a place. And they so clearly have given you the powers of the Wolf."

"I don't know," she said uneasily.

"Well, there's no hurry." He smiled, and let her hand go. "What is that?" Witgern pointed to the dully-gleaming serpent brooch securing her short cloak.

She covered Decius's fibula with her hand. "A thing of magic," she said. "It just *appeared* in my sack. Ragnhild says it was put there by the moss folk. I know it gave me protection yesterday."

"Ah. Good." He smiled, satisfied. "Be ready in the morn. Tomorrow, we go on a short journey together. Bring your battle prizes with you."

WITGERN HALTED BEFORE a low hill covered with goose grass, an uninteresting nob in the earth Avenahar never would have noticed, had she been a traveller passing by. He lit a mullein stem dipped in resin, pulled aside some thistles, and motioned for her to follow. Crouching, they made their way through a passage not unlike the vestibule of a Roman house, for soon it opened out into a spacious chamber.

The earthen floor was covered over with straw, back as far as the torchlight penetrated darkness, and she was uncertain what Witgern meant to show her. She started to step farther inside. Witgern roughly caught her shoulder and pulled her back.

"Do not step there."

He dropped to one knee and lifted a bit of straw. Avenahar dropped down beside him.

In a vast pit dug into the earth was a treasure-hoard of swords, laid out neatly by the hundreds. Most were the gem-studded and unique products of tribal forges, but there, too, were short swords of the Roman army. The torchlight infused the iron blades with cold life; it seemed many stern, watchful serpent eyes peered out at them. So alive. Here, dark power thickly swarmed, stored in earth as a steel seed that would sprout and break the earth one day like an oak—an oak of iron. Words of Ramis's wended their way into Avenahar's mind: *Iron and sorrow . . . they came into the world together.* Did Ramis mean there was once a race of men who didn't know war? That did not seem possible. Or was vengeance the "sorrow" she spoke of? Because there was no end to it?

"It is a marvel," she whispered.

"Here are more swords than we have ever possessed," Witgern said. "The Roman patrols pass this way every day and they do not know. These are waiting for the day, coming soon, when we will take back our land from the Cheruscan carrion. This is what your mother has done for us."

"These are the swords she—?" A nurturant warmth underlaid with biting sorrow overtook Avenahar. Her mother had, to the end of her days, dared what others would not, and Auriane seemed, just then, not a woman but a force, noble and flowing, some wind-horse of gods or pivot of hopes, her lifetime of deeds an endless song artfully sung—and when she was snuffed out, all she truly was would be unknown except to a pitiful few.

"Yes," Witgern continued. "She gave us this, and now, it seems, must give her life. This is why I will not hear people revile her."

Iron's "sorrow" is my mother, Avenahar thought then, *who again and again gave up her own hopes of peace to give shelter to those she loves.*

Avenahar's tears burnt a course down her face, hot as Greek fire. *My running off was a monstrous cruelty. How could I have struck her such a blow?*

The amulet of earth Auriane had given her—Ramis's amulet—seemed, then, to quicken at her breast; she caught it up in her hand. And in that moment, though the mechanism of the means remained veiled, Avenahar forgave her mother for Decius.

But not herself. His poison blood was still in her, blighting her hopes.

Witgern took the heavy cavalry swords she had brought and deposited them in the shallow pit. "The power in your deed flows into us all. You add your strength to ours. Come with me, I'll show you something greater still."

He guided her to a natural ledge at one side of the chamber, where some prize wrapped in a length of wool had been set aside. Witgern unwound it just far enough to show her the gem-studded hilt of a sword.

"Do you know this sword, Avenahar? You should. It holds the ghost of your line. It is your own grandfather's—the sword of Baldemar."

"How in the name of the gods—?"

"That fort we took last spring—Baldemar's sword was being kept there as a war trophy. This is why I still live on—I, an old man blind in one eye, who should be ending his days huddled comfortably before a hearthfire. This is why I am a Wolf. To heal us all by putting this sword back into the hands of our living shield—"

"My mother," she whispered.

"—who, one last time, must lead us out."

Fool with an impossible wish, came a harsh thought that Avenahar forced back before it was fully formed.

"Of course it cannot be, now," he said as if in response to her thought. "Only the moon could make it so. Yet, it waits here for her."

If I don't strive to live out her fate, I'm abandoning her . . . and all she did with her devotion. It might be as if she were not born.

"Witgern."

He held the mullein torch close to her face, to better see into her eyes.

"I will be a Wolf."

Chapter 23

The Ides of November

Arria Juliana was dressed in white silk. She travelled in a *reda* drawn by four dappled grays harnessed abreast. Through fringed curtains draped in a scallop pattern, she looked out on lightly frosted hills; a pull on a red tassel and she could close them if she wanted. It was cold. Steam from the horses' nostrils drifted back, thick as wool right off the sheep. Beside her was her nurse, Philomela; spread across their laps was her favorite old coverlet, pea green with five moth holes; she had counted them. Their carriage was not allowed to move fast as the grays could go, because then the eight *redas* filled with her trunks of clothes and all her treasures would not be able to keep up. Nor would the plainer carriages for the maid-servants, or the footmen, who had to run to stay up with them; she felt sorry for them. The fortunate grooms armed with staffs had horses, at least. Demaratos had a carriage all to himself, so he could better sulk. It was covered over with carvings of lotuses and vines, but still was not so fine as hers. She wondered what the countryside people thought of this grand parade as they peered from their thatched houses set along the edges of their fields. Surely they thought an important *matrona* was passing by.

She was journeying to Rome to live with her great-aunt who had her name—Arria Juliana. Philomela, soft as goosedown pillows and very old, was spinning wool, moving her padded hands as little as possible because they hurt her. Arria pulled an ivory comb through the silvery fur of her lap dog, who watched Philomela's spindle whorl with eyes like black beads. The maids who dressed her hair had taken extra time with it today, drawing it into a clever knot in the back; Arria liked the way the string of pearls they'd woven in were snowy against her hair's brown silk. From time to time she moved her head slightly so she could steal another look at herself, reflected in the silver mount of the carriage lamp. The wardrobe maid had dressed her in her best clothes. This was because they would be passing the first night at a fine villa. "The house of the procurator for the whole province, who administrates at the great town of Augusta Treverorum, so behave yourself and don't shout," Demaratos had said. Wherever it was possible, he'd arranged for their party to pass the night in the private houses of officials.

Journeying was almost as exciting as watching a horse race. Arria Juliana wanted to run alongside the carriage. She squirmed on her cushions, pulled at her pearl earrings, and counted the number of dappled-grays among the sleek horses in a passing field—that was her favorite color for a horse. Philomela gave her a nudge from time to time, to remind her not to rumple her heat-pressed clothes. She was excited and anxious because of the peacocks. She had heard this man kept peacocks in his gardens. They spread their tail feathers and it was like a gemstone fan. If she arrived after nightfall it would be too dark to see them.

Arria wished hard that her mother were here. At the thought of Auriane she pulled too sharply on the comb, hurting the dog so that he yelped. She apologized to her dog, and Philomela smiled. Thick smoke swirled about her mother, and Arria did not want to see what was causing that smoke. Somehow connected with this, Demaratos was snappish with everyone. The vileness clouded about her mother was the reason her father was gone, and this, she knew, was why everything was going badly. Philomela said Demaratos was angry for another cause, too—Brico, his *amica*, was not with him.

Arria knew why she must go away, because Demaratos had told her. The villa was no longer safe, and her father was not here to protect her. She had seen how frightened the servants had become. One night someone tried to set the barn alight. She would be better off in the household of her great-aunt, at least until her father's return from that far place. Someone had said eight months. She thought that was a long enough time for her to be taller when she saw her father again. She sensed more that was evil in her father's absence, beyond what Demaratos told her, but this, too, she shut her eyes against, and busied herself thinking of the wondrous life she'd have in the grandest of all the cities of the world. In Rome, palaces were stacked up on the hills. In Rome, Philomela told her, they spoke the language *properly*, not mispronouncing everything like the turnip-eating louts around here. In her mind's eye she ordered her future life like pins in a box. She would marry in four years. That was far off, but it would come, she was certain of that. She could remember four years *back*. At her wedding feast would be woodcocks in green sauce and nightingale tongues, or maybe something else, if something else was in fashion. The feast would go on for three days, and be written of in the *Acta Diurna*. She would wear a yellow silk veil, and the Arabian incense would be thick as clouds. The best augur in the city would take the auspices; the sheep's entrails would reveal remarkable omens for her coming happiness. Her groom-to-be was learned in many sciences, so famous philosophers would be there. She would open a door to a beautiful place as she put on the stola of a mistress of a great household. She would have two children, no more. Her husband might be angered at first, but maybe not—she could name six or seven old families in which the *matrona* had two children, and sometimes, only one. He would accept it better when he saw how useful she was to his advancement. She would establish a society of educated women, who would talk of poetry in her painted dining room, and she would curry the favor of the important families useful to her new husband.

She would have gardens with peacocks.

It was early afternoon, and she felt a steady upwelling of happiness like a warm spring, which bubbled down only when she worried over her father. But he *would* be there to see her eating her marriage-cakes steeped in wine.

They slowed, and just ahead, Arria could hear Demaratos, giving orders. Philomela leaned out to listen, then explained that Demaratos dispatched an understeward to ride ahead and inform their noble host of their arrival.

When they'd travelled a short distance farther, they turned off the paved road that went on to the town, and onto a road of dirt. Sharp words drifted back from the front of the train. Was this a shorter way, or the wrong way? From the look of the road, Arria supposed no one had travelled it recently. Demaratos left his carriage and strode past her, shouting angrily; she heard words about a lame horse that had had to be replaced. They'd lost so much time already, they might not reach the villa by dusk. That was why they must take this shorter way.

She felt prickly and irritated; now she wouldn't see the peacocks.

Soon, the road was not much more than two sets of deep wheel ruts. Once, the carriages stopped and started again, while grooms dragged away fallen tree limbs. She thought they would turn around, but they didn't.

As the carriage bumped onward, Arria began to feel frightened. She didn't know why—something just seemed wrong. The road was too deserted. Demaratos was too angry. The forest about was too quiet; she couldn't hear cattle lowing anymore.

It was upsetting and boring. No peacocks. She caved into Philomela's lap and slid into edgy sleep.

Shouts of outrage jerked her back into the world. She heard the fast crack of wood striking wood. *Fighting.*

Philomela's lap was a shivering aspic as she prayed to Juno, mixing up the words. Her voice sounded like a puppy crying.

Somewhere ahead of them, a ruthless stranger-voice spat out commands.

Demaratos cried out over the stranger's shouts. Demaratos's voice disturbed Arria; there was too much fear in it. It wasn't true that Demaratos feared nothing.

Arria huddled down and sat as still as she could. Philomela started dragging her to the back of the carriage. Arria reached for her dog. "No," Philomela whispered. "Quick. Put him out."

"I can't do it," she whispered, crushing her dog tightly to her chest. "I'll put my hand over his mouth so he won't make a sound."

Philomela drew the coverlet over them both. Pea green, with holes. Would the shouting strangers look beneath it?

A whip cracked. Her carriageman turned the *reda* about so sharply that it nearly tipped over; the curtain fell inward. Philomela yipped and grasped the carriage's sides. Arria slid across the floor, her dog scrambling in her hands. The carriage righted itself with a stomach-lurching bounce, then snapped her forward; she felt like a ball at the end of a string. Then it slowed again, to get round some obstacle. They were escaping—but from what?

So frightened she *had* to look, Arria jumped forward too fast for Philomela, parted the curtain, and looked behind them. And saw a sight she must try, hard as she could, to *wipe away,* like letters off a wax tablet: Two black-bearded men in leather tunics pummeled Demaratos, who reeled about, bleeding. Two others were on horseback; strips of black wool were wrapped round their heads, so that only their eyes could be seen. One struck Demaratos with a stave, hit him so hard on his head that he fell, slowly, to the ground. Another pulled him up, even though he couldn't walk any more, and pushed him forward, bellowing at him—"In here? Tell us. Or we gut you like a fish."

Bandits? Her fear rose to such a pitch, all flashed to whiteness. She began to tremble crazily, as if her bones had come apart. She had never seen so much as a dog mistreated. And now they were abusing Demaratos in a way her father would not have allowed a criminal to be used, kicking him even though he wasn't fighting back. Philomela dragged her back inside again, held to her so desperately that, all at once, Arria knew what Philomela knew already—these were not regular robbers intent on the jewel chest. These robbers wanted *her.*

Her carriage burst forward again; the bumpy road made it bounce in every direction like a madman skipping. Anyone could see them; how could they hide?

One of the bandits shot past them on horseback, shouting, "Halt, halt!" Arria heard a piteous shriek—and knew something dark and terrible had happened to her carriageman.

The *reda* jolted to a final stop.

It was no use hiding beneath a blanket. She crawled forward onto her cushions and made herself sit straight and proud, thinking this would help somehow—if they knew she were noble, then maybe they wouldn't hurt her. If Philomela had been praying for courage, Arria supposed Juno had listened. With great calm, Philomela pulled herself forward and sat beside her.

The man's voice was muffled through the cloth wrapped about his face.

"Ah. There she is. Pretty as her portrait."

Philomela put a pillowy arm about her.

A hairy hand ripped off the curtains, reached in, and tore Arria's trembling dog from her hands. The dog squealed in the ugly silence.

The door was thrown open.

It was like being grasped by a tentacle and pulled into the gaped jaws of a sea monster. The belly of the beast. She'd read a story once of a man lost at sea, swallowed by a monster, who actually lived inside its belly for a time. She didn't want to see, to know . . . hard, bony hands, lifting her . . . dark scents, and the cold . . . The cold struck her like a stinging slap.

Then darkness took her away somewhere, and that was good.

She next knew that someone had slung her like a grain sack across a horse's withers. She knew nothing else, for she was blindfolded. A cloth was tied over her mouth, too, and it hurt. Her hair hung loose and mussed; she knew the pearl-strings had been ripped away. Every part of her was sore.

Her first thought was for her poor dog, used to tucking himself into warm places, now all by himself in the bitter-cold forest. Who would care for him?

Demaratos. Horrible. They had hurt him so he would never get up again, she was certain of it.

Where was everyone else? Should she tell these men they'd better let her go, or her father would punish them? She decided to wait. With all her strength, she wished her mother here. It was Auriane she wanted most, now. Her mother could have saved her effortlessly. Auriane wouldn't have been frightened, as Demaratos had been. She would have risen up like Minerva with her shield and struck them all down.

Tears came, but she struggled against them because she didn't want to wet the blindfold.

After a long time of riding, the men halted and greeted someone.

"You've done well!" The new man's voice was gloating, and strange—it was a normal voice, but nervous, with a bit of apology in it. And, *familiar*. "I'll see that your guild prospers, for this."

She knew that voice.

He said *guild*. Understanding came like a tumble into a well. They were not highwaymen. They were stonemasons. Victorinus, when he had been magistrate, had used the stonemasons of Confluentes to threaten people in secret. Victorinus was gone, but people still feared his stonemasons.

Victorinus, whom her father had humbled, Victorinus, driven from his court in disgrace, an angry old man to whom no one listened anymore, who now sat brooding in his villa, the monster in the cave . . . he had sent out his tentacles . . .

"She'd better not be hurt." *Lucius*.

Victorinus's mean son.

A voice like the low growl of a mastiff said, "Don't worry, we were careful as a mother cat with her kittens."

"Tie her better." Lucius, again. "Bind her legs, too. We can't have her thrashing about when we take her through town."

"Pay us first."

Someone lifted her into a carriage or wagon.

Once, her blindfold slipped, and she saw Lucius's face.

She howled in terror and squeezed her eyes closed.

Lucius's nose was pounded flat; the flesh was curdled around his eyes. A blue-red scar overran one side of his face; it lifted one side of his mouth, as when a dog snarls.

But she knew about this. They'd heard of it from the tenant farmers. On that day when Lucius had played his cruel trick with the stones during the horse race, as he'd run through the woods, fleeing from Auriane, he'd fallen onto a rock slide. Normally Lucius wore a mask, so he wouldn't frighten people—but today, he did not. Rocks like flint daggers had carved Lucius's face into a thing no one wanted to see, but his injuries had made him, not a sea monster at all . . . but a human monster, who knew he was one.

Lucius reached out as if he feared, a little, to touch her, and put her blindfold back in place.

Poor Demaratos. She wished they would blindfold her mind's eye, as well.

The wagon smoothly moved forward, on a good road now.

But it was travelling in the wrong direction.

I was to go to Rome. Please, Mother Juno . . . someone has made a mistake.

Into the belly of a sea monster instead.

I will not die. I'll save myself somehow. I will get to my city. Where is my dog? I've lost the magic seeds my mother gave me. I'm to have a great house, a fine wedding, a garden with peacocks . . .

It will be well.

Mother. Help.

Her heart beat so hard and fast, it seemed a small, frenzied animal fought to get out of her chest. Then the smooth, welcome, pudding-warm blackness oozed over her again, bringing dark dreams.

Chapter 24

Gunora took a hare from a wicker cage and put it into a sack. It thrashed with startling vigor; she was always amazed by the strength of a hare. Smoke from a bonfire streamed above the nine thatched lodges ringed about an earthen temple enclosure that was Ramis's Summer Sanctuary. Gunora got her walking staff, departed her house built round an elm that grew alongside the community's common field, then set off into the hazed twilight of the deep forest.

That spirited smoke escaping off into the wood signified that Ramis's high sisters convened to cast lots to name the next Veleda. For Ramis must be counted as having perished off the earth. And Auriane, named by Ramis in the cradle, must be considered already among the dead. Gunora did not yield easily to despair, but that baleful smoke caused her to feel it cruelly on this eve. She came to a natural temple where a sleek fall of water streamed quietly into a deep stone bowl. Its depths glimmered with lunar fire, from offerings of silver cast in by the faithful through many generations. Gunora spoke words of consolation to the Nix of the pool, whom she heard murmuring worriedly. On a mossy altar stone she laid a bronze knife and a brush of broom twigs.

Gunora's first sacrifice was for Avenahar.

Gunora had just come from the midwinter Assembly of the Moon, the Chattian tribal law-gathering, which met despite a driving rain that sluiced off the fringed military cloaks of the Roman observers. Their centurion had demanded the names of the villains who ambushed four cavalrymen and murdered two, within a spear's throw of a village called the Raven's Nest. Gunora had sat grimly still among the thousand-times-three of her countrymen massed about the Assembly Oak, fearful one of them would offer up Avenahar's name. Finally, Sigibert had risen to answer. "My lord. It was one of Witgern's. They are outlaws who, as you know, are repudiated by us. They flow through the forest like a wind-stream. None will ever know the name of the men who did this."

But the centurion spoke again, promising freedom from the levy to the home village of any man who gave them the culprits' names. Gunora didn't know how long her countrymen could resist, so welcome a thing was it to be spared the hated burden of yielding sons for the Roman army. And when the Chattian Assembly had dispersed, a legionary cohort had been dispatched to the Raven's Nest. The soldiers found the longhouses empty—the villagers had fled into the forest. They burned the settlement to ash, then sought vengeance on a neighboring village to the west, taking its women and children into slavery.

Someone would weaken, and say Avenahar's name.

In a warbling monotone Gunora thanked the hare for giving its life. She took up the bronze knife. The little creature released its vigor quickly. "Let Avenahar live to grow into her fate," Gunora prayed, "for she was given the vision of the holy sisters of elder days." The alders rustled, as if to say, *We will*. She reddened the broom twig in sacrificial blood and gave the hare to the pool; now the spring was full of the clever, darting ghost of the little creature, and blessed. It shone like an eye in the dusk—a hare's eye.

Her second prayer was for the Holy Nine, meeting in mystery now, within the sanctuary's most hallowed inner enclosure.

"Lady of the Sun, let the seeresses name tonight any name but Sawitha's. Cross her will. She lusts. Inspire her sisters to resist her. The people will never love her as they do Ramis. About Sawitha, many of us have dreamed savage, unholy dreams."

*   *   *

THE BONFIRE HAD burned down to a troll's-eye glow. The women of the Holy Nine were seated on ox hides ringed about it; each gripped her yew staff as they joined their minds in silence. The remains of the sow they had offered to Fria lay in a shallow pit by the fire. The women's mantles were lined with wildcats' fur; along the hem, they glimmered with blood-stone and amber. Their booted feet were stuffed with straw to keep out cold and moisture. Their hoods were pulled back to expose masses of unbound hair, all in hues of winter—ice gray, sleet-white, sun-on-snow—except for the burnished-copper hair of their youngest member, Blithgund.

Blithgund rose to cast the Nine Herbs onto the fire. Her rumpled masses of spiraling locks fanned down her back like a bedraggled cape. Her brow was apple-smooth. Her eyes showed the faint fixedness of fear.

She planned to speak Auriane's case, even if Sawitha slew her for it.

Blithgund moved moonwise around the fire, chanting the Nine Herbs' holy names. "Soul of wormwood, ghost of centaury . . ." A lyrical flourish of her hand sent a scented cloud into the fire. As she moved past the ox hide that marked Ramis's empty place, she felt barren within. Ramis's presence always caused her to feel the closeness of the vast, sunny mystery of Fria herself.

She's made orphans of us. On this night we must hope all our spirits fused make one spirit as large as Ramis's.

"Ghosts of goatweed and mullein . . ." Blithgund moved past Sawitha. A gust of wind dragged a strand of Sawitha's dry, wispy hair across a face padded with flesh, still as a mask, blunt and square as a block—a face like a wall. Sawitha's hair was the gray of a wolf's coat—a closer look revealed it shot with varied shades of brown. Her eyes put Blithgund in mind of shining black beetles.

"Spirit of wolfsbane, soul of yarrow . . ."

Troubled clouds careened past the moon, hurrying off somewhere into the night. Blithgund wanted to go with them.

"Souls of water-mint, mother-herb, and moonwort . . . all be with us on this night . . ."

Blithgund then carried round the holy mead of the sanctuary—her charge, as youngest of them. It was strengthened with root of mandrake; tonight they would travel between nine realms and know the dead. As she offered Sawitha the horn, Blithgund read secret ecstasy in the face of this patient heir who had waited so long for Ramis's staff.

She gave it next to Sawitha's ally Sindgund, her formidable bulk settled comfortably on the ground. Sindgund's lichen-colored hair was tangled as a bramble thicket; her eyes were deep-set, morose, searching. She'd been a sorceress serving a distant snow-country tribe before Sawitha had seen to her elevation to the Nine. Sindgund drank with a noisy slurp. Blithgund then gave the horn to each in turn, moving with grave steps as if to add the weight of a few more years, keenly aware that, because of her youth, her voice counted least among them.

Blithgund herself took the last draught. As she resumed her place, she felt none of the lush consolation always there when Ramis was present.

The night was without a heart.

Sawitha struck a bronze bell and they intoned rhyming words of a thousand-year-old spell that invoked Fria and all her unearthly attendants. Sindgund beat a skin drum in a rhythm that was sinuous, whiplike, and beautiful as a water snake swimming a river; each stress of that rocking rhythm hoisted them farther into the night sky. Harmonizing voices shivered with silver. Blithgund felt herself a falcon streaming down a pathway beneath overarching arbors. She melted into mountains, then found herself dancing round a Tree . . . the Ash that ran down the center of every heart, every village, and harbored all the nations of the Nine Worlds in its roots, trunk, and leafy crown.

Once she stole a look at Sawitha. The elder seeress put her in mind of a hawk, sharply alert, feathers tightly together, eyes shining and empty. Those polished-mirror eyes gave a bright but distorted picture of the world about, while deflecting gazes from the world within. With her draught-honed senses, Blithgund could see a hard beak, a neat, feathered breast, leathery claws squeezing the life from prey. Blithgund sometimes wondered if the ever-unfathomable Ramis had kept Sawitha close all those years as some sort of teaching for the rest of them, perhaps to show them how *not* to behave among the people, or maybe as a whetstone on which to sharpen their wits, so often were they forced to counter Sawitha's subtle misapprehensions of everything Ramis said. Sawitha followed the proper order of the rites fixedly as the stars their courses, but for order's sake alone; she had no curiosity about the terrors and joys of the mysteries beneath those rites.

Sawitha lifted her staff for silence, exposing an arm-ring of silver depicting an Ancestress crowned with yew berries. An owl's call scudded into the attentive quiet.

There's still a measure of hope, Blithgund thought. *Sawitha cannot name herself.* Ramis had too often insisted that the woman who took her staff should not want it, that her eagerness for the office would prove she did not understand it. *I trust everyone has the good sense to confirm whoever Sawitha names.* Then Sawitha's ally Sindgund might never get a chance to propose Sawitha's name.

Sawitha had a harpist's voice, lush, rounded, possessed of the same emotionless calm as the owl's call.

"She who performed the rites that kept us all living, is gone. She who told us the time to place the first cakes in the furrow, is taken away. She who led the Lady's cart round the lake in spring, is among us no more. Ramis, highest of those who See, is stolen from us, and we must name another." Sawitha examined each of them in turn, as a chieftain might make a final survey of the enemy's lines. Then she said, "I propose that Algifu carry the staff."

Blithgund thought it a jest, in the instant before she caught Sawitha's purpose. None among them was less suitable. Algifu had little warrior-spirit in her. She was a woman who dreamed alone in quiet, a gentle creature unobtrusive as a straw cushion, whose glories were in the weavings of the mind.

The startled Algifu was like a shy maid dragged before multitudes. "Please, I do not want this."

Sawitha's head swiveled round like a prey-bird's. She regarded Algifu with bright scorn, affecting to believe Algifu but a canny actor making a convincing show of modesty.

Blithgund knew her sisters were alert to Sawitha's devices. But each in her separate fashion feared Sawitha just enough to clear from her path.

Sindgund was first to answer. "Algifu has never made treaties with our enemies. She has never led the great rites at Midsummer or at Eastre. She gives true oracles but a battle has never turned upon her advice. I say, *no.*"

One by one, they rejected Algifu. By Blithgund's turn, Algifu was struggling to look serenely into the fire, clearly humiliated by all this.

Blithgund was known for an errant spiritedness that flared brightly just as others dampened their fires. Blithgund herself thought of it as the times that misery drove her to courage.

Blithgund looked at Sawitha, who did not meet her gaze. "Ramis told us, 'A lust to stand above others is a trumpet in the ear that obscures the voices of the gods.' That disqualifies *some* of us—but not Algifu, who does not even know how clever and kind she is, and who has never plotted against her sisters . . . or done anyone harm. Perhaps she is the best of us. I reject her only because her powers lie elsewhere."

Blithgund felt Sawitha's gaze easing toward her, full of malign excitement, alert to her presence in a way she had not been before. Sawitha was a predator waiting for the prey to run. She liked the chase.

Next to propose a name was Sindgund.

"I put forth one whose council is sought on the eve of battle. She has negotiated five treaties with Rome. She is an adept who has mastered the skill of learning of future days by raising an Ancestress from the mound. This summer, she settled a dispute between our enemies the Hermundures that ended many years of raiding for salt along our river border.

"Most important, she is a woman who has never broken sacred law," Sindgund continued. "Never has she lain abed with a man of the Roman enemy. Nor has she abandoned our lands. Her Mother-line is strong as Auriane's. She has lived in Ramis's shadow longer than any of us. I name Sawitha."

Sawitha managed to look faintly disconcerted by all this praise.

"I will accept," Sawitha said in that chill, beautiful voice, "if I am accepted by you."

Sindgund responded, "Let it be."

As the next woman in order of precedence repeated, "Let it be," tension did not abate, for unanimity was required. Blithgund was certain she saw weary assent in several eyes, but Sawitha had prepared the ground well: To every one she'd built up obligations over time, through the granting of critical favors, or gifts to their families. When the gentle, much-loved Gerberga, the one woman Blithgund thought independent of Sawitha's machinations, also said, "Let it be," Blithgund felt a frantic sadness. Sawitha had made herself inevitable as spring flood.

Blithgund's turn came.

"I say no to Sawitha."

The flesh about Sawitha's eyes contracted slightly; other than this, she showed no emotion. But Blithgund's draught-sharpened senses could almost *see* red waves of rage rolling from her, the clenching hawk-feet.

Sindgund recovered herself first. "Blithgund, dear child. Why do you say no?"

Blithgund felt she stared straight through Sawitha's beetle-black eyes, and into the night beyond.

"Ramis chooses from dreams, and her dreams are greater than ours. To name another while Auriane still lives seems monstrous to me."

"But this is but the time between the raised blade and its falling on her neck," Sindgund replied.

"Then we should be working spells for Auriane's release instead of choosing another in her place." Blithgund forged her way further into the sharp silence. "Ramis herself named Auriane for the sacred mould that lay on our high altar—and are not destiny and name the same? And no one's spoken of Auriane's slaying of the white aurochs. Yet we know this bull was a marker of fate because it was death-colored. This aurochs had bested so many Roman hunters . . . it's a sign she's stronger than her masters. And might still get free."

At these last words, Blithgund saw Sawitha's gaze flick toward the fire, alert as a huntress. Blithgund thought it puzzling, but had little leisure to wonder over it, for Sindgund spoke.

"The rash, untried Blithgund knows the great signs and portents better than all of us."

"What's befallen Auriane is the just punishment of the Fates, Blithgund," Gerberga added in more placating tones. "She gave her flesh and spirit to a foreign murderer. She took their soul when she took their citizenship. Ramis chose Auriane as a babe, but a child can disappoint, in time's fullness."

"Do all of you mean to say, then, Ramis made a mistake?"

Several faces betrayed sharp discomfort. Sawitha continued to sit quietly, folded within herself.

Again, Sindgund recovered first. "Of course not. I don't know Ramis's reasons. I only speak from the needs of our present predicament. We cannot let the time of first planting come without our staff-carrier." She added with soft savagery, "It's a child's stubbornness that leads you to speak so, against all of us."

"And it's a shameless lack of gratitude that lets you spurn one who risked her life to shelter us," Blithgund said. She met each woman's gaze in turn. "Auriane sent us arms so we wouldn't starve. Now, they kill her for it. And all of you say, 'Go and take her. It's nothing to us. We'll just find another!'"

This roused Sawitha to reply. That little-used smile had the sweetness of mouldering fruit. "But Blithgund, supplying those swords was another of her crimes."

It was Blithgund's turn to feel jolted from her path. Sawitha spoke truly. Auriane should have had nothing to do with the transport of weapons of iron; it was an act of sacrilege against the elder gods.

"Loyalty and foolishness are married in you, Blithgund," Sindgund added. "But that is as it is. You are young." Sindgund traced in air runic signs to promote concord. "We must not fight among ourselves; we hold the world together. Think on all that's been said, and answer again, Blithgund. Do you confirm our choice, or not?"

The weight of her sisters' gazes upon her chest made it difficult for Blithgund to get a breath. *What right have I . . . ?* She sought refuge by looking into the calm, sunny center of their fire.

A log shifted; a mound of ash collapsed. And Blithgund saw something that before she had not—curving up from the low flames and living embers was the horn of a great aurochs, burnt black.

Why do we burn such a thing in our fire?

Blithgund poured the last of her strength into her reply. "I count it unholy to do this before Auriane is dead. I say 'no' to Sawitha."

Sawitha watched her with the serenity of a sated dragon.

"I've every vote but Blithgund's, it seems." Sawitha's voice conveyed only boredom. "The moon fades and dawn is near. Shall we propose another name? Or retire, purify ourselves, and meet again in three days' time?"

One by one, they agreed they should retire and meet again.

Blithgund could not pull her gaze from the fire. Burnt bone. *That is what Sawitha looked at, when I spoke of Auriane's singular deed . . .*

"Sawitha," Blithgund said.

Sawitha faintly raised her brows.

"What burns in our fire?"

Sindgund and Sawitha exchanged a discreet glance.

"I performed a rite known to the adept, for which you have no understanding," Sawitha said. "Ask me again in nine winters' time."

"That's the horns of the aurochs Auriane slew. You somehow laid your hands on the remains. You've cursed Auriane. And turned the white bull's power against her."

"I'll allow you to accuse me without warrant, just this one time—given your susceptibility to youthful passions," Sawitha said. "But you will never do it again."

As all rose to retire, Blithgund found herself trembling as though she'd carried the weight of a standing stone on her back. She hadn't realized how frightened she'd been.

Day came, and passed into night.

At a time poised between midnight and dawn, a clot of evil clouds covered the moon.

Blithgund lay sleeping on her straw mat, in her bare hut within the sanctuary. She dreamed that a wyrm glided up from the deep forest. It flowed beneath the sanctuary gate, then wended its way into her hut.

She felt its rough, heavy body sliding across her belly, her chest, as the muscular creature made its way toward her throat. Its mouth was gaped open; long fangs were poised like twin daggers.

Even as she dreamed, Blithgund remembered Sawitha had the power to call up serpents that struck while her victim slept.

Dry snakeskin, scaled hands, clenching tightly . . . all at once she could get no air. The terror of the abyss filled her lungs. She was awakened by her own rasping gasps. A man's strong hand was clamped about her neck, pinning her to the straw so she couldn't cry out.

Fangs struck, full of poison . . . not fangs, but a knife; it missed her throat, slashing across her cheek. Hot blood flooded out as she furiously writhed.

The serpent was a man and he smelled of swamp rot. His heaving breaths were rank on her cheek. Mute starlight glanced off a short blade, raised again. She saw the glint of a maddened eye. Hel was in that eye, Hel put into a man, through Sawitha's spell.

Blithgund thrashed with all her youthful strength; one flailing foot drove into a soft stomach. The iron hand's grip loosened. Someone scuffled, fell backward, grunted a curse in the thick darkness. She tried to shout for help but her voice was a mouse squeak. Then came the rapid beat of steps, fast fading, as a man sprinted for the sanctuary's gate.

Blithgund got to her feet to give chase, but stumbled on her long sleeping-dress and was pitched onto her hands and knees. The miasma of the dream still lay heavily on her; the poison memory of a snake's slick, cold body was bright and close as the low-hanging moon.

Sawitha. I thwarted her death-spell somehow—this time. But she'll try again.

On the third night, the Holy Nine convened again, even though the moon was waning now, and the time grown inauspicious.

An anguished Blithgund once again took her place round the fire, her voice quelled to a whisper from the near-throttling she'd been given.

On this night, Sawitha had had Ramis's staff brought from its place of safekeeping on the altar of the inner sanctuary, and the weighty, smooth-worn stave of yew wood, nearly the height of a man, lay on the ground before her. When Ramis had been taken off to Rome, she'd charged Algifu with bringing the Veleda's staff home to their lands. It was a dread thing, with its amber stones like yellow eyes, the world-parting runes carved down the shaft. In some way, it looked well there—Sawitha seemed a woman with the force of mind to carry it. *She is clever,* Blithgund thought; the effect was as though Sawitha sat upon a throne.

As the same ritual words were spoken, Blithgund bowed her head in a vain effort to conceal her face, torn and swollen from the slash of the knife. She knew, then, that there were ends to her courage.

She said "yes" to Sawitha.

Chapter 25

Dacia
Three days before the Nones of December

On the day Marcus Julianus's galley docked alongside Trajan's winter camp in Dacia, frost tinted the stony ground bone gray and leached what little color there was from a skeletal landscape. He found a land scored by rough gorges that might have been cleaved by the axe of some maddened bacchante seeking to destroy this country, a place void of the dimmest glimmer of the light of Greek learning, a land ridden with angry spirits that matched his bleakness of soul. *A place of no hope, as Auriane has none. A fitting stage on which to beg mercy for both of us, at the feet of the very man who tried to murder me in secret.*

A short distance farther down the black waters of the Danuvius were the arches of the famous stone bridge Trajan had built in this wilderness—the longest span on earth. It seized him in one moment as some ponderous concrete foot of man, brutishly imposed over struggling nature—and then as a disciplined beauty keeping at bay all that was wild, a portal to tranquil order. Wooden signal towers erected along the river were accompanied by log piles constructed of stout timbers, for bonfires that would light up the waters if the Dacians attempted a night crossing. To the north, darkly mottled with firs, were mountains marked *Transilvania Alpina* on his maps—their sinister profile seemed deflated beneath the weight of an ashy sky. Protected within their heart was the unknown Dacian enemy, a people counted barbarous by his countrymen in spite of their thriving towns, their trade networks that exported pottery prized at Rome—a judgment not improved by the ghastly tales filtering into Trajan's camp of the exotic tortures the Dacian women inflicted on captured legionaries. The wind seemed to carry their cries.

To the south, camped in unending rows as though the stars of the heavens made to align themselves in good order, was Rome's massive army of invasion—over fifty thousand men of war settled in to wait out the winter. The sight of such a multitude of men drawn together for one purpose caused him to think, *Here is yet another wonder of the world, no less than the Pyramids, the lighthouse at Pharos, if one doesn't count it inferior because of its impermanence.* Here were the full legions of the provinces of Moesia and Pannonia augmented by nine thousand Praetorian Guards from Rome, and an array of auxiliary forces bearing traditional weaponry—slingers from the Balearic islands, Palmyrene archers, Arab bowmen, Germanic natives who fought on horseback. Along with them were the engineers who maintained the engines for breaching fortifications, the scouts, interrogators, and craftsmen; here, too, were the Emperor's staff, High Council, and friends. The capital of the world had shifted to this waste. At snowmelt, when the first green shoots provided fodder for cavalry horses and pack animals, Trajan would send this prodigious force across the river, to close in upon the mountain stronghold of the rebellious Dacian king.

A small cavalry escort met Julianus as he debarked. His party rode between two tall stone guard houses, then began a quarter-hour journey down the wide central avenue of the Via Praetoria. They passed the tents of the regular legions, positioned round the camp's perimeter because they were counted more trustworthy than the foreign troops. Then came the hospital tents, a *veterinarium* for ailing horses, the grander tents of the legates and tribunes. The wind was raw with a penetrating cold that could best many layers of woolen tunics. As soon as he was assigned to quarters in the tents reserved for visiting dignitaries, he sent his request for an audience with the Emperor. An imperial freedman returned within the hour, informing him that his audience was set for three days' time, the Nones of December, at the eleventh hour of day. He got no succor from the swiftness of the reply; it was the Emperor's habit to discharge immediately any task he judged difficult or unpleasant.

Tellingly soon afterward, he received a request for a meeting from Lappius Blaesus, dispatched from the lavishly appointed tents housing the men of the Imperial Council. A suit for peace? A lure into ambush? *He must be in a fever of speculation, trying to calculate just how high I've traced that attempt on my life. If I do succeed in turning matters in my favor, doubtless, he's surmising someone highly placed must be sacrificed.*

Julianus sent Blaesus no reply.

Almost simultaneously came a summary command to report to the tent of Livianus, praefect of the Praetorian Guard. This, too, he carefully ignored, surmising that here was yet another man who knew entirely too much about a bungled murder attempt at an aurochs hunt. *His spies got wind of my death-bed interview of my would-be assassin—as I knew they would.* Julianus might have found it humorous but for the danger that obviously pressed close. He resolved to touch no food except that which was prepared by his own servants, and to go nowhere without a guard.

On the Nones of December, at the eleventh hour, Marcus Julianus pulled his mount to a halt before the great tent that was, temporarily, the center of the world. This was the Praetorium, which served as the Emperor's living quarters and place of council. A storm birthed deep within the mountain fastnesses was noisily invading the camp, heralded by errant wind-blasts of evil force. From behind him on the Via Praetoria came a momentary clamor of shouts, hollow bells, and lowing beasts, as slaves dragged to a more sheltered pen a complaining collection of boars, rams, and bulls reserved in camp for sacrifice to Mars. In this season night reached far into afternoon, and wintry darkness had already overtaken the camp. Resin torches whipped about in a bitter wind. Two Praetorian Guards in gold parade armor flanked the tent's entrance. Julianus dropped from his mount. One began a quick search for weapons, required of anyone admitted to the imperial presence in time of war.

Just above the rising trill of wind, Julianus heard the Guard say to him, "You are a dead man."

"Tell your master not to celebrate too quickly," Julianus replied.

I suppose I'd better make certain this interview goes well.

A loose portion of the closed tent-flap rattled urgently in the wintry gusts.

As the Guard opened the tent to admit Julianus, there came a rogue gust of wind. Within the tent, the lamps were snuffed out with one mighty breath.

He heard someone within muttering into the astonished silence, "Tartarus, who took the light?"—then came the placating whispers of servants, and a crash, as something ponderous—a map table?—overturned, prompting a chorus of servile apologies. Julianus fought to think it amusing, to banish a near-irresistible thought that it was an omen of ill, for how he might fare in this audience.

Lamps snuffed out as I enter. The wiliest augur could work nothing good from that.

Within, someone of the Emperor's staff commanded the Council members to depart. With more caution this time, the guardsman opened the tent, and five disgruntled members of the Imperial Council spilled out into the cold; their gazes raked over Julianus with sharp curiosity. Among them was a Dacian prince called Bikilis, striding along briskly as a camel, in a great hurry to get off; he was a figure outlandish to Roman eyes in a conical felt cap, full-legged black woolen trousers embroidered with serpents around the hems, a beard trained into a neat row of coiled locks to create an effect as intricate as any woman's coiffure. His cryptic gaze flicked fleetingly toward Julianus, who recoiled within; in the man's eyes he saw that same fathomless deadness he'd seen in the young Aelianus's, and it struck him cold. This disaffected prince had, Julianus knew, brought to Trajan's high council a map painted on sheepskin that purported to show the true location of the Dacian king's hastily stowed golden treasure. Trajan's ministers had long suspected that this golden hoard, if only they could find it, would pay the full cost of this war. The council members had the look of men who'd received a rough tongue-lashing, and Julianus surmised it because Trajan's chief mapmaker, needed to examine Bikilis's odd skin map for accuracy, was said to be hiding somewhere, sleeping off a carouse.

Flames materialized within as servants hurried to restore light. A debilitating desolation swept over Julianus then, not for his own predicament, which seemed secondary then, but for Auriane's, for whom sorrow pierced him through like a lance. As he groped for solace he was surprised to find himself calling up the stark face of that strangely disruptive woman he'd questioned in the Principia at Mogontiacum. Something he couldn't capture or name in the presence of Ramis brought a profounder peace than all the neatly reasoned discourses of Epictetus, or a hundred proofs of logic; her consolation was a sea.

Julianus stepped into close, pleasant-scented gloom, thick with smells of leather, oils, and resins. He discerned first, the Dacian's sheepskin treasure map, which was laid out in the best light, and was seduced into studying it for a moment, having freshly immersed himself in close geographical studies of this region during the long journey. Something in that painted pathway to gold urgently begged his attention, like a petitioner pulling at a cloak. But he had no leisure to consider it, for rising just beyond was the muscular form of Hercules, tall as a living man; the god's golden chest seemed to heave gently with his breathing, in the guttering lamp-glow. The image was draped in the pelt of a fresh-caught lynx that exuded a rank scent. The smoke of some burnt offering drifted magisterially past that cold, voluptuous face.

The altar of the golden god was meant to dominate the tent, but did not, because of the proud man quietly seated beside it.

The Emperor Trajan was watching him with a look that combined shrewdness, aggression, and openness. His long frame was folded onto a cross-legged chair too small for him, as most chairs were, and he sat with an easy grace Hercules might have adopted while on earth—while simultaneously seeming as trained on his purpose as the arrow poised to flash from the bow. Julianus had not seen the Emperor Trajan since the days of the citywide celebrations in Rome at his accession. That lean, bony face had changed little, though he did see signs of soft corrosion that were the work of wine: Beneath high cheekbones the flesh had begun to gently inflate, forming the beginnings of jowls. And that overbearing nose—the one part of him that seemed a mistake; surely the gods intended it for someone else—was flushed an angry scarlet. But such pleasures as this man took never blunted his vigilance; the lamplight glanced off eyes like polished steel. Here was a man most comfortable and alive in a war camp, content to bide here all winter, considering his prey, ready to spring on it at snowmelt. It was not surprising, Julianus had often thought, that the one blur of impracticality in that supremely practical mind was of a military nature—Trajan's Alexandrian passion of conquering the world. All had begun to suspect the Emperor would not stop at Dacia—Parthia, even distant India, beckoned.

Close by the Emperor was a silver wine service set on a table draped with a captured Dacian battle standard—a wind-sock of striped cloth; its gold-and-vermilion dragon with gaped mouth was a fierce beast, limp in defeat.

"Julianus!" the Emperor called out in that sturdy, all-embracing voice. "Come! Sit! What a pleasant surprise!"

Julianus inclined his head and began the formal greeting, alert to signs this was in fact an *un*pleasant surprise. But he discerned only solicitous reserve in the face of this man who ordered—or assented to—his death. He counted himself adept at reading men, but Trajan he had always found ultimately confounding, a difficult volume ever sealed in its bronze canister, showing to the world only a smooth, gleaming, outer shell.

"—and you only grow in greatness and esteem with each passing year."
Julianus concluded the greeting as he settled himself on a chair swung into
place by a nimble Egyptian youth he hadn't seen as he entered. More troubled thoughts intruded, just then, of the sheepskin map—*Nemesis, a land feature is missing, an important one*—but he disciplined himself to put them
aside.

"Let me be the first to say, Marcus Julianus, we all thank Providence you
are well!" Trajan's voice rang out convivially. "We heard a distressing tale of
an accident at an aurochs hunt. We are relieved you are fully recovered from
your injuries."

The brazen maneuver struck him like a thunderclap. Julianus carefully
suppressed his amazement. *He's telling me he knows that I know. But what's his
purpose—to startle me off a path of further investigation? Or to tell me he disowns
the shameful way the act was carried out?*

"It was no accident, my Lord," Julianus said, alert to the smallest shift in
those metallic eyes. "A junior officer of the Fortress attacked me, and was
himself fatally gored by the aurochs."

Julianus saw a minor disturbance there. It was not surprise.

"Truly? This was not known to me," Trajan said dismissively. "It was a
day of prodigies then, of odd but remarkable things—a man goes unac-
countably mad and attacks you. A woman takes the mantle of Hercules, and
slays the beast. Thank the gods every day is not like that! Let us drink to your
good fortune. This is from a forty-year-old vintage," he said as he took up a
slender glass wine jar from the table and expertly opened it with a small
knife, "from my own estates in Hispania." He poured the shining garnet liquid right to the brim of a chased silver cup—he had no plans to mix it with
water. The tales, then, were true; in the field, he drank wine neat, like a gladiator or a Scythian tribesman.

Julianus fought to keep his voice even. "The man lived for a day," he
pressed on. "I was able to interrogate him myself."

The Emperor halted a little too suddenly in pouring out the wine. *That,
apparently, he didn't know*, Julianus realized. *Which indicates he was kept somewhat distanced from the act.*

"How fortunate." Trajan's faint emphasis on each word was a reprimand, suggesting Julianus should be better aware of the decent moment to
let a matter drop. In a chill tone of challenge, he added, "Did you learn anything of worth?"

"In fact, yes. The man was, as it proved, a partisan of Domitian."

Julianus perceived a sudden, quiet attentiveness in the Emperor's face. *Kept somewhat distanced, perhaps . . . but he knew the plan, in outline.*

"Indeed?" the Emperor said carefully. "The tentacles of the tyrant are long, to wrap round his quarry so long after his death."

"Fanaticism never sleeps, it seems—or reasons, or forgets—even after so many years. It was the son of Casperius Aelianus."

Beautifully managed surprise came into the Emperor's face. Once again, Julianus felt he had slipped off that smooth, polished surface, and nearly found himself seduced into believing it true surprise.

"I learned something most distressing in that interview," Julianus pressed on, "that I thought must be brought to your attention."

The Emperor sat still as the golden image of Hercules. The wine was forgotten.

"The young fanatic had powerful friends, it seems," Julianus continued, "in . . . surprising places. He was but an arrow in a bow drawn by another."

Nothing moved but the smoke drifting languorously off the altar.

"Do continue."

It's gotten chill enough for frostbite in here, Julianus thought.

"He'd been provided with all he needed—lodgings, transportation by carriage, even a position at the Fortress—"

"Indeed? Disgraceful. Appalling! You should have come to me at once." The Emperor looked penetratingly into Julianus's eyes. "I shall start an investigation."

"That will be difficult . . . and somewhat awkward. I really think we had best let it go."

Trajan's eyes glittered darkly as obsidian.

"You speak as if this were a time of tyrants," the Emperor said with soft wrath. The Egyptian boy's eyes grew round with alarm. "I will not hear anyone speak so. This reign is dedicated to justice, and light, and openness. There will be no secret dealings, and the powerful are not exempt. Name the man, or men, and they will be put on trial."

Julianus was intrigued; there was something magnificent in the audacity of that leap into the fray. *It's almost as though he means to clear out any present darkness in the kingdom by sheer force of will,* he thought.

Shall I name him? It is almost as if he wishes me to. . . . It probably did not take much to turn him against me: I'm the author of one emperor's fall. He who opens the way to the throne must live out his life beneath a cloud of distrust.

"The dying Aelianus named higher accomplices, which enabled me to trace the act straight to . . ." *I have my answer. There's little to be gained by cornering the man with what he already knows I know.*

Time to ruin another, then. Why waste such a fine opportunity? ". . . Lappius Blaesus, my Lord."

The obsidian-glitter faded from the Emperor's eyes.

"—who has long been my enemy," Julianus continued, "and has spent many years harassing me in court, ever since, twenty years ago, I prosecuted him for setting brigands on Roman citizens in the province he was trusted to govern, after he'd squandered away his treasury—I'm sure you remember that case. I hesitated because it pained me to name a man who is your friend."

"You need not have, on that account! There is no immunity for my friends. I will look into the matter. Blaesus must know, the world must know: I refuse to allow such shameful plots in the dark. I'll aid you, if you wish to bring him to trial. But in truth, just between us, Blaesus has so many good family connections, the sentence the Senate will give him will be light, if he's convicted.

"Can we drink now to your coming," the Emperor said then, "regretfully delayed, as it is?" Trajan's smile was spare, ironic—and decidedly unamicable. "We all know this campaign is not a cause you believe in."

Bare civility, Julianus noted dispiritedly. *Often the herald of a man's ruin. I can't say this is going well.*

Both men reached, at last, for their wine cups. Julianus's hand stopped as if seized in mid-air. The sight of the Emperor poised to take a deep draught of the wine prompted a realization, born of a quick summing-up of all he'd seen and heard in the last quarter-hour, a fast calculation from the back of the mind, yielding up a total that was *wrong:* The lamps blown out. The Dacian prince, left unobserved in total darkness. The sheepskin treasure map, with a critical land feature missing. The nearness of their wine cups to the map table.

His next act was that of a madman.

He lunged from his seat and knocked the wine cup from the Emperor's hand.

What followed was as calm as a tavern brawl. The Egyptian boy shrieked words in his native tongue. The forecourt filled with armored men. Lamplight glanced off unsheathed steel. The plank floor resounded with booted feet. Two Praetorian guardsmen seized Julianus and thrust him, facedown, on the floor, pinning his arms behind his back. More Guards pressed in from outside, even though there was no more room; the lamp flames struggled at a brave horizontal. Imperial slaves edged in from the tent's inner chambers, their faces blank with amazement.

The Emperor sat very still, intently watching the wine cup as it rolled across the floor, then stopped. Thirty and more pairs of eyes followed his gaze; all saw the thick, grayish powder oozing from the tipped cup, so sinister in appearance it hardly needed testing by the camp's expert on poisons.

"Unhand him!" the Emperor trumpeted into the silence.

The Guards released Marcus Julianus. Grudgingly, one by one, they sheathed their swords. A servant of the chamber dropped to his knees and began wailing for his life, expecting to be held accountable simply because he was in attendance. Behind this noise was the high-pitched ramble of the Egyptian boy—". . . but the wine jar . . . it was just opened . . . It was sealed in gypsum . . ."

"The prince," Julianus said a little hoarsely, climbing painfully to his feet. "In the darkness he got it into the empty cup." The Guards examined the distance from the map table to wine service, considering the difficulty of pouring it into the cup in that confused darkness without spilling any—difficult, but not impossible.

A centurion of the Guard took Julianus's cup, poured it out into a bronze bowl, and found the same evil mud at its bottom. "It looks to be aconite," he said. Unwilling to wait for the official determination, he demanded a bit of hard bread, scooped a measure of the substance onto it, then exited to give it to one of the camp's dogs.

Trajan sat solemnly still; all that betrayed the agitation he must have felt was a greater than usual calm. "The Dacian prince," he said quietly to the Guards. "Put out the alarm at every guard tower. Ride him down."

The Guards quickly filed out; cavalry was dispatched in pursuit down the Via Principia. Julianus heard outraged shouts, fading off, as all along this wide way, men were roused. Within a remarkably short time, every last man in the vast encampment would know of this.

In the sudden, profoundly altered quiet, Julianus said as he resumed his seat, "My apologies for an unforgivable attack on your sacred person."

"Nonsense. How can you speak of it?"

The centurion of the Guard interrupted, admitting the wind's wail and flurries of snow. A servant slid in quietly behind him; in his arms was the limp body of a small red-and-white-spotted hound.

Trajan observed this grimly for a moment, then nodded for them to go.

"Enough poison to fell a good-sized bull! I should be flattered, I suppose."

Trajan said it jovially, but Julianus heard the faintest tremor of disquiet in that voice. The Emperor rested his gaze on Julianus for long moments, and slowly, a truce-filled peace crept into the room. "It is a humbling thing to owe one's life to the quickness of another," he said. "My good friend. What roused your suspicions?"

"The map." Julianus rose and moved to the map table. "There's a pass, here, that's not shown, a notorious place that's treacherous and narrow—it's overlooked by precipitous cliffs, and it's ideal for placing bowmen above, and indeed, has been used for ambush before, in times of these tribes' constant wars among each other. It could only have been left out deliberately. And this way through the pass—it's marked as the one route to the king's treasure hoard, which he indicates, here. They would have picked off our advance men like cattle in a pen."

"How came you to have such a close knowledge of a wild and distant country?"

"It was a long, dull journey, and I had little to do but study, and, as I've found philosophy . . . somewhat poisonous of late, I kept to a study of the tongues of this region—and the works of the Alexandrian geographers."

"So an assassin's warded off not by the sword, but by an insatiable pedant's need to make a close study of nearly everything, relevant to him or not! I've been unfair to you. I'm forgetting why I ever allowed you retire to the country."

Julianus saw a deep allegiance forming in those iron-gray eyes, and realized then that no subtle arguments, no fervent protestations of loyalty could have won trust so readily as this unintentioned event. He offered fervent thanks to Fortuna.

"Tomorrow, you are my guest of honor at dinner," the Emperor spoke on. "Come at the same hour. I must think of some proper way to thank you. I know you don't want any honors or posts."

Julianus found his senses could scarce keep apace with the suddenness of this restoration to favor. Few men were fortunate enough to outlive or outwit all their enemies, but it seemed he'd somehow managed it. The moment was not so honeyed as it might have been, however, for one dangling horror remained—the plight of Auriane.

"I wish no thanks," Julianus said, "What I did, any man not utterly base would have done. I wish only a sympathetic hearing of the case I travelled here to put to you."

"That can wait. First, we celebrate."

* * *

ON THE FOLLOWING day the chief priest made a thanksgiving sacrifice to Nemesis, who was—or so it was determined after long debate—the deity who had preserved the Emperor's life. The poisoner was not caught; he'd talked his way past the main gate's sentries moments before Trajan dispatched cavalry to hunt him, and the snowstorm covered his escape. Julianus restively endured seven courses of a banquet of celebration, centered on Danuvian carp grilled in date sauce with lovage and a Hispanian wine chosen because it was bottled in the year of his birth. Tedium peaked during locally-provided entertainment too rude for his taste—something announced as the "fire and sword dance," performed by skin-clad youths from a nearby village. If the senior tribunes were offended by the sight of a man who disapproved of Trajan's great war reclining in the place of honor, they disguised it well. Present, but distinctly nervous, was the Guards' praefect Livianus. *For now at least,* Julianus thought, *that panther is leashed.* Strikingly absent was Lappius Blaesus, and no one spoke his name; he'd been banished from the Emperor's side, and prepared to depart the camp in disgrace. Julianus couldn't say he was entirely pleased; he'd always held that having a dedicated enemy lurking about keeps the wits honed.

And so Marcus Julianus couldn't speak the cause for which he'd come until the first hour of the following day, when most of the banqueters were still sleeping off its effects. He returned to the Praetorium in dawn's sallow light, to find the Emperor Trajan as keen and clear of mind as if he'd drunk vinegar water the night before.

Julianus had scarce gotten beyond, "I would speak to you concerning the Chattian woman you know as Aurinia—" when Trajan interrupted him.

"If this is concerning that woman with whom you cohabit, who's been the author of so much mischief, and her confession before Maximus, rest your mind on *that* matter completely. I am not fool enough to believe, with some, that you had any knowledge of what she was doing."

He felt the first delicate touch of horror. "The woman with whom you cohabit" was a cold and cursory way to refer to Auriane. *This, then, is the cost of the trust I just won—this firm line of division he's drawn between Auriane and myself.*

I've never lost such a battle before. And now I grapple, not with a tyrant, but with a just ruler who favors me. Why, then, do I feel in the grip of a final sadness?

"It is of her I wish to speak," Julianus said carefully. "As you may already know, she will make a journey here to appeal to you."

Trajan frowned, and slowly nodded.

"You must forgive her," Julianus said.

The frown held; this did not augur well.

"Go on, make your case."

"I know she acted against the law, but she acted lawfully, even nobly, when considered as a woman of her own nation. Your reign is known for keeping alive reverence for the old virtues, but it's especially known for bringing forth new ones—"

"*New* ones? I've heard nothing of this."

"You push back not only the boundaries of the world, but the boundaries of what is good and right. I believe it is for these things that you will be remembered, and not so much for the new territories you win for the Empire. I refer to your measures for bringing education to greater numbers of citizens than ever before, and your system by which orphaned children are provided a dole from the interest farmers pay on money loaned them by the Treasury. These things are without precedent. Here is yet another new road for you to open, a boundary to push back, concerning what is good and right. For after all, did we not orphan *her*?"

Now the Emperor's frown seemed faintly clouded, suggesting a state of mind grown pensive, disturbed. Julianus pressed on.

"It appears she flouted the law in the gravest way, but it is really a matter of where one stands when you gaze upon her. She has always acted with a heroism one seldom sees in either women or men, in this quieter age. Considered as a daughter of her own beleaguered nation, her giving them arms was but a way to save them from starvation, for they'd no means to repel enemy raids. By the laws of her people, she hardly could have done otherwise."

"I know it's not necessary to remind you that no one may claim national custom if it has not been accepted in Roman law."

This blunt objection distressed him, but Julianus continued on. "Of course. But the law itself is in continuous evolution, as men make it—and has many refinements added by yourself. Consider that we were not in a state of war when she did this. Consider that she has been a noble friend to us, in every other way. And let us not forget how she saved Maximus's life, and the lives of five other men, when she bravely leapt upon the back of that beast—"

"This is true," the Emperor replied. "But the saving of several private persons' lives is of little consequence, weighed against her endangerment of the whole of the state."

"Consider that her people are besieged on every side, as Rome was, in its beginnings. She is one who has kinship with the heroes of our earliest days. She sought only to keep the Cheruscans from seizing the yearly grain crop. She never meant for those weapons to be directed at us.

"Always, we have respected the gods of other peoples," Julianus spoke on, "and it is not such a great step further to respect the actions mandated by these gods."

A distinct discomfort showed in Trajan's features.

I will not accept this, Julianus thought. *If she cannot be saved by persuasion, then, by Providence, I must find some other way.*

"You make an interesting case," Trajan said. "And you've long been an enemy of tyrants. If you tell me she is innocent, I am bound to believe it. So great is my debt to you, so strong is my natural desire to give you anything you ask—that this is agony to say. In this, you see, she has reached beyond herself. There are crimes that cannot be overlooked, for the sake of the safety of the frontier provinces, and all those who look to us for protection."

"But I give you my own assurance, she will do this no more. There is glory in leaving her alive. She would stand as a tribute to the greatness of this age."

"No," he said, and that voice was a firmly closing door. "It cannot be."

Julianus thought then, the malevolence of a tyrant could be battled more easily than this man's blunt, stubborn reasonableness.

"Marcus Julianus, you must let this matter go. It is even beyond me. If we look aside when citizens arm our enemies, it only serves as encouragement for others to do so. It does not even matter what her intention was. We must think, here, only of the greater good."

"But you'll hear her when she comes?" Julianus said with forced calm.

"Of course. It is the law." There was a moment's silence, then the Emperor added, "Is it not time to find a proper wife, one who's equal to your rank and eminence?"

This was an unpleasant blow from an unexpected direction. When Julianus had mastered surprise and grief, he answered solemnly, "You are correct that we are not equal in eminence. Hers is the greater. Might I go?"

A faint look of distress crossed the Emperor's face. "I tell you again, this opinion was an agony to give." The quiet between them was extended, unsatisfactory. The Emperor broke it. "I am going to found a school in your name, in Rome. I'll have a statue of you erected in its forecourt. You shall have unlimited monies for staffing it."

"That is most nobly generous," Julianus said flatly.

"Dio is speaking later. Did you know the court philosopher was here? You must entertain us by debating him."

Cannot he see I am too sick in heart to consider such things? Julianus realized suddenly that possibly Trajan didn't, that the Emperor may well have counted that impassioned defense as no more than what any patron might put forth for a client for whom he feels affection. Julianus considered then that few men had the means to understand that some fundamental bond of the spirit could flourish between two who stood at such different altitudes of society.

"I am sorry," Julianus said. "I debate no more, in these days. I care nothing of what Dio thinks, and indeed, I care nothing of what *I* think. The man could stretch half an idea across a stadium. He lives to provoke—choosing Ilium as a place to give a lecture that Troy never existed, and I . . . find myself full of unaccustomed emptiness. Which means I should keep silence. As a consequence, I want, no more, even to instruct others."

"What has so embittered you to philosophy?" Trajan added gravely, "I truly would like to know."

For some reason, Julianus told the truth.

"I met an old woman. And I have not been the same since."

"Ha!" He clapped a huge hand on Julianus's shoulder. "I like that answer. Our Dio causes Senators to interrupt meetings in the Curia so they can hear him, yet he has no effect on you. And an old woman does."

"Indeed. Because of her, philosophy seems senseless as counting grass blades. And tastes of dust."

"Well, that's tantalizingly odd. Can you tell me more?"

"Have you ever thought that perhaps it's not learning more and more, but unlearning what we think we know, that sets a man free?"

"Now I know I'm in a philosopher's company: You're making no sense. Who is this inestimable crone?"

"The great prophetess of the Chattians, who is called Ramis—"

"Who was just chastised by Maximus on my behalf, and sent to Rome."

"The same. There is a being who lives all those things of which the philosophers speak. And you know it in the blood when you stand before her."

"You've a formidable gift for goading the mind. I'll have an audience with her after this war's been won. You'll remind me, when I've returned home?"

It was said with the detachment of one who collects philosophies as some collect Corinthian bronzes, and warily, Julianus agreed. A moment later, as he was preparing to depart, Trajan seemed suddenly to remember a matter that had earlier been on his mind.

"I've a task before me that begs for your mastery of negotiation—you did say you'd remain here, long as I need you? Intelligence indicates that the eighty captives the Dacians took last spring have been transferred to a cave," Trajan continued, "where they're holding them, hopefully, for ransom. But this is a barbarous race, and they're as likely to slay them. There are men of rank among them. I want them back.

"Will you go at the head of a party to negotiate for their lives? I dislike asking; it's a perilous expedition that means journeying far into enemy lands. But I trust no one to do this better than I trust you."

Without spirit or interest, he agreed. Until Auriane was brought, he had no other desire but to remain in this country.

Chapter 26

The Fortress of Mogontiacum
The Nones of December

"Aurinia. You may sit in my presence." Maximus's comfortably settled features were tauter than usual, and there was a faintly anguished vagueness in his eyes. Tragedy's scent hung on the air like tainted perfume.

Slowly, warily, Auriane eased herself onto a bench. She'd been conducted from her prison rooms to this barren inner chamber of the Mogontiacum Fortress's headquarters, where the Governor awaited her alone—a thing that was alarming in itself, for a recorder or junior tribune was normally never far from his side. She prepared herself to hear that the Wolf Coats had fallen into an ambush, and a slain Avenahar had been pulled from the battlefield corpses. A mortifying cold began to spread through Auriane's stomach, her heart, as she wondered if he would give her leave to embrace her daughter's torn body before Avenahar was laid on the pyre.

At least, poor Arria is safe. Her mind's image of Arria happily cared for at the villa was the one warm, still place in all this storm and darkness. She'd not had words with Maximus since the day she'd been condemned. Her journey to Dacia, where she would make her final appeal before the Emperor, had been delayed until spring thaw, when the last detachments would be dispatched to Trajan's great war, so this Fortress would be her winter home. She had no way of knowing that Marcus Julianus's advance efforts on her behalf had, on this very day, failed.

"As you know," Maximus spoke on, "Marcus Julianus has asked me to look after your children."

Auriane felt something collapse within her.

"Yes. I've had no news of Arria Juliana for a month," Auriane broke in, trying to compel him to meet her eyes. In the last months she had felt herself some feral creature slinking about its cage, alert to nothing in life but some opening through which she might slip, wanting no nourishment but scraps of news of Arria, Avenahar, or Marcus. When there was a moon she felt stronger, and she would sit in her chamber's weed-ridden courtyard and say words to Fria, begging the Lady to give comfort to her children. Fria was silent, but often she thought she heard the whispered encouragements of Ramis in the wails of the winter winds scouring the rooftops. Under cover of darkness she would steal into the yard and practice swordfighting maneuvers with a stick broken from a hawthorn bush, or cast the stick at targets; her feral heart told her to stay limber and strong, as long as possible; she had always been a creature that survived by fighting. She was an amusing curiosity to the men quartered here, and a junior officer or two was discovered to be enlivening the tedium by practice-sparring with her in the barren courtyard—until Maximus had learned of it, and angrily stopped them. "I don't even know if Arria's gotten my letters," Auriane said. "I trust you've been watching over her well."

His focus shifted from the wall behind her to his ink pot, managing a deft swerve round her gaze. "I perceived a growing danger to your younger daughter in the last months." He spoke in his usual stately cadences, but the studied look of anguish deepened. "The vicious pranks of your neighbors had only gotten worse—as you know, petty folk can become emboldened, when they think a powerful man might fall. So I judged it best to remove Arria Juliana to Rome, to the household of her great-aunt—as Julianus insisted I do in his last instructions to me, if matters worsened. But it seems your daughter's met with some . . . misadventure."

"*Misadventure?*" Auriane rose weightlessly from the bench.

"Sit! Calm yourself. It seems your Arria Juliana's carriages were attacked by a band of highwaymen. She was kidnapped from her carriage."

"What sort of protection did you give her," Auriane said softly.

"I warn you, impertinence will not serve you. Members of your household have described the bandit party to us, and we're hunting them now. But I fear the steward of your estate, Demaratos, is dead."

"Gods below," she said, her throat tightening painfully. "No." She dropped her head into her hands and for an extended moment was mute in misery. *May ravens pluck out my eyes. Demaratos. Arria. It's all my doing. To the end of my days I'll flog myself for not being with her.*

"Others of your servants were injured, but most were unharmed, it seems, and—"

Abruptly she met his gaze. "*When* did this happen?"

Maximus calculated silently for a moment. "It must have been . . . eight . . . no, nine days ago."

"*Nine days?* Why have you taken so long to tell me?"

"Word was brought to me only today. Your servants were terrified and scattered over the countryside. An old woman called Philomela made her way to me, here, on foot—"

"Her nurse! You must take care of her, and provide her with a carriage. What did she report?"

"She's well enough, you can have speech with her, if you like. I'll send her back with the post carriage. She insists they didn't harm your Arria. They just bound your child and took her off on horseback. They took no plunder—it seems they wanted only your daughter."

"They want ransom, then."

"No demand for ransom has been brought to your villa, or to me."

"This is madness, it makes no sense whatsoever, why take only my poor babe and no jewelry or coin . . ." An upwelling of sick fear closed her throat. She wanted to claw at the ground, cry out, rip cloth, tear houses down.

"We will find her abductors," he said with an unctuous, complacent calm that angered her. "You have my assurance on that. That much, I owe Julianus. Rest your mind on one matter, at least—given the cautious way they handled her—whoever snatched her evidently wants her alive. You mustn't despair."

"Nine days," Auriane whispered, slowly shaking her head. "Time enough for every vile obscenity invented by man or goat to be committed on her."

She sat very still, her mind a huntress in the dark.

"I know where she is," Auriane said suddenly. "And I would wager a year's harvest upon it."

He frowned sharply and sat forward. "Tell me. I'll dispatch guardsmen there at once."

"Volusius Victorinus has her."

"*That* unsavory rascal?" The Governor put a meditative hand to his chin. ". . . Who sits at home, poisoned by his hatreds . . . Hmm . . . perhaps that's a road worth walking down. But could this man who's but a cockroach Julianus stepped upon have summoned the mettle to commit such a heinous act of vengeance? How would he dare?"

"I don't think it's vengeance," Auriane said. "It's a case of regular good sense overtaken by a satyr's itch, a carnal madness fixed upon my daughter."

ARRIA JULIANA HAD lost count of the days in this place. There were no days, actually, just one long night all run together, because the room they put her in had no windows.

Sometimes the room's lamp was lit, and she saw the belly of the beast.

She quickly learned to prefer darkness. For when the lamp burned, *he* was there. The room had one door through which a maidservant would come, bringing food that was never what she liked, and a larger door through which *he* would come, the man with scraggly hair and funny ears who was her father's enemy. Victorinus. That stubborn boy's face looked more like a sad flabby demon's, in the light of the one lamp on the floor. He watched her from his cave-corner, wanting to move toward her, but not yet able. As the run-together night went on and on, divided only by his coming, Victorinus started babbling stories while he sat there, telling her of himself as a child, talking of cruel doings that made no sense while he cried sick tears that terrified her. One time he moaned of the treachery of his wife, Decimina, who'd left him to return to her own family after Marcus Julianus wrecked their fortunes. Victorinus wanted her to say words of pity. He didn't seem to see that she was too frightened to say them.

He moved closer each time—slow, sneaky, and certain as a tide creeping up in the dark. Lapping up more and more ground. Eyes blurred with an unknown wanting. She was being pushed into a narrowing tunnel of darkness and it was harder to get a breath, locked in a room slowly filling up with mud, smelly slime that would force its way into her nose, her throat, and fill her up until she changed into something else, a creature made of swamp water and dung.

Room of darkness. Never allowed to leave it. Four walls with an alcove and a pallet on the floor. No nook to squeeze into where you couldn't be seen. She should have been a bird, then she could have flown up to the ceiling where no one could reach her.

Maybe she would become a swan.

The time came when she snapped awake to find Victorinus bent above her. *Mother, help.* But there was no one to help. She felt a fright so great she thought she would turn inside out. She wished herself small. He laid his flesh-of-a-worm palm on her belly—fearful of doing it, but doing it nevertheless. Skin of a rotted mushroom. Sliding flesh of a dead toad. He breathed strangely, like a winded dog. She thought herself into a thing of marble. It did little good.

Thinking only of the safety of darkness, she kicked the low stool on which he'd put the terra-cotta lamp. Light and dark leaped across the walls. The coverlet caught fire. He shrieked for the maidservants and shouted at her that she was a harpy's spawn. She saw that he had a greater-than-normal fear of fire. A mad fear, almost like a beast's.

The servants' door opened a cautious crack, then was thrown open amidst trilling voices as three womenservants rushed in. They flung their own cloaks on the flames to snuff them out.

She'd put Victorinus in an angry muddle and stopped him, this time.

But what of the next?

A swan. I'll be one of the snowy, kind ones that live on our river.

But the next time surprised her, for it was not at all the same. For the first time, a maidservant led her out of the dark room. She didn't want to go anywhere clad in nothing but a tunica of silk spun so fine she might as well have been naked—but the maidservant was strong as a bullock. Arria was thrust into a dingy dining hall, blinking from the lights of more lamps than she'd seen for many days. The dining chamber had no doors to outside gardens. If a room could be ill, this one was. Soot-blackened wall paintings glistened with grease. Fish bones from old meals crunched beneath her bare feet. Myrtle and bay were strewn there, too, but it didn't help the smell—a sweet foulness to cause you to look round and see who had a festering wound. The serving women wore rags, and were sad. In one corner a dwarf with muddy shoes played a reed pipe.

She turned about with a wail when she saw men reclining there, eating. But the maidservant forced her forward until she nearly stumbled over the low table before the couches where Victorinus and his dinner-friends lay, watching her the way a hound watches its meal being brought—two stout, brutish men with wrestlers' arms. Their brows glistened with spikenard oil. Two girls from some far-off place, Numidia or Cyrene, were captive in that room with her—limber maids with burnt-almond skin and kohl smeared thickly round their eyes. They were naked. They danced slowly, moving as if they were frightened. They were slaves, and she was ordered to say she was one, too—the daughter of one of Victorinus's carriagemen.

It was a dinner party from a fever dream. Boys hidden behind a curtain were singing shepherd songs, in thin, pretty voices.

Somehow, she knew it was to cover sounds she might make.

There was a monkey in that room, a prisoner like her, shrieking like a frightened boy in its wooden cage. A boy monkey, chattering. And a red-and-green parrot on a perch, which kept greeting Victorinus and speaking flatteries. Victorinus himself reclined on the first couch, in the place of honor. He was stupid from drink, blank-eyed—so much so, no one was home inside him now. So besotted, there was no one at the tiller.

Something told her that this was an exceedingly ill thing.

The man-guest with the blackened nails of a stonemason hooked a blistered paw in hers and dragged her close enough for a lover's embrace. He dipped his fingers in the spikenard oil and touched it to her lips, then, to his.

Victorinus told this man he could have her if he wanted her, he'd see that a room was prepared. The man-guest answered that she wasn't to his taste; his fires burnt only for Cappadocian youths—but he did believe that the monkey, over there, yearned to steer the chariot of Venus.

All three laughed loudly and long at this. A chorus of hissing and barking demons. They began nudging and goading Victorinus, who rose from his place, dribbling and wobbling. Blank-eyed and slobbering. No one at the tiller. He did their bidding, motioning to a manservant, who took the monkey from the cage.

A boy monkey. She knew the difference. The monkey screamed with blind rage as he was carried toward her. The man-guest held her so tightly she couldn't move. The youths behind the curtain sang louder. There came the fright that makes you float. Gods that come in tales sometimes appear as a golden mist—maybe one of them visited her then; she didn't know, but something warm and good wrapped about her then—and she knew what she must do. She saw, clearly as if it lay on the table before her, the fine weapon she held, good as a sword.

She told them her name.

They had had her whipped on her first day in this place, "just so that she would know what that was." And had promised her they would do it again, if she ever spoke her true name.

She shouted her name anyway.

And the name of her father. The man-guest on the couch lurched away from her as if she were a fire that blazed up in his face. He started shouting, too.

Everyone, suddenly, went quite mad.

She'd made *them* frightened. That was glorious.

Something told her to bolt off like a horse, even though she didn't know her way about. She dashed down the narrow passage through which the servants had entered. It was too dark. Too narrow. She collided, hard, with someone clammy and bony and sad.

Lucius.

Lucius with his mangled face, from playing the mean trick on her mother and sister. He must have been lurking there, watching it all.

All was lost.

Still she fought like a wild dog, biting, whipping about, scraping her arms against brick. No use. She was clamped in a vise. Now he would return her to the chamber.

Suddenly she realized she was wrong. He was struggling to drag her farther into the passage. Then he opened a small trapdoor, near the floor, and pushed her into it. She found herself on stone steps that led underground, beneath the house, where she saw a forest of brick columns stretching off in every direction. And softly roaring furnaces, giving out their strange, fuzzy light. Nice and warm. Down there, she found many good places to hide.

For what might have been a day and a night underground, no one came. When it seemed her stomach had shriveled to the size of a raisin, she heard scared footsteps. And Lucius was there. He'd hidden his monster face behind a cloth, but she could see his eyes, and they were worried and kind. He set an egg porridge behind one of the brick columns. Next to it, he laid neatly folded linen clothes. Kindness. How could this be? She guessed it must be far into night, when no slaves would come down to stoke the furnaces. She was astonished; she'd always thought him a boy ogre who only wanted to hurt people. But something else had been hiding in him, and now it was coming out.

Three or four egg porridges later, men from outside came. Rescuers sent by her father's friend, the Governor.

They arrested everyone in the house. Even the slaves, which to Arria did not seem fair.

They urged her to tell them all that had passed, but she wouldn't. She knew, then, she never would, for that was the only way to stop the evil pictures that rushed at her in a flood. She poured quicklime over the pictures and put them deep in the ground where worms and rotting things lived.

Lucius told her that he'd convinced his father she'd dashed out the door of the kitchens, then fled off into the night. He showed her the swollen cuts on his back, from the beatings Victorinus gave him for letting her get away.

And so, a new journey began. Well, the same journey, really—to Rome, to her great-aunt—but new because now she had a face that didn't fit her, inside. Like Lucius. In some strange way she couldn't name, she felt she'd won a race. Perhaps it was just because she'd known how to get free.

She'd found a weapon and made *them* afraid.

She wouldn't cry out for her mother again.

Once again, she was travelling in a carriage train. But now, everyone was different. A stranger-steward sent by the Governor took poor Demaratos's place. And now, there were many more guards, some, even, from the Fortress, with javelins and swords.

And Lucius was with her. She'd shouted at them until they agreed to let him come. For he had no father to stay with now, and his mother had left already, which made him an orphan. It was only right she should help him; he'd taken a cruel beating for her sake. Lucius had his own carriage, right behind hers.

All that was the same, now, was Philomela.

As the fine *reda* sped on, from time to time Arria looked out at the clean, white hills and wondered what had happened to her dog. Surely he lay stiff and cold somewhere in a grave of snow. She cried and couldn't stop herself when she thought of her dog, and Philomela didn't scold her. Philomela just looked sad.

But all that mattered was that once again she was travelling in the right direction. To the grandest, richest, most powerful city on earth.

Chapter 27

Germania Libera, The West Forest
Early Spring

Avenahar stood uneasily before Athelinda, the mother of her mother. Why had the great widow sent for her? The lady sat spiritedly still on the high seat of the hall of Baldemar, head faintly tilted as if she was listening to music. Her madder-red cloak was gathered majestically at her left shoulder; its silver wheel-form brooch glinted like a medallion awarded for valor. Sunlight from the smoke hole slanted in, singling her out for homage, melting her pearl-gray hair into liquid silver. Baldemar's shield hung on the wall behind her, forming a fearful nimbus about her head. The last time Athelinda had summoned Avenahar to this storied hall, Avenahar was certain she'd been visually appraised for some betrothal the lady had in mind, and found wanting. A new year had come; this was the moon of the ploughing of the loaves. A lifetime ago she would have called it *Februarius*, one of the days—who knew exactly which?—between the Nones and Ides. This time Avenahar was fortified by the lustrous gray-brown pelt of a wolf lying across her shoulders. Witgern had made her one of his own. She'd been given a nation—the nation of Wolves. It was a fine thing to no longer be lost between two worlds, to know that few dared spit on her now and call her Decius's daughter—but this pelt she fought so hard to win was both crown of victory and cloak of mourning. For she waited day by day to hear dread, final news of Auriane.

And now, what could this meddlesome, unbending woman want?

"I greet you, noble daughter of my daughter," Athelinda began liltingly, faintly inclining her head in greeting. "You've grown taller, since I saw you at Yule."

Athelinda motioned for Avenahar to come closer, a gesture delicate as a pale hand flowing over a lyre. An amethyst necklet glimmered at her intricately webbed throat. In Athelinda's youth, her great, lucid eyes had been said to shine like a Nix's behind a watery veil. In advanced age they'd only grown more brilliant in their soft nest of crinkled flesh, as if she hoarded her last store of life-force there. Avenahar had heard her grandmother had buckled from grief when she'd been told Auriane's fate, but it did not show. Athelinda stowed her private hurts as a queen stows them; she was too busied with managing the world.

"I greet you Athelinda, the Wise in Council," Avenahar responded, "daughter of Gandrida, wife of Baldemar . . . mother of Auriane." Her voice faltered over Auriane's name.

Athelinda squinted, delicately registering affront.

Now what have I done? The spear. Of course. How could I have been so unmannerly?

Avenahar deposited it too hastily on the plank floor, making a clatter that was an insult to the temple silence all about; it startled off a curious hen that strayed in from outside.

Wan humor passed across Athelinda's fine-boned face, there, and quickly gone. "You look fine and strong, child, even coated in—what is that all over you?"

"Honey . . . I was stalked here by men clad in Chariomer's colors. A farm wife stowed me in her mead shed last night and—"

Athelinda's laughter stopped Avenahar in place; it was surprisingly abandoned and kind. "How many maids of your tender years can say they're hunted by not one, but two armies? How celebrated you are," Athelinda went on musically; then her voice became sharp. ". . . And not yet old enough to kiss the bridal sword." *You've proven yourself to the world, perhaps, but not to me.*

"I'm . . . celebrated only among outcasts, Grandmother," Avenahar managed uncomfortably. "My deeds are paltry beside those of your husband."

"Modest, too. And you don't shrink from carnage. But how generous and bold are you, through the soul? Today will tell. Are you hungry, Avenahar? You certainly appear to be!"

Today will tell? Avenahar disliked the sound of that. The great lady gestured toward a settled old thrall woman who blended with the straw—a familiar spirit, Avenahar guessed, with whom the old widow had lived for a long time. Afflicted with some illness of the humors that thickened the limbs, the woman eased slowly from the secret shadows behind Athelinda's warp-weight loom. "The smokehouse is full," Athelinda was saying. "We slaughtered yesterday and offered a pig to the Lady. Mudrin's just made a porridge." The thrall called Mudrin set a bowl of thick barley porridge on the bench beside Avenahar. "Eat," the lady said. "If you were any thinner we could use you as a boundary post."

It was a command. Avenahar dutifully spooned gruel into her mouth.

"I've called you here because I've an important task for you," Athelinda went on. "There's a man hiding in my root cellar who can, possibly, be of extraordinary help to us all. He's hunted everywhere, so he'd best stay down there. He's lately escaped from Chariomer's camp, at fearful risk to himself—"

No, Avenahar thought, *it can't be . . .*

"—and as he had that Cheruscan bandit's trust, he has close knowledge of Chariomer's war plans. He knows much; he claims he can even name the days when the Cheruscans will strike again. He can't go abroad himself; our folk would recognize him, and, let us just say, wouldn't treat him gently. So we depend upon you, Avenahar, to carry what he knows back to Witgern's band."

"Grandmother, who is this man?"

"His name is Decius."

Avenahar disgraced herself and spewed out a mouthful of barley porridge. A jumble of questions arose—but she dared ask none of them. *Whose plan was this, yours or his?*—loomed chief among them. And, "Do you not know Decius is my natural father?" *She must. She can't have accepted that same bit of holy nonsense Ragnhild believes; she's too deep in knowledge to be fooled about such fundamental truths concerning her family.*

Gods below, she's conspired with him.

But why?

"Grandmother. I'm not certain I'm best for this task. Surely there are others who could—"

"Modesty's a vice, worn too heavily," Athelinda interrupted with a nip in her voice. "You carry our family's luck in abundance. You are greatly trusted by Witgern. You alone among his men can write, and so, can commit what this Decius says to parchment, to aid memory"—*she's got a voice that tightens about you like wet ropes,* Avenahar thought "—and because you lived outside our country for so long, your hatreds haven't festered—you can meet this man without rancor. You know, child—"

Without rancor? Was this some perverse jest?

"—that Chariomer, if he's not stopped, will have this farmstead next. Do you want Cheruscan carrion engaging in a filthy carouse around this very hearthfire where Baldemar gave heart to his men? Don't be nettlesome. I'll hear no griping from you on this matter, child."

THE WILLOW-WITHY LADDER swayed precariously as Avenahar lowered herself into the root cellar while striving to stave off murderous thoughts of Athelinda. Wattlework hurdles covered over with brushwood concealed this earthen pit from casual glances, for the root cellar had always served as the family's place of refuge during tribal raids. She found it not so cold as she might have expected, perhaps because down here, she was that much closer to the Earth Mother's heart. The place smelled of mold and apples.

She dropped to the hard-packed dirt floor. A man wrapped in marten furs stood quietly watching her in the speckled light filtering through hazelwood branches. That was the first surprise—he was just a man. Not tall. Not particularly wicked-looking—he looked more like someone waiting for slow-witted companions to catch onto a joke. His thick, curling hair was dark and glossy like hers where it wasn't salted with white. That seamed face was pleasantly boyish but for the sobering effect of the acerbic glimmer in his eyes. When young, he might have played an appealing Silenus in one of those dreadful comic dramas she'd seen on the town stage. It certainly wasn't the face of a man capable of great treachery or bloody deeds. She just stared for a moment, baffled to silence.

This is Decius.

He grinned—the smile of a trickster grown weary.

"Minerva's eyes! Behold, as fair a creature as ever stalked a battlefield— and she's every whit as beauteous as her clamorous mother! . . . Though perhaps, not as tidy. What's that mess all over your tunic?"

She quickly put a hand over the porridge stain.

"My apologies for being fourteen years late in meeting you," he went on. "But please understand, I was unavoidably detained." A slight huskiness came to his voice. "Avenahar. I've waited much, much too long for this day."

"You are my Roman father," she whispered, rather stupidly, she thought, as she stood stiffly, alternately battling a painful seizure of self-awareness, and fresh surges of anger at having been shoved into this snare. Just when she almost forgot she'd spoken, he answered.

"Well, yes . . . but you say 'Roman' as if all who bore that name were some mix of Circus procurer, professional poisoner and troll beneath a bridge." Cautiously he moved one step closer, and reached out his hands to her. "I hope I'm a *bit* better than that."

She took a step away. Moist earth pressed against her back.

"Ah, and is that my gift you're wearing?"

"Gift? What gift?"

"The golden fibula. It's bright as your eyes. It looks well there."

She put her hand to the golden brooch she had loved. "This was from *you*?"

"None other. Didn't your mother tell you where it came from? What are you doing? Don't take it off. You need a pin to fasten that thing."

"How dare you give me a gift," she managed hoarsely, flinging the brooch off as if it burned. It struck the dirt by his foot. It had tricked her into reverence. Her cloak slid from one shoulder, exposing the rough nettle-fiber shift beneath. She jerked it closed, while saying with exaggerated disdain, "I wore it only because I thought it a holy thing, from a woodwife or . . . or a god."

"I've been called many flattering things, mind you—but never a god. Unless you mean to slay me with that look, then deify me."

"You laid a trap for me. That was treacherous and base."

"Touchy as her mother, too. Sorry! 'Treacherous' and 'base' are two words that leave barely a scratch. From overuse, I suppose." He took another step toward her. "Avenahar—"

"Stay where you are." Her voice quavered. "Please."

"Be reasonable. Can you blame a father who wants to see his only child just once before he's packed off to Hades?"

"You desecrated my mother. Don't call yourself my father."

"Well, in this matter, it took two to desecrate."

"How dare you insult her!" Avenahar turned sharply away and stared hard at the earthen wall. But inwardly, she was surprised at herself. She'd always thought this moment, if it ever came, would be heroically simple—spit on him and walk away, leaving him to simmer in his own wretchedness. But she was finding she needed to work a bellows on the flames of her wrath. It was not just that this amiable, nimble-tongued rogue scarce seemed to breathe the same air as the Decius of her imaginings. It was also that he carried a strong imprint of her mother on him. Auriane's childhood was alive in this man's eyes. After seven months of standing alone against the world, Avenahar found she longed to keep close anything Auriane had touched or loved.

"That's a fine fit of pride!" Decius said to her back. "Gods, you're so like her, you'll bring me to maudlin tears—and the last time *I* cried was ten years ago when the last of the palatable wine ran out. Avenahar, you're not being fair."

"You deserted her when she was carrying me."

"Of course I did! I had half the Chattian tribe sprinting after me with axes in their hands!"

"You were the trained pet hound of Chariomer—"

"You sound as though you speak another's words. Speak your own."

"—and you helped him slaughter us, for years. All say so."

"Utter nonsense!" He shouted the words; his vehemence stopped her in place. "And I think I don't need an education in right conduct from a headstrong maid of fourteen who ran away from her noble parents, leaving them heartbroken, then galloped off to join a brawling band of wolf-men. Show some respect for your elders. Right now, maybe I don't want to claim fathering *you*. Sit down, be silent, and listen."

She found herself settling obediently onto the dirt floor. Decius took a place on an overturned pinewood barrel.

"Avenahar. Chariomer's battle plans are his own. I was his prisoner. Prisoner? I was his slave, always one jump ahead of death. Your Chattian folk never liked me and I think they invented a story or two, to make me worse. Such expert assistance as I gave him concerned only the building of his hall back in the Hart country. Who knows, but future ages may laud me as the man who brought steam heat to the barbarians. My war counsel was of no use among such backward folk. Tell them to hold men in reserve and they think you're insulting them, calling some of them cowards. Not to mention that simple discipline and the notion of fighting as one are ideas antithetical to the primitive mind. I can't force you to believe me. But it's the truth."

His voice became more gentle. "Avenahar, all those years, I wanted more than my freedom, just to look, once, upon your face. You may not be happy with me, but I'm certainly happy with you."

He reached out to touch her smoothed-back hair. Avenahar pulled away from him—but not so quickly as before.

"Poor child," he said in a voice surprisingly nurturant. "You are all I had hoped. And you'll be one in whom others place hopes. You are your mother, reborn."

She pulled the cloak more tightly about her, an unconscious act of warding. It seemed a fine joke on herself to hear the words she'd so long craved to hear, from *him*.

Then Decius leaned closer, and spoke in covered voice as if he feared the stored apples might overhear.

"Avenahar, I had another reason for coming." He put a hand beneath her chin, and lifted it. "Perhaps, just perhaps, I can help get your mother back."

"Please. Don't make jests about such things."

"No jest, my pretty. I know she goes to her appeal in that soon-to-be new Roman province, and that there will be no stay for her. But she has to cross through a bit of the country before she gets there, doesn't she?"

"You speak of . . . of some sort of rescue? Is it *possible*?"

"Anything is possible, pet."

She battled down a strong upsurge of elation—hope was the cruelest trap.

"I have close knowledge of the lands along her route—they'll have to take her along the Moenus, won't they? To pick up detachments from those forts? I did my second year of service in one of the first forts built along that river. I know that country like I know my father's house. It was there I got my first decoration. Did your mother tell you I was the youngest man, ever, in my legion, to be given the centurion's vine-stick? Don't forget, Avenahar, I know the weak points of a marching camp."

"How do I know you can be trusted? What's this you know of Chariomer? When will he strike?"

"Mercury's wings, do you think His Kingliness would divulge such a thing to *me*? He trusted me less than he trusted his wife."

"You tricked Athelinda. You're a mountebank and a fox."

"I own up to tricking a lot of people. But not Athelinda. I *do* have information about him—just not that. Athelinda was only keeping the truth close; the fewer who know this, the better. Chariomer may have turned a squinty eye toward me. But I listened. And I watched. And learned a thing or two of him."

Avenahar met this with a bored expression.

Decius dropped his voice, speaking scarce above a whisper. "Chariomer is superstitious about certain days. In fact, he counts some days so inauspicious, he'd never launch an attack at those times, and would be all in a muddle, were an enemy to attack him." He reached behind him and got a sheaf of thin sheets of beech bark bound with a leather thong, on which he'd inscribed Latin words in charcoal. "I've marked his bad days, here. You must commit them to memory."

Intrigued in spite of herself, Avenahar took the sheets from him and studied them.

"Avenahar, this is a man so fettered by a load of magical nonsense, if you know what he fears, you have him trussed and bound. For example, he counts the number 'five' as unlucky for him. Five days after the moon, five men riding; this terrifies him. When the north wind Boreas blows, he thinks it carries the ghosts of those he's put to death and he'll not even venture outside. A crow seen in the western part of the sky, this reduces him to aspic. I've seen it. He's distressed by the color red, or any man with red hair; he even wears red boots, thinking this will somehow reverse the effect—the examples go on and on."

"Gods, but that's useful," Avenahar whispered. She looked at him. "If it's true."

"Stop this, right now," he said curtly. "Do you think I would have risked so much to come here, simply to play you for a fool and pass false information on to you? What sort of man does that? Go now, if you think so little of me."

That burst of righteous wrath struck a mark within her. "I take those words back," Avenahar said softly, looking down at the sheets of beech bark. "Half of them, anyway. You *are* a fox. But you're not a mountebank."

"Ah, sweet words from a loving daughter are like the taste of warm honey cakes by a garden fountain."

"Please, Decius. Must you always speak with mockery?"

It was Decius's turn to feel knocked from his perch. This earnest young creature who was his daughter, so strong in some ways, so frail in others, turning those guileless eyes on him, expecting him to be simply and only what he was—somehow vaulted over every defensive ditch he'd ever dug about himself. For the first time his mocking words did seem faintly ridiculous, like a mime running out to fight an enemy no one around him could see.

"All right," he said. "Agreed. I'm sorry."

"You're not the ogre you want to be," she said then, not knowing what prompted her. "You're more like the god Hermes as a boy, who was a master of persuasion and tricks. . . . You know how he once stole some cows and made some shoes for them out of bark, which he tied onto their feet with plaited grass, so no one could follow their tracks." Avenahar frowned. "How did you persuade Athelinda to agree to draw me into this? She's got trusted messengers who could carry this information to Witgern."

"Perhaps she's wise enough to want us to make peace. Perhaps she thinks you're no good to us if you go through all your mortal days loathing where you came from. It unbalances the humors. It leads to melancholia. We don't want that, do we?"

Avenahar managed a half smile at this, then she cast her gaze down, still numbed somewhat by the swiftness with which all unfolded.

"Avenahar. If you can abide having anything to do with me—and if Witgern's game to make a try at snatching your mother back—will you act as messenger?"

"What's your reward in this?"

"The sight of you. That is all."

She was trembling. "You think there is a chance."

"Always, pet." He smiled. "Avenahar," he said then, his expression becoming more grave. "All these years, I've wanted to know something."

She waited, lulled by the sound of his voice. Surprisingly, there was humility in it.

"Were you and your mother content, at the villa of her high nobleman? Did Auriane have any good years of peace and happiness? I so wished it for her."

This broke Avenahar like a reed. She bent forward and softly cried, covering her face with her hands.

He put a comforting hand on her shoulder. She didn't push it off.

She managed to nod, *yes*.

"Avenahar, I thank you. I am most happy, knowing that."

He let her cry for a moment, while a new gentleness entered the root cellar. Then he grinned broadly, dispersing it. "Now, your mother listened to me and was the better for it, and as I believe gifts are passed on from mother to child, it's a good bet you're capable of the same, and so—"

"You said you'd stop that."

"Sorry, long habit. You still haven't answered me. Will you bring my instructions to Witgern, so we can, perhaps, cheat your mother's executioners?"

"Yes. How can I say no?"

"Good, then." He sat up straighter on his seat. "I suppose this is enough for one day. I don't want to overstrain this tenderly budding familial bond.

Go now. Help Athelinda serve the Assembly delegation, or whatever it is she's doing up there today."

As Avenahar got slowly to her feet, Decius retrieved the golden fibula, loudly blew the dirt from it, then held it out to her. "Please. Keep it. It looks good perched on that cloak."

She shook her head, *no*. But she seemed far less certain of herself this time.

"Am I *that* much an ogre?"

"No. But your people are. Most of them, anyway. I don't know what you are. I don't know what I am. I'm only half Chattian, that is hard enough to . . . That thing houses evil magic. I can't wear it, it would work against my fate."

"I'll take that rambling 'maybe' as a no. And I'll tell you what I'll do. I'll barter it for a small plot of land. It shall be yours, waiting for you, in some god-blessed future day when Chariomer is driven off and all is settled and safe for farming again. You can go there and live, when you're wearied of ransacking the earth with a wolf pack. You can take a fine husband. And perhaps . . . your old father could live somewhere near. In a house in back, or something."

"That's just folly. No place in all this land is safe, or ever will be."

"Don't tell the Fates their business, Avenahar." He ruffled her hair so that it fell into her face; she watched him forlornly through the cascade of hair, making no move to straighten it. "You'll pay me a visit tomorrow?" he said then. "It gets stupefyingly boring in this damp hole."

"Yes," she said hoarsely, tears forming in her eyes.

For an instant, he held out a mad hope she might embrace him.

But she turned suddenly, and started energetically climbing the rope ladder.

"Avenahar," he gaily called out after her. "Will you call me 'Father'?"

She paused, swaying, on the ladder.

"Would 'Uncle' keep you quiet?"

"Sorry, it's 'Father,' or nothing."

She just gave him a look of exasperation.

"Athelinda wouldn't have any books up there, would she?"

But he was speaking to her feet as she scrambled out of the root cellar. "Didn't think so," he muttered to himself as Avenahar dragged the hazel-wood branches in place and left him in gloom.

Chapter 28

The month of Maius

Auriane lay on the jolting floor of a *reda*, shorn of life-love and hope. Iron fetters dragged at her wrists. The four-wheeled travelling carriage had been stripped of all adornments and adapted to transport a prisoner—one side was boarded closed, the other, fitted with a bolted door. An aperture above the back board, not quite wide enough to thrust a head through, afforded the only light.

There had come the time of the breaking of ice—though Auriane scarce knew. With the first day of *Maius*, her journey to her appeal before the Emperor began. On this spring dawn, the march set out through the stone gate of the Mogontiacum Fortress; she travelled in the custody of four cohorts drawn from fortresses along the Rhenus, final detachments dispatched to the Dacian war. The first leg of their long journey would closely follow the meandering course of the Moenus, a lesser river that flowed into the Rhenus.

In Dacia, their destination far to the east, the Roman Army had crossed the Danuvius, and into shadow. The flow of letters from Marcus Julianus had ceased after the winter days of Saturnalia, last year. His silence was unsettling, for she knew well that had he his life, his freedom, and writing materials at hand, he would have written, often as he was able. Supply galleys travelled continuously to and from the army's base camp on the Danuvius, and it would not have been difficult to find someone to carry a letter. She felt certain some unknown shadow lay over him in that far land. And in the night's stillness, she knew in her blood that Marcus had not turned the Emperor's mind regarding her case. She accepted that she journeyed to her execution, to be carried out in that distant land.

Auriane's *reda* was positioned in the center of the march, amidst the legionary baggage and the two-wheeled carts hauling catapults and the larger ballistae. They travelled on a military road, no more than a well-cleared track. Fine dust lifted off the pathway and found its way inside the carriage, causing her to break into sporadic fits of coughing. From time to time she crawled to the back of the carriage, far as her fetters would allow, and looked out. Beyond the backs of a line of oxen and trudging men bent beneath loads, flowering hawthorn trees cast fragile veils across the green. Still farther in the distance were the gentle, maternal curves of the hills of her birth country, putting her in mind of the body of a kind mother, resting on her side.

A kind mother. Such as I am not. Ever since she'd been told of Arria's rescue from the household of Victorinus she was loath to close her eyes, for then would come bright, wretched imaginings she wanted to thrust off the edge of this iron-cold world. *Arria is well now. She is safe.* Or so Auriane had been told, when she'd been given letters detailing Arria's journey, and her supposedly happy arrival at her great-aunt's in Rome. Letters full of awful silence, as to what, precisely, had occurred in that fetid den. *Safe? No. She will never be. The nightly horrors I dream—who can heal them? A physician? Ramis? The sword?*

Perhaps only the sword that falls on my neck.

"You must want clear sight, more than refuge," Ramis had said. And now, Auriane wanted neither. That fleeting intoxication of hope she'd felt on that night on the quay had been driven off by her own unvoiced shrieks. *If only I could take Arria's hurts onto my body.* She wanted to fight a clamorous last battle that would bring a finish to all she knew. Or to slide underground, into eternal unknowing, taking with her the remnants of a sense that the Fates' workings were just.

Behind her, Brico drowsed atop a pile of soiled coverlets, seized occasionally with delicate, higher-pitched coughing spasms of her own. A sheet of dark amber hair fell across a creamy cheek; one voluptuous arm was curled about a four-string lyre she kept for plucking out tribal songs. The praefect of the march had allowed Auriane one trunk of possessions and a single maid. Brico had petitioned vigorously to be that maid. Auriane was reluctant to bring her on such a grueling journey, but knew Brico despised being confined to the villa, where she claimed to see the murdered Demaratos's ghost staring at her from the alcoves, begging her help. Brico was a sunny mystery with her rattling collection of beauty unguents, her durable trust in her gods—and that supple nature, venturesome and content as a puppy's, able to carve out a home anywhere. Auriane had stopped trying to understand her devotion and was content to be strongly grateful for her.

As they set out they would be passing close to the territories of the increasingly restive Chattians. This detachment numbered almost two thousand men, strung out over a distance of a half mile. At its head were regular cavalry troopers on proud Hispanian horses; they were a moving fortress wall as they rode at a decorous trot, two abreast. Their bronze-embossed helmets and the medallions on the horses' breast straps flashed across the meadows and fields like some mirror-signal announcing their menacing magnificence. Behind the cavalry were the men of the regular legions, marching row on row, six abreast. Trekking alongside Auriane's *reda* were the slaves of the legionaries, who shouldered the heavier equipment. Among them were a scattering of slave women, unassuming figures colored like earth in their hooded travelling cloaks; these served as cooks and washer women to the men of higher rank. Here, too, was a collection of camp followers, recognizable at once with their wine-dark lips, so harsh against faces whitened with cosmetic chalk, their tunicas of crimson or burnt orange, worn short enough to expose their glittering anklets of bright gold. The camp followers were a few hardy, nimble-witted young women of the Celtic tribe who dwelled in the native settlement by the Mogontiacum Fortress; they'd left to seek adventure, hoping to trade their embraces for a few coppers. They got no rations and thrived as best they could. All the noncombatant members of the march had been drilled in how to conduct themselves in the event of an attack, so they wouldn't interfere with the actions of the troops. Behind the ox-drawn baggage wagons marched two cohorts of veteran soldiers, protected by auxiliary cavalry serving as flank guards—barbarian attacks most commonly came from the rear. Horses, baggage, and legionaries were kept moving at a uniform speed so that the march could not easily be broken into sections. As it was counted unlikely a Chattian warband would attack a force of this size, the flank guards' vigilance was relaxed, and there was laughter and banter among the camp followers. Nevertheless, every dawn before they broke camp, a cavalry reconnaissance force would be sent ahead to search out ambushes.

But Auriane had no thought of ambushes—she noted only that the gray-blue forest that had swallowed Avenahar looked particularly benign on this day. All through winter she'd gotten no further news of Avenahar's fate. *Now I die not knowing if I have your love or even your understanding. I'd be drunken with happiness just to know you're contentedly living on.*

IT WAS THE time of the noon halt, on the first day of the march.

Brico had the freedom to move about, and Auriane had sent her to the medical orderlies' wagon, for coltsfoot leaves to ease their coughing spasms. When Brico returned she was like an overfull chalice spilling its contents.

"Mistress. The camp women are all talking of Avenahar. She's . . ." Brico paused to gasp for air; she had been running. ". . . in great trouble. She's wanted for murder and insurrection."

She lives still! Auriane found the knowledge disorienting and blinding, as if she'd been unexpectedly exposed to the sun after a time immured in a tomb. A moment passed before Brico's words turned her insides to pudding.

"It's all right, Brico, stay calm," Auriane said, though she herself had begun to shiver. Auriane grasped Brico's hand and pulled the girl into the carriage. "Tell me what she's done."

They sat close together in the gloom. "She's won great fame among Witgern's band," Brico whispered, fast as she could get the words out, "and there's a bounty on her head—"

"Gods, no."

"—for she has murdered two cavalrymen, from a patrol hated by your people because they robbed your villages. She used her woman's wiles and entered their camp at night and seduced them and gave them a draught and cut their throats while they lay sleeping—that's how the soldiers tell it, anyway—"

"To have such mean nonsense attached to her name," Auriane interrupted, "—woman's wiles? *Avenahar?* It means she must have struck deep and true."

"—but your people say she took the form of a black she-wolf and leapt upon the cavalrymen as they travelled, and with great strength, mangled them with teeth and claws."

Auriane battled nausea as the floor of the carriage began to roll in gentle, regular waves. *My fierce and foolish child. The life I feared you'd seek—you've embraced it with relish.*

Avenahar slew two cavalrymen. That, evidently, was the bare core of truth in the tale. With sword, dagger, or spear? Auriane tried to imagine it and couldn't. The thought was bewildering. *She's a hotheaded brawler, no more, she would never . . .* Then Auriane remembered that day in the grove, when she'd discovered that Avenahar had boldly defied her by keeping the fugitive sailor's sword. *There are chambers of her soul to which I've never had the key.*

Tears she had no will to stop streamed down, and she felt she bled from the eyes.

"Your people's Assembly declared her an outlaw," Brico said then. "Your own Chattian people. What does it mean?"

"Rome probably pressed them to do it. It means if anyone does her harm, my family can't avenge her." Auriane looked off at the forest. "She's just a babe. What sad madness. She's put up a mountain between herself and home!"

Auriane shut her eyes and rested her head against the carriage's side. "Her life's in Witgern's hands now," she said, all her strength running out. "I can do nothing. My poor child's on an island that grows smaller and smaller. I pray he's got the wit to protect her."

That night Auriane lay in a fever of wakefulness, struggling to wrap her mind protectively around Avenahar's, then Arria's, until shell-pink streaks lightened the eastern sky.

How can it have happened that in just one year our family's been quartered like some slaughtered beast? Avenahar has thrown herself on spears. My doom is certain. Some awful darkness lies over Marcus. Arria may well be all that's left of us. Live for us, Arria . . . my poor, dear, fragile-strong babe. Live for us in your new world.

They camped that night within the safety of the cleared land about one of the Moenus forts. On the second day she heard the trumpet-flourish of the army's salutation for greeting comrades—the march had been joined by a century of soldiers from the fort at Aquae Mattiaci. Not long after, Auriane was startled when one of the cavalrymen assigned to her carriage unbolted the side door, produced an iron key, and removed the fetters from her wrists and ankles. His manner was blunt and closed, suggesting he didn't approve of this; clearly, the order originated with someone above. The mystery over this small act of kindness lingered. And when their evening rations were brought, she and Brico got another surprise: Instead of barley mush, commonly thought fit only for geese, oxen, and slaves, they were given wheat porridge, hard-meal biscuits, and vinegar water—the same ration as the common soldier. Brico made a thanksgiving offering to her tribal goddess Sirona for these puzzling acts of good will, sprinkling a few crumbs from her meal biscuit onto the ground. And that eve, as the tents were being raised, Auriane saw that one of the centurions who had just joined the march watched her from a small distance—she would have known his rank by the proprietary sweep of his gaze as he surveyed the camp, even had she not seen the sword suspended from a baldric on his left side and his vine-stick of office. His bronzed cuirass was covered with the gold medallions awarded for valor. He seemed ready to approach and have words with her, but did not, and after a short time he moved on. She was near certain this man was responsible for their improved fortune. But the man was a stranger to her.

THE THIRD MORN blurred with the second. By day she found some obscure comfort in movement, even though it was movement toward death. Day was a narrow corridor, where all seemed bound in iron. By night, curiously, she was least afraid: Enfolded in darkness, the world fell open vastly; she sensed the ghosts of her people, thick in the forest. In night, she could float like some will-o'-the-wisp above her bones and flesh, and flit down avenues to other worlds.

In late afternoon, at a place where the trackway strayed close to a low ridge thick with beeches, Auriane and Brico heard a thin-voiced lament for the dead, sung out in the Chattian tongue. Gradually it grew fuller, entwining with the wind, seeming to drift from the sky. Brico was puzzled and alarmed. Auriane thought she heard her name. On the ridge above she saw gaunt human faces, tattered gray-brown cloaks. A collection of a hundred or more Chattian villagers had quietly massed there, doubtless feeling protected by the ridge's sheer face. Auriane felt a vaulting excitement as she recognized Gunora—but it proved only a woman who resembled her. The wind unfurled the women's long hair as they inclined their heads to look down upon the rank-upon-rank of passing soldiers. A cloud of petals and leaves spiraled down—they cast the Nine Herbs on the wind, as a last blessing. She squinted. Something else was there, too, fluttering like aspen keys—small tokens of wood, of the sort onto which runic letters were cut. Some charm for her release? How had the villagers known she would be passing by on this day? It was a mystery sometimes, how well news flew from Fortress to forest. As their wails ascended to the pitch of a gale, it brought her to a frenzy of stifled hope and longing. She wanted to stop her ears.

A detachment of ten cavalrymen cantered round the back of the ridge and drove the villagers off with shouts, despite the fact that their extended hands were empty of weapons.

That eve, when Brico returned from an errand, she brought Auriane one of these tokens. It was a strip of applewood. Brico had no comprehension of the sigils burned into the wood, so she watched raptly while Auriane struggled to work out the meaning.

Auriane recognized, first, the signs for the moon in eclipse. "It's not a charm," she said softly. "It's—" She had trouble with the next three signs, which indicated a name, employing the runes that corresponded to *S*, *Th*, and *A*. With a start of dismay she realized it was "Sawitha." This was followed by the sign for the Veleda, and the three runic letters that signified an enemy or wolf had stolen into the village.

She understood. Sawitha had been named Ramis's successor. Evidently, the women of the groves were not pleased. "It's a warning, and a plea." Grimly, she met Brico's gaze. "On a matter in which I can do nothing."

I resisted so long, another stepped forth and took my place. She felt she shed a great and uncomfortable burden. *Ramis, you hunted me all my life, but I eluded you. I'm sick with sadness to think what a disappointment I must have been. A part of me loved you, and did want to do your will.*

But I don't think I could have carried your staff. You were sadly mistaken, thinking I was the one.

Night came; the moon's gauzy orb was a ghost lantern lifted languorously above the sea of trees. Auriane felt it rise. Just as she crawled to the back of the carriage to meet its complex gaze, she heard a single cry of a wolf. There was a furtiveness in its tone—and a promise.

The man-wolf. Her breathing slowed.

She waited to hear it again, but was met with stubborn silence. Had it been conjured by her despair? She looked questioningly into the wild forest gloom beyond the cookfires. None in the camp paid it any mind; their attention was fixed upon their comforts and discomforts, not on forest and sky.

"Brico. Did you hear a wolf?"

"No, I didn't. How could I hear anything through all that carousing?" Brico indicated a half-drunken group of soldiers sitting round a nearby cookfire who were making animal sounds and yipping with laughter. "Maybe it was them."

"Perhaps you're right." Auriane was left with bleakness, and puzzlement—it must have been the cruel trick of a mind ravenous for reasons to hope.

No. She was certain she'd heard it.

Somewhere near, in the night-drenched forest, Witgern waited.

THAT EVE, THE legionary detachments camped at a site Auriane would not have chosen, had their men of rank taken counsel with her. The beech forest pressed too close. They had come to wilder country where native settlements were sparse; here, forts were more thinly spaced, and the forest, unknown and dense. A cleared strip of land alongside the trackway was punctuated with beech stumps; a previous legionary crew had begun cutting back the forest, but halted their work too soon. The country was broken with flinty projections of rock, which could afford cover for a warrior crawling on his belly. The nearby river was drunken and dangerous on spring. The narrowness of the open strip of ground between river and forest would make it difficult for their heavily equipped soldiers to maneuver. A bold enemy could do much with these land features. But she supposed the need to stay close to an abundant water source must have prevailed in their councils.

Night was just beginning to release its grip; a clear sky was paling to stone gray. The provisions master's slave had just brought their rations, so the door of their carriage was unbolted and open. Auriane watched as the camp broke apart in brisk, orderly fashion, amazed anew by how so many men could move in concert, each knowing his small place in the larger order. She'd abandoned her gruel bowl with her porridge half eaten. She felt agitated as the beast that knows the earth is poised to shake.

The eight-man divisions of each century, working with practiced ease, loaded onto muleback their long, rolled leather tents, the heavy millstones they carried for grinding their wheat. Then they began collecting up the construction tools each man carried on the march—pickax, turf cutters, sickle, and saw—and started stringing mess tins, buckets, clothing bags, and ration sacks onto the stout poles they used for carrying their soldier's kit. So they could move about with greater ease, they hadn't yet fastened on mail armor, or taken up helmets and shields. While one soldier from each eight-man unit doused the cookfire before his tent, another scattered a bit of meal onto the wind, as an offering to the local spirits. By the horse lines a row of glossy cavalry mounts, broad backs naked still, awaited the grooms, who worked in pairs as they brought up the heavy saddles and harness. Downstream, slaves were leading the last of the oxen and mules from a final drink at the river. At

the end of the *via quintana*—the wide avenue that sectioned off the rear portion of the camp, separating the legionary tents from the baggage—soldiers
rapidly pulled up the sharpened palisade stakes that had been driven into the
turf bank thrown up from the defensive ditch they'd dug about the encampment the night before.

It was a fleeting moment when the palisade was half dismantled and the
men had not yet begun to form up in marching order.

All at once she heard yelps of injury and surprise, accompanied by a reckless hammering of hooves. They issued from the dismantled place in the palisade, several hundred paces down the *via quintana*.

Brico sprang down from the *reda* to investigate, but Auriane caught
her arm and dragged her back. In the quarter of the camp where the Second
Cohort pitched their tents, men seemed to have broken into riot. Over their
angry shouts rose the bass-toned command of a centurion—*Get ropes, quick-
time, you lackwits, or I'll break those rampart stakes over your backs.*

The disorder was pressing closer to her carriage as men jostled each
other, fighting to escape some threat she could not see. Intrigued, Auriane
grasped the side of the *reda* and pulled herself up.

Above the brawling men was the dark blur of a horse's head, whipping
this way and that, ears flattened back, its eyes white-ringed and mad. A bristling mane stood up in a stubborn crest. The beast hurled itself about with
the ropy looseness of a serpent caught by the tail. As it heaved skyward, rav-
aging the air with its forehooves, she saw a stallion of brutish conformation—
short neck, heavy legs, stunted body. Its sorrel coat, still shaggy from winter,
was mottled with bare patches where it was scarred from battles with its own
kind. Men dropped to the ground as the stallion's hind legs ripped out in a
manic succession of kicks. The beast wheeled about like a top, spasmed sideways like a dancer on draughts, caught the end-flap of a tent with a hind
hoof and ripped it down. Then it bolted, dragging the heavy goathide tent
behind it while men dove out of its way.

Somehow a wild horse had gotten loose in the camp.

It was remarkable how disruptive this was. Nearly every man of the
camp abandoned his appointed task either to join in the effort to subdue the
horse, or to scramble off to escape from it. Others rushed to pull their equipment and possessions from the beast's unpredictable path. Order disintegrated faster than she would have believed possible. She was surprised by
how vulnerable the camp's machinery was to intrusions that were singular
and unexpected.

The horse continued to make its way like some equine puppet jerked about on ropes, whirling this way, frog-leaping that way, animated by demonic music only it could hear.

"Brico, get out, and get under the carriage," Auriane said in a low voice. "Quickly, before anyone bolts the door. If it's set afire you could be trapped inside."

"*Set afire?* Who would set it afire?" Disappointment showed in Brico's face. She wanted to enjoy the show.

"*Go!*"

"All right, but . . . what of you?"

"I think the camp has visitors. And they might need my help."

Brico seemed trapped in a trance of stubborn puzzlement.

"Get under it and stay there. Now."

Slowly, Brico obeyed, dismayed by the unreachable calm that had overtaken Auriane's face—she was more warrior than mistress now.

Neither their guards nor the *reda*'s mule master were anywhere about, so Auriane once again pulled herself up for a fuller view. The wild horse was hopelessly entangled in trailing tent-ropes, one of which was wound about a tree stump. The frantic animal gathered itself for a final leap, only to be jerked hard to its knees. By this time it had grievously wounded or killed a man; at a distance, two legionaries hurried off, bearing a limp, unmoving comrade.

Auriane was taut and alert as a runner waiting for a rope to drop.

From the dense beech wood beyond the camp, where all was still steeped in night-gloom, a trilling arose. At first it was low and unearthly. Then it spread and swelled, intensifying until it was ragged, shrill, and relentless, as disharmonious as shrieking flutes, unnerving as a wasp in the ear. It pressed into the brain like an ice shard. To the soldiers, it was a sound both rabid and barbarous—a song to drive men mad, like the horrible, inchoate noise of the Sirens. Some stopped their ears. The trilling did not seem to issue from multitudes of human throats, but most knew better: This was the dreaded *barritus*, produced by tribal warriors amplifying their voices against their shields.

It was the Chattian war cry.

Auriane heard it as a warm greeting.

Chapter 29

Native spears arced up in a mass, numerous as the long grasses. The sky darkened as if dawn had changed its mind. Auriane scuttled beneath the *reda,* where Brico clung to her like a bear cub to its mother. The horrific hail fell everywhere, penetrating soldiers' packs, clattering off hastily upraised shields, pinning mules to wagons, piercing limbs. The spears came and came, as if from an unquenchable source, thudding bluntly onto the *reda*'s roof, rocking it crazily. Brico was breathlessly sobbing. Auriane waited patiently through this as terror and rapture flooded through her together. The men of the camp scrambled about as if caught up in many small whirlwinds, seeking swords and javelins. As most had still not put on helmets or mail armor, several dozen paid with their lives.

A rescue. Auriane had not allowed herself to hope. A crack broke open in her prison wall. The miasmas that had settled on her were blown off as if by a gale. She found herself grabbing for life again.

From the cries she judged it a force greater than Witgern's; he must have united his Wolves with other Chattian warbands.

When the rain of spears began to slacken, Auriane tore off her cloak and wrapped it round Brico to conceal her, while mumbling a word or two of encouragement. Then Auriane crawled from beneath the carriage.

She lost herself in the chaos. No one had leisure to pay any mind to a tall woman in a belted tunic with loosened hair, an animal glint in the eye, running at a crouch as she flowed among confused soldiers, panicked slaves, heaps of toppled baggage, the wounded struggling along on the ground. She glided unseen behind an optio, second-in-command to a centurion, who was threatening a recruit too slow to get into battle formation. The legionaries saw only their centuries' signal flags, heard nothing but the shouts of their officers, the deep-throated blasts of the great, curved *cornu*—the Roman war trumpet—bleating commands in the language of horns, difficult to decipher beneath the competing trill of the Chattian warriors.

She was carried forth on a wave of fierce exultation. Battle is a door. She would force it wide. Her old forests would close round her like the arms of a beloved. This clash of wood and iron was a cauldron in which all would be transformed. She would rejoin Avenahar. She would have Arria brought to her—somehow. When the portals of everything swung wide, improbabilities seemed no more than wicked illusions. Of course, Marcus was well—and he would find her. All these reunitings flowed together in an impossible soup, a stew of things that could not coexist, that suddenly, she believed could be, just because of that joyous, mad trilling. *If Witgern has the mettle to do this, what cannot be done?*

The war-trill died off and she knew the attack must have come, though she saw only what was immediately before her. Just ahead, a century's Capricorn standard sagged, then straightened with the crispness of a salute as men of the First Minervia forged their way forward. On these men's left flank she saw the Bull emblem of a century of the Eighth Augusta, hoisted above helmeted heads as it closed in tightly beside the men of the First. The camp was rallying from surprise. From these units' positions, she determined the location of the thickest part of the fighting. She worked her way in that direction as an armored shoulder rammed into her back, a loosed pig darted between her legs, tripping her, a running soldier's hobnail-booted foot ground hers painfully into the dirt. She came to a row of twenty baggage wagons pulled tightly together to form a firewall against the onslaught. From the shadows beneath one wagon, a crouching camp follower, naked but for her breast band, grotesque with powdered antimony bleeding down her cheeks, watched Auriane with eyes sightless from terror. Auriane got a grip on the slatted side of the nearest wagon. Using its jammed back wheel as a step, she hauled herself up to survey the battle scene.

Two wagons had caught fire; Auriane was blinded by gusts of stinging smoke. It cleared to reveal, fifty paces off, a furiously churning mass of men, pressed so tightly together it was impossible to tell attacker from defender. She saw at first only the dully gleaming helmets of legionaries, crushed shoulder to shoulder. Then she discerned an irregular line where warrior met soldier, and the scene sorted itself into two waves of men in dreadful collision.

There they were, startlingly close at hand—long-maned warriors in loose, animal motion, manic and free as the stallion had been, bearing wickerwork shields daubed with red and blue images of Sun and Moon. The Wolf Coats. They were bestial and fearsome with their flapping pelts, swinging hair, naked shoulders, eyes spectral in faces darkened with charcoal and ash. Witgern's battle standard, a wolf's head with gaped jaws, bobbed about just above their roiling midst. They fought like wild dogs—for certain, frenzy mead coursed through their blood. She felt a start of amazement when she saw how far they penetrated into the camp. Their "swine's head" formation had broken up in the charge, and their best fighters had driven a spur into the mass of legionaries, puncturing the Romans' line like a long nail. In back of them, still spilling forth from the forest, were more warriors with blackened faces and flying hair. Through thickening smoke, she discerned a second battle standard hoisted above the chaos, one she knew only by report—the boar emblem of Sigibert.

She wanted to shout a victory song.

A heartbeat later she knew Witgern had made one grave mistake, which he hardly could have foreseen: His spur penetrated the part of the camp where the veterans made a stand. Their lines would hold.

A *tuba,* the long, straight horn that relayed centurions' commands, gave three brassy blasts, and the veterans of the First and the Eighth locked their great, rectangular shields. Their front rank was a moving wall of iron, pressing the native warriors back. On the left flank of these veteran cohorts, the *signifer*'s flag wrote a brisk command in air. And from the center ranks, a sheet of javelins shot forth, thrown almost levelly, with such precision they might have erupted from a single war engine. The heavy javelins tore into the mass of Witgern's men; some penetrated more than one body. It disrupted the onward press of Chattian warriors as if a chasm had opened beneath dozens of them. It caused such horror and distress that some broke and fled. Now Witgern's wounded formed a barrier that cut off the warriors at the front of his charge from those behind. The veteran cohort continued to push them back, a segmented monster protected, front and sides, by its shining carapace of shields.

A stray native spear whipped above Auriane's head, ripping out strands of her hair. She dropped down to save herself, and when she rose up again, for a tantalizingly brief moment she saw him at the forefront of the crush of trapped warriors—Witgern.

She felt a surge of wild sadness. He cut sweeping swaths with a longsword, fighting independently of his men, like some little god who expects to prevail through his own magic; there was no frenzy in his face, only an adamant calm. His men struggled to stay beside him, but they were being irrevocably pushed back. Witgern seemed to be fighting his way toward her—as though he knew where she was, through some inner sight.

She hesitated an instant longer, coughing in sooty smoke, searching for the one person she prayed she wouldn't see—Avenahar.

Fria and all the hosts of lesser gods, let her not be here. . . .

But she discerned no unbearded faces among them. While she felt a relief so encompassing that she nearly forgot where she was, organized activity to the west caught her attention: A hundred cavalrymen had formed into three long ranks on their tall, massively-built horses, their lances precisely aligned. They were colorful as a theater play with their dark scarlet cloaks, brazen helmets, gold-plumed horses, their blue signal flags whipping in the wind.

The camp was collecting its strength. Witgern's line was overstretched. The time for retreat had come—how quickly predator had become prey. The Wolf Coats at the back of the charge had already begun receding like a swift tide. At the forest line, escape was blocked; there, warriors' spears were bunched like upright bristles as the Wolf Coats crowded one another in a panicked retreat.

Now they had no room and no time.

A cavalry trumpet boomed through the dawn. As one, the cavalrymen's mounts broke into a menacing, slow-beat canter. They meant to charge into the side of Witgern's retreat and split it in two. The warriors stranded within the camp would be surrounded and massacred.

I must cover Witgern's retreat. Auriane sprang down from the wagon.

The earthquake she felt when she touched the ground was caused by the hooves of oncoming horses. *The wild horse, the tent ropes.* She bolted in that direction, darting round knots of men, parting dense smoke; five wagons were now afire. She found the wild horse, lying dead. One tent rope was still wound about a tree stump; she disentangled it from a limp hind leg and ran with it, dragging it across the path the cavalrymen must come. Somewhere behind her, she heard a man cry out—"The woman! She's broken loose!"—and she dropped behind an overturned ox cart to conceal herself, then rapidly turned over once, to avoid being crushed beneath a backward-rolling medical orderlies' wagon. Somehow she managed to keep her grip on the tent rope, while mess slaves and grooms hurrying out of the cavalrymen's path vaulted over her. She came to rest against another tree stump.

The clamor of hooves was a rockslide rumbling down a mountain.

An instant before the first rank of tall horsemen rushed by, she pulled hard on the rope and whipped it about the second stump, so it was stretched tight, from stump to stump. Six mounts in the first rank spasmed in midstride. The rope snapped, but the rank's relentless rhythm was broken; broad chestnut and bay hindquarters were pitched skyward. Their riders, too surprised to cry out, were flung over their mounts' bronze-armored necks. The second and third ranks collapsed into each other, causing a tangle of tumbling horses, mailed men, and cavalry shields. It disrupted the horsemen's whole front line, as those abreast of them slowed in confusion, for one of the groaning men trapped beneath his struggling horse was the officer who bore their signal-flag.

Would this give Witgern time to flee off? She sprinted back toward the center of the fighting, flinging herself into the curtains of smoke that veiled much from view, imagining herself a hawk winging through turbulent thunderclouds. She did not know it, but four soldiers had been dispatched in pursuit of her.

Had Witgern had the wit to leave fresh mounts tethered in the wood nearby? If not, the cavalry would hunt his band down like game, until every last man—and woman—was slain.

Avenahar. . . .

She snatched a fleeting, smoke-framed view of the Wolf Coats as they shrank into the forest, fencing with spears, scrambling over the bodies of their own. Witgern's wolf standard trailed the retreat, thrusting itself into the air with jaunty defiance. The long cavalry swords would drop on their necks like scythes, reaping a bloody harvest.

Find a weapon. Help him.

Only then did Auriane allow herself to know all hope of her own rescue was gone. But the fury of the moment left no time for grief.

Her four pursuers lost ground as a crew of ballista-men working to haul a catapult into position blocked their path. While a stubborn drift of smoke obscured her from their view, she stumbled over a fallen legionary soldier, clad only in the coarse woolen tunic they wore beneath their armor and his cold-weather breeches. She knelt beside him and turned him over. There, still in its scabbard, was his short sword; he'd not had time to unsheathe it before the gods bore him off.

A sword of iron. Her hand hesitated but briefly above the forbidden thing; had she not already drunk deeply of the transforming draughts of battle, she might have deliberated longer.

Gently, almost fearfully, she eased the soldier's *gladius* from its scabbard.

The corrugated bone grip fused to her hand like hot glass.

She wondered, once, at the boldness with which she made her own law. To that council within, protesting that women called by the seeresses should not touch iron, she answered only—*This one does.* Why would the gods give her a champion's skill, along with an admonition never to use it? And of what matter was it now, since she was doomed to die, and Sawitha had taken Ramis's place?

The stern weight of the sword in her hand brought a strong temblor of excitement as she got slowly to her feet. She lifted it to the sky so her war god could see it, while muttering a quick prayer to evict the spirit of the dead man from the blade, and infuse it with her family's soul.

She drew it once through air—a controlled, sure cut like the measured step of a dancer—to accustom herself to the balance, the striking distance. Something quiet and thunderous with the strength of horses gathered within her. She knew herself only as some fanged forest mother, poised to protect.

With the sword held low at her side, she slunk alongside the line of wagons, abandoning herself to the dark dance that killed.

She came to a break in the line of wagons. Through it streamed a more disorganized century made up of newer recruits, advancing at a slow trot in ragged files. They were driving Witgern's men ahead of them like cattle.

She fell upon their rear line, a lone predator gone gloriously mad.

It was as though a horse were dropped at full gallop into the midst of a race; she was already in furious motion as she landed among the last rank. A whip-fast lateral strike ripped across three mailed backs. The men she'd struck turned round to face a wheel already spinning, a dancer in frenzy. Before blank astonishment could fade from their faces, her powerful return cut struck a short sword's blade with a penetrating clang, dislodging it from a soldier's grip. The man she'd disarmed had no time to recover from the sight of his sword turning in air before she executed a series of deftly-modulated feints that drove his fellows back, then lashed out at serpent speed with her short sword's point—and he was slowly sinking forward onto his shield.

Dimly she was aware they yelped like dogs. One man thrust a javelin's point at her, but her sword flashed upward seemingly with its own mind—and the blade bit deeply into hard wood, knocking the javelin skyward. With a two-handed hold she tore her sword free, pulling this man off his feet. Then she was battering two blades at once, a frenetic staccato at racing speed—while a third man, emitting a hoarse bellow of rage, charged her from behind, meaning to maim her with the iron boss of his shield. Through the fury of this dance her mind rested somewhere in the sky; she saw all about her as if it were generated by one heart. Shifting forward in time with his movement, she broke the force of the blow as the shield struck. She missed the boss narrowly, lightly rolled off the iron-bound shield while, with animal fluidity, she lashed out with one foot, tripping him. He heaved sideways, pulling two men down with him as she fell seamlessly into the next rank of soldiers.

For long moments, surprise was her ally. No one expected an attack from behind their own lines, and even less, an ambush by a lone woman.

Through speed alone, she wove round herself a net of steel. Five men engaged her now, while dozens more waited their turn, barking encouragement to their fellows or simply gaping in disbelief at this Fury who erupted from the ground, this marvel wreaking baffling amounts of destruction with measured ferocity married to what seemed, astonishingly, displays of school-trained swordfighting skill. The very unlikeliness of it caused more and more in the ranks ahead to whip about and stare. "It's Bellona in possession of a woman," one sputtered out. A very few among them—men who had been in Rome at the time of the fall of Domitian—knew her history; this was that strange creature called Aurinia, who'd managed through sorcery and luck to slay a heavy-armed swordfighter who was Domitian's favorite, on the sands of the Great Amphitheater. These kept a careful distance from her, and strove to pull their fellows out of her path.

The forward movement of the unit was stuttering to a halt.

She had no plan but to fight until she died. She sensed the battle-spirits called the Choosers flocking above her, fierce and invisible, glad of her as they breathed strength into her hand. Memories long tamped down burst into day: *Musk of animals. Sprays of sand. Victory cries from thousands of throats.* Who would be mad enough to miss the arena as a lover? This was like being catapulted into the clouds, rediscovering a lost ability to fly. She'd once been told she owned battle; more right to say, battle owned her.

Gradually, the inevitable caught up with her. The bizarre disruption was drawing the attention of one of the veteran cohorts. Twenty and more abandoned their ranks in the fray ahead and began pouring in her direction at a jog-trot. After much jostling and confusion they formed a tight circle about her, great rectangular shields to the fore.

She had less and less room to maneuver; her sword broke against iron, sending sparks, as she found no more opponents, only shields. "Careful of her, stay aware," one man cautioned his fellows. A shield-boss ground into her back. As she spun round to meet it, a short sword lashed out at her from behind. She knew, and was too fast for it, but the blade caught in her flying hair and she was thrown to the ground with brutal force.

In fast succession a javelin struck the side of her head, a hobnail-booted foot delivered a blow to her spine with such force that a bright numbness flashed down her back. A second foot pinned her wrist to the ground while another man wrested the sword from her grasp.

By now, the four soldiers in pursuit of her had come up with the rest, and were giving an account of the mischief she'd committed with the tent rope. "Finish her," several began to shout. One lifted her beneath her arms, then heaved her into a blood-darkened puddle. As she finally lay still, another man crouched beside her, his manner that of a dumbfounded naturalist examining some unknown beast thrown up from the deep. "She cannot be mortal," this man muttered. "From where comes such mastery?"

Auriane withdrew into last darkness and acceptance, believing that death, this way, was no worse than the death sure to come later—and this, at least, was a useful expenditure of her life, if it divided their forces long enough to allow Witgern time to flee. "Live, Witgern," she whispered in her own tongue as another booted foot slammed into her chest, cracking a rib.

Hard hands sought purchase in her hair, pulling back her head to expose her throat. Of course they would slay her with the sword she stole from them. She had turned one of their own weapons against them; killing her with it would reverse the curse.

She waited for the quick, hot pain across the throat, and oblivion. A blind rabbit-fright gripped her, followed by a wretched twist of sadness at being cast down into gloomy realms where Marcus and her children were not, and finally, gratefulness, for she was seized with a sudden notion that, after death, all that passed would make sense.

"Fall back. Don't harm her." The words were spoken with the weary annoyance of a man accustomed to perfect obedience.

They let her drop like a grain sack. The soft blackness closed over her again; unconsciousness was a warm, comforting bed. Then someone was roughly hauling her to her feet; she clung to an armored shoulder while her knees turned to warm wax. Once, she thought she was in the hall of her father, and a warrior of his companions was politely addressing her at a feast. Then she realized one of their centurions was briskly, courteously, introducing himself to her.

Now she had gone mad, for certain.

She jumped within when he spoke his name—*Firmius Speratus*—though she could not, at first, recall why. Gradually, she discerned a familiar square, sun-weathered face, a narrow nose sharply interrupted, as if once broken. This was the man of many decorations for valor who had watched her from a distance, two days before—the man she believed responsible for her better treatment.

Two legionaries conducted her back to the *reda*, while this Firmius Speratus oversaw them closely; the soldiers would begin molesting her anew if she strayed more than an instant from his sight.

A memory came, then. Marcus had spoken this man's name. Firmius Speratus was the man Marcus rescued from disgrace, then saw promoted, during that inquiry last year, following Witgern's attack on the frontier fort. This was something she could understand, for it was in accord with the ways of her tribe: Marcus was this man's chieftain, his giver of gifts, and this man owed him fealty. And she, in the mind of Speratus, belonged to Marcus Julianus like a belt or a horse. For Marcus's sake, this Speratus would see her treated with decent respect—at least, until such time as a better man than he could dispose of her properly, when the sentence was carried out in that faraway land.

Before she sank once more into unknowing darkness she thought she heard the *barritus* again. She awakened to find herself within the *reda*, leg shackles chafing her ankles. Brico pressed close beside her. Auriane scarce recognized her maidservant. Brico's lips were a bloodless gray; damp hair clung to her glistening, swollen cheeks. Her eyes were as wide and fixed as a madwoman's.

And there was no quiet anywhere. Auriane did not know how much time had passed, but impossibly, she was rocking about in the midst of pitched battle. The clatter of swords falling on shields came crisp and fast as hailstones striking a roof. Shield bosses butted against the carriage's sides. The floor bucked like a horse. Javelins skidded off the top of the carriage. Witgern, or his allies, must have held men in reserve, even though such tactics were not common among her people. Auriane crawled to the back of the carriage. Two of Speratus's men were pushing it from behind, most likely to remove her from the path of danger. A mule gave out a pitiful squeal—she supposed it had caught a spear—and the carriage lurched as the animal kicked at the shafts in its death throes.

The *reda*'s door shuddered; someone struggled to remove the bolt. Brico was panting and clawing at the carriage's walls. All about were yips of pain, hoarsely shouted commands, the hollow shrieks of the *tubae*, and behind it all the deep, doomful booming of the *cornu*, insistent, almost continuous now—the shadow of a dark wing passing over the land. The haunted bellowing of the *cornu* was sure to rouse primitive terror in anyone who had ever met Rome in battle.

Auriane suspected that the *reda* was being employed as a fortification to hold the two forces apart. A Chattian warrior, beard matted with blood, sank against the rear window, dying, his arm linked over the backboard. His long red hair was flung into the carriage like a dirty mop. A short sword hacked downward, finishing him, bloodying Brico's cloak. She erupted into frenzied shrieks, but so overwhelming was the noise of battle, Brico seemed a mute taken off with spasms of madness. Auriane dragged her away from the opening and clamped a hand over the young woman's eyes. Struggling to ease her own terror, Auriane shut her eyes and strove to envision the calming flames of the Ritual of Fire, as Ramis had taught her so long ago.

But she soon gave it up and pulled furiously on her leg irons, cursing them—they were bolted to the *reda*'s floor. She wondered which warbands were taking part; all Witgern's men and all Sigibert's did not equal a band this size. Her numbed mind accepted that at least a quarter, or perhaps even half the men of her tribe fit for battle must have rallied for this rescue. Her people's Great Assembly must have had a part in laying plans for this. Only then did she let herself know how deeply her countrymen desired her return.

And then, just beyond the storm and confusion, Avenahar saw him—the Wolf warrior astride the fine bay stallion. The youth's face was smeared with mud from brow to chin, so that he wore a mask of night. He seemed to be urging his fellows to fall back to safety. Something in his demeanor caused her to feel her soul threw out an echo, and Auriane watched as though transfixed by a writhing flame in a darkened room.

Now he struggled to drag a wounded companion across the withers of his skittish stallion, a sturdy beauty that surely was cavalry-bred. Auriane looked more closely and felt a prickling on the skin. *Not a youth. A maid.*

Once the Wolf maid had gotten her injured companion securely positioned, she laid a length of rein across the horse's haunches, and the burdened stallion rocked forward, its stifled canter impeded by the crush of bodies, bringing its skin-clad riders within fifteen paces of the prison cart.

Gods below, no—let it not be.

But it was.

Auriane felt she'd been struck senseless by a fire bolt.

"Avenahar, no. Get out of here!" she cried out with such violence her lungs ached, even while knowing she couldn't compete with the clamor and distance. She pulled so hard at the leg shackles that she scored the flesh of her ankles. *Witgern, how can you have dragged my child into this slaughterhouse?*

"Avenahar! I am here." But her words were flung into the roar and lost. In a brutally brief instant she greedily took in every curve of that well-loved face she'd held to her breast, that stubborn chin, that proud and gracefully rounded brow. She wrapped herself tightly about Avenahar with a look, stretching out her hands in an embrace that could not be filled. She felt a bittersweet twist of the heart at the sight of Avenahar, so grown beyond what she had been, so at ease taking her place in a world that gave no quarter. *My babe is launched into the world-sea, with no need of me.*

"Avenahar!"

But it was as if they inhabited realms that, though tantalizingly close, could not touch. She might as well have observed her daughter's image in a bronze mirror—mute, small, but alive in another world. How thin she was—she'd never been that thin. *If only I could have her in my care, to nurse to health again.*

Avenahar . . . do you forgive me?

As Avenahar lurched forward in the saddle to keep her wounded companion from falling, Auriane saw something catch fire and go dim at her daughter's shoulder. A fibula with the low luster of purest gold secured Avenahar's loose wolfskin cloak.

She's wearing the brooch Decius gave her. Does she even know where she got it? I never had a chance to tell her.

"Get to safety! Get out of here," Auriane shrieked as Avenahar reined the half-bolting stallion behind a row of wagons, and she was lost again, a ghost in a dream.

My poor babe . . . we'll not be together again in this life.

She lay still against the backboard, her hand extended toward her vanished daughter. Some cruelly effective missile ploughed a furrow through the mass of native warriors, tearing a bloody avenue through densely-packed bodies. Auriane recognized it as the bolt of the war-engine called the scorpion.

The Wolf Coats bunched about the carriage reversed direction with the unanimity of a flock of birds, though with less grace. In the space they opened, Auriane saw a warrior of her people, taller by a head than his fellows, ramming his way through close-packed bodies, moving crossways against the human tide, forcing a path to the *reda*'s rear window. His naked chest was broad as a shield. This giant had no weapon in his hands, but that face was grotesque as the demon-masks of Charon she'd seen in Rome, worn by the men who dragged the dead from the arena—perhaps he depended upon frightening the enemy to death. He had a strangely pacific expression, as though he dreamed. Clamped beneath one heavy arm was a long linen-wrapped bundle, swaddled like a babe and bound with hemp rope; he held it upright, to ease his passage.

The fearful giant filled the narrow opening at the back of the *reda*. With one ring-girded arm he hauled the dead man away from the backboard. Then he began pushing his swaddled burden lengthways through the aperture, while gesturing sharply to Auriane, demanding her help.

Moving as if in a sleep-trance, Auriane joined in conspiracy with him, pulling on the cumbersome burden as he pushed. Once, she met his pale, slate-hued eyes; in them was the ecstasy mingled with the unreachable calm of the man who is ready to journey to the Sky Hall. Too wretched with grief to be curious as to the nature of the man's gift, she dragged the mysterious bundle across the floor, unlatched the cedar trunk, then pushed it within to conceal it. She looked back at the warrior, once. He held her gaze an instant longer, as if striving to take with him the image of her face, while quickly tracing in air the bird-foot shape of *algiz*, the rune of protection. Then he heaved himself away from the back of the carriage. A moment later, the gift-bearing giant stopped in place and began to sink slowly down, his eyes blank as a tablet on which nothing has yet been written. She never saw the weapon that struck him.

With horror's cup overfull, Auriane hid her face in her hands and sank to the floor of the carriage.

Avenahar. What great grace to know you're living. But for how long?
And do you despise me still?

Chapter 30

Auriane awakened to find the battle done, and a doleful quiet hanging all about. She heard forest sounds again—the dry rustling of interlaced branches wrestling in wind-rivers above, the Moenus's brisk song, the taunts of the ravens as they dropped from the sky to feast. When she moved to peer out, her head throbbed viciously. Debris was flung over the ground as if on a windstorm. The dead were strewn everywhere—mules, horses, men.

Avenahar, you were no mind-spectre—my most fevered imaginings wouldn't have conjured Decius's gift on your cloak. With great dread, Auriane examined the near-naked, blood-mottled bodies that lay near her carriage. Only her countrymen were left untended; the Roman dead had been respectfully collected up. Many of her tribesmen lay atop each other, and huge crows had taken possession, but gradually Auriane assured herself Avenahar was not among those lying within her sight. A measure of life-warmth started to flow through her again, but she didn't rejoice; her daughter might have been cut down somewhere in the wood.

At a small distance off in the forest, soldiers labored without helmets or shields, hacking at underbrush, dragging wood for pyres. The camp's wounded, legionaries and slaves, lay on the ground in neat rows, groaning softly beneath their blankets; their numbers had proved too great for the hospital tent. The rank tang of unwashed bodies mingled with the astringent smell of the terebinth resin the camp's *medicus* had employed to purify wounds.

The doomed warrior with the linen-wrapped bundle—had he been some battle apparition?

Auriane dared not unlatch the cedar chest, for fear of drawing the attention of the four grim-visaged cavalrymen posted by the back of the *reda*. A man had died to give that to her, whatever it was—surely his ghost watched her, to make certain she kept it safe. She imagined a netherworld light softly emanating from the trunk, by which she could warm herself against the bitter cold. Brico still lay curled against it, sleeping soundly. Auriane pulled a coverlet over her, not wanting to disturb her, knowing Brico desperately needed the brief succor brought by sleep.

When Brico finally sat up, wan and shivering, she nodded her head in solemn assent when Auriane asked her if she, too, had seen the warrior with the gift.

Auriane was left in shackles now, and she assumed they would keep her so. They'd even removed her wheelform brooch—evidently they didn't trust her in possession of anything sharp. Her unsecured woolen cloak kept slipping from one shoulder, and Brico would dutifully pull it back up.

At midday the *medicus* came, sent, doubtless, on Firmius Speratus's order—an impatient young Greek with a neatly trimmed black beard and the prideful manners of a cat. He examined Auriane with the brisk, competent indifference he might have shown an injured mule. With delicate distaste, he removed the dirty bandage Brico had applied to Auriane's head wound. After determining that her broken rib had not punctured a lung, he pressed a sponge soaked in vinegar and centaury wine to the abrasions at her temple. Then he gave to both women cups of warm red wine fortified with henbane and juice of the poppy. This worked so well to quell Brico's nervous affliction that afterward, Auriane sent her from the *reda* to offer aid where it might be needed—and learn what she could of Avenahar and Witgern.

While Auriane was alone she listened to the soldiers' mutterings as they worked near her in full armor, systematically stripping the bodies of her tribesmen of anything that might be of value—necklets of amber, fur cloaks, inlaid belts, bone daggers. They tormented her by saying nothing of the fates of Witgern's men; they spoke only of the treachery of Sigibert, whom all thought loyal to Rome, and of the deviousness inherent in the barbarian mind.

Brico returned after many hours, her cheeks smoldering with rouge, her ivory hairpin lost, her tumbled-down hair rumpled as a bed after a night's carouse, and—Auriane squinted—was her tunica on inside out?

"From the look of you, you spent your time in a tent," Auriane said as Brico bounded into the carriage with the durable buoyancy of youth. "You look like a happy stray cat! Who gave you the rouge?"

"Scylla, one of the camp girls. She's the only one who's kind."

"It's a fool's risk, Brico."

"What else was I to do? It was all they wanted of me. No babe will come of my wanderings; no one's wilier with the herbs than I am."

"That's not all you must worry over. Who was he?"

"A loose-lipped Adonis called Mago, of the Eighth Augusta."

How worldly the child's become, just since the march began. "Leave the men of the ranks alone—especially the Eighth; all say they couple with goats. Only the officers."

"Only the officers."

"You've learned something, your eyes are full of it."

"Yes. But nothing of Avenahar." Brico dropped her voice as she settled herself into the carriage. "Which is good. Sirona be thanked, it seems nobody even saw her."

"And no one found . . . the body of a maid, among all the dead?"

"I think they would have spoken of it. And Witgern got free. He lost . . . my man said they counted seventy-six—or did he say sixty-seven?—I mix up numbers. But you know how they exaggerate, to burnish their glory."

Auriane winced, and turned away. "Every blow my people ever struck, we've paid much more dearly than they."

"They despise Witgern even more now, because he was so very clever," Brico went on. "When the cavalry chased him into the woods, his men beat their spears against their shields to terrify the horses. Back in the forest he'd had a trench dug—he'd planted upright spears in it, and had the trench covered over with brushwood. Cavalrymen fell in and several died that way. Everyone in camp's in a stew of wrath about it."

"That doesn't sound like Witgern," Auriane said, more to herself. *It sounds . . . gods below, it sounds like Decius. I could almost believe Decius was at Witgern's side, doling out battle counsel. . . .*

Suddenly she considered anew the wild horse that had disrupted the camp. *That stratagem, for certain, bears the print of Decius's hand.* When she'd known the Decius of old, he'd even proposed such a thing once, as they'd laid plans for a raid on a Roman camp.

Decius is aligned with Witgern—I'd lay down my life it's so.

Perhaps, Avenahar, you did *know whose golden fibula you wore.*

Trapped in the eddies of these thoughts, Auriane was only half aware that Brico was speaking on.

"And all in camp fear they'll be pushed too hard on the march, to make up for the lost time. But Witgern is safe. Avenahar lives. You have done it." With a jester's smile she grasped Auriane's shoulders. "You rescued your rescuers."

Then her mobile face sobered with the quickness of a mime, and she sank back against the side of the *reda*. "But who, now, is going to rescue *you?*"

"No one, it seems," Auriane said wearily, looking off toward the forest. *And no more deliverers will come.* She remembered Gunora's dream. What were the elderwoman's words?—*"I saw nine fires. For this year, there was no fire. On this year, you either die, or return to us." It's no great feat now to guess which.*

Avenahar . . . carry on for me. Drive the Cheruscans off our land. Arria, know my ghost watches over you, always.

She felt herself an empty vessel filling up rapidly with all the needless griefs of the world. She'd taken a short crawl through a span that began and ended in mud and blood, its flashes of light in between so fleeting, she found it impossible to believe the gods counted their human children of greater nobility than flies buzzing about a midden. *My gods don't want me—that was proved when that great-hearted rescue try failed. Even Ramis would drive me off now—I polluted myself with death-dealing iron. Marcus's people* do *want me, but only to kill me. I thought I could satisfy all sides. I end satisfying none.*

Marcus, then, seemed the only balm; he had that deft ability to see sense where she saw only senselessness. His voice shielded her from the mist-ridden void. She mourned for his nurturant silences. Her life at the villa had shrunk off until it was distant, mythic as the Sky Hall.

"I suppose it was not to be," Auriane said while collecting up Brico's padded hand, struggling to hold fast to a blurred mind-picture of a mud-smeared Avenahar, and all the strength and promise in that face.

THROUGHOUT THE AFTERNOON, arrangements were made for the dead. The bodies of the men of rank were readied to be sent back to their home forts, so they could be given burials appropriate to their station. For the common soldiers, pyres were built by the bank of the river. At dusk, Auriane watched as a line of torches wended its way through the camp, and knew some sort of collective funeral procession was in progress. The sweetly exotic tang of incense wafted toward her. Thin strands of flute-song twined about one another in a wan lament, lost on the wind, then found again. By nightfall five pyres blazed, a frightful sight; the heat was as though Mother Sun had drifted too close to earth.

That night a double guard was set about the carriage. Auriane and Brico were brought spelt and fennel porridge, and the ever-present hard-meal biscuits. The men were given a generous ration of wine, and soon, she and Brico began to hear drunken voices chanting, "Punish the woman"—growing ever more bold. A half dozen of them ringed round their carriage, brandishing torches. One hurled a stone that rocked the *reda* as it struck.

After a harrowing length of time Auriane heard the voice of Firmius Speratus rising over the soldiers' chant, taking the men to task. This was a prisoner on her way to be tried in a higher court than theirs, she heard him admonishing them. How dare they usurp the Emperor's divine role as judge? They challenged the authority of the man to whom they'd sworn a sacred oath, and they should be ashamed. Any man who did her harm would be subject to that punishment in which a man was struck with cudgels by members of his own century. The naming of this brutal punishment sobered them.

Auriane and Brico listened in grateful amazement.

Auriane waited until the night was half spent before she dared open the cedar chest. Most of the camp slept fitfully—each tent housed at least one man who wailed with nightmares. But near dawn, all became so quiet she could hear the cavalry horses' hooves suctioning in wet ground as their sentries made rounds about the encampment. Of her own guards, one stared at the pyres as if in a trance, while two were intent on a dice game, heads together as they mumbled like lovers.

Auriane thought she'd made no sound as she unlatched the cedar chest, but Brico snapped awake like a startled squirrel, watching her with eyes that were limpid and shining.

Together, they lifted the bundle out. Brico helped her unwind the long strip of linen.

Bright blood sprang to Brico's finger as she nicked it on a steel blade.

"What is this?" Auriane whispered, though already, she knew.

It was the sword that had once been her own. And before that, her father, Baldemar's—with it, he had kept Rome at bay for a generation.

She lifted it out, still half bound in linen. Snakes of light wriggled up and down the length of a long, pattern-welded blade, so that it seemed to ripple with life. Dark-bright gemstones inset about the pommel and hilt glinted like falcons' eyes. The sword of Baldemar had been forged over a hundred years ago by a smith some tribes now honored as a god. She closed her hand round the grip, and its familiar weight brought an upsurge of tumultuous memories—of days of home and freedom, of months spent starving in a war camp, ending in fire. It was of no use to remind herself this sword opened the door to all she turned from: the separation of the world into things holy and unholy. Blind bondage to the age-old, unending oaths of vengeance—and all those passions so loathed as ignorant and unknowing, by Ramis.

Finally, she felt simple comfort, for her father's spirit was in the blade. She wouldn't be alone, in death.

"I never expected to see this again, in this life," Auriane whispered. "What's their purpose, Brico? The man who gave it to me—he must have seen the rescue was failing. I can't protect it from these men who hold me. The guards will find it—if not in the next days, then, surely, after my death. Witgern went to great trouble to rescue it from that fort—and now, all he's done is ensure it falls back into Roman hands again."

"Perhaps," Brico offered, "they thought you might work a spell with it and save yourself? Your folk must think there's powerful magic in reuniting you with it." She looked at Auriane, her eyes ardent. "They are not mad. They must have had a purpose."

"How trusting Witgern is of the goodness of the gods."

"Maybe it's the work of your father's ghost. I know many true stories of ghosts meddling in human affairs."

Auriane saw that two gemstones had been prised from the pommel, doubtless lost to grasping hands somewhere along the way to a Roman auction block. The empty sockets made her think of a man with his eyes gouged out. Baldemar's sightless eyes.

I am your living eyes, she spoke in silence to her long-dead father. *Your mind rests in mine. You have a last task for me. You want me to take this up, don't you? And rid your home of the Cheruscan marauders. But I'm a bound captive. I suppose ghosts don't consider that a thing might be simply impossible.*

Auriane wound the linen round the blade and returned it to the chest, concealing it beneath the neatly folded garments and clay jars of unguents before she closed the chest and latched it again.

"Brico, we've got to get rid of this before we've travelled too far from my lands."

"How can you! It's family treasure."

"I have it—at the river crossing that's coming up, you must toss it in. Rivers are full of spirits. Maybe it will find its way back to my father that way."

Brico slowly shook her head. "It's fearsome, I won't touch it. Please don't make me—"

"What's all this noise?" A man's voice cut in, rough as a saw blade.

One of their cavalry guards pressed his face to the opening at the back of the *reda*. Wine-soured breath quickly filled the enclosed place.

His gaze flashed to the cedar chest.

"What is in that trunk?"

Auriane cursed silently. Brico had been staring at it as if it were a snake—a sure way to draw someone's attention to it.

"*What's in the trunk?*" he repeated, rapping the boss of his shield against the backboard for emphasis. "Open it."

"Of course . . ." Auriane managed when she'd half mastered her fright. Obediently she crawled toward the trunk, and started fumbling, slowly, with the latch. Then she paused, and turned to meet his gaze. "But I must warn you, you're intruding upon women's matters."

He eased back with faint distaste.

"She's at her moon time," Auriane continued, nodding toward Brico, "and we put the rags in here so they wouldn't be left about before the slaves could take them away. I'll show you, if you wish—"

He grunted with displeasure and made a dismissive gesture.

"Just keep silent in there."

He moved off. Auriane dropped into dreamless sleep, pressed tightly against Brico to ward off the fierce cold.

ON THE THIRD day following the attack, the camp had recovered sufficiently, and the march began anew. A freezing, miserable rain came, which did little to dampen the ire of the men who still watched Auriane with barely-bridled rage. Brico learned one man of the Batavian cavalry was ready to pay whatever bribe was necessary for the privilege of witnessing her execution. It seemed a cavalryman Auriane had injured during the battle had died of wounds, and this man was his brother. Auriane understood this, and did not blame him.

They still followed the course of the Moenus, approaching ever closer to the place where the river arched away from her people's lands—within a day, they would cross over the Moenus, and her own country would be behind her forever.

At the noon halt, when Speratus came to determine if she was well, Auriane seized the chance to ask him what he knew of Marcus Julianus. If Speratus had had no official reports, perhaps he'd heard speculation or idle talk?

He said he'd heard nothing beyond that Julianus was, for certain, among Trajan's esteemed high council when the imperial forces left their Dacian base camp and crossed the Danuvius. The absence of news was to be expected—the war had begun. No tales coming from that rough country could be counted reliable. He himself had heard contradictory accounts: One claimed that Rome steadily overwhelmed the Dacian strongholds; Trajan's advance was so slow and thorough, the legions had halted to plant crops, to be reaped in early summer. Another held that the barbarous Dacian capitol in the mountains had fallen already, and winged dragons had flown from its dungeons. Soon, the muddy water would settle.

When she asked him of Witgern's fate, Speratus's manner became guarded. He would say only that a punitive expedition was to be carried out against the Chattians. This, she expected. When a board comes loose, one hammers it down. Among the settlements to be burned would be the little village of Witgern's birth.

But very soon after she put these questions to Speratus, news of Marcus Julianus did come.

She had only to wait a day. And when it came, it was given not just to her, but to the whole of the world. Marcus Julianus had become one of the heroes and mysteries of the Dacian war.

As THE SUN sank and the moon's pale orb appeared in a still-bright sky, two riders from the Imperial Post clattered noisily into camp. They'd been dispatched from the Dacian war; Trajan's military advisers sought to determine the speed of this company's progress. Immediately afterward, the camp was alive with fresh, and more accurate, tales of the war.

As cookfires illumined the dusk, two soldiers strode past Auriane's *reda*, debating whether "the noble Julianus could possibly have escaped." She fought to quell her alarm, thinking they could well be speaking of someone else—the name was not uncommon. Shortly afterward she heard his name again among fragments of talk, as another man declared, "What a magnificent end for a man such as Marcus Arrius Julianus was!"

She felt it as a well-placed punch to the stomach.

Her mind began a slow spiral down a fathomless well.

Battling off numbing anguish, she sent Brico out to learn more. But this
time the maidservant got into a scuffle with two of the camp followers—the
painted women had grown to resent the fact that Brico was peddling her
wares for free in territory they'd staked out as their own. When Brico returned bruised and soaking wet from a brawl that played out its end in a watering trough, she'd little more to add except for the assurance that the men
were indeed speaking of Auriane's own Julianus. Auriane spent the night
huddled on the floor of the carriage, feeling herself a brittle, dried, dead
thing sucked empty by a spider; and sleep, when it came, pitched her into
lurching nightmares.

On the following morn Auriane was unshackled. Two of Firmius Speratus's bodyguards escorted her down the wide avenue of the camp. She
moved through a gauntlet of hard stares as men paused in their morning
tasks to watch her with expressions ranging from curiosity to distaste. She
felt a burn of shame, knowing she must present a frightful sight with her
thin hands clutching at her unpinned cloak, the bloodied linen bandage
swaddling one arm, her hair so soiled it was several shades darker than it
truly was. She was naked before them—her throat bare of adornment, her
hands empty of even so much as a weapon of honor. *They could sculpt me to
personify my people's defeat—I've seen such miserable stone images, set above their
fortress gates.*

Speratus awaited her in his tent, seated on a camp bench. An errant vein
of kindness showed in those flinty eyes; he seemed a man in a battle against
his inclinations to gentleness. The greater-than-usual stubble on his chin was
turning to gray; she noted this at the same time she remembered his people
left off shaving when in mourning. *Mourning for Marcus Julianus, no doubt.*
But the sorrow in his face was sober and correct in the way of the professional mourner who walks in a funeral procession, rather than one who truly,
helplessly grieves.

His manner filled her with dread.

As she settled herself opposite him, he wordlessly offered her a battered
tin cup of unwatered wine. Oddly, she found his respectful treatment warming, though she knew it was inspired by no more than the man's sense of
duty toward Julianus.

"It is not good news," Speratus began. A light rain began to fall, its drumming amplified against the tightly stretched goathide of the tent. "Marcus Julianus was a great and good man, such as our country doesn't produce anymore, and now, I think him only the more so—"

"*Was* a great man?" She spilled some of the wine.

"In absolute truth, no one knows his exact fate. But from what I tell you, I fear you'll see . . . he cannot be living. Are you ready to hear it all?"

Her stomach gave a hard twist, but she forced out the words, "Yes. Spare me nothing."

He was momentarily silent, gathering strength to tell the tale.

"Julianus bravely volunteered to lead a final party of negotiation, right into the Dacian king's stronghold. It was believed by Trajan's counselors there was a fair chance the Dacian king might yield up his stronghold, and himself, without a single *ballista* ball thrown. So the Dacian king had little trouble getting Trajan to agree to this. It proved, however, but a treacherous ploy on old King Decabalus's part, to keep his wretched life and his gold."

Thunder sounded, faraway—a war in the sky, at a comfortable distance—*as that war is, to me,* she thought.

"Julianus's party of twenty set out through the gorges, believing they had an envoy's immunity. How bold he was, to go at all—that stronghold's in dismal mountain country where on nights of the full moon a plague of the dead rise up to prey on wayfarers. It sits high atop an outcropping of rock. There's a cloud of buzzards above it that never moves off. The gateway's decorated with captives' heads, and solid gold images of ravening monsters. You must be as proud of him as you can be—I'd sooner turn up at dinnertime at the stinking lair of Polyphemus."

Cannot he come more quickly to the end? But she didn't hurry him, for she was gratefully devouring every scrap.

"As Julianus's party arrived, the double-dealing rogues seized him and put him under guard. King Decabalus, you see, had heard that Julianus saved the Emperor's life last winter, for the tale's become famous—"

"*Saved the Emperor's life?* I did not know it," Auriane whispered. *Marcus, you've lived another lifetime in that country, of which I know nothing.*

"He did, indeed. A Dacian envoy somehow got aconite into our Lord's wine. The whole world is indebted to Julianus's quick thinking. And so, Decebalus thinks, What would a just and good ruler like Trajan *not* do, for the man who preserved his life? So the Dacian king believes he's got the golden fleece.

He sends one of our men back to Trajan with demands: He, Decabalus, is to be allowed to keep his own life, in exile. And he's to keep his wealth—that fabled hoard of gold he buried somewhere beneath a river. The king has twenty guards watching Marcus Julianus night and day, because the sly dog remembers how the last high-ranking Roman hostage managed to outfox him by taking poison."

Auriane put down the cup; her hand shivered too much to hold it. She felt she had no more substance than wind. She was frantic to hurry him on but bit back her words, suspecting that if she didn't hear the full tale now, from him, she might never hear it.

"This comes from the mouth of our only envoy who escaped alive," Speratus continued. "Julianus was kept in a filthy yard with pigs and the half-eaten bodies of prisoners who'd been left there to starve and rot. It had a low wall, to keep the beasts from tumbling down a sheer drop into a glen below. The guards were set at intervals along the wall.

"Julianus determined on the noblest course—ending his life, and sparing Trajan the cruel dilemma of having to decide whether to give in to the king's demands. He had no access to poison. So he waited for the first moonless night. He surprised a guard, and started bravely grappling with him—"

Auriane could not suppress a small cry.

"—and got the guard's *falx* into his hands, and made to turn it upon himself. There was a great and grim struggle that went on for long, and—"

Auriane shot restively to her feet, every muscle taut, feeling herself a being of air and fire, ready to hurl herself into battle to defend him. She edged toward the entryway to the tent, right hand clenched about the grip of an imagined sword as she looked out at the sea of forest rolling on forever to the east—to that place of dragons.

"You said you wanted to hear the whole tale," he said from behind her.

She returned to her place. "Forgive me. Go on."

"Good, then. I want someone who was dear to him to know what became of him.

"A clamor was raised throughout the barbarian compound," he continued. "King Decabalus himself flew there in a fury and promised to see them all flayed alive if Julianus was allowed to harm himself. Julianus took wound after wound; he fought like Hercules to get his hand upon that weapon again. But his jailers overwhelmed him, and stayed his hand. In the end, it was impossible to say whether Julianus leapt from the wall, or was pushed. But he fell. That is how he died. He perished in the forest below."

"What was the name of this witness?" Auriane closely examined Speratus's face, her voice tightly controlled. "How high was this place?" She knew she begged for more than he had to give. *"Might he have lived?"*

"I was not told these things, I am sorry. But it was a long drop. It's enemy country. And he'd lost much life-blood already. The only Roman witness said he died. And mark that King Decabalus himself evidently believed it—for directly afterward, Decabalus withdrew his ransom demands and fled for his life.

"Be grateful it was a hero's death," Speratus added, as a faint rumble of oratorical fullness started to creep into his tone, "well worthy of such a man. Can you call up a more fitting exit, after that lifetime of bold deeds? He outwitted one last tyrant. Marcus Julianus will be honored through all time."

Auriane said finally, while slowly shaking her head, "It's not a credible tale." In fact, it seemed not so much false as oversmooth—a public story whittled into overrefinement through repetition, its relation to truth like that of the portrait bust that renders its subject as a tranquil Apollo, to its living subject who sweats and fears. Would Marcus have been so quick to leave this life? Confronted with two evil alternatives, wouldn't he have sought out a third? "He lives," Auriane said with soft force. "I'll not hear you say otherwise."

Speratus said nothing. She glimpsed herself reflected in his eyes, and knew he thought her protest no more than the madness of grieving.

The rain drummed more urgently.

"I am sorry," Speratus offered again, turning up his palms as if to say, *I have no more to give.*

As she rose to leave, the thought that she would not see Marcus again in this world struck her a blow so jarring, so disorienting, that everyday life dropped off, shed like the flesh at death—and the veil that obscures future days dropped away.

And she saw the morrow, clear and sudden as the images of a wall painting in a darkened room, at the moment a torch is brought in. But that torch was whisked away before she had time to make full sense of what she saw.

Some unknown catastrophe comes.

"What is wrong?" Speratus said, watching her with great unease. Auriane was bent over like someone peering down a well. Her gray eyes seemed able to pierce stone. "Are you ill?"

"Something grievous comes to us. And very soon." She squinted, as if to better see. "As soon as . . . tomorrow."

"What are you saying?" A covert look crept over Speratus's face. He watched her with acute interest, for he believed that the single genius of her primitive countrymen lived in their women when they spoke in oracular voice. He dropped his voice, not wanting the man at guard to hear. "You've got spirits in you, don't you? You've an augur's powers—only yours are true. Tell me, is what comes of nature, or of man?"

"Of nature," Auriane whispered, "*and* of man. It is both."

He continued to stare at her, trapped in the hallowed silence while the rain sealed them in, their positions reversed now, as he was the one begging more than she had to give. She wrestled off the oddness of it first, and resumed her manner of polite distance. "I'm sorry. I can't see more."

The centurion rose to his feet, bringing their audience to a close; not quite knowing what else to say, he repeated, "Marcus Arrius Julianus was a great man. Be content with that."

Unexpectedly, those mild and meaningless words brought her to fury.

"Content? *Never.* Julianus believed that war was a stupid folly of overreaching, no more than organized rapine and murder, to seize a country so distant it can't possibly be held. If he has died, it was for a cause not his own, and it was a foul and miserable and meaningless death—"

"What impiety, how can you—"

".—as is *mine*—condemned to death for doing what any honorable woman of my people would have done. You praise him for love of country and kill me for the same. There is *no* meaning in all this. He died wretchedly. Do not tell me to go content."

"Grief has taken your mind. I'll not listen to such viciousness."

After a short, tortured silence, she turned away. "I sound ungrateful," she said in a voice gone flat. "And I shouldn't. You've been honorable and kind."

Auriane had little memory of being taken back through the camp.

Afterward she told and retold the tale of Marcus's death, sometimes to Brico, while stopping frequently to ask the girl what she thought, and sometimes in the silence of her mind. She was like some Alexandrian physician cutting into the body of a suspected poison victim to learn the truth of the crime, closely examining the color and shape of every part of the story Speratus had told her.

At midnight, she shook Brico awake and whispered, "He is alive. Why would he seize a *falx* to take his life, if the drop from this place was great enough to ensure death? Wouldn't leaping from the battlement have been easier than attacking a strong force of guards?"

As understanding slowly came into Brico's sleep-fogged face, so did helpless sadness.

"I suppose, but—"

"He must have judged that the fall might not have guaranteed death."

"I . . . I suppose that could be so." Brico, fully awake now, said no more, deciding it would be a cruelty to remind Auriane that the Dacian king himself had believed in Julianus's death.

"Brico, I *saw* something, on the eve Marcus and I parted for the last time. A sea of grass. Multitudes of men on horseback, men who roam the plains and do not farm. A tribe of riders. He is with them."

Brico's eyes glistened with tears and she turned away.

Auriane lay sleepless through the rest of the night, stunned beyond weeping. *We are two wings of a heron. If you were gone, Marcus, I would know.* She would have felt his death as a faint break of tension on invisible threads, as the Fates severed them. It would have been announced to her in the marked silences of the forest. She would have *seen* his absence from the world, as a sad interruption in the strings of stars across the night sky—one would have vanished, leaving a chill void.

When sleep finally overcame her near dawn, she dreamed of Ramis.

The seeress was serenely young, with gilded chestnut hair, a brow smooth as an alabaster vase. She wore a crown of marine blue flowers. Before her was a shallow bronze bowl in which hovered a still dagger of flame. Auriane smelled a rich incense that brought to mind honey and plums. A crawling in her stomach suggested that this vision might be the work of more than one dreaming mind. Ramis's spirit had never known distance, and Auriane felt it flooding with proprietary strength round her own.

Lady. Does Marcus live?

Ramis's frown was that of a schoolmaster enduring a pupil who isn't trying hard enough. *The living are water; the dead, snow. One is the companion of earth. The other eddies through air, leaving no tracks—and will become water again.* There was a serene silence, and then: *I cannot see him, Auriane. You're being asked to live as if he's gone.*

Black wings closed about Auriane. *Cannot you toss me a scrap of hope?*

You do not need hope, came voiceless words. *You do not even need me. You must learn, now, the power that lives in consenting to dissolution. Of letting yourself be pulled apart and reformed, over and over, like wind-borne clouds. Stop struggling against what's befallen Marcus. Or your children. Or yourself. Honor it all as if it were Fria herself.*

And it will bring a brilliance beyond the Sun.

Another silence. Then: *Auriane. You have no more time.*

The austere face, the aquamarine mantle, were smoothly swallowed back into dream-blackness. Auriane felt her body contract in a soundless shout—*Don't leave me.*

She awakened to a pulsing headache—and to Brico, bent over her worriedly.

"Mistress," Brico said plaintively. "We're moving. The river crossing, it's close."

The unsettling shadow of the dream roved along the edges of Auriane's consciousness, demanding to be remembered. She put a hand to her temple, feeling for the hotness of fever. Unease began a slow spider-crawl up her spine. For she *was* remembering, now—while struggling hard not to. Ramis's words throbbed through her like a potent headache, or some poison that her blood struggled to expel.

Embrace what's befallen us? What vicious counsel—it's villainous to ask such a thing. And what's the sense of telling a woman on her way to execution, You have no more time?

"Mistress," Brico tried again, her wide-open eyes like the water-filled bowls in which a sybil scries the future. "The river's high and and it's seething, and I heard someone say that a boatman drowned in it this morning. I'm . . . It's foolish, I know, but I'm frightened."

Brico's gaze strayed to the trunk. "I won't throw that thing in, you must not command me to do it."

Auriane sat up, finally shaking off the shackles of the dream. "Brico, Brico," she said with gentleness, pulling the young woman into a bleak embrace that knew no distinction between mistress and handmaid; they were two far-wanderers huddled together for solace. "Calm yourself. It doesn't matter. That sword will come to rest wherever it's meant to be. All will be well."

With one arm still draped about Brico, Auriane leaned forward to look through the aperture, but made no sense of the world outside as the row of ox carts alongside their carriage creaked pitiably, complaining of being forced into motion. She saw only Marcus, torn and bleeding in a cold, unknown forest. Arria, terrified beyond endurance from a thing the gods shouldn't allow. And Avenahar, lost to the killing life. And finally, her own horror at being the cause of it all.

Auriane had no room in her, just then, to remember the unknown catastrophe, "*. . . of nature, and of man,*" that she had foreseen for this day.

Chapter 31

The river roared softly. The wind was its coconspirator, gusting with warning fury. The sky was a cruel blue, and vast above the men in arms formed up before a trestle bridge. A thin thread of men marching six abreast separated from their formation and moved with patient slowness across the river. The *reda* that bore Auriane and Brico was stalled behind the ranks and files waiting their turn to cross. From this vantage, Auriane could see grassy earth arching down to a shining belt of black flecked with white. Normally this river was better behaved, but spring rains had swollen and maddened it, and it bucked and kicked, thwarted by its bed. It was a living stream fed through aeons with new souls straining for release, a spirit-flow teeming with ghosts strongly seeking the north. The froth-filled air above the waters sparked with rage. The bridge's five stone piers, brutish, permanent, were like evenly spaced teeth through which the black water flowed—or the high columns of some temple to the sprites. A more careful look revealed the piers delicately mottled with moss, which had been climbing the stone since the reign of Domitian, when men of the legions had built this bridge. *The piers are bone, the trestles, flesh,* she thought. The fine geometry of arches stretched delicately from bank to bank seemed some naive intrusion, no match for the river's young, muscular flow.

Four centurions had fallen out of the march, blood-colored cloaks rippling like pennants as they flanked the bridge's approach so they could observe the crossing. A unit of regular cavalry proceeded across at a slow trot. The bridge's roadway was floored with planks covered over with turf; the pounding of hooves raised a fine, stone-colored dust, which drifted to the horses' bellies.

Auriane felt a sharp unease she knew was shared by many of the men, and wondered why the army's priests did not offer a propitiatory sacrifice to the waters. Perhaps they knew nothing of the treacherous spirits that lived in northern rivers.

The sun glided deeper into the western sky. A century of the Eighth was crossing now, heads bare, helmets strapped to their right shoulders as they trudged over the bridge with the same indifference as the slaves and mules; the effulgence of glory soldiers envisioned about themselves when they passed a village was not in their minds now. Here, the world was not watching; they were men at labor, eager to strike camp before weariness overtook them. Sun glow softly ignited the far, fir-clad hills, so that the earth seemed to emit gauzy light from within, and Auriane felt the land spirits spoke her a final farewell. The Moenus's course switched back in this place, rushing northward into the heart of her lands, and had her soul not already begun its downward drift to Hel's realms, that road home would have looked fiercely inviting.

A *signifer* by the bridge's approach signed to a unit of Ubian auxiliaries to begin the crossing—two hundred and forty young recruits from Germania.

But their decurion dropped from his horse and soon after, every man of this unit dismounted with him. To a man, the tall Ubians set their shields before them, bent one knee to the ground, and remained solemnly still. *We will not move.* The brisk wind gracefully unfurled their heavy cloaks as they ignored, in turn, the threats of the two highest-ranking centurions, the calm pleading of Firmius Speratus.

Auriane knew their minds. The ways of the Ubians were not unlike those of her people—and they did know the ways of northern rivers. A recently made oath to a distant Emperor was easily forgotten before this show of enmity by spirits so much older than man.

The centurions and the praefect of the march met in an emergency council, to debate what must be done to induce the Ubians to cross. As threats of brutal punishments were proposed, Speratus happened to think of Auriane. Without consulting his colleagues, he left the council and sought her out.

"If you've some remedy we don't know of, you must tell me," he told her when his guard had unbolted the door of the *reda*.

Her first thought was, *Why aid them?* But nothing was to be gained by impeding the crossing. And matters wouldn't go well for these men of a brother-tribe if she stayed apart.

"They count you some sort of holy woman," Speratus pressed on. "Get them across somehow—inspire them, exhort them, tell them your gods say they've got to get to the other side—and I'll see both of you granted extra privileges for the rest of the journey."

"No one has performed the proper rites by the bank."

"What sort of rites?"

"The river must be given a small gift. The Nixes who live in this river—"

"The *who?*"

"The divine women who live naturally in the river—some call them sprites. They come on land sometimes, and if you've maddened them, they'll pull you down with them. The Nixes in this one are offended by thieves. If any among you has stolen anything, he must offer a part of it to the waters."

Speratus rubbed a hand across his chin. He had heard vague reports of watery beings that dwelled in northern rivers, rapacious and lustful creatures that looked human enough until you saw the duck feet or the fin down their backs. Their existence was not as definite to him as his own comfortably familiar Mars or Bellona—but who dared deny what might live, unseen, in a strange country?

"I suppose it would do no harm."

"It's a stilling-rite that's needed," Auriane said. "Your priests must first sing a river song to summon them, and then they must—"

"You know them?"

"I believe I remember one well enough. I watched my mother once, when the creek by our fields threatened to overflow her pea garden, but—"

"You'll do it, then. Our priests aren't schooled in these things. You succeed, and I'm a man of my word, you'll see better treatment."

"I'll need a mirror of bronze. And keep everything fashioned of iron covered from the river's sight."

He removed her fetters, then dispatched a slave to seek among the camp followers for a bronze mirror. As Auriane was conducted to the bank, walking with tedious slowness from the pain of her cracked rib, the tall Ubian horsemen looked on in profound silence. Some slowly nodded at her, then met one another's gaze with approval. Auriane remembered little of the stilling-rite, but for them, she wrestled off discouragement. At the riverbank, she removed her shoes so she could feel the heat of the earth fissuring up from the spirit realms underground.

The river in this place was half as wide as an ox field, surging onward with the wild energy of chariot teams closing on the finish. She closed her eyes, sank her mind into the river, and lifted the bronze mirror to entice the Nixes, who loved to see their own images. An alert quiet, partly baffled, partly amused, settled over the troops on both banks, as they watched the tall foreign woman in a torn cloak, her bronze hair collected into a braid that hung down in a heavy rope, as she performed some unknown rite by a river. The mighty rush of water was the only sound.

Her hands burned as she held them over the waters, as if that angry froth were hot steam. Tears of longing streamed down her face as she started to sing a song about rivers, half remembered from that remote time of red-gold contentment, when she was a loved child at her father's hall. She wasn't sure she'd spoken the verses in the correct order. Her imprecations felt fragile against the watery roar; this was like shouting into a riot.

But somewhere down in the river's living depths, she sensed a pricked ear. When she had finished, she dug up a clod from the earth beneath her feet and tossed it into the churning foam—not surprisingly, Speratus had found no one willing to admit to thieving anything, but she supposed the handful of earth would do, since his people had thieved all this land.

When it was done, the river raged on, and she felt rebuffed. However, the Ubians didn't seem to mind; one by one, they pulled themselves onto their mounts, and, trotting four abreast, began the crossing.

And afterward, though Speratus was careful to secure the *reda*'s door, to her relief he failed to put her back into the iron fetters. She'd no wish to pass over that river's snapping jaws while bound. He seemed to have simply neglected to do so, but she knew that sometimes a man's spirit gives a gift unknowingly, because the unseen folk tell him to.

Just ahead of her the heavier carts laden with *ballistae* and scaling ladders rumbled onto the bridge. At last, the *reda* was moving. For no reason she could name, she felt rising terror mingled with dark exultation.

The iron-bound tires of the carriage sank deeply into the soft turf of the roadway. Beyond the bridge's low, cross-timbered side rails, land abruptly fell away. The humid breath of the river enveloped them. The prickle of dread Auriane always felt when coming to an unholy place seized her then. Dark minds swarmed below. The waters, far from growing calmer, had risen—so much for her stilling-rite! She heard the screeching of powerful sprites, felt the firm tug of their strength—some were the ghosts of the drowned; others, the immortal Nixes, who had been denizens of the river since the world's beginning. The river was a boiling cauldron that would strip her bones. Rivers are the borders between worlds. Marcus had told her of the Styx, which the newly dead must cross. It washed the mind clean of all memory of the old life while it readied the soul for a fresh existence.

Her gaze was drawn, then, to the plain gold ring Marcus had given her when first they came together—that pitiful remembrance of their rich, fathomless storehouse of days. She felt the faint indentations on one side, where he'd had it inscribed with the words in his tongue, *Anima Mea*—"My Life." She heard the slight roughness in his voice as he spoke those words. And she thought she would give up the wretched few days she had left to look once more at the dear and noble contours of that face, to rest again in the womb-warmth of their nights, a last, exquisite coming-together that she might carry into eternity with her. The agony of his absence burned her to purest ash— but the ghost hovering above the pyre was, for a brief moment, strangely content. All whom she had loved inhabited her now. She didn't understand it, but she was not alone.

They passed over the second stone pier.

Her fevered senses saw a corona of amber light playing about the cedar trunk, as if the sword within reddened in agitation. Her father's sword didn't want to leave these lands. *It wants me to take it home.*

She was sharply conscious of the distance to the water; to fall, here, would be like leaping from a house of three stories. The time felt so marked, she thought herself an initiate waiting to be led into the cavern of the Mysteries. Embracing Brico, her unease grew. Both sat stone still, heads lifted— two birds in a flock, poised to wing off with one mind.

They were halfway across.

The elaborate, rolling *crack* was loud enough to split through the clamorous noise of water. Oddly it seemed to come from above, like some sky-borne whip in the hand of Wodan, striking out in unnaturally slow time as the god lashed on his windy steed. Deep in the structure of the trestles below, something shifted where it should not shift. Multiple crossed timbers shuddered and bowed. A woody groan shivered up.

There came a fast snapping of giants' bones. The timbers between the second and third piers began to buckle. Gently, horribly, the world heaved sideways.

Surprise suppressed the men to quiet—then, all found their voices at once. Yelps of fright, bellowed commands, competed with the frantic squeals of mules. Wagoners and men in armor fled past the *reda*, sprinting back the way they had come, to gain the safety of the bank. Brico was pitched into Auriane's lap. Behind them, an ox-drawn cart overturned; it was laden with the great, smooth stones thrown by the war engine called the *onager*. The roadway quaked as it was struck by a rain of ponderous stones designed to break down enemy walls. Some bounced; others streaked out, rattling and rumbling in every direction, cracking the spokes of wheels, breaking the cannon bones of mules, knocking men to their knees, before plummeting in silence into the river, far below.

The north side of the roadway was easing down by degrees. With a fresh jolt it sagged more sharply, yielding to the pummeling of the stones, the remorseless weight of massed wagons. At this frightful angle wagons started to slide, and men and beasts were sent scuffling and scrambling, until the whole moving mass was dammed against the bridge's cross-timbered side rails.

Auriane's *reda* moved with them. Men dangled from the rail, feet scrambling in emptiness as they shrieked the names of patron gods. Several lost their grip and dropped into the water below, to be drowned as the weight of their kit dragged them under. By the bridge's approach, it seemed battle had broken out as a jumble of wagons formed a barrier, and men trapped behind fought their way past, desperate to get off the bridge. It was a scene from the world's end, with chaos triumphant and the earth breaking apart to the cries of horns.

Within the gently lurching *reda* Auriane fought for balance while Brico clung to her as if to a stout post in a gale. The driver of the ox cart behind them was pitched, wailing, into the waters below. The frame of the *reda* bowed as it was crushed by the wagons collecting above it. The roadway between the second and third piers hung at an angle steep as the diagonal line a geometer draws across a square. The mule harnessed on the rail side rolled out into space, both forelegs broken; gradually, its agonized struggles pulled its companion-in-harness after—until their combined weight slowly upended the carriage. And there the *reda* hung, caught on the crossed timbers of the thin, splintering side rail.

Auriane acted from promptings too swift for thought, wholly inhabited by ghosts of family and tribe. She was upon the cedar trunk like a wildcat; with several savage movements she tore it open, freed her father's sword from its bindings, then sheathed it in the bronze-bound belt that girded her woolen tunic. It was done simply, naturally as putting on shoes, but another part of her felt as though she had pulled herself onto the back of some celestial horse for a ride into another world. At the last, she drew family, tribe, and fate about her like a cloak.

Then she got a firm grip around Brico's waist, and kicked hard at the carriage's door.

The bolt held.

"We must jump, Brico."

"No! I can't! Don't make me!"

"We must jump free of it or it will kill us!"

Where the *reda*'s side wall met its roof, it split open. They saw a strip of sky. Both women screamed. Again Auriane kicked the door, but it alone seemed secure while the frame of the carriage slowly buckled.

Then it no longer mattered. The wooden side rail cracked apart.

Carriage and mules shot down.

Horribly, impossibly, the heavy *reda* was airborne. It all happened so cruelly, so swiftly, the carriage might have been pounded down beneath a hammer of the gods. Plummeting mules writhed in air.

Fright pressed the screams from their throats; Auriane and Brico clutched one another, mute and braced. The cumbersome vehicle slammed into the swift-coursing river as though its waters were hard-packed earth. Auriane's head struck something ungiving; dense blackness claimed her. While she knew nothing of it, the carriage rocked on the surface for a moment, settled, then drifted swiftly toward the river bottom. The mules, still firmly attached by the harness, were pulled down after.

The men on the bank saw the river swallow the *reda* without a gulp; the sprites raised foamy hands and pulled it under. Two more souls were added to the sentient flow.

The roof of the carriage pressed its passengers deeper and deeper, as though it were a great stone thrusting them into the cold, smoky water. Silt exploded about the carriage as it struck the bottom.

Brought to consciousness once more by the shocking cold, Auriane whipped about like an eel in a net.

Who am I where am I—? Memories came like a fast series of blows: the world breaking apart . . . men's screams . . . herself and Brico, dropping through space. The roar of water still battered her ears—*impossible,* came the thought, for she was *in* the river. Locked alive in an underwater sarcophagus. Fright clamped round her like a vise. *The Nixes have us, they'll make us one of their own.* Calming herself was difficult as reining in a team of terrified horses, and she succeeded only gradually. Then she began systematically probing about in the frigid darkness, seeking a route of escape.

Her right hand shot out into open space. Hope vaulted.

She reached into the blackness and collected Brico, who had not been roused by the icy water. With her arms securely about her maidservant's waist, Auriane propelled the girl through the place where the *reda* had broken open.

The river grabbed them. While Auriane clung tightly to Brico, they tumbled end over end, in a current that was muscular and alive. A host of blurred terrors condensed into one shape: *the Nixes*. Auriane could see nothing in the murk but she knew they were there, flashing to organized attention like an excited school of fish, following her progress in eager swarms. Pallid hands prickly with scales reached for her, tentatively at first, growing bolder, stroking her face, pulling at her tunic . . . *hideous*. She and Brico were rolling and sliding toward their gaped maws. She would be mangled and ingested; she would become one of them, a she-fish wriggling on a river bottom in a gray, timeless forever.

Do I live still or did I slide down into the wet gullet of Hel herself?

Darkness pressed on her lungs.

I must be living—ghosts don't crave air.

The men above. Once they see I survived the fall, the chase begins.

Mind and body shrieked for air. But she was determined to stay beneath the surface as long as she could bear it, to put as much distance as possible between herself and the bridge.

She pushed off from the bottom and began undulating upward, moving toward the dim, distant glow above, following the direction of the sunlight cascading down. She felt she was being absorbed into light as she drifted, lungs ablaze, her ascent slowed by Brico's inert weight, Baldemar's sword sheathed at her side. She allowed only her face to break the water, and feasted greedily on air, praying the river's choppy wavelets would conceal her.

She had to look, just once, to see what the Fates had wrought.

Behind her was a sight as frightful as the wreckage of any battlefield. The bridge was broken into two parts; between bristling trestles, a vacant place stared back at her. Some clumsy giant might have slammed a foot down between the second and third piers. The timbered roadway was twisted about as if it were pliable as ribbon; debris and clothing fluttered from it sadly. A vast net was draped from a portion of the bridge like some webbed shroud, having been employed, no doubt, in attempts to rescue the drowning. Small, frantic figures hurried to and fro, carrying the injured, dragging the dead; some threw out lines to recover those still struggling in the water. Piteous cries reached her ears.

Was this the work of gods or men?

The current hadn't borne her as far as she'd thought; if they looked with care, she would be seen. Even as she hesitated, treading water, a dozen and more red-cloaked regular cavalrymen separated from the stunned groups of men collected about the approaches to the bridge and began trotting briskly up both banks. To free their arms they'd rid themselves of their shields; fishermen's nets were slung across their horses' withers. Though reason told her their purpose was to recover equipment and supplies borne off in the swift current, still she knew the blank fright of the rabbit before the hound.

She shifted Brico about so that the young woman floated on her back; only her face broke the waters. Auriane then cradled an arm beneath Brico's chin and swam vigorously on her side; in this fashion she was able to gently drag the smaller woman behind her. Auriane was almost glad of her panic; it helped to deaden the pounding pain of her multiple wounds.

Brico . . . dear Brico . . . why have you not yet been roused? Awaken now please . . . I know you can . . . I don't want to be alone.

She was a blind worm wriggling along, struggling to keep a companion afloat. She allowed herself to think only of the menace on the banks; if she thought of the Nixes below, terror would take her mind. The spirit of this river was mischievous, boisterous, and young—it would not do to show fear to it.

The river was a highway to freedom, or a grave.

Auriane wrenched herself around, once, to get a better grip on Brico— and the iron taste of blood filled her mouth. It collected about Brico in a doleful cloud. Auriane realized, then, that there was far too much of it. A long shudder passed through her, and she gave a small cry. Brico's chest had been nearly crushed, probably upon impact.

Auriane accepted, then, that her beloved maidservant and good companion was dead. Brico's goddess Sirona had taken her life swiftly and mercifully. Horror and grief came up in sharp fits and starts, but she vigorously pushed them off—there was no time.

The lead horsemen would soon be abreast of her. Panicked afresh, Auriane dropped beneath the surface, struggling along with Brico's chin still supported in the curve of one arm; she had no plan but to swim underwater until her tortured lungs could bear it no more. Good sense demanded she free herself of her burden, but she couldn't bring herself to release Brico's body to roll and tumble like some broken tree limb on the rough hands of the river. Brico deserved sacred rites, with those who loved her ringed round her pyre.

When Auriane came up gasping, a horseman with bright, needling eyes and a thick, stubbled neck was pointing her out with his decurion's staff, and bellowing. "Look, there's another. Is he living?" A pause, then—"It's the woman. Bring up the nets!"

"Are you addled?" came a shout from the opposite bank. "Nothing mortal could've survived that fall."

"It's one of our boys. Hurry on now, get ahead of him!"

Auriane spat out bloody water and swam hard, paddling frenziedly with one arm. The fishermen's nets were vast, and weighted with lead. *I'm done. Even if I weren't dragging poor Brico I can't outswim a galloping horse.*

The decurion of cavalry pulled his mount to an agitated halt; his embossed bronze cuirass glinted like a wolf's eye in firelight. Turning round to the horsemen coming up behind him, he roared, "It's the woman, I say! She gets free and I'll see every one of you demoted to the messenger service."

She had as much chance as the scurrying beetle beneath a descending foot.

This man gave his horse a hard kick; his armored and filleted mount broke into a heavy canter, taking him a short distance ahead of her. A horseman on the opposite bank kept apace. Then the whole company broke into a slow gallop, their sturdy mounts hurdling fallen alders, crashing noisily through hawthorn bushes, swerving round rockfall on the bank. The steady creak of leather, the sinister jingling of bits were alarmingly close at hand.

The insidious river was obliging them now, narrowing in this place; she felt she was swimming into the neck of a stoppered bottle. As more horsemen crowded alongside her, again she heard broken bits of their speech—

"Pull back! Let the Batavians have her. They need the commendation."

"That's not the woman—your eyes are failing!"

"—plenty of time to bicker over this *after* we've netted her—"

Just ahead, the nets flared out. They struck the water simultaneously, then floated out sinuously as some tentacled sea creature, entwining in one another, forming a single strand across the river.

Tentacles of death. *All hope's gone. They have me.*

Then came the appalling thought—*Give them Brico's body.* Auriane didn't think they had seen Brico at all; the maidservant was weighted down by the implements of iron she wore at her belt; her wan face scarce broke the surface. If the men lost time hauling in the wrong body, she might have some small chance of escaping. *But it would be a profane thing, for which men and gods would condemn me.*

The current propelled her rapidly toward the nets. When she was but a horse length away, Auriane released Brico to the river.

Dear Brico. I leave you among strangers. This is dreadful; they'll give you no rites.

She filled her lungs with a great reserve of air and dove straight down, like an otter. The muscular arms of the current gave her a powerful shove. She'd hoped to swim beneath the nets, but almost at once, she was struck by lead weights. She thrashed about, wrestling blindly with the stubborn webbing, then gave it up and dove deeper, while the net grabbed at her with light, eager hands.

Above her she felt several tugs as Brico's body was snagged, then began rolling in the net.

Auriane knifed into slimy river bottom. The feel of it repelled her—this was like plunging into a vat of viscera. A creature in serpent form glided across her back. Something jealous of the living, something half-human, half-fish, wormed up from the silt, fastening onto her arms and legs with pulpy, gray hands that were tentative, voracious. *Nixes. Fria, beloved Mother, keep them off me!*

It was not the Nixes; it was only a net. The lead weights brought it down and down until it molded itself about her, clinging like a skin.

The vigorous current dragged her onward; she was a plough cleaving a furrow through malign slime. But it wasn't enough to pluck her from the net's thousand hands; her every move delivered her deeper into their grasp. The tribe of fish-beings pressed close, sucking her warmth into their cold bodies.

Then her father's sword was in her hand. She had no memory of unsheathing it; it was simply there, quick as an old, loved memory. Bracing herself in mud, she executed a slow crosscut followed by a languorous upward strike through accumulating masses of net, carving a door through which she might escape.

She was a living woman in mortal combat with the Nixes.

The blade was keen; the net's tautness released at the barest touch. The Nixes flashed back as one before a weapon full of strong ghosts.

She fought with a wild, hopeful madness, through a time that felt infinitely extended, but allowed in fact for fewer than a dozen heartbeats. Her strength drained off as she encountered more, and ever more netting.

A hundred blind, watery horrors came for her. The Nixes' advantage was terrible—they could breathe; she could not. They could play with her until she drowned.

Night was on her lungs. Death-knowledge flashed through her limbs. A mute scream burst in her mind.

I die in muck. And it's only my due. I abandoned my people and lived in luxury with Marcus. And then, I betrayed him. My life is a desecration. Now I settle my debt for breaking sacred law . . .

Her panic was a phantom billowing ever larger until it condensed into one yawning Nix's mouth with fine, sharp teeth—but she didn't turn her face from it, even as a muscular throat forced her down into intestinal darkness. Death swallowed her; terror was triumphant. Fright swelled; her body could contain it no more—then it burst her open like some pod. And all dissolved into an exquisite, nurturant warmth, and she knew a rapture beyond what she'd thought possible in this world, a beauty greater than what babes knew at the breast, what lovers felt at the moment of honeyed flooding when they melted into one creature. All fears and sorrows she'd ever known seemed no more than shadows cast by oft-repeated dreams. Deep in the murk, she found a sun—a fiery face both majestic and maternal, that she could only call by the name of Fria, the deity she knew from her cradle. She felt she stood very close to the Fates.

There were no Nixes in the river now. They needed her fright to thrive.

She managed a ponderously slow cross-stroke that spun her about—*I thank every spirit that delivered this sword back to me*—and a dense clot of netting fell away. Then she executed a downward diagonal that looped back on itself—and she was free.

She spurted off like a squid, rejoining the determined current. The sunny warmth followed her. Rolling onto her back, briefly she exposed her face to the sky, and knew again the unbearable sweetness of air. Then she sank into the river and sped off again, propelling herself with strong frog kicks, speeding farther into a hallowed radiance that seemed to heal all wounds. *Honor all that's befallen you as if it were Fria herself*, Ramis had said—and in that moment, Auriane did so. And the radiance flashed out, vast and high as the World Tree, and she knew, then, what an encompassing peace lived in latching on to nothing, in being as naked and free of thought as the beast in the field. It was fighting to hold to one shape, one place, one course, one being, that brought pain like being flayed alive.

When Auriane broke the surface she found a stout tree limb and clung to it, gasping, feeling like a babe freshly pulled from the womb, wondering if she'd gone blessedly mad. A length of severed netting draped her head like a bridal veil, and wound round one arm like water weeds—one of her countrymen might have taken her for a fish woman.

The cavalrymen. Were they close?

Far upriver, the men huddled on the banks grew ever smaller as the current hurried her along. They seemed intent upon the efforts of a man with a grappling pole who probed at something caught in the nets. *Brico, beloved friend, how I misused you . . .*

But the ruse seemed a success.

I'm free. She whipped about and started swimming like a sprinting runner. The powerful current doubled her efforts, hurling her northward on fluid, nimble hands, back to her forest home. It seemed that all within her sight—from the blooming ramsons along the bank, to the mossy stones that jutted, glistening, from the shallows, to the fine lace of overarching branches above—were suffused with a numinous glow, a silver fire, as if the moon flowed into them. She was not aware she was seeing with a seeress's eyes. She just thought things had always been so.

She glided smoothly as a hawk on a shining sheet of black water, moving through the forest's striking silence while gods' eyes watched, unblinking, from the foliage. The water felt warm, like some heated bath or healing spring. Ramis's baffling words of last summer sounded in her mind—*If you do nothing, a river will decide.*

Had the Fates claimed her violently for some new life? A lawless river would be their perfect instrument. If so, it would be a fugitive freedom, in which she dared not ever again set foot on imperial lands. And a harshly cold one, bereft of Marcus, lived out in a land where Arria was so distant she might as well have been taken off by death. And where Avenahar—if Auriane could find her—might shun her mother in a fresh fit of wrath.

But in her holy fever Auriane saw only the beauty of all the fine, unseen webs, the kindness of this bloodstream of the Fates that bore her swiftly along, the nobility of the help one creature gives another—and behind them all, the fiery love of Fria herself, bright Mother of Light, spilling lavishly into all creatures, all things. She was stripped of every possession except for the plain gold ring that was a pledge of love from Marcus and a sword inhabited with her father's ghost. Yet she felt as wealthy as if she were mistress over a hundred estates.

There were no sounds in all the world but the ghostly rush of water. In this place, stands of gray alders lined the riverside—a forest of stilled dancers, elegant, stylus-thin, their bristling limbs outstretched in a mute shout of joy. This was well; the alders would shelter her when she gained the bank. She doubted her captors would be content to conclude that she'd drowned; they wouldn't move on before mounting a search of the countryside.

On a small spur of land jutting into the river course just ahead was a tree that stood alone—an ancient willow. The haunted, water-loving tree seemed to float in another world. Its shape was stark and peculiar, both droll and divine—masses of long, straight branches shot out of a bulbous trunk bunched like a defiant fist. It was great-breasted old crone with a fine fan of hair.

The dead lived in willows. She watched it in reverent silence.

The current dragged her closer. A solitary human figure stood beneath the willow.

Auriane almost dove beneath the surface again.

Fearful amazement broke through her tranquil haze.

It was Ramis.

She cannot be here. She is in Rome.

Ramis stood straight as a sword among the tangle of long grasses and aromatic agrimony stalks on the wilder bank. The lone willow seemed some spreading throne behind her, or a sky-door through which she'd come.

My eyes play tricks.

Perhaps I drowned and don't know it yet.

Auriane looked again and the old seeress was still there, impossible as a star in day, her image as solid as the willow's trunk—though her pale robe hung straight down, stately and still, in spite of the fact that a stiff wind was blowing. Somehow she was there but not there—she'd cast her mind across the world like some far-flung shadow. A smooth, graceful quiet lay round her, and the air about her crown of hair seemed oddly brighter than elsewhere. Such love and comfort were shed from her that Auriane began to swim in that direction; she could hardly help herself. Once, the shoal-riffled waters broke over her head, driving her under. In the watery silence Auriane felt a nimble consciousness fitting itself round her own; a familiar voice butted its way into her mind.

Ah. You're stronger than I thought. And I thought you couldn't surprise me anymore.

A pity you had to exhaust yourself so in that forty-year-long gallop away from me. Some fates are set, Auriane.

I tried to tell you.

Auriane scarce had the wit to consider those words' meaning; she just found herself helplessly glad of a companion. *By what deed of gods are you here?*

No deed of gods, came the mute reply. *You've opened a pathway for me.*

Auriane came up again and saw the falcon hanging in the sky above Ramis, beating powerful wings in a way that suggested surprise and joy; it dropped like a stone, then rushed at Auriane. Words poured into her mind and she did not know if they came from Ramis, the winged creature, or the rushing waters.

Auriane. I charge you to touch a living torch to the one that grows cold. And you will bear it on as long as you live, and give it over to the next of your line.

She gave a low cry of protest. She sensed spirits, the living and the dead, pressing the breath from her. The sole thought she could form was—*But it is too late. Your staff's been claimed by another.*

Ramis's answer was a smile like gentle summer.

All right, then. I battle you no more. Ramis, you have rightly won. Though I can't imagine being the eyes for so many when I've such a frail trust in my own sight. I'll never be as loved as you were, or as strong, but you would have me, so I'll take the oath on the sacred earth.

I'll do whatever I must, to be your successor.

A wavelet dashed itself into her eyes. When her blurred vision cleared, Ramis was gone.

Auriane swam toward the strange willow, suspecting that Ramis had shown herself in that place to tell her—*Come to the bank, here; in this place, it is safe.*

She ploughed through a rippling blanket of bogbean plants with their starlike flowers in crisp bloom. As she grasped an alder root and hauled herself from the water, the brisk wind found her wet clothes and she felt encased in ice. Shivering, she put a hand to her belt, relieved to discover she hadn't lost her fire-drill; she could make a fire when she needed to. Intent as an elk, she listened for the clink of iron on iron, horses' snorts, any sound that might signal the cavalrymen's approach. She was met with nothing but windy silence.

After a short search Auriane found some flowering hawthorn. She knelt by the riverbank and cast the petals into the water while intoning a prayer, asking the kindly spirits of this place to take Brico's ghost into their arms.

She was startled by the rattle-and-clatter of fast-beating wings from the opposite bank. Storks. As their ragged formation expanded across the sky, briefly they took the shape of the runic sign her people called *dagaz*—the advent of dawn.

The sign for rebirth.

She broke into bleak tears full of weakness and hurt, pressing Marcus's gold ring to her breast. *A break of day without you, Marcus.*

She was strongly aware, then, that this river gushed on until it poured into another, the Mother River, whose wide waters eventually intermingled with the Mosella, which wriggled backward to Marcus Julianus's villa—and her lost life. Somehow it brought a meager comfort to know all these waters were connected, just as this newborn life was the child of the one from which she'd been roughly exiled. Her life was proving to be a chain of worlds, each with a greater and louder ancestral chorus than the last.

For the last time, she looked toward the broken bridge. The men on the banks had grown so small, they had no nation or clan. Moving in concert, they were dragging the body of a woman from the waters. *Rest in Fria, poor Brico.*

Then her strength flowed out in a rush. Where the roots of the willow formed an earthen pocket, she crawled in, then covered herself with the wet cloak. There, in the lap of the guardian willow, she sank gratefully into a fathomless sleep.

SHE DID NOT awaken on her own. She was roused. The crackle of brisk, decisive footsteps through the grasses, the sharp mutterings of men, prodded her back into the world. Once again, she heard that loathsome jingling of bits . . .

Her mind still burdened with sleep, she fumbled for the grip of her father's sword. And made the discovery that she was too wearied to rise. Terror and acceptance claimed her together. *The exhausted prey awaits the wolf.*

Chapter 32

After the passage of thirty days

Witgern and Avenahar struggled through dog rose; hooked thorns tore at their woolen leggings. A hundred paces ahead, a green stone dominated the meadow, rising like a stark island in the weedy sea, a gargantuan surprise that seemed the lolling head of a primitive behemoth that had expired there at the time of the world's creation. "This is the place," Witgern said, extending an arm to stop her. "Stay here lest this be an ambush."

"But who else but my mother would have this ring?" Avenahar looked again at the warm, low-glowing beauty nested in her palm, with its pin-sharp inscription declaring, *Anima Mea*.

"Anyone could have stripped that ring from Auriane's drowned body. And the noblest of messengers can be corrupted by torture." Saddened by the undimmed light in Avenahar's eyes, he added more gently, "You must quell your hopes. The river was high. The banks were well watched. Don't lull yourself into believing she could be living, and free."

Conflicting tales of Auriane's end had filtered out into the forest.

The report that gave Avenahar no peace claimed that Auriane had survived the breaking of the bridge and managed an audacious escape, hurried along on the rough hands of the river. But as she lay on the bank depleted of all strength, she'd been seized by a Thracian auxiliary cavalry unit attached to the Twenty-second Legion.

To learn she was recaptured after such a noble swim, Avenahar thought. *It makes me want to have no more to do with this world.*

"So take that garland from your spear." Witgern's words came out hoarse and fierce; he, too, was feveredly hoping.

"Not yet. There's luck to be had in remaining hopeful."

The morning was majestic. Seemingly overnight all the willows of the land had clothed their bleak, reaching branches—the Mother Tree in glory. The wraith-ridden ground mist snaked back to its night coverts while the cresting sun inflamed the tops of trees, turning the freshly leafed-out willows into green lanterns.

From behind the colossal stone came a rush of meadow grouse.

Witgern fell to his hands and knees, roughly pulling Avenahar down beside him. "Something's there. Don't move."

He eased forward alone, ash spear positioned for a quick, hard throw.

As Avenahar waited, the dawn felt hollow and raw. Her mother was there or she was not. You couldn't beg mercy from the Fates; they'd no respect for human yearnings.

Finally she heard Witgern's shout, shuddering like a loose harp string— "Are you living woman or spirit!"

Then, the miracle of a reply. "Witgern." A living voice, a woman's, hurt and human. "Dearest of friends. Did . . . did not Avenahar come with you?"

Auriane.

Witgern again, gibbering now—". . . It cannot be, it's a vision conjured by all my cries to Hel to bring you back . . ."

Avenahar vaulted to her feet and sprinted round the stone, breathing heavily as a distance runner, fearful of looking, desperate to see.

She staggered to a halt next to Witgern, who stood with arms outstretched, rapt and still as if one of the Sun's daughters appeared before him. There, knee-deep in a pool of pale woodruff flowers, was Auriane.

She was garbed as a seeress of the people.

Avenahar found herself immobilized by the sight of the beloved and familiar married to the ancient and grand. The mantle of power fit her mother as comfortably as the supple sheath fits the knife. The spirit-calling stones lining Auriane's cloak glimmered with dark authority. The thin crescent moon at her forehead married her to the peaceful eternity of the night sky. In one instant Avenahar scarce knew her mother, then in the next, thought—*Yes, she has always been this*. Auriane's knotted elmwood staff was adorned with a spray of heron feathers—to speed an initiation begun so late? Her autumn-hued hair was unruly as a woodwife's. The subtly spotted wildcat pelt that lay across her shoulders matched a quiet, fierce soul. She seemed an epiphany of the wild in hues of granite, earth, stone dust, and bronze. *The forest saved her, then made her its own,* Avenahar thought as she began to shiver, eyes flooding as she stood in stunned gratitude.

"Of course I came," Avenahar managed. "This is too great a gift." The livid memory of the day she'd bolted off into the forest struck Avenahar a blinding blow. She felt a pain like a wasp sting on the heart. "I . . . uttered such vileness to you . . . killing words, that can't be called back. How your heart must have died as you searched for me. There is no way I can make amends."

"Avenahar, beloved. No."

The rich tranquillity in those words caused Avenahar to feel a flutter of communion with something shining and kind, and greater than them both. Still she turned from her mother in a fever of regret, pulling a section of her cloak over her head.

"Stop this," Auriane said urgently, striding swiftly to her daughter. "I raised you to be proud. What harm in a show of youthful fire? You are the daughter I prayed the gods for." She grasped Avenahar's shoulders and turned her about. "Avenahar. We've one soul between us. There's no need to beg forgiveness or accept it."

The balm in those words worked its way into Avenahar's mind, and she let the cloak drop back in place. The serpent-form fibula claimed Auriane's attention.

"Did you ever learn who gave you that?" Auriane whispered with dread.

Avenahar covered it with her hand. "'. . . A good and brave man who would have given me all he had, had fortune not taken him away,'" she quoted her mother's words. "I should have listened. My ears were shut and locked."

Auriane fiercely gathered Avenahar up and clung to her daughter as if she were the source of all life.

"Do you know now, there was no vileness in your birth?" Auriane said then. "How beloved you are of the gods . . . how beloved of me? . . . that you belong here . . . how wholly, gloriously, you belong?"

"Yes, but why did I have to become a loathsome daughter to learn it."

"No more of that." Auriane held to Avenahar so tightly she lifted her daughter from the ground. "Avenahar," she said, her face turned to the sky. "You will be great among our people."

The words filled Avenahar's breast with warm liquid gold.

"Ah, the sight of you two together," Witgern broke in grandly from behind them, "makes a man feel the horn is full, the fire lit, the hall crowded with good companions. Come, I've mead to share."

And then they sat, resting their backs against the stone that had brooded in the grass for millennia. The summer sun was in them. The wildflowers had grown high enough to wall them in from the eyes of the forest. Auriane related all she knew of Arria, of the baleful mystery of what had befallen Marcus—then told them, as she concluded the tale of her escape, ". . . and I lay there too weak to stir while cavalrymen combed the riverbank for me. Their horses nearly stepped on me. When they gave it up and dusk came, it was Gunora who found me and saw me carried to safety. Gunora nursed me to strength. She told me I'd collapsed in the one place along that stretch of the river where I was neatly hidden from the eyes of anyone scouring the banks. I had high protection, I think."

Witgern heard all this in silence, then said, "I thought I was your slayer. To find instead that I'm your deliverer . . ."

Auriane looked at him, baffled. "Why would you think yourself my slayer?"

"The bridge," Witgern said as if he expected her to know.

"What of the bridge? Witgern, you are saying . . . you caused the bridge to fall?"

"Last autumn I learned that a gaggle of Roman vermin bound for the great war were to cross that bridge on their way to the East. So I commanded my men to saw through the trestles. They worked all through the night, but—"

"You're jesting," Auriane said, laughing.

"—but the bridge refused to collapse, that day," Witgern said. "What vile luck I thought it, then. It just needed the winter rains to finish the work." His voice grew hoarse. "It waited, Auriane. The bridge waited. It fell for you."

"Gods above and below, that is wondrous," Auriane said, laughing while her face shone with tears of amazement. "Witgern. Your acts are blessed. I cannot believe this. No, I can. That was a haunted day, aswarm with marvels." She leaned back against the stone and said, "Witgern, you brought me home."

"And Baldemar's sword?" Witgern ventured, eyes narrowed, intent. "You have it still?"

"I have it. But not for war. I mean to return it to my father's barrow."

"No. Not yet! Auriane, what if you could go out in battle dress one final time, and *live*—then return to this new life you've set out upon?"

"There'll be no pardon if I thwart my birth fate again."

"The Fates went to a bit of trouble to unite you with it." Testily he added, "As did I."

"And without that sword, I would never have escaped the nets. It means you saved me from death twice, Witgern, and I owe you a debt that I can't repay in this life. But I've taken the oath at the forest altar."

"But Auriane, Chariomer has—"

"Witgern, let her be," Avenahar interjected firmly.

"Witgern, Ramis was ready to let her false accusers slay her," Auriane said with more patience, "just to preserve me to take her place. So I intend to try. I came today only because I wanted you to see me before I go to the caves. Avenahar can visit me there. But no man can." She dropped her voice. "You must tell no one I'm still living, not your First Companion, not a priest of the settlements, not a seeress, should she ask. You must let Sawitha believe I drowned. You'll not know me again until I've become adept in the ways of the seeing-women."

Avenahar saw the tautening of Witgern's jaw—he did not accept this. He looked hard toward the far hills of the north where Chariomer was camped; they were dark as basalt beneath scowling clouds, as though Wodan himself glowered down upon the invader. Snakes of wind moved through the woodruff flowers, promising unknown troubles to come.

But Witgern spoke no more of war that day.

When Auriane was ready to depart, mother and daughter walked alone along an elven path through flower-decked May trees. Avenahar felt a shy hope like that of the furred beast edging from its winter hole. Her life was here. There was no sadness in this. For her, the precarious future promised grand adventures, not terror and woe. She was a young Wolf who would seize peace and gift it to her people.

"Witgern doesn't believe you, you know," Avenahar said. "He's certain you'll take up that sword again when you hear the people cry out to you."

"And that would please you, too, I suppose."

"No. It wouldn't. I couldn't bear it."

"This must be someone borrowing Avenahar's skin."

"Promise me you'll stay away from war."

"What have you done with Avenahar? Her soul's trapped in a jar somewhere, isn't it?"

"Stop this! By every calculation of the wise, you shouldn't be alive. You weren't saved just so you could drive off a bandit chief. Though that needs doing. But leave that for Witgern and me. I sense the river was a last warning . . . a crossing of a dreaded precinct . . . and you don't mock these things." A silence, then Avenahar added with a thickening throat, "Yet, I fear you will."

"Well, my hotheaded daughter became an elderwoman while my back was turned."

Auriane said it smiling, but within, felt a shift of unease. *When lying beneath the willow I dreamed I went back to war.* She sensed the intrusion of something divine and not necessarily benign. But she lifted the elmwood staff and said, "This is my life now, Avenahar."

"Promise me you'll not let anything seduce you from it. Marcus . . . I believe Marcus would have wanted it so. I think that, wherever he is, he knows all these things, too."

A cry Auriane couldn't express—*Marcus, you are alive and I* will *see you again in this life*—swelled in her throat, stifling speech, so instead she caught her daughter's capable hand in her own, both seeking comfort and giving it.

THEY ARE THE *gold beneath a river, a knot tied by holy hands, an oracular gift,* Witgern thought as he watched Auriane and Avenahar grow small among the festive trees.

Auriane. You make me want to pick up a harp. I didn't save you. Your captors should have known you can't slay the blessed. You're one who ever makes anew with your soul. Somehow you will always be here, like the mountain ash. You'll haunt these rivers and forests a thousand summers from now.